THE OCTOPUS

FRANK NORRIS was born in Chicago in 1870. Moving to Oakland, California, in 1884, and shortly thereafter to San Francisco, he studied to become an artist and in 1887–89 worked in the studio of Guillaume Bouguereau at the Académie Julian in Paris. By the early 1890s, when a student at the University of California in Berkeley, however, he had turned to literature with the intention of becoming a professional author. His first book was a Sir Walter Scott-inspired poetical romance, *Yvernelle: A Legend of Feudal France* (1892). More modern influences such as Rudyard Kipling, Richard Harding Davis, and Robert Louis Stevenson soon became apparent in his short stories published in West Coast periodicals. By the mid-1890s his principal mentor was the notorious "father of literary Naturalism," French novelist Émile Zola. In *McTeague* (1899), *The Octopus* (1901), *The Pit* (1903), and *Vandover and the Brute* (1914), Norris employed Zola's theory and methods, fully initiating the American tradition of Naturalistic novel-writing and dramatically signaling his culture's rejection of Victorian values and tastes. Like Zola, whose post-Darwinian frankness about "the human animal" outraged puritanical American and English readers, Norris extended the scope of fictional representations of human experience in *McTeague*, shocking his contemporaries with his treatment of what he termed "the mystery of sex," as well as with his graphic depictions of abnormal behavior and psychological states. The posthumously published *Vandover*, begun at the same time as *McTeague*, even more unsqueamishly examines the irrational determinants at work in the lives of its characters. In *The Octopus*, one of the earliest muckraking novels of the Progressive Era, Norris exposed the operations of the ruthless *laissez-faire* capitalism sanctioned by turn-of-the-century Social Darwinists. *The Pit* continued this analysis, also offering a close psychological study similar to those of Gustave Flaubert in *Madame Bovary* and Kate Chopin in *The Awakening*. *The Pit* was published posthumously: Norris died in 1902 at the age of thirty-two, having written seven novels and over 200 poems, short stories, and essays.

KEVIN STARR teaches at the University of San Francisco and is active as a communications consultant in Northern California. Among his writings are *Americans and the California Dream*, 1805–1915; *Inventing the Dream: California Through the Progressive Era*; and the novel *Land's End*. Starr has also served as an All-ston Burr Senior Tutor at Harvard, the City Librarian of San Francisco, and a daily columnist for the *San Francisco Examiner*.

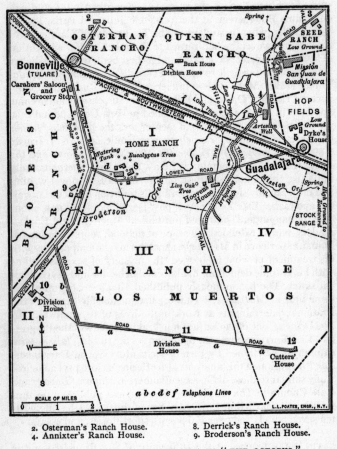

2. Osterman's Ranch House.   8. Derrick's Ranch House.
4. Annixter's Ranch House.   9. Broderson's Ranch House.

MAP OF THE COUNTRY DESCRIBED IN "THE OCTOPUS."

FRANK NORRIS

THE EPIC OF THE WHEAT

The Octopus

A STORY OF CALIFORNIA

With an Introduction by

KEVIN STARR

PENGUIN BOOKS

PENGUIN BOOKS
Published by the Penguin Group
Penguin Books USA Inc., 375 Hudson Street,
New York, New York 10014, U.S.A.
Penguin Books Ltd, 27 Wrights Lane, London W8 5TZ, England
Penguin Books Australia Ltd, Ringwood, Victoria, Australia
Penguin Books Canada Ltd, 10 Alcorn Avenue,
Toronto, Ontario, Canada M4V 3B2
Penguin Books (N.Z.) Ltd, 182–190 Wairau Road,
Auckland 10, New Zealand

Penguin Books Ltd, Registered Offices:
Harmondsworth, Middlesex, England

First published in the United States of America by
Doubleday, Page & Co. 1901
This edition with an introduction by Kevin Starr
first published in Penguin Books 1986
Reissued in Penguin Books 1994

3 5 7 9 10 8 6 4

LIBRARY OF CONGRESS CATALOGUING IN PUBLICATION DATA
Norris, Frank, 1870–1902.
The octopus: a story of California.
Includes bibliography.
I. Title.
PS2472.O3   1987   813′.4   85–31463
ISBN 0 14 01.8770 7

Printed in the United States of America
Set in Old Style

CONTENTS

A NOTE ON THE TEXT

In 1933 Willard E. Martin of the Harvard Library noted that there are no critical or textual problems involved in *The Octopus*. Norris was working for his publisher, Doubleday, Page & Co., at the time *The Octopus* was published and can be presumed to have seen his novel through the press personally. So, then: we begin in April 1901 with a text that represents the author's intentions. The first printing of the first edition, moreover, produced at the J. J. Little Press, contained only three typographical errors. These three errors were corrected in a 1901 reprinting of the first edition, printed by Grosset & Dunlap at The Country Life Press in Garden City, New York, using the original plates of the Doubleday, Page & Co. first edition. This 1901 Grosset & Dunlap reprinting is therefore (as far as eighty-plus years of scrutiny can ascertain) error free. The same is true of the subsequent reprintings from these original corrected plates issued by Doubleday, Page & Co. in 1903, 1906, 1914, and 1920. The text of this edition is based upon that of the second printing of the first American edition of April 1901. The three corrections made by the Grosset & Dunlap reprint of later that year have been incorporated into this text.

Since the manuscript of *The Octopus* has disappeared save for a few scattered sheets, these original plates are doubly authoritative. Any edition of *The Octopus* not based upon these plates—including the *Complete Edition* of 1928, with its spelling and punctuation revised long after Norris's death—is devoid of comparable authority.

INTRODUCTION

Around five in the morning sometime in March 1899, Bruce Porter, formerly of San Francisco, awoke in his apartment in The Benedict on Washington Square, New York City, to a pounding on his door. Opening to his unexpected visitor, Porter saw his friend the writer Frank Norris, likewise a former San Franciscan, who lived diagonally across the Square.

He had it, Norris told his friend excitedly. It had finally jelled in his mind—The Epic of the Wheat! In the weeks previous, Norris, fresh from the triumph of finishing his novel *McTeague* (1899) and from a stint as a combat correspondent in Cuba, had been using Porter as a sounding board for what he would be working on next. He wanted to write something big, Norris told Porter, something about business and the frontier and California, something not merely atmospheric but with guts in it. And now he had it: a trilogy of novels following the flow of wheat from its production in California, its brokerage and distribution in the commodities markets of Chicago, and its consumption in a famine-stricken Europe or Asia. It was, he wrote a friend, an idea as big as all outdoors.

The thirty-year-old Norris also announced his project to his mentor, William Dean Howells, who had just reviewed *McTeague* favorably in *Literature*. "I think," Norris wrote Howells from his rooms at 61 Washington Square South, "there is a chance for somebody to do some great work with the West and California as a background, and which will be at the same time thoroughly American. My idea is to write three novels around the one subject of *Wheat*. First, a story of California, (the producer), second, a story of Chicago (the distributor), third, a story of Europe (the consumer) and in each to keep to the idea of this huge Niagara of wheat rolling from West to

East. I think a big Epic trilogy could be made out of such a
subject, that at the same time would be modern and distinctly
American. The idea is so big that it frightens me at times but
I have about made up my mind to have a try at it."

Financially supported by his publishers, Doubleday &
McClure Co. (soon to be reorganized as Doubleday, Page &
Co.), Norris left for California in early April to research his
subject. The pivotal incident around which Norris was planning *The Octopus*, a bloody shoot-out between ranchers and a
sheriff's posse acting on behalf of the Southern Pacific Railroad,
had occurred nineteen years earlier on Henry Brewer's ranch,
Mussel Slough, in Tulare County, in the central San Joaquin
Valley. Brewer and his neighbors had been working leased land
for nearly a decade in the expectation of eventually buying it
from the Southern Pacific at a cost of $2.50 to $5 an acre, a
price originally quoted by the railroad. Together, the ranchers
had pooled their capital and excavated an irrigation system to
bring in water from the Kings River to their parched but po-
tentially fertile soil. By 1878 formerly arid tracts were blooming
in barley, wheat, and fruit trees. Quoting revised sale prices
of $17 to $40 an acre for the property, railroad land agents
demanded that the ranchers either buy their holdings at the
new rates or quit their improved properties altogether. Outraged, the ranchers organized themselves into a Settlers' Land
League and began preparing for armed resistance.

On the morning of May 11, 1880, United States Marshal
Alonzo W. Poole drove his buggy onto Henry Brewer's ranch.
In the marshal's pocket were eviction orders against Brewer
from the federal court. Poole and his deputies were escorting
onto the property the new legal owners, Walter J. Crow and
Mills D. Hart, who were most likely acting as dummy purchasers for the Southern Pacific. Poole and his associates were
confronted by some fifteen armed homesteaders on horseback.
Pulling up his buggy, Poole then alighted from the carriage as
the homesteaders encircled his party. This move probably
saved his life, for he was struck to the ground by a horse as
shots rang out. Walter J. Crow did most of the killing. While

still in his buggy, he shot one settler. Jumping to the ground, he blew two settlers off their horses with a shotgun. Reloading, he hit another three before fleeing into a nearby wheat field, where he was found dead the next day, shot in the back. All in all, eight men, including Crow and Hart, were killed in the gun battle.

Norris thoroughly researched the Mussel Slough incident, including the complicated efforts before the shoot-out by the Settlers' League to outmaneuver the Southern Pacific legally and politically. In both the courtroom and the legislative chambers of Washington and Sacramento, however, the settlers had lost out against the remorseless railroad machine.

These months in the spring and summer of 1899 were among the happiest of Frank Norris's all-too-brief life. He was in love with Jeannette Black, a tall, beautiful young woman, nine years his junior, whom he had met at a San Francisco sub-debutante dance in the late fall of 1896. Norris saw Miss Black assiduously throughout the spring of 1899, a courtship he recorded later in the year in the charming novella *Blix*. Together, the couple rambled about San Francisco. "It's a wonder I don't forget me own name these days," Norris wrote Ernest Peixotto and his wife (like himself, San Franciscans turned New Yorkers), "I'm having such a bully good time. Feel just as if I were out of doors playing after being in school for years. Jeanette and I spent the whole afternoon yesterday on the waterfront among the ships (*on* and all over *one* of them) came back and had tea and pickled ginger on the balcony of our own particular Chinese restaurant over the Plaza and wound up by dining at Luna's Mexican restaurant 'over in the Quarter.' "

After a decade of sporadic journalism and apprentice fiction, Norris's literary career was now in full swing. Published that February, *McTeague* had been favorably reviewed and was selling well. Grant Richards was publishing it in London. The fever Norris had contracted in Cuba had weakened him in the early part of the year; but now, busy with his new novel and very much in love, he regained his old buoyancy. In the early summer, he moved down to the Santa Anita Rancho in San

Benito county near Hollister, one hundred miles south of San
Francisco, in order to observe ranch operations firsthand. The
Peixottos had introduced Norris to the owners of the Santa
Anita, Gaston and Dulce Ashe, just the sort of smart young
modern couple Norris always admired. Made welcome by the
Ashes, Norris spent a full two months there, familiarizing himself with the details of ranch life, with special emphasis on the
production of wheat. At harvest time Norris took his turn on
the sacking platform of a harvester-thresher combine as it lumbered across the five thousand acres Gaston Ashe had planted
in wheat. Bending to his task, Norris felt himself part of an
exquisite orchestration of earth, men, animals, and steel. As
far as the eye could see, from the plains of Santa Anita to the
Coast Range in the distance, was wheat, ready for harvest.

Norris returned to New York in the fall of 1899. Jeannette
joined him there in early January of the new year, and they
were married at St. George's Episcopal Church on January 12,
1900. Supported by an $18-a-week advance against royalties,
supplemented by Norris's $12 a week in salary as a half-time
reader for Doubleday, Page & Co., the young couple moved
into two furnished rooms on the top floor of the Anglesea on
the south side of Washington Square, which the Peixottos had
occupied the previous winter. In October, seeking more room
and greater quiet, they moved to a six-room cottage in suburban
Roselle, New Jersey. Between January and December 15, 1900,
when he finished his manuscript, Frank Norris wrote *The Octopus*, if one is to judge from the few foolscap sheets that have
survived, almost as a single act of spontaneous composition,
with only a minimum of revision. When it came time to set
The Octopus in type, it was done (so it appears) directly from
the first-draft manuscript, no retyping being necessary.

Dedicated to Jeannette Norris, *The Octopus* was published
by Doubleday, Page & Co. in early April 1901, a month after
Norris's thirty-first birthday. In the months that followed,
The Octopus sold an impressive 33,000 copies in its first trade
edition. Many reviewers regarded *The Octopus* with mixed
feelings. Indeed, to read these contemporary reviews is to

encounter a pattern of response that has characterized more
than eighty years of critical commentary. Few major American
novels have been as simultaneously dismissed and respected.
Early reviewers and later academics alike have at once felt
superior to *The Octopus*—it is clumsy, verbose, repetitive, philosophically unresolved, lowbrow—while at the same time acknowledging it as a major American novel. Writing in *The
Atlantic Monthly* (May 1902), H. W. Boynton castigated *The
Octopus* for "the sort of romantic vulgarity of which only the
realist of the French school is capable." The compelling force
of many of Norris's characters, admitted Boynton in *The Atlantic Monthly*—the Derricks, Annixter, Hilma Tree—offset
Norris's tendency to Zolaesque vulgarity. For Frederic Taber
Cooper of the *Bookman* (May 1901) *The Octopus* was not re-
alistic enough. "The truth," Cooper wroter, "is that *The Octopus* is a sort of vast allegory, an example of symbolism pushed
to the extreme limit, rather than a picture of life." Railroad
agent S. Behrman's death in a ship's hold under a torrent of
cascading wheat, Cooper conceded, was equal to the best of
Zola. William M. Payne lambasted Norris in the *Dial* (September 1, 1901) for favoring the revolutionary ranchers over
the law-abiding Southern Pacific. ("We have little doubt, for
example, that if Mr. Norris were writing of an earlier generation in California, he would be on the side of the Vigilance
Committees rather than on the side of law and order.") Certain
episodes, agreed the otherwise critical Payne in the *Dial*, "are
presented with remarkable vividness and intensity of feeling."
The Athenaeum (October 5, 1901) took Norris to task for his
verbosity and repetition. However, *The Athenaeum* admitted
The Octopus was for all its faults "a powerful and tragic piece
of fiction." Norris, noted the *Independent* (May 16, 1901), had
almost hysterically lost control of *The Octopus* by the novel's
final pages. And yet, the *Independent* reviewer admitted, "*The
Octopus* has qualities that lift it out of the rank of commonplace
fiction." "Frank Norris," wrote Wallace Rice in *The Chicago
Literary and Art Review*, "has written a novel, as fascinating,

as repellent, as multifarious, as misshapen as the marine monster from which it gains its name . . ."

Thus reviewers gave with one hand and took with another,
as would their successors through three generations of academic
criticism. It was easy to criticize Norris's "multifarious, misshapen" book—so vast, so ambitious, so contradictory; yet no
one could deny its elemental power, the forward surge of Norris's narrative, the significance of his themes, the vividness of
his characters. *The Octopus*, wrote William Dean Howells in
Harper's Monthly Magazine (October 1901), "is a great book,
simple, sombre, large, and of a final authority as the record of
a tragical passage of American, of human events." *The Octopus*,
wrote B. O. Flower in the *Arena* (May 1902), "is a work of
genius."

Flower's review ("The Trust in Fiction: A Remarkable Social
Novel") first underscored one of the many reasons why no
reviewer could reduce *The Octopus* to the sum total of its faults.
Norris's social theme, the clash of frontier and trust, was at
the very center of turn-of-the-century American experience. As
Professor Frederick Jackson Turner of the University of Wis-
consin told the American Historical Association meeting in Chicago in July 1893, the frontier was over. No more free land
was available. While not strictly accurate in his timetable,
Turner's equation of free land, frontier, and dominant American identity provides insight into the nature of the power that
B. O. Flower felt pulsating through Norris's titanic novel. Led
by Magnus Derrick of Los Muertos Rancho, "the Governor,"
the very paragon of pre-Civil War, pre-corporate American
values, the ranchers of *The Octopus* take their central identity
from an America that is passing with the frontier. They are
self-made men, ruthless, exploitative, capable of using up their
lands in crop after crop of wheat with no thought for the future;
but they are also possessed of an ethic that prizes, if only as a
matter of myth and metaphor, honesty, self-reliance, fair play.
To describe them, one can easily employ Turner's catalog of
frontier traits. In Turner's language, the ranchers of the San
Joaquin show "that coarseness and strength combined with

acuteness and inquisitiveness; that practical, inventive turn of mind, quick to find expedients; that masterful grasp of material things, lacking in the artistic but powerful to effect great ends; that restless, nervous energy; that dominant individualism, working for good and for evil; and withal that buoyancy and exuberance which comes with freedom." The trust, by contrast (or to use the more modern phrase, the corporation), prized different virtues.

The trust wanted things consolidated, organized, predicated—and fixed. The trust wanted ownership, not freedom; conformity, not rugged individualism. In the second half of the nineteenth century, the frontier and all that it represented as fact and symbol was vanishing, and the trust was on the rise. From this encounter between land and capital, freedom and monopoly, arose a host of secondary socioeconomic and political issues which Norris so compellingly chronicles in *The Octopus:* class conflict between the middle classes and the plutocracy, the disposal of public lands, the corruption of government, the watering of stock, the suppression of labor, unemployment, price fixing, the blacklist.

Nowhere was this clash between frontier and trust more bold and more violent than in California. The wheat industry, as Norris correctly dramatizes, was a direct creation of the California frontier. The Gold Rush had taught Americans to employ technology to extract wealth from the land. The technology, infrastructure, and attitudes of the mining era led easily to the headlong, often ruthless wheat era that followed in the 1870s and lasted through the turn of the century. The famous plowing scene of *The Octopus* reflects the industrial model that soon characterized the wheat industry as plows grew larger and larger and pulling arrangements more intricate. One California plow, "the Leviathan," weighed a ton, cut a five-foot furrow three feet deep, and took eighty oxen to draw. Steam-propelled plows and harvesters began to appear in the late 1870s. Then harvesting and threshing were combined into one operation, the combine, either horse-drawn or steam-driven. A steam-driven combine could cut, thresh, and sack one hundred acres a day. Beginning in the 1880s, the sacked wheat was hauled off to shipping points by steam-powered road locomotives, capable of hauling thirty-five tons of wheat across the plains at three miles per hour. This technology enabled California wheat ranchers to utilize vast acreages. Even independent ranchers (such as the ranchers of *The Octopus*) could farm five to ten thousand acres. Holdings of ten to twenty thousand acres were common. The greater California wheat rancher of them all, Dr. Hugh J. Glenn, farmed some 55,000 acres in Colusa County, producing a half million bushels of wheat. After his death, Glenn's vast holdings were incorporated into a separate county.

Ironically, these frontier-miners-turned-wheat-ranchers were also big agribusinessmen, employing a large work force (a discharged bookkeeper dispatched Dr. Glenn with a shotgun), ever aware of trends on the world's grain markets, operating on borrowed money and leased land for a quick profit. "They had no love for their land," writes Norris of his ranchers. "They were not attached to the soil. They worked their ranches as a quarter of a century before they had worked their mines." The ranchers were as tough-minded and cynical as their counterparts who built and ran the railroad. The railroad/rancher clash at the center of *The Octopus* pits against each other comparable opponents, each capable of bribery and influence peddling and the public be damned.

The Central Pacific, later the Southern Pacific (called the Pacific and Southwestern in *The Octopus*), exacted significant compensation from the Federal government for building the railroad in California: ten sections of land extending up to twenty miles in alternate checkerboard patterns for each mile of track completed. That made the Southern Pacific the biggest landholder in the state. Much of this land was considered worthless, until it was improved and irrigated by railroad tenants. Added to its monopoly on rail transportation (not until the late 1890s was there an alternate inland route), the Southern Pacific controlled all major river traffic on the San Joaquin and Sacramento rivers and had rate agreements with all major oceanic shipping companies. Its political bureau in San Francisco controlled the politics of California through a skilled subsidy of party officials, free passes for politicians and judges, and outright bribes. Staffed by pro-railroad hacks, the California Railroad Commission, which Norris's ranchers seek to infiltrate, became derisively known as the Southern Pacific Literary Bureau.

Needless to say, the railroad was hated. Despite their resort to bloody vigilante action, a jury convicted the Mussel Slough survivors on only a minor charge of obstructing a federal officer, and sentenced them to short terms in a local prison in San Jose, where the jailer allowed them to come and go at will and where they dined off special provisions sent in by sympathizers from across the state. One settler found time to court and marry the jailer's daughter. Released after eight months, the Mussel Slough men were fêted at a barbecue, then escorted out of town in their buggies (they refused to return home on the SP) with a brass band. A crowd of three thousand gave them a rousing welcome when they arrived back home in Hanford. These Mussel Slough men, we must remember, were not Norris's agribusiness ranchers. They were little men (sandlappers, in California parlance) and their battle with the Southern Pacific impressed itself deeply on Californians; it distilled and dramatized the core conflict of the state, monopoly versus individual ownership. In California, as San Francisco journalist Henry George was pointing out in *Progress and Poverty* (1879), a handful of people, including the railroad, owned most of the land; since land was the ultimate source of wealth, they owned everything. In a post-*Octopus* essay, "The Literature of the West," published in the Boston *Evening Transcript* for January 8, 1902, Norris argued that the story of the West was both a story of Homeric daring, the exploration of a vast, uncharted half-continent by frontiersmen faced with persistent physical danger, and a more patient, peaceful story of settlement and city-building, a chronicle of business, stock reports, and ticker tape. *The Octopus* encapsulates all such successive levels of California experience. Led by Magnus Derrick, a for-

mer forty-niner, Norris's ranchers are mostly of the frontier
mining generation; yet they are raising wheat with the assistance of telephone, typewriters, ticker tapes, and corporate
managerial techniques. Into this area of Tulare County in the
lower portions of the San Joaquin Valley, Norris has consolidated a *mise-en-scène* suggestive of the composite elements of
the frontier California past. There are no inland missions or
Spanish settlements in California; but Norris brings a Mission,
San Juan de Guadalajara, over from the coast, a recreation of
Mission San Juan Bautista near the Santa Anita Rancho where
he had gathered facts and atmosphere in the late spring of
1899. The nearby town of San Juan Bautista, which in reality
is adjacent to the coastal Mission, Norris separates off as Guadalajara, a Mexican village still alive with the ambience and
memories of the Hispanic past. In a manner typical of his
generation of Californians, then in the beginnings of a Mission
Revival, Norris suffuses both mission and village with the
warmth of romance. Tolling the angelus at twilight, the ancient
Mission bells cast over the surrounding fields of seed flowers
and wheat "a note of the Old World, of the ancient regime, an
echo from the hillsides of medieval Europe, sounding there in
this new land, unfamiliar and strange at this end-of-the-century
time." In Guadalajara itself, Presley, a Norris *alter ego* who
speaks Spanish fluently, talks with a surviving centenarian of
the legends and glories of the vanished days of the Spanish and
their Mexican successors, an era, we are told, of spaciousness
and courtesy. Bonneville, by contrast, based on the real-life
town of Hollister near Santa Anita Rancho in San Benito
County, represents the urgent American present. Its crowded
sidewalks are paved in asphalt; and its central street is awhir
with passing bicycles, drayage carts, and two-wheeled sulkies.
The landscape and settlements of *The Octopus*—Guadalajara
and Bonneville, joined by the Pacific and Southwestern rail
line, the Mission and adjacent Seed Ranch, the great wheat
ranches extending out into a limitless distance, the county road,
irrigating ditch, telephone poles and lines, bunk and division

houses—function as a powerful force field keeping all elements
of *The Octopus* together.

For someone who argued so vigorously on behalf of a direct
apprehension of life and who postured (albeit not as flamboyantly as his contemporary Californian Jack London) so constantly as a despiser of the genteel, Frank Norris was a bookish
young man who had immersed himself in reading from his
Parisian student days onward. In the literary essays he wrote
while a journalist on the San Francisco *Wave* in the mid-1890s
and in those he wrote in such a rush as a literary columnist in
the year before his untimely death, Norris revealed himself as
a haphazard but energetically developing critic fully capable
of analyzing the patterns, premises, goals, and dynamics of
literature. He poured into *The Octopus* the literary ambitions
and influences of an assimilative, literary lifetime; and the resulting work of fiction shows strong signs of just about every
influence Norris had come under. In *The Octopus*, moreover,
are functioning a half dozen genres, held together by the forward rush of the narrative.

In terms of its literary architectonics, Kenneth Lynn argues,
The Octopus makes little sense. H. Willard Reninger claims it
possesses an Aristotelian structure: a clearly defined beginning,
middle, and end, together with characters who are at once
individuals while also representative of the universals of human
experience. Reninger argues that the book's theme, characters,
and action are in good proportion and energize interaction.
And Walter Taylor feels *The Octopus* is as elegantly structured
as *Tom Jones*.

The major influence on Norris's work and sense of literary
vocation can be traced to Émile Zola (1840–1902), the prodi-
giously energetic journalist, novelist, and social philosopher.
Fluent in French, Norris was rarely without a soft-cover Zola
novel in his jacket pocket during his undergraduate days at
Berkeley. Half humorously, but also with a significant gesture

of intent, he signed many of his letters "The Boy Zola." Zola
inspired in Norris the desire to write with sweep, scale, and
an abundance of accurate detail; to employ fiction as a remorseless engine of sociological diagnosis and as a chronicling
of men and women as biological creatures in their natural set-
tings. As Lars Ahnebrink points out, Norris was especially
indebted to three of Zola's novels in *The Octopus: Germinal*,
the story of a miners' strike; *La Bête humaine*, a railroad novel;
and *La Terre*, a novel of rural life. This influence encompasses
setting, subject matter, and such specific scenes as the spring
plowing, the barn dance, the harvest picnic, the personification
of the railroad (or rather its animalization), Dyke's flight across
the San Joaquin in a stolen railroad engine, and the elaborate
meal served at the Gerard mansion while Mrs. Hooven dies
from starvation on the streets of San Francisco. As Philip
Walker observes, Norris also adopts a number of Zolaesque
literary techniques: a mingling of realism and romanticism, for
example; a use of fixed Homeric epithet, repetition, and re-
current biological metaphor; the employment of an outsider for
the chief point of view; an extensive use of indirect discourse
to suggest motivation; and a proclivity toward thunderous language reaching out toward sublimity.

"The Wheat series," Norris promised literary journalist Isaac
Marcosson, "will be straight naturalism with all the guts I can
get into it." While overtly scientific in its attitudes and pro-
cedures, its relish for facts and unadorned behavior, naturalism, as Zola practiced it, was not a neutral philosophy of human
existence. Quite the contrary, Zola's naturalism sustained at
its center a romantic pessimism regarding human destiny. Despite their best efforts, Zola believed, their brave gestures and
private decencies, human beings were in the long run doomed:
biologically destined for extinction and in the brief intervals of
life that were allotted them crushed invariably by unjust economic and social institutions. Just about everyone in *The Octopus*, it must be noted, ends up dead, broken, sentenced to
life in prison, or, at minimum, badly shaken. Los Muertos
Rancho becomes literally that, the Ranch of the Dead Ones,

strewn with corpses. The women of *The Octopus* end up as
grieving widows, or dead from starvation, or forced into prostitution. Even the innocent female children are damaged, perhaps permanently, by the forces which have destroyed their
parents. All this defeat, incidentally, stands in contrast to the
mixed outcome of another naturalist novel, *Sister Carrie* by
Theodore Dreiser, which Norris, hard at work on *The Octopus*,
read in manuscript in May 1900 and vigorously sponsored for
publication at Doubleday. In *Sister Carrie*, the heroine at least
prevails. All this defeat seems also to work against Norris's
avowed intention—first expressed in a June 1896 essay for the
Wave, "Zola as a Romantic Writer"—to use naturalism as
a vehicle to underscore the essentially romantic nature of life,
by breaking through the pasteboard mark of the Howellsian
Realism ("small passions, restricted emotions, dramas of the
reception-room, tragedies of an afternoon call, crises involving
cups of tea") into broader, deeper, more compelling vistas. But
while Norris might admire the titanic romantic affirmations
and grand resolutions of Victor Hugo and Leo Tolstoy, his
attitude, so Alfred Kazin tells us, suggests "that romanticism
had not yet even begun to express itself fully in America when
it slipped into naturalism." After killing everybody off, Norris
would have a difficult time convincing his readers that since
the Wheat remained, everything was working inevitably for
the good. There is, however, in the symbol of the Wheat as
Norris employs it (as there is also in the huge gold tooth hanging
outside McTeague's dental parlors on Polk Street) something
partaking of the transcendental symbolism of earlier American
romances by Hawthorne, Melville, and Poe: a physical object,
that is, or a living creature (a black mask, a scarlet letter, a
white jacket, a white whale) possessed of mysterious significance almost beyond comprehension, a symbol transcending
plot and character, indeed barely attached to the action, but
containing within itself the final elusive meaning of the story.
As encountered in *The Octopus*, the Wheat is the Life Force,
Mother Nature herself; but how much this is supposed to mean
to all the dead or broken people remains problematic.

In a preface to his novel, Norris promised his readers a three-part Epic of the Wheat. Epics usually emerge just as the eras they celebrate are on the verge of passing forever or becoming transformed into something else. The epic is thus an elegiac form, an act of memory and celebration for what has just been accomplished—such as the frontier which Professor Turner officially announced as passing when Norris was a Berkeley undergraduate. Faced with the lack of challenge and heroic value in contemporary society, many young American intellectuals of Norris's generation, so Kenneth Lynn suggests, turned to either the Middle Ages or an idealized American frontier for imaginative release. Norris did both. In Paris, he haunted museums where he sketched and researched medieval armor, for an article in the *San Francisco Chronicle*. He had a huge canvas set up in his apartment, upon which he planned to execute a massive Battle of Crécy. He virtually memorized Froissart's *Chronicles* and learned enough Old French to enjoy *The Song of Roland* in the original. There was a boldness in the medieval epic, Norris believed, a capacity to present direct experience and heroic encounter, sadly lacking in most contemporary fiction. The American frontier challenged to a comparable epic treatment. In *The Octopus*, the poet Presley dreams of writing a verse epic song of the West that would tell the story of the frontier from the Dakotas to the Mexicos, from Winnipeg to Guadalupe, "a true and fearless setting forth of a passing phase of history." Why should Americans concern themselves exclusively with the epic traditions of Europe, Norris was writing just weeks before his death, when the story of the American frontier challenged writers to create a new *Song of Roland*? It is part of the complexity of *The Octopus* that in it Norris both challenges himself and performs in the matter of epic creation. Presley, the closest we have to a Norris *alter ego*, plans what Norris is also attempting in his novel, a great big frontier epic, energized in part, as Van Wyck Brooks asserts, by Norris's medievalism and by a sense that the frontier, being over, should now be transformed into literature.

Based in part upon the Bay Area poet and educator Edwin

Markham, whose poem of social protest, *The Man with the Hoe*, caused such a sensation when it appeared in the *San Francisco Examiner* on January 8, 1899, Presley is also Norris. Like Norris, Presley is high-strung, college-bred, upper-class; like Norris, Presley loathes the restraints and reticences of the genteel and the trivial bohemianism of San Francisco. He yearns to do something sweeping and bold in the way of literature. Emotionally swept up by the tragic events he witnesses, Presley writes *The Toilers*, a poem of social protest; but he has not yet managed to start *The Song of the West* as he sails for India at the novel's conclusion.

The three main male protagonists of the novel—Presley, Annixter, and Vanamee—dominate the action of *The Octopus* and are in dynamic relationship to each other. Each experiences personal transformations born of suffering in a manner that is typical of epic heroes. As *The Octopus* opens, Presley, Vanamee, and Annixter are each solitaries. Presley is without any love interest whatsoever; Annixter is incapable of love; and Vanamee is deprived of love by death. Annixter, a figure of pure action, experiences the most personal growth, from cynicism and calculating lust to love and marriage, but he does not live to enjoy his new-found happiness. There is a hint at the novel's conclusion that Presley and Annixter's widow Hilma might have a future together when Presley returns from India. Vanamee is thus the only one of the three central protagonists to attain any permanent fulfillment, united as he is with the daughter of his long-lost love in what is for Norris a symbol (somewhat overdone perhaps) of resurrected hope.

Annixter is pragmatic brainpower and energetic action, the essence of the mining and railroad engineers, ranchers, irrigationists, and business entrepreneurs who built the Far West in the last three decades of the nineteenth century. Vanamee embodies a West—in his case the desert and borderlands of the Spanish Southwest—that inspired in many American artists sojourning there an aesthetic mysticism that brought forward into the twentieth century a desert and arroyo version of the transcendentalist fervor of a half century earlier. Solitary, vi-

sionary, obsessed, Vanamee can trace his descent from a dozen
or more similar characters in the writings of Charles Brockden
Brown, Nathaniel Hawthorne, Edgar Allan Poe, and Herman
Melville: the outsider, possessed of extraordinary psychic powers, bearing the burden of a special sorrow.

The leading female characters, moreover—Hilma Tree, the
lost Angéle and her refound daughter, and Minna Hooven—
are also epic types. But it is the sheer scope and ambition of
The Octopus, as Ernest Marchand observes, its length and
largeness of design, its primitive color and cosmic energy, its
theme of the frontier dying before the onslaughts of an emerging
industrialism, that render it worthy of the name epic. Norris,
so Alfred Kazin writes in *On Native Grounds*,

> wrote as if men had never seen California before him, or
> known the joy of growing wheat in those huge fields that
> could take half a day to cross, or of piling enough flour
> on trains to feed a European nation. It is out of the surge
> and greed of that joy that his huge, restless characters
> grow, men so abundantly alive that the narrow life of cities
> and the constraints of the factory system can barely touch
> them. He was the poet of the bonanza, teeming with con-
> fidence, reckless in the face of that almost cosmological
> security that was California to him.

The novel, Frank Norris argued in *The World's Work* for
May 1902 ("The Novel with a Purpose"), comes in three classes:
those that merely tell something (*The Three Musketeers*), those
that both tell something and reveal the inner workings of temperament and character (*Romola*), and those, such as *Les Mis-
érables*, which simultaneously tell, show, and prove something
about society and the human condition. The novel with a purpose is the highest form of novel, writes Norris, because it
probes truth and preaches corrective action. The novel with a
purpose thus becomes "a great force, that works together with
the pulpit and the universities for the good of the people."
Frank Norris was obviously attempting a novel of this third

and higher order. Richard Hofstadter considers *The Octopus* a
major text in the era of investigative reporting, spearheaded
by Norris's former employer, S. S. McClure, that led to the
reforms of the early twentieth-century Progressive period. Experienced journalist that he was, Norris certainly began his
investigations in the field, notebook in hand, as did McClure's
muckraking team of Ida Tarbell, investigating Standard Oil;
Ray Stannard Baker, looking at labor; and Norris's fellow
Californian-turned-New Yorker, Lincoln Steffens, probing the
underlife of big-city political machines. Norris the reporter
got his story and skillfully employed its details. In his pio-
neering biography, Franklin Walker catalogs the real-life persons, places, and events that found their way into *The Octopus*.
But Norris was after more than verisimilitude. He wanted not
just to tell and show—but to prove as well.

The triviality of San Francisco, an important secondary
theme of *The Octopus*, relates directly to Norris's serious conviction of purpose. Although Norris loved San Francisco, re-
settling there just before his death, he savages it in *The Octopus*
with the bitter rejection of a young writer forced to expatriate
to New York to find an atmosphere of serious literary purpose.
Before his move to New York in 1898, Norris fell into a depression over his inability to pursue serious work in the city by the
Golden Gate. Once in New York, however, he stayed close to
his San Francisco friends, and in "Dying Fires" he wrote about
a West Coast writer (very much resembling himself) who ruins
his talent with an overdose of self-conscious New York literary
life. Norris found his vocation in New York and the sponsor-
ship of Howells, but he was still homesick for the city that had
in its own way nurtured him as an aspiring writer and where
he had set most of his fiction, including *McTeague*, which he
subtitled *A Story of San Francisco*. In the San Francisco scenes
of *The Octopus* Norris worked out his ambivalence through the
point of view of Presley. Don Graham has most usefully
mapped the full range and extent of Norris's San Francisco
critique, to include the virtually libelous (by contemporary standards) satirization of well-known San Francisco personalities.

A few years earlier Norris had been palling around San Francisco with *Les Jeunes*, a circle of young aesthetes who published
a charming but inconsequential little magazine, *The Lark*; but
now, in his thirtieth year, he was returning to judge and re-
pudiate idle aestheticism and studio art. Presley is all the more
savage in his judgments, Graham points out, because—like
Norris during his days as a dilatory San Francisco journalist
and would-be short story writer—he, too, had flirted danger-
ously with "the Fake, the eternal, irrepressible Sham" that in
swirls about Mrs. Cedarquist, a character based upon a prominent San Francisco social *doyenne* whom Norris had met
through his mother.

It was one thing, however, for Norris to describe the novel
with a purpose or to satirize those San Franciscans who pursued
a more trivial conception of art. It was another matter altogether to make his novel say something important and honest
about the events it had presented with such power. At the end
of it all—the violent deaths of some half dozen characters, the
eviction of the ranchers from their properties, a life sentence
for Dyke, the hop farmer forced into crime, the enforced prostitution of Minna Hooven, and the continuing triumph of the
railroad oligarchy, symbolized in the lavish dinner party at the
Gerard mansion, for which fresh asparagus is shipped across
the state without regard to cost—Presley tries to make sense
of it all, and fails. Driven to the edge of a total collapse after
the massacre, Presley at first accepts the radical revolutionary
explanation of the saloon keeper Caraher. Ineffectually, he
tries—and fails—to bomb the house of S. Behrman, the railroad's local representative. Presley then calls upon Shelgrim,
president of the P. and S. W., in his San Francisco office, just
as Norris had personally interviewed S. P. President Collis
P. Huntington in New York just months before Huntington's
death. Shelgrim tells Presley that railroads build themselves
just as the wheat grows itself. Rancher and railroader alike
must serve vast impersonal forces of supply and demand. "Men
have only little to do in the whole business," Shelgrim tells
Presley. "Can anyone stop the wheat? Well, then, no more can

I stop the road." Presley stumbles out of Shelgrim's office, his radical certainties shattered. He is next encountered at a railroad executive's dinner party.

There was in Frank Norris, writes Richard Chase, "a tension between Norris the liberal humanist and ardent democrat and Norris the protofascist, complete with a racist view of Anglo-Saxon supremacy, a myth of the superman, and a portentous nihilism" inspired by Kipling, nativism, and a misreading of Nietzsche. *Protofascist* is too strong a term, but Norris did have rightist leanings. As an upper-class Californian, Norris knew that without the Southern Pacific there would have been no established California economy of any significant proportions. As the character Cedarquist points out so convincingly to Presley, Magnus Derrick, and the other ranchers gathered over whiskies at the Bohemian Club in San Francisco, capitalistic economy could be abused, true; but properly employed, it created jobs and, in the example of a properly functioning California wheat industry, was capable of feeding the nations. And besides: if the railroad offered bribes, then so did the ranchers. Norris might have worked for *McClure's Magazine*, but he ultimately considered muckraking too simplistic. Like Presley, he did not have the instinct to betray his class.

Chase is justified, however, in catching more than a hint of racist attitudes in *The Octopus*. Norris heroes are all Americans of old British stock. The Spanish and the Portuguese are left to club to death the rounded-up jack rabbits, while the Anglo-Saxons draw back; for "the hot, degenerate blood of Portuguese, Mexican, and mixed Spaniard boiled up in excitement at this wholesale slaughter." If Stuart L. Burns is correct, then Norris came as close as he dared to suggest that the Mexican priest Father Sarria was the Other, responsible for Angéle Varian's rape and subsequent death in childbirth. The arch villain S. Behrman, a Jew, provides Norris with a figure who in the classic pattern of anti-Semitism can be scapegoated and punished while his non-Jewish employees are let off more easily. However distasteful, these flawed attitudes are not so central as to compromise the integrity of *The Octopus*.

The novel's conclusion, on the other hand, has since publication been faulted as at best a bromide and at worst a sellout. ". . . I've tried to accelerate it steadily," Norris wrote Isaac Marcosson on September 13, 1900, three months before completing his manuscript, "till at the last you are—I hope—just whirling and galloping and tearing along till you come *bang!* all of a sudden to a great big crushing END, something that will slam you right between your eyes and knock you off your feet . . ." What Norris ended up with, however, was something more complex and philosophical. In an effort to regain his health and perspective, a severely strained Presley sails to India aboard the wheat tanker *Swanhilda* while, unbeknownst to anyone, S. Behrman's body lies in the hold, buried under tons of wheat. Meditating alone on deck on a starry night as the *Swanhilda* sails past the south central California coast where the tragic events of the novel have recently transpired, Presley affirms to himself that, finally, no matter what has happened, the Wheat remained, truth in the end prevails, "and all things, surely, inevitably, resistlessly work together for good."

Such a conclusion, wrote Wallace Rice in the first major review *The Octopus* received, would "justify a Nero and damn an Antonine." A ridiculous theory, argues Granville Hicks; "it destroys the emotional effect of the book, for it means that the contemptible Behrman has worked as surely for good as the noble Derrick, the impulsive Annixter, or the violent Dyke." It has also been argued that the conslusion was Presley's, not Norris's, and should be viewed as a species of irony, Norris's little joke on the soft-headed, sentimental poet.

What Norris actually had in mind has been superbly set forth by Donald Pizer, Frank Norris's leading interpreter: As an undergraduate at Berkeley, Norris studied zoology and geology under the well-known scientist Joseph Le Conte (1823–1901). Trained at Harvard under Louis Agassiz, Le Conte exercised great influence at Berkeley through natural history courses in which he attempted to reconcile evolution and Christianity. According to Le Conte's philosophy of evolutionary theism— articulated in such books as *Religion and Science* (1874) and

Evolution, Its Nature, Its Evidences, and Its Relations to Religious Thought (1888)—the Divine Will was operative in nature through the evolutionary mechanism. Science offered one perspective on nature; religion, another; but both science and religion sought to comprehend the will of God in the natural universe. Evil, Le Conte believed—the disappearance of a species, a tidal wave, an exploding volcano, the deaths of ranchers defending their property against the railroad—could never be considered as an isolated phenomenon. Nature might break some, but only for a long-range evolutionary good. "Greed, cruelty, selfishness, and inhumanity are short-lived," thus Le Conte's student writes at the conclusion to *The Octopus:* "the individual suffers, but the race goes on. Annixter dies, but in a far distant corner of the world a thousand lives are saved. The larger view always and through all shams, all wickednesses, discovers the Truth that will, in the end, prevail, and all things, surely, inevitably, resistlessly work together for good."

Facile optimism or profound acceptance? Whatever assessment is made, Le Conte's ideas influenced Norris as he sought to prove something in his novel of purpose. For Norris, the Wheat was at once the product and the symbol of the Divine Force sustaining all creation. The Wheat prevailed, instructed—and healed. On the very same spring night that the wheat sprouts through the soil, Presley writes his poem, Vanamee has a new Angéle restored to him, and Annixter experiences a breakthrough in his blocked emotional and moral life. Each has learned a special lesson from the Wheat, which is to say, nature herself. Each has been reconciled and made more complete. From this perspective, S. Behrman's death by wheat is no mere accident, or even gratuitous melodrama, but only the result of natural justice.

While not directly in the main line of action, the Vanamee/Angéle subplot advances Norris's most philosophically (even theologically) ambitious gloss on the problem of evil that proves so personally shattering to Presley. It is Vanamee who personally experiences the truth of First Corinthians, 15:36–44, cited to him by Father Sarria in the Mission garden: that what is most enduring in human beings never dies, whatever happens to their mortal bodies; that the wheat, dying under the winter ground, brings forth new life in the spring. "The whole," Vanamee tells Presley in their final meeting, "is, in the end, perfect."

Presley, however, struggles with his doubts, as do the vast majority of Norris's readers. While neither dishonest nor fatuous as some critics would have it, Norris's resolutions as voiced through Vanamee and in the last paragraphs by Presley are doomed to dissatisfy because no novel or novelist can answer such profound questions—or prove them, to use Norris's special terminology. A novelist can only probe the human condition through plot, character, action, symbol, idea, and the other resources of fiction, to include the capacity of the novel to recreate the world anew according to a specific poetic vision, and thereby prove by indirection. Critics have been overly harsh on Norris for using Presley as a vehicle through which to struggle toward assent. What would they prefer? That Presley collapse completely under the burden of his confusion? Or curse God and die, his face turned to the wall? Or cope bleakly in a posture of existentialist resignation? In recent times, there have been novels aplenty with such resolutions. *The Octopus* must be judged on its own terms. These terms are partly Zolaesque naturalist; hence vast impersonal forces turn the wheels of fate and innocent people suffer. But Norris's premises are also Romantic; hence nature regenerates and heals as well as destroys. And since Norris was a believer, his premises are Judeo-Christian as well; hence faith and hope are always possibilities. *The Octopus* has been described, justifiably, as the most ambitious novel up to its time since *Moby-Dick:* ambitious in terms of its mighty social and philosophical themes—the clash of frontier and monopoly, the impersonal forces represented by technology and corporate structures, the problem of social justice, and the reconciling power of nature.

In July 1902 Frank and Jeanette Norris, accompanied by their six-month-old daughter, Jeannette Junior (whom they nicknamed Billy), moved back to San Francisco permanently. "Happiness in this world," Frank had recently told his younger brother, Charles, "is being able to devote all your time to the work you love; nothing else matters." With the comparative success of *McTeague* and the sales of *The Octopus* pushing past 33,000 by the middle of 1902, Norris felt that the profession of full-time authorship was at long last within his grasp. As early as March 1899, Norris was admitting to a plan, suggested by William Dean Howells, first to establish his literary connections in New York, then to set up as a writer based in San Francisco. With reputation and income established, Howells had told Norris, a literary man could work anywhere that was personally congenial. Having just completed the second volume of the Wheat trilogy, *The Pit* (posthumously published in 1903 and selling 95,000 copies in its first trade edition), Norris planned to sail with Jeannette around the world on a tramp steamer to gather material for *The Wolf*, the last of the Wheat series. *The Wolf* completed, Norris intended to write a trilogy of novels set around the Battle of Gettysburg, which he considered the supreme moment in American history. Frank and Jeanette also purchased ten acres and a log cabin in the redwoods of the Santa Cruz Mountains south of San Francisco. They named the cabin *Quien Sabe*, after Annixter's ranch in *The Octopus*. Norris intended to use *Quien Sabe* as a summer writing studio before eventually enlarging it into a permanent home.

When Jeannette suffered an attack of appendicitis in late September, Norris postponed their tramp steamer voyage until his wife could recover. On the evening of October 20, 1902, at the couple's home at 1921 Broderick Street, San Francisco, Frank Norris suffered an acute attack of indigestion. He resisted Jeannette's suggestion that he go to the hospital. At three the next morning, Norris awoke in agony. Jeannette had him rushed to Mount Zion Hospital. For three days Norris struggled against an advanced state of general peritonitis, complicated by gangrene and a perforated appendix. The fevers he had suffered in South Africa and Cuba, however, had severely weakened his constitution. Jeannette spent the night of October 24–25 at his bedside. Frank Norris, aged thirty-two, died of a ruptured appendix and kidney failure at 9:15 on Saturday morning the 25th. The funeral was held the following Monday at St. Luke's Episcopal Church in San Francisco. Internment was at the Mountain View Cemetery in Oakland.

Hearing of Frank Norris's death, Hamlin Garland wanted to confront Norris's physician and say: "See what an irreparable injury to American literature you have wrought!" Had Norris lived, his talent might very well have continued to grow and to express itself down through the 1940s. Theodore Dreiser, whom Norris had discovered while working as a reader at Doubleday, might have had good company; and F. Scott Fitzgerald, who admired Norris's work enormously, might have had the same sort of friend and mentor Norris enjoyed in Howells. All this, however, is speculation. Norris died at thirty-two and a major career was tragically ended. Left behind was an astonishingly rich and diverse legacy for a writer dying so young: seven novels (two published posthumously), 74 short stories, 154 articles and sketches, some poetry, four translations from the French, and a book of posthumously published letters.

Norris believed that *McTeague* ("The Dentist," he called it) was his best work to date. Most obituary assessments, however, ranked *McTeague* and *The Octopus* equally. Writing in the *North American Review*, William Dean Howells was first to compare *The Octopus*—which Howells praised for its Homeric breadth, its powerful play of passion and ideas—with *Moby-Dick*. *The Octopus*, Jack London believed, was the fully achieved Epic of the West that his generation of writers felt compelled to produce. There had been doubts that Norris could pull it off, London admitted (". . . who is this Presley but Norris, grappling in keen travail with his problem of *The Octopus*, and doubting often, as we of the West have doubted?"); but Norris had "produced results, Titantic results." Whatever faults *The Octopus* might possess, as a whole it is greater than any fault in its parts. It is, as Kenneth Lynn observes, a penetration "to the heart of the American consciousness at a crucial moment in history." Frank Norris was after the big questions, the major issues of American life. He believed that the novel provided the best twentieth-century forum for such investigations. He possessed, observes Alfred Kazin, "an energy almost worthy of the teeming, world-changing forces of the new century." In *The Octopus* Frank Norris greeted the new century with the salute—and the challenge—of ambitious literature.

KEVIN STARR

The Octopus

BOOK I

I

Just after passing Caraher's saloon, on the County Road that ran south from Bonneville, and that divided the Broderson ranch from that of Los Muertos, Presley was suddenly aware of the faint and prolonged blowing of a steam whistle that he knew must come from the railroad shops near the depot at Bonneville. In starting out from the ranch house that morning, he had forgotten his watch, and was now perplexed to know whether the whistle was blowing for twelve or for one o'clock. He hoped the former. Early that morning he had decided to make a long excursion through the neighbouring country, partly on foot and partly on his bicycle, and now noon was come already, and as yet he had hardly started. As he was leaving the house after breakfast, Mrs. Derrick had asked him to go for the mail at Bonneville, and he had not been able to refuse.

He took a firmer hold of the cork grips of his handlebars—the road being in a wretched condition after the recent hauling of the crop—and quickened his pace. He told himself that, no matter what the time was, he would not stop for luncheon at the ranch house, but would push on to Guadalajara and have a Spanish dinner at Solotari's, as he had originally planned.

There had not been much of a crop to haul that year. Half of the wheat on the Broderson ranch had failed entirely, and Derrick himself had hardly raised more than enough to supply seed for the winter's sowing. But such little hauling as there had been had reduced the roads thereabouts to a lamentable condition, and, during the dry season of the past few months, the layer of dust had deepened and thickened to such an extent that more than once Presley was obliged to dismount and trudge along on foot, pushing his bicycle in front of him.

It was the last half of September, the very end of the dry season, and all Tulare County, all the vast reaches of the San Joaquin Valley—in fact all South Central California, was bone dry, parched, and baked and crisped after four months of cloudless weather, when the day seemed always at noon, and the sun blazed white hot over the valley from the Coast Range in the west to the foothills of the Sierras in the east.

As Presley drew near to the point where what was known as the Lower Road struck off through the Rancho de Los Muertos, leading on to Guadalajara, he came upon one of the county watering-tanks, a great, iron-hooped tower of wood, straddling clumsily on its four uprights by the roadside. Since the day of its completion, the storekeepers and retailers of Bonneville had painted their advertisements upon it. It was a landmark. In that reach of level fields, the white letters upon it could be read for miles. A watering-trough stood near by, and, as he was very thirsty, Presley resolved to stop for a moment to get a drink.

He drew abreast of the tank and halted there, leaning his bicycle against the fence. A couple of men in white overalls were repainting the surface of the tank, seated on swinging platforms that hung by hooks from the roof. They were painting a sign—an advertisement. It was all but finished and read, " S. Behrman, Real Estate, Mortgages, Main Street, Bonneville, Opposite the Post Office." On the horse-trough that stood in the shadow of the tank was another freshly painted inscription: " S. Behrman Has Something To Say To *You*."

As Presley straightened up after drinking from the faucet at one end of the horse-trough, the watering-cart itself laboured into view around the turn of the Lower Road. Two mules and two horses, white with dust, strained leisurely in the traces, moving at a snail's pace, their limp ears marking the time; while perched high upon the seat, under a yellow cotton wagon umbrella, Presley recognised Hooven, one of Derrick's tenants, a German, whom every one called " Bismarck," an excitable little man with a perpetual grievance and an endless flow of broken English.

" Hello, Bismarck," said Presley, as Hooven brought his team to a standstill by the tank, preparatory to re-filling.

" Yoost der men I look for, Mist'r Praicely," cried the other, twisting the reins around the brake. " Yoost one minute, you wait, hey? I wanta talk mit you."

Presley was impatient to be on his way again. A little more time wasted, and the day would be lost. He had nothing to do with the management of the ranch, and if Hooven wanted any advice from him, it was so much breath wasted. These uncouth brutes of farm-hands and petty ranchers, grimed with the soil they worked upon, were odious to him beyond words. Never could he feel in sympathy with them, nor with their lives, their ways, their marriages, deaths, bickerings, and all the monotonous round of their sordid existence.

" Well, you must be quick about it, Bismarck," he answered sharply. " I'm late for dinner, as it is."

" Soh, now. Two minuten, und I be mit you." He

drew down the overhanging spout of the tank to the
vent in the circumference of the cart and pulled the chain
that let out the water. Then he climbed down from the
seat, jumping from the tire of the wheel, and taking Presley by the arm led him a few steps down the road.

"Say," he began. "Say, I want to hef some converzations mit you. Yoost der men I want to see. Say,
Caraher, he tole me dis morgen—say, he tole me Mist'r
Derrick gowun to farm der whole demn rench hisseluf der
next yahr. No more tenants. Say, Caraher, he tole me
all der tenants get der sach; Mist'r Derrick gowun to
work der whole demn rench hisseluf, hey? *Me*, I get der
sach alzoh, hey? You hef hear about dose ting? Say,
me, I hef on der ranch been sieben yahr—seven yahr.
Do I alzoh——"

"You'll have to see Derrick himself or Harran about
that, Bismarck," interrupted Presley, trying to draw
away. "That's something outside of me entirely."

But Hooven was not to be put off. No doubt he had
been meditating his speech all the morning, formulating
his words, preparing his phrases.

"Say, no, no," he continued. "Me, I wanta stay bei
der place; seven yahr I hef stay. Mist'r Derrick, he
doand want dot I should be ge-sacked. Who, den, will
der ditch ge-tend? Say, you tell 'um Bismarck hef gotta
sure stay bei der place. Say, you hef der pull mit der
Governor. You speak der gut word for me."

"Harran is the man that has the pull with his father,
Bismarck," answered Presley. "You get Harran to
speak for you, and you're all right."

"Sieben yahr I hef stay," protested Hooven, "and
who will der ditch ge-tend, und alle dem cettles drive?"

"Well, Harran's your man," answered Presley, preparing to mount his bicycle.

"Say, you hef hear about dose ting?"

"I don't hear about anything, Bismarck. I don't know the first thing about how the ranch is run."

"*Und der pipe-line ge-mend*," Hooven burst out, suddenly remembering a forgotten argument. He waved an arm. "Ach, der pipe-line bei der Mission Greek, und der waäter-hole for dose cettles. Say, he doand doo ut *himselluf*, berhaps, I doand tink."

"Well, talk to Harran about it."

"Say, he doand farm der whole demn rench bei hisseluf. Me, I gotta stay."

But on a sudden the water in the cart gushed over the sides from the vent in the top with a smart sound of splashing. Hooven was forced to turn his attention to it. Presley got his wheel under way.

"I hef some converzations mit Herran," Hooven called after him. "He doand doo ut bei hisseluf, den, Mist'r Derrick; ach, no. I stay bei der rench to drive dose cettles."

He climbed back to his seat under the wagon umbrella, and, as he started his team again with great cracks of his long whip, turned to the painters still at work upon the sign and declared with some defiance:

"Sieben yahr; yais, sir, seiben yahr I hef been on dis rench. Git oop, you mule you, hoop!"

Meanwhile Presley had turned into the Lower Road. He was now on Derrick's land, division No. 1, or, as it was called, the Home ranch, of the great Los Muertos Rancho. The road was better here, the dust laid after the passage of Hooven's watering-cart, and, in a few minutes, he had come to the ranch house itself, with its white picket fence, its few flower beds, and grove of eucalyptus trees. On the lawn at the side of the house, he saw Harran in the act of setting out the automatic sprinkler. In the shade of the house, by the porch, were two or three of the greyhounds, part of the pack that were used to hunt down jack-rabbits, and Godfrey, Harran's prize deerhound.

Presley wheeled up the driveway and met Harran by the horse-block. Harran was Magnus Derrick's youngest son, a very well-looking young fellow of twenty-three or twenty-five. He had the fine carriage that marked his father, and still further resembled him in that he had the Derrick nose—hawk-like and prominent, such as one sees in the later portraits of the Duke of Wellington. He was blond, and incessant exposure to the sun had, instead of tanning him brown, merely heightened the colour of his cheeks. His yellow hair had a tendency to curl in a forward direction, just in front of the ears.

Beside him, Presley made the sharpest of contrasts. Presley seemed to have come of a mixed origin; appeared to have a nature more composite, a temperament more complex. Unlike Harran Derrick, he seemed more of a character than a type. The sun had browned his face till it was almost swarthy. His eyes were a dark brown, and his forehead was the forehead of the intellectual, wide and high, with a certain unmistakable lift about it that argued education, not only of himself, but of his people before him. The impression conveyed by his mouth and chin was that of a delicate and highly sensitive nature, the lips thin and loosely shut together, the chin small and rather receding. One guessed that Presley's refinement had been gained only by a certain loss of strength. One expected to find him nervous, introspective, to discover that his mental life was not at all the result of impressions and sensations that came to him from without, but rather of thoughts and reflections germinating from within. Though morbidly sensitive to changes in his physical surroundings, he would be slow to act upon such sensations, would not prove impulsive, not because he was sluggish, but because he was merely irresolute. It could be foreseen that morally he was of that sort who avoid evil through good taste, lack of decision, and want of opportunity. His temperament was that of the poet; when he told himself he had been thinking, he deceived himself. He had, on such occasions, been only brooding.

Some eighteen months before this time, he had been threatened with consumption, and, taking advantage of a standing invitation on the part of Magnus Derrick, had come to stay in the dry, even climate of the San Joaquin for an indefinite length of time. He was thirty years old, and had graduated and post-graduated with high honours from an Eastern college, where he had devoted himself to a passionate study of literature, and, more especially, of poetry.

It was his insatiable ambition to write verse. But up to this time, his work had been fugitive, ephemeral, a note here and there, heard, appreciated, and forgotten. He was in search of a subject; something magnificent, he did not know exactly what; some vast, tremendous theme, heroic, terrible, to be unrolled in all the thundering progression of hexameters.

But whatever he wrote, and in whatever fashion, Presley was determined that his poem should be of the West, that world's frontier of Romance, where a new race, a new people—hardy, brave, and passionate—were building an empire; where the tumultuous life ran like fire from dawn to dark, and from dark to dawn again, primitive, brutal, honest, and without fear. Something (to his idea not much) had been done to catch at that life in passing, but its poet had not yet arisen. The few sporadic attempts, thus he told himself, had only touched the keynote. He strove for the diapason, the great song that should embrace in itself a whole epoch, a complete era, the voice of an entire people, wherein all people

should be included—they and their legends, their folk
lore, their fightings, their loves and their lusts, their
blunt, grim humour, their stoicism under stress, their
adventures, their treasures found in a day and gambled
in a night, their direct, crude speech, their generosity and
cruelty, their heroism and bestiality, their religion and
profanity, their self-sacrifice and obscenity—a true and
fearless setting forth of a passing phase of history, uncompromising, sincere; each group in its proper environment; the valley, the plain, and the mountain; the ranch,
the range, and the mine—all this, all the traits and types
of every community from the Dakotas to the Mexicos,
from Winnipeg to Guadalupe, gathered together, swept
together, welded and riven together in one single,
mighty song, the Song of the West. That was what he
dreamed, while things without names—thoughts for
which no man had yet invented words, terrible formless
shapes, vague figures, colossal, monstrous, distorted—
whirled at a gallop through his imagination.

As Harran came up, Presley reached down into the
pouches of the sun-bleached shooting coat he wore and
drew out and handed him the packet of letters and
papers.

"Here's the mail. I think I shall go on."

"But dinner is ready," said Harran; "we are just,
sitting down."

Presley shook his head. "No, I'm in a hurry. Perhaps I shall have something to eat at Guadalajara. I
shall be gone all day."

He delayed a few moments longer, tightening a loose
nut on his forward wheel, while Harran, recognising his
father's handwriting on one of the envelopes, slit it open
and cast his eye rapidly over its pages.

"The Governor is coming home," he exclaimed, " to-
morrow morning on the early train; wants me to meet

him with the team at Guadalajara; *and*," he cried between his clenched teeth, as he continued to read, " we've lost the case."

" What case? Oh, in the matter of rates? "

Harran nodded, his eyes flashing, his face growing suddenly scarlet.

" Ulsteen gave his decision yesterday," he continued, reading from his father's letter. " He holds, Ulsteen does, that ' grain rates as low as the new figure would amount to confiscation of property, and that, on such a basis, the railroad could not be operated at a legitimate profit. As he is powerless to legislate in the matter, he can only put the rates back at what they originally were before the commissioners made the cut, and it is so ordered.' That's our friend S. Behrman again," added Harran, grinding his teeth. " He was up in the city the whole of the time the new schedule was being drawn, and he and Ulsteen and the Railroad Commission were as thick as thieves. He has been up there all this last week, too, doing the railroad's dirty work, and backing Ulsteen up. ' Legitimate profit, legitimate profit,' " he broke out. " Can we raise wheat at a legitimate profit with a tariff of four dollars a ton for moving it two hundred miles to tide-water, with wheat at eighty-seven cents? Why not hold us up with a gun in our faces, and say, ' hands up,' and be done with it? "

He dug his boot-heel into the ground and turned away to the house abruptly, cursing beneath his breath.

" By the way," Presley called after him, " Hooven wants to see you. He asked me about this idea of the Governor's of getting along without the tenants this year. Hooven wants to stay to tend the ditch and look after the stock. I told him to see you."

Harran, his mind full of other things, nodded to say he understood. Presley only waited till he had disap-

peared indoors, so that he might not seem too indifferent
to his trouble; then, remounting, struck at once into a
brisk pace, and, turning out from the carriage gate, held
on swiftly down the Lower Road, going in the direction
of Guadalajara. These matters, these eternal fierce
bickerings between the farmers of the San Joaquin and
the Pacific and Southwestern Railroad irritated him and
wearied him. He cared for none of these things. They
did not belong to his world. In the picture of that huge
romantic West that he saw in his imagination, these
dissensions made the one note of harsh colour that refused to enter into the great scheme of harmony. It
was material, sordid, deadly commonplace. But, however he strove to shut his eyes to it or his ears to it, the
thing persisted and persisted. The romance seemed
complete up to that point. There it broke, there it
failed, there it became realism, grim, unlovely, unyield-
ing. To be true—and it was the first article of his creed
to be unflinchingly true—he could not ignore it. All the
noble poetry of the ranch—the valley—seemed in his
mind to be marred and disfigured by the presence of
certain immovable facts. Just what he wanted, Presley
hardly knew. On one hand, it was his ambition to
portray life as he saw it—directly, frankly, and through
no medium of personality or temperament. But, on the
other hand, as well, he wished to see everything through
a rose-coloured mist—a mist that dulled all harsh outlines, all crude and violent colours. He told himself
that, as a part of the people, he loved the people and
sympathised with their hopes and fears, and joys and
griefs; and yet Hooven, grimy and perspiring, with his
perpetual grievance and his contracted horizon, only revolted him. He had set himself the task of giving true,
absolutely true, poetical expression to the life of the
ranch, and yet, again and again, he brought up against

the railroad, that stubborn iron barrier against which
his romance shattered itself to froth and disintegrated,
flying spume. His heart went out to the people, and his
groping hand met that of a slovenly little Dutchman,
whom it was impossible to consider seriously. He
searched for the True Romance, and, in the end, found
grain rates and unjust freight tariffs.

"But the stuff is *here*," he muttered, as he sent his
wheel rumbling across the bridge over Broderson
Creek. "The romance, the real romance, is here somewhere. I'll get hold of it yet."

He shot a glance about him as if in search of the inspiration. By now he was not quite half way across the
northern and narrowest corner of Los Muertos, at this
point some eight miles wide. He was still on the Home
ranch. A few miles to the south he could just make out
the line of wire fence that separated it from the third division; and to the north, seen faint and blue through the
haze and shimmer of the noon sun, a long file of telegraph poles showed the line of the railroad and marked
Derrick's northeast boundary. The road over which
Presley was travelling ran almost diametrically straight.
In front of him, but at a great distance, he could make
out the giant live-oak and the red roof of Hoven's barn
that stood near it.

All about him the country was flat. In all directions
he could see for miles. The harvest was just over.
Nothing but stubble remained on the ground. With the
one exception of the live-oak by Hooven's place, there
was nothing green in sight. The wheat stubble was of
a dirty yellow; the ground, parched, cracked, and dry,
of a cheerless brown. By the roadside the dust lay thick
and grey, and, on either hand, stretching on toward the
horizon, losing itself in a mere smudge in the distance,
ran the illimitable parallels of the wire fence. And that

was all; that and the burnt-out blue of the sky and the
steady shimmer of the heat.

The silence was infinite. After the harvest, small
though that harvest had been, the ranches seemed
asleep. It was as though the earth, after its period of
reproduction, its pains of labour, had been delivered of
the fruit of its loins, and now slept the sleep of exhaustion.

It was the period between seasons, when nothing was
being done, when the natural forces seemed to hang
suspended. There was no rain, there was no wind,
there was no growth, no life; the very stubble had no
force even to rot. The sun alone moved.

Toward two o'clock, Presley reached Hooven's
place, two or three grimy frame buildings, infested with
a swarm of dogs. A hog or two wandered aimlessly
about. Under a shed by the barn, a broken-down seeder
lay rusting to its ruin. But overhead, a mammoth live-
oak, the largest tree in all the country-side, towered
superb and magnificent. Grey bunches of mistletoe and
festoons of trailing moss hung from its bark. From its
lowest branch hung Hooven's meat-safe, a square box,
faced with wire screens.

What gave a special interest to Hooven's was the fact
that here was the intersection of the Lower Road and
Derrick's main irrigating ditch, a vast trench not yet
completed, which he and Annixter, who worked the
Quien Sabe ranch, were jointly constructing. It ran directly across the road and at right angles to it, and lay a
deep groove in the field between Hooven's and the town
of Guadalajara, some three miles farther on. Besides
this, the ditch was a natural boundary between two divisions of the Los Muertos ranch, the first and fourth.

Presley now had the choice of two routes. His ob-
jective point was the spring at the headwaters of Broder-

son Creek, in the hills on the eastern side of the Quien
Sabe ranch. The trail afforded him a short cut thitherward. As he passed the house, Mrs. Hooven came to
the door, her little daughter Hilda, dressed in a boy's
overalls and clumsy boots, at her skirts. Minna, her
oldest daughter, a very pretty girl, whose love affairs
were continually the talk of all Los Muertos, was visible
through a window of the house, busy at the week's
washing. Mrs. Hooven was a faded, colourless woman,
middle-aged and commonplace, and offering not the
least characteristic that would distinguish her from a
thousand other women of her class and kind. She
nodded to Presley, watching him with a stolid gaze from
under her arm, which she held across her forehead to
shade her eyes.

But now Presley exerted himself in good earnest.
His bicycle flew. He resolved that after all he would go
to Guadalajara. He crossed the bridge over the irrigating ditch with a brusque spurt of hollow sound, and shot
forward down the last stretch of the Lower Road that
yet intervened between Hooven's and the town. He was
on the fourth division of the ranch now, the only one
whereon the wheat had been successful, no doubt because of the Little Mission Creek that ran through it.
But he no longer occupied himself with the landscape.
His only concern was to get on as fast as possible. He
had looked forward to spending nearly the whole day on
the crest of the wooded hills in the northern corner of
the Quien Sabe ranch, reading, idling, smoking his pipe.
But now he would do well if he arrived there by the middle of the afternoon. In a few moments he had reached
the line fence that marked the limits of the ranch. Here
were the railroad tracks, and just beyond—a huddled
mass of roofs, with here and there an adobe house on its
outskirts—the little town of Guadalajara. Nearer at

hand, and directly in front of Presley, were the freight and passenger depots of the P. and S. W., painted in the grey and white, which seemed to be the official colours of all the buildings owned by the corporation. The station was deserted. No trains passed at this hour. From the direction of the ticket window, Presley heard the unsteady chittering of the telegraph key. In the shadow of one of the baggage trucks upon the platform, the great yellow cat that belonged to the agent dozed complacently, her paws tucked under her body. Three flat cars, loaded with bright-painted farming machines, were on the siding above the station, while, on the switch below, a huge freight engine that lacked its cowcatcher sat back upon its monstrous driving-wheels, motionless, solid, drawing long breaths that were punctuated by the subdued sound of its steam-pump clicking at exact intervals.

But evidently it had been decreed that Presley should be stopped at every point of his ride that day, for, as he was pushing his bicycle across the tracks, he was surprised to hear his name called. "Hello, there, Mr. Presley. What's the good word?"

Presley looked up quickly, and saw Dyke, the engineer, leaning on his folded arms from the cab window of the freight engine. But at the prospect of this further delay, Presley was less troubled. Dyke and he were well acquainted and the best of friends. The picturesqueness of the engineer's life was always attractive to Presley, and more than once he had ridden on Dyke's engine between Guadalajara and Bonneville. Once, even, he had made the entire run between the latter town and San Francisco in the cab.

Dyke's home was in Guadalajara. He lived in one of the remodelled 'dobe cottages, where his mother kept house for him. His wife had died some five years before this time, leaving him a little daughter, Sidney, to bring up as best he could. Dyke himself was a heavy built, well-looking fellow, nearly twice the weight of Presley, with great shoulders and massive, hairy arms, and a tremendous, rumbling voice.

" Hello, old man," answered Presley, coming up to the engine. " What are you doing about here at this time of day? I thought you were on the night service this month."

" We've changed about a bit," answered the other. " Come up here and sit down, and get out of the sun. They've held us here to wait orders," he explained, as Presley, after leaning his bicycle against the tender, climbed to the fireman's seat of worn green leather. " They are changing the run of one of the crack passenger engines down below, and are sending her up to Fresno. There was a smash of some kind on the Bakersfield division, and she's to hell and gone behind her time. I suppose when she comes, she'll come a-humming. It will be stand clear and an open track all the way to Fresno. They have held me here to let her go by."

He took his pipe, an old T. D. clay, but coloured to a beautiful shiny black, from the pocket of his jumper and filled and lit it.

" Well, I don't suppose you object to being held here," observed Presley. " Gives you a chance to visit your mother and the little girl."

" And precisely they choose this day to go up to Sacramento," answered Dyke. " Just my luck. Went up to visit my brother's people. By the way, my brother may come down here—locate here, I mean—and go into the hop-raising business. He's got an option on five hundred acres just back of the town here. He says there's going to be money in hops. I don't know; maybe I'll go in with him."

"Why, what's the matter with railroading?"

Dyke drew a couple of puffs on his pipe, and fixed Presley with a glance.

"There's this the matter with it," he said; "I'm fired."

"Fired! You!" exclaimed Presley, turning abruptly toward him.

"That's what I'm telling you," returned Dyke grimly.

"You don't mean it. Why, what for, Dyke?"

"Now, *you* tell me what for," growled the other savagely. "Boy and man, I've worked for the P. and S. W. for over ten years, and never one yelp of a complaint did I ever hear from them. They know damn well they've not got a steadier man on the road. And more than that, more than that, I don't belong to the Brotherhood. And when the strike came along, I stood by them —stood by the company. *You* know that. And you know, and they know, that at Sacramento that time, I ran my train according to schedule, with a gun in each hand, never knowing when I was going over a mined culvert, and there was talk of giving me a gold watch at the time. To hell with their gold watches! I want ordinary justice and fair treatment. And now, when hard times come along, and they are cutting wages, what do they do? Do they make any discrimination in my case? Do they remember the man that stood by them and risked his life in their service? No. They cut my pay down just as off-hand as they do the pay of any dirty little wiper in the yard. Cut me along with—listen to this—cut me along with men that they had *black-listed;* strikers that they took back because they were short of hands." He drew fiercely on his pipe. "I went to them, yes, I did; I went to the General Office, and ate dirt. I told them I was a family man, and that I didn't see how

I was going to get along on the new scale, and I reminded them of my service during the strike. The swine told me that it wouldn't be fair to discriminate in favour of one man, and that the cut must apply to all their employees alike. Fair! " he shouted with laughter. "Fair! Hear the P. and S. W. talking about fairness and discrimination. That's good, that is. Well, I got furious. I was a fool, I suppose. I told them that, in justice to myself, I wouldn't do first-class work for third-class pay. And they said, ' Well, Mr. Dyke, you know what you can do.' Well, I did know. I said, ' I'll ask for my time, if you please,' and they gave it to me just as if they were glad to be shut of me. So there you are, Presley. That's the P. & S. W. Railroad Company of California. I am on my last run now."

" Shameful," declared Presley, his sympathies all aroused, now that the trouble concerned a friend of his. " It's shameful, Dyke. But," he added, an idea occurring to him, " that don't shut you out from work. There are other railroads in the State that are not controlled by the P. and S. W."

Dyke smote his knee with his clenched fist.

" *Name one.*"

Presley was silent. Dyke's challenge was unanswerable. There was a lapse in their talk, Presley drumming on the arm of the seat, meditating on this injustice; Dyke looking off over the fields beyond the town, his frown lowering, his teeth rasping upon his pipestem. The station agent came to the door of the depot, stretching and yawning. On ahead of the engine, the empty rails of the track, reaching out toward the horizon, threw off visible layers of heat. The telegraph key clicked incessantly.

" So I'm going to quit," Dyke remarked after a while, his anger somewhat subsided. " My brother and I will take up this hop ranch. I've saved a good deal in the last ten years, and there ought to be money in hops."

Presley went on, remounting his bicycle, wheeling silently through the deserted streets of the decayed and dying Mexican town. It was the hour of the siesta. Nobody was about. There was no business in the town. It was too close to Bonneville for that. Before the railroad came, and in the days when the raising of cattle was the great industry of the country, it had enjoyed a fierce and brilliant life. Now it was moribund. The drug store, the two bar-rooms, the hotel at the corner of the old Plaza, and the shops where Mexican "curios" were sold to those occasional Eastern tourists who came to visit the Mission of San Juan, sufficed for the town's activity.

At Solotari's, the restaurant on the Plaza, diagonally across from the hotel, Presley ate his long-deferred Mexican dinner—an omelette in Spanish-Mexican style, frijoles and tortillas, a salad, and a glass of white wine. In a corner of the room, during the whole course of his dinner, two young Mexicans (one of whom was astonishingly handsome, after the melodramatic fashion of his race) and an old fellow, the centenarian of the town, decrepit beyond belief, sang an interminable love-song to the accompaniment of a guitar and an accordion.

These Spanish-Mexicans, decayed, picturesque, vicious, and romantic, never failed to interest Presley. A few of them still remained in Guadalajara, drifting from the saloon to the restaurant, and from the restaurant to the Plaza, relics of a former generation, standing for a different order of things, absolutely idle, living God knew how, happy with their cigarette, their guitar, their glass of mescal, and their siesta. The centenarian remembered Fremont and Governor Alvarado, and the bandit Jésus Tejéda, and the days when Los Muertos

was a Spanish grant, a veritable principality, leagues in
extent, and when there was never a fence from Visalia
to Fresno. Upon this occasion, Presley offered the old
man a drink of mescal, and excited him to talk of the
things he remembered. Their talk was in Spanish, a
language with which Presley was familiar.

" De La Cuesta held the grant of Los Muertos in those
days," the centenarian said; "a grand man. He had
the power of life and death over his people, and there was
no law but his word. There was no thought of wheat
then, you may believe. It was all cattle in those days,
sheep, horses—steers, not so many—and if money was
scarce, there was always plenty to eat, and clothes
enough for all, and wine, ah, yes, by the vat, and oil too;
the Mission Fathers had that. Yes, and there was wheat
as well, now that I come to think; but a very little—in the
field north of the Mission where now it is the Seed ranch;
wheat fields were there, and also a vineyard, all on Mission grounds. Wheat, olives, and the vine; the Fathers
planted those, to provide the elements of the Holy Sacrament—bread, oil, and wine, you understand. It was like
that, those industries began in California—from the
Church; and now," he put his chin in the air, "what
would Father Ullivari have said to such a crop as Señor
Derrick plants these days? Ten thousand acres of
wheat! Nothing but wheat from the Sierra to the Coast
Range. I remember when De La Cuesta was married.
He had never seen the young lady, only her miniature
portrait, painted "—he raised a shoulder—" I do not
know by whom, small, a little thing to be held in the palm.
But he fell in love with that, and marry her he would.
The affair was arranged between him and the girl's
parents. But when the time came that De La Cuesta
was to go to Monterey to meet and marry the girl, behold, Jésus Tejéda broke in upon the small rancheros

near Terrabella.   It was no time for De La Cuesta to
be away, so he sent his brother Esteban to Monterey
to marry the girl by proxy for him.   I went with Esteban.
We were a company, nearly a hundred men.   And De La
Cuesta sent a horse for the girl to ride, white, pure white;
and the saddle was of red leather; the head-stall, the bit,
and buckles, all the metal work, of virgin silver.   Well,
there was a ceremony in the Monterey Mission, and Esteban, in the name of his brother, was married to the girl.
On our way back, De La Cuesta rode out to meet us.
His company met ours at Agatha dos Palos.   Never
will I forget De La Cuesta's face as his eyes fell upon the
girl.   It was a look, a glance, come and gone like *that*,"
he snapped his fingers.   " No one but I saw it, but I was
close by.   There was no mistaking that look.   De La
Cuesta was disappointed."

" And the girl? " demanded Presley.

" She never knew.   Ah, he was a grand gentleman, De
La Cuesta.   Always he treated her as a queen.   Never
was husband more devoted, more respectful, more chiv-
alrous.   But love? "   The old fellow put his chin in the
air, shutting his eyes in a knowing fashion.   " It was not
there.   I could tell.   They were married over again at
the Mission San Juan de Guadalajara—*our* Mission—and
for a week all the town of Guadalajara was in *fête*.   There
were bull-fights in the Plaza—this very one—for five
days, and to each of his tenants-in-chief, De La Cuesta
gave a horse, a barrel of tallow, an ounce of silver, and
half an ounce of gold dust.   Ah, those were days.   That
was a gay life.   This "—he made a comprehensive gesture with his left hand—" this is stupid."

" You may well say that," observed Presley moodily,
discouraged by the other's talk.   All his doubts and uncertainty had returned to him.   Never would he grasp
the subject of his great poem.   To-day, the life was

colourless. Romance was dead. He had lived too late.
To write of the past was not what he desired. Reality
was what he longed for, things that he had seen. Yet
how to make this compatible with romance. He rose,
putting on his hat, offering the old man a cigarette. The
centenarian accepted with the air of a grandee, and extended his horn snuff-box. Presley shook his head.

" I was born too late for that," he declared, " for that,
and for many other things. *Adios.*"

" You are travelling to-day, señor? "

" A little turn through the country, to get the kinks
out of the muscles," Presley answered. " I go up into
the Quien Sabe, into the high country beyond the Mission."

" Ah, the Quien Sabe rancho. The sheep are grazing there this week."

Solotari, the keeper of the restaurant, explained:

" Young Annixter sold his wheat stubble on the
ground to the sheep raisers off yonder; " he motioned
eastward toward the Sierra foothills. " Since Sunday the
herd has been down. Very clever, that young Annixter.
He gets a price for his stubble, which else he would have
to burn, and also manures his land as the sheep move
from place to place. A true Yankee, that Annixter, a
good gringo."

After his meal, Presley once more mounted his bicycle,
and leaving the restaurant and the Plaza behind him,
held on through the main street of the drowsing town—
the street that farther on developed into the road which
turned abruptly northward and led onward through the
hop-fields and the Quien Sabe ranch toward the Mission
of San Juan.

The Home ranch of the Quien Sabe was in the little
triangle bounded on the south by the railroad, on the
northwest by Broderson Creek, and on the east by the

hop fields and the Mission lands. It was traversed in all directions, now by the trail from Hooven's, now by the irrigating ditch—the same which Presley had crossed earlier in the day—and again by the road upon which Presley then found himself. In its centre were Annixter's ranch house and barns, topped by the skeleton-like tower of the artesian well that was to feed the irrigating ditch. Farther on, the course of Broderson Creek was marked by a curved line of grey-green willows, while on the low hills to the north, as Presley advanced, the ancient Mission of San Juan de Guadalajara, with its belfry tower and red-tiled roof, began to show itself over the crests of the venerable pear trees that clustered in its garden.

When Presley reached Annixter's ranch house, he found young Annixter himself stretched in his hammock behind the mosquito-bar on the front porch, reading "David Copperfield," and gorging himself with dried prunes.

Annixter—after the two had exchanged greetings—complained of terrific colics all the preceding night. His stomach was out of whack, but you bet he knew how to take care of himself; the last spell, he had consulted a doctor at Bonneville, a gibbering busy-face who had filled him up to the neck with a dose of some hogwash stuff that had made him worse—a healthy lot the doctors knew, anyhow. *His* case was peculiar. *He* knew; prunes were what he needed, and by the pound.

Annixter, who worked the Quien Sabe ranch—some four thousand acres of rich clay and heavy loams—was a very young man, younger even than Presley, like him a college graduate. He looked never a year older than he was. He was smooth-shaven and lean built. But his youthful appearance was offset by a certain male cast of countenance, the lower lip thrust out, the chin large and deeply cleft. His university course had hardened rather than polished him. He still remained one of the people, rough almost to insolence, direct in speech, intolerant in his opinions, relying upon absolutely no one but himself; yet, with all this, of an astonishing degree of intelligence, and possessed of an executive ability little short of positive genius. He was a ferocious worker, allowing himself no pleasures, and exacting the same degree of energy from all his subordinates. He was widely hated, and as widely trusted. Every one spoke of his crusty temper and bullying disposition, invariably qualifying the statement with a commendation of his resources and capabilities. The devil of a driver, a hard man to get along with, obstinate, contrary, cantankerous; but brains! No doubt of that; brains to his boots. One would like to see the man who could get ahead of him on a deal. Twice he had been shot at, once from ambush on Osterman's ranch, and once by one of his own men whom he had kicked from the sacking platform of his harvester for gross negligence. At college, he had specialised on finance, political economy, and scientific agriculture. After his graduation (he stood almost at the very top of his class) he had returned and obtained the degree of civil engineer. Then suddenly he had taken a notion that a practical knowledge of law was indispensable to a modern farmer. In eight months he did the work of three years, studying for his bar examinations. His method of study was characteristic. He reduced all the material of his text-books to notes. Tearing out the leaves of these note-books, he pasted them upon the walls of his room; then, in his shirt-sleeves, a cheap cigar in his teeth, his hands in his pockets, he walked around and around the room, scowling fiercely at his notes, memorising, devouring, digesting. At intervals, he drank great cupfuls of unsweetened, black coffee. When the

bar examinations were held, he was admitted at the very
head of all the applicants, and was complimented by the
judge.   Immediately afterwards, he collapsed with
nervous prostration; his stomach " got out of whack,"
and he all but died in a Sacramento boarding-house, obstinately refusing to have anything to do with doctors,
whom he vituperated as a rabble of quacks, dosing himself with a patent medicine and stuffing himself almost
to bursting with liver pills and dried prunes.

He had taken a trip to Europe after this sickness to
put himself completely to rights.   He intended to be
gone a year, but returned at the end of six weeks, fulminating abuse of European cooking.   Nearly his entire
time had been spent in Paris; but of this sojourn he had
brought back but two souvenirs, an electro-plated bill-
hook and an empty bird cage which had tickled his fancy
immensely.

He was wealthy.   Only a year previous to this his
father—a widower, who had amassed a fortune in land
speculation—had died, and Annixter, the only son, had
come into the inheritance.

For Presley, Annixter professed a great admiration,
holding in deep respect the man who could rhyme words,
deferring to him whenever there was question of literature or works of fiction.   No doubt, there was not much
use in poetry, and as for novels, to his mind, there were
only Dickens's works.   Everything else was a lot of lies.
But just the same, it took brains to grind out a poem.   It
wasn't every one who could rhyme " brave " and
" glaive," and make sense out of it.   Sure not.

But Presley's case was a notable exception.   On no
occasion was Annixter prepared to accept another man's
opinion without reserve.   In conversation with him, it
was almost impossible to make any direct statement,
however trivial, that he would accept without either modi-

fication or open contradiction. He had a passion for violent discussion. He would argue upon every subject in the range of human knowledge, from astronomy to the tariff, from the doctrine of predestination to the height of a horse. Never would he admit himself to be mistaken; when cornered, he would intrench himself behind the remark, " Yes, that's all very well. In some ways, it is, and then, again, in some ways, it *isn't*."

Singularly enough, he and Presley were the best of friends. More than once, Presley marvelled at this state of affairs, telling himself that he and Annixter had nothing in common. In all his circle of acquaintances, Presley was the one man with whom Annixter had never quarrelled. The two men were diametrically opposed in temperament. Presley was easy-going; Annixter, alert. Presley was a confirmed dreamer, irresolute, inactive, with a strong tendency to melancholy; the young farmer was a man of affairs, decisive, combative, whose only reflection upon his interior economy was a morbid concern in the vagaries of his stomach. Yet the two never met without a mutual pleasure, taking a genuine interest in each other's affairs, and often putting themselves to great inconvenience to be of trifling service to help one another.

As a last characteristic, Annixter pretended to be a woman-hater, for no other reason than that he was a very bull-calf of awkwardness in feminine surroundings. Feemales! Rot! There was a fine way for a man to waste his time and his good money, lally gagging with a lot of feemales. No, thank you; none of it in *his*, if you please. Once only he had an affair—a timid, little creature in a glove-cleaning establishment in Sacramento, whom he had picked up, Heaven knew how. After his return to his ranch, a correspondence had been maintained between the two, Annixter taking the precaution to typewrite his letters, and never affixing his signature, in an excess of prudence. He furthermore made carbon copies of all his letters, filing them away in a compartment of his safe. Ah, it would be a clever feemale who would get him into a mess. Then, suddenly smitten with a panic terror that he had committed himself, that he was involving himself too deeply, he had abruptly sent the little woman about her business. It was his only love affair. After that, he kept himself free. No petticoats should ever have a hold on him. Sure not.

As Presley came up to the edge of the porch, pushing his bicycle in front of him, Annixter excused himself for not getting up, alleging that the cramps returned the moment he was off his back.

"What are you doing up this way?" he demanded.

"Oh, just having a look around," answered Presley. "How's the ranch?"

"Say," observed the other, ignoring his question, "what's this I hear about Derrick giving his tenants the bounce, and working Los Muertos himself—working *all* his land?"

Presley made a sharp movement of impatience with his free hand. "I've heard nothing else myself since morning. I suppose it must be so."

"Huh!" grunted Annixter, spitting out a prune stone. "You give Magnus Derrick my compliments and tell him he's a fool."

"What do you mean?"

"I suppose Derrick thinks he's still running his mine, and that the same principles will apply to getting grain out of the earth as to getting gold. Oh, let him go on and see where he brings up. That's right, there's your Western farmer," he exclaimed contemptuously. "Get the guts out of your land; work it to death; never give it a rest. Never alternate your crop, and then when your soil is exhausted, sit down and roar about hard times."

"I suppose Magnus thinks the land has had rest enough these last two dry seasons," observed Presley. "He has raised no crop to speak of for two years. The land has had a good rest."

"Ah, yes, that sounds well," Annixter contradicted, unwilling to be convinced. "In a way, the land's been rested, and then, again, in a way, it hasn't."

But Presley, scenting an argument, refrained from answering, and bethought himself of moving on.

"I'm going to leave my wheel here for a while, Buck," he said, "if you don't mind. I'm going up to the spring, and the road is rough between here and there."

"Stop in for dinner on your way back," said Annixter. "There'll be a venison steak. One of the boys got a deer over in the foothills last week. Out of season, but never mind that. I can't eat it. This stomach of mine wouldn't digest sweet oil to-day. Get here about six."

"Well, maybe I will, thank you," said Presley, moving off. "By the way," he added, "I see your barn is about done."

"You bet," answered Annixter. "In about a fortnight now she'll be all ready."

"It's a big barn," murmured Presley, glancing around the angle of the house toward where the great structure stood.

"Guess we'll have to have a dance there before we move the stock in," observed Annixter. "That's the custom all around here."

Presley took himself off, but at the gate Annixter called after him, his mouth full of prunes, "Say, take a look at that herd of sheep as you go up. They are right off here to the east of the road, about half a mile from here. I guess that's the biggest lot of sheep *you* ever

saw. You might write a poem about 'em. Lamb—ram;
sheep graze—sunny days. Catch on? "

Beyond Broderson Creek, as Presley advanced,
tramping along on foot now, the land opened out again
into the same vast spaces of dull brown earth,
sprinkled with stubble, such as had been characteristic
of Derrick's ranch. To the east the reach seemed infinite, flat, cheerless, heat-ridden, unrolling like a gigantic
scroll toward the faint shimmer of the distant horizons,
with here and there an isolated live-oak to break the
sombre monotony. But bordering the road to the westward, the surface roughened and raised, clambering up
to the higher ground, on the crest of which the old Mission and its surrounding pear trees were now plainly
visible.

Just beyond the Mission, the road be..t abruptly eastward, striking off across the Seed ranch. But Presley
left the road at this point, going on across the open
fields. There was no longer any trail. It was toward
three o'clock. The sun still spun, a silent, blazing disc,
high in the heavens, and tramping through the clods of
uneven, broken plough was fatiguing work. The slope
of the lowest foothills begun, the surface of the country
became rolling, and, suddenly, as he topped a higher
ridge, Presley came upon the sheep.

Already he had passed the larger part of the herd—an
intervening rise of ground having hidden it from sight.
Now, as he turned half way about, looking down into the
shallow hollow between him and the curve of the creek,
he saw them very plainly. The fringe of the herd was
some two hundred yards distant, but its farther side, in
that illusive shimmer of hot surface air, seemed miles
away. The sheep were spread out roughly in the shape
of a figure eight, two larger herds connected by a
smaller, and were headed to the southward, moving

slowly, grazing on the wheat stubble as they proceeded. But the number seemed incalculable. Hundreds upon hundreds upon hundreds of grey, rounded backs, all exactly alike, huddled, close-packed, alive, hid the earth from sight. It was no longer an aggregate of individuals. It was a mass—a compact, solid, slowly moving mass, huge, without form, like a thick-pressed growth of mushrooms, spreading out in all directions over the earth. From it there arose a vague murmur, confused, inarticulate, like the sound of very distant surf, while all the air in the vicinity was heavy with the warm, ammoniacal odour of the thousands of crowding bodies.

All the colours of the scene were sombre—the brown of the earth, the faded yellow of the dead stubble, the grey of the myriad of undulating backs. Only on the far side of the herd, erect, motionless—a single note of black, a speck, a dot—the shepherd stood, leaning upon an empty water-trough, solitary, grave, impressive.

For a few moments, Presley stood, watching. Then, as he started to move on, a curious thing occurred. At first, he thought he had heard some one call his name. He paused, listening; there was no sound but the vague noise of the moving sheep. Then, as this first impression passed, it seemed to him that he had been beckoned to. Yet nothing stirred; except for the lonely figure beyond the herd there was no one in sight. He started on again, and in half a dozen steps found himself looking over his shoulder. Without knowing why, he looked toward the shepherd; then halted and looked a second time and a third. Had the shepherd called to him? Presley knew that he had heard no voice. Brusquely, all his attention seemed riveted upon this distant figure. He put one forearm over his eyes, to keep off the sun, gazing across the intervening herd. Surely, the shepherd had called him. But at the next instant he started, uttering an ex-

clamation under his breath. The far-away speck of
black became animated. Presley remarked a sweeping
gesture. Though the man had not beckoned to him before, there was no doubt that he was beckoning now.
Without any hesitation, and singularly interested in the
incident, Presley turned sharply aside and hurried on
toward the shepherd, skirting the herd, wondering all
the time that he should answer the call with so little
question, so little hesitation.

But the shepherd came forward to meet Presley, followed by one of his dogs. As the two men approached
each other, Presley, closely studying the other, began to
wonder where he had seen him before. It must have
been a very long time ago, upon one of his previous visits
to the ranch. Certainly, however, there was something
familiar in the shepherd's face and figure. When they
came closer to each other, and Presley could see him
more distinctly, this sense of a previous acquaintance
was increased and sharpened.

The shepherd was a man of about thirty-five. He was
very lean and spare. His brown canvas overalls were
thrust into laced boots. A cartridge belt without any
cartridges encircled his waist. A grey flannel shirt, open
at the throat, showed his breast, tanned and ruddy. He
wore no hat. His hair was very black and rather long.
A pointed beard covered his chin, growing straight and
fine from the hollow cheeks. The absence of any covering for his head was, no doubt, habitual with him, for his
face was as brown as an Indian's—a ruddy brown—quite
different from Presley's dark olive. To Presley's morbidly keen observation, the general impression of the
shepherd's face was intensely interesting. It was un-
common to an astonishing degree. Presley's vivid imagination chose to see in it the face of an ascetic, of a
recluse, almost that of a young seer. So must have

appeared the half-inspired shepherds of the Hebraic legends, the younger prophets of Israel, dwellers in the wilderness, beholders of visions, having their existence in a continual dream, talkers with God, gifted with strange powers.

Suddenly, at some twenty paces distant from the approaching shepherd, Presley stopped short, his eyes riveted upon the other.

" Vanamee ! " he exclaimed.

The shepherd smiled and came forward, holding out his hands, saying, " I thought it was you. When I saw you come over the hill, I called you."

" But not with your voice," returned Presley. " I knew that some one wanted me. I felt it. I should have remembered that you could do that kind of thing."

" I have never known it to fail. It helps with the sheep."

" With the sheep? "

" In a way. I can't tell exactly how. We don't understand these things yet. There are times when, if I close my eyes and dig my fists into my temples, I can hold the entire herd for perhaps a minute. Perhaps, though, it's imagination, who knows? But it's good to see you again. How long has it been since the last time? Two, three, nearly five years."

It was more than that. It was six years since Presley and Vanamee had met, and then it had been for a short time only, during one of the shepherd's periodical brief returns to that part of the country. During a week he and Presley had been much together, for the two were devoted friends. Then, as abruptly, as mysteriously as he had come, Vanamee disappeared. Presley awoke one morning to find him gone. Thus, it had been with Vanamee for a period of sixteen years. He lived his life in

3

the unknown, one could not tell where—in the desert, in
the mountains, throughout all the vast and vague Southwest, solitary, strange. Three, four, five years passed.
The shepherd would be almost forgotten. Never the
most trivial scrap of information as to his whereabouts
reached Los Muertos. He had melted off into the
surface-shimmer of the desert, into the mirage; he sank
below the horizons; he was swallowed up in the waste of
sand and sage. Then, without warning, he would reap-
pear, coming in from the wilderness, emerging from the
unknown. No one knew him well. In all that country-
side he had but three friends, Presley, Magnus Derrick,
and the priest at the Mission of San Juan de Guadalajara, Father Sarria. He remained always a mystery,
living a life half-real, half-legendary. In all those years
he did not seem to have grown older by a single day.
At this time, Presley knew him to be thirty-six years of
age. But since the first day the two had met, the shepherd's face and bearing had, to his eyes, remained the
same. At this moment, Presley was looking into the
same face he had first seen many, many years ago. It
was a face stamped with an unspeakable sadness, a deathless grief, the permanent imprint of a tragedy long past,
but yet a living issue. Presley told himself that it was
impossible to look long into Vanamee's eyes without
knowing that here was a man whose whole being had
been at one time shattered and riven to its lowest depths,
whose life had suddenly stopped at a certain moment of
its development.

The two friends sat down upon the ledge of the watering-trough, their eyes wandering incessantly toward the
slow moving herd, grazing on the wheat stubble, moving
southward as they grazed.

"Where have you come from this time?" Presley had
asked. "Where have you kept yourself?"

The other swept the horizon to the south and east with a vague gesture.

" Off there, down to the south, very far off. So many places that I can't remember. I went the Long Trail this time; a long, long ways. Arizona, The Mexicos, and, then, afterwards, Utah and Nevada, following the horizon, travelling at hazard. Into Arizona first, going in by Monument Pass, and then on to the south, through the country of the Navajos, down by the Aga Thia Needle—a great blade of red rock jutting from out the desert, like a knife thrust. Then on and on through The Mexicos, all through the Southwest, then back again in a great circle by Chihuahua and Aldama to Laredo, to Torreon, and Albuquerque. From there across the Uncompahgre plateau into the Uintah country; then at last due west through Nevada to California and to the valley of the San Joaquin."

His voice lapsed to a monotone, his eyes becoming fixed; he continued to speak as though half awake, his thoughts elsewhere, seeing again in the eye of his mind the reach of desert and red hill, the purple mountain, the level stretch of alkali, leper white, all the savage, gorgeous desolation of the Long Trail.

He ignored Presley for the moment, but, on the other hand, Presley himself gave him but half his attention. The return of Vanamee had stimulated the poet's memory. He recalled the incidents of Vanamee's life, reviewing again that terrible drama which had uprooted his soul, which had driven him forth a wanderer, a shunner of men, a sojourner in waste places. He was, strangely enough, a college graduate and a man of wide reading and great intelligence, but he had chosen to lead his own life, which was that of a recluse.

Of a temperament similar in many ways to Presley's, there were capabilities in Vanamee that were not ordinarily to be found in the rank and file of men. Living close to nature, a poet by instinct, where Presley was but a poet by training, there developed in him a great sensitiveness to beauty and an almost abnormal capacity for great happiness and great sorrow; he felt things intensely, deeply. He never forgot. It was when he was eighteen or nineteen, at the formative and most impressionable period of his life, that he had met Angéle Varian. Presley barely remembered her as a girl of sixteen, beautiful almost beyond expression, who lived with an aged aunt on the Seed ranch back of the Mission. At this moment he was trying to recall how she looked, with her hair of gold hanging in two straight plaits on either side of her face, making three-cornered her round, white forehead; her wonderful eyes, violet blue, heavy lidded, with their astonishing upward slant toward the temples, the slant that gave a strange, oriental cast to her face, perplexing, enchanting. He remembered the Egyptian fulness of the lips, the strange balancing movement of her head upon her slender neck, the same movement that one sees in a snake at poise. Never had he seen a girl more radiantly beautiful, never a beauty so strange, so troublous, so out of all accepted standards. It was small wonder that Vanamee had loved her, and less wonder, still, that his love had been so intense, so passionate, so part of himself. Angéle had loved him with a love no less th n his own. It was one of those legendary passions that sometimes occur, idyllic, untouched by civilisation, spontaneous as the growth of trees, natural as dew-fall, strong as the firm-seated mountains.

At the time of his meeting with Angéle, Vanamee was living on the Los Muertos ranch. It was there he had chosen to spend one of his college vacations. But he preferred to pass it in out-of-door work, sometimes herding cattle, sometimes pitching hay, sometimes working with pick and dynamite-stick on the ditches in the fourth division of the ranch, riding the range, mending breaks in the wire fences, making himself generally useful. College bred though he was, the life pleased him. He was, as he desired, close to nature, living the full measure of life, a worker among workers, taking enjoyment in simple pleasures, healthy in mind and body. He believed in an existence passed in this fashion in the country, working hard, eating full, drinking deep, sleeping dreamlessly.

But every night, after supper, he saddled his pony and rode over to the garden of the old Mission. The 'dobe dividing wall on that side, which once had separated the Mission garden and the Seed ranch, had long since crumbled away, and the boundary between the two pieces of ground was marked only by a line of venerable pear trees. Here, under these trees, he found Angéle awaiting him, and there the two would sit through the hot, still evening, their arms about each other, watching the moon rise over the foothills, listening to the trickle of the water in the moss-encrusted fountain in the garden, and the steady croak of the great frogs that lived in the damp north corner of the enclosure. Through all one summer the enchantment of that new-found, wonderful love, pure and untainted, filled the lives of each of them with its sweetness. The summer passed, the harvest moon came and went. The nights were very dark. In the deep shade of the pear trees they could no longer see each other. When they met at the rendezvous, Vanamee found her only with his groping hands. They did not speak, mere words were useless between them. Silently as his reaching hands touched her warm body, he took her in his arms, searching for her lips with his. Then one night the tragedy had suddenly

leaped from out the shadow with the abruptness of an
explosion.

It was impossible afterwards to reconstruct the manner of its occurrence. To Angéle's mind—what there
was left of it—the matter always remained a hideous
blur, a blot, a vague, terrible confusion. No doubt they
two had been watched; the plan succeeded too well for
any other supposition. One moonless night, Angéle,
arriving under the black shadow of the pear trees a little
earlier than usual, found the apparently familiar figure
waiting for her. All unsuspecting she gave herself to
the embrace of a strange pair of arms, and Vanamee arriving but a score of moments later, stumbled over her
prostrate body, inert and unconscious, in the shadow of
the overspiring trees.

Who was the Other? Angéle was carried to her home
on the Seed ranch, delirious, all but raving, and Vanamee, with knife and revolver ready, ranged the country-
side like a wolf. He was not alone. The whole county
rose, raging, horror-struck. Posse after posse was
formed, sent out, and returned, without so much as a
clue. Upon no one could even the shadow of suspicion
be thrown. The Other had withdrawn into an impenetrable mystery. There he remained. He never was
found; he never was so much as heard of. A legend
arose about him, this prowler of the night, this strange,
fearful figure, with an unseen face, swooping in there
from out the darkness, come and gone in an instant, but
leaving behind him a track of terror and death and rage
and undying grief. Within the year, in giving birth to
the child, Angéle had died.

The little babe was taken by Angéle's parents, and
Angéle was buried in the Mission garden near to the
aged, grey sun dial. Vanamee stood by during the ceremony, but half conscious of what was going forward.

At the last moment he had stepped forward, looked long into the dead face framed in its plaits of gold hair, the hair that made three-cornered the round, white forehead; looked again at the closed eyes, with their perplexing upward slant toward the temples, oriental, bizarre; at the lips with their Egyptian fulness; at the sweet, slender neck; the long, slim hands; then abruptly turned about. The last clods were filling the grave at a time when he was already far away, his horse's head turned toward the desert.

For two years no syllable was heard of him. It was believed that he had killed himself. But Vanamee had no thought of that. For two years he wandered through Arizona, living in the desert, in the wilderness, a recluse, a nomad, an ascetic. But, doubtless, all his heart was in the little coffin in the Mission garden. Once in so often he must come back thither. One day he was seen again in the San Joaquin. The priest, Father Sarria, returning from a visit to the sick at Bonneville, met him on the Upper Road.

Eighteen years had passed since Angéle had died, but the thread of Vanamee's life had been snapped. Nothing remained now but the tangled ends. He had never forgotten. The long, dull ache, the poignant grief had now become a part of him. Presley knew this to be so.

While Presley had been reflecting upon all this, Vanamee had continued to speak. Presley, however, had not been wholly inattentive. While his memory was busy reconstructing the details of the drama of the shepherd's life, another part of his brain had been swiftly registering picture after picture that Vanamee's monotonous flow of words struck off, as it were, upon a steadily moving scroll. The music of the unfamiliar names that occurred in his recital was a stimulant to the poet's imagination. Presley had the poet's passion for expressive, sonorous names. As these came and went in Vanamee's monotonous undertones, like little notes of harmony in a musical progression, he listened, delighted with their resonance. Navajo, Quijotoa, Uintah, Sonora, Laredo, Uncompahgre—to him they were so many symbols. It was his West that passed, unrolling there before the eye of his mind: the open, heat-scourged round of desert; the mesa, like a vast altar, shimmering purple in the royal sunset; the still, gigantic mountains, heaving into the sky from out the cañons; the strenuous, fierce life of isolated towns, lost and forgotten, down there, far off, below the horizon. Abruptly his great poem, his Song of the West, leaped up again in his imagination. For the moment, he all but held it. It was there, close at hand. In another instant he would grasp it.

" Yes, yes," he exclaimed, " I can see it all. The desert, the mountains, all wild, primordial, untamed. How I should have loved to have been with you. Then, perhaps, I should have got hold of my idea."

" Your idea? "

" The great poem of the West. It's that which I want to write. Oh, to put it all into hexameters; strike the great iron note; sing the vast, terrible song; the song of the People; the forerunners of empire! "

Vanamee understood him perfectly. He nodded gravely.

" Yes, it is there. It is Life, the primitive, simple, direct Life, passionate, tumultuous. Yes, there is an epic there."

Presley caught at the word. It had never before occurred to him.

" Epic, yes, that's it. It is the epic I'm searching for. And *how* I search for it. You don't know. It is sometimes almost an agony. Often and often I can feel it right there, there, at my finger-tips, but I never quite catch it. It always eludes me. I was born too late. Ah, to get back to that first clear-eyed view of things, to see as Homer saw, **as Beowulf saw,** as the Nibelungen poets saw. The life is here, the same as then; the Poem is here; my West is here; the primeval, epic life is here, here under our hands, in the desert, in the mountain, on the ranch, all over here, from Winnipeg to Guadalupe. It is the man who is lacking, the poet; we have been educated away from it all. We are out of touch. We are out of tune."

Vanamee heard him to the end, his grave, sad face thoughtful and attentive. Then he rose.

"I am going over to the Mission," he said, "to see Father Sarria. I have not seen him yet."

"How about the sheep?"

"The dogs will keep them in hand, and I shall not be gone long. Besides that, I have a boy here to help. He is over yonder on the other side of the herd. We can't see him from here."

Presley wondered at the heedlessness of leaving the sheep so slightly guarded, but made no comment, and the two started off across the field in the direction of the Mission church.

"Well, yes, it is there—your epic," observed Vanamee, as they went along. "But why write? Why not *live* in it? Steep oneself in the heat of the desert, the glory of the sunset, the blue haze of the mesa and the cañon."

"As you have done, for instance?"

Vanamee nodded.

"No, I could not do that," declared Presley; "I want to go back, but not so far as you. I feel that I must compromise. I must find expression. I could not lose myself like that in your desert. When its vastness overwhelmed me, or its beauty dazzled me, or its loneliness weighed down upon me, I should have to record my impressions. Otherwise, I should suffocate."

" Each to his own life," observed Vanamee.

The Mission of San Juan, built of brown 'dobe blocks, covered with yellow plaster, that at many points had dropped away from the walls, stood on the crest of a low rise of the ground, facing to the south. A covered colonnade, paved with round, worn bricks, from whence opened the doors of the abandoned cells, once used by the monks, adjoined it on the left. The roof was of tiled half-cylinders, split longitudinally, and laid in alternate rows, now concave, now convex. The main body of the church itself was at right angles to the colonnade, and at the point of intersection rose the belfry tower, an ancient campanile, where swung the three cracked bells, the gift of the King of Spain. Beyond the church was the Mission garden and the graveyard that overlooked the Seed ranch in a little hollow beyond.

Presley and Vanamee went down the long colonnade to the last door next the belfry tower, and Vanamee pulled the leather thong that hung from a hole in the door, setting a little bell jangling somewhere in the interior. The place, but for this noise, was shrouded in a Sunday stillness, an absolute repose. Only at intervals, one heard the trickle of the unseen fountain, and the liquid cooing of doves in the garden.

Father Sarria opened the door. He was a small man, somewhat stout, with a smooth and shiny face. He wore a frock coat that was rather dirty, slippers, and an old yachting cap of blue cloth, with a broken leather vizor. He was smoking a cheap cigar, very fat and black.

But instantly he recognised Vanamee. His face went all alight with pleasure and astonishment. It seemed as if he would never have finished shaking both his hands;

and, as it was, he released but one of them, patting him affectionately on the shoulder with the other. He was voluble in his welcome, talking partly in Spanish, partly in English.

So he had come back again, this great fellow, tanned as an Indian, lean as an Indian, with an Indian's long, black hair. But he had not changed, not in the very least. His beard had not grown an inch. Aha! The rascal, never to give warning, to drop down, as it were, from out the sky. Such a hermit! To live in the desert! A veritable Saint Jerome. Did a lion feed him down there in Arizona, or was it a raven, like Elijah? The good God had not fattened him, at any rate, and, apropos, he was just about to dine himself. He had made a salad from his own lettuce. The two would dine with him, eh? For this, my son, that was lost is found again.

But Presley excused himself. Instinctively, he felt that Sarria and Vanamee wanted to talk of things concerning which he was an outsider. It was not at all unlikely that Vanamee would spend half the night before the high altar in the church.

He took himself away, his mind still busy with Vanamee's extraordinary life and character. But, as he descended the hill, he was startled by a prolonged and raucous cry, discordant, very harsh, thrice repeated at exact intervals, and, looking up, he saw one of Father Sarria's peacocks balancing himself upon the topmost wire of the fence, his long tail trailing, his neck outstretched, filling the air with his stupid outcry, for no reason than the desire to make a noise.

About an hour later, toward four in the afternoon, Presley reached the spring at the head of the little cañon in the northeast corner of the Quien Sabe ranch, the point toward which he had been travelling since early in the forenoon. The place was not without its charm.

Innumerable live-oaks overhung the cañon, and Broderson Creek—there a mere rivulet, running down from
the spring—gave a certain coolness to the air. It was
one of the few spots thereabouts that had survived the
dry season of the last year. Nearly all the other springs
had dried completely, while Mission Creek on Derrick's
ranch was nothing better than a dusty cutting in the
ground, filled with brittle, concave flakes of dried and
sun-cracked mud.

Presley climbed to the summit of one of the hills—the
highest—that rose out of the cañon, from the crest of
which he could see for thirty, fifty, sixty miles down the
valley, and, filling his pipe, smoked lazily for upwards of
an hour, his head empty of thought, allowing himself to
succumb to a pleasant, gentle inanition, a little drowsy,
comfortable in his place, prone upon the ground, warmed
just enough by such sunlight as filtered through the live-
oaks, soothed by the good tobacco and the prolonged
murmur of the spring and creek. By degrees, the sense
of his own personality became blunted, the little wheels
and cogs of thought moved slower and slower; consciousness dwindled to a point, the animal in him
stretched itself, purring. A delightful numbness invaded his mind and his body. He was not asleep, he was
not awake, stupefied merely, lapsing back to the state
of the faun, the satyr.

After a while, rousing himself a little, he shifted his
position and, drawing from the pocket of his shooting
coat his little tree-calf edition of the Odyssey, read far
into the twenty-first book, where, after the failure of all
the suitors to bend Ulysses's bow, it is finally put, with
mockery, into his own hands. Abruptly the drama of
the story roused him from all his languor. In an instant,
he was the poet again, his nerves tingling, alive to every
sensation, responsive to every impression. The desire

of creation, of composition, grew big within him. Hexameters of his own clamoured, tumultuous, in his brain.
Not for a long time had he " felt his poem," as he called
this sensation, so poignantly. For an instant he told
himself that he actually held it.

It was, no doubt, Vanamee's talk that had stimulated
him to this point. The story of the Long Trail, with its
desert and mountain, its cliff-dwellers, its Aztec ruins, its
colour, movement, and romance, filled his mind with
picture after picture. The epic defiled before his vision
like a pageant. Once more, he shot a glance about him,
as if in search of the inspiration, and this time he all but
found it. He rose to his feet, looking out and off below
him.

As from a pinnacle, Presley, from where he now stood,
dominated the entire country. The sun had begun to
set, everything in the range of his vision was overlaid
with a sheen of gold.

First, close at hand, it was the Seed ranch, carpeting
the little hollow behind the Mission with a spread of
greens, some dark, some vivid, some pale almost to yel-
lowness. Beyond that was the Mission itself, its venerable campanile, in whose arches hung the Spanish King's
bells, already glowing ruddy in the sunset. Farther on,
he could make out Annixter's ranch house, marked by
the skeleton-like tower of the artesian well, and, a little
farther to the east, the huddled, tiled roofs of Guadalajara. Far to the west and north, he saw Bonneville very
plain, and the dome of the courthouse, a purple silhouette against the glare of the sky. Other points detached
themselves, swimming in a golden mist, projecting blue
shadows far before them; the mammoth live-oak by
Hooven's, towering superb and magnificent; the line of
eucalyptus trees, behind which he knew was the Los
Muertos ranch house—his home; the watering-tank, the

great iron-hooped tower of wood that stood at the joining of the Lower Road and the County Road; the long
wind-break of poplar trees and the white walls of Caraher's saloon on the County Road.

But all this seemed to be only foreground, a mere
array of accessories—a mass of irrelevant details. Beyond Annixter's, beyond Guadalajara, beyond the Lower
Road, beyond Broderson Creek, on to the south and
west, infinite, illimitable, stretching out there under the
sheen of the sunset forever and forever, flat, vast, unbroken, a huge scroll, unrolling between the horizons,
spread the great stretches of the ranch of Los Muertos, bare of crops, shaved close in the recent harvest.
Near at hand were hills, but on that far southern horizon
only the curve of the great earth itself checked the view.
Adjoining Los Muertos, and widening to the west,
opened the Broderson ranch. The Osterman ranch to
the northwest carried on the great sweep of landscape;
ranch after ranch. Then, as the imagination itself expanded under the stimulus of that measureless range of
vision, even those great ranches resolved themselves
into mere foreground, mere accessories, irrelevant details. Beyond the fine line of the horizons, over the
curve of the globe, the shoulder of the earth, were other
ranches, equally vast, and beyond these, others, and beyond these, still others, the immensities multiplying,
lengthening out vaster and vaster. The whole gigantic
sweep of the San Joaquin expanded, Titanic, before the
eye of the mind, flagellated with heat, quivering and
shimmering under the sun's red eye. At long intervals,
a faint breath of wind out of the south passed slowly
over the levels of the baked and empty earth, accentuat-
ing the silence, marking off the stillness. It seemed to
exhale from the land itself, a prolonged sigh as of deep
fatigue. It was the season after the harvest, and the

great earth, the mother, after its period of reproduction, its pains of labour, delivered of the fruit of its loins, slept the sleep of exhaustion, the infinite repose of the colossus, benignant, eternal, strong, the nourisher of nations, the feeder of an entire world.

Ha! there it was, his epic, his inspiration, his West, his thundering progression of hexameters. A sudden uplift, a sense of exhilaration, of physical exaltation appeared abruptly to sweep Presley from his feet. As from a point high above the world, he seemed to dominate a universe, a whole order of things. He was dizzied, stunned, stupefied, his morbid supersensitive mind reeling, drunk with the intoxication of mere immensity. Stupendous ideas for which there were no names drove headlong through his brain. Terrible, formless shapes, vague figures, gigantic, monstrous, distorted, whirled at a gallop through his imagination.

He started homeward, still in his dream, descending from the hill, emerging from the cañon, and took the short cut straight across the Quien Sabe ranch, leaving Guadalajara far to his left. He tramped steadily on through the wheat stubble, walking fast, his head in a whirl.

Never had he so nearly grasped his inspiration as at that moment on the hill-top. Even now, though the sunset was fading, though the wide reach of valley was shut from sight, it still kept him company. Now the details came thronging back—the component parts of his poem, the signs and symbols of the West. It was there, close at hand, he had been in touch with it all day. It was in the centenarian's vividly coloured reminiscences—De La Cuesta, holding his grant from the Spanish crown, with his power of life and death; the romance of his marriage; the white horse with its pillion of red leather and silver bridle mountings; the bull-fights in the

Plaza; the gifts of gold dust, and horses and tallow. It
was in Vanamee's strange history, the tragedy of his
love; Angéle Varian, with her marvellous loveliness; the
Egyptian fulness of her lips, the perplexing upward slant
of her violet eyes, bizarre, oriental; her white forehead
made three cornered by her plaits of gold hair; the mystery of the Other; her death at the moment of her child's
birth. It was in Vanamee's flight into the wilderness;
the story of the Long Trail; the sunsets behind the altar-
like mesas, the baking desolation of the deserts; the
strenuous, fierce life of forgotten towns, down there, far
off, lost below the horizons of the southwest; the sonorous music of unfamiliar names—Quijotoa, Uintah, Sonora, Laredo, Uncompahgre. It was in the Mission, with
its cracked bells, its decaying walls, its venerable sun dial,
its fountain and old garden, and in the Mission Fathers
themselves, the priests, the padres, planting the first
wheat and oil and wine to produce the elements of the
Sacrament—a trinity of great industries, taking their
rise in a religious rite.

Abruptly, as if in confirmation, Presley heard the
sound of a bell from the direction of the Mission itself.
It was the *de Profundis*, a note of the Old World; of the
ancient régime, an echo from the hillsides of mediæval
Europe, sounding there in this new land, unfamiliar and
strange at this end-of-the-century time.

By now, however, it was dark. Presley hurried forward. He came to the line fence of the Quien Sabe
ranch. Everything was very still. The stars were all
out. There was not a sound other than the *de Profundis*, still sounding from very far away. At long intervals
the great earth sighed dreamily in its sleep. All about,
the feeling of absolute peace and quiet and security and
untroubled happiness and content seemed descending
from the stars like a benediction. The beauty of his

poem, its idyl, came to him like a caress; that alone
had been lacking.   It was that, perhaps, which had left
it hitherto incomplete.   At last he was to grasp his song
in all its entity.

But suddenly there was an interruption.   Presley had
climbed the fence at the limit of the Quien Sabe ranch.
Beyond was Los Muertos, but between the two ran the
railroad.   He had only time to jump back upon the
embankment when, with a quivering of all the earth, a
locomotive, single, unattached, shot by him with a roar,
filling the air with the reek of hot oil, vomiting smoke
and sparks; its enormous eye, cyclopean, red, throwing
a glare far in advance, shooting by in a sudden crash of
confused thunder; filling the night with the terrific
clamour of its iron hoofs.

Abruptly Presley remembered.   This must be the
crack passenger engine of which Dyke had told him, the
one delayed by the accident on the Bakersfield division
and for whose passage the track had been opened all the
way to Fresno.

Before Presley could recover from the shock of the
irruption, while the earth was still vibrating, the rails
still humming, the engine was far away, flinging the echo
of its frantic gallop over all the valley.   For a brief instant it roared with a hollow diapason on the Long
Trestle over Broderson Creek, then plunged into a cutting farther on, the quivering glare of its fires losing itself in the night, its thunder abruptly diminishing to a
subdued and distant humming.   All at once this ceased.
The engine was gone.

But the moment the noise of the engine lapsed, Presley—about to start forward again—was conscious of a
confusion of lamentable sounds that rose into the night
from out the engine's wake.   Prolonged cries of agony,
sobbing wails of infinite pain, heart-rending, pitiful.

The noises came from a little distance. He ran down the track, crossing the culvert, over the irrigating ditch, and at the head of the long reach of track—between the culvert and the Long Trestle—paused abruptly, held immovable at the sight of the ground and rails all about him.

In some way, the herd of sheep—Vanamee's herd— had found a breach in the wire fence by the right of way and had wandered out upon the tracks. A band had been crossing just at the moment of the engine's passage. The pathos of it was beyond expression.   It was a slaughter, a massacre of innocents.   The iron monster had charged full into the midst, merciless, inexorable. To the right and left, all the width of the right of way, the little bodies had been flung; backs were snapped against the fence posts; brains knocked out.   Caught in the barbs of the wire, wedged in, the bodies hung suspended.   Under foot it was terrible.   The black blood, winking in the starlight, seeped down into the clinkers between the ties with a prolonged sucking murmur.

Presley turned away, horror-struck, sick at heart, overwhelmed with a quick burst of irresistible compassion for this brute agony he could not relieve.   The sweetness was gone from the evening, the sense of peace, of security, and placid contentment was stricken from the landscape.   The hideous ruin in the engine's path drove all thought of his poem from his mind.   The inspiration vanished like a mist.   The *de Profundis* had ceased to ring.

He hurried on across the Los Muertos ranch, almost running, even putting his hands over his ears till he was out of hearing distance of that all but human distress. Not until he was beyond ear-shot did he pause, looking back, listening.   The night had shut down again.   For a moment the silence was profound, unbroken.

Then, faint and prolonged, across the levels of the ranch, he heard the engine whistling for Bonneville. Again and again, at rapid intervals in its flying course, it whistled for road crossings, for sharp curves, for trestles; ominous notes, hoarse, bellowing, ringing with the accents of menace and defiance; and abruptly Presley saw again, in his imagination, the galloping monster, the terror of steel and steam, with its single eye, cyclopean, red, shooting from horizon to horizon; but saw it now as the symbol of a vast power, huge, terrible, flinging the echo of its thunder over all the reaches of the valley, leaving blood and destruction in its path; the leviathan, with tentacles of steel clutching into the soil, the soulless Force, the iron-hearted Power, the monster, the Colossus, the Octopus.

II

On the following morning, Harran Derrick was up and about by a little after six o'clock, and a quarter of an hour later had breakfast in the kitchen of the ranch house, preferring not to wait until the Chinese cook laid the table in the regular dining-room. He scented a hard day's work ahead of him, and was anxious to be at it betimes. He was practically the manager of Los Muertos, and, with the aid of his foreman and three division superintendents, carried forward nearly the entire direction of the ranch, occupying himself with the details of his father's plans, executing his orders, signing contracts, paying bills, and keeping the books.

For the last three weeks little had been done. The crop—such as it was—had been harvested and sold, and there had been a general relaxation of activity for upwards of a month. Now, however, the fall was coming on, the dry season was about at its end; any time after the twentieth of the month the first rains might be expected, softening the ground, putting it into condition for the plough. Two days before this, Harran had notified his superintendents on Three and Four to send in such grain as they had reserved for seed. On Two the wheat had not even shown itself above the ground, while on One, the Home ranch, which was under his own immediate supervision, the seed had already been graded and selected.

It was Harran's intention to commence blue-stoning his seed that day, a delicate and important process which prevented rust and smut appearing in the crop when the wheat should come up. But, furthermore, he wanted to find time to go to Guadalajara to meet the Governor on the morning train. His day promised to be busy.

But as Harran was finishing his last cup of coffee, Phelps, the foreman on the Home ranch, who also looked after the storage barns where the seed was kept, presented himself, cap in hand, on the back porch by the kitchen door.

" I thought I'd speak to you about the seed from Four, sir," he said. " That hasn't been brought in yet."

Harran nodded.

" I'll see about it. You've got all the blue-stone you want, have you, Phelps?" and without waiting for an answer he added, " Tell the stableman I shall want the team about nine o'clock to go to Guadalajara. Put them in the buggy. The bays, you understand."

When the other had gone, Harran drank off the rest of his coffee, and, rising, passed through the dining-room and across a stone-paved hallway with a glass roof into the office just beyond.

The office was the nerve-centre of the entire ten thousand acres of Los Muertos, but its appearance and furnishings were not in the least suggestive of a farm. It was divided at about its middle by a wire railing, painted green and gold, and behind this railing were the high desks where the books were kept, the safe, the letter-press and letter-files, and Harran's typewriting machine. A great map of Los Muertos with every water-course, depression, and elevation, together with indications of the varying depths of the clays and loams in the soil, accurately plotted, hung against the wall between the windows, while near at hand by the safe was the telephone.

But, no doubt, the most significant object in the office

was the ticker.   This was an innovation in the San Joaquin, an idea of shrewd, quick-witted young Annixter,
which Harran and Magnus Derrick had been quick to
adopt, and after them Broderson and Osterman, and
many others of the wheat growers of the county.   The
offices of the ranches were thus connected by wire with
San Francisco, and through that city with Minneapolis,
Duluth, Chicago, New York, and at last, and most important of all, with Liverpool.   Fluctuations in the price
of the world's crop during and after the harvest thrilled
straight to the office of Los Muertos, to that of the
Quien Sabe, to Osterman's, and to Broderson's.   During a flurry in the Chicago wheat pits in the August of
that year, which had affected even the San Francisco
market, Harran and Magnus had sat up nearly half of one
night watching the strip of white tape jerking unsteadily
from the reel.   At such moments they no longer felt
their individuality.   The ranch became merely the part
of an enormous whole, a unit in the vast agglomera-
tion of wheat land the whole world round, feeling the
effects of causes thousands of miles distant—a drought
on the prairies of Dakota, a rain on the plains of India,
a frost on the Russian steppes, a hot wind on the llanos
of the Argentine.

Harran crossed over to the telephone and rang six
bells, the call for the division house on Four.   It was the
most distant, the most isolated point on all the ranch,
situated at its far southeastern extremity, where few
people ever went, close to the line fence, a dot, a speck,
lost in the immensity of the open country.   By the road
it was eleven miles distant from the office, and by the
trail to Hooven's and the Lower Road all of nine.

"How about that seed?" demanded Harran when he
had got Cutter on the line.

The other made excuses for an unavoidable delay, and

was adding that he was on the point of starting out, when
Harran cut in with:

"You had better go the trail. It will save a little
time and I am in a hurry. Put your sacks on the horses'
backs. And, Cutter, if you see Hooven when you go by
his place, tell him I want him, and, by the way, take a
look at the end of the irrigating ditch when you get to
it. See how they are getting along there and if Billy
wants anything. Tell him we are expecting those new
scoops down to-morrow or next day and to get along
with what he has until then. . . . How's everything
on Four? . . . All right, then. Give your seed to
Phelps when you get here if I am not about. I am going
to Guadalajara to meet the Governor. He's coming
down to-day. And that makes me think; we lost the
case, you know. I had a letter from the Governor
yesterday. . . . Yes, hard luck. S. Behrman did us
up. Well, good-bye, and don't lose any time with that
seed. I want to blue-stone to-day."

After telephoning Cutter, Harran put on his hat, went
over to the barns, and found Phelps. Phelps had already cleaned out the vat which was to contain the solu-
tion of blue-stone, and was now at work regrading the
seed. Against the wall behind him ranged the row of
sacks. Harran cut the fastenings of these and examined
the contents carefully, taking handfuls of wheat from
each and allowing it to run through his fingers, or nip-
ping the grains between his nails, testing their hardness.

The seed was all of the white varieties of wheat and
of a very high grade, the berries hard and heavy, rigid
and swollen with starch.

"If it was all like that, sir, hey?" observed Phelps.

Harran put his chin in the air.

"Bread would be as good as cake, then," he answered,

going from sack to sack, inspecting the contents and consulting the tags affixed to the mouths.

"Hello," he remarked, "here's a red wheat. Where did this come from?"

"That's that red Clawson we sowed to the piece on Four, north the Mission Creek, just to see how it would do here. We didn't get a very good catch."

"We can't do better than to stay by White Sonora and Propo," remarked Harran. "We've got our best results with that, and European millers like it to mix with the Eastern wheats that have more gluten than ours. That is, if we have any wheat at all next year."

A feeling of discouragement for the moment bore down heavily upon him. At intervals this came to him and for the moment it was overpowering. The idea of "what's-the-use" was upon occasion a veritable oppression. Everything seemed to combine to lower the price of wheat. The extension of wheat areas always exceeded increase of population; competition was growing fiercer every year. The farmer's profits were the object of attack from a score of different quarters. It was a flock of vultures descending upon a common prey—the commission merchant, the elevator combine, the mixing-house ring, the banks, the warehouse men, the labouring man, and, above all, the railroad. Steadily the Liverpool buyers cut and cut and cut. Everything, every element of the world's markets, tended to force down the price to the lowest possible figure at which it could be profitably farmed. Now it was down to eighty-seven. It was at that figure the crop had sold that year; and to think that the Governor had seen wheat at two dollars and five cents in the year of the Turko-Russian War!

He turned back to the house after giving Phelps final directions, gloomy, disheartened, his hands deep in his pockets, wondering what was to be the outcome. So narrow had the margin of profit shrunk that a dry season meant bankruptcy to the smaller farmers throughout all the valley. He knew very well how widespread had been the distress the last two years. With their own tenants on Los Muertos, affairs had reached the stage of desperation. Derrick had practically been obliged to " carry " Hooven and some of the others. The Governor himself had made almost nothing during the last season; a third year like the last, with the price steadily sagging, meant nothing else but ruin.

But here he checked himself. Two consecutive dry seasons in California were almost unprecedented; a third would be beyond belief, and the complete rest for nearly all the land was a compensation. They had made no money, that was true; but they had lost none. Thank God, the homestead was free of mortgage; one good season would more than make up the difference.

He was in a better mood by the time he reached the driveway that led up to the ranch house, and as he raised his eyes toward the house itself, he could not but feel that the sight of his home was cheering. The ranch house was set in a great grove of eucalyptus, oak, and cypress, enormous trees growing from out a lawn that was as green, as fresh, and as well-groomed as any in a garden in the city. This lawn flanked all one side of the house, and it was on this side that the family elected to spend most of its time. The other side, looking out upon the Home ranch toward Bonneville and the railroad, was but little used. A deep porch ran the whole length of the house here, and in the lower branches of a live-oak near the steps Harran had built a little summer house for his mother. To the left of the ranch house itself, toward the County Road, was the bunk-house and kitchen for some of the hands. From the steps of the porch the

view to the southward expanded to infinity.   There was
not so much as a twig to obstruct the view.   In one leap
the eye reached the fine, delicate line where earth and
sky met, miles away.   The flat monotony of the land,
clean of fencing, was broken by one spot only, the roof
of the Division Superintendent's house on Three—a mere
speck, just darker than the ground.   Cutter's house on
Four was not even in sight.   That was below the
horizon.

As Harran came up he saw his mother at breakfast.
The table had been set on the porch and Mrs. Derrick,
stirring her coffee with one hand, held open with the
other the pages of Walter Pater's " Marius."   At her
feet, Princess Nathalie, the white Angora cat, sleek,
over-fed, self-centred, sat on her haunches, industriously
licking at the white fur of her breast, while near at hand,
by the railing of the porch, Presley pottered with a new
bicycle lamp, filling it with oil, adjusting the wicks.

Harran kissed his mother and sat down in a wicker
chair on the porch, removing his hat, running his fingers
through his yellow hair.

Magnus Derrick's wife looked hardly old enough to
be the mother of two such big fellows as Harran and
Lyman Derrick.   She was not far into the fifties, and
her brown hair still retained much of its brightness.   She
could yet be called pretty.   Her eyes were large and
easily assumed a look of inquiry and innocence, such as
one might expect to see in a young girl.   By disposition
she was retiring; she easily obliterated herself.   She was
not made for the harshness of the world, and yet she had
known these harshnesses in her younger days.   Magnus
had married her when she was twenty-one years old, at
a time when she was a graduate of some years' standing
from the State Normal School and was teaching literature, music, and penmanship in a seminary in the town

of Marysville. She overworked herself here continually, loathing the strain of teaching, yet clinging to it
with a tenacity born of the knowledge that it was her
only means of support. Both her parents were dead;
she was dependent upon herself. Her one ambition was
to see Italy and the Bay of Naples. The " Marble
Faun," Raphael's " Madonnas " and " Il Trovatore "
were her beau ideals of literature and art. She dreamed
of taly, Rome, Naples, and the world's great " art-
centres." There was no doubt that her affair with Magnus had been a love-match, but Annie Payne would have
loved any man who would have taken her out of the
droning, heart-breaking routine of the class and music
room. She had followed his fortunes unquestioningly.
First at Sacramento, during the turmoil of his political
career, later on at Placerville in El Dorado County, after
Derrick had interested himself in the Corpus Christi
group of mines, and finally at Los Muertos, where, after
selling out his fourth interest in Corpus Christi, he had
turned rancher and had " come in " on the new tracts
of wheat land just thrown open by the railroad. She
had lived here now for nearly ten years. But never for
one moment since the time her glance first lost itself in
the unbroken immensity of the ranches had she known
a moment's content. Continually there came into her
pretty, wide-open eyes—the eyes of a young doe—a look
of uneasiness, of distrust, and aversion. Los Muertos
frightened her. She remembered the dɛys of her young
girlhood passed on a farm in eastern Ohio—five hundred
acres, neatly partitioned into the water lot, the cow pas-
ture, the corn lot, the barley field, and wheat farm; cosey,
comfortable, home-like; where the farmers loved their
land, caressing it, coaxing it, nourishing it as though it
were a thing almost conscious; where the seed was sown
by hand, and a single two-horse plough was sufficient

for the entire farm; where the scythe sufficed to cut the harvest and the grain was thrashed with flails.

But this new order of things—a ranch bounded only by the horizons, where, as far as one could see, to the north, to the east, to the south and to the west, was all one holding, a principality ruled with iron and steam, bullied into a yield of three hundred and fifty thousand bushels, where even when the land was resting, unploughed, unharrowed, and unsown, the wheat came up —troubled her, and even at times filled her with an undefinable terror. To her mind there was something inordinate about it all; something almost unnatural. The direct brutality of ten thousand acres of wheat, nothing but wheat as far as the eye could see, stunned her a little. The one-time writing-teacher of a young ladies' seminary, with her pretty deer-like eyes and delicate fingers, shrank from it. She did not want to look at so much wheat. There was something vaguely indecent in the sight, this food of the people, this elemental force, this basic energy, weltering here under the sun in all the unconscious nakedness of a sprawling, primordial Titan.

The monotony of the ranch ate into her heart hour by hour, year by year. And with it all, when was she to see Rome, Italy, and the Bay of Naples? It was a different prospect truly. Magnus had given her his promise that once the ranch was well established, they two should travel. But continually he had been obliged to put her off, now for one reason, now for another; the machine would not as yet run of itself, he must still feel his hand upon the lever; next year, perhaps, when wheat should go to ninety, or the rains were good. She did not insist. She obliterated herself, only allowing, from time to time, her pretty, questioning eyes to meet his. In the meantime she retired within herself. She surrounded herself with books. Her taste was of the delicacy of point lace.

She knew her Austin Dobson by heart. She read poems, essays, the ideas of the seminary at Marysville persisting in her mind. "Marius the Epicurean," "The Essays of Elia," "Sesame and Lilies," "The Stones of Venice," and the little toy magazines, full of the flaccid banalities of the "Minor Poets," were continually in her hands.

When Presley had appeared on Los Muertos, she had welcomed his arrival with delight. Here at last was a congenial spirit. She looked forward to long conversations with the young man on literature, art, and ethics. But Presley had disappointed her. That he—outside of his few chosen deities—should care little for literature, shocked her beyond words. His indifference to "style," to elegant English, was a positive affront. His savage abuse and open ridicule of the neatly phrased rondeaux and sestinas and chansonettes of the little magazines was to her mind a wanton and uncalled-for cruelty. She found his Homer, with its slaughters and hecatombs and barbaric feastings and headstrong passions, violent and coarse. She could not see with him any romance, any poetry in the life around her; she looked to Italy for that. His "Song of the West," which only once, incoherent and fierce, he had tried to explain to her, its swift, tumultous life, its truth, its nobility and savagery, its heroism and obscenity, had revolted her.

"But, Presley," she had murmured, "that is not literature."

"No," he had cried between his teeth, "no, thank God, it is not."

A little later, one of the stablemen brought the buggy with the team of bays up to the steps of the porch, and Harran, putting on a different coat and a black hat, took himself off to Guadalajara.

The morning was fine; there was no cloud in the sky,

but as Harran's buggy drew away from the grove of trees about the ranch house, emerging into the open country on either side of the Lower Road, he caught himself looking sharply at the sky and the faint line of hills beyond the Quien Sabe ranch. There was a certain indefinite cast to the landscape that to Harran's eye was not to be mistaken. Rain, the first of the season, was not far off.

"That's good," he muttered, touching the bays with the whip, " we can't get our ploughs to hand any too soon."

These ploughs Magnus Derrick had ordered from an Eastern manufacturer some months before, since he was dissatisfied with the results obtained from the ones he had used hitherto, which were of local make. However, there had been exasperating and unexpected delays in their shipment. Magnus and Harran both had counted upon having the ploughs in their implement barns that very week, but a tracer sent after them had only resulted in locating them, still *en route*, somewhere between The Needles and Bakersfield. Now there was likelihood of rain within the week. Ploughing could be undertaken immediately afterward, so soon as the ground was softened, but there was a fair chance that the ranch would lie idle for want of proper machinery.

It was ten minutes before train time when Harran reached the depot at Guadalajara. The San Francisco papers of the preceding day had arrived on an earlier train. He bought a couple from the station agent and looked them over till a distant and prolonged whistle announced the approach of the down train.

In one of the four passengers that alighted from the train, he recognised his father. He half rose in his seat, whistling shrilly between his teeth, waving his hand, and Magnus Derrick, catching sight of him, came forward quickly.

Magnus—the Governor—was all of six feet tall, and though now well toward his sixtieth year, was as erect as an officer of cavalry. He was broad in proportion, a fine commanding figure, imposing an immediate respect, impressing one with a sense of gravity, of dignity and a certain pride of race. He was smooth-shaven, thin-lipped, with a broad chin, and a prominent hawk-like nose—the characteristic of the family—thin, with a high bridge, such as one sees in the later portraits of the Duke of Wellington. His hair was thick and iron-grey, and had a tendency to curl in a forward direction just in front of his ears. He wore a top-hat of grey, with a wide brim, and a frock coat, and carried a cane with a yellowed ivory head.

As a young man it had been his ambition to represent his native State—North Carolina—in the United States Senate. Calhoun was his " great man," but in two successive campaigns he had been defeated. His career checked in this direction, he had come to California in the fifties. He had known and had been the intimate friend of such men as Terry, Broderick, General Baker, Lick, Alvarado, Emerich, Larkin, and, above all, of the unfortunate and misunderstood Ralston. Once he had been put forward as the Democratic candidate for governor, but failed of election. After this Magnus had definitely abandoned politics and had invested all his money in the Corpus Christi mines. Then he had sold out his interest at a small profit—just in time to miss his chance of becoming a multi-millionaire in the Comstock boom—and was looking for reinvestments in other lines when the news that " wheat had been discovered in California " was passed from mouth to mouth. Practically it amounted to a discovery. Dr. Glenn's first harvest of wheat in Colusa County, quietly undertaken but suddenly realised with dramatic abruptness, gave a new matter for reflection to the thinking men of the New West. California suddenly leaped unheralded into the world's market as a competitor in wheat production. In a few years her output of wheat exceeded the value of her output of gold, and when, later on, the Pacific and Southwestern Railroad threw open to settlers the rich lands of Tulare County—conceded to the corporation by the government as a bonus for the construction of the road—Magnus had been quick to seize the opportunity and had taken up the ten thousand acres of Los Muertos. Wherever he had gone, Magnus had taken his family with him. Lyman had been born at Sacramento during the turmoil and excitement of Derrick's campaign for governor, and Harran at Shingle Springs, in El Dorado County, six years later.

But Magnus was in every sense the "prominent man." In whatever circle he moved he was the chief figure. Instinctively other men looked to him as the leader. He himself was proud of this distinction; he assumed the grand manner very easily and carried it well. As a public speaker he was one of the last of the followers of the old school of orators. He even carried the diction and manner of the rostrum into private life. It was said of him that his most colloquial conversation could be taken down in shorthand and read off as an admirable specimen of pure, well-chosen English. He loved to do things upon a grand scale, to preside, to dominate. In his good humour there was something Jovian. When angry, everybody around him trembled. But he had not the genius for detail, was not patient. The certain grandiose lavishness of his disposition occupied itself more with results than with means. He was always ready to take chances, to hazard everything on the hopes of colossal returns. In the mining days at Placerville there was no more redoubtable poker player in the county.

He had been as lucky in his mines as in his gambling, sinking shafts and tunnelling in violation of expert theory and finding " pay " in every case. Without knowing it, he allowed himself to work his ranch much as if he was still working his mine. The old-time spirit of '49, hap-hazard, unscientific, persisted in his mind. Everything was a gamble—who took the greatest chances was most apt to be the greatest winner. The idea of manuring Los Muertos, of husbanding his great resources, he would have scouted as niggardly, Hebraic, ungenerous.

Magnus climbed into the buggy, helping himself with Harran's outstretched hand which he still held. The two were immensely fond of each other, proud of each other. They were constantly together and Magnus kept no secrets from his favourite son.

" Well, boy."

" Well, Governor."

" I am very pleased you came yourself, Harran. I feared that you might be too busy and send Phelps. It was thoughtful."

Harran was about to reply, but at that moment Magnus caught sight of the three flat cars loaded with bright-painted farming machines which still remained on the siding above the station. He laid his hands on the reins and Harran checked the team.

" Harran," observed Magnus, fixing the machinery with a judicial frown, " Harran, those look singularly like our ploughs. Drive over, boy."

The train had by this time gone on its way and Harran brought the team up to the siding.

" Ah, I was right," said the Governor. " ' Magnus Derrick, Los Muertos, Bonneville, from Ditson & Co., Rochester.' These are ours, boy."

Harran breathed a sigh of relief.

" At last," he answered, " and just in time, too. We'll
have rain before the week is out. I think, now that I am
here, I will telephone Phelps to send the wagon right
down for these. I started blue-stoning to-day."

Magnus nodded a grave approval.

" That was shrewd, boy. As to the rain, I think you
are well informed; we will have an early season. The
ploughs have arrived at a happy moment."

" It means money to us, Governor," remarked Harran.

But as he turned the horses to allow his father to get
into the buggy again, the two were surprised to hear a
thick, throaty voice wishing them good-morning, and
turning about were aware of S. Behrman, who had come
up while they were examining the ploughs. Harran's
eyes flashed on the instant and through his nostrils he
drew a sharp, quick breath, while a certain rigour of carriage stiffened the set of Magnus Derrick's shoulders
and back. Magnus had not yet got into the buggy, but
stood with the team between him and S. Behrman, eyeing him calmly across the horses' backs. S. Behrman
came around to the other side of the buggy and faced
Magnus.

He was a large, fat man, with a great stomach; his
cheek and the upper part of his thick neck ran together
to form a great tremulous jowl, shaven and blue-grey in
colour; a roll of fat, sprinkled with sparse hair, moist
with perspiration, protruded over the back of his collar.
He wore a heavy black moustache. On his head was a
round-topped hat of stiff brown straw, highly varnished.
A light-brown linen vest, stamped with innumerable interlocked horseshoes, covered his protuberant stomach,
upon which a heavy watch chain of hollow links rose
and fell with his difficult breathing, clinking against the
vest buttons of imitation mother-of-pearl.

S. Behrman was the banker of Bonneville. But besides this he was many other things. He was a real estate agent. He bought grain; he dealt in mortgages. He was one of the local political bosses, but more important than all this, he was the representative of the Pacific and Southwestern Railroad in that section of Tulare County. The railroad did little business in that part of the country that S. Behrman did not supervise, from the consignment of a shipment of wheat to the management of a damage suit, or even to the repair and maintenance of the right of way. During the time when the ranchers of the county were fighting the grain-rate case, S. Behrman had been much in evidence in and about the San Francisco court rooms and the lobby of the legislature in Sacramento. He had returned to Bonneville only recently, a decision adverse to the ranchers being foreseen. The position he occupied on the salary list of the Pacific and Southwestern could not readily be defined, for he was neither freight agent, passenger agent, attorney, real-estate broker, nor political servant, though his influence in all these offices was undoubted and enormous. But for all that, the ranchers about Bonneville knew whom to look to as a source of trouble. There was no denying the fact that for Osterman, Broderson, Annixter and Derrick, S. Behrman was the railroad.

"Mr. Derrick, good-morning," he cried as he came up. "Good-morning, Harran. Glad to see you back, Mr. Derrick." He held out a thick hand.

Magnus, head and shoulders above the other, tall, thin, erect, looked down upon S. Behrman, inclining his head, failing to see his extended hand.

"Good-morning, sir," he observed, and waited for S. Behrman's further speech.

"Well, Mr. Derrick," continued S. Behrman, wiping the back of his neck with his handkerchief, "I saw in the city papers yesterday that our case had gone against you."

"I guess it wasn't any great news to *you*," commented Harran, his face scarlet. "I guess you knew which way Ulsteen was going to jump after your very first interview with him. You don't like to be surprised in this sort of thing, S. Behrman."

"Now, you know better than that, Harran," remonstrated S. Behrman blandly. "I know what you mean to imply, but I ain't going to let it make me get mad. I wanted to say to your Governor—I wanted to say to you, Mr. Derrick—as one man to another—letting alone for the minute that we were on opposite sides of the case —that I'm sorry you didn't win. Your side made a good fight, but it was in a mistaken cause. That's the whole trouble. Why, you could have figured out before you ever went into the case that such rates are confiscation of property. You must allow us—must allow the railroad—a fair interest on the investment. You don't want us to go into the receiver's hands, do you now, Mr. Derrick?"

"The Board of Railroad Commissioners was bought," remarked Magnus sharply, a keen, brisk flash glinting in his eye.

"It was part of the game," put in Harran, "for the Railroad Commission to cut rates to a ridiculous figure, far below a *reasonable* figure, just so that it *would* be confiscation. Whether Ulsteen is a tool of yours or not, he had to put the rates back to what they were originally."

"If you enforced those rates, Mr. Harran," returned S. Behrman calmly, "we wouldn't be able to earn sufficient money to meet operating expenses or fixed charges, to say nothing of a surplus left over to pay dividends——"

"Tell me when the P. and S. W. ever paid dividends."

"The lowest rates," continued S. Behrman, "that the legislature can establish must be such as will secure us a fair interest on our investment."

"Well, what's your standard? Come, let's hear it. Who is to say what's a fair rate? The railroad has its own notions of fairness sometimes."

"The laws of the State," returned S. Behrman, "fix the rate of interest at seven per cent. That's a good enough standard for us. There is no reason, Mr. Harran, why a dollar invested in a railroad should not earn as much as a dollar represented by a promissory note— seven per cent. By applying your schedule of rates we would not earn a cent; we would be bankrupt."

"Interest on your investment!" cried Harran, furious. "It's fine to talk about fair interest. *I* know and *you* know that the total earnings of the P. and S. W.—their main, branch and leased lines for last year—was between nineteen and twenty millions of dollars. Do you mean to say that twenty million dollars is seven per cent. of the original cost of the road?"

S. Behrman spread out his hands, smiling.

"That was the gross, not the net figure—and how can you tell what was the original cost of the road?"

"Ah, that's just it," shouted Harran, emphasising each word with a blow of his fist upon his knee, his eyes sparkling, "you take cursed good care that we don't know anything about the original cost of the road. But we know you are bonded for treble your value; and we know this: that the road *could* have been built for fifty-four thousand dollars per mile and that you *say* it cost you eighty-seven thousand. It makes a difference, S. Behrman, on which of these two figures you are basing your seven per cent."

"That all may show obstinacy, Harran," observed S. Behrman vaguely, "but it don't show common sense."

"We are threshing out old straw, I believe, gentlemen," remarked Magnus. "The question was thoroughly sifted in the courts."

"Quite right," assented S. Behrman. "The best way is that the railroad and the farmer understand each other and get along peaceably. We are both dependent on each other. Your ploughs, I believe, Mr. Derrick." S. Behrman nodded toward the flat cars.

"They are consigned to me," admitted Magnus.

"It looks a trifle like rain," observed S. Behrman, easing his neck and jowl in his limp collar. "I suppose you will want to begin ploughing next week."

"Possibly," said Magnus.

"I'll see that your ploughs are hurried through for you then, Mr. Derrick. We will route them by fast freight for you and it won't cost you anything extra."

"What do you mean?" demanded Harran. "The ploughs are here. We have nothing more to do with the railroad. I am going to have my wagons down here this afternoon."

"I am sorry," answered S. Behrman, "but the cars are going north, not, as you thought, coming *from* the north. They have not been to San Francisco yet."

Magnus made a slight movement of the head as one who remembers a fact hitherto forgotten. But Harran was as yet unenlightened.

"To San Francisco!" he answered, "we want them here—what are you talking about?"

"Well, you know, of course, the regulations," answered S. Behrman. "Freight of this kind coming from the Eastern points into the State must go first to one of our common points and be reshipped from there."

Harran did remember now, but never before had the

matter so struck home. He leaned back in his seat in dumb amazement for the instant. Even Magnus had turned a little pale. Then, abruptly, Harran broke out violent and raging.

"What next? My God, why don't you break into our houses at night? Why don't you steal the watch out of my pocket, steal the horses out of the harness, hold us up with a shot-gun; yes, 'stand and deliver; your money or your life.' Here we bring our ploughs from the East over your lines, but you're not content with your long-haul rate between Eastern points and Bonneville. You want to get us under your ruinous short-haul rate between Bonneville and San Francisco, *and return.* Think of it! Here's a load of stuff for Bonneville that can't stop at Bonneville, where it is consigned, but has got to go up to San Francisco first *by way of* Bonneville, at forty cents per ton and then be reshipped from San Francisco back to Bonneville again at *fifty-one* cents per ton, the short-haul rate. And we have to pay it all or go without. Here are the ploughs right here, in sight of the land they have got to be used on, the season just ready for them, and we can't touch them. Oh," he exclaimed in deep disgust, "isn't it a pretty mess! Isn't it a farce! the whole dirty business!"

S. Behrman listened to him unmoved, his little eyes blinking under his fat forehead, the gold chain of hollow links clicking against the pearl buttons of his waistcoat as he breathed.

"It don't do any good to let loose like that, Harran," he said at length. "I am willing to do what I can for you. I'll hurry the ploughs through, but I can't change the freight regulation of the road."

"What's your blackmail for this?" vociferated Harran. "How much do you want to let us go? How much have we got to pay you to be *allowed* to use our own ploughs—what's your figure? Come, spit it out."

"I see you are trying to make me angry, Harran," returned S. Behrman, "but you won't succeed. Better give up trying, my boy. As I said, the best way is to have the railroad and the farmer get along amicably. It is the only way we can do business. Well, s'long, Governor, I must trot along. S'long, Harran." He took himself off.

But before leaving Guadalajara Magnus dropped into the town's small grocery store to purchase a box of cigars of a certain Mexican brand, unprocurable elsewhere. Harran remained in the buggy.

While he waited, Dyke appeared at the end of the street, and, seeing Derrick's younger son, came over to shake hands with him. He explained his affair with the P. and S. W., and asked the young man what he thought of the expected rise in the price of hops.

"Hops ought to be a good thing," Harran told him. "The crop in Germany and in New York has been a dead failure for the last three years, and so many people have gone out of the business that there's likely to be a shortage and a stiff advance in the price. They ought to go to a dollar next year. Sure, hops ought to be a good thing. How's the old lady and Sidney, Dyke?"

"Why, fairly well, thank you, Harran. They're up to Sacramento just now to see my brother. I was thinking of going in with my brother into this hop business. But I had a letter from him this morning. He may not be able to meet me on this proposition. He's got other business on hand. If he pulls out—and he probably will —I'll have to go it alone, but I'll have to borrow. I had thought with his money and mine we would have enough to pull off the affair without mortgaging anything. As it is, I guess I'll have to see S. Behrman."

"I'll be cursed if I would!" exclaimed Harran.

"Well, S. Behrman is a screw," admitted the engineer, "and he is 'railroad' to his boots; but business is business, and he would have to stand by a contract in black and white, and this chance in hops is too good to let slide. I guess we'll try it on, Harran. I can get a good foreman that knows all about hops just now, and if the deal pays—well, I want to send Sid to a seminary up in San Francisco."

"Well, mortgage the crops, but don't mortgage the homestead, Dyke," said Harran. "And, by the way, have you looked up the freight rates on hops?"

"No, I haven't yet," answered Dyke, "and I had better be sure of *that*, hadn't I? I hear that the rate is reasonable, though."

"You be sure to have a clear understanding with the railroad first about the rate," Harran warned him.

When Magnus came out of the grocery store and once more seated himself in the buggy, he said to Harran, "Boy, drive over here to Annixter's before we start home. I want to ask him to dine with us to-night. Osterman and Broderson are to drop in, I believe, and I should like to have Annixter as well."

Magnus was lavishly hospitable. Los Muertos's doors invariably stood open to all the Derricks' neighbours, and once in so often Magnus had a few of his intimates to dinner.

As Harran and his father drove along the road toward Annixter's ranch house, Magnus asked about what had happened during his absence.

He inquired after his wife and the ranch, commenting upon the work on the irrigating ditch. Harran gave him the news of the past week, Dyke's discharge, his resolve to raise a crop of hops; Vanamee's return, the killing of the sheep, and Hooven's petition to remain upon the

ranch as Magnus's tenant. It needed only Harran's rec-
ommendation that the German should remain to have
Magnus consent upon the instant.

"You know more about it than I, boy," he said, "and
whatever you think is wise shall be done."

Harran touched the bays with the whip, urging them
to their briskest pace. They were not yet at Annixter's
and he was anxious to get back to the ranch house to
supervise the blue-stoning of his seed.

"By the way, Governor," he demanded suddenly,
"how is Lyman getting on?"

Lyman, Magnus's eldest son, had never taken kindly
toward ranch life. He resembled his mother more than
he did Magnus, and had inherited from her a distaste for
agriculture and a tendency toward a profession. At a
time when Harran was learning the rudiments of farming, Lyman was entering the State University, and,
graduating thence, had spent three years in the study
of law. But later on, traits that were particularly his
father's developed. Politics interested him. He told
himself he was a born politician, was diplomatic, approachable, had a talent for intrigue, a gift of making
friends easily and, most indispensable of all, a veritable
genius for putting influential men under obligations to
himself. Already he had succeeded in gaining for himself two important offices in the municipal administration
of San Francisco—where he had his home—sheriff's attorney, and, later on, assistant district attorney. But
with these small achievements he was by no means satisfied. The largeness of his father's character, modified
in Lyman by a counter-influence of selfishness, had produced in him an inordinate ambition. Where his father
during his political career had considered himself only
as an exponent of principles he strove to apply, Lyman
saw but the office, his own personal aggrandisement.

He belonged to the new school, wherein objects were attained not by orations before senates and assemblies, but by sessions of committees, caucuses, compromises and expedients. His goal was to be in fact what Magnus was only in name—governor. Lyman, with shut teeth, had resolved that some day he would sit in the gubernatorial chair in Sacramento.

"Lyman is doing well," answered Magnus. "I could wish he was more pronounced in his convictions, less willing to compromise, but I believe him to be earnest and to have a talent for government and civics. His ambition does him credit, and if he occupied himself a little more with means and a little less with ends, he would, I am sure, be the ideal servant of the people. But I am not afraid. The time will come when the State will be proud of him."

As Harran turned the team into the driveway that led up to Annixter's house, Magnus remarked:

"Harran, isn't that young Annixter himself on the porch?"

Harran nodded and remarked:

"By the way, Governor, I wouldn't seem too cordial in your invitation to Annixter. He will be glad to come, I know, but if you seem to want him too much, it is just like his confounded obstinacy to make objections."

"There is something in that," observed Magnus, as Harran drew up at the porch of the house. "He is a queer, cross-grained fellow, but in many ways sterling."

Annixter was lying in the hammock on the porch, precisely as Presley had found him the day before, reading "David Copperfield" and stuffing himself with dried prunes. When he recognised Magnus, however, he got up, though careful to give evidence of the most poignant discomfort. He explained his difficulty at great length, protesting that his stomach was no better than a sponge-

bag. Would Magnus and Harran get down and have
a drink? There was whiskey somewhere about.

Magnus, however, declined. He stated his errand,
asking Annixter to come over to Los Muertos that evening for seven o'clock dinner. Osterman and Broderson
would be there.

At once Annixter, even to Harran's surprise, put his
chin in the air, making excuses, fearing to compromise
himself if he accepted too readily. No, he did not think
he could get around—was sure of it, in fact. There were
certain businesses he had on hand that evening. He
had practically made an appointment with a man at
Bonneville; then, too, he was thinking of going up to
San Francisco to-morrow and needed his sleep; would
go to bed early; and besides all that, he was a very sick
man; his stomach was out of whack; if he moved about
it brought the gripes back. No, they must get along
without him.

Magnus, knowing with whom he had to deal, did not
urge the point, being convinced that Annixter would
argue over the affair the rest of the morning. He re-
settled himself in the buggy and Harran gathered up
the reins.

"Well," he observed, "you know your business best.
Come if you can. We dine at seven."

"I hear you are going to farm the whole of Los Muertos this season," remarked Annixter, with a certain note
of challenge in his voice.

"We are thinking of it," replied Magnus.

Annixter grunted scornfully.

"Did you get the message I sent you by Presley?"
he began.

Tactless, blunt, and direct, Annixter was quite capable
of calling even Magnus a fool to his face. But before
he could proceed, S. Behrman in his single buggy turned

into the gate, and driving leisurely up to the porch
halted on the other side of Magnus's team.

"Good-morning, gentlemen," he remarked, nodding
to the two Derricks as though he had not seen them
earlier in the day. "Mr. Annixter, how do you do?"

"What in hell do *you* want?" demanded Annixter
with a stare.

S. Behrman hiccoughed slightly and passed a fat hand
over his waistcoat.

"Why, not very much, Mr. Annixter," he replied,
ignoring the belligerency in the young ranchman's voice,
"but I will have to lodge a protest against you, Mr.
Annixter, in the matter of keeping your line fence in
repair. The sheep were all over the track last night,
this side the Long Trestle, and I am afraid they have seriously disturbed our ballast along there. We—the railroad—can't fence along our right of way. The farmers
have the prescriptive right of that, so we have to look
to you to keep your fence in repair. I am sorry, but I
shall have to protest——"

Annixter returned to the hammock and stretched himself out in it to his full length, remarking tranquilly:

"Go to the devil!"

"It is as much to your interest as to ours that the
safety of the public——"

"You heard what I said. Go to the devil!"

"That all may show obstinacy, Mr. Annixter, but——"

Suddenly Annixter jumped up again and came to the
edge of the porch; his face flamed scarlet to the roots of
his stiff yellow hair. He thrust out his jaw aggressively,
clenching his teeth.

"*You*," he vociferated, "I'll tell you what you are.
You're a—a—a *pip!*"

To his mind it was the last insult, the most outrageous
calumny. He had no worse epithet at his command.

" ——may show obstinacy," pursued S. Behrman, bent upon finishing the phrase, " but it don't show common sense."

" I'll mend my fence, and then, again, maybe I won't mend my fence," shouted Annixter. " I know what you mean—that wild engine last night. Well, you've no right to run at that speed in the town limits."

" How the town limits? The sheep were this side the Long Trestle."

" Well, that's in the town limits of Guadalajara."

" Why, Mr. Annixter, the Long Trestle is a good two miles out of Guadalajara.

Annixter squared himself, leaping to the chance of an argument.

" Two miles! It's not a mile and a quarter. No, it's not a mile. I'll leave it to Magnus here."

" Oh, I know nothing about it," declared Magnus, refusing to be involved.

" Yes, you do. Yes, you do, too. Any fool knows how far it is from Guadalajara to the Long Trestle. It's about five-eighths of a mile."

" From the depot of the town," remarked S. Behrman placidly, " to the head of the Long Trestle is about two miles."

" That's a lie and you know it's a lie," shouted the other, furious at S. Behrman's calmness, " and I can prove it's a lie. I've walked that distance on the Upper Road, and I know just how fast I walk, and if I can walk four miles in one hour——"

Magnus and Harran drove on, leaving Annixter trying to draw S. Behrman into a wrangle.

When at length S. Behrman as well took himself away, Annixter returned to his hammock, finished the rest of his prunes and read another chapter of " Copperfield."

Then he put the book, open, over his face and went to sleep.

An hour later, toward noon, his own terrific snoring woke him up suddenly, and he sat up, rubbing his face and blinking at the sunlight. There was a bad taste in his mouth from sleeping with it wide open, and going into the dining-room of the house, he mixed himself a drink of whiskey and soda and swallowed it in three great gulps. He told himself that he felt not only better but hungry, and pressed an electric button in the wall near the sideboard three times to let the kitchen—situated in a separate building near the ranch house—know that he was ready for his dinner. As he did so, an idea occurred to him. He wondered if Hilma Tree would bring up his dinner and wait on the table while he ate it.

In connection with his ranch, Annixter ran a dairy farm on a very small scale, making just enough butter and cheese for the consumption of the ranch's *personnel*. Old man Tree, his wife, and his daughter Hilma looked after the dairy. But there was not always work enough to keep the three of them occupied and Hilma at times made herself useful in other ways. As often as not she lent a hand in the kitchen, and two or three times a week she took her mother's place in looking after Annixter's house, making the beds, putting his room to rights, bringing his meals up from the kitchen. For the last summer she had been away visiting with relatives in one of the towns on the coast. But the week previous to this she had returned and Annixter had come upon her suddenly one day in the dairy, making cheese, the sleeves of her crisp blue shirt waist rolled back to her very shoulders. Annixter had carried away with him a clear-cut recollection of these smooth white arms of hers, bare to the shoulder, very round and cool and fresh. He

would not have believed that a girl so young should
have had arms so big and perfect. To his surprise he
found himself thinking of her after he had gone to bed
that night, and in the morning when he woke he was
bothered to know whether he had dreamed about
Hilma's fine white arms over night. Then abruptly he
had lost patience with himself for being so occupied with
the subject, raging and furious with all the breed of feemales—a fine way for a man to waste his time. He
had had his experience with the timid little creature in
the glove-cleaning establishment in Sacramento. That
was enough. Feemales! Rot! None of them in *his*,
thank you. *He* had seen Hilma Tree give him a look in
the dairy. Aha, he saw through her! She w s trying
to get a hold on him, was she? He would show her.
Wait till he saw her again. He would send her about
her business in a hurry. He resolved upon a terrible
demeanour in the presence of the dairy girl—a great
show of indifference, a fierce masculine nonchalance; and
when, the next morning, she brought him his breakfast,
he had been smitten dumb as soon as she entered the
room, glueing his eyes upon his plate, his elbows close
to his side, awkward, clumsy, overwhelmed with constraint.

While true to his convictions as a woman-hater and
genuinely despising Hilma both as a girl and as an in-
ferior, the idea of her worried him. Most of all, he was
angry with himself because of his inane sheepishness
when she was about. He at first had told himself that
he was a fool not to be able to ignore her existence as
hitherto, and then that he was a greater fool not to take
advantage of his position. Certainly he had not the
remotest idea of any affection, but Hilma was a fine
looking girl. He imagined an affair with her.

As he reflected upon the matter now, scowling abstractedly at the button of the electric bell, turning the whole business over in his mind, he remembered that to-day was butter-making day and that Mrs. Tree would be occupied in the dairy. That meant that Hilma would take her place. He turned to the mirror of the sideboard, scrutinising his reflection with grim disfavour. After a moment, rubbing the roughened surface of his chin the wrong way, he muttered to his image in the glass:

"What a mug! Good Lord! what a looking mug!" Then, after a moment's silence, "Wonder if that fool feemale will be up here to-day."

He crossed over into his bedroom and peeped around the edge of the lowered curtain. The window looked out upon the skeleton-like tower of the artesian well and the cook-house and dairy-house close beside it. As he watched, he saw Hilma come out from the cook-house and hurry across toward the kitchen. Evidently, she was going to see about his dinner. But as she passed by the artesian well, she met young Delaney, one of Annixter's hands, coming up the trail by the irrigating ditch, leading his horse toward the stables, a great coil of barbed wire in his gloved hands and a pair of nippers thrust into his belt. No doubt, he had been mending the break in the line fence by the Long Trestle. Annixter saw him take off his wide-brimmed hat as he met Hilma, and the two stood there for some moments talking together. Annixter even heard Hilma laughing very gayly at something Delaney was saying. She patted his horse's neck affectionately, and Delaney, drawing the nippers from his belt, made as if to pinch her arm with them. She caught at his wrist and pushed him away, laughing again. To Annixter's mind the pair seemed astonishingly intimate. Brusquely his anger flamed up.

Ah, that was it, was it? Delaney and Hilma had an

understanding between themselves. They carried on their affair right out there in the open, under his very eyes. It was absolutely disgusting. Had they no sense of decency, those two? Well, this ended it. He would stop that sort of thing short off; none of that on *his* ranch if he knew it. No, sir. He would pack that girl off before he was a day older. He wouldn't have that kind about the place. Not much! She'd have to get out. He would talk to old man Tree about it this afternoon. Whatever happened, *he* insisted upon morality.

"And my dinner!" he suddenly exclaimed. "I've got to wait and go hungry—and maybe get sick again—while they carry on their disgusting love-making."

He turned about on the instant, and striding over to the electric bell, rang it again with all his might.

"When that feemale gets up here," he declared, "I'll just find out why I've got to wait like this. I'll take her down, to the Queen's taste. I'm lenient enough, Lord knows, but I don't propose to be imposed upon *all* the time."

A few moments later, while Annixter was pretending to read the county newspaper by the window in the dining-room, Hilma came in to set the table. At the time Annixter had his feet cocked on the window ledge and was smoking a cigar, but as soon as she entered the room he—without premeditation—brought his feet down to the floor and crushed out the lighted tip of his cigar under the window ledge. Over the top of the paper he glanced at her covertly from time to time.

Though Hilma was only nineteen years old, she was a large girl with all the development of a much older woman. There was a certain generous amplitude to the full, round curves of her hips and shoulders that suggested the precocious maturity of a healthy, vigorous animal life passed under the hot southern sun of a half-tropical country. She was, one knew at a glance, warm-blooded, full-blooded, with an even, comfortable balance of temperament. Her neck was thick, and sloped to her shoulders, with full, beautiful curves, and under her chin and under her ears the flesh was as white and smooth as floss satin, shading exquisitely to a faint delicate brown on her nape at the roots of her hair. Her throat rounded to meet her chin and cheek, with a soft swell of the skin, tinted pale amber in the shadows, but blending by barely perceptible gradations to the sweet, warm flush of her cheek. This colour on her temples was just touched with a certain blueness where the flesh was thin over the fine veining underneath. Her eyes were light brown, and so wide open that on the slightest provocation the ful disc of the pupil was disclosed; the lids—just a fraction of a shade darker than the hue of her face—were edged with lashes that were almost black. While these lashes were not long, they were thick and rimmed her eyes with a fine, thin line. Her mouth was rather large, the lips shut tight, and nothing could have been more graceful, more charming than the outline of these full lips of hers, and her round white chin, modulating downward with a certain delicious roundness to her neck, her throat and the sweet feminine amplitude of her breast. The slightest movement of her head and shoulders sent a gentle undulation through all this beauty of soft outlines and smooth surfaces, the delicate amber shadows deepening or fading or losing themselves imperceptibly in the pretty rose-colour of her cheeks, or the dark, warm-tinted shadow of her thick brown hair.

Her hair seemed almost to have a life of its own, almost Medusa-like, thick, glossy and moist, lying in heavy, sweet-smelling masses over her forehead, over her small ears with their pink lobes, and far down upon her nape. Deep in between the coils and braids it was

of a bitumen brownness, but in the sunlight it vibrated
with a sheen like tarnished gold.

Like most large girls, her movements were not hurried, and this indefinite deliberateness of gesture, this
slow grace, this certain ease of attitude, was a charm
that was all her own.

But Hilma's greatest charm of all was her simplicity—
a simplicity that was not only in the calm regularity of
her face, with its statuesque evenness of contour, its
broad surface of cheek and forehead and the masses of
her straight smooth hair, but was apparent as well in
the long line of her carriage, from her foot to her waist
and the single deep swell from her waist to her shoulder.
Almost unconsciously she dressed in harmony with this
note of simplicity, and on this occasion wore a skirt of
plain dark blue calico and a white shirt waist crisp from
the laundry.

And yet, for all the dignity of this rigourous simplicity,
there were about Hilma small contradictory suggestions
of feminine daintiness, charming beyond words.   Even
Annixter could not help noticing that her feet were
narrow and slender, and that the little steel buckles of
her low shoes were polished bright, and that her finger-
tips and nails were of a fine rosy pink.

He found himself wondering how it was that a girl in
Hilma's position should be able to keep herself so pretty,
so trim, so clean and feminine, but he reflected that her
work was chiefly in the dairy, and even there of the lightest order.   She was on the ranch more for the sake of
being with her parents than from any necessity of employment.   Vaguely he seemed to understand that, in
that great new land of the West, in the open-air, healthy
life of the ranches, where the conditions of earning a live-
lihood were of the easiest, refinement among the
younger women was easily to be found—not the refine-

ment of education, nor culture, but the natural, intuitive
refinement of the woman, not as yet defiled and crushed
out by the sordid, strenuous life-struggle of over-popu-
lated districts. It was the original, intended and natural
delicacy of an elemental existence, close to nature, close
to life, close to the great, kindly earth.

As Hilma laid the table-spread, her arms opened to
their widest reach, the white cloth setting a little glisten
of reflected light underneath the chin, Annixter stirred
in his place uneasily.

"Oh, it's you, is it, Miss Hilma?" he remarked, for
the sake of saying something. "Good-morning. How
do you do?"

"*Good*-morning, sir," she answered, looking up, resting for a moment on her outspread palms. "I hope you
are better."

Her voice was low in pitch and of a velvety huskiness,
seeming to come more from her chest than from her
throat.

"Well, I'm some better," growled Annixter. Then
suddenly he demanded, "Where's that dog?"

A decrepit Irish setter sometimes made his appearance
in and about the ranch house, sleeping under the bed
and eating when anyone about the place thought to give
him a plate of bread.

Annixter had no particular interest in the dog. For
weeks at a time he ignored its existence. It was not
his dog. But to-day it seemed as if he could not let the
subject rest. For no reason that he could explain even
to himself, he recurred to it continually. He questioned
Hilma minutely all about the dog. Who owned him?
How old did she think he was? Did she imagine the dog
was sick? Where had he got to? Maybe he had
crawled off to die somewhere. He recurred to the subject all through the meal; apparently, he could talk of

nothing else, and as she finally went away after clearing off the table, he went onto the porch and called after her:

"Say, Miss Hilma."

"Yes, sir."

"If that dog turns up again you let me know."

"Very well, sir."

Annixter returned to the dining-room and sat down in the chair he had just vacated.

"To hell with the dog!" he muttered, enraged, he could not tell why.

When at length he allowed his attention to wander from Hilma Tree, he found that he had been staring fixedly at a thermometer upon the wall opposite, and this made him think that it had long been his intention to buy a fine barometer, an instrument that could be accurately depended on. But the barometer suggested the present condition of the weather and the likelihood of rain. In such case, much was to be done in the way of getting the seed ready and overhauling his ploughs and drills. He had not been away from the house in two days. It was time to be up and doing. He determined to put in the afternoon "taking a look around," and have a late supper. He would not go to Los Muertos; he would ignore Magnus Derrick's invitation. Possibly, though, it might be well to run over and see what was up.

"If I do," he said to himself, "I'll ride the buckskin."

The buckskin was a half-broken broncho that fought like a fiend under the saddle until the quirt and spur brought her to her senses. But Annixter remembered that the Trees' cottage, next the dairy-house, looked out upon the stables, and perhaps Hilma would see him while he was mounting the horse and be impressed with his courage.

"Huh!" grunted Annixter under his breath, "I should like to see that fool Delaney try to bust that bronch. That's what *I'd* like to see."

However, as Annixter stepped from the porch of the ranch house, he was surprised to notice a grey haze over all the sky; the sunlight was gone; there was a sense of coolness in the air; the weather-vane on the barn—a fine golden trotting horse with flamboyant mane and tail— was veering in a southwest wind. Evidently the expected rain was close at hand.

Annixter crossed over to the stables reflecting that he could ride the buckskin to the Trees' cottage and tell Hilma that he would not be home to supper. The conference at Los Muertos would be an admirable excuse for this, and upon the spot he resolved to go over to the Derrick ranch house, after all.

As he passed the Trees' cottage, he observed with satisfaction that Hilma was going to and fro in the front room. If he busted the buckskin in the yard before the stable she could not help but see. Annixter found the stableman in the back of the barn greasing the axles of the buggy, and ordered him to put the saddle on the buckskin.

"Why, I don't think she's here, sir," answered the stableman, glancing into the stalls. "No, I remember now. Delaney took her out just after dinner. His other horse went lame and he wanted to go down by the Long Trestle to mend the fence. He started out, but had to come back."

"Oh, Delaney got her, did he?"

"Yes, sir. He had a circus with her, but he busted her right enough. When it comes to horse, Delaney can wipe the eye of any cow-puncher in the county, I guess."

"He can, can he?" observed Annixter. Then after

a silence, " Well, all right, Billy; put my saddle on whatever you've got here. I'm going over to Los Muertos
this afternoon."

" Want to look out for the rain, Mr. Annixter," remarked Billy. " Guess we'll have rain before night."

" I'll take a rubber coat," answered Annixter. " Bring
the horse up to the ranch house when you're ready."

Annixter returned to the house to look for his rubber
coat in deep disgust, not permitting himself to glance
toward the dairy-house and the Trees' cottage. But
as he reached the porch he heard the telephone ringing
his call. It was Presley, who rang up from Los Muertos. He had heard from Harran that Annixter was,
perhaps, coming over that evening. If he came, would
he mind bringing over his—Presley's—bicycle. He had
left it at the Quien Sabe ranch the day before and had
forgotten to come back that way for it.

" Well," objected Annixter, a surly note in his voice,
" I *was* going to *ride* over."

" Oh, never mind, then, " returned Presley easily. " I
was to blame for forgetting it. Don't bother about it.
I'll come over some of these days and get it myself."

Annixter hung up the transmitter with a vehement
wrench and stamped out of the room, banging the door.
He found his rubber coat hanging in the hallway and
swung into it with a fierce movement of the shoulders that
all but started the seams. Everything seemed to con-
spire to thwart him. It was just like that absent-minded,
crazy poet, Presley, to forget his wheel. Well, he could
come after it himself. He, Annixter, would ride *some*
horse, anyhow. When he came out upon the porch he
saw the wheel leaning against the fence where Presley
had left it. If it stayed there much longer the rain would
catch it. Annixter ripped out an oath. At every moment his ill-humour was increasing. Yet, for all that, he

went back to the stable, pushing the bicycle before him, and countermanded his order, directing the stableman to get the buggy ready. He himself carefully stowed Presley's bicycle under the seat, covering it with a couple of empty sacks and a tarpaulin carriage cover.

While he was doing this, the stableman uttered an exclamation and paused in the act of backing the horse into the shafts, holding up a hand, listening.

From the hollow roof of the barn and from the thick velvet-like padding of dust over the ground outside, and from among the leaves of the few nearby trees and plants there came a vast, monotonous murmur that seemed to issue from all quarters of the horizon at once, a prolonged and subdued rustling sound, steady, even, persistent.

"There's your rain," announced the stableman. "The first of the season."

"And I got to be out in it," fumed Annixter, "and I suppose those swine will quit work on the big barn now."

When the buggy was finally ready, he put on his rubber coat, climbed in, and without waiting for the stableman to raise the top, drove out into the rain, a new-lit cigar in his teeth. As he passed the dairy-house, he saw Hilma standing in the doorway, holding out her hand to the rain, her face turned upward toward the grey sky, amused and interested at this first shower of the wet season. She was so absorbed that she did not see Annixter, and his clumsy nod in her direction passed unnoticed.

"She did it on purpose," Annixter told himself, chewing fiercely on his cigar. "Cuts me now, hey? Well, this *does* settle it. She leaves this ranch before I'm a day older."

He decided that he would put off his tour of inspection

till the next day. Travelling in the buggy as he did, he must keep to the road which led to Derrick's, in very roundabout fashion, by way of Guadalajara. This rain would reduce the thick dust of the road to two feet of viscid mud. It would take him quite three hours to reach the ranch house on Los Muertos. He thought of Delaney and the buckskin and ground his teeth. And all this trouble, if you please, because of a fool feemale girl. A fine way for him to waste his time. Well, now he was done with it. His decision was taken now. She should pack.

Steadily the rain increased. There was no wind. The thick veil of wet descended straight from sky to earth, blurring distant outlines, spreading a vast sheen of grey over all the landscape. Its volume became greater, the prolonged murmuring note took on a deeper tone. At the gate to the road which led across Dyke's hop-fields toward Guadalajara, Annixter was obliged to descend and raise the top of the buggy. In doing so he caught the flesh of his hand in the joint of the iron elbow that supported the top and pinched it cruelly. It was the last misery, the culmination of a long train of wretchedness. On the instant he hated Hilma Tree so fiercely that his sharply set teeth all but bit his cigar in two.

While he was grabbing and wrenching at the buggy-top, the water from his hat brim dripping down upon his nose, the horse, restive under the drench of the rain, moved uneasily.

"Yah-h-h you!" he shouted, inarticulate with exasperation. "You—you—Gor-r-r, wait till I get hold of you. *Whoa*, you!"

But there was an interruption. Delaney, riding the buckskin, came around a bend in the road at a slow trot and Annixter, getting into the buggy again, found himself face to face with him.

" Why, hello, Mr. Annixter," said he, pulling up.
" Kind of sort of wet, isn't it? "

Annixter, his face suddenly scarlet, sat back in his
place abruptly, exclaiming:

" Oh—oh, there you are, are you? "

" I've been down there," explained Delaney, with a
motion of his head toward the railroad, " to mend that
break in the fence by the Long Trestle and I thought
while I was about it I'd follow down along the fence
toward Guadalajara to see if there were any more breaks.
But I guess it's all right."

" Oh, you guess it's all right, do you? " observed Annixter through his teeth.

" Why—why—yes," returned the other, bewildered at
the truculent ring in Annixter's voice. " I mended that
break by the Long Trestle just now and——"

" Well, why didn't you mend it a week ago? " shouted
Annixter wrathfully. " I've been looking for you all the
morning, I have, and who told you you could take that
buckskin? And the sheep were all over the right of
way last night because of that break, and here that filthy
pip, S. Behrman, comes down here this morning and
wants to make trouble for me." Suddenly he cried out,
" What do I *feed* you for? What do I keep you around
here for? Think it's just to fatten up your carcass, hey? "

" Why, Mr. Annixter——" began Delaney.

" And don't *talk* to me," vociferated the other, exciting
himself with his own noise. "Don't you say a word to
me even to apologise. If I've spoken to you once about
that break, I've spoken fifty times."

" Why, sir," declared Delaney, beginning to get in-
dignant, " the sheep did it themselves last night."

" I told you not to *talk* to me," clamoured Annixter.

" But, say, look here——"

" Get off the ranch. You get off the ranch. And

taking that buckskin against my express orders.   I
won't have your kind about the place, not much.   I'm
easy-going enough, Lord knows, but I don't propose to
be imposed on *all* the time.   Pack off, you understand,
and do it lively.   Go to the foreman and tell him I told
him to pay you off and then clear out.   And, you hear
me," he concluded, with a menacing outthrust of his
lower jaw, " you hear me, if I catch you hanging around
the ranch house after this, or if I so much as see you on
Quien Sabe, I'll show you the way off of it, my friend, at
the toe of my boot.   Now, then, get out of the way and
let me pass."

Angry beyond the power of retort, Delaney drove the
spurs into the buckskin and passed the buggy in a single
bound.   Annixter gathered up the reins and drove on,
muttering to himself, and occasionally looking back to
observe the buckskin flying toward the ranch house in
a spattering shower of mud, Delaney urging her on, his
head bent down against the falling rain.

" Huh," grunted Annixter with grim satisfaction, a
certain sense of good humour at length returning to him,
" that just about takes the saleratus out of *your* dough,
my friend."

A little farther on, Annixter got out of the buggy a
second time to open another gate that let him out upon
the Upper Road, not far distant from Guadalajara.   It
was the road that connected that town with Bonneville,
and that ran parallel with the railroad tracks.   On the
other side of the track he could see the infinite extension
of the brown, bare land of Los Muertos, turning now to
a soft, moist welter of fertility under the insistent caressing of the rain.   The hard, sun-baked clods were de-
composing, the crevices between drinking the wet with
an eager, sucking noise.   But the prospect was dreary;
the distant horizons were blotted under drifting mists

of rain; the eternal monotony of the earth lay open to the sombre low sky without a single adornment, without a single variation from its melancholy flatness. Near at hand the wires between the telegraph poles vibrated with a faint humming under the multitudinous fingering of the myriad of falling drops, striking among them and dripping off steadily from one to another. The poles themselves were dark and swollen and glistening with wet, while the little cones of glass on the transverse bars reflected the dull grey light of the end of the afternoon.

As Annixter was about to drive on, a freight train passed, coming from Guadalajara, going northward toward Bonneville, Fresno and San Francisco. It was a long train, moving slowly, methodically, with a measured coughing of its locomotive and a rhythmic cadence of its .trucks over the interstices of the rails. On two or three of the flat cars near its end, Annixter plainly saw Magnus Derrick's ploughs, their bright coating of red and green paint setting a single brilliant note in all this array of grey and brown.

Annixter halted, watching the train file past, carrying Derrick's ploughs away from his ranch, at this very time of the first rain, when they would be most needed. He watched it, silent, thoughtful, and without articulate comment. Even after it passed he sat in his place a long time, watching it lose itself slowly in the distance, its prolonged rumble diminishing to a faint murmur. Soon he heard the engine sounding its whistle for the Long Trestle.

But the moving train no longer carried with it that impression of terror and destruction that had so thrilled Presley's imagination the night before. It passed slowly on its way with a mournful roll of wheels, like the passing of a cortege, like a file of artillery-caissons charioting dead bodies; the engine's smoke enveloping it in a mournful veil, leaving a sense of melancholy in its wake, moving past there, lugubrious, lamentable, infinitely sad, under the grey sky and under the grey mist of rain which continued to fall with a subdued, rustling sound, steady, persistent, a vast monotonous murmur that seemed to come from all quarters of the horizon at once.

III

When Annixter arrived at the Los Muertos ranch house that same evening, he found a little group already assembled in the dining-room. Magnus Derrick, wearing the frock coat of broadcloth that he had put on for the occasion, stood with his back to the fireplace. Harran sat close at hand, one leg thrown over the arm of his chair. Presley lounged on the sofa, in corduroys and high laced boots, smoking cigarettes. Broderson leaned on his folded arms at one corner of the dining table, and Genslinger, editor and proprietor of the principal newspaper of the county, the " Bonneville Mercury," stood with his hat and driving gloves under his arm, opposite Derrick, a half-emptied glass of whiskey and water in his hand.

As Annixter entered he heard Genslinger observe: " I'll have a leader in the ' Mercury ' to-morrow that will interest you people. There's some talk of your ranch lands being graded in value this winter. I suppose you will all buy? "

In an instant the editor's words had riveted upon him the attention of every man in the room. Annixter broke the moment's silence that followed with the remark:

" Well, it's about time they graded these lands of theirs."

The question in issue in Genslinger's remark was of the most vital interest to the ranchers around Bonneville and Guadalajara. Neither Magnus Derrick, Broderson, Annixter, nor Osterman actually owned all the ranches which they worked. As yet, the vast majority of these wheat lands were the property of the P. and S. W. The explanation of this condition of affairs went back to the early history of the Pacific and Southwestern, when, as a bonus for the construction of the road, the national government had granted to the company the odd numbered sections of land on either side of the proposed line of route for a distance of twenty miles. Indisputably, these sections belonged to the P. and S. W. The even-numbered sections being government property could be and had been taken up by the ranchers, but the railroad sections, or, as they were called, the " alternate sections," would have to be purchased direct from the railroad itself.

But this had not prevented the farmers from "coming in" upon that part of the San Joaquin. Long before this the railroad had thrown open these lands, and, by means of circulars, distributed broadcast throughout the State, had expressly invited settlement thereon. At that time patents had not been issued to the railroad for their odd-numbered sections, but as soon as the land was patented the railroad would grade it in value and offer it for sale, the first occupants having the first chance of purchase. The price of these lands was to be fixed by the price the government put upon its own adjoining lands—about two dollars and a half per acre.

With cultivation and improvement the ranches must inevitably appreciate in value. There was every chance to make fortunes. When the railroad lands about Bonneville had been thrown open, there had been almost a rush in the matter of settlement, and Broderson, An-nixter, Derrick, and Osterman, being foremost with their claims, had secured the pick of the country. But the land once settled upon, the P. and S. W. seemed to be in no hurry as to fixing exactly the value of its sections

included in the various ranches and offering them for
sale. The matter dragged along from year to year, was
forgotten for months together, being only brought to
mind on such occasions as this, when the rumour spread
that the General Office was about to take definite action
in the affair.

"As soon as the railroad wants to talk business with
me," observed Annixter, "about selling me their interest
in Quien Sabe, I'm ready. The land has more than
quadrupled in value. I'll bet I could sell it to-morrow for fifteen dollars an acre, and if I buy of the railroad for two and a half an acre, there's boodle in the
game."

"For two and a half!" exclaimed Genslinger. "You
don't suppose the railroad will let their land go for any
such figure as that, do you? Wherever did you get that
idea?"

"From the circulars and pamphlets," answered Harran, "that the railroad issued to us when they opened
these lands. They are pledged to that. Even the P. and
S. W. couldn't break such a pledge as that. You are new
in the country, Mr. Genslinger. You don't remember
the conditions upon which we took up this land."

"And our improvements," exclaimed Annixter.
"Why, Magnus and I have put about five thousand dollars between us into that irrigating ditch already. I
guess we are not improving the land just to make it
valuable for the railroad people. No matter how much
we improve the land, or how much it increases in value,
they have got to stick by their agreement on the basis of
two-fifty per acre. Here's one case where the P. and
S. W. *don't* get everything in sight."

Genslinger frowned, perplexed.

"I *am* new in the country, as Harran says," he answered, "but it seems to me that there's no fairness in

7

that proposition.   The presence of the railroad has
helped increase the value of your ranches quite as much
as your improvements. Why should you get all the benefit of the rise in value and the railroad nothing?   The
fair way would be to share it between you."

" I don't care anything about that," declared Annixter.
" They agreed to charge but two-fifty, and they've got to
stick to it."

" Well," murmured Genslinger, " from what I know of
the affair, I don't believe the P. and S. W. intends to sell
for two-fifty an acre, at all. The managers of the road
want the best price they can get for everything in these
hard times."

" Times aren't ever very hard for the railroad," haz-
ards old Broderson.

Broderson was the oldest man in the room. He was
about sixty-five years of age, venerable, with a white
beard, his figure bent earthwards with hard work.

He was a narrow-minded man, painfully conscientious
in his statements lest he should be unjust to somebody;
a slow thinker, unable to let a subject drop when once
he had started upon it. He had no sooner uttered
his remark about hard times than he was moved to
qualify it.

" Hard times," he repeated, a troubled, perplexed note
in his voice; " well, yes—yes. I suppose the road *does*
have hard times, maybe. Everybody does—of course.
I didn't mean that exactly. I believe in being just and
fair to everybody. I mean that we've got to use their
lines and pay their charges good years *and* bad years,
the P. and S. W. being the only road in the State.   That
is—well, when I say the only road—no, I won't say the
only road. Of course there are other roads. There's the
D. P. and M. and the San Francisco and North Pacific,
that runs up to Ukiah. I got a brother-in-law in Ukiah.

That's not much of a wheat country round Ukiah, though they *do* grow *some* wheat there, come to think. But I guess it's too far north. Well, of course there isn't *much*. Perhaps sixty thousand acres in the whole county—if you include barley and oats. I don't know; maybe it's nearer forty thousand. I don't remember very well. That's a good many years ago. I——"

But Annixter, at the end of all patience, turned to Genslinger, cutting short the old man:

"Oh, rot! Of course the railroad will sell at two-fifty," he cried. "We've got the contracts."

"Look to them, then, Mr. Annixter," retorted Genslinger significantly, "look to them. Be sure that you are protected."

Soon after this Genslinger took himself away, and Derrick's Chinaman came in to set the table.

"What do you suppose he meant?" asked Broderson, when Genslinger was gone.

"About this land business?" said Annixter. "Oh, I don't know. Some tom fool idea. Haven't we got their terms printed in black and white in their circulars? There's their pledge."

"Oh, as to pledges," murmured Broderson, "the railroad is not always *too* much hindered by those."

"Where's Osterman?" demanded Annixter, abruptly changing the subject as if it were not worth discussion. "Isn't that goat Osterman coming down here to-night?"

"You telephoned him, didn't you, Presley?" inquired Magnus.

Presley had taken Princess Nathalie upon his knee, stroking her long, sleek hair, and the cat, stupefied with beatitude, had closed her eyes to two fine lines, clawing softly at the corduroy of Presley's trousers with alternate paws.

" Yes, sir," returned Presley. " He said he would be here."

And as he spoke, young Osterman arrived.

He was a young fellow, but singularly inclined to baldness. His ears, very red and large, stuck out at right angles from either side of his head, and his mouth, too, was large—a great horizontal slit beneath his nose. His cheeks were of a brownish red, the cheek bones a little salient. His face was that of a comic actor, a singer of songs, a man never at a loss for an answer, continually striving to make a laugh. But he took no great interest in ranching and left the management of his land to his superintendents and foremen, he, himself, living in Bonneville. He was a poser, a wearer of clothes, forever acting a part, striving to create an impression, to draw attention to himself. He was not without a certain energy, but he devoted it to small ends, to perfecting himself in little accomplishments, continually running after some new thing, incapable of persisting long in any one course. At one moment his mania would be fencing; the next, sleight-of-hand tricks; the next, archery. For upwards of one month he had devoted himself to learning how to play two banjos simultaneously, then abandoning this had developed a sudden passion for stamped leather work and had made a quantity of purses, tennis belts, and hat bands, which he presented to young ladies of his acquaintance. It was his policy never to make an enemy. He was liked far better than he was respected. People spoke of him as " that goat Osterman," or " that fool Osterman kid," and invited him to dinner. He was of the sort who somehow cannot be ignored. If only because of his clamour he made himself important. If he had one abiding trait, it was his desire of astonishing people, and in some way, best known to himself, managed to cause the circulation of the most extraordinary stories wherein he, himself, was the chief actor. He was glib, voluble, dexterous, ubiquitous, a teller of funny stories, a cracker of jokes.

Naturally enough, he was heavily in debt, but carried the burden of it with perfect nonchalance. The year before S. Behrman had held mortgages for fully a third of his crop and had squeezed him viciously for interest. But for all that, Osterman and S. Behrman were continually seen arm-in-arm on the main street of Bonneville. Osterman was accustomed to slap S. Behrman on his fat back, declaring:

"You're a good fellow, old jelly-belly, after all, hey?"

As Osterman entered from the porch, after hanging his cavalry poncho and dripping hat on the rack outside, Mrs. Derrick appeared in the door that opened from the dining-room into the glass-roofed hallway just beyond. Osterman saluted her with effusive cordiality and with ingratiating blandness.

"I am not going to stay," she explained, smiling pleasantly at the group of men, her pretty, wide-open brown eyes, with their look of inquiry and innocence, glancing from face to face, "I only came to see if you wanted anything and to say how do you do."

She began talking to old Broderson, making inquiries as to his wife, who had been sick the last week, and Osterman turned to the company, shaking hands all around, keeping up an incessant stream of conversation.

"Hello, boys and girls. Hello, Governor. Sort of a gathering of the clans to-night. Well, if here isn't that man Annixter. Hello, Buck. What do you know? Kind of dusty out to-night."

At once Annixter began to get red in the face, retiring towards a corner of the room, standing in an awkward position by the case of stuffed birds, shambling and confused, while Mrs. Derrick was present, standing rigidly on both feet, his elbows close to his sides. But he was angry with Osterman, muttering imprecations to himself, horribly vexed that the young fellow should call him " Buck " before Magnus's wife. This goat Osterman! Hadn't he any sense, that fool? Couldn't he ever learn how to behave before a feemale? Calling him " Buck " like that while Mrs. Derrick was there. Why a stable-boy would know better; a hired man would have better manners.

All through the dinner that followed Annixter was out of sorts, sulking in his place, refusing to eat by way of vindicating his self-respect, resolving to bring Osterman up with a sharp turn if he called him " Buck " again.

The Chinaman had made a certain kind of plum pudding for dessert, and Annixter, who remembered other dinners at the Derrick's, had been saving himself for this, and had meditated upon it all through the meal. No doubt, it would restore all his good humour, and he believed his stomach was so far recovered as to be able to stand it.

But, unfortunately, the pudding was served with a sauce that he abhorred—a thick, gruel-like, colourless mixture, made from plain water and sugar. Before he could interfere, the Chinaman had poured a quantity of it upon his plate.

" Faugh! " exclaimed Annixter. " It makes me sick. Such—such *sloop*. Take it away. I'll have mine straight, if you don't mind."

" That's good for your stomach, Buck," observed young Osterman; " makes it go down kind of sort of slick; don't you see? Sloop, hey? That's a good name."

" Look here, don't you call me Buck. You don't seem to have any sense, and, besides, it *isn't* good for my stomach. I know better. What do *you* know about my stomach, anyhow? Just looking at sloop like that makes me sick."

A little while after this the Chinaman cleared away the dessert and brought in coffee and cigars. The whiskey bottle and the syphon of soda-water reappeared. The men eased themselves in their places, pushing back from the table, lighting their cigars, talking of the beginning of the rains and the prospects of a rise in wheat. Broderson began an elaborate mental calculation, trying to settle in his mind the exact date of his visit to Ukiah, and Osterman did sleight-of-hand tricks with bread pills. But Princess Nathalie, the cat, was uneasy. Annixter was occupying her own particular chair in which she slept every night. She could not go to sleep, but spied upon him continually, watching his every movement with her lambent, yellow eyes, clear as amber.

Then, at length, Magnus, who was at the head of the table, moved in his place, assuming a certain magisterial attitude. "Well, gentlemen," he observed, "I have lost my case against the railroad, the grain-rate case. Ulsteen decided against me, and now I hear rumours to the effect that rates for the hauling of grain are to be advanced."

When Magnus had finished, there was a moment's silence, each member of the group maintaining his attitude of attention and interest. It was Harran who first spoke.

"S. Behrman manipulated the whole affair. There's a big deal of some kind in the air, and if there is, we all know who is back of it; S. Behrman, of course, but who's back of him? It's Shelgrim."

Shelgrim! The name fell squarely in the midst of the conversation, abrupt, grave, sombre, big with suggestion, pregnant with huge associations. No one in the group who was not familiar with it; no one, for that matter, in the county, the State, the whole reach of the West, the entire Union, that did not entertain convictions as to the man who carried it; a giant figure in the end-of-the-century finance, a product of circumstance, an inevitable result of conditions, characteristic, typical, symbolic of ungovernable forces. In the New Movement, the New Finance, the reorganisation of capital, the amalgamation of powers, the consolidation of enormous enterprises— no one individual was more constantly in the eye of the world; no one was more hated, more dreaded, no one more compelling of unwilling tribute to his commanding genius, to the colossal intellect operating the width of an entire continent than the president and owner of the Pacific and Southwestern.

" I don't think, however, he has moved yet," said Magnus.

" The thing for us, then," exclaimed Osterman, " is to stand from under before he does."

" Moved yet ! " snorted Annixter. " He's probably moved so long ago that we've never noticed it."

" In any case," hazarded Magnus, " it is scarcely probable that the deal—whatever it is to be—has been consummated. If we act quickly, there may be a chance."

" Act quickly ! How ? " demanded Annixter. " Good Lord ! what can you do? We're cinched already. It all amounts to just this : *You can't buck against the railroad.* We've tried it and tried it, and we are stuck every time. You, yourself, Derrick, have just lost your grain-rate case. S. Behrman did you up. Shelgrim owns the courts. He's got men like Ulsteen in his pocket. He's got the Railroad Commission in his pocket. He's got the Governor of the State in his pocket. He keeps a million-dollar lobby at Sacramento every minute of the time the legislature is in session; he's got his own men on the floor of the United States Senate. He has the whole thing organised like an army corps. What *are* you going to do? He sits in his office in San Francisco and pulls the strings and we've got to dance."

"But—well—but," hazarded Broderson, "but there's the Interstate Commerce Commission. At least on long-haul rates they——"

"Hoh, yes, the Interstate Commerce Commission," shouted Annixter, scornfully, "that's great, ain't it? The greatest Punch and Judy show on earth. It's almost as good as the Railroad Commission. There never was and there never will be a California Railroad Commission not in the pay of the P. and S. W."

"It is to the Railroad Commission, nevertheless," remarked Magnus, "that the people of the State must look for relief. That is our only hope. Once elect Commissioners who would be loyal to the people, and the whole system of excessive rates falls to the ground."

"Well, why not *have* a Railroad Commission of our own, then?" suddenly declared young Osterman.

"Because it can't be done," retorted Annixter. "*You can't buck against the railroad* and if you could you can't organise the farmers in the San Joaquin. We tried it once, and it was enough to turn your stomach. The railroad quietly bought delegates through S. Behrman and did us up."

"Well, that's the game to play," said Osterman decisively, "buy delegates."

"It's the only game that seems to win," admitted Harran gloomily.

"Or ever will win," exclaimed Osterman, a sudden excitement seeming to take possession of him. His face—the face of a comic actor, with its great slit of mouth and stiff, red ears—went abruptly pink.

"Look here," he cried, "this thing is getting desperate. We've fought and fought in the courts and out and we've tried agitation and—and all the rest of it and S. Behrman sacks us every time. Now comes the time when there's a prospect of a big crop ; we've had no rain for two years and the land has had a long rest. If there is any rain at all this winter, we'll have a bonanza year, and just at this very moment when we've got our chance —a chance to pay off our mortgages and get clear of debt and make a strike—here is Shelgrim making a deal to cinch us and put up rates. And now here's the primaries coming off and a new Railroad Commission going in. That's why Shelgrim chose this time to make his deal. If we wait till Shelgrim pulls it off, we're done for, that's flat. I tell you we're in a fix if we don't keep an eye open. Things are getting desperate. Magnus has just said that the key to the whole thing is the Railroad Commission. Well, why not have a Commission of our own? Never mind how we get it, let's get it. If it's got to be bought, let's buy it and put our own men on it and dictate what the rates will be. Suppose it costs a hundred thousand dollars. Well, we'll get back more than that in cheap rates."

" Mr. Osterman," said Magnus, fixing the young man with a swift glance, " Mr. Osterman, you are proposing a scheme of bribery, sir."

" I am proposing," repeated Osterman, " a scheme of bribery. Exactly so."

" And a crazy, wild-eyed scheme at that," said Annixter gruffly. " Even supposing you bought a Railroad Commission and got your schedule of low rates, what happens? The P. and S. W. crowd get out an injunction and tie you up."

" They would tie themselves up, too. Hauling at low rates is better than no hauling at all. The wheat has got to be moved."

" Oh, rot!" cried Annixter. " Aren't you ever going

to learn any sense? Don't you know that cheap transportation would benefit the Liverpool buyers and not
us? Can't it be *fed* into you that you can't buck against
the railroad? When you try to buy a Board of Commissioners don't you see that you'll have to bid against
the railroad, bid against a corporation that can chuck
out millions to our thousands? Do you think you can
bid against the P. and S. W.?"

" The railroad don't need to know we are in the game
against them till we've got our men seated."

" And when you've got them seated, what's to prevent
the corporation buying them right over your head?"

" If we've got the right kind of men in they could not
be bought that way," interposed Harran. "I don't
know but what there's something in what Osterman
says. We'd have the naming of the Commission and
we'd name honest men."

Annixter struck the table with his fist in exasperation.

" Honest men!" he shouted; "the kind of men you
could get to go into such a scheme would have to be *dis*-
honest to begin with."

Broderson, shifting uneasily in his place, fingering his
beard with a vague, uncertain gesture, spoke again:

" It would be the *chance* of them—our Commissioners
—selling out against the certainty of Shelgrim doing us
up. That is," he hastened to add, " *almost* a certainty;
pretty near a certainty."

" Of course, it would be a chance," exclaimed Osterman. " But it's come to the point where we've got to
take chances, risk a big stake to make a big strike, and
risk is better than sure failure."

" I can be no party to a scheme of avowed bribery
and corruption, Mr. Osterman," declared Magnus, a
ring of severity in his voice. "I am surprised, sir, that
you should even broach the subject in my hearing."

" And," cried Annixter, " it can't be done."

" I don't know," muttered Harran, " maybe it just wants a little spark like this to fire the whole train."

Magnus glanced at his son in considerable surprise. He had not expected this of Harran. But so great was his affection for his son, so accustomed had he become to listening to his advice, to respecting his opinions, that, for the moment, after the first shock of surprise and disappointment, he was influenced to give a certain degree of attention to this new proposition. He in no way countenanced it. At any moment he was prepared to rise in his place and denounce it and Osterman both. It was trickery of the most contemptible order, a thing he believed to be unknown to the old school of politics and statesmanship to which he was proud to belong; but since Harran, even for one moment, considered it, he, Magnus, who trusted Harran implicitly, would do likewise—if it was only to oppose and defeat it in its very beginnings.

And abruptly the discussion began. Gradually Osterman, by dint of his clamour, his strident reiteration, the plausibility of his glib, ready assertions, the ease with which he extricated himself when apparently driven to a corner, completely won over old Broderson to his way of thinking. Osterman bewildered him with his volubility, the lightning rapidity with which he leaped from one subject to another, garrulous, witty, flamboyant, terrifying the old man with pictures of the swift approach of ruin, the imminence of danger.

Annixter, who led the argument against him—loving argument though he did—appeared to poor advantage, unable to present his side effectively. He called Osterman a fool, a goat, a senseless, crazy-headed jackass, but was unable to refute his assertions. His debate was the clumsy heaving of brickbats, brutal, direct. He con-

tradicted everything Osterman said as a matter of principle, made conflicting assertions, declarations that were
absolutely inconsistent, and when Osterman or Harran
used these against him, could only exclaim:

" Well, in a way it's so, and then again in a way it
isn't."

But suddenly Osterman discovered a new argument.
" If we swing this deal," he cried, " we've got old jelly-
belly Behrman right where we want him."

" He's the man that does us every time," cried Harran.
" If there is dirty work to be done in which the railroad
doesn't wish to appear, it is S. Behrman who does it.
If the freight rates are to be ' adjusted ' to squeeze us a
little harder, it is S. Behrman who regulates what we can
stand. If there's a judge to be bought, it is S. Behrman
who does the bargaining. If there is a jury to be bribed,
it is S. Behrman who handles the money. If there is an
election to be jobbed, it is S. Behrman who manipulates
it. It's Behrman here and Behrman there. It is Behrman we come against every time we make a move. It is
Behrman who has the grip of us and will never let go
till he has squeezed us bone dry. Why, when I think
of it all sometimes I wonder I keep my hands off the
man."

Osterman got on his feet; leaning across the table,
gesturing wildly with his right hand, his serio-comic face,
with its bald forehead and stiff, red ears, was inflamed
with excitement. He took the floor, creating an impression, attracting all attention to himself, playing to the
gallery, gesticulating, clamourous, full of noise.

"Well, now is your chance to get even," he vociferated.
" It is now or never. You can take it and save the situation for yourselves and all California or you can leave
it and rot on your own ranches. Buck, I know you. I
know you're not afraid of anything that wears skin.

I know you've got sand all through you, and I know if I showed you how we could put our deal through and seat a Commission of our own, you wouldn't hang back. Governor, you're a brave man. You know the advantage of prompt and fearless action. You are not the sort to shrink from taking chances. To play for big stakes is just your game—to stake a fortune on the turn of a card. You didn't get the reputation of being the strongest poker player in El Dorado County for nothing. Now, here's the biggest gamble that ever came your way. If we stand up to it like men with guts in us, we'll win out. If we hesitate, we're lost."

" I don't suppose you can help playing the goat, Osterman," remarked Annixter, " but what's your idea? What do you think we can do? I'm not saying," he hastened to interpose, " that you've anyways convinced me by all this cackling. I know as well as you that we are in a hole. But I knew that before I came here to-night. *You've* not done anything to make me change my mind. But just what do you propose? Let's hear it."

" Well, I say the first thing to do is to see Disbrow. He's the political boss of the Denver, Pueblo, and Mojave road. We will have to get in with the machine some way and that's particularly why I want Magrus with us. He knows politics better than any of us and if we don't want to get sold again we will have to have some one that's in the know to steer us."

" The only politics I understand, Mr. Osterman," answered Magnus sternly, " are honest politics. You must look elsewhere for your political manager. I refuse to have any part in this matter. If the Railroad Commission can be nominated legitimately, if your arrangements can be made without bribery, I am with you to the last iota of my ability."

"Well, you can't get what you want without paying for it," contradicted Annixter.

Broderson was about to speak when Osterman kicked his foot under the table. He, himself, held his peace. He was quick to see that if he could involve Magnus and Annixter in an argument, Annixter, for the mere love of contention, would oppose the Governor and, without knowing it, would commit himself to his—Osterman's—scheme.

This was precisely what happened. In a few moments Annixter was declaring at top voice his readiness to mortgage the crop of Quien Sabe, if necessary, for the sake of "busting S. Behrman." He could see no great obstacle in the way of controlling the nominating convention so far as securing the naming of two Railroad Commissioners was concerned. Two was all they needed. Probably it *would* cost money. You didn't get something for nothing. It would cost them all a good deal more if they sat like lumps on a log and played tiddledy-winks while Shelgrim sold out from under them. Then there was this, too: the P. and S. W. were hard up just then. The shortage on the State's wheat crop for the last two years had affected them, too. They were retrenching in expenditures all along the line. Hadn't they just cut wages in all departments? There was this affair of Dyke's to prove it. The railroad didn't always act as a unit, either. There was always a party in it that opposed spending too much money. He would bet that party was strong just now. He was kind of sick himself of being kicked by S. Behrman. Hadn't that pip turned up on his ranch that very day to bully him about his own line fence? Next he would be telling him what kind of clothes he ought to wear. Harran had the right idea. Somebody had got to be busted mighty soon now and he didn't propose that it should be he.

" Now you are talking something like sense," observed Osterman.   " I thought you would see it like that when you got my idea."

" Your idea, *your* idea! " cried Annixter.   " Why, I've had this idea myself for over three years."

" What about Disbrow? " asked Harran, hastening to interrupt.   " Why do we want to see Disbrow? "

" Disbrow is the political man for the Denver, Pueblo, and Mojave," answered Osterman, " and you see it's like this: the Mojave road don't run up into the valley at all. Their terminus is way to the south of us, and they don't care anything about grain rates through the San Joaquin. They don't care how anti-railroad the Commission is, because the Commission's rulings can't affect them.   But they divide traffic with the P. and S. W. in the southern part of the State and they have a good deal of influence with that road.   I want to get the Mojave road, through Disbrow, to recommend a Commissioner of our choosing to the P. and S. W. and have the P. and S. W. adopt him as their own."

" Who, for instance? "

" Darrell, that Los Angeles man—remember? "

" Well, Darrell is no particular friend of Disbrow," said Annixter.   " Why should Disbrow take him up? "

" *Prec*-cisely," cried Osterman.   " We make it worth Disbrow's while to do it.   We go to him and say, ' Mr. Disbrow, you manage the politics for the Mojave railroad, and what you say goes with your Board of Directors.   We want you to adopt our candidate for Railroad Commissioner for the third district.   How much do you want for doing it? '   I *know* we can buy Disbrow.   That gives us one Commissioner.   We need not bother about that any more.   In the first district we don't make any move at all.   We let the political managers of the P. and S. W. nominate whoever they like.   Then we concentrate all our efforts to putting in our man in the second district. There is where the big fight will come."

"I see perfectly well what you mean, Mr. Osterman," observed Magnus, "but make no mistake, sir, as to my attitude in this business. You may count me as out of it entirely."

"Well, suppose we win," put in Annixter truculently, already acknowledging himself as involved in the proposed undertaking; "suppose we win and get low rates for hauling grain. How about you, then? You count yourself *in* then, don't you? You get all the benefit of lower rates without sharing any of the risks *we* take to secure them. No, nor any of the expense, either. No, you won't dirty your fingers with helping us put this deal through, but you won't be so cursed particular when it comes to sharing the profits, will you?"

Magnus rose abruptly to his full height, the nostrils of his thin, hawk-like nose vibrating, his smooth-shaven face paler than ever.

"Stop right where you are, sir," he exclaimed. "You forget yourself, Mr. Annixter. Please understand that I tolerate such words as you have permitted yourself to make use of from no man, not even from my guest. I shall ask you to apologise."

In an instant he dominated the entire group, imposing a respect that was as much fear as admiration. No one made response. For the moment he was the Master again, the Leader. Like so many delinquent school-boys, the others cowered before him, ashamed, put to confusion, unable to find their tongues. In that brief instant of silence following upon Magnus's outburst, and while he held them subdued and over-mastered, the fabric of their scheme of corruption and dishonesty trembled to its base. It was the last protest of the Old School, rising up there in denunciation of the new order of things, the statesman opposed to the politician; honesty, rectitude, uncompromising integrity, prevailing for the last time against the devious manœuvring, the evil communications, the rotten expediency of a corrupted institution.

For a few seconds no one answered. Then, Annixter, moving abruptly and uneasily in his place, muttered:

"I spoke upon provocation. If you like, we'll consider it unsaid. *I* don't know what's going to become of us—go out of business, I presume."

"I understand Magnus all right," put in Osterman. "He don't have to go into this thing, if it's against his conscience. That's all right. Magnus can stay out if he wants to, but that won't prevent us going ahead and seeing what we can do. Only there's this about it." He turned again to Magnus, speaking with every degree of earnestness, every appearance of conviction. "I did not deny, Governor, from the very start that this would mean bribery. But you don't suppose that *I* like the idea either. If there was one legitimate hope that was yet left untried, no matter how forlorn it was, I would try it. But there's not. It is literally and soberly true that every means of help—every honest means—has been attempted. Shelgrim is going to cinch us. Grain rates are increasing, while, on the other hand, the price of wheat is sagging lower and lower all the time. If we don't do something we are ruined."

Osterman paused for a moment, allowing precisely the right number of seconds to elapse, then altering and lowering his voice, added:

"I respect the Governor's principles. I admire them. They do him every degree of credit." Then, turning directly to Magnus, he concluded with, "But I only want you to ask yourself, sir, if, at such a crisis, one ought to think of oneself, to consider purely personal motives in

such a desperate situation as this? Now, we want you
with us, Governor; perhaps not openly, if you don't
wish it, but tacitly, at least. I won't ask you for an
answer to-night, but what I do ask of you is to consider
this matter seriously and think over the whole business.
Will you do it?"

Osterman ceased definitely to speak, leaning forward
across the table, his eyes fixed on Magnus's face. There
was a silence. Outside, the rain fell continually with
an even, monotonous murmur. In the group of men
around the table no one stirred nor spoke. They looked
steadily at Magnus, who, for the moment, kept his glance
fixed thoughtfully upon the table before him. In another moment he raised his head and looked from face
to face around the group. After all, these were his
neighbours, his friends, men with whom he had been
upon the closest terms of association. In a way they
represented what now had come to be his world. His
single swift glance took in the men, one after another.
Annixter, rugged, crude, sitting awkwardly and uncom-
fortably in his chair, his unhandsome face, with its out-
thrust lower lip and deeply cleft masculine chin, flushed
and eager, his yellow hair disordered, the one tuft on the
crown standing stiffly forth like the feather in an Indian's
scalp lock; Broderson, vaguely combing at his long
beard with a persistent maniacal gesture, distressed,
troubled and uneasy; Osterman, with his comedy face,
the face of a music-hall singer, his head bald and set off
by his great red ears, leaning back in his place, softly
cracking the knuckle of a forefinger, and, last of all and
close to his elbow, his son, his support, his confidant and
companion, Harran, so like himself, with his own erect,
fine carriage, his thin, beak-like nose and his blond hair,
with its tendency to curl in a forward direction in front
of the ears, young, strong, courageous, full of the prom-

ise of the future years. His blue eyes looked straight into his father's with what Magnus could fancy a glance of appeal. Magnus could see that expression in the faces of the others very plainly. They looked to him as their natural leader, their chief who was to bring them out from this abominable trouble which was closing in upon them, and in them all he saw many types. They —these men around his table on that night of the first rain of a coming season—seemed to stand in his imagination for many others—all the farmers, ranchers, and wheat growers of the great San Joaquin. Their words were the words of a whole community; their distress, the distress of an entire State, harried beyond the bounds of endurance, driven to the wall, coerced, exploited, harassed to the limits of exasperation.

"I will think of it," he said, then hastened to add, "but I can tell you beforehand that you may expect only a refusal."

After Magnus had spoken, there was a prolonged silence. The conference seemed of itself to have come to an end for that evening. Presley lighted another cigarette from the butt of the one he had been smoking, and the cat, Princess Nathalie, disturbed by his movement and by a whiff of drifting smoke, jumped from his knee to the floor and picking her way across the room to Annixter, rubbed gently against his legs, her tail in the air, her back delicately arched. No doubt she thought it time to settle herself for the night, and as Annixter gave no indication of vacating his chair, she chose this way of cajoling him into ceding his place to her. But Annixter was irritated at the Princess's attentions, misunderstanding their motive.

"Get out!" he exclaimed, lifting his feet to the rung of the chair. "Lord love me, but I sure do hate a cat."

"By the way," observed Osterman, "I passed Gen-slinger by the gate as I came in to-night. Had he been here?"

"Yes, he was here," said Harran, "and—" but An-nixter took the words out of his mouth.

"He says there's some talk of the railroad selling us their sections this winter."

"Oh, he did, did he?" exclaimed Osterman, interested at once. "Where did he hear that?"

"Where does a railroad paper get its news? From the General Office, I suppose."

"I hope he didn't get it straight from headquarters that the land was to be graded at twenty dollars an acre," murmured Broderson.

"What's that?" demanded Osterman. "Twenty dollars! Here, put me on, somebody. What's all up? What did Genslinger say?"

"Oh, you needn't get scared," said Annixter. "Gen-slinger don't know, that's all. He thinks there was no understanding that the price of the land should not be advanced when the P. and S. W. came to sell to us."

"Oh," muttered Osterman relieved. Magnus, who had gone out into the office on the other side of the glass-roofed hallway, returned with a long, yellow envelope in his hand, stuffed with newspaper clippings and thin, closely printed pamphlets.

"Here is the circular," he remarked, drawing out one of the pamphlets. "The conditions of settlement to which the railroad obligated itself are very explicit."

He ran over the pages of the circular, then read aloud:

"'The Company invites settlers to go upon its lands before patents are issued or the road is completed, and intends in such cases to sell to them in preference to any other applicants and at a price based upon the value of the land without improvements,' and on the other page here," he remarked, "they refer to this

again. '*In ascertaining the value of the lands, any improvements that a settler or any other person may have on the lands
will not be taken into consideration, neither will the price be
increased in consequence thereof. . . . Settlers are thus
insured that in addition to being accorded the first privilege of
purchase, at the graded price, they will also be protected in
their improvements.*'   And here," he commented, "in Section IX. it reads, ' *The lands are not uniform in price, but
are offered at various figures from* $2.50 *upward per acre.
Usually land covered with tall timber is held at* $5.00 *per acre,
and that with pine at* $10.00.   *Most is for sale at* $2.50 *and*
$5.00.*"

"When you come to read that carefully," hazarded old
Broderson, "it—it's not so *very* reassuring. '*Most* is
for sale at two-fifty an acre,' it says. That don't mean
'*all*,' that only means *some*. I wish now that I had secured a more iron-clad agreement from the P. and S. W.
when I took up its sections on my ranch, and—and Genslinger is in a position to know the intentions of the railroad. At least, he—he—he is in *touch* with them. All
newspaper men are. Those, I mean, who are subsidised
by the General Office. But, perhaps, Genslinger isn't
subsidised, I don't know. I—I am not sure. Maybe—
perhaps——"

"Oh, you don't know and you do know, and maybe
and perhaps, and you're not so sure," vociferated Annixter. "How about ignoring the value of our improvements? Nothing hazy about *that* statement, I guess. It
says in so many words that any improvements we make
will not be considered when the land is appraised and
that's the same thing, isn't it? The unimproved land is
worth two-fifty an acre; only timber land is worth more
and there's none too much timber about here."

"Well, one thing at a time," said Harran. "The thing
for us now is to get into this primary election and the

convention and see if we can push our men for Railroad Commissioners."

"Right," declared Annixter. He rose, stretching his arms above his head. "I've about talked all the wind out of me," he said. "Think I'll be moving along. It's pretty near midnight."

But when Magnus's guests turned their attention to the matter of returning to their different ranches, they abruptly realised that the downpour had doubled and trebled in its volume since earlier in the evening. The fields and roads were veritable seas of viscid mud, the night absolutely black-dark; assuredly not a night in which to venture out. Magnus insisted that the three ranchers should put up at Los Muertos. Osterman accepted at once, Annixter, after an interminable discussion, allowed himself to be persuaded, in the end accepting as though granting a favour. Broderson protested that his wife, who was not well, would expect him to return that night and would, no doubt, fret if he did not appear. Furthermore, he lived close by, at the junction of the County and Lower Road. He put a sack over his head and shoulders, persistently declining Magnus's offered umbrella and rubber coat, and hurried away, remarking that he had no foreman on his ranch and had to be up and about at five the next morning to put his men to work.

"Fool!" muttered Annixter when the old man had gone. "Imagine farming a ranch the size of his without a foreman."

Harran showed Osterman and Annixter where they were to sleep, in adjoining rooms. Magnus soon afterward retired.

Osterman found an excuse for going to bed, but Annixter and Harran remained in the latter's room, in a haze of blue tobacco smoke, talking, talking. But at length, at the end of all argument, Annixter got up, remarking:

"Well, *I'm* going to turn in.　It's nearly two o'clock."

He went to his room, closing the door, and Harran, opening his window to clear out the tobacco smoke, looked out for a moment across the country toward the south.

The darkness was profound, impenetrable; the rain fell with an uninterrupted roar.　Near at hand one could hear the sound of dripping eaves and foliage and the eager, sucking sound of the drinking earth, and abruptly while Harran stood looking out, one hand upon the upraised sash, a great puff of the outside air invaded the room, odourous with the reek of the soaking earth, redolent with fertility, pungent, heavy, tepid.　He closed the window again and sat for a few moments on the edge of the bed, one shoe in his hand, thoughtful and absorbed, wondering if his father would involve himself in this new scheme, wondering if, after all, he wanted him to.

But suddenly he was aware of a commotion, issuing from the direction of Annixter's room, and the voice of Annixter himself upraised in expostulation and exasperation.　The door of the room to which Annixter had been assigned opened with a violent wrench and an angry voice exclaimed to anybody who would listen:

"Oh, yes, funny, isn't it?　In a way, it's funny, and then, again, in a way it isn't."

The door banged to so that all the windows of the house rattled in their frames.

Harran hurried out into the dining-room and there met Presley and his father, who had been aroused as well by Annixter's clamour.　Osterman was there, too, his bald head gleaming like a bulb of ivory in the light of the lamp that Magnus carried.

"What's all up?" demanded Osterman. "Whatever in the world is the matter with Buck?"

Confused and terrible sounds came from behind the door of Annixter's room. A prolonged monologue of grievance, broken by explosions of wrath and the vague noise of some one in a furious hurry. All at once and before Harran had a chance to knock on the door, Annixter flung it open. His face was blazing with anger, his outthrust lip more prominent than ever, his wiry, yellow hair in disarray, the tuft on the crown sticking straight into the air like the upraised hackles of an angry hound. Evidently he had been dressing himself with the most headlong rapidity; he had not yet put on his coat and vest, but carried them over his arm, while with his disengaged hand he kept hitching his suspenders over his shoulders with a persistent and hypnotic gesture. Without a moment's pause he gave vent to his indignation in a torrent of words.

"Ah, yes, in my bed, sloop, aha! I know the man who put it there," he went on, glaring at Osterman, "and that man is a *pip*. Sloop! Slimy, disgusting stuff; you heard me say I didn't like it when the Chink passed it to me at dinner—and just for that reason you put it in my bed, and I stick my feet into it when I turn in. Funny, isn't it? Oh, yes, too funny for any use. I'd laugh a little louder if I was you."

"Well, Buck," protested Harran, as he noticed the hat in Annixter's hand, "you're not going home just for——"

Annixter turned on him with a shout.

"I'll get plumb out of here," he trumpeted. "I won't stay here another minute."

He swung into his waistcoat and coat, scrabbling at the buttons in the violence of his emotions. "And I don't know but what it will make me sick again to go

out in a night like this. *No,* I won't stay. Some things
are funny, and then, again, there are some things that are
not. Ah, yes, sloop! Well, that's all right. I can be
funny, too, when you come to that. You don't get a
cent of money out of me. You can do your dirty bribery
in your own dirty way. I won't come into this scheme
at all. I wash my hands of the whole business. It's
rotten and it's wild-eyed; it's dirt from start to finish;
and you'll all land in State's prison. You can count *me*
out."

"But, Buck, look here, you crazy fool," cried Harran,
"I don't know who put that stuff in your bed, but I'm
not going to let you go back to Quien Sabe in a rain like
this."

"*I* know who put it in," clamoured the other, shaking
his fists, "and don't call me Buck and I'll do as I please.
I *will* go back home. I'll get plumb out of here. Sorry
I came. Sorry I ever lent myself to such a disgusting,
dishonest, dirty bribery game as this all to-night. I won't
put a dime into it, no, not a penny."

He stormed to the door leading out upon the porch,
deaf to all reason. Harran and Presley followed him,
trying to dissuade him from going home at that time of
night and in such a storm, but Annixter was not to be
placated. He stamped across to the barn where his
horse and buggy had been stabled, splashing through the
puddles under foot, going out of his way to drench himself, refusing even to allow Presley and Harran to help
him harness the horse.

"What's the use of making a fool of yourself, Annixter?" remonstrated Presley, as Annixter backed the
horse from the stall. "You act just like a ten-year-old
boy. If Osterman wants to play the goat, why should
you help him out?"

"He's a *pip,*" vociferated Annixter. "You don't

understand, Presley. It runs in my family to hate anything sticky. It's—it's—it's heredity. How would you like to get into bed at two in the morning and jam your feet down into a slimy mess like that? Oh, no. It's not so funny then. And you mark my words, Mr. Harran Derrick," he continued, as he climbed into the buggy, shaking the whip toward Harran, "this business we talked over to-night—I'm *out* of it. It's yellow. It's too *cursed* dishonest."

He cut the horse across the back with the whip and drove out into the pelting rain. In a few seconds the sound of his buggy wheels was lost in the muffled roar of the downpour.

Harran and Presley closed the barn and returned to the house, sheltering themselves under a tarpaulin carriage cover. Once inside, Harran went to remonstrate with Osterman, who was still up. Magnus had again retired. The house had fallen quiet again.

As Presley crossed the dining-room on the way to his own apartment in the second story of the house, he paused for a moment, looking about him. In the dull light of the lowered lamps, the redwood panelling of the room showed a dark crimson as though stained with blood. On the massive slab of the dining table the half-emptied glasses and bottles stood about in the confusion in which they had been left, reflecting themselves deep into the polished wood; the glass doors of the case of stuffed birds was a subdued shimmer; the many-coloured Navajo blanket over the couch seemed a mere patch of brown.

Around the table the chairs in which the men had sat throughout the evening still ranged themselves in a semicircle, vaguely suggestive of the conference of the past few hours, with all its possibilities of good and evil, its significance of a future big with portent. The room was

still.   Only on the cushions of the chair that Annixter
had occupied, the cat, Princess Nathalie, at last comfortably settled in her accustomed place, dozed complacently,
her paws tucked under her breast, filling the deserted
room with the subdued murmur of her contented purr.

IV

On the Quien Sabe ranch, in one of its western divisions, near the line fence that divided it from the Osterman holding, Vanamee was harnessing the horses to the plough to which he had been assigned two days before, a stable-boy from the division barn helping him.

Promptly discharged from the employ of the sheep-raisers after the lamentable accident near the Long Trestle, Vanamee had presented himself to Harran, asking for employment. The season was beginning; on all the ranches work was being resumed. The rain had put the ground into admirable condition for ploughing, and Annixter, Broderson, and Osterman all had their gangs at work. Thus, Vanamee was vastly surprised to find Los Muertos idle, the horses still in the barns, the men gathering in the shade of the bunk-house and eating-house, smoking, dozing, or going aimlessly about, their arms dangling. The ploughs for which Magnus and Harran were waiting in a fury of impatience had not yet arrived, and since the management of Los Muertos had counted upon having these in hand long before this time, no provision had been made for keeping the old stock in repair; many of these old ploughs were useless, broken, and out of order; some had been sold. It could not be said definitely when the new ploughs would arrive. Harran had decided to wait one week longer, and then, in case of their non-appearance, to buy a consignment of the old style of plough from the dealers in Bonneville. He could afford to lose the money better than he could afford to lose the season.

Failing of work on Los Muertos, Vanamee had gone to Quien Sabe. Annixter, whom he had spoken to first, had sent him across the ranch to one of his division superintendents, and this latter, after assuring himself of Vanamee's familiarity with horses and his previous experience—even though somewhat remote—on Los Muertos, had taken him on as a driver of one of the gang ploughs, then at work on his division.

The evening before, when the foreman had blown his whistle at six o'clock, the long line of ploughs had halted upon the instant, and the drivers, unharnessing their teams, had taken them back to the division barns—leaving the ploughs as they were in the furrows. But an hour after daylight the next morning the work was resumed. After breakfast, Vanamee, riding one horse and leading the others, had returned to the line of ploughs together with the other drivers. Now he was busy harnessing the team. At the division blacksmith shop—temporarily put up—he had been obliged to wait while one of his lead horses was shod, and he had thus been delayed quite five minutes. Nearly all the other teams were harnessed, the drivers on their seats, waiting for the foreman's signal.

" All ready here? " inquired the foreman, driving up to Vanamee's team in his buggy.

" All ready, sir," answered Vanamee, buckling the last strap.

He climbed to his seat, shaking out the reins, and turning about, looked back along the line, then all around him at the landscape inundated with the brilliant glow of the early morning.

The day was fine. Since the first rain of the season, there had been no other. Now the sky was without a cloud, pale blue, delicate, luminous, scintillating with morning. The great brown earth turned a huge flank to it, exhaling the moisture of the early dew. The atmosphere, washed clean of dust and mist, was translucent as crystal. Far off to the east, the hills on the other side of Broderson Creek stood out against the pallid saffron of the horizon as flat and as sharply outlined as if pasted on the sky. The campanile of the ancient Mission of San Juan seemed as fine as frost work. All about between the horizons, the carpet of the land unrolled itself to infinity. But now it was no longer parched with heat, cracked and warped by a merciless sun, powdered with dust. The rain had done its work; not a clod that was not swollen with fertility, not a fissure that did not exhale the sense of fecundity. One could not take a dozen steps upon the ranches without the brusque sensation that underfoot the land was alive; roused at last from its sleep, palpitating with the desire of reproduction. Deep down there in the recesses of the soil, the great heart throbbed once more, thrilling with passion, vibrating with desire, offering itself to the caress of the plough, insistent, eager, imperious. Dimly one felt the deepseated trouble of the earth, the uneasy agitation of its members, the hidden tumult of its womb, demanding to be made fruitful, to reproduce, to disengage the eternal renascent germ of Life that stirred and struggled in its loins.

The ploughs, thirty-five in number, each drawn by its team of ten, stretched in an interminable line, nearly a quarter of a mile in length, behind and ahead of Vanamee. They were arranged, as it were, *en echelon*, not in file—not one directly behind the other, but each succeeding plough its own width farther in the field than the one in front of it. Each of these ploughs held five shears, so that when the entire company was in motion, one hundred and seventy-five furrows were made at the same instant. At a distance, the ploughs resembled a great column of field **artillery.** Each driver was in his place, his glance alternating between his horses and the foreman nearest at hand. Other foremen, in their buggies or buckboards, were at intervals along the line, like battery lieutenants. Annixter himself, on horseback, in boots and campaign hat, a cigar in his teeth, overlooked the scene.

The division superintendent, on the opposite side of the line, galloped past to a position at the head. For a long moment there was a silence. A sense of preparedness ran from end to end of the column. All things were ready, each man in his place. The day's work was about to begin.

Suddenly, from a distance at the head of the line came the shrill trilling of a whistle. At once the foreman nearest Vanamee repeated it, at the same time turning down the line, and waving one arm. The signal was repeated, whistle answering whistle, till the sounds lost themselves in the distance. At once the line of ploughs lost its immobility, moving forward, getting slowly under way, the horses straining in the traces. A prolonged movement rippled from team to team, disengaging in its passage a multitude of sounds—the click of buckles, the creak of straining leather, the subdued clash of machinery, the cracking of whips, the deep breathing of nearly four hundred horses, the abrupt commands and cries of the drivers, and, last of all, the prolonged, soothing murmur of the thick brown earth turning steadily from the multitude of advancing shears.

The ploughing thus commenced, continued. The sun rose higher. Steadily the hundred iron hands kneaded and furrowed and stroked the brown, humid earth, the hundred iron teeth bit deep into the Titan's flesh. Perched on his seat, the moist living reins slipping and tugging in his hands, Vanamee, in the midst of this steady confusion of constantly varying sensation, sight interrupted by sound, sound mingling with sight, on this swaying, vibrating seat, quivering with the prolonged thrill of the earth, lapsed to a sort of pleasing numbness, in a sense, hypnotised by the weaving maze of things in which he found himself involved. To keep his team at an even, regular gait, maintaining the precise interval, to run his furrows as closely as possible to those already made by the plough in front—this for the moment was the entire sum of his duties. But while one part of his brain, alert and watchful, took cognisance of these matters, all the greater part was lulled and stupefied with the long monotony of the affair.

The ploughing, now in full swing, enveloped him in a vague, slow-moving whirl of things. Underneath him was the jarring, jolting, trembling machine; not a clod was turned, not an obstacle encountered, that he did not receive the swift impression of it through all his body, the very friction of the damp soil, sliding incessantly from the shiny surface of the shears, seemed to reproduce itself in his finger-tips and along the back of his head. He heard the horse-hoofs by the myriads crushing down easily, deeply, into the loam, the prolonged clinking of trace-chains, the working of the smooth brown flanks in the harness, the clatter of wooden hames, the champing of bits, the click of iron shoes against pebbles, the brittle stubble of the surface ground crackling and snapping as the furrows turned, the sonorous, steady breaths wrenched from the deep, labouring chests, strap-bound, shining with sweat, and all along the line the voices of the men talking to the horses. Everywhere there were visions of glossy brown backs, straining, heaving, swollen with muscle; harness streaked with specks of froth, broad, cup-shaped hoofs, heavy with brown loam, men's faces red with tan, blue overalls spotted with axle-grease; muscled hands, the knuckles whitened in their grip on the reins, and through it all the ammoniacal smell of the horses, the bitter reek of perspiration of beasts and men, the aroma of warm leather, the scent of dead stubble—and stronger and more penetrating than everything else, the heavy, enervating odour of the upturned, living earth.

At intervals, from the tops of one of the rare, low swells of the land, Vanamee overlooked a wider horizon. On the other divisions of Quien Sabe the same work was in progress. Occasionally he could see another column of ploughs in the adjoining division—sometimes so close at hand that the subdued murmur of its movements reached his ear; sometimes so distant that it resolved itself into a long, brown streak upon the grey of the ground. Farther off to the west on the Osterman ranch other columns came and went, and, once, from the crest of the highest swell on his division, Vanamee caught a distant glimpse of the Broderson ranch. There, too, moving specks indicated that the ploughing was under way. And farther away still, far off there beyond the fine line of the horizons, over the curve of the globe, the shoulder of the earth, he knew were other ranches, and beyond these others, and beyond these still others, the immensities multiplying to infinity.

Everywhere throughout the great San Joaquin, unseen and unheard, a thousand ploughs up-stirred the land, tens of thousands of shears clutched deep into the warm, moist soil.

It was the long stroking caress, vigorous, male, powerful, for which the Earth seemed panting. The heroic embrace of a multitude of iron hands, gripping deep into the brown, warm flesh of the land that quivered responsive and passionate under this rude advance, so robust as to be almost an assault, so violent as to be veritably brutal. There, under the sun and under the speckless sheen of the sky, the wooing of the Titan began, the vast primal passion, the two world-forces, the elemental Male and Female, locked in a colossal embrace, at grapples in the throes of an infinite desire, at once terrible and divine, knowing no law, untamed, savage, natural, sublime.

From time to time the gang in which Vanamee worked halted on the signal from foreman or overseer. The horses came to a standstill, the vague clamour of the work lapsed away. Then the minutes passed. The whole work hung suspended. All up and down the line one demanded what had happened. The division superintendent galloped past, perplexed and anxious. For the moment, one of the ploughs was out of order, a bolt had slipped, a lever refused to work, or a machine had become immobilised in heavy ground, or a horse had lamed himself. Once, even, toward noon, an entire plough was taken out of the line, so out of gear that a messenger had to be sent to the division forge to summon the machinist.

Annixter had disappeared. He had ridden farther on to the other divisions of his ranch, to watch the work in progress there. At twelve o'clock, according to his orders, all the division superintendents put themselves in communication with him by means of the telephone wires that connected each of the division houses, reporting the condition of the work, the number of acres covered, the prospects of each plough traversing its daily average of twenty miles.

At half-past twelve, Vanamee and the rest of the drivers ate their lunch in the field, the tin buckets having been distributed to them that morning after breakfast. But in the evening, the routine of the previous day was repeated, and Vanamee, unharnessing his team, riding one horse and leading the others, returned to the division barns and bunk-house.

It was between six and seven o'clock. The half hundred men of the gang threw themselves upon the supper the Chinese cooks had set out in the shed of the eating-house, long as a bowling alley, unpainted, crude, the seats benches, the table covered with oil cloth. Overhead a half-dozen kerosene lamps flared and smoked.

The table was taken as if by assault; the clatter of iron knives upon the tin plates was as the reverberation of hail upon a metal roof. The ploughmen rinsed their throats with great draughts of wine, and, their elbows wide, their foreheads flushed, resumed the attack upon the beef and bread, eating as though they would never have enough. All up and down the long table, where the kerosene lamps reflected themselves deep in the oil-cloth cover, one heard the incessant sounds of mastication, and saw the uninterrupted movement of great jaws. At every moment one or another of the men demanded a fresh portion of beef, another pint of wine, another half-loaf of bread. For upwards of an hour the gang ate. It was no longer a supper. It was a veritable barbecue, a crude and primitive feasting, barbaric, homeric.

But in all this scene Vanamee saw nothing repulsive. Presley would have abhorred it—this feeding of the People, this gorging of the human animal, eager for its meat. Vanamee, simple, uncomplicated, living so close to nature and the rudimentary life, understood its significance. He knew very well that within a short half-hour after this meal the men would throw themselves down in their bunks to sleep without moving, inert and stupefied with fatigue, till the morning. Work, food, and sleep, all life reduced to its bare essentials, uncomplex, honest, healthy. They were strong, these men,

with the strength of the soil they worked, in touch with
the essential things, back again to the starting point of
civilisation, coarse, vital, real, and sane.

For a brief moment immediately after the meal, pipes
were lit, and the air grew thick with fragrant tobacco
smoke. On a corner of the dining-room table, a game
of poker was begun. One of the drivers, a Swede, produced an accordion; a group on the steps of the bunk-
house listened, with alternate gravity and shouts of
laughter, to the acknowledged story-teller of the gang.
But soon the men began to turn in, stretching themselves at full length on the horse blankets in the racklike
bunks. The sounds of heavy breathing increased steadily, lights were put out, and before the afterglow had
faded from the sky, the gang was asleep.

Vanamee, however, remained awake. The night was
fine, warm; the sky silver-grey with starlight. By and
by there would be a moon. In the first watch after the
twilight, a faint puff of breeze came up out of the south.
From all around, the heavy penetrating smell of the new-
turned earth exhaled steadily into the darkness. After
a while, when the moon came up, he could see the vast
brown breast of the earth turn toward it. Far off, distant objects came into view: The giant oak tree at
Hooven's ranch house near the irrigating ditch on Los
Muertos, the skeleton-like tower of the windmill on Annixter's Home ranch, the clump of willows along Broderson Creek close to the Long Trestle, and, last of all, the
venerable tower of the Mission of San Juan on the high
ground beyond the creek.

Thitherward, like homing pigeons, Vanamee's
thoughts turned irresistibly. Near to that tower, just
beyond, in the little hollow, hidden now from his sight,
was the Seed ranch where Angéle Varian had lived.
Straining his eyes, peering across the intervening levels,

Vanamee fancied he could almost see the line of venerable pear trees in whose shadow she had been accustomed to wait for him. On many such a night as this
he had crossed the ranches to find her there. His mind
went back to that wonderful time of his life sixteen
years before this, when Angéle was alive, when they two
were involved in the sweet intricacies of a love so fine,
so pure, so marvellous that it seemed to them a miracle,
a manifestation, a thing veritably divine, put into the life
of them and the hearts of them by God Himself. To
that they had been born. For this love's sake they had
come into the world, and the mingling of their lives was
to be the Perfect Life, the intended, ordained union of
the soul of man with the soul of woman, indissoluble,
harmonious as music, beautiful beyond all thought, a
foretaste of Heaven, a hostage of immortality.

No, he, Vanamee, could never, never forget; never was
the edge of his grief to lose its sharpness; never would
the lapse of time blunt the tooth of his pain. Once
more, as he sat there, looking off across the ranches, his
eyes fixed on the ancient campanile of the Mission
church, the anguish that would not die leaped at his
throat, tearing at his heart, shaking him and rending
him with a violence as fierce and as profound as if it all
had been but yesterday. The ache returned to his heart,
a physical keen pain; his hands gripped tight together,
twisting, interlocked, his eyes filled with tears, his whole
body shaken and riven from head to heel.

He had lost her. God had not meant it, after all. The
whole matter had been a mistake. That vast, wonderful
love that had come upon them had been only the flimsiest
mockery. Abruptly Vanamee rose. He knew the night
that was before him. At intervals throughout the course
of his prolonged wanderings, in the desert, on the mesa,
deep in the cañon, lost and forgotten on the flanks of

unnamed mountains, alone under the stars and under the moon's white eye, these hours came to him, his grief recoiling upon him like the recoil of a vast and terrible engine. Then he must fight out the night, wrestling with his sorrow, praying sometimes, incoherent, hardly conscious, asking "Why" of the night and of the stars.

Such another night had come to him now. Until dawn he knew he must struggle with his grief, torn with memories, his imagination assaulted with visions of a vanished happiness. If this paroxysm of sorrow was to assail him again that night, there was but one place for him to be. He would go to the Mission—he would see Father Sarria; he would pass the night in the deep shadow of the aged pear trees in the Mission garden.

He struck out across Quien Sabe, his face, the face of an ascetic, lean, brown, infinitely sad, set toward the Mission church. In about an hour he reached and crossed the road that led northward from Guadalajara toward the Seed ranch, and, a little farther on, forded Broderson Creek where it ran through one corner of the Mission land. He climbed the hill and halted, out of breath from his brisk wall, at the end of the colonnade of the Mission itself.

Until this moment Vanamee had not trusted himself to see the Mission at night. On the occasion of his first daytime visit with Presley, he had hurried away even before the twilight had set in, not daring for the moment to face the crowding phantoms that in his imagination filled the Mission garden after dark. In the daylight, the place had seemed strange to him. None of his associations with the old building and its surroundings were those of sunlight and brightness. Whenever, during his long sojourns in the wilderness of the Southwest, he had called up the picture in the eye of his mind, it had always appeared to him in the dim mystery of moonless nights, the venerable pear trees black with shadow, the fountain a thing to be heard rather than seen.

But as yet he had not entered the garden. That lay on the other side of the Mission. Vanamee passed down the colonnade, with its uneven pavement of worn red bricks, to the last door by the belfry tower, and rang the little bell by pulling the leather thong that hung from a hole in the door above the knob.

But the maid-servant, who, after a long interval, opened the door, blinking and confused at being roused from her sleep, told Vanamee that Sarria was not in his room. Vanamee, however, was known to her as the priest's *protégé* and great friend, and she allowed him to enter, telling him that, no doubt, he would find Sarria in the church itself. The servant led the way down the cool adobe passage to a larger room that occupied the entire width of the bottom of the belfry tower, and whence a flight of aged steps led upward into the dark. At the foot of the stairs was a door opening into the church. The servant admitted Vanamee, closing the door behind her.

The interior of the Mission, a great oblong of white-washed adobe with a flat ceiling, was lighted dimly by the sanctuary lamp that hung from three long chains just over the chancel rail at the far end of the church, and by two or three cheap kerosene lamps in brackets of imitation bronze. All around the walls was the inevitable series of pictures representing the Stations of the Cross. They were of a hideous crudity of design and composition, yet were wrought out with an innocent, unquestioning sincerity that was not without its charm. Each picture framed alike in gilt, bore its suitable inscription in staring black letters. " Simon, The Cyrenean, Helps Jesus to Carry His Cross." " Saint Veronica Wipes the

Face of Jesus." " Jesus Falls for the Fourth Time," and so on. Half-way up the length of the church the pews began, coffin-like boxes of blackened oak, shining from years of friction, each with its door; while over them, and built out from the wall, was the pulpit, with its tarnished gilt sounding-board above it, like the raised cover of a great hat-box. Between the pews, in the aisle, the violent vermilion of a strip of ingrain carpet assaulted the eye. Farther on were the steps to the altar, the chancel rail of worm-riddled oak, the high altar, with its napery from the bargain counters of a San Francisco store, the massive silver candlesticks, each as much as one man could lift, the gift of a dead Spanish queen, and, last, the pictures of the chancel, the Virgin in a glory, a Christ in agony on the cross, and St. John the Baptist, the patron saint of the Mission, the San Juan Bautista, of the early days, a gaunt grey figure, in skins, two fingers upraised in the gesture of benediction.

The air of the place was cool and damp, and heavy with the flat, sweet scent of stale incense smoke. It was of a vault-like stillness, and the closing of the door behind Vanamee reëchoed from corner to corner with a prolonged reverberation of thunder.

However, Father Sarria was not in the church. Vanamee took a couple of turns the length of the aisle, looking about into the chapels on either side of the chancel. But the building was deserted. The priest had been there recently, nevertheless, for the altar furniture was in disarray, as though he had been rearranging it but a moment before. On both sides of the church and half-way up their length, the walls were pierced by low archways, in which were massive wooden doors, clamped with iron bolts. One of these doors, on the pulpit side of the church, stood ajar, and stepping to it and pushing it wide open, Vanamee looked diagonally across a little

patch of vegetables—beets, radishes, and lettuce—to the
rear of the building that had once contained the cloisters,
and through an open window saw Father Sarria dili-
gently polishing the silver crucifix that usually stood on
the high altar. Vanamee did not call to the priest. Putting a finger to either temple, he fixed his eyes steadily
upon him for a moment as he moved about at his work.
In a few seconds he closed his eyes, but only part way.
The pupils contracted; his forehead lowered to an expression of poignant intensity. Soon afterward he saw
the priest pause abruptly in the act of drawing the cover
over the crucifix, looking about him from side to side.
He turned again to his work, and again came to a stop,
perplexed, curious. With uncertain steps, and evidently
wondering why he did so, he came to the door of the
room and opened it, looking out into the night. Vanamee, hidden in the deep shadow of the archway, did not
move, but his eyes closed, and the intense expression
deepened on his face. The priest hesitated, moved forward a step, turned back, paused again, then came
straight across the garden patch, brusquely colliding
with Vanamee, still motionless in the recess of the archway.

Sarria gave a great start, catching his breath.

"Oh—oh, it's you. Was it you I heard calling? No,
I could not have heard—I remember now. What a
strange power! I am not sure that it is right to do this
thing, Vanamee. I—I *had* to come. I do not know why.
It is a great force—a power—I don't like it. Vanamee,
sometimes it frightens me."

Vanamee put his chin in the air.

"If I had wanted to, sir, I could have made you come
to me from back there in the Quien Sabe ranch."

The priest shook his head.

"It troubles me," he said, "to think that my own will

can count for so little. Just now I could not resist. If a deep river had been between us, I must have crossed it. Suppose I had been asleep now?"

"It would have been all the easier," answered Vanamee. "I understand as little of these things as you. But I think if you had been asleep, your power of resistance would have been so much the more weakened."

"Perhaps I should not have waked. Perhaps I should have come to you in my sleep."

"Perhaps."

Sarria crossed himself. "It is occult," he hazarded. "No; I do not like it. Dear fellow," he put his hand on Vanamee's shoulder, "don't—call me that way again; promise. See," he held out his hand, "I am all of a tremble. There, we won't speak of it further. Wait for me a moment. I have only to put the cross in its place, and a fresh altar cloth, and then I am done. Tomorrow is the feast of The Holy Cross, and I am preparing against it. The night is fine. We will smoke a cigar in the cloister garden."

A few moments later the two passed out of the door on the other side of the church, opposite the pulpit, Sarria adjusting a silk skull cap on his tonsured head. He wore his cassock now, and was far more the churchman in appearance than when Vanamee and Presley had seen him on a former occasion.

They were now in the cloister garden. The place was charming. Everywhere grew clumps of palms and magnolia trees. A grapevine, over a century old, occupied a trellis in one angle of the walls which surrounded the garden on two sides. Along the third side was the church itself, while the fourth was open, the wall having crumbled away, its site marked only by a line of eight great pear trees, older even than the grapevine, gnarled, twisted, bearing no fruit. Directly opposite

the pear trees, in the south wall of the garden, was a
round, arched portal, whose gate giving upon the espla-
nade in front of the Mission was always closed. Small
gravelled walks, well kept, bordered with mignonette,
twisted about among the flower beds, and underneath
the magnolia trees. In the centre was a little fountain
in a stone basin green with moss, while just beyond,
between the fountain and the pear trees, stood what was
left of a sun dial, the bronze gnomon, green with the
beatings of the weather, the figures on the half-circle
of the dial worn away, illegible.

But on the other side of the fountain, and directly opposite the door of the Mission, ranged against the wall,
were nine graves—three with headstones, the rest with
slabs. Two of Sarria's predecessors were buried here;
three of the graves were those of Mission Indians. One
was thought to contain a former alcalde of Guadalajara;
two more held the bodies of De La Cuesta and his young
wife (taking with her to the grave the illusion of her
husband's love), and the last one, the ninth, at the end of
the line, nearest the pear trees, was marked by a little
headstone, the smallest of any, on which, together with
the proper dates—only sixteen years apart—was cut the
name " Angéle Varian."

But the quiet, the repose, the isolation of the little
cloister garden was infinitely delicious. It was a tiny
corner of the great valley that stretched in all directions
around it—shut off, discreet, romantic, a garden of
dreams, of enchantments, of illusions. Outside there,
far off, the great grim world went clashing through its
grooves, but in here never an echo of the grinding of its
wheels entered to jar upon the subdued modulation of
the fountain's uninterrupted murmur.

Sarria and Vanamee found their way to a stone bench
against the side wall of the Mission, near the door from

which they had just issued, and sat down, Sarria lighting a cigar, Vanamee rolling and smoking cigarettes in
Mexican fashion.

All about them widened the vast calm night. All the
stars were out. The moon was coming up. There was
no wind, no sound. The insistent flowing of the fountain
seemed only as the symbol of the passing of time, a
thing that was understood rather than heard, inevitable,
prolonged. At long intervals, a faint breeze, hardly
more than a breath, found its way into the garden over
the enclosing walls, and passed overhead, spreading
everywhere the delicious, mingled perfume of magnolia
blossoms, of mignonette, of moss, of grass, and all the
calm green life silently teeming within the enclosure of
the walls.

From where he sat, Vanamee, turning his head, could
look out underneath the pear trees to the north. Close
at hand, a little valley lay between the high ground on
which the Mission was built, and the line of low hills just
beyond Broderson Creek on the Quien Sabe. In here
was the Seed ranch, which Angéle's people had cultivated, a unique and beautiful stretch of five hundred
acres, planted thick with roses, violets, lilies, tulips, iris,
carnations, tube-roses, poppies, heliotrope—all manner
and description of flowers, five hundred acres of them,
solid, thick, exuberant; blooming and fading, and leaving their seed or slips to be marketed broadcast all over
the United States. This had been the vocation of
Angéle's parents—raising flowers for their seeds. All
over the country the Seed ranch was known. Now it
was arid, almost dry, but when in full flower, toward the
middle of summer, the sight of these half-thousand acres
royal with colour—vermilion, azure, flaming yellow—
was a marvel. When an east wind blew, men on the
streets of Bonneville, nearly twelve miles away, could

catch the scent of this valley of flowers, this chaos of perfume.

And into this life of flowers, this world of colour, this atmosphere oppressive and clogged and cloyed and thickened with sweet odour, Angéle had been born. There she had lived her sixteen years. There she had died. It was not surprising that Vanamee, with his intense, delicate sensitiveness to beauty, his almost abnormal capacity for great happiness, had been drawn to her, had loved her so deeply.

She came to him from out of the flowers, the smell of the roses in her hair of gold, that hung in two straight plaits on either side of her face; the reflection of the violets in the profound dark blue of her eyes, perplexing, heavy-lidded, almond-shaped, oriental; the aroma and the imperial red of the carnations in her lips, with their almost Egyptian fulness; the whiteness of the lilies, the perfume of the lilies, and the lilies' slender balancing grace in her neck. Her hands disengaged the odour of the heliotropes. The folds of her dress gave off the enervating scent of poppies. Her feet were redolent of hyacinths.

For a long time after sitting down upon the bench, neither the priest nor Vanamee spoke. But after a while Sarria took his cigar from his lips, saying:

" How still it is ! This is a beautiful old garden, peaceful, very quiet. Some day I shall be buried here. I like to remember that; and you, too, Vanamee."

" *Quien sabe?* "

" Yes, you, too. Where else? No, it is better here, yonder, by the side of the litle girl."

" I am not able to look forward yet, sir. The things that are to be are somehow nothing to me at all. For me they amount to nothing."

" They amount to everything, my boy."

" Yes, to one part of me, but not to the part of me that belonged to Angéle—the best part. Oh, you don't know," he exclaimed with a sudden movement, " no one can understand. What is it to me when you tell me that sometime after I shall die too, somewhere, in a vague place you call Heaven, I shall see her again? Do you think that the idea of that ever made any one's sorrow easier to bear? Ever took the edge from any one's grief?"

" But you believe that——"

" Oh, believe, believe!" echoed the other. " What do I believe? I don't know. I believe, or I don't believe. I can remember what she *was*, but I cannot hope what she will be. Hope, after all, is only memory seen reversed. When I try to see her in another life—whatever you call it—in Heaven—beyond the grave—this vague place of yours; when I try to see her there, she comes to my imagination only as what she was, material, earthly, as I loved her. Imperfect, you say; but that is as I saw her, and as I saw her, I loved her; and as she *was*, material, earthly, imperfect, she loved me. It's that, that I want," he exclaimed. " I don't want her changed. I don't want her spiritualised, exalted, glorified, celestial. I want *her*. I think it is only this feeling that has kept me from killing myself. I would rather be unhappy in the memory of what she actually was, than be happy in the realisation of her transformed, changed, made celestial. I am only human. Her soul! That was beautiful, no doubt. But, again, it was something very vague, intangible, hardly more than a phrase. But the touch of her hand was real, the sound of her voice was real, the clasp of her arms about my neck was real. Oh," he cried, shaken with a sudden wrench of passion, " give those back to me. Tell your God to give those back to me—the sound of her voice, the touch of her hand, the clasp of her dear arms, *real*, *real*, and then you may talk to me of Heaven."

Sarria shook his head. "But when you meet her again," he observed, "in Heaven, you, too, will be changed. You will see her spiritualised, with spiritual eyes. As she is now, she does not appeal to you. I understand that. It is because, as you say, you are only human, while she is divine. But when you come to be like her, as she is now, you will know her as she really is, not as she seemed to be, because her voice was sweet, because her hair was pretty, because her hand was warm in yours. Vanamee, your talk is that of a foolish child. You are like one of the Corinthians to whom Paul wrote. Do you remember? Listen now. I can recall the words, and such words, beautiful and terrible at the same time, such a majesty. They march like soldiers with trumpets. ' But some man will say '—as you have said just now— ' How are the dead raised up? And with what body do they come? Thou fool! That which thou sowest is not quickened except it die, and that which thou sowest, thou sowest not that body that shall be, but bare grain. It may chance of wheat, or of some other grain. But God giveth it a body as it hath pleased him, and to every seed his own body. . . . It is sown a natural body; it is raised a spiritual body.' It is because you are a natural body that you cannot understand her, nor wish for her as a spiritual body, but when you are both spiritual, then you shall know each other as you are—know as you never knew before. Your grain of wheat is your symbol of immortality. You bury it in the earth. It dies, and rises again a thousand times more beautiful. Vanamee, your dear girl was only a grain of humanity that we have buried here, and the end is not yet. But all this is so old, so old. The world learned it a thousand years ago, and yet each man that has ever stood by the open grave of any one he loved must learn it all over again from the beginning."

Vanamee was silent for a moment, looking off with unseeing eyes between the trunks of the pear trees, over the little valley.

"That may all be as you say," he answered after a while. "I have not learned it yet, in any case. Now, I only know that I love her—oh, as if it all were yesterday—and that I am suffering, suffering, always."

He leaned forward, his head supported on his clenched fists, the infinite sadness of his face deepening like a shadow, the tears brimming in his deep-set eyes. A question that he must ask, which involved the thing that was scarcely to be thought of, occurred to him at this moment. After hesitating for a long moment, he said:

"I have been away a long time, and I have had no news of this place since I left. Is there anything to tell, Father? Has any discovery been made, any suspicion developed, as to—the Other?"

The priest shook his head.

"Not a word, not a whisper. It is a mystery. It always will be."

Vanamee clasped his head between his clenched fists, rocking himself to and fro.

"Oh, the terror of it," he murmured. "The horror of it. And she—think of it, Sarria, only sixteen, a little girl; so innocent, that she never knew what wrong meant, pure as a little child is pure, who believed that all things were good; mature only in her love. And to be struck down like that, while your God looked down from Heaven and would not take her part." All at once he seemed to lose control of himself. One of those furies of impotent grief and wrath that assailed him from time to time, blind, insensate. incoherent, suddenly took pos-

session of him. A torrent of words issued from his
lips, and he flung out an arm, the fist clenched, in a fierce,
quick gesture, partly of despair, partly of defiance, partly
of supplication.

" No, your God would not take her part. Where was
God's mercy in that? Where was Heaven's protection
in that? Where was the loving kindness you preach
about? Why did God give her life if it was to be
stamped out? Why did God give her the power of love
if it was to come to nothing? Sarria, listen to me. Why
did God make her so divinely pure if He permitted that
abomination? Ha!" he exclaimed bitterly, " your God!
Why, an Apache buck would have been more merciful.
Your God! There is no God. There is only the Devil.
The Heaven you pray to is only a joke, a wretched trick,
a delusion. It is only Hell that is real."

Sarria caught him by the arm.

" You are a fool and a child," he exclaimed, " and it is
blasphemy that you are saying. I forbid it. You understand? I forbid it."

Vanamee turned on him with a sudden cry.

" Then, tell your God to give her back to me!"

Sarria started away from him, his eyes widening in
astonishment, surprised out of all composure by the
other's outburst. Vanamee's swarthy face was pale,
the sunken cheeks and deep-set eyes were marked with
great black shadows. The priest no longer recognised
him. The face, that face of the ascetic, lean, framed in
its long black hair and pointed beard, was quivering with
the excitement of hallucination. It was the face of the
inspired shepherds of the Hebraic legends, living close
to nature, the younger prophets of Israel, dwellers in the
wilderness, solitary, imaginative, believing in the
Vision, having strange delusions, gifted wth strange
powers. In a brief second of thought, Sarria under-

stood. Out into the wilderness, the vast arid desert
of the Southwest, Vanamee had carried his grief. For
days, for weeks, months even, he had been alone, a solitary speck lost in the immensity of the horizons; continually he was brooding, haunted with his sorrow,
thinking, thinking, often hard put to it for food. The
body was ill-nourished, and the mind, concentrated forever upon one subject, had recoiled upon itself, had
preyed upon the naturally nervous temperament, till the
imagination had become exalted, morbidly active, diseased, beset with hallucinations, forever in search of the
manifestation, of the miracle. It was small wonder that,
bringing a fancy so distorted back to the scene of a vanished happiness, Vanamee should be racked with the
most violent illusions, beset in the throes of a veritable
hysteria.

"Tell your God to give her back to me," he repeated
with fierce insistence.

It was the pitch of mysticism, the imagination harassed and goaded beyond the normal round, suddenly
flipping from the circumference, spinning off at a tan-
gent, out into the void, where all things seemed possible,
hurtling through the dark there, groping for the supernatural, clamouring for the miracle. And it was also the
human, natural protest against the inevitable, the irre-
vocable; the spasm of revolt under the sting of death,
the rebellion of the soul at the victory of the grave.

"He can give her back to me if He only will," Vanamee cried. "Sarria, you must help me. I tell you—I
warn you, sir, I can't last much longer under it. My
head is all wrong with it—I've no more hold on my
mind. Something must happen or I shall lose my senses.
I am breaking down under it all, my body and my mind
alike. Bring her to me; make God show her to me. If
all tales are true, it would not be the first time. If I

cannot have her, at least let me see her as she was, real, earthly, not her spirit, her ghost. I want her real self, undefiled again. If this is dementia, then let me be demented. But help me, you and your God; create the delusion, do the miracle."

"Stop!" cried the priest again, shaking him roughly by the shoulder. "Stop. Be yourself. This *is* dementia; but I shall *not* let you be demented. Think of what you are saying. Bring her back to you! Is that the way of God? I thought you were a man; this is the talk of a weak-minded girl."

Vanamee stirred abruptly in his place, drawing a long breath and looking about him vaguely, as if he came to himself.

"You are right," he muttered. "I hardly know what I am saying at times. But there are moments when my whole mind and soul seem to rise up in rebellion against what has happened; when it seems to me that I am stronger than death, and that if I only knew how to use the strength of my will, concentrate my power of thought—volition—that I could—I don't know—not call her back—but—something——"

"A diseased and distorted mind is capable of hallucinations, if that is what you mean," observed Sarria.

"Perhaps that is what I mean. Perhaps I want only the delusion, after all."

Sarria did not reply, and there was a long silence. In the damp south corners of the walls a frog began to croak at exact intervals. The little fountain rippled monotonously, and a magnolia flower dropped from one of the trees, falling straight as a plummet through the motionless air, and settling upon the gravelled walk with a faint rustling sound. Otherwise the stillness was profound.

A little later, the priest's cigar, long since out, slipped

from his fingers to the ground. He began to nod gently.
Vanamee touched his arm.

" Asleep, sir? "

The other started, rubbing his eyes.

" Upon my word, I believe I was."

" Better go to bed, sir. I am not tired. I think I shall
sit out here a little longer."

" Well, perhaps I would be better off in bed. *Your*
bed is always ready for you here whenever you want to
use it."

" No—I shall go back to Quien Sabe—later. Good-
night, sir."

" Good-night, my boy."

Vanamee was left alone. For a long time he sat
motionless in his place, his elbows on his knees, his chin
propped in his hands. The minutes passed—then the
hours. The moon climbed steadily higher among the
stars. Vanamee rolled and smoked cigarette after cigarette, the blue haze of smoke hanging motionless above
his head, or drifting in slowly weaving filaments across
the open spaces of the garden.

But the influence of the old enclosure, this corner of
romance and mystery, this isolated garden of dreams,
savouring of the past, with its legends, its graves, its
crumbling sun dial, its fountain with its rime of moss,
was not to be resisted. Now that the priest had left him,
the same exaltation of spirit that had seized upon Vanamee earlier in the evening, by degrees grew big again
in his mind and imagination. His sorrow assaulted him
like the flagellations of a fine whiplash, and his love for
Angéle rose again in his heart, it seemed to him never
so deep, so tender, so infinitely strong. No doubt, it
was his familiarity with the Mission garden, his clear-cut
remembrance of it, as it was in the days when he had met
Angéle there, tallying now so exactly with the reality

there under his eyes, that brought her to his imagination so vividly. As yet he dared not trust himself near her grave, but, for the moment, he rose and, his hands clasped behind him, walked slowly from point to point amid the tiny gravelled walks, recalling the incidents of eighteen years ago. On the bench he had quitted he and Angéle had often sat. Here by the crumbling sun dial, he recalled the night when he had kissed her for the first time. Here, again, by the rim of the fountain, with its fringe of green, she once had paused, and, baring her arm to the shoulder, had thrust it deep into the water, and then withdrawing it, had given it to him to kiss, all wet and cool; and here, at last, under the shadow of the pear trees they had sat, evening after evening, looking off over the little valley below them, watching the night build itself, dome-like, from horizon to zenith.

Brusquely Vanamee turned away from the prospect. The Seed ranch was dark at this time of the year, and flowerless. Far off toward its centre, he had caught a brief glimpse of the house where Angéle had lived, and a faint light burning in its window. But he turned from it sharply. The deep-seated travail of his grief abruptly reached the paroxysm. With long strides he crossed the garden and reëntered the Mission church itself, plunging into the coolness of its atmosphere as into a bath. What he searched for he did not know, or, rather, did not define. He knew only that he was suffering, that a longing for Angéle, for some object around which his great love could enfold itself, was tearing at his heart with iron teeth. He was ready to be deluded; craved the hallucination; begged pitifully for the illusion; anything rather than the empty, tenantless night, the voiceless silence, the vast loneliness of the overspanning arc of the heavens.

Before the chancel rail of the altar, under the sanctuary lamp, Vanamee sank upon his knees, his arms folded upon the rail, his head bowed down upon them. He prayed, with what words he could not say, for what he did not understand—for help, merely, for relief, for an Answer to his cry.

It was upon that, at length, that his disordered mind concentrated itself, an Answer—he demanded, he implored an Answer. Not a vague visitation of Grace, not a formless sense of Peace; but an Answer, something real, even if the reality were fancied, a voice out of the night, responding to his, a hand in the dark clasping his groping fingers, a breath, human, warm, fragrant, familiar, like a soft, sweet caress on his shrunken cheeks. Alone there in the dim half-light of the decaying Mission, with its crumbling plaster, its naïve crudity of ornament and picture, he wrestled fiercely with his desires—words, fragments of sentences, inarticulate, incoherent, wrenched from his tight-shut teeth.

But the Answer was not in the church. Above him, over the high altar, the Virgin in a glory, with downcast eyes and folded hands, grew vague and indistinct in the shadow, the colours fading, tarnished by centuries of incense smoke. The Christ in agony on the Cross was but a lamentable vision of tormented anatomy, grey flesh, spotted with crimson. The St. John, the San Juan Bautista, patron saint of the Mission, the gaunt figure in skins, two fingers upraised in the gesture of benediction, gazed stolidly out into the half-gloom under the ceiling, ignoring the human distress that beat itself in vain against the altar rail below, and Angéle remained as before—only a memory, far distant, intangible, lost.

Vanamee rose, turning his back upon the altar with a

vague gesture of despair. He crossed the church, and issuing from the low-arched door opposite the pulpit, once more stepped out into the garden. Here, at least, was reality. The warm, still air descended upon him like a cloak, grateful, comforting, dispelling the chill that lurked in the damp mould of plaster and crumbling adobe.

But now he found his way across the garden on the other side of the fountain, where, ranged against the eastern wall, were nine graves. Here Angéle was buried, in the smallest grave of them all, marked by the little headstone, with its two dates, only sixteen years apart. To this spot, at last, he had returned, after the years spent in the desert, the wilderness—after all the wanderings of the Long Trail. Here, if ever, he must have a sense of her nearness. Close at hand, a short four feet under that mound of grass, was the form he had so often held in the embrace of his arms; the face, the very face he had kissed, that face with the hair of gold making three-cornered the round white forehead, the violet-blue eyes, heavy-lidded, with their strange oriental slant upward toward the temples; the sweet full lips, almost Egyptian in their fulness—all that strange, perplexing, wonderful beauty, so troublous, so enchanting, so out of all accepted standards.

He bent down, dropping upon one knee, a hand upon the headstone, and read again the inscription. Then instinctively his hand left the stone and rested upon the low mound of turf, touching it with the softness of a caress; and then, before he was aware of it, he was stretched at full length upon the earth, beside the grave, his arms about the low mound, his lips pressed against the grass with which it was covered. The pent-up grief of nearly twenty years rose again within his heart, and overflowed, irresistible, violent, passionate. There was

no one to see, no one to hear. Vanamee had no thought
of restraint. He no longer wrestled with his pain—
strove against it. There was even a sense of relief in
permitting himself to be overcome. But the reaction
from this outburst was equally violent. His revolt
against the inevitable, his protest against the grave,
shook him from head to foot, goaded him beyond all
bounds of reason, hounded him on and into the domain of hysteria, dementia. Vanamee was no longer
master of himself—no longer knew what he was doing.

At first, he had been content with merely a wild, unreasoned cry to Heaven that Angéle should be restored
to him, but the vast egotism that seems to run through
all forms of disordered intelligence gave his fancy
another turn. He forgot God. He no longer reckoned
with Heaven. He arrogated their powers to himself—
struggled to be, of his own unaided might, stronger than
death, more powerful than the grave. He had demanded
of Sarria that God should restore Angéle to him, but
now he appealed directly to Angéle herself. As he lay
there, his arms clasped about her grave, she seemed so
near to him that he fancied she *must* hear. And suddenly, at this moment, his recollection of his strange
compelling power—the same power by which he had
called Presley to him half-way across the Quien Sabe
ranch, the same power which had brought Sarria to his
side that very evening—recurred to him. Concentrat-
ing his mind upon the one object with which it had so
long been filled, Vanamee, his eyes closed, his face buried
in his arms, exclaimed:

"Come to me—Angéle—don't you hear? Come to
me."

But the Answer was not in the Grave. Below him the
voiceless Earth lay silent, moveless, withholding the
secret, jealous of that which it held so close in its grip,

refusing to give up that which had been confided to its keeping, untouched by the human anguish that above there, on its surface, clutched with despairing hands at a grave long made. The Earth that only that morning had been so eager, so responsive to the lightest summons, so vibrant with Life, now at night, holding death within its embrace, guarding inviolate the secret of the Grave, was deaf to all entreaty, refused the Answer, and Angéle remained as before, only a memory, far distant, intangible, lost.

Vanamee lifted his head, looking about him with unseeing eyes, trembling with the exertion of his vain effort. But he could not as yet allow himself to despair. Never before had that curious power of attraction failed him. He felt himself to be so strong in this respect that he was persuaded if he exerted himself to the limit of his capacity, something—he could not say what—*must* come of it. If it was only a self-delusion, an hallucination, he told himself that he would be content.

Almost of its own accord, his distorted mind concentrated itself again, every thought, all the power of his will riveting themselves upon Angéle. As if she were alive, he summoned her to him. His eyes, fixed upon the name cut into the headstone, contracted, the pupils growing small, his fists shut tight, his nerves braced rigid.

For a few seconds he stood thus, breathless, expectant, awaiting the manifestation, the Miracle. Then, without knowing why, hardly conscious of what was transpiring, he found that his glance was leaving the headstone, was turning from the grave. Not only this, but his whole body was following the direction of his eyes. Before he knew it, he was standing with his back to Angéle's grave, was facing the north, facing the line of pear trees and the little valley where the Seed ranch lay. At first,

he thought this was because he had allowed his will to
weaken, the concentrated power of his mind to grow
slack. And once more turning toward the grave, he
banded all his thoughts together in a consummate effort,
his teeth grinding together, his hands pressed to his forehead. He forced himself to the notion that Angéle was
alive, and to this creature of his imagination he addressed
himself:

"Angéle!" he cried in a low voice; "Angéle, I am
calling you—do you hear? Come to me—come to me
now, now."

Instead of the Answer he demanded, that inexplicable
counter-influence cut across the current of his thought.
Strive as he would against it, he must veer to the north,
toward the pear trees. Obeying it, he turned, and, still
wondering, took a step in that direction, then another
and another. The next moment he came abruptly to
himself, in the black shadow of the pear trees themselves, and, opening his eyes, found himself looking off
over the Seed ranch, toward the little house in the
centre where Angéle had once lived.

Perplexed, he returned to the grave, once more calling
upon the resources of his will, and abruptly, so soon as
these reached a certain point, the same cross-current
set in. He could no longer keep his eyes upon the
headstone, could no longer think of the grave and what
it held. He must face the north; he must be drawn toward the pear trees, and there left standing in their
shadow, looking out aimlessly over the Seed ranch,
wondering, bewildered. Farther than this the influence
never drew him, but up to this point—the line of pear
trees—it was not to be resisted.

For a time the peculiarity of the affair was of more
interest to Vanamee than even his own distress of spirit,
and once or twice he repeated the attempt, almost experi-

mentally, and invariably with the same result: so soon as he seemed to hold Angéle in the grip of his mind, he was moved to turn about toward the north, and hurry toward the pear trees on the crest of the hill that over-looked the little valley.

But Vanamee's unhappiness was too keen this night for him to dwell long upon the vagaries of his mind. Submitting at length, and abandoning the grave, he flung himself down in the black shade of the pear trees, his chin in his hands, and resigned himself finally and definitely to the inrush of recollection and the exquisite grief of an infinite regret.

To his fancy, she came to him again. He put himself back many years. He remembered the warm nights of July and August, profoundly still, the sky encrusted with stars, the little Mission garden exhaling the mingled perfumes that all through the scorching day had been distilled under the steady blaze of a summer's sun. He saw himself as another person, arriving at this, their rendezvous. All day long she had been in his mind. All day long he had looked forward to this quiet hour that belonged to her. It was dark. He could see nothing, but, by and by, he heard a step, a gentle rustle of the grass on the slope of the hill pressed under an advancing foot. Then he saw the faint gleam of pallid gold of her hair, a barely visible glow in the starlight, and heard the murmur of her breath in the lapse of the over-passing breeze. And then, in the midst of the gentle perfumes of the garden, the perfumes of the magnolia flowers, of the mignonette borders, of the crumbling walls, there expanded a new odour, or the faint mingling of many odours, the smell of the roses that lingered in her hair, of the lilies that exhaled from her neck, of the heliotrope that disengaged itself from her hands and arms, and of the hyacinths with which her little feet were redolent.

And then, suddenly, it was herself—her eyes, heavy-lidded, violet blue, full of the love of him; her sweet full lips speaking his name; her hands clasping his hands, his shoulders, his neck—her whole dear body giving itself into his embrace; her lips against his; her hands holding his head, drawing his face down to hers.

Vanamee, as he remembered all this, flung out an arm with a cry of pain, his eyes searching the gloom, all his mind in strenuous mutiny against the triumph of Death. His glance shot swiftly out across the night, unconsciously following the direction from which Angéle used to come to him.

"Come to me now," he exclaimed under his breath, tense and rigid with the vast futile effort of his will. "Come to me now, now. Don't you hear me, Angéle? You must, you must come."

Suddenly Vanamee returned to himself with the abruptness of a blow. His eyes opened. He half raised himself from the ground. Swiftly his scattered wits readjusted themselves. Never more sane, never more himself, he rose to his feet and stood looking off into the night across the Seed ranch.

"What was it?" he murmured, bewildered.

He looked around him from side to side, as if to get in touch with reality once more. He looked at his hands, at the rough bark of the pear tree next which he stood, at the streaked and rain-eroded walls of the Mission and garden. The exaltation of his mind calmed itself; the unnatural strain under which he laboured slackened. He became thoroughly master of himself again, matter-of-fact, practical, keen.

But just so sure as his hands were his own, just so sure as the bark of the pear tree was rough, the mouldering adobe of the Mission walls damp—just so sure had Something occurred. It was vague, intangible, appealing only to some strange, nameless sixth sense, but none the less perceptible. His mind, his imagination, sent out from him across the night, across the little valley below him, speeding hither and thither through the dark, lost, confused, had suddenly paused, hovering, had found Something. It had not returned to him empty-handed. It had come back, but now there was a change—mysterious, illusive. There were no words for this that had transpired. But for the moment, one thing only was certain. The night was no longer voiceless, the dark was no longer empty. Far off there, beyond the reach of vision, unlocalised, strange, a ripple had formed on the still black pool of the night, had formed, flashed one instant to the stars, then swiftly faded again. The night shut down once more. There was no sound—nothing stirred.

For the moment, Vanamee stood transfixed, struck rigid in his place, stupefied, his eyes staring, breathless with utter amazement. Then, step by step, he shrank back into the deeper shadow, treading with the infinite precaution of a prowling leopard. A qualm of something very much like fear seized upon him. But immediately on the heels of this first impression came the doubt of his own senses. Whatever had happened had been so ephemeral, so faint, so intangible, that now he wondered if he had not deceived himself, after all. But the reaction followed. Surely, there had been Something. And from that moment began for him the most poignant uncertainty of mind. Gradually he drew back into the garden, holding his breath, listening to every faintest sound, walking upon tiptoe. He reached the fountain, and wetting his hands, passed them across his forehead and eyes. Once more he stood listening. The silence was profound.

Troubled, disturbed, Vanamee went away, passing out

of the garden, descending the hill. 'He forded Broderson Creek where it intersected the road to Guadalajara, and went on across Quien Sabe, walking slowly, his head bent down, his hands clasped behind his back, thoughtful, perplexed.

V

At seven o'clock, in the bedroom of his ranch house, in the white-painted iron bedstead with its blue-grey army blankets and red counterpane, Annixter was still asleep, his face red, his mouth open, his stiff yellow hair in wild disorder. On the wooden chair at the bed-head, stood the kerosene lamp, by the light of which he had been reading the previous evening. Beside it was a paper bag of dried prunes, and the limp volume of " Copperfield," the place marked by a slip of paper torn from the edge of the bag.

Annixter slept soundly, making great work of the business, unable to take even his rest gracefully. His eyes were shut so tight that the skin at their angles was drawn into puckers. Under his pillow, his two hands were doubled up into fists. At intervals, he gritted his teeth ferociously, while, from time to time, the abrupt sound of his snoring dominated the brisk ticking of the alarm clock that hung from the brass knob of the bed-post, within six inches of his ear.

But immediately after seven, this clock sprung its alarm with the abruptness of an explosion, and within the second, Annixter had hurled the bed-clothes from him and flung himself up to a sitting posture on the edge of the bed, panting and gasping, blinking at the light, rubbing his head, dazed and bewildered, stupefied at the hideous suddenness with which he had been wrenched from his sleep.

His first act was to take down the alarm clock and stifle its prolonged whirring under the pillows and blankets. But when this had been done, he continued to sit stupidly on the edge of the bed, curling his toes away from the cold of the floor; his half-shut eyes, heavy with sleep, fixed and vacant, closing and opening by turns. For upwards of three minutes he alternately dozed and woke, his head and the whole upper half of his body sagging abruptly sideways from moment to moment. But at length, coming more to himself, he straightened up, ran his fingers through his hair, and with a prodigious yawn, murmured vaguely:

" Oh, Lord!   Oh-h, *Lord!* "

He stretched three or four times, twisting about in his place, curling and uncurling his toes, muttering from time to time between two yawns:

" Oh, Lord!   Oh, Lord! "

He stared about the room, collecting his thoughts, readjusting himself for the day's work.

The room was barren, the walls of tongue-and-groove sheathing—alternate brown and yellow boards—like the walls of a stable, were adorned with two or three unframed lithographs, the Christmas " souvenirs " of weekly periodicals, fastened with great wire nails; a bunch of herbs or flowers, lamentably withered and grey with dust, was affixed to the mirror over the black walnut washstand by the window, and a yellowed photograph of Annixter's combined harvester—himself and his men in a group before it—hung close at hand. On the floor, at the bedside and before the bureau, were two oval rag-carpet rugs. In the corners of the room were muddy boots, a McClellan saddle, a surveyor's transit, an empty coal-hod and a box of iron bolts and nuts. On the wall over the bed, in a gilt frame, was Annixter's college diploma, while on the bureau, amid a litter of hair-brushes, dirty collars, driving gloves, cigars and the like, stood a broken machine for loading shells.

It was essentially a man's room, rugged, uncouth, virile, full of the odours of tobacco, of leather, of rusty iron; the bare floor hollowed by the grind of hob-nailed boots, the walls marred by the friction of heavy things of metal. Strangely enough, Annixter's clothes were disposed of on the single chair with the precision of an old maid. Thus he had placed them the night before; the boots set carefully side by side, the trousers, with the overalls still upon them, neatly folded upon the seat of the chair, the coat hanging from its back.

The Quien Sabe ranch house was a six-room affair, all on one floor. By no excess of charity could it have been called a home. Annixter was a wealthy man; he could have furnished his dwelling with quite as much elegance as that of Magnus Derrick. As it was, however, he considered his house merely as a place to eat, to sleep, to change his clothes in; as a shelter from the rain, an office where business was transacted—nothing more.

When he was sufficiently awake, Annixter thrust his feet into a pair of wicker slippers, and shuffled across the office adjoining his bedroom, to the bathroom just beyond, and stood under the icy shower a few minutes, his teeth chattering, fulminating oaths at the coldness of the water. Still shivering, he hurried into his clothes, and, having pushed the button of the electric bell to announce that he was ready for breakfast, immediately plunged into the business of the day. While he was thus occupied, the butcher's cart from Bonneville drove into the yard with the day's supply of meat. This cart also brought the Bonneville paper and the mail of the previous night. In the bundle of correspondence that the butcher handed to Annixter that morning, was a telegram from Osterman, at that time on his second trip to Los Angeles. It read:

"Flotation of company in this district assured. Have secured services of desirable party. Am now in position to sell you your share stock, as per original plan."

Annixter grunted as he tore the despatch into strips. "Well," he muttered, "that part is settled, then."

He made a little pile of the torn strips on the top of the unlighted stove, and burned them carefully, scowling down into the flicker of fire, thoughtful and preoccupied.

He knew very well what Osterman referred to by "Flotation of company," and also who was the "desirable party" he spoke of.

Under protest, as he was particular to declare, and after interminable argument, Annixter had allowed himself to be reconciled with Osterman, and to be persuaded to reënter the proposed political "deal." A committee had been formed to finance the affair—Osterman, old Broderson, Annixter himself, and, with reservations, hardly more than a looker-on, Harran Derrick. Of this committee, Osterman was considered chairman. Magnus Derrick had formally and definitely refused his adherence to the scheme. He was trying to steer a middle course. His position was difficult, anomalous. If freight rates were cut through the efforts of the members of the committee, he could not very well avoid taking advantage of the new schedule. He would be the gainer, though sharing neither the risk nor the expense. But, meanwhile, the days were passing; the primary elections were drawing nearer. The committee could not afford to wait, and by way of a beginning, Osterman had gone to Los Angeles, fortified by a large sum of money—a purse to which Annixter, Broderson and himself had contributed. He had put himself in touch with Disbrow, the political man of the Denver, Pueblo and Mojave road, and had had two interviews with him. The telegram that Annixter received that morning was to say that Disbrow had been bought over, and would adopt Darrell as the D., P. and M. candidate for Railroad Commissioner from the third district.

One of the cooks brought up Annixter's breakfast that morning, and he went through it hastily, reading his mail at the same time and glancing over the pages of the "Mercury," Genslinger's paper. The "Mercury," Annixter was persuaded, received a subsidy from the Pacific and Southwestern Railroad, and was hardly better than the mouthpiece by which Shelgrim and the General Office spoke to ranchers about Bonneville.

An editorial in that morning's issue said:

"It would not be surprising to the well-informed, if the long-deferred re-grade of the value of the railroad sections included in the Los Muertos, Quien Sabe, Osterman and Broderson properties was made before the first of the year. Naturally, the tenants of these lands feel an interest in the price which the railroad will put upon its holdings, and it is rumoured they expect the land will be offered to them for two dollars and fifty cents per acre. It needs no seventh daughter of a seventh daughter to foresee that these gentlemen will be disappointed."

"Rot!" vociferated Annixter to himself as he finished. He rolled the paper into a wad and hurled it from him.

"Rot! rot! What does Genslinger know about it? I stand on my agreement with the P. and S. W.—from two fifty to five dollars an acre—there it is in black and white. The road *is* obligated. And my improvements! I made the land valuable by improving it, irrigating it, draining it, and cultivating it. Talk to *me*. I know better."

The most abiding impression that Genslinger's editorial made upon him was, that possibly the "Mercury" was not subsidised by the corporation after all. If it was, Genslinger would not have been led into making his mistake as to the value of the land. He would have known that the railroad was under contract to sell at two dollars and a half an acre, and not only this, but that when the land was put upon the market, it was to be offered to the present holders first of all. Annixter called to mind the explicit terms of the agreement between himself and the railroad, and dismissed the matter from his mind. He lit a cigar, put on his hat and went out.

The morning was fine, the air nimble, brisk. On the summit of the skeleton-like tower of the artesian well, the windmill was turning steadily in a breeze from the southwest. The water in the irrigating ditch was well up. There was no cloud in the sky. Far off to the east and west, the bulwarks of the valley, the Coast Range and the foothills of the Sierras stood out, pale amethyst against the delicate pink and white sheen of the horizon. The sunlight was a veritable flood, crystal, limpid, sparkling, setting a feeling of gayety in the air, stirring up an effervescence in the blood, a tumult of exuberance in the veins.

But on his way to the barns, Annixter was obliged to pass by the open door of the dairy-house. Hilma Tree was inside, singing at her work; her voice of a velvety huskiness, more of the chest than of the throat, mingling with the liquid dashing of the milk in the vats and churns, and the clear, sonorous clinking of the cans and pans. Annixter turned into the dairy-house, pausing on the threshold, looking about him. Hilma stood bathed from head to foot in the torrent of sunlight that poured in upon her from the three wide-open windows. She was charming, delicious, radiant of youth, of health, of well-being. Into her eyes, wide open, brown, rimmed with their fine, thin line of intense black lashes, the sun set a

diamond flash; the same golden light glowed all around
her thick, moist hair, lambent, beautiful, a sheen of almost metallic lustre, and reflected itself upon her wet
lips, moving with the words of her singing. The white-
ness of her skin under the caress of this hale, vigorous
morning light was dazzling, pure, of a fineness beyond
words. Beneath the sweet modulation of her chin, the
reflected light from the burnished copper vessel she was
carrying set a vibration of pale gold. Overlaying the
flush of rose in her cheeks, seen only when she stood
against the sunlight, was a faint sheen of down, a lustrous
floss, delicate as the pollen of a flower, or the impalpable
powder of a moth's wing. She was moving to and fro
about her work, alert, joyous, robust; and from all the
fine, full amplitude of her figure, from her thick white
neck, sloping downward to her shoulders, from the deep,
feminine swell of her breast, the vigorous maturity of
her hips, there was disengaged a vibrant note of gayety,
of exuberant animal life, sane, honest, strong. She wore
a skirt of plain blue calico and a shirtwaist of pink linen,
clean, trim; while her sleeves turned back to her shoulders, showed her large, white arms, wet with milk, redolent and fragrant with milk, glowing and resplendent
in the early morning light.

On the threshold, Annixter took off his hat.

" Good morning, Miss Hilma."

Hilma, who had set down the copper can on top of the
vat, turned about quickly.

"Oh, *good* morning, sir;" and, unconsciously, she
made a little gesture of salutation with her hand, raising
it part way toward her head, as a man would have done.

"Well," began Annixter vaguely, "how are you getting along down here?"

"Oh, very fine. To-day, there is not so much to do.
We drew the whey hours ago, and now we are just done

putting the curd to press. I have been cleaning. See my pans. Wouldn't they do for mirrors, sir? And the copper things. I have scrubbed and scrubbed. Oh, you can look into the tiniest corners, everywhere, you won't find so much as the littlest speck of dirt or grease. I love *clean* things, and this room is my own particular place. Here I can do just as I please, and that is, to keep the cement floor, and the vats, and the churns and the separators, and especially the cans and coppers, clean; clean, and to see that the milk is pure, oh, so that a little baby could drink it; and to have the air always sweet, and the sun—oh, lots and lots of sun, morning, noon and afternoon, so that everything shines. You know, I never see the sun set that it don't make me a little sad; yes, always, just a little. Isn't it funny? I should want it to be day all the time. And when the day is gloomy and dark, I am just as sad as if a very good friend of mine had left me. Would you believe it? Just until within a few years, when I was a big girl, sixteen and over, mamma had to sit by my bed every night before I could go to sleep. I was afraid in the dark. Sometimes I am now. Just imagine, and now I am nineteen—a young lady."

"You were, hey?" observed Annixter, for the sake of saying something. "Afraid in the dark? What of— ghosts?"

"N-no; I don't know what. I wanted the light, I wanted——" She drew a deep breath, turning towards the window and spreading her pink finger-tips to the light. "Oh, the *sun*. I love the sun. See, put your hand there—here on the top of the vat—like that. Isn't it warm? Isn't it fine? And don't you love to see it coming in like that through the windows, floods of it; and all the little dust in it shining? Where there is lots of sunlight, I think the people must be very good. It's only wicked people that love the dark. And the wicked things are always done and planned in the dark, I think. Perhaps, too, that's why I hate things that are mysterious—things that I can't see, that happen in the dark." She wrinkled her nose with a little expression of aversion. "I hate a mystery. Maybe that's why I am afraid in the dark—or was. I shouldn't like to think that anything could happen around me that I couldn't see or understand or explain."

She ran on from subject to subject, positively garrulous, talking in her low-pitched voice of velvety huskiness for the mere enjoyment of putting her ideas into speech, innocently assuming that they were quite as interesting to others as to herself. She was yet a great child, ignoring the fact that she had ever grown up, taking a child's interest in her immediate surroundings, direct, straightforward, plain. While speaking, she continued about her work, rinsing out the cans with a mixture of hot water and soda, scouring them bright, and piling them in the sunlight on top of the vat.

Obliquely, and from between his narrowed lids, Annixter scrutinised her from time to time, more and more won over by her adorable freshness, her clean, fine youth. The clumsiness that he usually experienced in the presence of women was wearing off. Hilma Tree's direct simplicity put him at his ease. He began to wonder if he dared to kiss Hilma, and if he did dare, how she would take it. A spark of suspicion flickered up in his mind. Did not her manner imply, vaguely, an invitation? One never could tell with feemales. That was why she was talking so much, no doubt, holding him there, affording the opportunity. Aha! She had best look out, or he would take her at her word.

"Oh, I had forgotten," suddenly exclaimed Hilma, "the very thing I wanted to show you—the new press.

You remember I asked for one last month? This is it. See, this is how it works. Here is where the curds go; look. And this cover is screwed down like this, and then you work the lever this way." She grasped the lever in both hands, throwing her weight upon it, her smooth, bare arm swelling round and firm with the effort, one slim foot, in its low shoe set off with the bright, steel buckle, braced against the wall.

" My, but that takes strength," she panted, looking up at him and smiling. " But isn't it a fine press? Just what we needed."

" And," Annixter cleared his throat, " and where do you keep the cheeses and the butter?" He thought it very likely that these were in the cellar of the dairy.

" In the cellar," answered Hilma. " Down here, see?" She raised the flap of the cellar door at the end of the room. " Would you like to see? Come down; I'll show you."

She went before him down into the cool obscurity underneath, redolent of new cheese and fresh butter. Annixter followed, a certain excitement beginning to gain upon him. He was almost sure now that Hilma wanted him to kiss her. At all events, one could but try. But, as yet, he was not absolutely sure. Suppose he had been mistaken in her; suppose she should consider herself insulted and freeze him with an icy stare. Annixter winced at the very thought of it. Better let the whole business go, and get to work. He was wasting half the morning. Yet, if she *did* want to give him the opportunity of kissing her, and he failed to take advantage of it, what a ninny she would think him; she would despise him for being afraid. He afraid! He, Annixter, afraid of a fool, feemale girl. Why, he owed it to himself as a man to go as far as he could. He told himself that that goat Osterman would have kissed Hilma Tree weeks ago. To test

his state of mind, he imagined himself as having decided
to kiss her, after all, and at once was surprised to experience a poignant qualm of excitement, his heart beating
heavily, his breath coming short. At the same time, his
courage remained with him. He was not afraid to try.
He felt a greater respect for himself because of this. His
self-assurance hardened within him, and as Hilma turned
to him, asking him to taste a cut from one of the ripe
cheeses, he suddenly stepped close to her, throwing an
arm about her shoulders, advancing his head.

But at the last second, he bungled, hesitated; Hilma
shrank from him, supple as a young reed; Annixter
clutched harshly at her arm, and trod his full weight upon
one of her slender feet, his cheek and chin barely touching the delicate pink lobe of one of her ears, his lips
brushing merely a fold of her shirt waist between neck
and shoulder. The thing was a failure, and at once he
realised that nothing had been further from Hilma's
mind than the idea of his kissing her.

She started back from him abruptly, her hands nervously clasped against her breast, drawing in her breath
sharply and holding it with a little, tremulous catch of
the throat that sent a quivering vibration the length of
her smooth, white neck. Her eyes opened wide with a
childlike look, more of astonishment than anger. She
was surprised, out of all measure, discountenanced, taken
all aback, and when she found her breath, gave voice to a
great "Oh" of dismay and distress.

For an instant, Annixter stood awkwardly in his place,
ridiculous, clumsy, murmuring over and over again:

"Well—well—that's all right—who's going to hurt
you? You needn't be afraid—who's going to hurt you—
that's all right."

Then, suddenly, with a quick, indefinite gesture of one
arm, he exclaimed:

" Good-bye, I—I'm sorry."

He turned away, striding up the stairs, crossing the dairy-room, and regained the open air, raging and furious. He turned toward the barns, clapping his hat upon his head, muttering the while under his breath:

" Oh, you goat! You beastly fool *pip*. Good *Lord*, what an ass you've made of yourself now! "

Suddenly he resolved to put Hilma Tree out of his thoughts. The matter was interfering with his work. This kind of thing was sure not earning any money. He shook himself as though freeing his shoulders of an irksome burden, and turned his entire attention to the work nearest at hand.

The prolonged rattle of the shinglers' hammers upon the roof of the big barn attracted him, and, crossing over between the ranch house and the artesian well, he stood for some time absorbed in the contemplation of the vast building, amused and interested with the confusion of sounds—the clatter of hammers, the cadenced scrape of saws, and the rhythmic shuffle of planes—that issued from the gang of carpenters who were at that moment putting the finishing touches upon the roof and rows of stalls. A boy and two men were busy hanging the great sliding door at the south end, while the painters—come down from Bonneville early that morning—were engaged in adjusting the spray and force engine, by means of which Annixter had insisted upon painting the vast surfaces of the barn, condemning the use of brushes and pots for such work as old-fashioned and out-of-date.

He called to one of the foremen, to ask when the barn would be entirely finished, and was told that at the end of the week the hay and stock could be installed.

" And a precious long time you've been at it, too," Annixter declared.

" Well, you know the rain——"

" Oh, rot the rain! *I* work in the rain. You and your unions make me sick."

" But, Mr. Annixter, we couldn't have begun painting in the rain. The job would have been spoiled."

" Hoh, yes, spoiled. That's all very well. Maybe it would, and then, again, maybe it wouldn't."

But when the foreman had left him, Annixter could not forbear a growl of satisfaction. It could not be denied that the barn was superb, monumental even. Almost any one of the other barns in the county could be swung, bird-cage fashion, inside of it, with room to spare. In every sense, the barn was precisely what Annixter had hoped of it. In his pleasure over the success of his idea, even Hilma for the moment was forgotten.

" And, now," murmured Annixter, " I'll give that dance in it. I'll make 'em sit up."

It occurred to him that he had better set about sending out the invitations for the affair. He was puzzled to decide just how the thing should be managed, and resolved that it might be as well to consult Magnus and Mrs. Derrick.

" I want to talk of this telegram of the goat's with Magnus, anyhow," he said to himself reflectively, " and there's things I got to do in Bonneville before the first of the month."

He turned about on his heel with a last look at the barn, and set off toward the stable. He had decided to have his horse saddled and ride over to Bonneville by way of Los Muertos. He would make a day of it, would see Magnus, Harran, old Broderson and some of the business men of Bonneville.

A few moments later, he rode out of the barn and the stable-yard, a fresh cigar between his teeth, his hat slanted over his face against the rays of the sun, as yet low in the east. He crossed the irrigating ditch and gained the trail—the short cut over into Los Muertos, by way of Hooven's. It led south and west into the low ground overgrown by grey-green willows by Broderson Creek, at this time of the rainy season a stream of considerable volume, farther on dipping sharply to pass underneath the Long Trestle of the railroad. On the other side of the right of way, Annixter was obliged to open the gate in Derrick's line fence. He managed this without dismounting, swearing at the horse the while, and spurring him continually. But once inside the gate he cantered forward briskly.

This part of Los Muertos was Hooven's holding, some five hundred acres enclosed between the irrigating ditch and Broderson Creek, and half the way across, Annixter came up with Hooven himself, busily at work replacing a broken washer in his seeder. Upon one of the horses hitched to the machine, her hands gripped tightly upon the harness of the collar, Hilda, his little daughter, with her small, hob-nailed boots and boy's canvas overalls, sat, exalted and petrified with ecstasy and excitement, her eyes wide opened, her hair in a tangle.

" Hello, Bismarck," said Annixter, drawing up beside him. " What are *you* doing here? I thought the Governor was going to manage without his tenants this year."

" Ach, Meest'r Ennixter," cried the other, straightening up. " Ach, dat's you, eh? Ach, you bedt he doand menege mitout me. Me, I gotta stay. I talk der straighd talk mit der Governor. I fix 'em. Ach, you bedt. Sieben yahr I hef bei der rench ge-stopped; yais, sir. Efery oder sohn-of-a-guhn bei der plaice ged der sach bud me. Eh? Wat you tink von dose ting?"

" I think that's a crazy-looking monkey-wrench you've got there," observed Annixter, glancing at the instrument in Hooven's hand.

"Ach, dot wrainch," returned Hooven. "Soh! Wail, I tell you dose ting now whair I got 'em. Say, you see dot wrainch. Dat's not Emericen wrainch at alle. I got 'em at Gravelotte der day we licked der stuffun oudt der Frainch, ach, you bedt. Me, I pelong to der Würtemberg redgimend, dot dey use to suppord der batterie von der Brince von Hohenlohe. Alle der day we lay down bei der stomach in der feildt behindt der batterie, und der schells von der Frainch cennon hef eggsblode— *ach, donnerwetter!*—I tink efery schell eggsblode bei der beckside my neck. Und dat go on der whole day, noddun else, noddun aber der Frainch schell, b-r-r, b-r-r, b-r-r, b-r-*am*, und der smoag, und unzer batterie, dat go off slow, steady, yoost like der glock, eins, zwei, boom! eins, zwei, boom! yoost like der glock, ofer und ofer again, alle der day. Den vhen der night come dey say we hev der great victorie made. I doand know. Vhat do I see von der bettle? Noddun. Den we gedt oop und maerch und maerch alle night, und in der morgen we hear dose cennon egain, hell oaf der way, far-off, I doand know vhair. Budt, nef'r mindt. Bretty quick, ach, Gott—" his face flamed scarlet, "*Ach, du lieber Gott!* Bretty zoon, dere wass der Kaiser, glose bei, und Fritz, Unzer Fritz. Bei Gott, den I go grazy, und yell, ach, you bedt, der whole redgimend: 'Hoch der Kaiser! Hoch der Vaterland!' Und der dears come to der eyes, I doand know because vhy, und der mens gry und shaike der hend, und der whole redgimend maerch off like dat, fairy broudt, bei Gott, der head oop high, und sing 'Die Wacht am Rhein.' Dot wass Gravelotte."

"And the monkey-wrench?"

"Ach, I pick 'um oop vhen der batterie go. Der cennoniers hef forgedt und leaf 'um. I carry 'um in der sack. I tink I use 'um vhen I gedt home in der business. I was maker von vagons in Carlsruhe, und I nef'r gedt

home again. Vhen der war hef godt over, I go beck to
Ulm und gedt marriet, und den I gedt demn sick von der
armie. Vhen I gedt der release, I clair oudt, you bedt.
I come to Emerica. First, New Yor-ruk; den Milwau-
kee; den Sbringfieldt-Illinoy; den Galifornie, und heir I
stay."

"And the Fatherland? Ever want to go back?"

"Wail, I tell you dose ting, Meest'r Ennixter. Alle-
ways, I tink a lot oaf Shairmany, und der Kaiser, und
nef'r I forgedt Gravelotte. Budt, say, I tell you dose ting.
Vhair der wife is, und der kinder—der leedle girl Hilda—
dere is der Vaterland. Eh? Emerica, dat's my gountry
now, und dere," he pointed behind him to the house
under the mammoth oak tree on the Lower Road, "dat's
my home. Dat's goot enough Vaterland for me."

Annixter gathered up the reins, about to go on.

"So you like America, do you, Bismarck?" he said.
"Who do you vote for?"

"Emerica? I doand know," returned the other, in-
sistently. "Dat's my home yonder. Dat's my Vaterland. Alle von we Shairmens yoost like dot. Shairmany,
dot's hell oaf some fine plaice, sure. Budt der Vaterland
iss vhair der home und der wife und kinder iss. Eh?
Yes? Voad? Ach, no. Me, I nef'r voad. I doand bod-
der der haid mit dose ting. I maig der wheat grow, und
ged der braid fur der wife und Hilda, dot's all. Dot's me;
dot's Bismarck."

"Good-bye," commented Annixter, moving off.

Hooven, the washer replaced, turned to his work
again, starting up the horses. The seeder advanced,
whirring.

"Ach, Hilda, leedle girl," he cried, "hold tight bei der
shdrap on. Hey *mule!* Hoop! Gedt oop, you."

Annixter cantered on. In a few moments, he had
crossed Broderson Creek and had entered upon the

Home ranch of Los Muertos. Ahead of him, but so far off that the greater portion of its bulk was below the horizon, he could see the Derricks' home, a roof or two between the dull green of cypress and eucalyptus. Nothing else was in sight. The brown earth, smooth, unbroken, was as a limitless, mud-coloured ocean. The silence was profound.

Then, at length, Annixter's searching eye made out a blur on the horizon to the northward; the blur concentrated itself to a speck; the speck grew by steady degrees to a spot, slowly moving, a note of dull colour, barely darker than the land, but an inky black silhouette as it topped a low rise of ground and stood for a moment outlined against the pale blue of the sky. Annixter turned his horse from the road and rode across the ranch land to meet this new object of interest. As the spot grew larger, it resolved itself into constituents, a collection of units; its shape grew irregular, fragmentary. A disintegrated, nebulous confusion advanced toward Annixter, preceded, as he discovered on nearer approach, by a medley of faint sounds. Now it was no longer a spot, but a column, a column that moved, accompanied by spots. As Annixter lessened the distance, these spots resolved themselves into buggies or men on horseback that kept pace with the advancing column. There were horses in the column itself. At first glance, it appeared as if there were nothing else, a riderless squadron tramping steadily over the upturned plough land of the ranch. But it drew nearer. The horses were in lines, six abreast, harnessed to machines. The noise increased, defined itself. There was a shout or two; occasionally a horse blew through his nostrils with a prolonged, vibrating snort. The click and clink of metal work was incessant, the machines throwing off a continual rattle of wheels and cogs and clashing springs. The column approached

nearer; was close at hand. The noises mingled to a subdued uproar, a bewildering confusion; the impact of innumerable hoofs was a veritable rumble. Machine after
machine appeared; and Annixter, drawing to one side,
remained for nearly ten minutes watching and interested,
while, like an array of chariots—clattering, jostling,
creaking, clashing, an interminable procession, machine
succeeding machine, six-horse team succeeding six-
horse team — bustling, hurried — Magnus Derrick's
thirty-three grain drills, each with its eight hoes, went
clamouring past, like an advance of military, seeding the
ten thousand acres of the great ranch; fecundating the
living soil; implanting deep in the dark womb of the
Earth the germ of life, the sustenance of a whole world,
the food of an entire People.

When the drills had passed, Annixter turned and rode
back to the Lower Road, over the land now thick with
seed. He did not wonder that the seeding on Los
Muertos seemed to be hastily conducted. Magnus and
Harran Derrick had not yet been able to make up the
time lost at the beginning of the season, when they had
waited so long for the ploughs to arrive. They had been
behindhand all the time. On Annixter's ranch, the land
had not only been harrowed, as well as seeded, but in
some cases, cross-harrowed as well. The labour of putting in the vast crop was over. Now there was nothing to
do but wait, while the seed silently germinated; nothing
to do but watch for the wheat to come up.

When Annixter reached the ranch house of Los
Muertos, under the shade of the cypress and eucalyptus
trees, he found Mrs. Derrick on the porch, seated in a
long wicker chair. She had been washing her hair, and
the light brown locks that yet retained so much of their
brightness, were carefully spread in the sun over the
back of her chair. Annixter could not but remark that,

spite of her more than fifty years, Annie Derrick was yet
rather pretty. Her eyes were still those of a young girl,
just touched with an uncertain expression of innocence
and inquiry, but as her glance fell upon him, he found
that that expression changed to one of uneasiness, of
distrust, almost of aversion.

The night before this, after Magnus and his wife had
gone to bed, they had lain awake for hours, staring up
into the dark, talking, talking. Magnus had not long
been able to keep from his wife the news of the coalition
that was forming against the railroad, nor the fact that
this coalition was determined to gain its ends by any
means at its command. He had told her of Osterman's
scheme of a fraudulent election to seat a Board of Railroad Commissioners, who should be nominees of the
farming interests. Magnus and his wife had talked this
matter over and over again; and the same discussion,
begun immediately after supper the evening before, had
lasted till far into the night.

At once, Annie Derrick had been seized with a sudden
terror lest Magnus, after all, should allow himself to be
persuaded; should yield to the pressure that was every
day growing stronger. None better than she knew the
iron integrity of her husband's character. None better
than she remembered how his dearest ambition, that of
political preferment, had been thwarted by his refusal to
truckle, to connive, to compromise with his ideas of
right. Now, at last, there seemed to be a change. Long
continued oppression, petty tyranny, injustice and extortion had driven him to exasperation. S. Behrman's
insults still rankled. He seemed nearly ready to countenance Osterman's scheme. The very fact that he was
willing to talk of it to her so often and at such great
length, was proof positive that it occupied his mind.
The pity of it, the tragedy of it! He, Magnus, the

" Governor," who had been so staunch, so rigidly upright, so loyal to his convictions, so bitter in his denunciation of the New Politics, so scathing in his attacks on
bribery and corruption in high places; was it possible
that now, at last, he could be brought to withhold his
condemnation of the devious intrigues of the unscrupulous, going on there under his very eyes? That Magnus
should not command Harran to refrain from all inter-
course with the conspirators, had been a matter of vast
surprise to Mrs. Derrick. Time was when Magnus
would have forbidden his son to so much as recognise
a dishonourable man.

But besides all this, Derrick's wife trembled at the
thought of her husband and son engaging in so desperate
a grapple with the railroad—that great monster, iron-
hearted, relentless, infinitely powerful. Always it had
issued triumphant from the fight; always S. Behrman,
the Corporation's champion, remained upon the field
as victor, placid, unperturbed, unassailable. But now a
more terrible struggle than any hitherto loomed menacing over the rim of the future; money was to be spent
like water; personal reputations were to be hazarded in
the issue; failure meant ruin in all directions, financial
ruin, moral ruin, ruin of prestige, ruin of character.
Success, to her mind, was almost impossible. Annie
Derrick feared the railroad. At night, when everything
else was still, the distant roar of passing trains echoed
across Los Muertos, from Guadalajara, from Bonneville,
or from the Long Trestle, straight into her heart. At
such moments she saw very plainly the galloping terror
of steam and steel, with its single eye, cyclopean, red,
shooting from horizon to horizon, symbol of a vast
power, huge and terrible; the leviathan with tentacles of
steel, to oppose which meant to be ground to instant destruction beneath the clashing wheels. No, it was better

to submit, to resign oneself to the inevitable. She obliterated herself, shrinking from the harshness of the
world, striving, with vain hands, to draw her husband
back with her.

Just before Annixter's arrival, she had been sitting,
thoughtful, in her long chair, an open volume of poems
turned down upon her lap, her glance losing itself in the
immensity of Los Muertos that, from the edge of the
lawn close by, unrolled itself, gigantic, toward the far,
southern horizon, wrinkled and serrated after the season's ploughing. The earth, hitherto grey with dust,
was now upturned and brown. As far as the eye could
reach, it was empty of all life, bare, mournful, absolutely
still; and, as she looked, there seemed to her morbid
imagination—diseased and disturbed with long brooding,
sick with the monotony of repeated sensation—to be
disengaged from all this immensity, a sense of a vast
oppression, formless, disquieting. The terror of sheer
bigness grew slowly in her mind; loneliness beyond
words gradually enveloped her. She was lost in all these
limitless reaches of space. Had she been abandoned in
mid-ocean, in an open boat, her terror could hardly have
been greater. She felt vividly that certain uncongeniality
which, when all is said, forever remains between humanity
and the earth which supports it. She recognised the
colossal indifference of nature, not hostile, even kindly
and friendly, so long as the human ant-swarm was sub-
missive, working with it, hurrying along at its side in the
mysterious march of the centuries. Let, however, the
insect rebel, strive to make head against the power of
this nature, and at once it became relentless, a gigantic
engine, a vast power, huge, terrible; a leviathan with a
heart of steel, knowing no compunction, no forgiveness,
no tolerance; crushing out the human atom with sound-
less calm, the agony of destruction sending never a jar,

never the faintest tremour through all that prodigious
mechanism of wheels and cogs.

Such thoughts as these did not take shape distinctly in
her mind. She could not have told herself exactly what
it was that disquieted her. She only received the vague
sensation of these things, as it were a breath of wind
upon her face, confused, troublous, an indefinite sense
of hostility in the air.

The sound of hoofs grinding upon the gravel of the
driveway brought her to herself again, and, withdrawing
her gaze from the empty plain of Los Muertos, she saw
young Annixter stopping his horse by the carriage steps.
But the sight of him only diverted her mind to the other
trouble. She could not but regard him with aversion.
He was one of the conspirators, was one of the leaders
in the battle that impended; no doubt, he had come to
make a fresh attempt to win over Magnus to the unholy
alliance.

However, there was little trace of enmity in her greeting. Her hair was still spread, like a broad patch of
brown sea-weed, upon the white towel over the chair-
back, and she made that her excuse for not getting up.
In answer to Annixter's embarrassed inquiry after Magnus, she sent the Chinese cook to call him from the office;
and Annixter, after tying his horse to the ring driven
into the trunk of one of the eucalyptus trees, came up to
the porch, and, taking off his hat, sat down upon the
steps.

" Is Harran anywhere about? " he asked. " I'd like to
see Harran, too."

" No," said Mrs. Derrick, " Harran went to Bonneville early this morning."

She glanced toward Annixter nervously, without
turning her head, lest she should disturb her outspread
hair.

"What is it you want to see Mr. Derrick about?" she inquired hastily. "Is it about this plan to elect a Railroad Commission? Magnus does not approve of it," she declared with energy. "He told me so last night."

Annixter moved about awkwardly where he sat, smoothing down with his hand the one stiff lock of yellow hair that persistently stood up from his crown like an Indian's scalp-lock. At once his suspicions were all aroused. Ah! this feemale woman was trying to get a hold on him, trying to involve him in a petticoat mess, trying to cajole him. Upon the instant, he became very crafty; an excess of prudence promptly congealed his natural impulses. In an actual spasm of caution, he scarcely trusted himself to speak, terrified lest he should commit himself to something. He glanced about apprehensively, praying that Magnus might join them speedily, relieving the tension.

"I came to see about giving a dance in my new barn," he answered, scowling into the depths of his hat, as though reading from notes he had concealed there. "I wanted to ask how I should send out the *in*vites. I thought of just putting an ad. in the 'Mercury.'"

But as he spoke, Presley had come up behind Annixter in time to get the drift of the conversation, and now observed:

"That's nonsense, Buck. You're not giving a public ball. You *must* send out invitations."

"Hello, Presley, you there?" exclaimed Annixter, turning round. The two shook hands.

"Send out invitations?" repeated Annixter uneasily. "Why must I?"

"Because that's the only way to do."

"It is, is it?" answered Annixter, perplexed and troubled. No other man of his acquaintance could have so contradicted Annixter without provoking a quarrel upon the instant. Why the young rancher, irascible, obstinate, belligerent, should invariably defer to the poet, was an inconsistency never to be explained. It was with great surprise that Mrs. Derrick heard him continue:

" Well, I suppose you know what you're talking about, Pres. Must have written *in*vites, hey?"

" Of course."

" Typewritten?"

" Why, what an ass you are, Buck," observed Presley calmly. " Before you get through with it, you will probably insult three-fourths of the people you intend to invite, and have about a hundred quarrels on your hands, and a lawsuit or two."

However, before Annixter could reply, Magnus came out on the porch, erect, grave, freshly shaven. Without realising what he was doing, Annixter instinctively rose to his feet. It was as though Magnus was a commander-in-chief of an unseen army, and he a subaltern. There was some little conversation as to the proposed dance, and then Annixter found an excuse for drawing the Governor aside. Mrs. Derrick watched the two with eyes full of poignant anxiety, as they slowly paced the length of the gravel driveway to the road gate, and stood there, leaning upon it, talking earnestly; Magnus tall, thin-lipped, impassive, one hand in the breast of his frock coat, his head bare, his keen, blue eyes fixed upon Annixter's face. Annixter came at once to the main point.

" I got a wire from Osterman this morning, Governor, and, well—we've got Disbrow. That means that the Denver, Pueblo and Mojave is back of us. There's half the fight won, first off."

" Osterman bribed him, I suppose," observed Magnus.

Annixter raised a shoulder vexatiously.

" You've got to pay for what you get," he returned. " You don't get something for nothing, I guess. Gov-

ernor," he went on, " I don't see how you can stay out of
this business much longer. You see how it will be.
We're going to win, and I don't see how you can feel
that it's right of you to let us do all the work and stand
all the expense. There's never been a movement of any
importance that went on around you that you weren't the
leader in it. All Tulare County, all the San Joaquin, for
that matter, knows you. They want a leader, and they
are looking to you. I know how you feel about politics
nowadays. But, Governor, standards have changed
since your time; everybody plays the game now as we
are playing it—the most honourable men. You can't
play it any other way, and, pshaw! if the right wins out
in the end, that's the main thing. We want you in this
thing, and we want you bad. You've been chewing on
this affair now a long time. Have you made up your
mind? Do you come in? I tell you what, you've got to
look at these things in a large way. You've got to judge
by results. Well, now, what do you think? Do you
come in?"

Magnus's glance left Annixter's face, and for an instant sought the ground. His frown lowered, but now it
was in perplexity, rather than in anger. His mind was
troubled, harassed with a thousand dissensions.

But one of Magnus's strongest instincts, one of his
keenest desires, was to be, if only for a short time, the
master. To control men had ever been his ambition;
submission of any kind, his greatest horror. His energy
stirred within him, goaded by the lash of his anger, his
sense of indignity, of insult. Oh for one moment to be
able to strike back, to crush his enemy, to defeat the railroad, hold the Corporation in the grip of his fist, put
down S. Behrman, rehabilitate himself, regain his self-
respect. To be once more powerful, to command, to
dominate. His thin lips pressed themselves together,

the nostrils of his prominent hawk-like nose dilated, his erect, commanding figure stiffened unconsciously. For a moment, he saw himself controlling the situation, the foremost figure in his State, feared, respected, thousands of men beneath him, his ambition at length gratified; his career, once apparently brought to naught, completed; success a palpable achievement. What if this were his chance, after all, come at last after all these years. His chance! The instincts of the old-time gambler, the most redoubtable poker player of El Dorado County, stirred at the word. Chance! To know it when it came, to recognise it as it passed fleet as a wind-flurry, grip at it, catch at it, blind, reckless, staking all upon the hazard of the issue, that was genius. Was this his Chance? All of a sudden, it seemed to him that it was. But his honour! His cherished, lifelong integrity, the unstained purity of his principles? At this late date, were they to be sacrificed? Could he now go counter to all the firm built fabric of his character? How, afterward, could he bear to look Harran and Lyman in the face? And, yet—and, yet—back swung the pendulum—to neglect his Chance meant failure; a life begun in promise, and ended in obscurity, perhaps in financial ruin, poverty even. To seize it meant achievement, fame, influence, prestige, possibly great wealth.

"I am so sorry to interrupt," said Mrs. Derrick, as she came up. "I hope Mr. Annixter will excuse me, but I want Magnus to open the safe for me. I have lost the combination, and I must have some money. Phelps is going into town, and I want him to pay some bills for me. Can't you come right away, Magnus? Phelps is ready and waiting."

Annixter struck his heel into the ground with a suppressed oath. Always these fool feemale women came between him and his plans, mixing themselves up in his

affairs. Magnus had been on the very point of saying
something, perhaps committing himself to some course
of action, and, at precisely the wrong moment, his wife
had cut in. The opportunity was lost. The three returned toward the ranch house; but before saying good-
bye, Annixter had secured from Magnus a promise to the
effect that, before coming to a definite decision in the
matter under discussion, he would talk further with him.

Presley met him at the porch. He was going into
town with Phelps, and proposed to Annixter that he
should accompany them.

"I want to go over and see old Broderson," Annixter
objected.

But Presley informed him that Broderson had gone
to Bonneville earlier in the morning. He had seen him
go past in his buckboard. The three men set off, Phelps
and Annixter on horseback, Presley on his bicycle.

When they had gone, Mrs. Derrick sought out her
husband in the office of the ranch house. She was at
her prettiest that morning, her cheeks flushed with excitement, her innocent, wide-open eyes almost girlish.
She had fastened her hair, still moist, with a black ribbon tied at the back of her head, and the soft mass of
light brown reached to below her waist, making her look
very young.

"What was it he was saying to you just now," she
exclaimed, as she came through the gate in the green-
painted wire railing of the office. "What was Mr. Annixter saying? I know. He was trying to get you to
join him, trying to persuade you to be dishonest, wasn't
that it? Tell me, Magnus, wasn't that it?"

Magnus nodded.

His wife drew close to him, putting a hand on his
shoulder.

"But you won't, will you? You won't listen to him

again; you won't so much as allow him—*anybody*—to even suppose you would lend yourself to bribery? Oh, Magnus, I don't know what has come over you these last few weeks. Why, before this, you would have been insulted if any one thought you would even consider anything like dishonesty. Magnus, it would break my heart if you joined Mr. Annixter and Mr. Osterman. Why, you couldn't be the same man to me afterward; you, who have kept yourself so clean till now. And the boys; what would Lyman say, and Harran, and every one who knows you and respects you, if you lowered yourself to be just a political adventurer!"

For a moment, Derrick leaned his head upon his hand, avoiding her gaze. At length, he said, drawing a deep breath:

"I am troubled, Annie. These are the evil days. I have much upon my mind."

"Evil days or not," she insisted, "promise me this one thing, that you will not join Mr. Annixter's scheme."

She had taken his hand in both of hers and was looking into his face, her pretty eyes full of pleading.

"Promise me," she repeated; "give me your word. Whatever happens, let me always be able to be proud of you, as I always have been. Give me your word. I know you never seriously thought of joining Mr. Annixter, but I am so nervous and frightened sometimes. Just to relieve my mind, Magnus, give me your word."

"Why—you are right," he answered. "No, I never thought seriously of it. Only for a moment, I was ambitious to be—I don't know what—what I had hoped to be once—well, that is over now. Annie, your husband is a disappointed man."

"Give me your word," she insisted. "We can talk about other things afterward."

Again Magnus wavered, about to yield to his better

instincts and to the entreaties of his wife. He began to
see how perilously far he had gone in this business. He
was drifting closer to it every hour. Already he was
entangled, already his foot was caught in the mesh that
was being spun. Sharply he recoiled. Again all his
instincts of honesty revolted. No, whatever happened,
he would preserve his integrity. His wife was right.
Always she had influenced his better side. At that moment, Magnus's repugnance of the proposed political
campaign was at its pitch of intensity. He wondered
how he had ever allowed himself to so much as entertain
the idea of joining with the others. Now, he would
wrench free, would, in a single instant of power, clear
himself of all compromising relations. He turned to his
wife. Upon his lips trembled the promise she implored.
But suddenly there came to his mind the recollection of
his new-made pledge to Annixter. He had given his
word that before arriving at a decision he would have a
last interview with him. To Magnus, his given word
was sacred. Though now he wanted to, he could not as
yet draw back, could not promise his wife that he would
decide to do right. The matter must be delayed a few
days longer.

Lamely, he explained this to her. Annie Derrick
made but little response when he had done. She kissed
his forehead and went out of the room, uneasy, de-
pressed, her mind thronging with vague fears, leaving
Magnus before his office desk, his head in his hands,
thoughtful, gloomy, assaulted by forebodings.

Meanwhile, Annixter, Phelps, and Presley continued
on their way toward Bonneville. In a short time they
had turned into the County Road by the great watering-
tank, and proceeded onward in the shade of the interminable line of poplar trees, the wind-break that
stretched along the roadside bordering the Broderson

ranch. But as they drew near to Caraher's saloon and grocery, about half a mile outside of Bonneville, they recognised Harran's horse tied to the railing in front of it. Annixter left the others and went in to see Harran.

"Harran," he said, when the two had sat down on either side of one of the small tables, "you've got to make up your mind one way or another pretty soon. What are you going to do? Are you going to stand by and see the rest of the Committee spending money by the bucketful in this thing and keep your hands in your pockets? If we win, you'll benefit just as much as the rest of us. I suppose you've got some money of your own—you have, haven't you? You are your father's manager, aren't you?"

Disconcerted at Annixter's directness, Harran stammered an affirmative, adding:

"It's hard to know just what to do. It's a mean position for me, Buck. I want to help you others, but I do want to play fair. I don't know how to play any other way. I should like to have a line from the Governor as to how to act, but there's no getting a word out of him these days. He seems to want to let me decide for myself."

"Well, look here," put in Annixter. "Suppose you keep out of the thing till it's all over, and then share and share alike with the Committee on campaign expenses."

Harran fell thoughtful, his hands in his pockets, frowning moodily at the toe of his boot. There was a silence. Then:

"I don't like to go it blind," he hazarded. "I'm sort of sharing the responsibility of what you do, then. I'm a silent partner. And, then—I don't want to have any difficulties with the Governor. We've always got along well together. He wouldn't like it, *you* know, if I did anything like that."

"Say," exclaimed Annixter abruptly, " if the Governor says he will keep his hands off, and that you can do as you please, will you come in? For God's sake, let us ranchers act together for once. Let's stand in with each other in *one* fight."

Without knowing it, Annixter had touched the right spring.

" I don't know but what you're right," Harran murmured vaguely. His sense of discouragement, that feeling of what's-the-use, was never more oppressive. All fair means had been tried. The wheat grower was at last with his back to the wall. If he chose his own means of fighting, the responsibility must rest upon his enemies, not on himself.

" It's the only way to accomplish anything," he continued, " standing in with each other . . . well, . . . go ahead and see what you can do. If the Governor is willing, I'll come in for my share of the campaign fund."

" That's some sense," exclaimed Annixter, shaking him by the hand. " Half the fight is over already. We've got Disbrow you know; and the next thing is to get hold of some of those rotten San Francisco bosses. Osterman will——" But Harran interrupted him, making a quick gesture with his hand.

" Don't tell me about it," he said. " I don't want to know what you and Osterman are going to do. If I did, I shouldn't come in."

Yet, for all this, before they said good-bye Annixter had obtained Harran's promise that he would attend the next meeting of the Committee, when Osterman should return from Los Angeles and make his report. Harran went on toward Los Muertos. Annixter mounted and rode into Bonneville.

Bonneville was very lively at all times. It was a little

city of some twenty or thirty thousand inhabitants, where, as yet, the city hall, the high school building, and the opera house were objects of civic pride. It was well governed, beautifully clean, full of the energy and strenuous young life of a new city. An air of the briskest activity pervaded its streets and sidewalks. The business portion of the town, centring about Main Street, was always crowded. Annixter, arriving at the Post Office, found himself involved in a scene of swiftly shifting sights and sounds. Saddle horses, farm wagons—the inevitable Studebakers—buggies grey with the dust of country roads, buckboards with squashes and grocery packages stowed under the seat, two-wheeled sulkies and training carts, were hitched to the gnawed railings and zinc-sheathed telegraph poles along the curb. Here and there, on the edge of the sidewalk, were bicycles, wedged into bicycle racks painted with cigar advertisements. Upon the asphalt sidewalk itself, soft and sticky with the morning's heat, was a continuous movement. Men with large stomachs, wearing linen coats but no vests, laboured ponderously up and down. Girls in lawn skirts, shirt waists, and garden hats, went to and fro, invariably in couples, coming in and out of the drug store, the grocery store, and haberdasher's, or lingering in front of the Post Office, which was on a corner under the I.O.O.F. hall. Young men, in shirt sleeves, with brown, wicker cuff-protectors over their forearms, and pencils behind their ears, bustled in front of the grocery store, anxious and preoccupied. A very old man, a Mexican, in ragged white trousers and bare feet, sat on a horse-block in front of the barber shop, holding a horse by a rope around its neck. A Chinaman went by, teetering under the weight of his market baskets slung on a pole across his shoulders. In the neighbourhood of the hotel, the Yosemite House, travelling salesmen, drum-

mers for jewelry firms of San Francisco, commercial
agents, insurance men, well-dressed, metropolitan, debonair, stood about cracking jokes, or hurried in and
out of the flapping white doors of the Yosemite bar-
room. The Yosemite 'bus and City 'bus passed up the
street, on the way from the morning train, each with its
two or three passengers. A very narrow wagon, belonging to the Cole & Colemore Harvester Works, went
by, loaded with long strips of iron that made a horrible
din as they jarred over the unevenness of the pavement.
The electric car line, the city's boast, did a brisk business,
its cars whirring from end to end of the street, with a
jangling of bells and a moaning plaint of gearing. On
the stone bulkheads of the grass plat around the new
City Hall, the usual loafers sat, chewing tobacco, swap-
ping stories. In the park were the inevitable array of
nursemaids, skylarking couples, and ragged little boys.
A single policeman, in grey coat and helmet, friend and
acquaintance of every man and woman in the town, stood
by the park entrance, leaning an elbow on the fence post,
twirling his club.

But in the centre of the best business block of the
street was a three-story building of rough brown stone,
set off with plate glass windows and gold-lettered signs.
One of these latter read, "Pacific and Southwestern Railroad, Freight and Passenger Office," while another,
much smaller, beneath the windows of the second story,
bore the inscription, " P. and S. W. Land Office."

Annixter hitched his horse to the iron post in front of
this building, and tramped up to the second floor, letting
himself into an office where a couple of clerks and book-
keepers sat at work behind a high wire screen. One of
these latter recognised him and came forward.

" Hello," said Annixter abruptly, scowling the while.
" Is your boss in? Is Ruggles in? "

The bookkeeper led Annixter to the private office in an adjoining room, ushering him through a door, on the frosted glass of which was painted the name, " Cyrus Blakelee Ruggles." Inside, a man in a frock coat, shoe-string necktie, and Stetson hat, sat writing at a roller-top desk. Over this desk was a vast map of the railroad holdings in the country about Bonneville and Guadala-jara, the alternate sections belonging to the Corporation accurately plotted.

Ruggles was cordial in his welcome of Annixter. He had a way of fiddling with his pencil continually while he talked, scribbling vague lines and fragments of words and names on stray bits of paper, and no sooner had Annixter sat down than he had begun to write, in full-bellied script, *Ann Ann* all over his blotting pad.

" I want to see about those lands of mine—I mean of yours—of the railroad's," Annixter commenced at once. " I want to know when I can buy. I'm sick of fooling along like this."

" Well, Mr. Annixter," observed Ruggles, writing a great *L* before the *Ann*, and finishing it off with a flourishing *d*. " The lands "—he crossed out one of the *n's* and noted the effect with a hasty glance—" the lands are practically yours. You have an option on them in-definitely, and, as it is, you don't have to pay the taxes."

" Rot your option! I want to own them," Annixter declared. " What have you people got to gain by putting off selling them to us. Here this thing has dragged along for over eight years. When I came in on Quien Sabe, the understanding was that the lands—your alter-nate sections—were to be conveyed to me within a few months."

" The land had not been patented to us then," an-swered Ruggles.

" Well, it has been now, I guess," retorted Annixter.

"I'm sure I couldn't tell you, Mr. Annixter."

Annixter crossed his legs weariedly.

"Oh, what's the good of lying, Ruggles? You know better than to talk that way to me."

Ruggles's face flushed on the instant, but he checked his answer and laughed instead.

"Oh, if you know so much about it—" he observed.

"Well, when are you going to sell to me?"

"I'm only acting for the General Office, Mr. Annixter," returned Ruggles. "Whenever the Directors are ready to take that matter up, I'll be only too glad to put it through for you."

"As if you didn't know. Look here, you're not talking to old Broderson. Wake up, Ruggles. What's all this talk in Genslinger's rag about the grading of the value of our lands this winter and an advance in the price?"

Ruggles spread out his hands with a deprecatory gesture.

"I don't own the 'Mercury,'" he said.

"Well, your company does."

"If it does, I don't know anything about it."

"Oh, rot! As if you and Genslinger and S. Behrman didn't run the whole show down here. Come on, let's have it, Ruggles. What does S. Behrman pay Genslinger for inserting that three-inch ad. of the P. and S. W. in his paper? Ten thousand a year, hey?"

"Oh, why not a hundred thousand and be done with it?" returned the other, willing to take it as a joke.

Instead of replying, Annixter drew his check-book from his inside pocket.

"Let me take that fountain pen of yours," he said. Holding the book on his knee he wrote out a check, tore it carefully from the stub, and laid it on the desk in front of Ruggles.

" What's this? " asked Ruggles.

" Three-fourths payment for the sections of railroad land included in my ranch, based on a valuation of two dollars and a half per acre.   You can have the balance in sixty-day notes."

Ruggles shook his head, drawing hastily back from the check as though it carried contamination.

" I can't touch it," he declared.   " I've no authority to sell to you yet."

" I don't understand you people," exclaimed Annixter.   " I offered to buy of you the same way four years ago and you sang the same song.   Why, it isn't business. You lose the interest on your money.   Seven per cent. of that capital for four years—you can figure it out. It's big money."

" Well, then, I don't see why you're so keen on parting with it.   You can get seven per cent. the same as us."

" I want to own my own land," returned Annixter. " I want to feel that every lump of dirt inside my fence is my personal property.   Why, the very house I live in now—the ranch house—stands on railroad ground."

" But, you've an option——"

" I tell you I don't want your cursed option.   I want ownership; and it's the same with Magnus Derrick and old Broderson and Osterman and all the ranchers of the county.   We want to own our land, want to feel we can do as we blame please with it.   Suppose I should want to sell Quien Sabe.   I can't sell it as a whole till I've bought of you.   I can't give anybody a clear title.   The land has doubled in value ten times over again since I came in on it and improved it.   It's worth easily twenty an acre now.   But I can't take advantage of that rise in value so long as you won't sell, so long as I don't own it.   You're blocking me."

" But, according to you, the railroad can't take advantage of the rise in any case. According to you, you can sell for twenty dollars, but *we* can only get two and a half."

"Who made it worth twenty?" cried Annixter. "I've improved it up to that figure. Genslinger seems to have that idea in his nut, too. Do you people think you can hold that land, untaxed, for speculative purposes until it goes up to thirty dollars and then sell out to some one else—sell it over our heads? You and Genslinger weren't in office when those contracts were drawn. You ask your boss, you ask S. Behrman, *he* knows. The General Office is pledged to sell to us in preference to any one else, for two and a half."

"Well," observed Ruggles decidedly, tapping the end of his pencil on his desk and leaning forward to emphasise his words, "we're not selling *now*. That's said and signed, Mr. Annixter."

"Why not? Come, spit it out. What's the bunco game this time?"

"Because we're not ready. Here's your check."

"You won't take it?"

"No."

"I'll make it a cash payment, money down—the whole of it—payable to Cyrus Blakelee Ruggles, for the P. and S. W."

"No."

"Third and last time."

"No."

"Oh, go to the devil!"

"I don't like your tone, Mr. Annixter," returned Ruggles, flushing angrily.

"I don't give a curse whether you like it or not," retorted Annixter, rising and thrusting the check into his pocket, "but never you mind, Mr. Ruggles, you and S. Behrman and Genslinger and Shelgrim and the whole gang of thieves of you—you'll wake this State of California up some of these days by going just one little bit *too* far, and there'll be an election of Railroad Commissioners of, by, and for the people, that'll get a twist of you, my bunco-steering friend—you and your backers and cappers and swindlers and thimble-riggers, and *smash* you, lock, stock, and barrel. That's my tip to you and be damned to you, Mr. Cyrus Blackleg Ruggles."

Annixter stormed out of the room, slamming the door behind him, and Ruggles, trembling with anger, turned to his desk and to the blotting pad written all over with the words *Lands, Twenty dollars, Two and a half, Option,* and, over and over again, with great swelling curves and flourishes, *Railroad, Railroad, Railroad.*

But as Annixter passed into the outside office, on the other side of the wire partition he noted the figure of a man at the counter in conversation with one of the clerks. There was something familiar to Annixter's eye about the man's heavy built frame, his great shoulders and massive back, and as he spoke to the clerk in a tremendous, rumbling voice, Annixter promptly recognised Dyke.

There was a meeting. Annixter liked Dyke, as did every one else in and about Bonneville. He paused now to shake hands with the discharged engineer and to ask about his little daughter, Sidney, to whom he knew Dyke was devotedly attached.

" Smartest little tad in Tulare County," asserted Dyke. " She's getting prettier every day, Mr. Annixter. *There's* a little tad that was just born to be a lady. Can recite the whole of ' Snow Bound ' without ever stopping. You don't believe that, maybe, hey? Well, it's true. She'll be just old enough to enter the Seminary up at Marysville next winter, and if my hop business pays two per cent. on the investment, there's where she's going to go."

"How's it coming on?" inquired Annixter.

"The hop ranch? Prime. I've about got the land
in shape, and I've engaged a foreman who knows all
about hops. I've been in luck. Everybody will go into
the business next year when they see hops go to a dollar,
and they'll overstock the market and bust the price.
But I'm going to get the cream of it now. I say two per
cent. Why, Lord love you, it will pay a good deal more
than that. It's got to. It's cost more than I figured
to start the thing, so, perhaps, I may have to borrow
somewheres; but then on such a sure game as this—and
I do want to make something out of that little tad of
mine."

"Through here?" inquired Annixter, making ready
to move off.

"In just a minute," answered Dyke. "Wait for me
and I'll walk down the street with you."

Annixter grumbled that he was in a hurry, but waited,
nevertheless, while Dyke again approached the clerk.

"I shall want some empty cars of you people this
fall," he explained. "I'm a hop-raiser now, and I just
want to make sure what your rates on hops are. I've
been told, but I want to make sure. Savvy?"

There was a long delay while the clerk consulted the
tariff schedules, and Annixter fretted impatiently. Dyke,
growing uneasy, leaned heavily on his elbows, watching
the clerk anxiously. If the tariff was exorbitant, he saw
his plans brought to naught, his money jeopardised, the
little tad, Sidney, deprived of her education. He began
to blame himself that he had not long before determined
definitely what the railroad would charge for moving his
hops. He told himself he was not much of a business
man; that he managed carelessly.

"Two cents," suddenly announced the clerk with a
certain surly indifference.

" Two cents a pound? "

" Yes, two cents a pound—that's in car-load lots, of course.   I won't give you that rate on smaller consignments."

" Yes, car-load lots, of course . . . two cents. Well, all right."

He turned away with a great sigh of relief.

" He sure did have me scared for a minute," he said to Annixter, as the two went down to the street, "fiddling and fussing so long. Two cents is all right, though. Seems fair to me. That fiddling of his was all put on. I know 'em, these railroad heelers. He knew I was a discharged employee first off, and he played the game just to make me seem small because I had to ask favours of him. I don't suppose the General Office tips its slavees off to act like swine, but there's the feeling through the whole herd of them. ' Ye got to come to us. We let ye live only so long as we choose, and what are ye going to do about it? If ye don't like it, git out.' "

Annixter and the engineer descended to the street and had a drink at the Yosemite bar, and Annixter went into the General Store while Dyke bought a little pair of red slippers for Sidney. Before the salesman had wrapped them up, Dyke slipped a dime into the toe of each with a wink at Annixter.

" Let the little tad find 'em there," he said behind his hand in a hoarse whisper. " That'll be one on Sid."

" Where to now? " demanded Annixter as they regained the street. " I'm going down to the Post Office and then pull out for the ranch.   Going my way? "

Dyke hesitated in some confusion, tugging at the ends of his fine blonde beard.

" No, no. I guess I'll leave you here. I've got—got other things to do up the street. So long."

The two separated, and Annixter hurried through the crowd to the Post Office, but the mail that had come in on that morning's train was unusually heavy. It was nearly half an hour before it was distributed. Naturally enough, Annixter placed all the blame of the delay upon the railroad, and delivered himself of some pointed remarks in the midst of the waiting crowd. He was irritated to the last degree when he finally emerged upon the sidewalk again, cramming his mail into his pockets. One cause of his bad temper was the fact that in the bundle of Quien Sabe letters was one to Hilma Tree in a man's handwriting.

"Huh!" Annixter had growled to himself, "that pip Delaney. Seems now that I'm to act as go-between for 'em. Well, maybe that feemale girl gets this letter, and then, again, maybe she don't."

But suddenly his attention was diverted. Directly opposite the Post Office, upon the corner of the street, stood quite the best business building of which Bonneville could boast. It was built of Colusa granite, very solid, ornate, imposing. Upon the heavy plate of the window of its main floor, in gold and red letters, one read the words: "Loan and Savings Bank of Tulare County." It was of this bank that S. Behrman was president. At the street entrance of the building was a curved sign of polished brass, fixed upon the angle of the masonry; this sign bore the name, "S. Behrman," and under it in smaller letters were the words, "Real Estate, Mortgages."

As Annixter's glance fell upon this building, he was surprised to see Dyke standing upon the curb in front of it, apparently reading from a newspaper that he held in his hand. But Annixter promptly discovered that he was not reading at all. From time to time the former engineer shot a swift glance out of the corner of his eye up and down the street. Annixter jumped at a conclusion. An idea suddenly occurred to him. Dyke was watching to see if he was observed—was waiting an opportunity when no one who knew him should be in sight. Annixter stepped back a little, getting a telegraph pole somewhat between him and the other. Very interested, he watched what was going on. Pretty soon Dyke thrust the paper into his pocket and sauntered slowly to the windows of a stationery store, next the street entrance of S. Behrman's offices. For a few seconds he stood there, his back turned, seemingly absorbed in the display, but eyeing the street narrowly nevertheless; then he turned around, gave a last look about and stepped swiftly into the doorway by the great brass sign. He disappeared. Annixter came from behind the telegraph pole with a flush of actual shame upon his face. There had been something so slinking, so mean, in the movements and manner of this great, burly honest fellow of an engineer, that he could not help but feel ashamed for him. Circumstances were such that a simple business transaction was to Dyke almost culpable, a degradation, a thing to be concealed.

" Borrowing money of S. Behrman," commented Annixter, " mortgaging your little homestead to the railroad, putting your neck in the halter. Poor fool! The pity of it. Good Lord, your hops must pay you big, now, old man."

Annixter lunched at the Yosemite Hotel, and then later on, toward the middle of the afternoon, rode out of the town at a canter by the way of the Upper Road that paralleled the railroad tracks and that ran diametrically straight between Bonneville and Guadalajara. About half-way between the two places he overtook Father Sarria trudging back to San Juan, his long cassock powdered with dust. He had a wicker crate in one hand, and in the other, in a small square valise, the materials for the Holy Sacrament. Since early morning the priest had covered nearly fifteen miles on foot, in order to administer Extreme Unction to a moribund good-for-nothing, a greaser, half Indian, half Portuguese, who lived in a remote corner of Osterman's stock range, at the head of a cañon there. But he had returned by way of Bonneville to get a crate that had come for him from San Diego. He had been notified of its arrival the day before.

Annixter pulled up and passed the time of day with the priest.

"I don't often get up your way," he said, slowing down his horse to accommodate Sarria's deliberate plodding. Sarria wiped the perspiration from his smooth, shiny face.

"You? Well, with you it is different," he answered. "But there are a great many Catholics in the county— some on your ranch. And so few come to the Mission. At High Mass on Sundays, there are a few—Mexicans and Spaniards from Guadalajara mostly; but weekdays, for matins, vespers, and the like, I often say the offices to an empty church—'the voice of one crying in the wilderness.' You Americans are not good churchmen. Sundays you sleep—you read the newspapers."

"Well, there's Vanamee," observed Annixter. "I suppose he's there early and late."

Sarria made a sharp movement of interest.

"Ah, Vanamee—a strange lad; a wonderful character, for all that. If there were only more like him. I am troubled about him. You know I am a very owl at night. I come and go about the Mission at all hours. Within the week, three times I have seen Vanamee in the little garden by the Mission, and at the dead of night. He had come without asking for me. He did not see

me. It was strange. Once, when I had got up at dawn
to ring for early matins, I saw him stealing away out of
the garden. He must have been there all the night. He
is acting queerly. He is pale; his cheeks are more
sunken than ever. There is something wrong with him.
I can't make it out. It is a mystery. Suppose you ask
him?"

"Not I. I've enough to bother myself about. Vanamee is crazy in the head. Some morning he will turn
up missing again, and drop out of sight for another
three years. Best let him alone, Sarria. He's a crank.
How is that greaser of yours up on Osterman's stock
range?"

"Ah, the poor fellow—the poor fellow," returned the
other, the tears coming to his eyes. "He died this
morning—as you might say, in my arms, painfully, but
in the faith, in the faith. A good fellow."

"A lazy, cattle-stealing, knife-in-his-boot Dago."

"You misjudge him. A really good fellow on better
acquaintance."

Annixter grunted scornfully. Sarria's kindness and
good-will toward the most outrageous reprobates of
the ranches was proverbial. He practically supported
some half-dozen families that lived in forgotten cabins,
lost and all but inaccessible, in the far corners of stock
range and cañon. This particular greaser was the lazi-
est, the dirtiest, the most worthless of the lot. But in
Sarria's mind, the lout was an object of affection, sincere, unquestioning. Thrice a week the priest, with a
basket of provisions—cold ham, a bottle of wine, olives,
loaves of bread, even a chicken or two—toiled over the
interminable stretch of country between the Mission
and his cabin. Of late, during the rascal's sickness,
these visits had been almost daily. Hardly once did
the priest leave the bedside that he did not slip a half-

dollar into the palm of his wife or oldest daughter. And this was but one case out of many.

His kindliness toward animals was the same. A horde of mange-corroded curs lived off his bounty, wolfish, ungrateful, often marking him with their teeth, yet never knowing the meaning of a harsh word. A burro, over-fed, lazy, incorrigible, browsed on the hill back of the Mission, obstinately refusing to be harnessed to Sarria's little cart, squealing and biting whenever the attempt was made; and the priest suffered him, submitting to his humour, inventing excuses for him, alleging that the burro was foundered, or was in need of shoes, or was feeble from extreme age. The two peacocks, magnificent, proud, cold-hearted, resenting all familiarity, he served with the timorous, apologetic affection of a queen's lady-in-waiting, resigned to their disdain, happy if only they condescended to enjoy the grain he spread for them.

At the Long Trestle, Annixter and the priest left the road and took the trail that crossed Broderson Creek by the clumps of grey-green willows and led across Quien Sabe to the ranch house, and to the Mission far-ther on. They were obliged to proceed in single file here, and Annixter, who had allowed the priest to go in front, promptly took notice of the wicker basket he car-ried. Upon his inquiry, Sarria became confused. "It was a basket that he had had sent down to him from the city."

"Well, I know—but what's in it?"

"Why—I'm sure—ah, poultry—a chicken or two."

"Fancy breed?"

"Yes, yes, that's it, a fancy breed."

At the ranch house, where they arrived toward five o'clock, Annixter insisted that the priest should stop long enough for a glass of sherry. Sarria left the basket and his small black valise at the foot of the porch steps, and sat down in a rocker on the porch itself, fanning himself with his broad-brimmed hat, and shaking the dust from his cassock. Annixter brought out the decanter of sherry and glasses, and the two drank to each other's health.

But as the priest set down his glass, wiping his lips with a murmur of satisfaction, the decrepit Irish setter that had attached himself to Annixter's house came out from underneath the porch, and nosed vigorously about the wicker basket. He upset it. The little peg holding down the cover slipped, the basket fell sideways, opening as it fell, and a cock, his head enclosed in a little chamois bag such as are used for gold watches, struggled blindly out into the open air. A second, similarly hooded, followed. The pair, stupefied in their headgear, stood rigid and bewildered in their tracks, clucking uneasily. Their tails were closely sheared. Their legs, thickly muscled, and extraordinarily long, were furnished with enormous cruel-looking spurs. The breed was unmistakable. Annixter looked once at the pair, then shouted with laughter.

"'Poultry'—'a chicken or two'—'fancy breed'—ho! yes, I should think so. Game cocks! Fighting cocks! Oh, you old rat! You'll be a dry nurse to a burro, and keep a hospital for infirm puppies, but you will fight game cocks. Oh, Lord! Why, Sarria, this is as good a grind as I ever heard. There's the Spanish cropping out, after all."

Speechless with chagrin, the priest bundled the cocks into the basket and catching up the valise, took himself abruptly away, almost running till he had put himself out of hearing of Annixter's raillery. And even ten minutes later, when Annixter, still chuckling, stood upon the porch steps, he saw the priest, far in the distance, climbing the slope of the high ground, in the direction of the Mission, still hurrying on at a great pace, his cassock flapping behind him, his head bent; to Annixter's notion the very picture of discomfiture and confusion.

As Annixter turned about to reënter the house, he found himself almost face to face with Hilma Tree. She was just going in at the doorway, and a great flame of the sunset, shooting in under the eaves of the porch, enveloped her from her head, with its thick, moist hair that hung low over her neck, to her slim feet, setting a golden flash in the little steel buckles of her low shoes. She had come to set the table for Annixter's supper. Taken all aback by the suddenness of the encounter, Annixter ejaculated an abrupt and senseless, " Excuse me." But Hilma, without raising her eyes, passed on unmoved into the dining-room, leaving Annixter trying to find his breath, and fumbling with the brim of his hat, that he was surprised to find he had taken from his head. Resolutely, and taking a quick advantage of his opportunity, he followed her into the dining-room.

" I see that dog has turned up," he announced with brisk cheerfulness. " That Irish setter I was asking about."

Hilma, a swift, pink flush deepening the delicate rose of her cheeks, did not reply, except by nodding her head. She flung the table-cloth out from under her arms across the table, spreading it smooth, with quick little caresses of her hands. There was a moment's silence. Then Annixter said:

" Here's a letter for you." He laid it down on the table near her, and Hilma picked it up. " And see here, Miss Hilma," Annixter continued, " about that—this morning—I suppose you think I am a first-class mucker. If it will do any good to apologise, why, I will. I want to be friends with you. I made a bad mistake, and started in the wrong way. I don't know much about

women people. I want you to forget about that—this
morning, and not think I am a galoot and a mucker. Will
you do it? Will you be friends with me?"

Hilma set the plate and coffee cup by Annixter's place
before answering, and Annixter repeated his question.
Then she drew a deep, quick breath, the flush in her
cheeks returning.

"I think it was—it was so wrong of you," she murmured. "Oh! you don't know how it hurt me. I cried
—oh, for an hour."

"Well, that's just it," returned Annixter vaguely,
moving his head uneasily. "I didn't know what kind
of a girl you were—I mean, I made a mistake. I thought
it didn't make much difference. I thought all feemales
were about alike."

"I hope you know now," murmured Hilma ruefully.
"I've paid enough to have you find out. I cried—you
don't know. Why, it hurt me worse than anything I can
remember. I hope you know now."

"Well, I do know now," he exclaimed.

"It wasn't so much that you tried to do—what you
did," answered Hilma, the single deep swell from her
waist to her throat rising and falling in her emotion.
"It was that you thought that you could—that anybody
could that wanted to—that I held myself so cheap.
Oh!" she cried, with a sudden sobbing catch in her
throat, "I never can forget it, and you don't know what
it means to a girl."

"Well, that's just what I do want," he repeated. "I
want you to forget it and have us be good friends."

In his embarrassment, Annixter could think of no
other words. He kept reiterating again and again during the pauses of the conversation:

"I want you to forget it. Will you? Will you forget
it—that—this morning, and have us be good friends?"

He could see that her trouble was keen. He was astonished that the matter should be so grave in her estimation. After all, what was it that a girl should be kissed? But he wanted to regain his lost ground.

"Will you forget it, Miss Hilma? I want you to like me."

She took a clean napkin from the sideboard drawer and laid it down by the plate.

"I—I do want you to like me," persisted Annixter. "I want you to forget all about this business and like me."

Hilma was silent. Annixter saw the tears in her eyes.

"How about that? Will you forget it? Will you—will—will you *like* me?"

She shook her head.

"No," she said.

"No what? You won't like me? Is that it?"

Hilma, blinking at the napkin through her tears, nodded to say, Yes, that was it.

Annixter hesitated a moment, frowning, harassed and perplexed.

"You don't like me at all, hey?"

At length Hilma found her speech. In her low voice, lower and more velvety than ever, she said:

"No—I don't like you at all."

Then, as the tears suddenly overpowered her, she dashed a hand across her eyes, and ran from the room and out of doors.

Annixter stood for a moment thoughtful, his protruding lower lip thrust out, his hands in his pocket.

"I suppose she'll quit now," he muttered. "Suppose she'll leave the ranch—if she hates me like that. Well, she can go—that's all—she can go. Fool feemale girl," he muttered between his teeth, "petticoat mess."

He was about to sit down to his supper when his eye

fell upon the Irish setter, on his haunches in the doorway. There was an expectant, ingratiating look on the dog's face. No doubt, he suspected it was time for eating.

" Get out—*you!* " roared Annixter in a tempest of wrath.

The dog slunk back, his tail shut down close, his ears drooping, but instead of running away, he lay down and rolled supinely upon his back, the very image of submission, tame, abject, disgusting. It was the one thing to drive Annixter to a fury. He kicked the dog off the porch in a rolling explosion of oaths, and flung himself down to his seat before the table, fuming and panting.

" Damn the dog and the girl and the whole rotten business—and *now*," he exclaimed, as a sudden fancied qualm arose in his stomach, " *now*, it's all made me sick. Might have known it. Oh, it only lacked that to wind up the whole day. Let her go, I don't care, and the sooner the better."

He countermanded the supper and went to bed before it was dark. lighting his lamp, on the chair near the head of the bed, and opening his " Copperfield " at the place marked by the strip of paper torn from the bag of prunes. For upward of an hour he read the novel, methodically swallowing one prune every time he reached the bottom of a page. About nine o'clock he blew out the lamp and, punching up his pillow, settled himself for the night.

Then, as his mind relaxed in that strange, hypnotic condition that comes just before sleep, a series of pictures of the day's doings passed before his imagination like the roll of a kinetoscope.

First, it was Hilma Tree, as he had seen her in the dairy-house—charming, delicious, radiant of youth, her thick, white neck with its pale amber shadows under the chin; her wide, open eyes rimmed with fine, black lashes;

the deep swell of her breast and hips, the delicate, lustrous floss on her cheek, impalpable as the pollen of a flower. He saw her standing there in the scintillating light of the morning, her smooth arms wet with milk, redolent and fragrant of milk, her whole, desirable figure moving in the golden glory of the sun, steeped in a lambent flame, saturated with it, glowing with it, joyous as the dawn itself.

Then it was Los Muertos and Hooven, the sordid little Dutchman, grimed with the soil he worked in, yet vividly remembering a period of military glory, exciting himself with recollections of Gravelotte and the Kaiser, but contented now in the country of his adoption, defining the Fatherland as the place where wife and children lived. Then came the ranch house of Los Muertos, under the grove of cypress and eucalyptus, with its smooth, gravelled driveway and well-groomed lawns; Mrs. Derrick with her wide-opened eyes, that so easily took on a look of uneasiness, of innocence, of anxious inquiry, her face still pretty, her brown hair that still retained so much of its brightness spread over her chair back, drying in the sun; Magnus, erect as an officer of cavalry, smooth-shaven, grey, thin-lipped, imposing, with his hawk-like nose and forward-curling grey hair; Presley with his dark face, delicate mouth and sensitive, loose lips, in corduroys and laced boots, smoking cigarettes—an interesting figure, suggestive of a mixed origin, morbid, excitable, melancholy, brooding upon things that had no names. Then it was Bonneville, with the gayety and confusion of Main Street, the whirring electric cars, the zinc-sheathed telegraph poles, the buckboards with squashes stowed under the seats; Ruggles in frock coat, Stetson hat and shoe-string necktie, writing abstractedly upon his blotting pad; Dyke, the engineer, big-boned, powerful, deep-voiced, good-natured, with his fine blonde beard and massive arms, rehearsing the praises of his little daughter Sidney, guided only by the one ambition that she should be educated at a seminary, slipping a dime into the toe of her diminutive slipper, then, later, overwhelmed with shame, slinking into S. Behrman's office to mortgage his homestead to the heeler of the corporation that had discharged him. By suggestion, Annixter saw S. Behrman, too, fat, with a vast stomach, the check and neck meeting to form a great, tremulous jowl, the roll of fat over his collar, sprinkled with sparse, stiff hairs; saw his brown, round-topped hat of varnished straw, the linen vest stamped with innumerable interlocked horseshoes, the heavy watch chain, clinking against the pearl vest buttons; invariably placid, unruffled, never losing his temper, serene, unassailable, enthroned.

Then, at the end of all, it was the ranch again, seen in a last brief glance before he had gone to bed; the fecundated earth, calm at last, nursing the emplanted germ of life, ruddy with the sunset, the horizons purple, the small clamour of the day lapsing into quiet, the great, still twilight, building itself, dome-like, toward the zenith. The barn fowls were roosting in the trees near the stable, the horses crunching their fodder in the stalls, the day's work ceasing by slow degrees; and the priest, the Spanish churchman, Father Sarria, relic of a departed régime, kindly, benign, believing in all goodness, a lover of his fellows and of dumb animals, yet, for all that, hurrying away in confusion and discomfiture, carrying in one hand the vessels of the Holy Communion and in the other a basket of game cocks.

VI

It was high noon, and the rays of the sun, that hung poised directly overhead in an intolerable white glory, fell straight as plummets upon the roofs and streets of Guadalajara. The adobe walls and sparse brick sidewalks of the drowsing town radiated the heat in an oily, quivering shimmer. The leaves of the eucalyptus trees around the Plaza drooped motionless, limp and relaxed under the scorching, searching blaze. The shadows of these trees had shrunk to their smallest circumference, contracting close about the trunks. The shade had dwindled to the breadth of a mere line. The sun was everywhere. The heat exhaling from brick and plaster and metal met the heat that steadily descended blanketwise and smothering, from the pale, scorched sky. Only the lizards—they lived in chinks of the crumbling adobe and in interstices of the sidewalk—remained without, motionless, as if stuffed, their eyes closed to mere slits, basking, stupefied with heat. At long intervals the prolonged drone of an insect developed out of the silence, vibrated a moment in a soothing, somnolent, long note, then trailed slowly into the quiet again. Somewhere in the interior of one of the 'dobe houses a guitar snored and hummed sleepily. On the roof of the hotel a group of pigeons cooed incessantly with subdued, liquid murmurs, very plaintive; a cat, perfectly white, with a pink nose and thin, pink lips, dozed complacently on a fence rail, full in the sun. In a corner of the Plaza three hens wallowed in the baking hot dust, their wings fluttering, clucking comfortably.

And this was all. A Sunday repose prevailed the whole moribund town, peaceful, profound. A certain pleasing numbness, a sense of grateful enervation exhaled from the scorching plaster. There was no movement, no sound of human business. The faint hum of the insect, the intermittent murmur of the guitar, the mellow complainings of the pigeons, the prolonged purr of the white cat, the contented clucking of the hens—all these noises mingled together to form a faint, drowsy bourdon, prolonged, stupefying, suggestive of an infinite quiet, of a calm, complacent life, centuries old, lapsing gradually to its end under the gorgeous loneliness of a cloudless, pale blue sky and the steady fire of an interminable sun.

In Solotari's Spanish-Mexican restaurant, Vanamee and Presley sat opposite each other at one of the tables near the door, a bottle of white wine, tortillas, and an earthen pot of frijoles between them. They were the sole occupants of the place. It was the day that Annixter had chosen for his barn-dance and, in consequence, Quien Sabe was in *fête* and work suspended. Presley and Vanamee had arranged to spend the day in each other's company, lunching at Solotari's and taking a long tramp in the afternoon. For the moment they sat back in their chairs, their meal all but finished. Solotari brought black coffee and a small carafe of mescal, and retiring to a corner of the room, went to sleep.

All through the meal Presley had been wondering over a certain change he observed in his friend. He looked at him again.

Vanamee's lean, spare face was of an olive pallor. His long, black hair, such as one sees in the saints and evangelists of the pre-Raphaelite artists, hung over his ears. Presley again remarked his pointed beard, black and fine, growing from the hollow cheeks. He looked at his face, a face like that of a young seer, like a half-inspired shepherd of the Hebraic legends, a dweller in the wilderness, gifted with strange powers. He was dressed as when Presley had first met him, herding his sheep, in brown canvas overalls, thrust into top boots; grey flannel shirt, open at the throat, showing the breast ruddy with tan; the waist encircled with a cartridge belt, empty of cartridges.

But now, as Presley took more careful note of him, he was surprised to observe a certain new look in Vanamee's deep-set eyes. He remembered now that all through the morning Vanamee had been singularly reserved. He was continually drifting into reveries, abstracted, distrait. Indubitably, something of moment had happened.

At length Vanamee spoke. Leaning back in his chair, his thumbs in his belt, his bearded chin upon his breast, his voice was the even monotone of one speaking in his sleep.

He told Presley in a few words what had happened during the first night he had spent in the garden of the old Mission, of the Answer, half-fancied, half-real, that had come to him.

"To no other person but you would I speak of this," he said, "but you, I think, will understand—will be sympathetic, at least, and I feel the need of unburdening myself of it to some one. At first I would not trust my own senses. I was sure I had deceived myself, but on a second night it happened again. Then I was afraid—or no, not afraid, but disturbed—oh, shaken to my very heart's core. I resolved to go no further in the matter, never again to put it to test. For a long time I stayed away from the Mission, occupying myself with my work, keeping it out of my mind. But the temptation was too strong. One night I found myself there again, under the black shadow of the pear trees calling for Angéle, summoning her from out the dark, from out the night.

This time the Answer was prompt, unmistakable. I cannot explain to you what it was, nor how it came to me, for there was no sound. I saw absolutely nothing but the empty night. There was no moon. But somewhere off there over the little valley, far off, the darkness was troubled; that *me* that went out upon my thought—out from the Mission garden, out over the valley, calling for her, searching for her, found, I don't know what, but found a resting place—a companion. Three times since then I have gone to the Mission garden at night. Last night was the third time."

He paused, his eyes shining with excitement. Presley leaned forward toward him, motionless with intense absorption.

"Well—and last night," he prompted.

Vanamee stirred in his seat, his glance fell, he drummed an instant upon the table.

"Last night," he answered, "there was—there was a change. The Answer was—" he drew a deep breath—"nearer."

"You are sure?"

The other smiled with absolute certainty.

"It was not that I found the Answer sooner, easier. I could not be mistaken. No, that which has troubled the darkness, that which has entered into the empty night—is coming nearer to me—physically nearer, actually nearer."

His voice sank again. His face like the face of younger prophets, the seers, took on a half-inspired expression. He looked vaguely before him with unseeing eyes.

"Suppose," he murmured, "suppose I stand there under the pear trees at night and call her again and again, and each time the Answer comes nearer and nearer and I wait until at last one night, the supreme night of all, she—she——"

Suddenly the tension broke. With a sharp cry and a

violent uncertain gesture of the hand Vanamee came to himself.

"Oh," he exclaimed, "what is it? Do I dare? What does it mean? There are times when it appals me and there are times when it thrills me with a sweetness and a happiness that I have not known since she died. The vagueness of it! How can I explain it to you, this that happens when I call to her across the night—that faint, far-off, unseen tremble in the darkness, that intangible, scarcely perceptible stir. Something neither heard nor seen, appealing to a sixth sense only. Listen, it is something like this: On Quien Sabe, all last week, we have been seeding the earth. The grain is there now under the earth buried in the dark, in the black stillness, under the clods. Can you imagine the first—the very first little quiver of life that the grain of wheat must feel after it is sown, when it answers to the call of the sun, down there in the dark of the earth, blind, deaf; the very first stir from the inert, long, long before any physical change has occurred,—long before the microscope could discover the slightest change,—when the shell first tightens with the first faint premonition of life? Well, it is something as illusive as that." He paused again, dreaming, lost in a reverie, then, just above a whisper, murmured:

"'That which thou sowest is not quickened except it die,' . . . and she, Angéle . . . died."

"You could not have been mistaken?" said Presley. "You were sure that there was something? Imagination can do so much and the influence of the surroundings was strong. How impossible it would be that anything *should* happen. And you say you heard nothing, saw nothing."

"I believe," answered Vanamee, "in a sixth sense, or, rather, a whole system of other unnamed senses beyond the reach of our understanding. People who live much

alone and close to nature experience the sensation of it.
Perhaps it is something fundamental that we share with
plants and animals. The same thing that sends the
birds south long before the first colds, the same thing that
makes the grain of wheat struggle up to meet the sun.
And this sense never deceives. You may see wrong,
hear wrong, but once touch this sixth sense and it acts
with absolute fidelity, you are certain. No, I hear nothing in the Mission garden. I see nothing, nothing
touches me, but I am *certain* for all that."

Presley hesitated for a moment, then he asked:
" Shall you go back to the garden again? Make the
test again?"

" I don't know."

" Strange enough," commented Presley, wondering.

Vanamee sank back in his chair, his eyes growing
vacant again:

"Strange enough," he murmured.

There was a long silence. Neither spoke nor moved.
There, in that moribund, ancient town, wrapped in its
siesta, flagellated with heat, deserted, ignored, baking in
a noon-day silence, these two strange men, the one a poet
by nature, the other by training, both out of tune with
their world, dreamers, introspective, morbid, lost and unfamiliar at that end-of-the-century time, searching for a
sign, groping and baffled amidst the perplexing obscurity
of the Delusion, sat over empty wine glasses, silent with
the pervading silence that surrounded them, hearing only
the cooing of doves and the drone of bees, the quiet so
profound, that at length they could plainly distinguish at
intervals the puffing and coughing of a locomotive
switching cars in the station yard of Bonneville.

It was, no doubt, this jarring sound that at length
roused Presley from his lethargy. The two friends rose;
Solotari very sleepily came forward; they paid for the

luncheon, and stepping out into the heat and glare of the
streets of the town, passed on through it and took the
road that led northward across a corner of Dyke's hop
fields. They were bound for the hills in the northeastern
corner of Quien Sabe. It was the same walk which
Presley had taken on the previous occasion when he had
first met Vanamee herding the sheep. This encompassing detour around the whole country-side was a favorite
pastime of his and he was anxious that Vanamee should
share his pleasure in it.

But soon after leaving Guadalajara, they found themselves upon the land that Dyke had bought and upon
which he was to raise his famous crop of hops. Dyke's
house was close at hand, a very pleasant little cottage,
painted white, with green blinds and deep porches, while
near it and yet in process of construction, were two great
storehouses and a drying and curing house, where the
hops were to be stored and treated. All about were evidences that the former engineer had already been hard at
work. The ground had been put in readiness to receive
the crop and a bewildering, innumerable multitude of
poles, connected with a maze of wire and twine, had been
set out. Farther on at a turn of the road, they came upon
Dyke himself, driving a farm wagon loaded with more
poles. He was in his shirt sleeves, his massive, hairy
arms bare to the elbow, glistening with sweat, red with
heat. In his bell-like, rumbling voice, he was calling to
his foreman and a boy at work in stringing the poles
together. At sight of Presley and Vanamee he hailed
them jovially, addressing them as "boys," and insisting
that they should get into the wagon with him and drive
to the house for a glass of beer. His mother had only
the day before returned from Marysville, where she had
been looking up a seminary for the little tad. She would
be delighted to see the two boys; besides, Vanamee must

see how the little tad had grown since he last set eyes on her; wouldn't know her for the same little girl; and the beer had been on ice since morning. Presley and Vanamee could not well refuse.

They climbed into the wagon and jolted over the uneven ground through the bare forest of hop-poles to the house. Inside they found Mrs. Dyke, an old lady with a very gentle face, who wore a cap and a very old-fashioned gown with hoop skirts, dusting the what-not in a corner of the parlor. The two men were presented and the beer was had from off the ice.

"Mother," said Dyke, as he wiped the froth from his great blond beard, "ain't Sid anywheres about? I want Mr. Vanamee to see how she has grown. Smartest little tad in Tulare County, boys. Can recite the whole of 'Snow Bound,' end to end, without skipping or looking at the book. Maybe you don't believe that. Mother, ain't I right—without skipping a line, hey?"

Mrs. Dyke nodded to say that it was so, but explained that Sidney was in Guadalajara. In putting on her new slippers for the first time the morning before, she had found a dime in the toe of one of them and had had the whole house by the ears ever since till she could spend it.

"Was it for licorice to make her licorice water?" inquired Dyke gravely.

"Yes," said Mrs. Dyke. "I made her tell me what she was going to get before she went, and it was licorice."

Dyke, though his mother protested that he was foolish and that Presley and Vanamee had no great interest in "young ones," insisted upon showing the visitors Sidney's copy-books. They were monuments of laborious, elaborate neatness, the trite moralities and ready-made aphorisms of the philanthropists and publicists, repeated from page to page with wearying insistence. "I, too, am an American Citizen. S. D.," "As the Twig is Bent the

Tree is Inclined," "Truth Crushed to Earth Will Rise
Again," "As for Me, Give Me Liberty or Give Me
Death," and last of all, a strange intrusion amongst the
mild, well-worn phrases, two legends. "My motto—
Public Control of Public Franchises," and "The P. and
S. W. is an Enemy of the State."

"I see," commented Presley, "you mean the little tad
to understand 'the situation' early."

"I told him he was foolish to give that to Sid to copy,"
said Mrs. Dyke, with indulgent remonstrance. "What
can she understand of public franchises?"

"Never mind," observed Dyke, "she'll remember it
when she grows up and when the seminary people have
rubbed her up a bit, and then she'll begin to ask questions
and understand. And don't you make any mistake,
mother," he went on, "about the little tad not knowing
who her dad's enemies are. What do you think, boys?
Listen, here. Precious little I've ever told her of the
railroad or how I was turned off, but the other day I was
working down by the fence next the railroad tracks and
Sid was there. She'd brought her doll rags down and
she was playing house behind a pile of hop poles. Well,
along comes a through freight—mixed train from Mis-
souri points and a string of empties from New Orleans,—
and when it had passed, what do you suppose the tad did?
She didn't know I was watching her. She goes to the
fence and spits a little spit after the caboose and puts out
her little head and, if you'll believe me, *hisses* at the
train; and mother says she does that same every time
she sees a train go by, and never crosses the tracks that
she don't spit her little spit on 'em. What do you *think*
of *that?*"

"But I correct her every time," protested Mrs. Dyke
seriously. "Where she picked up the trick of hissing I
don't know. No, it's not funny. It seems dreadful to

see a little girl who's as sweet and gentle as can be in
every other way, so venomous. She says the other little
girls at school and the boys, too, are all the same way.
Oh, dear," she sighed, " why will the General Office be
so unkind and unjust? Why, I couldn't be happy, with
all the money in the world, if I thought that even one
little child hated me—hated me so that it would spit and
hiss at me. And it's not one child, it's all of them, so
Sidney says; and think of all the grown people who hate
the road, women and men, the whole county, the whole
State, thousands and thousands of people. Don't the
managers and the directors of the road ever think of
that? Don't they ever think of all the hate that surrounds
them, everywhere, everywhere, and the good people that
just grit their teeth when the name of the road is mentioned? Why do they want to make the people hate them?
No," she murmured, the tears starting to her eyes, " No,
I tell you, Mr. Presley, the men who own the railroad are
wicked, bad-hearted men who don't care how much the
poor people suffer, so long as the road makes its eighteen
million a year. They don't care whether the people hate
them or love them, just so long as they are afraid of
them. It's not right and God will punish them sooner or
later."

A little after this the two young men took themselves
away, Dyke obligingly carrying them in the wagon as far
as the gate that opened into the Quien Sabe ranch. On
the way, Presley referred to what Mrs. Dyke had said and
led Dyke, himself, to speak of the P. and S. W.

"Well," Dyke said, " it's like this, Mr. Presley. I,
personally, haven't got the right to kick. With you
wheat-growing people I guess it's different, but hops, you
see, don't count for much in the State. It's such a little
business that the road don't want to bother themselves to
tax it. It's the wheat growers that the road cinches.

The rates on hops *are fair*. I've got to admit that; I was in to Bonneville a while ago to find out. It's two cents a pound, and Lord love you, that's reasonable enough to suit any man. No," he concluded, "I'm on the way to make money now. The road sacking me as they did was, maybe, a good thing for me, after all. It came just at the right time. I had a bit of money put by and here was the chance to go into hops with the certainty that hops would quadruple and quintuple in price inside the year. No, it was my chance, and though they didn't mean it by a long chalk, the railroad people did me a good turn when they gave me my time—and the tad'll enter the seminary next fall."

About a quarter of an hour after they had said good-bye to the one-time engineer, Presley and Vanamee, tramping briskly along the road that led northward through Quien Sabe, arrived at Annixter's ranch house. At once they were aware of a vast and unwonted bustle that revolved about the place. They stopped a few moments looking on, amused and interested in what was going forward.

The colossal barn was finished. Its freshly white-washed sides glared intolerably in the sun, but its interior was as yet innocent of paint and through the yawning vent of the sliding doors came a delicious odour of new, fresh wood and shavings. A crowd of men—Annixter's farm hands—were swarming all about it. Some were balanced on the topmost rounds of ladders, hanging festoons of Japanese lanterns from tree to tree, and all across the front of the barn itself. Mrs. Tree, her daughter Hilma and another woman were inside the barn cutting into long strips bolt after bolt of red, white and blue cambric and directing how these strips should be draped from the ceiling and on the walls; everywhere resounded the tapping of tack hammers. A farm wagon drove up loaded to overflowing with evergreens and with great bundles of palm leaves, and these were immediately seized upon and affixed as supplementary decorations to the tri-coloured cambric upon the inside walls of the barn. Two of the larger evergreen trees were placed on either side the barn door and their tops bent over to form an arch. In the middle of this arch it was proposed to hang a mammoth pasteboard escutcheon with gold letters, spelling the word *Welcome*. Piles of chairs, rented from I.O.O.F. hall in Bonneville, heaped themselves in an apparently hopeless entanglement on the ground; while at the far extremity of the barn a couple of carpenters clattered about the impromptu staging which was to accommodate the band.

There was a strenuous gayety in the air; everybody was in the best of spirits. Notes of laughter continually interrupted the conversation on every hand. At every moment a group of men involved themselves in uproarious horse-play. They passed oblique jokes behind their hands to each other—grossly veiled double-meanings meant for the women—and bellowed with laughter thereat, stamping on the ground. The relations between the sexes grew more intimate, the women and girls pushing the young fellows away from their sides with vigorous thrusts of their elbows. It was passed from group to group that Adela Vacca, a division superintendent's wife, had lost her garter; the daughter of the foreman of the Home ranch was kissed behind the door of the dairy-house.

Annixter, in execrable temper, appeared from time to time, hatless, his stiff yellow hair in wild disorder. He hurried between the barn and the ranch house, carrying now a wickered demijohn, now a case of wine, now a basket of lemons and pineapples. Besides general supervision, he had elected to assume the responsibility of

composing the punch—something stiff, by jingo, a punch
that would raise you right out of your boots; a regular
hairlifter.

The harness room of the barn he had set apart for
himself and intimates. He had brought a long table
down from the house and upon it had set out boxes of
cigars, bottles of whiskey and of beer and the great
china bowls for the punch. It would be no fault of his,
he declared, if half the number of his men friends were
not uproarious before they left. His barn dance would
be the talk of all Tulare County for years to come. For
this one day he had resolved to put all thoughts of business out of his head. For the matter of that, things were
going well enough. Osterman was back from Los Angeles with a favourable report as to his affair with Disbrow and Darrell. There had been another meeting of
the committee. Harran Derrick had attended. Though
he had taken no part in the discussion, Annixter was
satisfied. The Governor had consented to allow Harran
to "come in," if he so desired, and Harran had pledged
himself to share one-sixth of the campaign expenses,
providing these did not exceed a certain figure.

As Annixter came to the door of the barn to shout
abuse at the distraught Chinese cook who was cutting up
lemons in the kitchen, he caught sight of Presley and
Vanamee and hailed them.

"Hello, Pres," he called. "Come over here and see
how she looks;" he indicated the barn with a movement
of his head. "Well, we're getting ready for you to-
night," he went on as the two friends came up. "But
how we are going to get straightened out by eight o'clock
I don't know. Would you believe that pip Caraher is
short of lemons—at this last minute and I told him I'd
want three cases of 'em as much as a month ago, and
here, just when I want a good lively saddle horse to get

around on, somebody hikes the buckskin out the corral. *Stole* her, by jingo. I'll have the law on that thief if it breaks me—and a sixty-dollar saddle 'n' head-stall gone with her; and only about half the number of Jap lanterns that I ordered have shown up and not candles enough for those. It's enough to make a dog sick. There's nothing done that you don't do yourself, unless you stand over these loafers with a club. I'm sick of the whole business —and I've lost my hat; wish to God I'd never dreamed of givin' this rotten fool dance. Clutter the whole place up with a lot of feemales. I sure did lose my presence of mind when I got *that* idea."

Then, ignoring the fact that it was he, himself, who had called the young men to him, he added:

"Well, this is my busy day. Sorry I can't stop and talk to you longer."

He shouted a last imprecation at the Chinaman and turned back into the barn. Presley and Vanamee went on, but Annixter, as he crossed the floor of the barn, all but collided with Hilma Tree, who came out from one of the stalls, a box of candles in her arms.

Gasping out an apology, Annixter reëntered the harness room, closing the door behind him, and forgetting all the responsibility of the moment, lit a cigar and sat down in one of the hired chairs, his hands in his pockets, his feet on the table, frowning thoughtfully through the blue smoke.

Annixter was at last driven to confess to himself that he could not get the thought of Hilma Tree out of his mind. Finally she had " got a hold on him." The thing that of all others he most dreaded had happened. A feemale girl had got a hold on him, and now there was no longer for him any such thing as peace of mind. The idea of the young woman was with him continually. He went to bed with it; he got up with it. At every moment

of the day he was pestered with it. It interfered with
his work, got mixed up in his business. What a miserable confession for a man to make; a fine way to waste
his time. Was it possible that only the other day he had
stood in front of the music store in Bonneville and seriously considered making Hilma a present of a music-
box? Even now, the very thought of it made him flush
with shame, and this after she had told him plainly that
she did not like him. He was running after her—he,
Annixter! He ripped out a furious oath, striking the
table with his boot heel. Again and again he had resolved to put the whole affair from out his mind. Once
he had been able to do so, but of late it was becoming
harder and harder with every successive day. He had
only to close his eyes to see her as plain as if she stood
before him; he saw her in a glory of sunlight that set a
fine tinted lustre of pale carnation and gold on the silken
sheen of her white skin, her hair sparkled with it, her
thick, strong neck, sloping to her shoulders with beautiful, full curves, seemed to radiate the light; her eyes,
brown, wide, innocent in expression, disclosing the full
disc of the pupil upon the slightest provocation, flashed
in this sunlight like diamonds.

Annixter was all bewildered. With the exception of
the timid little creature in the glove-cleaning establishment in Sacramento, he had had no acquaintance with
any woman. His world was harsh, crude, a world of
men only—men who were to be combatted, opposed—
his hand was against nearly every one of them. Women
he distrusted with the instinctive distrust of the overgrown
schoolboy. Now, at length, a young woman had come
into his life. Promptly he was struck with discomfiture,
annoyed almost beyond endurance, harassed, bedevilled,
excited, made angry and exasperated. He was suspicious
of the woman, yet desired her, totally ignorant of how to

approach her, hating the sex, yet drawn to the individual, confusing the two emotions, sometimes even hating Hilma as a result of this confusion, but at all times disturbed, vexed, irritated beyond power of expression.

At length, Annixter cast his cigar from him and plunged again into the work of the day. The afternoon wore to evening, to the accompaniment of wearying and clamorous endeavour. In some unexplained fashion, the labour of putting the great barn in readiness for the dance was accomplished; the last bolt of cambric was hung in place from the rafters. The last evergreen tree was nailed to the joists of the walls; the last lantern hung, the last nail driven into the musicians' platform. The sun set. There was a great scurry to have supper and dress. Annixter, last of all the other workers, left the barn in the dusk of twilight. He was alone; he had a saw under one arm, a bag of tools was in his hand. He was in his shirt sleeves and carried his coat over his shoulder; a hammer was thrust into one of his hip pockets. He was in execrable temper. The day's work had fagged him out. He had not been able to find his hat.

"And the buckskin with sixty dollars' worth of saddle gone, too," he groaned. "Oh, ain't it sweet?"

At his house, Mrs. Tree had set out a cold supper for him, the inevitable dish of prunes serving as dessert. After supper Annixter bathed and dressed. He decided at the last moment to wear his usual town-going suit, a sack suit of black, made by a Bonneville tailor. But his hat was gone. There were other hats he might have worn, but because this particular one was lost he fretted about it all through his dressing and then decided to have one more look around the barn for it.

For over a quarter of an hour he pottered about the barn, going from stall to stall, rummaging the harness room and feed room, all to no purpose. At last he came out again upon the main floor, definitely giving up the search, looking about him to see if everything was in order.

The festoons of Japanese lanterns in and around the barn were not yet lighted, but some half-dozen lamps, with great, tin reflectors, that hung against the walls, were burning low. A dull half light pervaded the vast interior, hollow, echoing, leaving the corners and roof thick with impenetrable black shadows. The barn faced the west and through the open sliding doors was streaming a single bright bar from the after-glow, incongruous and out of all harmony with the dull flare of the kerosene lamps.

As Annixter glanced about him, he saw a figure step briskly out of the shadows of one corner of the building, pause for the fraction of one instant in the bar of light, then, at sight of him, dart back again. There was a sound of hurried footsteps.

Annixter, with recollections of the stolen buckskin in his mind, cried out sharply:

" Who's there? "

There was no answer. In a second his pistol was in his hand.

" Who's there?   Quick, speak up or I'll shoot."

" No, no, no, don't shoot," cried an answering voice. " Oh, be careful.   It's I—Hilma Tree."

Annixter slid the pistol into his pocket with a great qualm of apprehension. He came forward and met Hilma in the doorway.

" Good Lord," he murmured, " that sure did give me a start. If I *had* shot——"

Hilma stood abashed and confused before him. She was dressed in a white organdie frock of the most rigorous simplicity and wore neither flower nor ornament. The severity of her dress made her look even larger than usual, and even as it was her eyes were on a level with

Annixter's. There was a certain fascination in the contradiction of stature and character of Hilma—a great girl, half-child as yet, but tall as a man for all that.

There was a moment's awkward silence, then Hilma explained:

"I—I came back to look for my hat. I thought I left it here this afternoon."

"And I was looking for *my* hat," cried Annixter. "Funny enough, hey?"

They laughed at this as heartily as children might have done. The constraint of the situation was a little relaxed and Annixter, with sudden directness, glanced sharply at the young woman and demanded:

"Well, Miss Hilma, hate me as much as ever?"

"Oh, no, sir," she answered, "I never said I hated you."

"Well,—dislike me, then; I know you said that."

"I—I disliked what you did—*tried* to do. It made me angry and it hurt me. I shouldn't have said what I did that time, but it was your fault."

"You mean you shouldn't have said you didn't like me?" asked Annixter. "Why?"

"Well, well,—I don't—I don't *dis*like anybody," admitted Hilma.

"Then I can take it that you don't dislike *me?* Is that it?"

"I don't dislike anybody," persisted Hilma.

"Well, I asked you more than that, didn't I?" queried Annixter uneasily. "I asked you to like me, remember, the other day. I'm asking you that again, now. I want you to like me."

Hilma lifted her eyes inquiringly to his. In her words was an unmistakable ring of absolute sincerity. Innocently she inquired:

"Why?"

Annixter was struck speechless. In the face of such candour, such perfect ingenuousness, he was at a loss for any words.

"Well—well," he stammered, "well—I don't know," he suddenly burst out. "That is," he went on, groping for his wits, "I can't quite say why." The idea of a colossal lie occurred to him, a thing actually royàl.

"I like to have the people who are around me like me," he declared. "I—I like to be popular, understand? Yes, that's it," he continued, more reassured. "I don't like the idea of any one disliking me. That's the way I am. It's my nature."

"Oh, then," returned Hilma, "you needn't bother. No, I don't dislike you."

"Well, that's good," declared Annixter judicially. "That's good. But hold on," he interrupted, "I'm forgetting. It's not enough to not dislike me. I want you to like me. How about *that?*"

Hilma paused for a moment, glancing vaguely out of the doorway toward the lighted window of the dairy-house, her head tilted.

"I don't know that I ever thought about that," she said.

"Well, think about it now," insisted Annixter.

"But I never thought about liking anybody particularly," she observed. "It's because I like everybody, don't you see?"

"Well, you've got to like some people more than other people," hazarded Annixter, "and I want to be one of those 'some people,' savvy? Good Lord, I don't know how to say these fool things. I talk like a galoot when I get talking to feemale girls and I can't lay my tongue to anything that sounds right. It isn't my nature. And look here, I lied when I said I liked to have people like me—to be popular. Rot! I don't care a curse about people's opinions of me. But there's a few people that are more to me than most others—that chap Presley, for instance—and those people I *do* want to have like me. What they think counts. Pshaw! I know I've got enemies; piles of them. I could name you half a dozen men right now that are naturally itching to take a shot at me. How about this ranch? Don't I know, can't I hear the men growling oaths under their breath after I've gone by? And in business ways, too," he went on, speaking half to himself, " in Bonneville and all over the county there's not a man of them wouldn't howl for joy if they got a chance to down Buck Annixter. Think I care? Why, I *like* it. I run my ranch to suit myself and I play my game my own way. I'm a 'driver,' I know it, and a 'bully,' too. Oh, I know what they call me—' a brute beast, with a twist in my temper that would rile up a new-born lamb,' and I'm 'crusty' and 'pig-headed' and 'obstinate.' They say all that, but they've *got* to say, too, that I'm cleverer than any man-jack in the running. There's nobody can get ahead of me." His eyes snapped. " Let 'em grind their teeth. They can't 'down' me. When I shut my fist there's not one of them can open it. No, not with a *chisel*." He turned to Hilma again. " Well, when a man's hated as much as that, it stands to reason, don't it, Miss Hilma, that the few friends he has got he wants to keep? I'm not such an entire swine to the people that know me best—that jackass, Presley, for instance. I'd put my hand in the fire to do him a real service. Sometimes I get kind of lonesome; wonder if you would understand? It's my fault, but there's not a horse about the place that don't lay his ears back when I get on him; there's not a dog don't put his tail between his legs as soon as I come near him. The cayuse isn't foaled yet here on Quien Sabe that can throw me, nor the dog whelped that would dare show

his teeth at me. I kick that Irish setter every time I
see him—but wonder what I'd do, though, if he didn't
slink so much, if he wagged his tail and was glad to see
me? So it all comes to this: I'd like to have you—well,
sort of feel that I was a good friend of yours and like
me because of it."

The flame in the lamp on the wall in front of Hilma
stretched upward tall and thin and began to smoke. She
went over to where the lamp hung and, standing on tiptoe, lowered the wick. As she reached her hand up,
Annixter noted how the sombre, lurid red of the lamp
made a warm reflection on her smooth, round arm.

"Do you understand?" he queried.

"Yes, why, yes," she answered, turning around. "It's
very good of you to want to be a friend of mine. I
didn't think so, though, when you tried to kiss me. But
maybe it's all right since you've explained things. You
see I'm different from you. I like everybody to like me
and I like to like everybody. It makes one so much
happier. You wouldn't believe it, but you ought to try
it, sir, just to see. It's so good to be good to people and
to have people good to you. And everybody has always
been so good to me. Mamma and papa, of course, and
Billy, the stableman, and Montalegre, the Portugee foreman, and the Chinese cook, even, and Mr. Delaney—only
he went away—and Mrs. Vacca and her little——"

"Delaney, hey?" demanded Annixter abruptly. "You
and he were pretty good friends, were you?"

"Oh, yes," she answered. "He was just as *good* to
me. Every day in the summer time he used to ride over
to the Seed ranch back of the Mission and bring me a
great armful of flowers, the prettiest things, and I used
to pretend to pay him for them with dollars made of
cheese that I cut out of the cheese with a biscuit cutter.
It was such fun. We were the best of friends."

"There's another lamp smoking," growled Annixter. "Turn it down, will you?—and see that somebody sweeps this floor here. It's all littered up with pine needles. I've got a lot to do. Good-bye."

"Good-bye, sir."

Annixter returned to the ranch house, his teeth clenched, enraged, his face flushed.

"Ah," he muttered, "Delaney, hey? Throwing it up to me that I fired him." His teeth gripped together more fiercely than ever. "The best of friends, hey? By God, I'll have that girl yet. I'll show that cow-puncher. Ain't I her employer, her boss? I'll show her—and Delaney, too. It would be easy enough—and then Delaney can have her—if he wants her—after me."

An evil light flashing from under his scowl, spread over his face. The male instincts of possession, unreasoned, treacherous, oblique, came twisting to the surface. All the lower nature of the man, ignorant of women, racked at one and the same time with enmity and desire, roused itself like a hideous and abominable beast. And at the same moment, Hilma returned to her house, humming to herself as she walked, her white dress glowing with a shimmer of faint saffron light in the last ray of the after-glow.

A little after half-past seven, the first carry-all, bearing the druggist of Bonneville and his women-folk, arrived in front of the new barn. Immediately afterward an express wagon loaded down with a swarming family of Spanish-Mexicans, gorgeous in red and yellow colours, followed. Billy, the stableman, and his assistant took charge of the teams, unchecking the horses and hitching them to a fence back of the barn. Then Caraher, the saloon-keeper, in "derby" hat, "Prince Albert" coat, pointed yellow shoes and inevitable red necktie, drove into the yard on his buckboard, the delayed box of lemons under the seat. It looked as if the whole array of invited guests was to arrive in one unbroken procession, but for a long half-hour nobody else appeared. Annixter and Caraher withdrew to the harness room and promptly involved themselves in a wrangle as to the make-up of the famous punch. From time to time their voices could be heard uplifted in clamorous argument.

"Two quarts and a half and a cupful of chartreuse."

"Rot, rot, I know better. Champagne straight and a dash of brandy."

The druggist's wife and sister retired to the feed room, where a bureau with a swinging mirror had been placed for the convenience of the women. The druggist stood awkwardly outside the door of the feed room, his coat collar turned up against the draughts that drifted through the barn, his face troubled, debating anxiously as to the propriety of putting on his gloves. The Spanish-Mexican family, a father, mother and five children and sister-in-law, sat rigid on the edges of the hired chairs, silent, constrained, their eyes lowered, their elbows in at their sides, glancing furtively from under their eyebrows at the decorations or watching with intense absorption young Vacca, son of one of the division superintendents, who wore a checked coat and white thread gloves and who paced up and down the length of the barn, frowning, very important, whittling a wax candle over the floor to make it slippery for dancing.

The musicians arrived, the City Band of Bonneville— Annixter having managed to offend the leader of the "Dirigo" Club orchestra, at the very last moment, to such a point that he had refused his services. These members of the City Band repaired at once to their platform in the corner. At every instant they laughed uproariously among themselves, joshing one of their number, a Frenchman, whom they called "Skeezicks." Their hilarity reverberated in a hollow, metallic roll among the rafters overhead. The druggist observed to young Vacca as he passed by that he thought them pretty fresh, just the same.

"I'm busy, I'm very busy," returned the young man, continuing on his way, still frowning and paring the stump of candle.

"Two quarts 'n' a half. Two quarts 'n' a half."

"Ah, yes, in a way, that's so; and then, again, in a way, it *isn't*. I know better."

All along one side of the barn were a row of stalls, fourteen of them, clean as yet, redolent of new cut wood, the sawdust still in the cracks of the flooring. Deliberately the druggist went from one to the other, pausing contemplatively before each. He returned down the line and again took up his position by the door of the feed room, nodding his head judicially, as if satisfied. He decided to put on his gloves.

By now it was quite dark. Outside, between the barn and the ranch houses one could see a group of men on step-ladders lighting the festoons of Japanese lanterns. In the darkness, only their faces appeared here and there, high above the ground, seen in a haze of red, strange, grotesque. Gradually as the multitude of lanterns were lit, the light spread. The grass underfoot looked like green excelsior. Another group of men invaded the barn itself, lighting the lamps and lanterns there. Soon the whole place was gleaming with points of light. Young Vacca, who had disappeared, returned with his pockets full of wax candles. He resumed his whittling, refusing to answer any questions, vociferating that he was busy.

Outside there was a sound of hoofs and voices. More guests had arrived. The druggist, seized with confusion, terrified lest he had put on his gloves too soon, thrust his

hands into his pockets.   It was Cutter, Magnus Derrick's
division superintendent, who came, bringing his wife and
her two girl cousins.   They had come fifteen miles by
the trail from the far distant division house on " Four "
of Los Muertos and had ridden on horseback instead of
driving.   Mrs. Cutter could be heard declaring that she
was nearly dead and felt more like going to bed than
dancing.   The two girl cousins, in dresses of dotted
Swiss over blue sateen, were doing their utmost to pacify
her.   She could be heard protesting from moment to
moment.   One distinguished the phrases " straight to my
bed," " back nearly broken in two," " never wanted to
come in the first place."   The druggist, observing Cutter take a pair of gloves from Mrs. Cutter's reticule,
drew his hands from his pockets.

But abruptly there was an interruption.   In the musicians' corner a scuffle broke out.   A chair was overturned.   There was a noise of imprecations mingled
with shouts of derision.   Skeezicks, the Frenchman, had
turned upon the joshers.

" Ah, no," he was heard to exclaim, " at the end of the
end it is too much.   Kind of a bad canary—we will go to
see about that.   Aha, let him close up his face before I
demolish it with a good stroke of the fist."

The men who were lighting the lanterns were obliged
to intervene before he could be placated.

Hooven and his wife and daughters arrived.   Minna
was carrying little Hilda, already asleep, in her arms.
Minna looked very pretty, striking even, with her black
hair, pale face, very red lips and greenish-blue eyes.
She was dressed in what had been Mrs. Hooven's wedding gown, a cheap affair of " farmer's satin."   Mrs.
Hooven had pendent earrings of imitation jet in her
ears.   Hooven was wearing an old frock coat of Magnus
Derrick's, the sleeves too long, the shoulders absurdly too

wide. He and Cutter at once entered into an excited conversation as to the ownership of a certain steer.

"Why, the brand——"

"Ach, Gott, der brendt," Hooven clasped his head, "ach, der brendt, dot maks me laugh some laughs. Dot's goot—der brendt—doand I see um—shoor der boole mit der bleck star bei der vore-head in der middle oaf. Any someones you esk tell you dot is mein boole. You esk any someones. Der brendt? To hell mit der brendt. You aindt got some memorie aboudt does ting I guess nodt."

"Please step aside, gentlemen," said young Vacca, who was still making the rounds of the floor.

Hooven whirled about. "Eh? What den," he exclaimed, still excited, willing to be angry at any one for the moment. "Doand you push soh, you. I tink berhapz you doand *own* dose barn, hey?"

"I'm busy, I'm very busy." The young man pushed by with grave preoccupation.

"Two quarts 'n' a half. Two quarts 'n' a half."

"I know better. That's all rot."

But the barn was filling up rapidly. At every moment there was a rattle of a newly arrived vehicle from outside. Guest after guest appeared in the doorway, singly or in couples, or in families, or in garrulous parties of five and six. Now it was Phelps and his mother from Los Muertos, now a foreman from Broderson's with his family, now a gayly apparelled clerk from a Bonneville store, solitary and bewildered, looking for a place to put his hat, now a couple of Spanish-Mexican girls from Guadalajara with coquettish effects of black and yellow about their dress, now a group of Osterman's tenants, Portuguese, swarthy, with plastered hair and curled mustaches, redolent of cheap perfumes. Sarria arrived, his smooth, shiny face glistening with perspira-

tion. He wore a new cassock and carried his broad-
brimmed hat under his arm. His appearance made quite
a stir. He passed from group to group, urbane, affable,
shaking hands right and left; he assumed a set smile of
amiability which never left his face the whole evening.

But abruptly there was a veritable sensation. From
out the little crowd that persistently huddled about the
doorway came Osterman. He wore a dress-suit with a
white waistcoat and patent leather pumps—what a wonder! A little qualm of excitement spread around the
barn. One exchanged nudges of the elbow with one's
neighbour, whispering earnestly behind the hand. What
astonishing clothes! Catch on to the coat-tails! It was
a masquerade costume, maybe; that goat Osterman was
such a josher, one never could tell what he would do
next.

The musicians began to tune up. From their corner
came a medley of mellow sounds, the subdued chirps of
the violins, the dull bourdon of the bass viol, the liquid
gurgling of the flageolet and the deep-toned snarl of the
big horn, with now and then a rasping stridulating of the
snare drum. A sense of gayety began to spread throughout the assembly. At every moment the crowd increased.
The aroma of new-sawn timber and sawdust began to be
mingled with the feminine odour of sachet and flowers.
There was a babel of talk in the air—male baritone and
soprano chatter—varied by an occasional note of laughter and the swish of stiffly starched petticoats. On the
row of chairs that went around three sides of the wall
groups began to settle themselves. For a long time the
guests huddled close to the doorway; the lower end of
the floor was crowded, the upper end deserted; but by degrees the lines of white muslin and pink and blue sateen
extended, dotted with the darker figures of men in black
suits. The conversation grew louder as the timidity of

the early moments wore off. Groups at a distance called
back and forth; conversations were carried on at top
voice. Once, even a whole party hurried across the
floor from one side of the barn to the other.

Annixter emerged from the harness room, his face red
with wrangling. He took a position to the right of the
door, shaking hands with newcomers, inviting them over
and over again to cut loose and whoop it along. Into
the ears of his more intimate male acquaintances he
dropped a word as to punch and cigars in the harness
room later on, winking with vast intelligence.

Ranchers from remoter parts of the country appeared:
Garnett, from the Ruby rancho, Keast, from the ranch
of the same name, Gethings, of the San Pablo, Chattern,
of the Bonanza, and others and still others, a score of
them—elderly men, for the most part, bearded, slow of
speech, deliberate, dressed in broadcloth. Old Broderson, who entered with his wife on his arm, fell in with
this type, and with them came a certain Dabney, of
whom nothing but his name was known, a silent old
man, who made no friends, whom nobody knew or spoke
to, who was seen only upon such occasions as this, coming
from no one knew where, going, no one cared to inquire
whither.

Between eight and half-past, Magnus Derrick and his
family were seen. Magnus's entry caused no little impression. Some said: "There's the Governor," and called
their companions' attention to the thin, erect figure, commanding, imposing, dominating all in his immediate
neighbourhood. Harran came with him, wearing a cutaway suit of black. He was undeniably handsome, young
and fresh looking, his cheeks highly coloured, quite the
finest looking of all the younger men; blond, strong,
with that certain courtliness of manner that had always
made him liked. He took his mother upon his arm

and conducted her to a seat by the side of Mrs.
Broderson.

Annie Derrick was very pretty that evening. She
was dressed in a grey silk gown with a collar of pink
velvet. Her light brown hair that yet retained so much
of its brightness was transfixed by a high, shell comb,
very Spanish. But the look of uneasiness in her large
eyes—the eyes of a young girl—was deepening every
day. The expression of innocence and inquiry which
they so easily assumed, was disturbed by a faint suggestion of aversion, almost of terror. She settled herself in
her place, in the corner of the hall, in the rear rank of
chairs, a little frightened by the glare of lights, the hum
of talk and the shifting crowd, glad to be out of the
way, to attract no attention, willing to obliterate herself.

All at once Annixter, who had just shaken hands with
Dyke, his mother and the little tad, moved abruptly in
his place, drawing in his breath sharply. The crowd
around the great, wide-open main door of the barn had
somewhat thinned out and in the few groups that still
remained there he had suddenly recognised Mr. and
Mrs. Tree and Hilma, making their way towards some
empty seats near the entrance of the feed room.

In the dusky light of the barn earlier in the evening,
Annixter had not been able to see Hilma plainly. Now,
however, as she passed before his eyes in the glittering
radiance of the lamps and lanterns, he caught his breath
in astonishment. Never had she appeared more beautiful
in his eyes. It did not seem possible that this was the
same girl whom he saw every day in and around the
ranch house and dairy, the girl of simple calico frocks
and plain shirt waists, who brought him his dinner, who
made up his bed. Now he could not take his eyes from
her. Hilma, for the first time, was wearing her hair
done high upon her head. The thick, sweet-smelling

masses, bitumen brown in the shadows, corruscated like golden filaments in the light. Her organdie frock was long, longer than any she had yet worn. It left a little of her neck and breast bare and all of her arm.

Annixter muttered an exclamation. Such arms! How did she manage to keep them hid on ordinary occasions. Big at the shoulder, tapering with delicious modulations to the elbow and wrist, overlaid with a delicate, gleaming lustre. As often as she turned her head the movement sent a slow undulation over her neck and shoulders, the pale amber-tinted shadows under her chin, coming and going over the creamy whiteness of the skin like the changing moire of silk. The pretty rose colour of her cheek had deepened to a pale carnation. Annixter, his hands clasped behind him, stood watching.

In a few moments Hilma was surrounded by a group of young men, clamouring for dances. They came from all corners of the barn, leaving the other girls precipitately, almost rudely. There could be little doubt as to who was to be the belle of the occasion. Hilma's little triumph was immediate, complete. Annixter could hear her voice from time to time, its usual velvety huskiness vibrating to a note of exuberant gayety.

All at once the orchestra swung off into a march—the Grand March. There was a great rush to secure "partners." Young Vacca, still going the rounds, was pushed to one side. The gayly apparelled clerk from the Bonneville store lost his head in the confusion. He could not find his "partner." He roamed wildly about the barn, bewildered, his eyes rolling. He resolved to prepare an elaborate programme card on the back of an old envelope. Rapidly the line was formed, Hilma and Harran Derrick in the lead, Annixter having obstinately refused to engage in either march, set or dance the whole evening. Soon the confused shuffling of feet settled to a measured cadence; the orchestra blared and wailed, the snare drum, rolling at exact intervals, the cornet marking the time. It was half-past eight o'clock.

Annixter drew a long breath:

" Good," he muttered, " the thing is under way at last."

Singularly enough, Osterman also refused to dance. The week before he had returned from Los Angeles, bursting with the importance of his mission. He had been successful. He had Disbrow " in his pocket." He was impatient to pose before the others of the committee as a skilful political agent, a manipulator. He forgot his attitude of the early part of the evening when he had drawn attention to himself with his wonderful clothes. Now his comic actor's face, with its brownish-red cheeks, protuberant ears and horizontal slit of a mouth, was overcast with gravity. His bald forehead was seamed with the wrinkles of responsibility. He drew Annixter into one of the empty stalls and began an elaborate explanation, glib, voluble, interminable, going over again in detail what he had reported to the committee in outline.

" I managed — I schemed — I kept dark — I lay low——"

But Annixter refused to listen.

" Oh, rot your schemes. There's a punch in the harness room that will make the hair grow on the top of your head in the place where the hair ought to grow. Come on, we'll round up some of the boys and walk into it."

They edged their way around the hall outside " The Grand March," toward the harness room, picking up on their way Caraher, Dyke, Hooven and old Broderson. Once in the harness room, Annixter shot the bolt.

" That affair outside," he observed, " will take care of itself, but here's a little orphan child that gets lonesome without company."

Annixter began ladling the punch, filling the glasses.

Osterman proposed a toast to Quien Sabe and the Biggest Barn. Their elbows crooked in silence. Old Broderson set down his glass, wiping his long beard and remarking:

"That—that certainly is very—very agreeable. I remember a punch I drank on Christmas day in '83, or no, it was '84—anyhow, that punch—it was in Ukiah—'twas '83—" He wandered on aimlessly, unable to stop his flow of speech, losing himself in details, involving his talk in a hopeless maze of trivialities to which nobody paid any attention.

"I don't drink myself," observed Dyke, "but just a taste of that with a lot of water wouldn't be bad for the little tad. She'd think it was lemonade." He was about to mix a glass for Sidney, but thought better of it at the last moment.

"It's the chartreuse that's lacking," commented Caraher, lowering at Annixter. The other flared up on the instant.

"Rot, rot. I know better. In some punches it goes; and then, again, in others it don't."

But it was left to Hooven to launch the successful phrase:

"*Gesundheit*," he exclaimed, holding out his second glass. After drinking, he replaced it on the table with a long breath. "Ach Gott!" he cried, "dat poonsch, say I tink dot poonsch mek some demn goot vertilizer, hey?"

Fertiliser! The others roared with laughter.

"Good eye, Bismarck," commented Annixter. The name had a great success. Thereafter throughout the evening the punch was invariably spoken of as the "Fertiliser." Osterman, having spilt the bottom of a glassful on the floor, pretended that he saw shoots of grain coming up on the spot. Suddenly he turned upon old Broderson.

"I'm bald, ain't I? Want to know how I lost my hair? Promise you won't ask a single other question and I'll tell you. Promise your word of honour."

"Eh? What—wh—I—I don't understand. Your hair? Yes, I'll promise. How *did* you lose it?"

"It was bit off."

The other gazed at him stupefied; his jaw dropped. The company shouted, and old Broderson, believing he had somehow accomplished a witticism, chuckled in his beard, wagging his head. But suddenly he fell grave, struck with an idea. He demanded:

"Yes—I know—but—but what bit it off?"

"Ah," vociferated Osterman, "that's *just* what you promised not to ask."

The company doubled up with hilarity. Caraher leaned against the door, holding his sides, but Hooven, all abroad, unable to follow, gazed from face to face with a vacant grin, thinking it was still a question of his famous phrase.

"Vertilizer, hey? Dots some fine joke, hey? You bedt."

What with the noise of their talk and laughter, it was some time before Dyke, first of all, heard a persistent knocking on the bolted door. He called Annixter's attention to the sound. Cursing the intruder, Annixter unbolted and opened the door. But at once his manner changed.

"Hello. It's Presley. Come in, come in, Pres."

There was a shout of welcome from the others. A spirit of effusive cordiality had begun to dominate the gathering. Annixter caught sight of Vanamee back of Presley, and waiving for the moment the distinction of employer and employee, insisted that both the friends should come in.

"Any friend of Pres is my friend," he declared.

But when the two had entered and had exchanged greetings, Presley drew Annixter aside.

"Vanamee and I have just come from Bonneville," he explained. "We saw Delaney there. He's got the buckskin, and he's full of bad whiskey and dago-red. You should see him; he's wearing all his cow-punching outfit, hair trousers, sombrero, spurs and all the rest of it, and he has strapped himself to a big revolver. He says he wasn't invited to your barn dance but that he's coming over to shoot up the place. He says you promised to show him off Quien Sabe at the toe of your boot and that he's going to give you the chance to-night!"

"Ah," commented Annixter, nodding his head, "he is, is he?"

Presley was disappointed. Knowing Annixter's irascibility, he had expected to produce a more dramatic effect. He began to explain the danger of the business. Delaney had once knifed a greaser in the Panamint country. He was known as a "bad" man. But Annixter refused to be drawn.

"All right," he said, "that's all right. Don't tell anybody else. You might scare the girls off. Get in and drink."

Outside the dancing was by this time in full swing. The orchestra was playing a polka. Young Vacca, now at his fiftieth wax candle, had brought the floor to the slippery surface of glass. The druggist was dancing with one of the Spanish-Mexican girls with the solemnity of an automaton, turning about and about, always in the same direction, his eyes glassy, his teeth set. Hilma Tree was dancing for the second time with Harran Derrick. She danced with infinite grace. Her cheeks were bright red, her eyes half-closed, and through her parted lips she drew from time to time a long, tremulous breath of pure delight. The music, the weaving colours, the heat of the air, by now a little oppressive, the monotony of repeated sensation, even the pain of physical fatigue had exalted all her senses. She was in a dreamy lethargy of happiness. It was her "first ball." She could have danced without stopping until morning. Minna Hooven and Cutter were "promenading." Mrs. Hooven, with little Hilda already asleep on her knees, never took her eyes from her daughter's gown. As often as Minna passed near her she vented an energetic "pst! pst!" The metal tip of a white draw string was showing from underneath the waist of Minna's dress. Mrs. Hooven was on the point of tears.

The solitary gayly apparelled clerk from Bonneville was in a fever of agitation. He had lost his elaborate programme card. Bewildered, beside himself with trepidation, he hurried about the room, jostled by the dancing couples, tripping over the feet of those who were seated; he peered distressfully under the chairs and about the floor, asking anxious questions.

Magnus Derrick, the centre of a listening circle of ranchers—Garnett from the Ruby rancho, Keast from the ranch of the same name, Gethings and Chattern of the San Pablo and Bonanza—stood near the great open doorway of the barn, discussing the possibility of a shortage in the world's wheat crop for the next year.

Abruptly the orchestra ceased playing with a roll of the snare drum, a flourish of the cornet and a prolonged growl of the bass viol. The dance broke up, the couples hurrying to their seats, leaving the gayly apparelled clerk suddenly isolated in the middle of the floor, rolling his eyes. The druggist released the Spanish-Mexican girl with mechanical precision out amidst the crowd of dancers. He bowed, dropping his chin upon his cravat; throughout the dance neither had hazarded a word. The girl found her way alone to a chair, but the druggist, sick from continually revolving in the same direction, walked unsteadily toward the wall. All at once the barn reeled around him; he fell down. There was a great laugh, but he scrambled to his feet and disappeared abruptly out into the night through the doorway of the barn, deathly pale, his hand upon his stomach.

Dabney, the old man whom nobody knew, approached the group of ranchers around Magnus Derrick and stood, a little removed, listening gravely to what the governor was saying, his chin sunk in his collar, silent, offering no opinions.

But the leader of the orchestra, with a great gesture of his violin bow, cried out:

"All take partners for the lancers and promenade around the hall!"

However, there was a delay. A little crowd formed around the musicians' platform; voices were raised; there was a commotion. Skeezicks, who played the big horn, accused the cornet and the snare-drum of stealing his cold lunch. At intervals he could be heard expostulating:

"Ah, no! at the end of the end! Render me the sausages, you, or less I break your throat! Aha! I know you. You are going to play me there a bad farce. My sausages and the pork sandwich, else I go away from this place!"

He made an exaggerated show of replacing his big horn in its case, but the by-standers raised a great protest. The sandwiches and one sausage were produced; the other had disappeared. In the end Skeezichs allowed himself to be appeased. The dance was resumed.

Half an hour later the gathering in the harness room was considerably reinforced. It was the corner of the barn toward which the male guests naturally gravitated. Harran Derrick, who only cared to dance with Hilma

Tree, was admitted. Garnett from the Ruby rancho and
Gethings from the San Pablo, came in a little afterwards.
A fourth bowl of punch was mixed, Annixter and Caraher clamouring into each other's face as to its ingre-
dients. Cigars were lighted. Soon the air of the room
became blue with an acrid haze of smoke. It was very
warm. Ranged in their chairs around the side of the
room, the guests emptied glass after glass.

Vanamee alone refused to drink. He sat a little to
one side, disassociating himself from what was going
forward, watching the others calmly, a little contemptuously, a cigarette in his fingers.

Hooven, after drinking his third glass, however, was
afflicted with a great sadness; his breast heaved with
immense sighs. He asserted that he was "obbressed;"
Cutter had taken his steer. He retired to a corner and
seated himself in a heap on his chair, his heels on the
rungs, wiping the tears from his eyes, refusing to be com-
forted.

Old Broderson startled Annixter, who sat next to him,
out of all measure by suddenly winking at him with
infinite craftiness.

"When I was a lad in Ukiah," he whispered hoarsely,
"I was a devil of a fellow with the girls; but Lordy!"
he nudged him slyly, "I wouldn't have it known!"

Of those who were drinking, Annixter alone retained
all his wits. Though keeping pace with the others, glass
for glass, the punch left him solid upon his feet, clear-
headed. The tough, cross-grained fibre of him seemed
proof against alcohol. Never in his life had he been
drunk. He prided himself upon his power of resistance.
It was his nature.

"Say!" exclaimed old Broderson, gravely addressing
the company, pulling at his beard uneasily—"say! I—I
—listen! I'm a devil of a fellow with the girls." He

wagged his head doggedly, shutting his eyes in a knowing fashion. "Yes, sir, I am. There was a young lady
in Ukiah—that was when I was a lad of seventeen. We
used to meet in the cemetery in the afternoons. I was
to go away to school at Sacramento, and the afternoon
I left we met in the cemetery and we stayed so long I
almost missed the train. Her name was Celestine."

There was a pause. The others waited for the rest of
the story.

"And afterwards?" prompted Annixter.

"Afterwards? Nothing afterwards. I never saw her
again. Her name was Celestine."

The company raised a chorus of derision, and Osterman cried ironically:

"Say! *that's* a pretty good one! Tell us another."

The old man laughed with the rest, believing he had
made another hit. He called Osterman to him, whispering in his ear:

"Sh! Look here! Some night you and I will go up
to San Francisco—hey? We'll go skylarking. We'll be
gay. Oh, I'm a—a—a rare old *buck*, I am! I ain't too
old. You'll see."

Annixter gave over the making of the fifth bowl of
punch to Osterman, who affirmed that he had a recipe
for a "fertiliser" from Solotari that would take the
plating off the ladle. He left him wrangling with Caraher, who still persisted in adding chartreuse, and stepped
out into the dance to see how things were getting on.

It was the interval between two dances. In and around
a stall at the farther end of the floor, where lemonade
was being served, was a great throng of young men.
Others hurried across the floor singly or by twos and
threes, gingerly carrying overflowing glasses to their
"partners," sitting in long rows of white and blue and
pink against the opposite wall, their mothers and older

sisters in a second dark-clothed rank behind them. A babel of talk was in the air, mingled with gusts of laughter. Everybody seemed having a good time. In the increasing heat the decorations of evergreen trees and festoons threw off a pungent aroma that suggested a Sunday-school Christmas festival. In the other stalls, lower down the barn, the young men had brought chairs, and in these deep recesses the most desperate love-making was in progress, the young man, his hair neatly parted, leaning with great solicitation over the girl, his "partner" for the moment, fanning her conscientiously, his arm carefully laid along the back of her chair.

By the doorway, Annixter met Sarria, who had stepped out to smoke a fat, black cigar. The set smile of amiability was still fixed on the priest's smooth, shiny face; the cigar ashes had left grey streaks on the front of his cassock. He avoided Annixter, fearing, no doubt, an allusion to his game cocks, and took up his position back of the second rank of chairs by the musicians' stand, beaming encouragingly upon every one who caught his eye.

Annixter was saluted right and left as he slowly went the round of the floor. At every moment he had to pause to shake hands and to listen to congratulations upon the size of his barn and the success of his dance. But he was distrait, his thoughts elsewhere; he did not attempt to hide his impatience when some of the young men tried to engage him in conversation, asking him to be introduced to their sisters, or their friends' sisters. He sent them about their business harshly, abominably rude, leaving a wake of angry disturbance behind him, sowing the seeds of future quarrels and renewed unpopularity. He was looking for Hilma Tree.

When at last he came unexpectedly upon her, standing near where Mrs. Tree was seated, some half-dozen young men hovering uneasily in her neighbourhood, all his audacity was suddenly stricken from him; his gruffness, his overbearing insolence vanished with an abruptness that left him cold. His old-time confusion and embarrassment returned to him. Instead of speaking to her as he intended, he affected not to see her, but passed by, his head in the air, pretending a sudden interest in a Japanese lantern that was about to catch fire.

But he had had a single distinct glimpse of her, definite, precise, and this glimpse was enough. Hilma had changed. The change was subtle, evanescent, hard to define, but not the less unmistakable. The excitement, the enchanting delight, the delicious disturbance of "the first ball," had produced its result. Perhaps there had only been this lacking. It was hard to say, but for that brief instant of time Annixter was looking at Hilma, the woman. She was no longer the young girl upon whom he might look down, to whom he might condescend, whose little, infantile graces were to be considered with amused toleration.

When Annixter returned to the harness room, he let himself into a clamour of masculine hilarity. Osterman had, indeed, made a marvellous "fertiliser," whiskey for the most part, diluted with champagne and lemon juice. The first round of this drink had been welcomed with a salvo of cheers. Hooven, recovering his spirits under its violent stimulation, spoke of "heving ut oudt mit Cudder, bei Gott," while Osterman, standing on a chair at the end of the room, shouted for a "few moments quiet, gentlemen," so that he might tell a certain story he knew.

But, abruptly, Annixter discovered that the liquors— the champagne, whiskey, brandy, and the like—were running low. This would never do. He felt that he would stand disgraced if it could be said afterward that he had not provided sufficient drink at his entertainment. He slipped out, unobserved, and, finding two of his ranch hands near the doorway, sent them down to the ranch house to bring up all the cases of "stuff" they found there.

However, when this matter had been attended to, Annixter did not immediately return to the harness room. On the floor of the barn a square dance was under way, the leader of the City Band calling the figures. Young Vacca indefatigably continued the rounds of the barn, paring candle after candle, possessed with this single idea of duty, pushing the dancers out of his way, refusing to admit that the floor was yet sufficiently slippery. The druggist had returned indoors, and leaned dejected and melancholy against the wall near the doorway, unable to dance, his evening's enjoyment spoiled. The gayly apparelled clerk from Bonneville had just involved himself in a deplorable incident. In a search for his handkerchief, which he had lost while trying to find his programme card, he had inadvertently wandered into the feed room, set apart as the ladies' dressing room, at the moment when Mrs. Hooven, having removed the waist of Minna's dress, was relacing her corsets. There was a tremendous scene. The clerk was ejected forcibly, Mrs. Hooven filling all the neighbourhood with shrill expostulation. A young man, Minna's "partner," who stood near the feed room door, waiting for her to come out, had invited the clerk, with elaborate sarcasm, to step outside for a moment; and the clerk, breathless, stupefied, hustled from hand to hand, remained petrified, with staring eyes, turning about and about, looking wildly from face to face, speechless, witless, wondering what had happened.

But the square dance was over. The City Band was just beginning to play a waltz. Annixter assuring himself that everything was going all right, was picking his way across the floor, when he came upon Hilma Tree quite alone, and looking anxiously among the crowd of dancers.

"Having a good time, Miss Hilma?" he demanded, pausing for a moment.

"Oh, am I, *just!*" she exclaimed. "The best time— but I don't know what has become of my partner. See! I'm left all alone—the only time this whole evening," she added proudly. "Have you seen him—my partner, sir? I forget his name. I only met him this evening, and I've met *so* many I can't begin to remember half of them. He was a young man from Bonneville—a clerk, I think, because I remember seeing him in a store there, and he wore the prettiest clothes!"

"I guess he got lost in the shuffle," observed Annixter. Suddenly an idea occurred to him. He took his resolution in both hands. He clenched his teeth.

"Say! look here, Miss Hilma. What's the matter with you and I stealing this one for ourselves? I don't mean to dance. I don't propose to make a jumping-jack of myself for some galoot to give me the laugh, but we'll walk around. Will you? What do you say?"

Hilma consented.

"I'm not so *very* sorry I missed my dance with that— that—little clerk," she said guiltily. "I suppose that's very bad of me, isn't it?"

Annixter fulminated a vigorous protest.

"I *am* so warm!" murmured Hilma, fanning herself with her handkerchief; "and, oh! *such* a good time as I have had! I was so afraid that I would be a wall-flower and sit up by mamma and papa the whole evening; and as it is, I have had every single dance, and even some dances I had to split. Oh-h!" she breathed, glancing lovingly around the barn, noting again the festoons of tri-coloured cambric, the Japanese lanterns, flaring lamps, and "decorations" of evergreen; "oh-h! it's all so lovely, just like a fairy story; and to think that it can't last but for one little evening, and that to-morrow morning one must wake up to the every-day things again!"

"Well," observed Annixter doggedly, unwilling that she should forget whom she ought to thank, "I did my best, and my best is as good as another man's, I guess."

Hilma overwhelmed him with a burst of gratitude which he gruffly pretended to deprecate. Oh, that was all right. It hadn't cost him much. He liked to see people having a good time himself, and the crowd did seem to be enjoying themselves. What did *she* think? Did things look lively enough? And how about herself —was she enjoying it?

Stupidly Annixter drove the question home again, at his wits' end as to how to make conversation. Hilma protested volubly she would never forget this night, adding:

"Dance! Oh, you don't know how I love it! I didn't know myself. I could dance all night and never stop once!"

Annixter was smitten with uneasiness. No doubt this "promenading" was not at all to her taste. Wondering what kind of a spectacle he was about to make of himself, he exclaimed:

"Want to dance now?"

"Oh, yes!" she returned.

They paused in their walk, and Hilma, facing him, gave herself into his arms. Annixter shut his teeth, the perspiration starting from his forehead. For five years he had abandoned dancing. Never in his best days had it been one of his accomplishments.

They hesitated a moment, waiting to catch the time from the musicians. Another couple bore down upon

them at precisely the wrong moment, jostling them out of
step. Annixter swore under his breath. His arm still
about the young woman, he pulled her over to one corner.
"Now," he muttered, "we'll try again."

A second time, listening to the one-two-three, one-two-
three cadence of the musicians, they endeavoured to get
under way. Annixter waited the fraction of a second
too long and stepped on Hilma's foot. On the third
attempt, having worked out of the corner, a pair of
dancers bumped into them once more, and as they were
recovering themselves another couple caromed violently
against Annixter so that he all but lost his footing. He
was in a rage. Hilma, very embarrassed, was trying not
to laugh, and thus they found themselves, out in the
middle of the floor, continually jostled from their position, holding clumsily to each other, stammering excuses
into one another's faces, when Delaney arrived.

He came with the suddenness of an explosion. There
was a commotion by the doorway, a rolling burst of
oaths, a furious stamping of hoofs, a wild scramble of
the dancers to either side of the room, and there he was.
He had ridden the buckskin at a gallop straight through
the doorway and out into the middle of the floor of the
barn.

Once well inside, Delaney hauled up on the cruel spade-
bit, at the same time driving home the spurs, and the
buckskin, without halting in her gait, rose into the air
upon her hind feet, and coming down again with a
thunder of iron hoofs upon the hollow floor, lashed out
with both heels simultaneously, her back arched, her head
between her knees. It was the running buck, and had
not Delaney been the hardest buster in the county, would
have flung him headlong like a sack of sand. But he
eased off the bit, gripping the mare's flanks with his
knees, and the buckskin, having long since known her

master, came to hand quivering, the bloody spume dripping from the bit upon the slippery floor.

Delaney had arrayed himself with painful elaboration,
determined to look the part, bent upon creating the impression, resolved that his appearance at least should
justify his reputation of being "bad." Nothing was
lacking—neither the campaign hat with up-turned brim,
nor the dotted blue handkerchief knotted behind the neck,
nor the heavy gauntlets stitched with red, nor—this above
all—the bear-skin "chaparejos," the hair trousers of the
mountain cowboy, the pistol holster low on the thigh. But
for the moment this holster was empty, and in his right
hand, the hammer at full cock, the chamber loaded, the
puncher flourished his teaser, an army Colt's, the lamp-
light dully reflected in the dark blue steel.

In a second of time the dance was a bedlam. The
musicians stopped with a discord, and the middle of the
crowded floor bared itself instantly. It was like sand
blown from off a rock; the throng of guests, carried
by an impulse that was not to be resisted, bore back
against the sides of the barn, overturning chairs, tripping
upon each other, falling down, scrambling to their feet
again, stepping over one another, getting behind each
other, diving under chairs, flattening themselves against
the wall—a wild, clamouring pell-mell, blind, deaf, panic-
stricken; a confused tangle of waving arms, torn muslin,
crushed flowers, pale faces, tangled legs, that swept in
all directions back from the centre of the floor, leaving
Annixter and Hilma, alone, deserted, their arms about
each other, face to face with Delaney, mad with alcohol,
bursting with remembered insult, bent on evil, reckless
of results.

After the first scramble for safety, the crowd fell quiet
for the fraction of an instant, glued to the walls, afraid
to stir, struck dumb and motionless with surprise and

terror, and in the instant's silence that followed Annixter, his eyes on Delaney, muttered rapidly to Hilma:

"Get back, get away to one side. The fool *might* shoot."

There was a second's respite afforded while Delaney occupied himself in quieting the buckskin, and in that second of time, at this moment of crisis, the wonderful thing occurred. Hilma, turning from Delaney, her hands clasped on Annixter's arm, her eyes meeting his, exclaimed:

"You, too!"

And that was all; but to Annixter it was a revelation. Never more alive to his surroundings, never more observant, he suddenly understood. For the briefest lapse of time he and Hilma looked deep into each other's eyes, and from that moment on, Annixter knew that Hilma cared.

The whole matter was brief as the snapping of a finger. Two words and a glance and all was done. But as though nothing had occurred, Annixter pushed Hilma from him, repeating harshly:

"Get back, I tell you. Don't you see he's got a gun? Haven't I enough on my hands without you?"

He loosed her clasp and his eyes once more on Delaney, moved diagonally backwards toward the side of the barn, pushing Hilma from him. In the end he thrust her away so sharply that she gave back with a long stagger; somebody caught her arm and drew her in, leaving Annixter alone once more in the middle of the floor, his hands in his coat pockets, watchful, alert, facing his enemy.

But the cow-puncher was not ready to come to grapples yet. Fearless, his wits gambolling under the lash of the alcohol, he wished to make the most of the occasion, maintaining the suspense, playing for the gallery. By touches of the hand and knee he kept the buckskin in continual, nervous movement, her hoofs clattering, snorting, tossing her head, while he, himself, addressing himself to Annixter, poured out a torrent of invective.

"Well, strike me blind if it ain't old Buck Annixter! He was going to show me off Quien Sabe at the toe of his boot, was he? Well, here's your chance,—with the ladies to see you do it. Gives a dance, does he, highfalutin' hoe-down in his barn and forgets to invite his old broncho-bustin' friend. But his friend don't forget him; no, he don't. He remembers little things, does his broncho-bustin' friend. Likes to see a dance hisself on occasion, his friend does. Comes anyhow, trustin' his welcome will be hearty; just to see old Buck Annixter dance, just to show Buck Annixter's friends how Buck can dance—dance all by hisself, a little hen-on-a-hot-plate dance when his broncho-bustin' friend asks him so polite. A little dance for the ladies, Buck. This feature of the entertainment is alone worth the price of admission. Tune up, Buck. Attention now! I'll give you the key."

He "fanned" his revolver, spinning it about his index finger by the trigger-guard with incredible swiftness, the twirling weapon a mere blur of blue steel in his hand. Suddenly and without any apparent cessation of the movement, he fired, and a little splinter of wood flipped into the air at Annixter's feet.

"Time!" he shouted, while the buckskin reared to the report. "Hold on—wait a minute. This place is too light to suit. That big light yonder is in my eyes. Look out, I'm going to throw lead."

A second shot put out the lamp over the musicians' stand. The assembled guests shrieked, a frantic, shrinking quiver ran through the crowd like the huddling of frightened rabbits in their pen.

Annixter hardly moved. He stood some thirty paces

from the buster, his hands still in his coat pockets, his eyes glistening, watchful.

Excitable and turbulent in trifling matters, when actual bodily danger threatened he was of an abnormal quiet.

"I'm watching you," cried the other. "Don't make any mistake about that. Keep your hands in your *coat* pockets, if you'd like to live a little longer, understand? And don't let me see you make a move toward your hip or your friends will be asked to identify you at the morgue to-morrow morning. When I'm bad, I'm called the Undertaker's Friend, so I am, and I'm that bad to-night that I'm scared of myself. They'll have to revise the census returns before I'm done with this place. Come on, now, I'm getting tired waiting. I come to see a dance."

"Hand over that horse, Delaney," said Annixter, without raising his voice, "and clear out."

The other affected to be overwhelmed with infinite astonishment, his eyes staring. He peered down from the saddle.

"Wh-a-a-t!" he exclaimed; "wh-a-a-t did you say? Why, I guess you must be looking for trouble; that's what I guess."

"There's where you're wrong, m'son," muttered Annixter, partly to Delaney, partly to himself. "If I was looking for trouble there wouldn't be any guess-work about it."

With the words he began firing. Delaney had hardly entered the barn before Annixter's plan had been formed. Long since his revolver was in the pocket of his coat, and he fired now through the coat itself, without withdrawing his hands.

Until that moment Annixter had not been sure of himself. There was no doubt that for the first few moments of the affair he would have welcomed with joy any reasonable excuse for getting out of the situation. But the sound of his own revolver gave him confidence. He whipped it from his pocket and fired again.

Abruptly the duel began, report following report, spurts of pale blue smoke jetting like the darts of short spears between the two men, expanding to a haze and drifting overhead in wavering strata. It was quite probable that no thought of killing each other suggested itself to either Annixter or Delaney. Both fired without aiming very deliberately. To empty their revolvers and avoid being hit was the desire common to both. They no longer vituperated each other. The revolvers spoke for them.

Long after, Annixter could recall this moment. For years he could with but little effort reconstruct the scene —the densely packed crowd flattened against the sides of the barn, the festoons of lanterns, the mingled smell of evergreens, new wood, sachets, and powder smoke; the vague clamour of distress and terror that rose from the throng of guests, the squealing of the buckskin, the uneven explosions of the revolvers, the reverberation of trampling hoofs, a brief glimpse of Harran Derrick's excited face at the door of the harness room, and in the open space in the centre of the floor, himself and Delaney, manœuvring swiftly in a cloud of smoke.

Annixter's revolver contained but six cartridges. Already it seemed to him as if he had fired twenty times. Without doubt the next shot was his last. Then what? He peered through the blue haze that with every discharge thickened between him and the buster. For his own safety he must "place" at least one shot. Delaney's chest and shoulders rose suddenly above the smoke close upon him as the distraught buckskin reared again. Annixter, for the first time during the fight, took definite aim, but before he could draw the trigger there was a great shout and he was aware of the buckskin, the bridle trailing, the saddle empty, plunging headlong across the floor, crashing into the line of chairs. Delaney was scrambling off the floor. There was blood on the buster's wrist and he no longer carried his revolver. Suddenly he turned and ran. The crowd parted right and left before him as he made toward the doorway. He disappeared.

Twenty men promptly sprang to the buckskin's head, but she broke away, and wild with terror, bewildered, blind, insensate, charged into the corner of the barn by the musicians' stand. She brought up against the wall with cruel force and with impact of a sack of stones; her head was cut. She turned and charged again, bull-like, the blood streaming from her forehead. The crowd, shrieking, melted before her rush. An old man was thrown down and trampled. The buckskin trod upon the dragging bridle, somersaulted into a confusion of chairs in one corner, and came down with a terrific clatter in a wild disorder of kicking hoofs and splintered wood. But a crowd of men fell upon her, tugging at the bit, sitting on her head, shouting, gesticulating. For five minutes she struggled and fought; then, by degrees, she recovered herself, drawing great sobbing breaths at long intervals that all but burst the girths, rolling her eyes in bewildered, supplicating fashion, trembling in every muscle, and starting and shrinking now and then like a young girl in hysterics. At last she lay quiet. The men allowed her to struggle to her feet. The saddle was removed and she was led to one of the empty stalls, where she remained the rest of the evening, her head low, her pasterns quivering, turning her head apprehensively from time to time, showing the white of one eye and at long intervals heaving a single prolonged sigh.

And an hour later the dance was progressing as evenly as though nothing in the least extraordinary had occurred. The incident was closed—that abrupt swoop of terror and impending death dropping down there from out the darkness, cutting abruptly athwart the gayety of the moment, come and gone with the swiftness of a thunderclap. Many of the women had gone home, taking their men with them; but the great bulk of the crowd still remained, seeing no reason why the episode should interfere with the evening's enjoyment, resolved to hold the ground for mere bravado, if for nothing else. Delaney would not come back, of that everybody was persuaded, and in case he should, there was not found wanting fully half a hundred young men who would give him a dressing down, by jingo! They had been too surprised to act when Delaney had first appeared, and before they knew where they were at, the buster had cleared out. In another minute, just another second, they would have shown him—yes, sir, by jingo!—ah, you bet!

On all sides the reminiscences began to circulate. At least one man in every three had been involved in a gun fight at some time of his life. "Ah, you ought to have seen in Yuba County one time—" "Why, in Butte County in the early days—" "Pshaw! this to-night wasn't anything! Why, once in a saloon in Arizona when I was there—" and so on, over and over again. Osterman solemnly asserted that he had seen a greaser sawn in two in a Nevada sawmill. Old Broderson had witnessed a Vigilante lynching in '55 on California Street in San Francisco. Dyke recalled how once in his engineering days he had run over a drunk at a street crossing. Gethings of the San Pablo had taken a shot at a highwayman. Hooven had bayonetted a French *Chasseur* at Sedan. An old Spanish-Mexican, a centenarian from Guadalajara, remembered Fremont's stand

on a mountain top in San Benito County. The druggist
had fired at a burglar trying to break into his store one
New Year's eve. Young Vacca had seen a dog shot in
Guadalajara. Father Sarria had more than once admin-
istered the sacraments to Portuguese desperadoes dying
of gunshot wounds. Even the women recalled terrible
scenes. Mrs. Cutter recounted to an interested group
how she had seen a claim jumped in Placer County in
1851, when three men were shot, falling in a fusillade of
rifle shots, and expiring later upon the floor of her kitchen
while she looked on. Mrs. Dyke had been in a stage
hold-up, when the shotgun messenger was murdered.
Stories by the hundreds went the round of the company.
The air was surcharged with blood, dying groans, the
reek of powder smoke, the crack of rifles. All the
legends of '49, the violent, wild life of the early days,
were recalled to view, defiling before them there in an
endless procession under the glare of paper lanterns and
kerosene lamps.

But the affair had aroused a combative spirit amongst
the men of the assembly. Instantly a spirit of aggression, of truculence, swelled up underneath waistcoats
and starched shirt bosoms. More than one offender was
promptly asked to " step outside." It was like young
bucks excited by an encounter of stags, lowering their
horns upon the slightest provocation, showing off before
the does and fawns. Old quarrels were remembered.
One sought laboriously for slights and insults, veiled in
ordinary conversation. The sense of personal honour became refined to a delicate, fine point. Upon the slightest
pretext there was a haughty drawing up of the figure,
a twisting of the lips into a smile of scorn. Caraher
spoke of shooting S. Behrman on sight before the end
of the week. Twice it became necessary to separate
Hooven and Cutter, renewing their quarrel as to the

ownership of the steer. All at once Minna Hooven's "partner" fell upon the gayly apparelled clerk from Bonneville, pummelling him with his fists, hustling him out of the hall, vociferating that Miss Hooven had been grossly insulted. It took three men to extricate the clerk from his clutches, dazed, gasping, his collar unfastened and sticking up into his face, his eyes staring wildly into the faces of the crowd.

But Annixter, bursting with pride, his chest thrown out, his chin in the air, reigned enthroned in a circle of adulation. He was the Hero. To shake him by the hand was an honour to be struggled for. One clapped him on the back with solemn nods of approval. " There's the *boy* for you;" " There was nerve for you;" " What's the matter with Annixter?" " How about *that* for sand, and how was *that* for a *shot?*" " Why, Apache Kid couldn't have bettered that." " Cool enough." " Took a steady eye and a sure hand to make a shot like that." " There was a shot that would be told about in Tulare County fifty years to come."

Annixter had refrained from replying, all ears to this conversation, wondering just what had happened. He knew only that Delaney had run, leaving his revolver and a spatter of blood behind him. By degrees, however, he ascertained that his last shot but one had struck Delaney's pistol hand, shattering it and knocking the revolver from his grip. He was overwhelmed with astonishment. Why, after the shooting began he had not so much as seen Delaney with any degree of plainness. The whole affair was a whirl.

" Well, where did *you* learn to shoot *that* way?" some one in the crowd demanded. Annixter moved his shoulders with a gesture of vast unconcern.

" Oh," he observed carelessly, " it's not my *shooting* that ever worried *me,* m'son."

The crowd gaped with delight. There was a great wagging of heads.

" Well, I guess not."

" No, sir, not much."

" Ah, no, you bet not."

When the women pressed around him, shaking his hands, declaring that he had saved their daughters' lives, Annixter assumed a pose of superb deprecation, the modest self-obliteration of the chevalier. He delivered himself of a remembered phrase, very elegant, refined. It was Lancelot after the tournament, Bayard receiving felicitations after the battle.

" Oh, don't say anything about it," he murmured. " I only did what any man would have done in my place."

To restore completely the equanimity of the company, he announced supper. This he had calculated as a tremendous surprise. It was to have been served at midnight, but the irruption of Delaney had dislocated the order of events, and the tables were brought in an hour ahead of time. They were arranged around three sides of the barn and were loaded down with cold roasts of beef, cold chickens and cold ducks, mountains of sandwiches, pitchers of milk and lemonade, entire cheeses, bowls of olives, plates of oranges and nuts. The advent of this supper was received with a volley of applause. The musicians played a quick step. The company threw themselves upon the food with a great scraping of chairs and a vast rustle of muslins, tarletans, and organdies; soon the clatter of dishes was a veritable uproar. The tables were taken by assault. One ate whatever was nearest at hand, some even beginning with oranges and nuts and ending with beef and chicken. At the end the paper caps were brought on, together with the ice cream. All up and down the tables the pulled " crackers " snapped continually like the discharge of innumerable tiny rifles.

The caps of tissue paper were put on—" Phrygian Bonnets," " Magicians' Caps," " Liberty Caps; " the young
girls looked across the table at their vis-a-vis with bursts
of laughter and vigorous clapping of the hands.

The harness room crowd had a table to themselves, at
the head of which sat Annixter and at the foot Harran.
The gun fight had sobered Presley thoroughly. He sat
by the side of Vanamee, who ate but little, preferring
rather to watch the scene with calm observation, a little
contemptuous when the uproar around the table was too
boisterous, savouring of intoxication. Osterman rolled
bullets of bread and shot them with astonishing force
up and down the table, but the others—Dyke, old Broderson, Caraher, Harran Derrick, Hooven, Cutter, Garnett
of the Ruby rancho, Keast from the ranch of the same
name, Gethings of the San Pablo, and Chattern of the
Bonanza—occupied themselves with eating as much as
they could before the supper gave out. At a corner of
the table, speechless, unobserved, ignored, sat Dabney,
of whom nothing was known but his name, the silent
old man who made no friends. He ate and drank
quietly, dipping his sandwich in his lemonade.

Osterman ate all the olives he could lay his hands on,
a score of them, fifty of them, a hundred of them. He
touched no crumb of anything else. Old Broderson
stared at him, his jaw fallen. Osterman declared he had
once eaten a thousand on a bet. The men called each
others' attention to him. Delighted to create a sensation, Osterman persevered. The contents of an entire
bowl disappeared in his huge, reptilian slit of a mouth.
His cheeks of brownish red were extended, his bald forehead glistened. Colics seized upon him. His stomach
revolted. It was all one with him. He was satisfied,
contented. He was astonishing the people.

"Once I swallowed a tree toad," he told old Broderson, "by mistake. I was eating grapes, and the beggar lived in me three weeks. In rainy weather he would sing. You don't believe that," he vociferated. "Haven't I got the toad at home now in a bottle of alcohol."

And the old man, never doubting, his eyes starting, wagged his head in amazement.

"Oh, yes," cried Caraher, the length of the table, "that's a pretty good one. Tell us another."

"That reminds me of a story," hazarded old Broderson uncertainly; "once when I was a lad in Ukiah, fifty years——"

"Oh, yes," cried half a dozen voices, "*that's* a pretty good one. Tell us another."

"Eh—wh—what?" murmured Broderson, looking about him. "I—I don't know. It *was* Ukiah. You—you—you mix me all up."

As soon as supper was over, the floor was cleared again. The guests clamoured for a Virginia reel. The last quarter of the evening, the time of the most riotous fun, was beginning. The young men caught the girls who sat next to them. The orchestra dashed off into a rollicking movement. The two lines were formed. In a second of time the dance was under way again; the guests still wearing the Phrygian bonnets and liberty caps of pink and blue tissue paper.

But the group of men once more adjourned to the harness room. Fresh boxes of cigars were opened; the seventh bowl of fertiliser was mixed. Osterman poured the dregs of a glass of it upon his bald head, declaring that he could feel the hair beginning to grow.

But suddenly old Broderson rose to his feet.

"Aha," he cackled, "*I'm* going to have a dance, I am. Think I'm too old? I'll show you young fellows. I'm a regular old *rooster* when I get started."

He marched out into the barn, the others following,

holding their sides. He found an aged Mexican woman by the door and hustled her, all confused and giggling, into the Virginia reel, then at its height. Every one crowded around to see. Old Broderson stepped off with the alacrity of a colt, snapping his fingers, slapping his thigh, his mouth widening in an excited grin. The entire company of the guests shouted. The City Band redoubled their efforts; and the old man, losing his head, breathless, gasping, dislocated his stiff joints in his efforts. He became possessed, bowing, scraping, advancing, retreating, wagging his beard, cutting pigeons' wings, distraught with the music, the clamour, the applause, the effects of the fertiliser.

Annixter shouted:

" Nice eye, Santa Claus."

But Annixter's attention wandered. He searched for Hilma Tree, having still in mind the look in her eyes at that swift moment of danger. He had not seen her since then. At last he caught sight of her. She was not dancing, but, instead, was sitting with her " partner " at the end of the barn near her father and mother, her eyes wide, a serious expression on her face, her thoughts, no doubt, elsewhere. Annixter was about to go to her when he was interrupted by a cry.

Old Broderson, in the midst of a double shuffle, had clapped his hand to his side with a gasp, which he followed by a whoop of anguish. He had got a stitch or had started a twinge somewhere. With a gesture of resignation, he drew himself laboriously out of the dance, limping abominably, one leg dragging. He was heard asking for his wife. Old Mrs. Broderson took him in charge. She jawed him for making an exhibition of himself, scolding as though he were a ten-year-old.

" Well, I want to know ! " she exclaimed, as he hobbled off, dejected and melancholy, leaning upon her arm, "thought he had to dance, indeed! What next? A gay old grandpa, this. He'd better be thinking of his coffin."

It was almost midnight. The dance drew towards its close in a storm of jubilation. The perspiring musicians toiled like galley slaves; the guests singing as they danced.

The group of men reassembled in the harness room. Even Magnus Derrick condescended to enter and drink a toast. Presley and Vanamee, still holding themselves aloof, looked on, Vanamee more and more disgusted. Dabney, standing to one side, overlooked and forgotten, continued to sip steadily at his glass, solemn, reserved. Garnett of the Ruby rancho, Keast from the ranch of the same name, Gethings of the San Pablo, and Chattern of the Bonanza, leaned back in their chairs, their waistcoats unbuttoned, their legs spread wide, laughing—they could not tell why. Other ranchers, men whom Annixter had never seen, appeared in the room, wheat growers from places as far distant as Goshen and Pixley; young men and old, proprietors of veritable principalities, hundreds of thousands of acres of wheat lands, a dozen of them, a score of them; men who were strangers to each other, but who made it a point to shake hands with Magnus Derrick, the "prominent man" of the valley. Old Broderson, whom every one had believed had gone home, returned, though much sobered, and took his place, refusing, however, to drink another spoonful.

Soon the entire number of Annixter's guests found themselves in two companies, the dancers on the floor of the barn, frolicking through the last figures of the Virginia reel and the boisterous gathering of men in the harness room, downing the last quarts of fertiliser. Both assemblies had been increased. Even the older people had joined in the dance, while nearly every one of the men who did not dance had found their way into the harness room. The two groups rivalled each other in their noise. Out on the floor of the barn was a very whirlwind of gayety, a tempest of laughter, hand-clapping and cries of amusement. In the harness room the confused shouting and singing, the stamping of heavy feet, set a quivering reverberation in the oil of the kerosene lamps, the flame of the candles in the Japanese lanterns flaring and swaying in the gusts of hilarity. At intervals, between the two, one heard the music, the wailing of the violins, the vigorous snarling of the cornet, and the harsh, incessant rasping of the snare drum.

And at times all these various sounds mingled in a single vague note, huge, clamorous, that rose up into the night from the colossal, reverberating compass of the barn and sent its echoes far off across the unbroken levels of the surrounding ranches, stretching out to infinity under the clouded sky, calm, mysterious, still.

Annixter, the punch bowl clasped in his arms, was pouring out the last spoonful of liquor into Caraher's glass when he was aware that some one was pulling at the sleeve of his coat. He set down the punch bowl.

"Well, where did *you* come from?" he demanded.

It was a messenger from Bonneville, the uniformed boy that the telephone company employed to carry messages. He had just arrived from town on his bicycle, out of breath and panting.

"Message for you, sir. Will you sign?"

He held the book to Annixter, who signed the receipt, wondering.

The boy departed, leaving a thick envelope of yellow paper in Annixter's hands, the address typewritten, the word "Urgent" written in blue pencil in one corner.

Annixter tore it open. The envelope contained other sealed envelopes, some eight or ten of them, addressed to Magnus Derrick, Osterman, Broderson, Garnett, Keast, Gethings, Chattern, Dabney, and to Annixter himself,

Still puzzled, Annixter distributed the envelopes, muttering to himself:

"What's up now?"

The incident had attracted attention. A comparative quiet followed, the guests following the letters with their eyes as they were passed around the table. They fancied that Annixter had arranged a surprise.

Magnus Derrick, who sat next to Annixter, was the first to receive his letter. With a word of excuse he opened it.

"Read it, read it, Governor," shouted a half-dozen voices. "No secrets, you know. Everything above board here to-night."

Magnus cast a glance at the contents of the letter, then rose to his feet and read:

Magnus Derrick,
     Bonneville, Tulare Co., Cal.

Dear Sir:

By regrade of October 1st, the value of the railroad land you occupy, included in your ranch of Los Muertos, has been fixed at $27.00 per acre. The land is now for sale at that price to any one.

                    Yours, etc.,
          Cyrus Blakelee Ruggles,
                    Land Agent, P. and S. W. R. R.

     S. Behrman,
          Local Agent, P. and S. W. R. R.

In the midst of the profound silence that followed, Osterman was heard to exclaim grimly:

"*That's* a pretty good one. Tell us another."

But for a long moment this was the only remark.

The silence widened, broken only by the sound of torn

paper as Annixter, Osterman, old Broderson, Garnett, Keast, Gethings, Chattern, and Dabney opened and read their letters. They were all to the same effect, almost word for word like the Governor's. Only the figures and the proper names varied. In some cases the price per acre was twenty-two dollars. In Annixter's case it was thirty.

"And—and the company promised to sell to me, to—to all of us," gasped old Broderson, "at *two dollars and a half* an acre."

It was not alone the ranchers immediately around Bonneville who would be plundered by this move on the part of the Railroad. The "alternate section" system applied throughout all the San Joaquin. By striking at the Bonneville ranchers a terrible precedent was established. Of the crowd of guests in the harness room alone, nearly every man was affected, every man menaced with ruin. All of a million acres was suddenly involved.

Then suddenly the tempest burst. A dozen men were on their feet in an instant, their teeth set, their fists clenched, their faces purple with rage. Oaths, curses, maledictions exploded like the firing of successive mines. Voices quivered with wrath, hands flung upward, the fingers hooked, prehensile, trembled with anger. The sense of wrongs, the injustices, the oppression, extortion, and pillage of twenty years suddenly culminated and found voice in a raucous howl of execration. For a second there was nothing articulate in that cry of savage exasperation, nothing even intelligent. It was the human animal hounded to its corner, exploited, harried to its last stand, at bay, ferocious, terrible, turning at last with bared teeth and upraised claws to meet the death grapple. It was the hideous squealing of the tormented brute, its back to the wall, defending its lair, its mate and its whelps, ready to bite, to rend, to trample, to batter out the life of The Enemy in a primeval, bestial welter of blood and fury.

The roar subsided to intermittent clamour, in the pauses of which the sounds of music and dancing made themselves audible once more.

" S. Behrman again," vociferated Harran Derrick.

" Chose his moment well," muttered Annixter. " Hits his hardest when we're all rounded up having a good time."

" Gentlemen, this is ruin."

" What's to be done now? "

" *Fight!* My God! do you think we are going to stand this? Do you think we *can?* "

The uproar swelled again. The clearer the assembly of ranchers understood the significance of this move on the part of the Railroad, the more terrible it appeared, the more flagrant, the more intolerable. Was it possible, was it within the bounds of imagination that this tyranny should be contemplated? But they knew—past years had driven home the lesson—the implacable, iron monster with whom they had to deal, and again and again the sense of outrage and oppression lashed them to their feet, their mouths wide with curses, their fists clenched tight, their throats hoarse with shouting.

" Fight! How fight? What *are* you going to do? "

" If there's a law in this land——"

" If there is, it is in Shelgrim's pocket. Who owns the courts in California? Ain't it Shelgrim? "

" God damn him."

" Well, how long are you going to stand it? How long before you'll settle up accounts with six inches of plugged gas-pipe? "

" And our contracts, the solemn pledges of the corporation to sell to us first of all——"

"And now the land is for sale to anybody."

"Why, it is a question of my home. Am I to be turned
out? Why, I have put eight thousand dollars into improving this land."

"And I six thousand, and now that I have, the Railroad grabs it."

"And the system of irrigating ditches that Derrick
and I have been laying out. There's thousands of dollars
in that!"

"I'll fight this out till I've spent every cent of my
money."

"Where? In the courts that the company owns?"

"Think I am going to give in to this? Think I am to
get off my land? By God, gentlemen, law or no law,
railroad or no railroad, *I—will—not.*"

"Nor I."

"Nor I."

"Nor I."

"This is the last. Legal means first; if those fail—
the shotgun."

"They can kill me. They can shoot me down, but
I'll die—die fighting for my home—before I'll give in to
this."

At length Annixter made himself heard:

"All out of the room but the ranch owners," he
shouted. "Hooven, Caraher, Dyke, you'll have to clear
out. This is a family affair. Presley, you and your
friend can remain."

Reluctantly the others filed through the door. There
remained in the harness room—besides Vanamee and
Presley—Magnus Derrick, Annixter, old Broderson,
Harran, Garnett from the Ruby rancho, Keast from the
ranch of the same name, Gethings of the San Pablo,
Chattern of the Bonanza, about a score of others, ranchers from various parts of the county, and, last of all,

Dabney, ignored, silent, to whom nobody spoke and who, as yet, had not uttered a word.

But the men who had been asked to leave the harness room spread the news throughout the barn. It was repeated from lip to lip. One by one the guests dropped out of the dance. Groups were formed. By swift degrees the gayety lapsed away. The Virginia reel broke up. The musicians ceased playing, and in the place of the noisy, effervescent revelry of the previous half hour, a subdued murmur filled all the barn, a mingling of whispers, lowered voices, the coming and going of light footsteps, the uneasy shifting of positions, while from behind the closed doors of the harness room came a prolonged, sullen hum of anger and strenuous debate. The dance came to an abrupt end. The guests, unwilling to go as yet, stunned, distressed, stood clumsily about, their eyes vague, their hands swinging at their sides, looking stupidly into each others' faces. A sense of impending calamity, oppressive, foreboding, gloomy, passed through the air overhead in the night, a long shiver of anguish and of terror, mysterious, despairing.

In the harness room, however, the excitement continued unchecked. One rancher after another delivered himself of a torrent of furious words. There was no order, merely the frenzied outcry of blind fury. One spirit alone was common to all—resistance at whatever cost and to whatever lengths.

Suddenly Osterman leaped to his feet, his bald head gleaming in the lamp-light, his red ears distended, a flood of words filling his great, horizontal slit of a mouth, his comic actor's face flaming. Like the hero of a melodrama, he took stage with a great sweeping gesture.

"*Organisation*," he shouted, "that must be our watchword. The curse of the ranchers is that they fritter away their strength. Now, we must stand together, now,

now. Here's the crisis, here's the moment. Shall we
meet it? *I call for the League.* Not next week, not to-
morrow, not in the morning, but now, now, now, this
very moment, before we go out of that door. Every one
of us here to join it, to form the beginnings of a vast
organisation, banded together to death, if needs be, for
the protection of our rights and homes. Are you ready?
Is it now or never? I call for the League."

Instantly there was a shout. With an actor's instinct,
Osterman had spoken at the precise psychological moment.
He carried the others off their feet, glib, dexterous, voluble. Just what was meant by the League the others did
not know, but it was something, a vague engine, a machine with which to fight. Osterman had not done speaking before the room rang with outcries, the crowd of
men shouting, for what they did not know.

"The League! The League!"

"Now, to-night, this moment; sign our names before
we leave."

"He's right. Organisation! The League!"

"We have a committee at work already," Osterman
vociferated. "I am a member, and also Mr. Broderson,
Mr. Annixter, and Mr. Harran Derrick. What our aims
are we will explain to you later. Let this committee be
the nucleus of the League—temporarily, at least. Trust
us. We are working for you and with you. Let this
committee be merged into the larger committee of the
League, and for President of the League "—he paused
the fraction of a second—" for President there can be
but one name mentioned, one man to whom we all must
look as leader—Magnus Derrick."

The Governor's name was received with a storm of
cheers. The harness room reëchoed with shouts of:

"Derrick! Derrick!"

"Magnus for President!"

"Derrick, our natural leader."

"Derrick, Derrick, Derrick for President."

Magnus rose to his feet. He made no gesture. Erect as a cavalry officer, tall, thin, commanding, he dominated the crowd in an instant. There was a moment's hush.

"Gentlemen," he said, "if organisation is a good word, moderation is a better one. The matter is too grave for haste. I would suggest that we each and severally return to our respective homes for the night, sleep over what has happened, and convene again to-morrow, when we are calmer and can approach this affair in a more judicious mood. As for the honour with which you would inform me, I must affirm that that, too, is a matter for grave deliberation. This League is but a name as yet. To accept control of an organisation whose principles are not yet fixed is a heavy responsibility. I shrink from it——"

But he was allowed to proceed no farther. A storm of protest developed. There were shouts of:

"No, no. The League to-night and Derrick for President."

"We have been moderate too long."

"The League first, principles afterward."

"We can't wait," declared Osterman. "Many of us cannot attend a meeting to-morrow. Our business affairs would prevent it. Now we are all together. I propose a temporary chairman and secretary be named and a ballot be taken. But first the League. Let us draw up a set of resolutions to stand together, for the defence of our homes, to death, if needs be, and each man present affix his signature thereto."

He subsided amidst vigorous applause. The next quarter of an hour was a vague confusion, every one talking at once, conversations going on in low tones in

various corners of the room. Ink, pens, and a sheaf of
foolscap were brought from the ranch house. A set of
resolutions was draughted, having the force of a pledge,
organising the League of Defence. Annixter was the
first to sign. Others followed, only a few holding back,
refusing to join till they had thought the matter over.
The roll grew; the paper circulated about the table;
each signature was welcomed by a salvo of cheers. At
length, it reached Harran Derrick, who signed amid
tremendous uproar. He released the pen only to shake
a score of hands.

"Now, Magnus Derrick."

"Gentlemen," began the Governor, once more rising,
"I beg of you to allow me further consideration. Gentlemen——"

He was interrupted by renewed shouting.

"No, no, now or never. Sign, join the League."

"Don't leave us. We look to you to help."

But presently the excited throng that turned their
faces towards the Governor were aware of a new face at
his elbow. The door of the harness room had been left
unbolted and Mrs. Derrick, unable to endure the heart-
breaking suspense of waiting outside, had gathered up
all her courage and had come into the room. Trembling,
she clung to Magnus's arm, her pretty light-brown hair
in disarray, her large young girl's eyes wide with terror
and distrust. What was about to happen she did not
understand, but these men were clamouring for Magnus
to pledge himself to something, to some terrible course
of action, some ruthless, unscrupulous battle to the death
with the iron-hearted monster of steel and steam. Nerved
with a coward's intrepidity, she, who so easily obliterated
herself, had found her way into the midst of this frantic
crowd, into this hot, close room, reeking of alcohol and
tobacco smoke, into this atmosphere surcharged with

hatred and curses. She seized her husband's arm imploring, distraught with terror.

"No, no," she murmured; "no, don't sign."

She was the feather caught in the whirlwind. *En masse,* the crowd surged toward the erect figure of the Governor, the pen in one hand, his wife's fingers in the other, the roll of signatures before him. The clamour was deafening; the excitement culminated brusquely. Half a hundred hands stretched toward him; thirty voices, at top pitch, implored, expostulated, urged, almost commanded. The reverberation of the shouting was as the plunge of a cataract.

It was the uprising of The People; the thunder of the outbreak of revolt; the mob demanding to be led, aroused at last, imperious, resistless, overwhelming. It was the blind fury of insurrection, the brute, many-tongued, red-eyed, bellowing for guidance, baring its teeth, unsheathing its claws, imposing its will with the abrupt, resistless pressure of the relaxed piston, inexorable, knowing no pity.

"No, no," implored Annie Derrick. "No, Magnus, don't sign."

"He *must,*" declared Harran, shouting in her ear to make himself heard, "he must. Don't you understand?"

Again the crowd surged forward, roaring. Mrs. Derrick was swept back, pushed to one side. Her husband no longer belonged to her. She paid the penalty for being the wife of a great man. The world, like a colossal iron wedge, crushed itself between. She was thrust to the wall. The throng of men, stamping, surrounded Magnus; she could no longer see him, but, terror-struck, she listened. There was a moment's lull, then a vast thunder of savage jubilation. Magnus had signed.

Harran found his mother leaning against the wall, her hands shut over her ears; her eyes, dilated with fear, brimming with tears. He led her from the harness room to the outer room, where Mrs. Tree and Hilma took charge of her, and then, impatient, refusing to answer the hundreds of anxious questions that assailed him, hurried back to the harness room.

Already the balloting was in progress, Osterman acting as temporary chairman. On the very first ballot he was made secretary of the League *pro tem.,* and Magnus unanimously chosen for its President. An executive committee was formed, which was to meet the next day at the Los Muertos ranch house.

It was half-past one o'clock. In the barn outside the greater number of the guests had departed. Long since the musicians had disappeared. There only remained the families of the ranch owners involved in the meeting in the harness room. These huddled in isolated groups in corners of the garish, echoing barn, the women in their wraps, the young men with their coat collars turned up against the draughts that once more made themselves felt.

For a long half hour the loud hum of eager conversation continued to issue from behind the door of the harness room. Then, at length, there was a prolonged scraping of chairs. The session was over. The men came out in groups, searching for their families.

At once the homeward movement began. Every one was worn out. Some of the ranchers' daughters had gone to sleep against their mothers' shoulders.

Billy, the stableman, and his assistant were awakened, and the teams were hitched up. The stable yard was full of a maze of swinging lanterns and buggy lamps. The horses fretted, champing the bits; the carry-alls creaked with the straining of leather and springs as they received their loads. At every instant one heard the rattle of wheels, as vehicle after vehicle disappeared in the night.

A fine, drizzling rain was falling, and the lamps began to show dim in a vague haze of orange light.

Magnus Derrick was the last to go. At the doorway of the barn he found Annixter, the roll of names—which it had been decided he was to keep in his safe for the moment—under his arm. Silently the two shook hands. Magnus departed. The grind of the wheels of his carryall grated sharply on the gravel of the driveway in front of the ranch house, then, with a hollow roll across a little plank bridge, gained the roadway. For a moment the beat of the horses' hoofs made itself heard on the roadway. It ceased. Suddenly there was a great silence.

Annixter, in the doorway of the great barn, stood looking about him for a moment, alone, thoughtful. The barn was empty. That astonishing evening had come to an end. The whirl of things and people, the crowd of dancers, Delaney, the gun fight, Hilma Tree, her eyes fixed on him in mute confession, the rabble in the harness room, the news of the regrade, the fierce outburst of wrath, the hasty organising of the League, all went spinning confusedly through his recollection. But he was exhausted. Time enough in the morning to think it all over. By now it was raining sharply. He put the roll of names into his inside pocket, threw a sack over his head and shoulders, and went down to the ranch house.

But in the harness room, lighted by the glittering lanterns and flaring lamps, in the midst of overturned chairs, spilled liquor, cigar stumps, and broken glasses, Vanamee and Presley still remained talking, talking. At length, they rose, and came out upon the floor of the barn and stood for a moment looking about them.

Billy, the stableman, was going the rounds of the walls, putting out light after light. By degrees, the vast interior was growing dim. Upon the roof overhead the rain drummed incessantly, the eaves dripping. The floor was littered with pine needles, bits of orange peel, ends and fragments of torn organdies and muslins and bits of tissue paper from the " Phrygian Bonnets " and " Liberty Caps." The buckskin mare in the stall, dozing on three legs, changed position with a long sigh. The sweat stiffening the hair upon her back and loins, as it dried, gave off a penetrating, ammoniacal odour that mingled with the stale perfume of sachet and wilted flowers.

Presley and Vanamee stood looking at the deserted barn. There was a long silence. Then Presley said:

" Well . . . what do you think of it all? "

" I think," answered Vanamee slowly, " I think that there was a dance in Brussels the night before Waterloo."

BOOK II

I

In his office at San Francisco, seated before a massive desk of polished redwood, very ornate, Lyman Derrick sat dictating letters to his typewriter, on a certain morning early in the spring of the year. The subdued monotone of his voice proceeded evenly from sentence to sentence, regular, precise, businesslike.

" I have the honour to acknowledge herewith your favour of the 14th instant, and in reply would state——"

" Please find enclosed draft upon New Orleans to be applied as per our understanding——"

" In answer to your favour No. 1107, referring to the case of the City and County of San Francisco against Excelsior Warehouse & Storage Co., I would say——"

His voice continued, expressionless, measured, distinct. While he spoke, he swung slowly back and forth in his leather swivel chair, his elbows resting on the arms, his pop eyes fixed vaguely upon the calendar on the opposite wall, winking at intervals when he paused, searching for a word.

" That's all for the present," he said at length.

Without reply, the typewriter rose and withdrew, thrusting her pencil into the coil of her hair, closing the door behind her, softly, discreetly.

When she had gone, Lyman rose, stretching himself, putting up three fingers to hide his yawn. To further loosen his muscles, he took a couple of turns the length of the room, noting with satisfaction its fine appointments, the padded red carpet, the dull olive green tint of the walls, the few choice engravings—portraits of Marshall, Taney, Field, and a coloured lithograph—excellently done—of the Grand Cañon of the Colorado—the deep-seated leather chairs, the large and crowded bookcase (topped with a bust of James Lick, and a huge greenish globe), the waste basket of woven coloured grass, made by Navajo Indians, the massive silver inkstand on the desk, the elaborate filing cabinet, complete in every particular, and the shelves of tin boxes, padlocked, impressive, grave, bearing the names of clients, cases and estates.

He was between thirty-one and thirty-five years of age. Unlike Harran, he resembled his mother, but he was much darker than Annie Derrick and his eyes were much fuller, the eyeball protruding, giving him a pop-eyed, foreign expression, quite unusual and unexpected. His hair was black, and he wore a small, tight, pointed mustache, which he was in the habit of pushing delicately upward from the corners of his lips with the ball of his thumb, the little finger extended. As often as he made this gesture, he prefaced it with a little twisting gesture of the forearm in order to bring his cuff into view, and, in fact, this movement by itself was habitual.

He was dressed carefully, his trousers creased, a pink rose in his lapel. His shoes were of patent leather, his cutaway coat was of very rough black cheviot, his double-breasted waistcoat of tan covert cloth with buttons of smoked pearl. An Ascot scarf—a great puff of heavy black silk—was at his neck, the knot transfixed by a tiny golden pin set off with an opal and four small diamonds.

At one end of the room were two great windows of plate glass, and pausing at length before one of these, Lyman selected a cigarette from his curved box of oxydized silver, lit it and stood looking down and out, willing to be idle for a moment, amused and interested in the view.

His office was on the tenth floor of the *Exchange Building*, a beautiful, tower-like affair of white stone, that stood on the corner of Market Street near its inter-section with Kearney, the most imposing office building of the city.

Below him the city swarmed tumultuous through its grooves, the cable-cars starting and stopping with a gay jangling of bells and a strident whirring of jostled glass windows. Drays and carts clattered over the cobbles, and an incessant shuffling of thousands of feet rose from the pavement. Around Lotta's fountain the baskets of the flower sellers, crammed with chrysanthemums, violets, pinks, roses, lilies, hyacinths, set a brisk note of colour in the grey of the street.

But to Lyman's notion the general impression of this centre of the city's life was not one of strenuous business activity. It was a continuous interest in small things, a people ever willing to be amused at trifles, refusing to consider serious matters—good-natured, allowing them-selves to be imposed upon, taking life easily—generous, companionable, enthusiastic; living, as it were, from day to day, in a place where the luxuries of life were had without effort; in a city that offered to consideration the restlessness of a New York, without its earnestness; the serenity of a Naples, without its languor; the romance of a Seville, without its picturesqueness.

As Lyman turned from the window, about to resume his work, the office boy appeared at the door.

"The man from the lithograph company, sir," an-nounced the boy.

"Well, what does he want?" demanded Lyman, add-ing, however, upon the instant: "Show him in."

A young man entered, carrying a great bundle, which he deposited on a chair, with a gasp of relief, exclaiming, all out of breath:

" From the Standard Lithograph Company."

" What is? "

" Don't know," replied the other.　" Maps, I guess."

" I don't want any maps.　Who sent them?　I guess you're mistaken."

Lyman tore the cover from the top of the package, drawing out one of a great many huge sheets of white paper, folded eight times.　Suddenly, he uttered an exclamation:

"Ah, I see.　They *are* maps.　But these should not have come here.　They are to go to the regular office for distribution."　He wrote a new direction on the label of the package: " Take them to that address," he went on. " I'll keep this one here.　The others go to that address. If you see Mr. Darrell, tell him that Mr. Derrick—you get the name—Mr. Derrick may not be able to get around this afternoon, but to go ahead with any business just the same."

The young man departed with the package and Lyman, spreading out the map upon the table, remained for some time studying it thoughtfully.

It was a commissioner's official railway map of the State of California, completed to March 30th of that year. Upon it the different railways of the State were accurately plotted in various colours, blue, green, yellow. However, the blue, the yellow, and the green were but brief traceries, very short, isolated, unimportant.　At a little distance these could hardly be seen.　The whole map was gridironed by a vast, complicated network of red lines marked P. and S. W. R. R.　These centralised at San Francisco and thence ramified and spread north, east, and south, to every quarter of the State.　From

Coles, in the topmost corner of the map, to Yuma in the lowest, from Reno on one side to San Francisco on the other, ran the plexus of red, a veritable system of blood circulation, complicated, dividing, and reuniting, branching, splitting, extending, throwing out feelers, off-shoots, tap roots, feeders—diminutive little blood suckers that shot out from the main jugular and went twisting up into some remote county, laying hold upon some forgotten village or town, involving it in one of a myriad branching coils, one of a hundred tentacles, drawing it, as it were, toward that centre from which all this system sprang.

The map was white, and it seemed as if all the colour which should have gone to vivify the various counties, towns, and cities marked upon it had been absorbed by that huge, sprawling organism, with its ruddy arteries converging to a central point. It was as though the State had been sucked white and colourless, and against this pallid background the red arteries of the monster stood out, swollen with life-blood, reaching out to infinity, gorged to bursting; an excrescence, a gigantic parasite fattening upon the life-blood of an entire commonwealth.

However, in an upper corner of the map appeared the names of the three new commissioners: Jones McNish for the first district, Lyman Derrick for the second, and James Darrell for the third.

Nominated in the Democratic State convention in the fall of the preceding year, Lyman, backed by the coteries of San Francisco bosses in the pay of his father's political committee of ranchers, had been elected together with Darrell, the candidate of the Pueblo and Mojave road, and McNish, the avowed candidate of the Pacific and Southwestern. Darrell was rabidly against the P. and S. W., McNish rabidly for it. Lyman was supposed to be the conservative member of the board, the ranchers' candidate, it was true, and faithful to their interests, but a calm man, deliberative, swayed by no such violent emotions as his colleagues.

Osterman's dexterity had at last succeeded in entangling Magnus inextricably in the new politics. The famous League, organised in the heat of passion the night of Annixter's barn dance, had been consolidated all through the winter months. Its executive committee, of which Magnus was chairman, had been, through Osterman's manipulation, merged into the old committee composed of Broderson, Annixter, and himself. Promptly thereat he had resigned the chairmanship of this committee, thus leaving Magnus at its head. Precisely as Osterman had planned, Magnus was now one of them. The new committee accordingly had two objects in view : to resist the attempted grabbing of their lands by the Railroad, and to push forward their own secret scheme of electing a board of railroad commissioners who should regulate wheat rates so as to favour the ranchers of the San Joaquin. The land cases were promptly taken to the courts and the new grading—fixing the price of the lands at twenty and thirty dollars an acre instead of two—bitterly and stubbornly fought. But delays occurred, the process of the law was interminable, and in the intervals the committee addressed itself to the work of seating the "Ranchers' Commission," as the projected Board of Commissioners came to be called.

It was Harran who first suggested that his brother, Lyman, be put forward as the candidate for this district. At once the proposition had a great success. Lyman seemed made for the place. While allied by every tie of blood to the ranching interests, he had never been identified with them. He was city-bred. The Railroad would not be over-suspicious of him. He was a good lawyer, a good business man, keen, clear-headed, farsighted, had already some practical knowledge of politics, having served a term as assistant district attorney, and even at the present moment occupying the position of sheriff's attorney. More than all, he was the son of Magnus Derrick; he could be relied upon, could be trusted implicitly to remain loyal to the ranchers' cause.

The campaign for Railroad Commissioner had been very interesting. At the very outset Magnus's committee found itself involved in corrupt politics. The primaries had to be captured at all costs and by any means, and when the convention assembled it was found necessary to buy outright the votes of certain delegates. The campaign fund raised by contributions from Magnus, Annixter, Broderson, and Osterman was drawn upon to the extent of five thousand dollars.

Only the committee knew of this corruption. The League, ignoring ways and means, supposed as a matter of course that the campaign was honorably conducted.

For a whole week after the consummation of this part of the deal, Magnus had kept to his house, refusing to be seen, alleging that he was ill, which was not far from the truth. The shame of the business, the loathing of what he had done, were to him things unspeakable. He could no longer look Harran in the face. He began a course of deception with his wife. More than once, he had resolved to break with the whole affair, resigning his position, allowing the others to proceed without him. But now it was too late. He was pledged. He had joined the League. He was its chief, and his defection might mean its disintegration at the very time when it needed all its strength to fight the land cases. More than a mere deal in bad politics was involved. There was the land grab. His withdrawal from an unholy cause would mean the weakening, perhaps the collapse, of another cause that he believed to be righteous as truth itself. He was hopelessly caught in the mesh. Wrong seemed indissolubly knitted into the texture of Right. He was blinded, dizzied, overwhelmed, caught in the current of events, and hurried along he knew not where. He resigned himself.

In the end, and after much ostentatious opposition on the part of the railroad heelers, Lyman was nominated and subsequently elected.

When this consummation was reached Magnus, Osterman, Broderson, and Annixter stared at each other. Their wildest hopes had not dared to fix themselves upon so easy a victory as this. It was not believable that the corporation would allow itself to be fooled so easily, would rush open-eyed into the trap. How had it happened?

Osterman, however, threw his hat into the air with wild whoops of delight. Old Broderson permitted himself a feeble cheer. Even Magnus beamed satisfaction. The other members of the League, present at the time, shook hands all around and spoke of opening a few bottles on the strength of the occasion. Annixter alone was recalcitrant.

"It's too easy," he declared. "No, I'm not satisfied. Where's Shelgrim in all this? Why don't he show his hand, damn his soul? The thing is yellow, I tell you. There's a big fish in these waters somewheres. I don't know his name, and I don't know his game, but he's moving round off and on, just out of sight. If you think you've netted him, I *don't,* that's all I've got to say."

But he was jeered down as a croaker. There was the Commission. He couldn't get around that, could he? There was Darrell and Lyman Derrick, both pledged to the ranches. Good Lord, he was never satisfied. He'd be obstinate till the very last gun was fired. Why, if he got drowned in a river he'd float up-stream just to be contrary.

In the course of time, the new board was seated. For the first few months of its term, it was occupied in clearing up the business left over by the old board and in the completion of the railway map. But now, the decks were cleared. It was about to address itself to the consideration of a revision of the tariff for the carriage of grain between the San Joaquin Valley and tide-water.

Both Lyman and Darrell were pledged to an average ten per cent. cut of the grain rates throughout the entire State.

The typewriter returned with the letters for Lyman to sign, and he put away the map and took up his morning's routine of business, wondering, the while, what would become of his practice during the time he was involved in the business of the Ranchers' Railroad Commission.

But towards noon, at the moment when Lyman was drawing off a glass of mineral water from the siphon that stood at his elbow, there was an interruption. Some one rapped vigorously upon the door, which was immediately after opened, and Magnus and Harran came in, followed by Presley.

" Hello, hello! " cried Lyman, jumping up, extending his hands, " why, here's a surprise. I didn't expect you all till to-night. Come in, come in and sit down. Have a glass of sizz-water, Governor."

The others explained that they had come up from Bonneville the night before, as the Executive Committee of the League had received a despatch from the lawyers it had retained to fight the Railroad, that the judge of the court in San Francisco, where the test cases were being tried, might be expected to hand down his decision the next day.

Very soon after the announcement of the new grading of the ranchers' lands, the corporation had offered, through S. Behrman, to lease the disputed lands to the ranchers at a nominal figure. The offer had been angrily rejected, and the Railroad had put up the lands for sale at Ruggles's office in Bonneville. At the exorbitant price named, buyers promptly appeared—dummy buyers, beyond shadow of doubt, acting either for the Railroad or for S. Behrman—men hitherto unknown in the county, men without property, without money, adventurers, heelers. Prominent among them, and bidding for the railroad's holdings included on Annixter's ranch, was Delaney.

The farce of deeding the corporation's sections to these fictitious purchasers was solemnly gone through with at Ruggles's office, the Railroad guaranteeing them possession. The League refused to allow the supposed buyers to come upon the land, and the Railroad, faithful to its pledge in the matter of guaranteeing its dummies possession, at once began suits in ejectment in the district court in Visalia, the county seat.

It was the preliminary skirmish, the reconnaisance in force, the combatants feeling each other's strength, willing to proceed with caution, postponing the actual deathgrip for a while till each had strengthened its position and organised its forces.

During the time the cases were on trial at Visalia, S. Behrman was much in evidence in and about the courts. The trial itself, after tedious preliminaries, was brief. The ranchers lost. The test cases were immediately carried up to the United States Circuit Court in San Francisco. At the moment the decision of this court was pending.

"Why, this is news," exclaimed Lyman, in response to the Governor's announcement; "I did not expect them to be so prompt. I was in court only last week and there seemed to be no end of business ahead. I suppose you are very anxious?"

Magnus nodded. He had seated himself in one of Lyman's deep chairs, his grey top-hat, with its wide brim, on the floor beside him. His coat of black broadcloth that had been tightly packed in his valise, was yet wrinkled and creased; his trousers were strapped under his high boots. As he spoke, he stroked the bridge of his hawklike nose with his bent forefinger.

Leaning back in his chair, he watched his two sons with secret delight. To his eye, both were perfect specimens of their class, intelligent, well-looking, resourceful. He was intensely proud of them. He was never happier, never more nearly jovial, never more erect, more military, more alert, and buoyant than when in the company of his two sons. He honestly believed that no finer examples of young manhood existed throughout the entire nation.

"I think we should win in this court," Harran observed, watching the bubbles break in his glass. "The investigation has been much more complete than in the Visalia trial. Our case this time is too good. It has made too much talk. The court would not dare render a decision for the Railroad. Why, there's the agreement in black and white—and the circulars the Railroad issued. How *can* one get around those?"

"Well, well, we shall know in a few hours now," remarked Magnus.

"Oh," exclaimed Lyman, surprised, "it is for this morning, then. Why aren't you at the court?"

"It seemed undignified, boy," answered the Governor. "We shall know soon enough."

"Good God!" exclaimed Harran abruptly, "when I think of what is involved. Why, Lyman, it's our home, the ranch house itself, nearly all Los Muertos, practically our whole fortune, and just now when there is promise of an enormous crop of wheat. And it is not only us.

There are over half a million acres of the San Joaquin involved. In some cases of the smaller ranches, it is the confiscation of the whole of the rancher's land. If this thing goes through, it will absolutely beggar nearly a hundred men. Broderson wouldn't have a thousand acres to his name. Why, it's monstrous."

"But the corporations offered to lease these lands," remarked Lyman. "Are any of the ranchers taking up that offer—or are any of them buying outright?"

"Buying! At the new figure!" exclaimed Harran, "at twenty and thirty an acre! Why, there's not one in ten that *can*. They are land-poor. And as for leasing —leasing land they virtually own—no, there's precious few are doing that, thank God! That would be acknowledging the railroad's ownership right away—forfeiting their rights for good. None of the *Leaguers* are doing it, I know. That would be the rankest treachery."

He paused for a moment, drinking the rest of the mineral water, then interrupting Lyman, who was about to speak to Presley, drawing him into the conversation through politeness, said: "Matters are just romping right along to a crisis these days. It's a make or break for the wheat growers of the State now, no mistake. Here are the land cases and the new grain tariff drawing to a head at about the same time. If we win our land cases, there's your new freight rates to be applied, and then all is beer and skittles. Won't the San Joaquin go wild if we pull it off, and I believe we will."

"How we wheat growers are exploited and trapped and deceived at every turn," observed Magnus sadly. "The courts, the capitalists, the railroads, each of them in turn hoodwinks us into some new and wonderful scheme, only to betray us in the end. Well," he added, turning to Lyman, "one thing at least we can depend on. We will cut their grain rates for them, eh, Lyman?"

Lyman crossed his legs and settled himself in his office chair.

"I have wanted to have a talk with you about that, sir," he said. "Yes, we will cut the rates—an average 10 per cent. cut throughout the State, as we are pledged. But I am going to warn you, Governor, and you, Harran; don't expect too much at first. The man who, even after twenty years' training in the operation of railroads, can draw an equitable, smoothly working schedule of freight rates between shipping point and common point, is capable of governing the United States. What with main lines, and leased lines, and points of transfer, and the laws governing common carriers, and the rulings of the Inter-State Commerce Commission, the whole matter has become so confused that Vanderbilt himself couldn't straighten it out. And how can it be expected that railroad commissions who are chosen—well, let's be frank—as ours was, for instance, from out a number of men who don't know the difference between a switching charge and a differential rate, are going to regulate the whole business in six months' time? Cut rates; yes, any fool can do that; any fool can write one dollar instead of two, but if you cut too low by a fraction of one per cent. and if the railroad can get out an injunction, tie you up and show that your new rate prevents the road being operated at a profit, how are you any better off?"

"Your conscientiousness does you credit, Lyman," said the Governor. "I respect you for it, my son. I know you will be fair to the railroad. That is all we want. Fairness to the corporation is fairness to the farmer, and we won't expect you to readjust the whole matter out of hand. Take your time. We can afford to wait."

"And suppose the next commission is a railroad board, and reverses all our figures?"

The one-time mining king, the most redoubtable poker

player of Calaveras County, permitted himself a momentary twinkle of his eyes.

"By then it will be too late. We will, all of us, have made our fortunes by then."

The remark left Presley astonished out of all measure. He never could accustom himself to these strange lapses in the Governor's character. Magnus was by nature a public man, judicious, deliberate, standing firm for principle, yet upon rare occasion, by some such remark as this, he would betray the presence of a sub-nature of recklessness, inconsistent, all at variance with his creeds and tenets.

At the very bottom, when all was said and done, Magnus remained the Forty-niner. Deep down in his heart the spirit of the Adventurer yet persisted. "We will all of us have made fortunes by then." That was it precisely. "After us the deluge." For all his public spirit, for all his championship of justice and truth, his respect for law, Magnus remained the gambler, willing to play for colossal stakes, to hazard a fortune on the chance of winning a million. It was the true California spirit that found expression through him, the spirit of the West, unwilling to occupy itself with details, refusing to wait, to be patient, to achieve by legitimate plodding; the miner's instinct of wealth acquired in a single night prevailed, in spite of all. It was in this frame of mind that Magnus and the multitude of other ranchers of whom he was a type, farmed their ranches. They had no love for their land. They were not attached to the soil. They worked their ranches as a quarter of a century before they had worked their mines. To husband the resources of their marvellous San Joaquin, they considered niggardly, petty, Hebraic. To get all there was out of the land, to squeeze it dry, to exhaust it, seemed their policy. When, at last, the land worn out, would refuse to yield, they would invest their money in something else; by then, they would all have made fortunes. They did not care. "After us the deluge."

Lyman, however, was obviously uneasy, willing to change the subject. He rose to his feet, pulling down his cuffs.

"By the way," he observed, "I want you three to lunch with me to-day at my club. It is close by. You can wait there for news of the court's decision as well as anywhere else, and I should like to show you the place. I have just joined."

At the club, when the four men were seated at a small table in the round window of the main room, Lyman's popularity with all classes was very apparent. Hardly a man entered that did not call out a salutation to him, some even coming over to shake his hand. He seemed to be every man's friend, and to all he seemed equally genial. His affability, even to those whom he disliked, was unfailing.

"See that fellow yonder," he said to Magnus, indicating a certain middle-aged man, flamboyantly dressed, who wore his hair long, who was afflicted with sore eyes, and the collar of whose velvet coat was sprinkled with dandruff, "that's Hartrath, the artist, a man absolutely devoid of even the commonest decency. How he got in here is a mystery to me."

Yet, when this Hartrath came across to say "How do you do" to Lyman, Lyman was as eager in his cordiality as his warmest friend could have expected.

"Why the devil are you so chummy with him, then?" observed Harran when Hartrath had gone away.

Lyman's explanation was vague. The truth of the matter was, that Magnus's oldest son was consumed by inordinate ambition. Political preferment was his dream, and to the realisation of this dream popularity was an essential. Every man who could vote, blackguard or gentleman, was to be conciliated, if possible. He made it his study to become known throughout the entire community—to put influential men under obligations to himself. He never forgot a name or a face. With everybody he was the hail-fellow-well-met. His ambition was not trivial. In his disregard for small things, he resembled his father. Municipal office had no attraction for him. His goal was higher. He had planned his life twenty years ahead. Already Sheriff's Attorney, Assistant District Attorney and Railroad Commissioner, he could, if he desired, attain the office of District Attorney itself. Just now, it was a question with him whether or not it would be politic to fill this office. Would it advance or sidetrack him in the career he had outlined for himself? Lyman wanted to be something better than District Attorney, better than Mayor, than State Senator, or even than member of the United States Congress. He wanted to be, in fact, what his father was only in name—to succeed where Magnus had failed. He wanted to be governor of the State. He had put his teeth together, and, deaf to all other considerations, blind to all other issues, he worked with the infinite slowness, the unshakable tenacity of the coral insect to this one end.

After luncheon was over, Lyman ordered cigars and liqueurs, and with the three others returned to the main room of the club. However, their former place in the round window was occupied. A middle-aged man, with iron grey hair and moustache, who wore a frock coat and a white waistcoat, and in some indefinable manner suggested a retired naval officer, was sitting at their table smoking a long, thin cigar. At sight of him, Presley became animated. He uttered a mild exclamation:

"Why, isn't that Mr. Cedarquist?"

"Cedarquist?" repeated Lyman Derrick. "I know

him well. Yes, of course, it is," he continued. "Governor, you must know him. He is one of our representative men. You would enjoy talking to him. He was the head of the big Atlas Iron Works. They have shut down recently, you know. Not failed exactly, but just ceased to be a paying investment, and Cedarquist closed them out. He has other interests, though. He's a rich man—a capitalist."

Lyman brought the group up to the gentleman in question and introduced them.

"Mr. Magnus Derrick, of course," observed Cedarquist, as he took the Governor's hand. "I've known you by repute for some time, sir. This is a great pleasure, I assure you." Then, turning to Presley, he added: "Hello, Pres, my boy. How is the great, the very great Poem getting on?"

"It's not getting on at all, sir," answered Presley, in some embarrassment, as they all sat down. "In fact, I've about given up the idea. There's so much interest in what you might call 'living issues' down at Los Muertos now, that I'm getting further and further from it every day."

"I should say as much," remarked the manufacturer, turning towards Magnus. "I'm watching your fight with Shelgrim, Mr. Derrick, with every degree of interest." He raised his drink of whiskey and soda. "Here's success to you."

As he replaced his glass, the artist Hartrath joined the group uninvited. As a pretext, he engaged Lyman in conversation. Lyman, he believed, was a man with a "pull" at the City Hall. In connection with a projected Million-Dollar Fair and Flower Festival, which at that moment was the talk of the city, certain statues were to be erected, and Hartrath bespoke Lyman's influence to further the pretensions of a sculptor friend of his, who

wished to be Art Director of the affair. In the matter of
this Fair and Flower Festival, Hartrath was not lacking
in enthusiasm. He addressed the others with extravagant gestures, blinking his inflamed eyelids.

"A million dollars," he exclaimed. "Hey! think of
that. Why, do you know that we have five hundred
thousand practically pledged already? Talk about public spirit, gentlemen, this is the most public-spirited city
on the continent. And the money is not thrown away.
We will have Eastern visitors here by the thousands—
capitalists—men with money to invest. The million we
spend on our fair will be money in our pockets. Ah,
you should see how the women of this city are taking
hold of the matter. They are giving all kinds of little
entertainments, teas, ' Olde Tyme Singing Skules,' ama-
teur theatricals, gingerbread *fêtes*, all for the benefit of
the fund, and the business men, too—pouring out their
money like water. It is splendid, splendid, to see a community so patriotic."

The manufacturer, Cedarquist, fixed the artist with a
glance of melancholy interest.

"And how much," he remarked, " will they contrib-
ute—your gingerbread women and public-spirited capitalists, towards the blowing up of the ruins of the Atlas
Iron Works? "

"Blowing up? I don't understand," murmured the
artist, surprised.

"When you get your Eastern capitalists out here with
your Million-Dollar Fair," continued Cedarquist, "you
don't propose, do you, to let them see a Million-Dollar
Iron Foundry standing idle, because of the indifference
of San Francisco business men? They might ask perti-
nent questions, your capitalists, and we should have to
answer that our business men preferred to invest their
money in corner lots and government bonds, rather than

to back up a legitimate, industrial enterprise. We don't want fairs. We want active furnaces. We don't want public statues, and fountains, and park extensions and gingerbread *fêtes*. We want business enterprise. Isn't it like us? Isn't it like us?" he exclaimed sadly. "What a melancholy comment! San Francisco! It is not a city —it is a Midway Plaisance. California likes to be fooled. Do you suppose Shelgrim could convert the whole San Joaquin Valley into his back yard otherwise? Indifference to public affairs—absolute indifference, it stamps us all. Our State is the very paradise of fakirs. You and your Million-Dollar Fair!" He turned to Hartrath with a quiet smile. "It is just such men as you, Mr. Hartrath, that are the ruin of us. You organise a sham of tinsel and pasteboard, put on fool's cap and bells, beat a gong at a street corner, and the crowd cheers you and drops nickels into your hat. Your gingerbread *fête;* yes, I saw it in full blast the other night on the grounds of one of your women's places on Sutter Street. I was on my way home from the last board meeting of the Atlas Company. A *gingerbread fête*, my God! and the Atlas plant shutting down for want of financial backing. A million dollars spent to attract the Eastern investor, in order to show him an abandoned rolling mill, wherein the only activity is the sale of remnant material and scrap steel."

Lyman, however, interfered. The situation was becoming strained. He tried to conciliate the three men— the artist, the manufacturer, and the farmer, the warring elements. But Hartrath, unwilling to face the enmity that he felt accumulating against him, took himself away. A picture of his—"A Study of the Contra Costa Foothills"—was to be raffled in the club rooms for the benefit of the Fair. He, himself, was in charge of the matter. He disappeared.

Cedarquist looked after him with contemplative interest. Then, turning to Magnus, excused himself for the acridity of his words.

"He's no worse than many others, and the people of this State and city are, after all, only a little more addle-headed than other Americans." It was his favourite topic. Sure of the interest of his hearers, he unburdened himself.

"If I were to name the one crying evil of American life, Mr. Derrick," he continued, "it would be the indifference of the better people to public affairs. It is so in all our great centres. There are other great trusts, God knows, in the United States besides our own dear P. and S.W. Railroad. Every State has its own grievance. If it is not a railroad trust, it is a sugar trust, or an oil trust, or an industrial trust, that exploits the People, *because the People allow it*. The indifference of the People is the opportunity of the despot. It is as true as that the whole is greater than the part, and the maxim is so old that it is trite—it is laughable. It is neglected and disused for the sake of some new ingenious and complicated theory, some wonderful scheme of reorganisation, but the fact remains, nevertheless, simple, fundamental, everlasting. The People have but to say 'No,' and not the strongest tyranny, political, religious, or financial, that was ever organised, could survive one week."

The others, absorbed, attentive, approved, nodding their heads in silence as the manufacturer finished.

"That's one reason, Mr. Derrick," the other resumed after a moment, "why I have been so glad to meet you. You and your League are trying to say 'No' to the trust. I hope you will succeed. If your example will rally the People to your cause, you will. Otherwise—" he shook his head.

"One stage of the fight is to be passed this very day," observed Magnus. "My sons and myself are expecting hourly news from the City Hall, a decision in our case is pending."

"We are both of us fighters, it seems, Mr. Derrick," said Cedarquist. "Each with his particula. enemy. We are well met, indeed, the farmer and the manufacturer, both in the same grist between the two millstones of the lethargy of the Public and the aggression of the Trust, the two great evils of modern America. Pres, my boy, there is your epic poem ready to hand."

But Cedarquist was full of another idea. Rarely did so favourable an opportunity present itself for explaining his theories, his ambitions. Addressing himself to Magnus, he continued:

"Fortunately for myself, the Atlas Company was not my only investment. I have other interests. The building of ships—steel sailing ships—has been an ambition of mine,—for this purpose, Mr. Derrick, to carry American wheat. For years, I have studied this question of American wheat, and at last, I have arrived at a theory. Let me explain. At present, all our California wheat goes to Liverpool, and from that port is distributed over the world. But a change is coming. I am sure of it. You young men," he turned to Presley, Lyman, and Harran, "will live to see it. Our century is about done. The great word of this nineteenth century has been Production. The great word of the twentieth century will be— listen to me, you youngsters—Markets. As a market for our Production—or let me take a concrete example—as a market for our *Wheat*, Europe is played out. Population in Europe is not increasing fast enough to keep up with the rapidity of our production. In some cases, as in France, the population is stationary. *We,* however, have gone on producing wheat at a tremendous rate.

The result is over-production. We supply more than Europe can eat, and down go the prices. The remedy is *not* in the curtailing of our wheat areas, but in this, we *must have new markets, greater markets*. For years we have been sending our wheat from East to West, from California to Europe. But the time will come when we must send it from West to East. We must march with the course of empire, not against it. I mean, we must look to China. Rice in China is losing its nutritive quality. The Asiatics, though, must be fed; if not on rice, then on wheat. Why, Mr. Derrick, if only one-half the population of China ate a half ounce of flour per man per day all the wheat areas in California could not feed them. Ah, if I could only hammer that into the brains of every rancher of the San Joaquin, yes, and of every owner of every bonanza farm in Dakota and Minnesota. Send your wheat to China; handle it yourselves; do away with the middleman; break up the Chicago wheat pits and elevator rings and mixing houses. When in feeding China you have decreased the European shipments, the effect is instantaneous. Prices go up in Europe without having the least effect upon the prices in China. We hold the key, we have the wheat,—infinitely more than we ourselves can eat. Asia and Europe must look to America to be fed. What fatuous neglect of opportunity to continue to deluge Europe with our surplus food when the East trembles upon the verge of starvation!"

The two men, Cedarquist and Magnus, continued the conversation a little further. The manufacturer's idea was new to the Governor. He was greatly interested. He withdrew from the conversation. Thoughtful, he leaned back in his place, stroking the bridge of his beak-like nose with a crooked forefinger.

Cedarquist turned to Harran and began asking details

as to the conditions of the wheat growers of the San Joaquin. Lyman still maintained an attitude of polite aloofness, yawning occasionally behind three fingers, and Presley was left to the company of his own thoughts.

There had been a day when the affairs and grievances of the farmers of his acquaintance—Magnus, Annixter, Osterman, and old Broderson—had filled him only with disgust. His mind full of a great, vague epic poem of the West, he had kept himself apart, disdainful of what he chose to consider their petty squabbles. But the scene in Annixter's harness room had thrilled and uplifted him. He was palpitating with excitement all through the succeeding months. He abandoned the idea of an epic poem. In six months he had not written a single verse. Day after day he trembled with excitement as the relations between the Trust and League became more and more strained. He saw the matter in its true light. It was typical. It was the world-old war between Freedom and Tyranny, and at times his hatred of the railroad shook him like a crisp and withered reed, while the languid indifference of the people of the State to the quarrel filled him with a blind exasperation.

But, as he had once explained to Vanamee, he must find expression. He felt that he would suffocate otherwise. He had begun to keep a journal. As the inclination spurred him, he wrote down his thoughts and ideas in this, sometimes every day, sometimes only three or four times a month. Also he flung aside his books of poems—Milton, Tennyson, Browning, even Homer— and addressed himself to Mill, Malthus, Young, Poushkin, Henry George, Schopenhauer. He attacked the subject of Social Inequality with unbounded enthusiasm. He devoured, rather than read, and emerged from the affair, his mind a confused jumble of conflicting notions,

sick with over-effort, raging against injustice and oppression, and with not one sane suggestion as to remedy
or redress.

The butt of his cigarette scorched his fingers and
roused him from his brooding. In the act of lighting
another, he glanced across the room and was surprised to
see two very prettily dressed young women in the company of an older gentleman, in a long frock coat, standing before Hartrath's painting, examining it, their heads
upon one side.

Presley uttered a murmur of surprise. He, himself,
was a member of the club, and the presence of women
within its doors, except on special occasions, was not
tolerated. He turned to Lyman Derrick for an explanation, but this other had also seen the women and abruptly exclaimed:

"I declare, I had forgotten about it. Why, this is
Ladies' Day, of course."

"Why, yes," interposed Cedarquist, glancing at the
women over his shoulder. "Didn't you know? They let
'em in twice a year, you remember, and this is a double
occasion. They are going to raffle Hartrath's picture,—
for the benefit of the Gingerbread Fair. Why, you are
not up to date, Lyman. This is a sacred and religious
rite,—an important public event."

"Of course, of course," murmured Lyman. He found
means to survey Harran and Magnus. Certainly, neither
his father nor his brother were dressed for the function
that impended. He had been stupid. Magnus invariably
attracted attention, and now with his trousers strapped
under his boots, his wrinkled frock coat—Lyman twisted
his cuffs into sight with an impatient, nervous movement of his wrists, glancing a second time at his brother's
pink face, forward curling, yellow hair and clothes of a
country cut. But there was no help for it. He wondered

what were the club regulations in the matter of bringing
in visitors on Ladies' Day.

"Sure enough, Ladies' Day," he remarked, "I am very
glad you struck it, Governor. We can sit right where
we are. I guess this is as good a place as any to see the
crowd. It's a good chance to see all the big guns of the
city. Do you expect your people here, Mr. Cedarquist?"

"My wife may come, and my daughters," said the
manufacturer.

"Ah," murmured Presley, "so much the better. I
was going to give myself the pleasure of calling upon
your daughters, Mr. Cedarquist, this afternoon."

"You can save your carfare, Pres," said Cedarquist,
"you will see them here."

No doubt, the invitations for the occasion had appointed one o'clock as the time, for between that hour
and two, the guests arrived in an almost unbroken
stream. From their point of vantage in the round window of the main room, Magnus, his two sons, and Presley looked on very interested. Cedarquist had excused
himself, affirming that he must look out for his women
folk.

Of every ten of the arrivals, seven, at least, were ladies.
They entered the room—this unfamiliar masculine
haunt, where their husbands, brothers, and sons spent so
much of their time—with a certain show of hesitancy
and little, nervous, oblique glances, moving their heads
from side to side like a file of hens venturing into a
strange barn. They came in groups, ushered by a single
member of the club, doing the honours with effusive
bows and polite gestures, indicating the various objects
of interest, pictures, busts, and the like, that decorated
the room.

Fresh from his recollections of Bonneville, Guadalajara, and the dance in Annixter's barn, Presley was as-

tonished at the beauty of these women and the elegance
of their toilettes. The crowd thickened rapidly. A murmur of conversation arose, subdued, gracious, mingled
with the soft rustle of silk, grenadines, velvet. The scent
of delicate perfumes spread in the air, Violet de Parme,
Peau d'Espagne. Colours of the most harmonious blends
appeared and disappeared at intervals in the slowly moving press, touches of lavender-tinted velvets, pale violet
crêpes and cream-coloured appliquéd laces.

There seemed to be no need of introductions. Everybody appeared to be acquainted. There was no awkwardness, no constraint. The assembly disengaged an
impression of refined pleasure. On every hand, innumerable dialogues seemed to go forward easily and naturally,
without break or interruption, witty, engaging, the
couple never at a loss for repartee. A third party was
gracefully included, then a fourth. Little groups were
formed,—groups that divided themselves, or melted into
other groups, or disintegrated again into isolated pairs,
or lost themselves in the background of the mass,—all
without friction, without embarrassment,—the whole affair going forward of itself, decorous, tactful, well-bred.

At a distance, and not too loud, a stringed orchestra
sent up a pleasing hum. Waiters, with brass buttons on
their full dress coats, went from group to group, silent,
unobtrusive, serving salads and ices.

But the focus of the assembly was the little space before Hartrath's painting. It was called " A Study of the
Contra Costa Foothills," and was set in a frame of natural redwood, the bark still adhering. It was conspicu-
ously displayed on an easel at the right of the entrance to
the main room of the club, and was very large. In the
foreground, and to the left, under the shade of a live-oak,
stood a couple of reddish cows, knee-deep in a patch of
yellow poppies, while in the right-hand corner, to bal-

ance the composition, was placed a girl in a pink dress
and white sunbonnet, in which the shadows were indicated by broad dashes of pale blue paint. The ladies and
young girls examined the production with little murmurs
of admiration, hazarding remembered phrases, searching
for the exact balance between generous praise and critical discrimination, expressing their opinions in the mild
technicalities of the Art Books and painting classes.
They spoke of atmospheric effects, of middle distance, of
" *chiaro-oscuro*," of fore-shortening, of the decomposition
of light, of the subordination of individuality to fidelity
of interpretation.

One tall girl, with hair almost white in its blondness,
having observed that the handling of the masses reminded her strongly of Corot, her companion, who carried a gold lorgnette by a chain around her neck, answered:

" Ah! *Millet*, perhaps, but not Corot."

This verdict had an immediate success. It was passed
from group to group. It seemed to imply a delicate distinction that carried conviction at once. It was decided
formally that the reddish brown cows in the picture were
reminiscent of Daubigny, and that the handling of the
masses was altogether Millet, but that the general effect
was *not quite* Corot.

Presley, curious to see the painting that was the subject of so much discussion, had left the group in the
round window, and stood close by Hartrath, craning his
head over the shoulders of the crowd, trying to catch a
glimpse of the reddish cows, the milk-maid and the blue
painted foothills. He was suddenly aware of Cedarquist's
voice in his ear, and, turning about, found himself face
to face with the manufacturer, his wife and his two
daughters.

.There was a meeting. Salutations were exchanged,

Presley shaking hands all around, expressing his delight at seeing his old friends once more, for he had known the family from his boyhood, Mrs. Cedarquist being his aunt. Mrs. Cedarquist and her two daughters declared that the air of Los Muertos must certainly have done him a world of good. He was stouter, there could be no doubt of it. A little pale, perhaps. He was fatiguing himself with his writing, no doubt. Ah, he must take care. Health was everything, after all. Had he been writing any more verse? Every month they scanned the magazines, looking for his name.

Mrs. Cedarquist was a fashionable woman, the president or chairman of a score of clubs. She was forever running after fads, appearing continually in the society wherein she moved with new and astounding *protégés*— fakirs whom she unearthed no one knew where, discovering them long in advance of her companions. Now it was a Russian Countess, with dirty finger nails, who travelled throughout America and borrowed money; now an Æsthete who possessed a wonderful collection of topaz gems, who submitted decorative schemes for the interior arrangement of houses and who "received" in Mrs. Cedarquist's drawing-rooms dressed in a white velvet cassock; now a widow of some Mohammedan of Bengal or Rajputana, who had a blue spot in the middle of her forehead and who solicited contributions for her sisters in affliction; now a certain bearded poet, recently back from the Klondike; now a decayed musician who had been ejected from a young ladies' musical conservatory of Europe because of certain surprising pamphlets on free love, and who had come to San Francisco to introduce the community to the music of Brahms; now a Japanese youth who wore spectacles and a grey flannel shirt and who, at intervals, delivered himself of the most astonishing poems, vague, unrhymed, unmetrical lucubrations, incoherent, bizarre; now a Christian Scientist, a lean, grey woman, whose creed was neither Christian nor scientific; now a university professor, with the bristling beard of an anarchist chief-of-section, and a roaring, guttural voice, whose intenseness left him gasping and apoplectic; now a civilised Cherokee with a mission; now a female elocutionist, whose forte was Byron's Songs of Greece; now a high caste Chinaman; now a miniature painter; now a tenor, a pianiste, a mandolin player, a missionary, a drawing master, a virtuoso, a collector, an Armenian, a botanist with a new flower, a critic with a new theory, a doctor with a new treatment.

And all these people had a veritable mania for declamation and fancy dress. The Russian Countess gave talks on the prisons of Siberia, wearing the headdress and pinchbeck ornaments of a Slav bride; the Æsthete, in his white cassock, gave readings on obscure questions of art and ethics. The widow of India, in the costume of her caste, described the social life of her people at home. The bearded poet, perspiring in furs and boots of reindeer skin, declaimed verses of his own composition about the wild life of the Alaskan mining camps. The Japanese youth, in the silk robes of the *Samurai* two-sworded nobles, read from his own works—"The flat-bordered earth, nailed down at night, rusting under the darkness," " The brave, upright rains that came down like errands from iron-bodied yore-time." The Christian Scientist, in funereal, impressive black, discussed the contra-will and pan-psychic hylozoism. The university professor put on a full dress suit and lisle thread gloves at three in the afternoon and before literary clubs and circles bellowed extracts from Goethe and Schiler in the German, shaking his fists, purple with vehemence. The Cherokee, arrayed in fringed buckskin and blue beads, rented from a costumer, intoned folk songs of his people in the vernacu-

lar. The elocutionist in cheese-cloth toga and tin brace-
lets, rendered " The Isles of Greece, where burning Sap-
pho loved and sung." The Chinaman, in the robes of a
mandarin, lectured on Confucius. The Armenian, in fez
and baggy trousers, spoke of the Unspeakable Turk. The
mandolin player, dressed like a bull fighter, held musical *conversazioni*, interpreting the peasant songs of
Andalusia.

It was the Fake, the eternal, irrepressible Sham; glib,
nimble, ubiquitous, tricked out in all the paraphernalia
of imposture, an endless defile of charlatans that passed
interminably before the gaze of the city, marshalled by
" lady presidents," exploited by clubs of women, by literary societies, reading circles, and culture organisations.
The attention the Fake received, the time devoted to it,
the money which it absorbed, were incredible. It was all
one that impostor after impostor was exposed; it was all
one that the clubs, the circles, the societies were proved
beyond doubt to have been swindled. The more the Philistine press of the city railed and guyed, the more the
women rallied to the defence of their *protégé* of the hour.
That their favourite was persecuted, was to them a
veritable rapture. Promptly they invested the apostle of
culture with the glamour of a martyr.

The fakirs worked the community as shell-game tricksters work a county fair, departing with bursting pocket-
books, passing on the word to the next in line, assured
that the place was not worked out, knowing well that
there was enough for all.

More frequently the public of the city, unable to think
of more than one thing at one time, prostrated itself at the
feet of a single apostle, but at other moments, such as the
present, when a Flower Festival or a Million-Dollar Fair
aroused enthusiasm in all quarters, the occasion was one
of gala for the entire Fake. The decayed professors,

virtuosi, litterateurs, and artists thronged to the place *en masse*. Their clamour filled all the air. On every hand one heard the scraping of violins, the tinkling of mandolins, the suave accents of "art talks," the incoherencies of poets, the declamation of elocutionists, the inarticulate wanderings of the Japanese, the confused mutterings of the Cherokee, the guttural bellowing of the German university professor, all in the name of the Million-Dollar Fair. Money to the extent of hundreds of thousands was set in motion.

Mrs. Cedarquist was busy from morning until night. One after another, she was introduced to newly arrived fakirs. To each poet, to each litterateur, to each professor she addressed the same question:

"How long have you known you had this power?"

She spent her days in one quiver of excitement and jubilation. She was "in the movement." The people of the city were awakening to a Realisation of the Beautiful, to a sense of the higher needs of life. This was Art, this was Literature, this was Culture and Refinement. The Renaissance had appeared in the West.

She was a short, rather stout, red-faced, very much over-dressed little woman of some fifty years. She was rich in her own name, even before her marriage, being a relative of Shelgrim himself and on familiar terms with the great financier and his family. Her husband, while deploring the policy of the railroad, saw no good reason for quarrelling with Shelgrim, and on more than one occasion had dined at his house.

On this occasion, delighted that she had come upon a "minor poet," she insisted upon presenting him to Hartrath.

"You two should have so much in common," she explained.

Presley shook the flaccid hand of the artist, murmuring conventionalities, while Mrs. Cedarquist hastened to say:

"I am sure you know Mr. Presley's verse, Mr. Hartrath. You should, believe me. You two have much in common. I can see so much that is alike in your modes of interpreting nature. In Mr. Presley's sonnet, 'The Better Part,' there is the same note as in your picture, the same sincerity of tone, the same subtlety of touch, the same *nuances*,—ah."

"Oh, my dear Madame," murmured the artist, interrupting Presley's impatient retort; "I am a mere bungler. You don't mean quite that, I am sure. I am *too* sensitive. It is my cross. Beauty," he closed his sore eyes with a little expression of pain, "beauty unmans me."

But Mrs. Cedarquist was not listening. Her eyes were fixed on the artist's luxuriant hair, a thick and glossy mane, that all but covered his coat collar.

"Leonine!" she murmured—"leonine! Like Samson of old."

However, abruptly bestirring herself, she exclaimed a second later:

"But I must run away. I am selling tickets for you this afternoon, Mr. Hartrath. I am having such success. Twenty-five already. Mr. Presley, you will take two chances, I am sure, and, oh, by the way, I have such good news. You know I am one of the lady members of the subscription committee for our Fair, and you know we approached Mr. Shelgrim for a donation to help along. Oh, such a liberal patron, a real Lorenzo di' Medici. In the name of the Pacific and Southwestern he has subscribed, think of it, five thousand dollars; and yet they will talk of the meanness of the railroad."

"Possibly it is to his interest," murmured Presley. "The fairs and festivals bring people to the city over his railroad."

But the others turned on him, expostulating.

"Ah, you Philistine," declared Mrs. Cedarquist. "And this from *you*, Presley; to attribute such base motives——"

"If the poets become materialised, Mr. Presley," declared Hartrath, "what can we say to the people?"

"And Shelgrim encourages your million-dollar fairs and *fêtes*," said a voice at Presley's elbow, "because it is throwing dust in the people's eyes."

The group turned about and saw Cedarquist, who had come up unobserved in time to catch the drift of the talk. But he spoke without bitterness; there was even a good-humoured twinkle in his eyes.

"Yes," he continued, smiling, "our dear Shelgrim promotes your fairs, not only as Pres says, because it is money in his pocket, but because it amuses the people, distracts their attention from the doings of his railroad. When Beatrice was a baby and had little colics, I used to jingle my keys in front of her nose, and it took her attention from the pain in her tummy; so Shelgrim."

The others laughed good-humouredly, protesting, nevertheless, and Mrs. Cedarquist shook her finger in warning at the artist and exclaimed:

"The Philistines be upon thee, Samson!"

"By the way," observed Hartrath, willing to change the subject, "I hear you are on the Famine Relief Committee. Does your work progress?"

"Oh, most famously, I assure you," she said. "Such a movement as we have started. Those poor creatures. The photographs of them are simply dreadful. I had the committee to luncheon the other day and we passed them around. We are getting subscriptions from all over the State, and Mr. Cedarquist is to arrange for the ship."

The Relief Committee in question was one of a great number that had been formed in California—and all over

the Union, for the matter of that—to provide relief for
the victims of a great famine in Central India. The whole
world had been struck with horror at the reports of suffering and mortality in the affected districts, and had
hastened to send aid. Certain women of San Francisco,
with Mrs. Cedarquist at their head, had organised a
number of committees, but the manufacturer's wife
turned the meetings of these committees into social affairs—luncheons, teas, where one discussed the ways and
means of assisting the starving Asiatics over teacups and
plates of salad.

Shortly afterward a mild commotion spread throughout the assemblage of the club's guests. The drawing of
the numbers in the raffle was about to be made. Hartrath, in a flurry of agitation, excused himself. Cedarquist took Presley by the arm.

"Pres, let's get out of this," he said. "Come into the
wine room and I will shake you for a glass of sherry."

They had some difficulty in extricating themselves.
The main room where the drawing was to take place
suddenly became densely thronged. All the guests
pressed eagerly about the table near the picture, upon
which one of the hall boys had just placed a ballot box
containing the numbers. The ladies, holding their tickets
in their hands, pushed forward. A staccato chatter of
excited murmurs arose.

"What became of Harran and Lyman and the Governor?" inquired Presley.

Lyman had disappeared, alleging a business engagement, but Magnus and his younger son had retired to
the library of the club on the floor above. It was almost
deserted. They were deep in earnest conversation.

"Harran," said the Governor, with decision, "there is
a deal, there, in what Cedarquist says. Our wheat to
China, hey, boy?"

" It is certainly worth thinking of, sir."

" It appeals to me, boy; it appeals to me. It's big and there's a fortune in it. Big chances mean big returns; and I know—your old father isn't a back number yet, Harran—I may not have so wide an outlook as our friend Cedarquist, but I am quick to see my chance. Boy, the whole East is opening, disintegrating before the Anglo-Saxon. It is time that bread stuffs, as well, should make markets for themselves in the Orient. Just at this moment, too, when Lyman will scale down freight rates so we can haul to tidewater at little cost."

Magnus paused again, his frown beetling, and in the silence the excited murmur from the main room of the club, the soprano chatter of a multitude of women, found its way to the deserted library.

" I believe it's worth looking into, Governor," asserted Harran.

Magnus rose, and, his hands behind him, paced the floor of the library a couple of times, his imagination all stimulated and vivid. The great gambler perceived his Chance, the kaleidoscopic shifting of circumstances that made a Situation. It had come silently, unexpectedly. He had not seen its approach. Abruptly he woke one morning to see the combination realised. But also he saw a vision. A sudden and abrupt revolution in the Wheat. A new world of markets discovered, the matter as important as the discovery of America. The torrent of wheat was to be diverted, flowing back upon itself in a sudden, colossal eddy, stranding the middleman, the *entre-preneur*, the elevator- and mixing-house men dry and despairing, their occupation gone. He saw the farmer suddenly emancipated, the world's food no longer at the mercy of the speculator, thousands upon thousands of men set free of the grip of Trust and ring and monopoly acting for themselves, selling their own wheat, organising into one gigantic trust, themselves, sending their agents to all the entry ports of China. Himself, Annixter, Broderson and Osterman would pool their issues. He would convince them of the magnificence of the new movement. They would be its pioneers. Harran would be sent to Hong Kong to represent the four. They would charter—probably buy—a ship, perhaps one of Cedarquist's, American built, the nation's flag at the peak, and the sailing of that ship, gorged with the crops from Broderson's and Osterman's ranches, from Quien Sabe and Los Muertos, would be like the sailing of the caravels from Palos. It would mark a new era; it would make an epoch.

With this vision still expanding before the eye of his mind, Magnus, with Harran at his elbow, prepared to depart.

They descended to the lower floor and involved themselves for a moment in the throng of fashionables that blocked the hallway and the entrance to the main room, where the numbers of the raffle were being drawn. Near the head of the stairs they encountered Presley and Cedarquist, who had just come out of the wine room.

Magnus, still on fire with the new idea, pressed a few questions upon the manufacturer before bidding him good-bye. He wished to talk further upon the great subject, interested as to details, but Cedarquist was vague in his replies. He was no farmer, he hardly knew wheat when he saw it, only he knew the trend of the world's affairs; he felt them to be setting inevitably eastward.

However, his very vagueness was a further inspiration to the Governor. He swept details aside. He saw only the grand *coup*, the huge results, the East conquered, the march of empire rolling westward, finally arriving at its starting point, the vague, mysterious Orient.

He saw his wheat, like the crest of an advancing billow, crossing the Pacific, bursting upon Asia, flooding the Orient in a golden torrent. It was the new era. He had lived to see the death of the old and the birth of the new; first the mine, now the ranch; first gold, now wheat. Once again he became the pioneer, hardy, brilliant, taking colossal chances, blazing the way, grasping a fortune —a million in a single day. All the bigness of his nature leaped up again within him. At the magnitude of the inspiration he felt young again, indomitable, the leader at last, king of his fellows, wresting from fortune at this eleventh hour, before his old age, the place of high command which so long had been denied him. At last he could achieve.

Abruptly Magnus was aware that some one had spoken his name. He looked about and saw behind him, at a little distance, two gentlemen, strangers to him. They had withdrawn from the crowd into a little recess. Evidently having no women to look after, they had lost interest in the afternoon's affair. Magnus realised that they had not seen him. One of them was reading aloud to his companion from an evening edition of that day's newspaper. It was in the course of this reading that Magnus caught the sound of his name. He paused, listening, and Presley, Harran and Cedarquist followed his example. Soon they all understood. They were listening to the report of the judge's decision, for which Magnus was waiting—the decision in the case of the League vs. the Railroad. For the moment, the polite clamour of the raffle hushed itself—the winning number was being drawn. The guests held their breath, and in the ensuing silence Magnus and the others heard these words distinctly:

" . . . . It follows that the title to the lands in question is in the plaintiff—the Pacific and Southwestern Railroad, and the defendants have no title, and their possession is wrongful. There must be findings and judgment for the plaintiff, and it is so ordered."

In spite of himself, Magnus paled. Harran shut his teeth with an oath. Their exaltation of the previous moment collapsed like a pyramid of cards. The vision of the new movement of the wheat, the conquest of the East, the invasion of the Orient, seemed only the flimsiest mockery. With a brusque wrench, they were snatched back to reality. Between them and the vision, between the fecund San Joaquin, reeking with fruitfulness, and the millions of Asia crowding toward the verge of starvation, lay the iron-hearted monster of steel and steam, implacable, insatiable, huge—its entrails gorged with the life blood that it sucked from an entire commonwealth, its ever hungry maw glutted with the harvests that should have fed the famished bellies of the whole world of the Orient.

But abruptly, while the four men stood there, gazing into each other's faces, a vigorous hand-clapping broke out. The raffle of Hartrath's picture was over, and as Presley turned about he saw Mrs. Cedarquist and her two daughters signalling eagerly to the manufacturer, unable to reach him because of the intervening crowd. Then Mrs. Cedarquist raised her voice and cried:

" I've won. I've won."

Unnoticed, and with but a brief word to Cedarquist, Magnus and Harran went down the marble steps leading to the street door, silent, Harran's arm tight around his father's shoulder.

At once the orchestra struck into a lively air. A renewed murmur of conversation broke out, and Cedarquist, as he said good-bye to Presley, looked first at the retreating figures of the ranchers, then at the gayly dressed throng of beautiful women and debonair young men, and indicating the whole scene with a single gesture, said, smiling sadly as he spoke:

"Not a city, Presley, not a city, but a Midway Plaisance."

II

Underneath the Long Trestle where Broderson Creek cut the line of the railroad and the Upper Road, the ground was low and covered with a second growth of grey green willows. Along the borders of the creek were occasional marshy spots, and now and then Hilma Tree came here to gather water-cresses, which she made into salads.

The place was picturesque, secluded, an oasis of green shade in all the limitless, flat monotony of the surrounding wheat lands. The creek had eroded deep into the little gully, and no matter how hot it was on the baking, shimmering levels of the ranches above, down here one always found one's self enveloped in an odorous, moist coolness. From time to time, the incessant murmur of the creek, pouring over and around the larger stones, was interrupted by the thunder of trains roaring out upon the trestle overhead, passing on with the furious gallop of their hundreds of iron wheels, leaving in the air a taint of hot oil, acrid smoke, and reek of escaping steam.

On a certain afternoon, in the spring of the year, Hilma was returning to Quien Sabe from Hooven's by the trail that led from Los Muertos to Annixter's ranch houses, under the trestle. She had spent the afternoon with Minna Hooven, who, for the time being, was kept indoors because of a wrenched ankle. As Hilma descended into the gravel flats and thickets of willows underneath the trestle, she decided that she would gather some cresses for her supper that night. She found a spot around the base of one of the supports of the trestle where the cresses grew thickest, and plucked a couple of handfuls, washing them in the creek and pinning them up in her handkerchief. It made a little, round, cold bundle, and Hilma, warm from her walk, found a delicious enjoyment in pressing the damp ball of it to her cheeks and neck.

For all the change that Annixter had noted in her upon the occasion of the barn dance, Hilma remained in many things a young child. She was never at loss for enjoyment, and could always amuse herself when left alone. Just now, she chose to drink from the creek, lying prone on the ground, her face half-buried in the water, and this, not because she was thirsty, but because it was a new way to drink. She imagined herself a belated traveller, a poor girl, an outcast, quenching her thirst at the wayside brook, her little packet of cresses doing duty for a bundle of clothes. Night was coming on. Perhaps it would storm. She had nowhere to go. She would apply at a hut for shelter.

Abruptly, the temptation to dabble her feet in the creek presented itself to her. Always she had liked to play in the water. What a delight now to take off her shoes and stockings and wade out into the shallows near the bank! She had worn low shoes that afternoon, and the dust of the trail had filtered in above the edges. At times, she felt the grit and grey sand on the soles of her feet, and the sensation had set her teeth on edge. What a delicious alternative the cold, clean water suggested, and how easy it would be to do as she pleased just then, if only she were a little girl. In the end, it was stupid to be grown up.

Sitting upon the bank, one finger tucked into the heel of her shoe, Hilma hesitated. Suppose a train should come! She fancied she could see the engineer leaning from the cab with a great grin on his face, or the brakeman shouting gibes at her from the platform. Abruptly she blushed scarlet. The blood throbbed in her temples. Her heart beat.

Since the famous evening of the barn dance, Annixter had spoken to her but twice. Hilma no longer looked after the ranch house these days. The thought of setting foot within Annixter's dining-room and bed-room terrified her, and in the end her mother had taken over that part of her work. Of the two meetings with the master of Quien Sabe, one had been a mere exchange of good mornings as the two happened to meet over by the artesian well; the other, more complicated, had occurred in the dairy-house again, Annixter, pretending to look over the new cheese press, asking about details of her work. When this had happened on that previous occasion, ending with Annixter's attempt to kiss her, Hilma had been talkative enough, chattering on from one subject to another, never at a loss for a theme. But this last time was a veritable ordeal. No sooner had Annixter appeared than her heart leaped and quivered like that of the hound-harried doe. Her speech failed her. Throughout the whole brief interview she had been miserably tongue-tied, stammering monosyllables, confused, horribly awkward, and when Annixter had gone away, she had fled to her little room, and bolting the door, had flung herself face downward on the bed and wept as though her heart were breaking, she did not know why.

That Annixter had been overwhelmed with business all through the winter was an inexpressible relief to Hilma. His affairs took him away from the ranch continually. He was absent sometimes for weeks, making trips to San Francisco, or to Sacramento, or to Bonneville. Perhaps he was forgetting her, overlooking her;

and while, at first, she told herself that she asked nothing better, the idea of it began to occupy her mind. She began to wonder if it was really so.

She knew his trouble. Everybody did. The news of the sudden forward movement of the Railroad's forces, inaugurating the campaign, had flared white-hot and blazing all over the country side. To Hilma's notion, Annixter's attitude was heroic beyond all expression. His courage in facing the Railroad, as he had faced Delaney in the barn, seemed to her the pitch of sublimity. She refused to see any auxiliaries aiding him in his fight. To her imagination, the great League, which all the ranchers were joining, was a mere form. Single-handed, Annixter fronted the monster. But for him the corporation would gobble Quien Sabe, as a whale would a minnow. He was a hero who stood between them all and destruction. He was a protector of her family. He was her champion. She began to mention him in her prayers every night, adding a further petition to the effect that he would become a *good* man, and that he should not swear so much, and that he should never meet Delaney again.

However, as Hilma still debated the idea of bathing her feet in the creek, a train did actually thunder past overhead—the regular evening Overland,—the through express, that never stopped between Bakersfield and Fresno. It stormed by with a deafening clamour, and a swirl of smoke, in a long succession of way-coaches, and chocolate coloured Pullmans, grimy with the dust of the great deserts of the Southwest. The quivering of the trestle's supports set a tremble in the ground underfoot. The thunder of wheels drowned all sound of the flowing of the creek, and also the noise of the buckskin mare's hoofs descending from the trail upon the gravel about the creek, so that Hilma, turning about after the passage

of the train, saw Annixter close at hand, with the abruptness of a vision.

He was looking at her, smiling as he rarely did, the
firm line of his out-thrust lower lip relaxed good-
humouredly. He had taken off his campaign hat to her,
and though his stiff, yellow hair was twisted into a
bristling mop, the little persistent tuft on the crown,
usually defiantly erect as an Apache's scalp-lock, was
nowhere in sight.

"Hello, it's you, is it, Miss Hilma?" he exclaimed,
getting down from the buckskin, and allowing her to
drink.

Hilma nodded, scrambling to her feet, dusting her
skirt with nervous pats of both hands.

Annixter sat down on a great rock close by and, the
loop of the bridle over his arm, lit a cigar, and began to
talk. He complained of the heat of the day, the bad
condition of the Lower Road, over which he had come
on his way from a committee meeting of the League at
Los Muertos; of the slowness of the work on the irrigating ditch, and, as a matter of course, of the general
hard times.

"Miss Hilma," he said abruptly, "never you marry a
ranchman. He's never out of trouble."

Hilma gasped, her eyes widening till the full round
of the pupil was disclosed. Instantly, a certain, inexplicable guiltiness overpowered her with incredible confusion.
Her hands trembled as she pressed the bundle of cresses
into a hard ball between her palms.

Annixter continued to talk. He was disturbed and excited himself at this unexpected meeting. Never through
all the past winter months of strenuous activity, the fever
of political campaigns, the harrowing delays and ultimate
defeat in one law court after another, had he forgotten
the look in Hilma's face as he stood with one arm around

her on the floor of his barn, in peril of his life from the
buster's revolver. That dumb confession of Hilma's
wide-open eyes had been enough for him. Yet, somehow, he never had had a chance to act upon it. During
the short period when he could be on his ranch Hilma
had always managed to avoid him. Once, even, she had
spent a month, about Christmas time, with her mother's
father, who kept a hotel in San Francisco.

Now, to-day, however, he had her all to himself. He
would put an end to the situation that troubled him, and
vexed him, day after day, month after month. Beyond
question, the moment had come for something definite,
he could not say precisely what. Readjusting his cigar
between his teeth, he resumed his speech. It suited
his humour to take the girl into his confidence, following an instinct which warned him that this would bring
about a certain closeness of their relations, a certain intimacy.

"What do you think of this row, anyways, Miss Hilma,
—this railroad fuss in general? Think Shelgrim and his
rushers are going to jump Quien Sabe—are going to run
us off the ranch?"

"Oh, no, sir," protested Hilma, still breathless. "Oh,
no, indeed not."

"Well, what then?"

Hilma made a little uncertain movement of ignorance.

"I don't know what."

"Well, the League agreed to-day that if the test cases
were lost in the Supreme Court—you know we've appealed to the Supreme Court, at Washington—we'd
fight."

"Fight?"

"Yes, fight."

"Fight like—like you and Mr. Delaney that time with
—oh, dear—with guns?"

"I don't know," grumbled Annixter vaguely. "What do *you* think?"

Hilma's low-pitched, almost husky voice trembled a little as she replied, " Fighting—with guns—that's so terrible. Oh, those revolvers in the barn! I can hear them yet. Every shot seemed like the explosion of tons of powder."

" Shall we clear out, then? Shall we let Delaney have possession, and S. Behrman, and all that lot? Shall we give in to them?"

" Never, never," she exclaimed, her great eyes flashing.

" *You* wouldn't like to be turned out of your home, would you, Miss Hilma, because Quien Sabe *is* your home isn't it? You've lived here ever since you were as big as a minute. You wouldn't like to have S. Behrman and the rest of 'em turn you out?"

" N-no," she murmured. " No, I shouldn't like that. There's mamma and——"

" Well, do you think for one second I'm going to *let* 'em?" cried Annixter, his teeth tightening on his cigar. " You stay right where you are. I'll take care of you, right enough. Look here," he demanded abruptly, " you've no use for that roaring lush, Delaney, have you?"

" I think he is a wicked man," she declared. " I know the Railroad has pretended to sell him part of the ranch, and he lets Mr. S. Behrman and Mr. Ruggles just use him."

" Right. I thought you wouldn't be keen on him."

There was a long pause. The buckskin began blowing among the pebbles, nosing for grass, and Annixter shifted his cigar to the other corner of his mouth.

" Pretty place," he muttered, looking around him. Then he added: " Miss Hilma, see here, I want to have a kind of talk with you, if you don't mind. I don't know

just how to say these sort of things, and if I get all balled
up as I go along, you just set it down to the fact that
I've never had any experience in dealing with feemale
girls; understand? You see, ever since the barn dance—
yes, and long before then—I've been thinking a lot about
you. Straight, I have, and I guess you know it. You're
about the only girl that I ever knew well, and I guess,"
he declared deliberately, "you're about the only one I
want to know. It's my nature. You didn't say anything that time when we stood there together and Delaney was playing the fool, but, somehow, I got the idea
that you didn't want Delaney to do for me one little bit;
that if he'd got me then you would have been sorrier
than if he'd got any one else. Well, I felt just that way
about you. I would rather have had him shoot any other
girl in the room than you; yes, or in the whole State.
Why, if anything should happen to you, Miss Hilma—
well, I wouldn't care to go on with anything. S. Behrman could jump Quien Sabe, and welcome. And Delaney
could shoot me full of holes whenever he got good and
ready. I'd quit. I'd lay right down. I wouldn't care a
whoop about anything any more. You are the only girl
for me in the whole world. I didn't think so at first. I
didn't want to. But seeing you around every day, and
seeing how pretty you were, and how clever, and hearing
your voice and all, why, it just got all inside of me somehow, and now I can't think of anything else. I hate to
go to San Francisco, or Sacramento, or Visalia, or even
Bonneville, for only a day, just because you aren't there,
in any of those places, and I just rush what I've got to
do so as I can get back here. While you were away
that Christmas time, why, I was as lonesome as—oh, you
don't know anything about it. I just scratched off the
days on the calendar every night, one by one, till you got
back. And it just comes to this, I want you with me all

the time. I want you should have a home that's my
home, too. I want to take care of you, and have you all
for myself, you understand. What do you say?"

Hilma, standing up before him, retied a knot in her
handkerchief bundle with elaborate precaution, blinking
at it through her tears.

"What do you say, Miss Hilma?" Annixter repeated.
"How about that? What do you say?"

Just above a whisper, Hilma murmured:

"I—I don't know."

"Don't know what? Don't you think we could hit it
off together?"

"I don't know."

"I know we could, Hilma. I don't mean to scare you.
What are you crying for?"

"I don't know."

Annixter got up, cast away his cigar, and dropping
the buckskin's bridle, came and stood beside her, putting a hand on her shoulder. Hilma did not move, and he
felt her trembling. She still plucked at the knot of the
handkerchief.

"I can't do without you, little girl," Annixter continued, "and I want you. I want you bad. I don't get
much fun out of life ever. It, sure, isn't my nature, I
guess. I'm a hard man. Everybody is trying to down
me, and now I'm up against the Railroad. I'm fighting
'em all, Hilma, night and day, lock, stock, and barrel, and
I'm fighting now for my home, my land, everything I
have in the world. If I win out, I want somebody to be
glad with me. If I don't—I want somebody to be sorry
for me, sorry with me,—and that somebody is you. I am
dog-tired of going it alone. I want some one to back me
up. I want to feel you alongside of me, to give me a
touch of the shoulder now and then. I'm tired of fighting
for *things*—land, property, money. I want to fight for

some *person*—somebody beside myself. Understand? I
want to feel that it isn't all selfishness—that there are
other interests than mine in the game—that there's some
one dependent on me, and that's thinking of me as I'm
thinking of them—some one I can come home to at night
and put my arm around—like this, and have her put her
two arms around me—like—" He paused a second, and
once again, as it had been in that moment of imminent
peril, when he stood with his arm around her, their eyes
met,—" put her two arms around me," prompted Annixter, half smiling, " like—like what, Hilma?"

" I don't know."

" Like what, Hilma?" he insisted.

" Like—like this?" she questioned. With a movement
of infinite tenderness and affection she slid her arms
around his neck, still crying a little.

The sensation of her warm body in his embrace, the
feeling of her smooth, round arm, through the thinness
of her sleeve, pressing against his cheek, thrilled Annixter with a delight such as he had never known. He bent
his head and kissed her upon the nape of her neck, where
the delicate amber tint melted into the thick, sweet smell-
ing mass of her dark brown hair. She shivered a little,
holding him closer, ashamed as yet to look up. Without
speech, they stood there for a long minute, holding each
other close. Then Hilma pulled away from him, mopping her tear-stained cheeks with the little moist ball of
her handkerchief.

" What do you say? Is it a go?" demanded Annixter
jovially.

" I thought I hated you all the time," she said, and
the velvety huskiness of her voice never sounded so sweet
to him.

" And I thought it was that crockery smashing goat of
a lout of a cow-puncher."

"Delaney? The idea! Oh, dear! I think it must always have been you."

"Since when, Hilma?" he asked, putting his arm around her. "Ah, but it is good to have you, my girl," he exclaimed, delighted beyond words that she permitted this freedom. "Since when? Tell us all about it."

"Oh, since always. It was ever so long before I came to think of you—to, well, to think about—I mean to remember—oh, you know what I mean. But when I did, oh, *then!* "

"Then what?"

"I don't know—I haven't thought—that way long enough to know."

"But you said you thought it must have been me always."

"I know; but that was different—oh, I'm all mixed up. I'm so nervous and trembly now. Oh," she cried suddenly, her face overcast with a look of earnestness and great seriousness, both her hands catching at his wrist, "Oh, you *will* be good to me, now, won't you? I'm only a little, little child in so many ways, and I've given myself to you, all in a minute, and I can't go back of it now, and it's for always. I don't know how it happened or why. Sometimes I think I didn't wish it, but now it's done, and I am glad and happy. But *now* if you weren't good to me—oh, think of how it would be with me. You are strong, and big, and rich, and I am only a servant of yours, a little nobody, but I've given all I had to you—myself—and you must be so good to me now. Always remember that. Be good to me and be gentle and kind to me in *little* things,—in everything, or you will break my heart."

Annixter took her in his arms. He was speechless. No words that he had at his command seemed adequate. All he could say was:

"That's all right, little girl. Don't you be frightened. I'll take care of you. That's all right, that's all right."

For a long time they sat there under the shade of the great trestle, their arms about each other, speaking only at intervals. An hour passed. The buckskin, finding no feed to her taste, took the trail stablewards, the bridle dragging. Annixter let her go. Rather than to take his arm from around Hilma's waist he would have lost his whole stable. At last, however, he bestirred himself and began to talk. He thought it time to formulate some plan of action.

"Well, now, Hilma, what are we going to do?"

"Do?" she repeated. "Why, must we do anything? Oh, isn't this enough?"

"There's better ahead," he went on. "I want to fix you up somewhere where you can have a bit of a home all to yourself. Let's see; Bonneville wouldn't do. There's always a lot of yaps about there that know us, and they would begin to cackle first off. How about San Francisco. We might go up next week and have a look around. I would find rooms you could take somewheres, and we would fix 'em up as lovely as how-do-you-do."

"Oh, but why go away from Quien Sabe?" she protested. "And, then, so soon, too. Why must we have a wedding trip, now that you are so busy? Wouldn't it be better—oh, I tell you, we could go to Monterey after we were married, for a little week, where mamma's people live, and then come back here to the ranch house and settle right down where we are and let me keep house for you. I wouldn't even want a single servant."

Annixter heard and his face grew troubled.

"Hum," he said, "I see."

He gathered up a handful of pebbles and began snapping them carefully into the creek. He fell thoughtful. Here was a phase of the affair he had not planned in the

least. He had supposed all the time that Hilma took
his meaning. His old suspicion that she was trying to
get a hold on him stirred again for a moment. There was
no good of such talk as that. Always these feemale girls
seemed crazy to get married, bent on complicating the
situation.

"Isn't that best?" said Hilma, glancing at him.

"I don't know," he muttered gloomily.

"Well, then, let's not. Let's come right back to Quien
Sabe without going to Monterey. Anything that you
want I want."

"I hadn't thought of it in just that way," he observed.

"In what way, then?"

"Can't we—can't we wait about this marrying business?"

"That's just it," she said gayly. "I said it was too
soon. There would be so much to do between whiles.
Why not say at the end of the summer?"

"Say what?"

"Our marriage, I mean."

"Why get married, then? What's the good of all that
fuss about it? I don't go anything upon a minister
puddling round in my affairs. What's the difference,
anyhow? We understand each other. Isn't that enough?
Pshaw, Hilma, *I'm* no marrying man."

She looked at him a moment, bewildered, then slowly
she took his meaning. She rose to her feet, her eyes
wide, her face paling with terror. He did not look at
her, but he could hear the catch in her throat.

"Oh!" she exclaimed, with a long, deep breath, and
again "Oh!" the back of her hand against her lips.

It was a quick gasp of a veritable physical anguish.
Her eyes brimmed over. Annixter rose, looking at her.

"Well?" he said, awkwardly, "Well?"

Hilma leaped back from him with an instinctive recoil

of her whole being, throwing out her hands in a gesture
of defence, fearing she knew not what. There was as yet
no sense of insult in her mind, no outraged modesty. She
was only terrified. It was as though searching for wild
flowers she had come suddenly upon a snake.

She stood for an instant, spellbound, her eyes wide,
her bosom swelling; then, all at once, turned and fled,
darting across the plank that served for a foot bridge
over the creek, gaining the opposite bank and disappearing with a brisk rustle of underbrush, such as might have
been made by the flight of a frightened fawn.

Abruptly Annixter found himself alone. For a moment he did not move, then he picked up his campaign
hat, carefully creased its limp crown and put it on his
head and stood for a moment, looking vaguely at the
ground on both sides of him. He went away without
uttering a word, without change of countenance, his
hands in his pockets, his feet taking great strides along
the trail in the direction of the ranch house.

He had no sight of Hilma again that evening, and the
next morning he was up early and did not breakfast at
the ranch house. Business of the League called him to
Bonneville to confer with Magnus and the firm of lawyers
retained by the League to fight the land-grabbing cases.
An appeal was to be taken to the Supreme Court at
Washington, and it was to be settled that day which of
the cases involved should be considered as test cases.

Instead of driving or riding into Bonneville, as he
usually did, Annixter took an early morning train, the
Bakersfield-Fresno local at Guadalajara, and went to
Bonneville by rail, arriving there at twenty minutes after
seven and breakfasting by appointment with Magnus
Derrick and Osterman at the Yosemite House, on Main
Street.

The conference of the committee with the lawyers took

place in a front room of the Yosemite, one of the latter bringing with him his clerk, who made a stenographic report of the proceedings and took carbon copies of all letters written. The conference was long and complicated, the business transacted of the utmost moment, and it was not until two o'clock that Annixter found himself at liberty.

However, as he and Magnus descended into the lobby of the hotel, they were aware of an excited and interested group collected about the swing doors that opened from the lobby of the Yosemite into the bar of the same name. Dyke was there—even at a distance they could hear the reverberation of his deep-toned voice, uplifted in wrath and furious expostulation. Magnus and Annixter joined the group wondering, and all at once fell full upon the first scene of a drama.

That same morning Dyke's mother had awakened him according to his instructions at daybreak. A consignment of his hop poles from the north had arrived at the freight office of the P. and S. W. in Bonneville, and he was to drive in on his farm wagon and bring them out. He would have a busy day.

" Hello, hello," he said, as his mother pulled his ear to arouse him; " morning, mamma."

" It's time," she said, " after five already. Your breakfast is on the stove."

He took her hand and kissed it with great affection. He loved his mother devotedly, quite as much as he did the little tad. In their little cottage, in the forest of green hops that surrounded them on every hand, the three led a joyous and secluded life, contented, industrious, happy, asking nothing better. Dyke, himself, was a big-hearted, jovial man who spread an atmosphere of good-humour wherever he went. In the evenings he played with Sidney like a big boy, an older brother, lying on the bed, or the sofa, taking her in his arms. Between them they had invented a great game. The ex-engineer, his boots removed, his huge legs in the air, hoisted the little tad on the soles of his stockinged feet like a circus acrobat, dandling her there, pretending he was about to let her fall. Sidney, choking with delight, held on nervously, with little screams and chirps of excitement, while he shifted her gingerly from one foot to another, and thence, the final act, the great gallery play, to the palm of one great hand. At this point Mrs. Dyke was called in, both father and daughter, children both, crying out that she was to come in and look, look. She arrived out of breath from the kitchen, the potato masher in her hand.

"Such children," she murmured, shaking her head at them, amused for all that, tucking the potato masher under her arm and clapping her hands.

In the end, it was part of the game that Sidney should tumble down upon Dyke, whereat he invariably vented a great bellow as if in pain, declaring that his ribs were broken. Gasping, his eyes shut, he pretended to be in the extreme of dissolution—perhaps he was dying. Sidney, always a little uncertain, amused but distressed, shook him nervously, tugging at his beard, pushing open his eyelid with one finger, imploring him not to frighten her, to wake up and be good.

On this occasion, while yet he was half-dressed, Dyke tiptoed into his mother's room to look at Sidney fast asleep in her little iron cot, her arm under her head, her lips parted. With infinite precaution he kissed her twice, and then finding one little stocking, hung with its mate very neatly over the back of a chair, dropped into it a dime, rolled up in a wad of paper. He winked all to himself and went out again, closing the door with exaggerated carefulness.

He breakfasted alone, Mrs. Dyke pouring his coffee and handing him his plate of ham and eggs, and half an hour later took himself off in his springless, skeleton wagon, humming a tune behind his beard and cracking the whip over the backs of his staid and solid farm horses.

The morning was fine, the sun just coming up. He left Guadalajara, sleeping and lifeless, on his left, and going across lots, over an angle of Quien Sabe, came out upon the Upper Road, a mile below the Long Trestle. He was in great spirits, looking about him over the brown fields, ruddy with the dawn. Almost directly in front of him, but far off, the gilded dome of the court-house at Bonneville was glinting radiant in the first rays of the sun, while a few miles distant, toward the north, the venerable campanile of the Mission San Juan stood silhouetted in purplish black against the flaming east. As he proceeded, the great farm horses jogging forward, placid, deliberate, the country side waked to another day. Crossing the irrigating ditch further on, he met a gang of Portuguese, with picks and shovels over their shoulders, just going to work. Hooven, already abroad, shouted him a "Goot mornun" from behind the fence of Los Muertos. Far off, toward the southwest, in the bare expanse of the open fields, where a clump of eucalyptus and cypress trees set a dark green note, a thin stream of smoke rose straight into the air from the kitchen of Derrick's ranch houses.

But a mile or so beyond the Long Trestle he was surprised to see Magnus Derrick's *protégé*, the one-time shepherd, Vanamee, coming across Quien Sabe, by a trail from one of Annixter's division houses. Without knowing exactly why, Dyke received the impression that the young man had not been in bed all of that night.

As the two approached each other, Dyke eyed the

young fellow. He was distrustful of Vanamee, having
the country-bred suspicion of any person he could not
understand. Vanamee was, beyond doubt, no part of the
life of ranch and country town. He was an alien, a vagabond, a strange fellow who came and went in mysterious
fashion, making no friends, keeping to himself. Why
did he never wear a hat, why indulge in a fine, black,
pointed beard, when either a round beard or a mustache
was the invariable custom? Why did he not cut his hair?
Above all, why did he prowl about so much at night?
As the two passed each other, Dyke, for all his good-
nature, was a little blunt in his greeting and looked back
at the ex-shepherd over his shoulder.

Dyke was right in his suspicion. Vanamee's bed had
not been disturbed for three nights. On the Monday of
that week he had passed the entire night in the garden of
the Mission, overlooking the Seed ranch, in the little valley. Tuesday evening had found him miles away from
that spot, in a deep arroyo in the Sierra foothills to the
eastward, while Wednesday he had slept in an abandoned
'dobe on Osterman's stock range, twenty miles from his
resting place of the night before.

The fact of the matter was that the old restlessness
had once more seized upon Vanamee. Something began
tugging at him; the spur of some unseen rider touched
his flank. The instinct of the wanderer woke and moved.
For some time now he had been a part of the Los Muertos
staff. On Quien Sabe, as on the other ranches, the slack
season was at hand. While waiting for the wheat to
come up no one was doing much of anything. Vanamee
had come over to Los Muertos and spent most of his
days on horseback, riding the range, rounding up and
watching the cattle in the fourth division of the ranch.
But if the vagabond instinct now roused itself in the
strange fellow's nature, a counter influence had also set in.

More and more Vanamee frequented the Mission garden after nightfall, sometimes remaining there till the dawn began to whiten, lying prone on the ground, his chin on his folded arms, his eyes searching the darkness over the little valley of the Seed ranch, watching, watching. As the days went by, he became more reticent than ever. Presley often came to find him on the stock range, a lonely figure in the great wilderness of bare, green hillsides, but Vanamee no longer took him into his confidence. Father Sarria alone heard his strange stories.

Dyke drove on toward Bonneville, thinking over the whole matter. He knew, as every one did in that part of the country, the legend of Vanamee and Angéle, the romance of the Mission garden, the mystery of the Other, Vanamee's flight to the deserts of the southwest, his periodic returns, his strange, reticent, solitary character, but, like many another of the country people, he accounted for Vanamee by a short and easy method. No doubt, the fellow's wits were turned. That was the long and short of it.

The ex-engineer reached the Post Office in Bonneville towards eleven o'clock, but he did not at once present his notice of the arrival of his consignment at Ruggles's office. It entertained him to indulge in an hour's lounging about the streets. It was seldom he got into town, and when he did he permitted himself the luxury of enjoying his evident popularity. He met friends everywhere, in the Post Office, in the drug store, in the barber shop and around the court-house. With each one he held a moment's conversation; almost invariably this ended in the same way:

"Come on 'n have a drink."

"Well, I don't care if I do."

And the friends proceeded to the Yosemite bar, pledging each other with punctilious ceremony. Dyke, how-

ever, was a strictly temperate man. His life on the engine
had trained him well. Alcohol he never touched, drinking
instead ginger ale, sarsaparilla-and-iron—soft drinks.

At the drug store, which also kept a stock of miscel-
laneous stationery, his eye was caught by a " transparent
slate," a child's toy, where upon a little pane of frosted
glass one could trace with considerable elaboration outline figures of cows, ploughs, bunches of fruit and even
rural water mills that were printed on slips of paper underneath.

" Now, there's an idea, Jim," he observed to the boy
behind the soda-water fountain; " I know a little tad
that would just about jump out of her skin for that.
Think I'll have to take it with me."

" How's Sidney getting along?" the other asked, while
wrapping up the package.

Dyke's enthusiasm had made of his little girl a
celebrity throughout Bonneville.

The ex-engineer promptly became voluble, assertive,
doggedly emphatic.

" Smartest little tad in all Tulare County, and more
fun! A regular whole show in herself."

" And the hops?" inquired the other.

" Bully," declared Dyke, with the good-natured man's
readiness to talk of his private affairs to any one who
would listen. " Bully. I'm dead sure of a bonanza
crop by now. The rain came *just* right. I actually don't
know as I can store the crop in those barns I built, it's
going to be so big. That foreman of mine was a daisy.
Jim, I'm going to make money in that deal. After I've
paid off the mortgage—you know I had to mortgage, yes,
crop and homestead both, but I can pay it off and all
the interest to boot, lovely,—well, and as I was saying,
after all expenses are paid off I'll clear big money, m'
son. Yes, sir. I *knew* there was boodle in hops. You

know the crop is contracted for already. Sure, the foreman managed that. He's a daisy. Chap in San Francisco will take it all and at the advanced price. I wanted
to hang on, to see if it wouldn't go to six cents, but the
foreman said, ' No, that's good enough.' So I signed.
Ain't it bully, hey?"

"Then what'll you do?"

"Well, I don't know. I'll have a lay-off for a month
or so and take the little tad and mother up and show 'em
the city—'Frisco—until it's time for the schools to open,
and then we'll put Sid in the seminary at Marysville.
Catch on?"

"I suppose you'll stay right by hops now?"

"Right you are, m'son. I know a good thing when
I see it. There's plenty others going into hops next
season. I set 'em the example. Wouldn't be surprised
if it came to be a regular industry hereabouts. I'm planning ahead for next year already. I can let the foreman
go, now that I've learned the game myself, and I think
I'll buy a piece of land off Quien Sabe and get a bigger
crop, and build a couple more barns, and, by George, in
about five years time I'll have things humming. I'm
going to make *money*, Jim."

He emerged once more into the street and went up the
block leisurely, planting his feet squarely. He fancied
that he could feel he was considered of more importance
nowadays. He was no longer a subordinate, an employee. He was his own man, a proprietor, an owner of
land, furthering a successful enterprise. No one had
helped him; he had followed no one's lead. He had
struck out unaided for himself, and his success was due
solely to his own intelligence, industry, and foresight.
He squared his great shoulders till the blue gingham of
his jumper all but cracked. Of late, his great blond beard
had grown and the work in the sun had made his face

very red. Under the visor of his cap—relic of his engineering days—his blue eyes twinkled with vast good-nature. He felt that he made a fine figure as he went by a group of young girls in lawns and muslins and garden hats on their way to the Post Office. He wondered if they looked after him, wondered if they had heard that he was in a fair way to become a rich man.

But the chronometer in the window of the jewelry store warned him that time was passing. He turned about, and, crossing the street, took his way to Ruggles's office, which was the freight as well as the land office of the P. and S. W. Railroad.

As he stood for a moment at the counter in front of the wire partition, waiting for the clerk to make out the order for the freight agent at the depot, Dyke was surprised to see a familiar figure in conference with Ruggles himself, by a desk inside the railing.

The figure was that of a middle-aged man, fat, with a great stomach, which he stroked from time to time. As he turned about, addressing a remark to the clerk, Dyke recognised S. Behrman. The banker, railroad agent, and political manipulator seemed to the ex-engineer's eyes to be more gross than ever. His smooth-shaven jowl stood out big and tremulous on either side of his face; the roll of fat on the nape of his neck, sprinkled with sparse, stiff hairs, bulged out with greater prominence. His great stomach, covered with a light brown linen vest, stamped with innumerable interlocked horseshoes, protruded far in advance, enormous, aggressive. He wore his inevitable round-topped hat of stiff brown straw, varnished so bright that it reflected the light of the office windows like a helmet, and even from where he stood Dyke could hear his loud breathing and the clink of the hollow links of his watch chain upon the vest buttons of imitation pearl, as his stomach rose and fell.

Dyke looked at him with attention. There was the enemy, the representative of the Trust with which Derrick's League was locking horns. The great struggle had begun to invest the combatants with interest. Daily, almost hourly, Dyke was in touch with the ranchers, the wheat-growers. He heard their denunciations, their growls of exasperation and defiance. Here was the other side—this placid, fat man, with a stiff straw hat and linen vest, who never lost his temper, who smiled affably upon his enemies, giving them good advice, commiserating with them in one defeat after another, never ruffled, never excited, sure of his power, conscious that back of him was the Machine, the colossal force, the inexhaustible coffers of a mighty organisation, vomiting millions to the League's thousands.

The League was clamorous, ubiquitous, its objects known to every urchin on the streets, but the Trust was silent, its ways inscrutable, the public saw only results. It worked on in the dark, calm, disciplined, irresistible. Abruptly Dyke received the impression of the multitudinous ramifications of the colossus. Under his feet the ground seemed mined; down there below him in the dark the huge tentacles went silently twisting and advancing, spreading out in every direction, sapping the strength of all opposition, quiet, gradual, biding the time to reach up and out and grip with a sudden unleashing of gigantic strength.

"I'll be wanting some cars of you people before the summer is out," observed Dyke to the clerk as he folded up and put away the order that the other had handed him. He remembered perfectly well that he had arranged the matter of transporting his crop some months before, but his rôle of proprietor amused him and he liked to busy himself again and again with the details of his undertaking.

"I suppose," he added, "you'll be able to give 'em to me. There'll be a big wheat crop to move this year and I don't want to be caught in any car famine."

"Oh, you'll get your cars," murmured the other.

"I'll be the means of bringing business your way," Dyke went on; "I've done so well with my hops that there are a lot of others going into the business next season. Suppose," he continued, struck with an idea, "suppose we went into some sort of pool, a sort of shippers' organisation, could you give us special rates, cheaper rates—say a cent and a half?"

The other looked up.

"A cent and a half! Say *four* cents and a half and maybe I'll talk business with you."

"Four cents and a half," returned Dyke, "I don't see it. Why, the regular rate is only two cents."

"No, it isn't," answered the clerk, looking him gravely in the eye, "it's five cents."

"Well, there's where you are wrong, m'son," Dyke retorted, genially. "You look it up. You'll find the freight on hops from Bonneville to 'Frisco is two cents a pound for car load lots. You told me that yourself last fall."

"That was last fall," observed the clerk. There was a silence. Dyke shot a glance of suspicion at the other. Then, reassured, he remarked:

"You look it up. You'll see I'm right."

S. Behrman came forward and shook hands politely with the ex-engineer.

"Anything I can do for you, Mr. Dyke?"

Dyke explained. When he had done speaking, the clerk turned to S. Behrman and observed, respectfully:

"Our regular rate on hops is five cents."

"Yes," answered S. Behrman, pausing to reflect; "yes, Mr. Dyke, that's right—five cents."

The clerk brought forward a folder of yellow paper and handed it to Dyke. It was inscribed at the top "Tariff Schedule No. 8," and underneath these words, in brackets, was a smaller inscription, *"Supersedes No. 7 of Aug. 1."*

"See for yourself," said S. Behrman. He indicated an item under the head of "Miscellany."

"The following rates for carriage of hops in car load lots," read Dyke, "take effect June 1, and will remain in force until superseded by a later tariff. Those quoted beyond Stockton are subject to changes in traffic arrangements with carriers by water from that point."

In the list that was printed below, Dyke saw that the rate for hops between Bonneville or Guadalajara and San Francisco was five cents.

For a moment Dyke was confused. Then swiftly the matter became clear in his mind. The Railroad had raised the freight on hops from two cents to five.

All his calculations as to a profit on his little investment he had based on a freight rate of two cents a pound. He was under contract to deliver his crop. He could not draw back. The new rate ate up every cent of his gains. He stood there ruined.

"Why, what do you mean?" he burst out. "You promised me a rate of two cents and I went ahead with my business with that understanding. What do you mean?"

S. Behrman and the clerk watched him from the other side of the counter.

"The rate is five cents," declared the clerk doggedly.

"Well, that ruins me," shouted Dyke. "Do you understand? I won't make fifty cents. *Make!* Why, I will *owe*,—I'll be—be— That ruins me, do you understand?"

The other raised a shoulder.

"We don't force you to ship. You can do as you like. The rate is five cents."

"Well—but—damn you, I'm under contract to deliver. What am I going to do? Why, you told me—you promised me a two-cent rate."

"I don't remember it," said the clerk. "I don't know anything about that. But I know this; I know that hops have gone up. I know the German crop was a failure and that the crop in New York wasn't worth the hauling. Hops have gone up to nearly a dollar. You don't suppose we don't know that, do you, Mr. Dyke?"

"What's the price of hops got to do with you?"

"It's got *this* to do with us," returned the other with a sudden aggressiveness, "that the freight rate has gone up to meet the price. We're not doing business for our health. My orders are to raise your rate to five cents, and I think you are getting off easy."

Dyke stared in blank astonishment. For the moment, the audacity of the affair was what most appealed to him. He forgot its personal application.

"Good Lord," he murmured, "good Lord! What will you people do next? Look here. What's your basis of applying freight rates, anyhow?" he suddenly vociferated with furious sarcasm. "What's your rule? What are you guided by?"

But at the words, S. Behrman, who had kept silent during the heat of the discussion, leaned abruptly forward. For the only time in his knowledge, Dyke saw his face inflamed with anger and with the enmity and contempt of all this farming element with whom he was contending.

"Yes, what's your rule? What's your basis?" demanded Dyke, turning swiftly to him.

S. Behrman emphasised each word of his reply with a tap of one forefinger on the counter before him:

" All—the—traffic—will—bear."

The ex-engineer stepped back a pace, his fingers on the ledge of the counter, to steady himself. He felt himself grow pale, his heart became a mere leaden weight in his chest, inert, refusing to beat.

In a second the whole affair, in all its bearings, went speeding before the eye of his imagination like the rapid unrolling of a panorama. Every cent of his earnings was sunk in this hop business of his. More than that, he had borrowed money to carry it on, certain of success— borrowed of S. Behrman, offering his crop and his little home as security. Once he failed to meet his obligations, S. Behrman would foreclose. Not only would the Railroad devour every morsel of his profits, but also it would take from him his home; at a blow he would be left penniless and without a home. What would then become of his mother—and what would become of the little tad? She, whom he had been planning to educate like a veritable lady. For all that year he had talked of his ambition for his little daughter to every one he met. All Bonneville knew of it. What a mark for gibes he had made of himself. The workingman turned farmer! What a target for jeers—he who had fancied he could elude the Railroad! He remembered he had once said the great Trust had overlooked his little enterprise, disdaining to plunder such small fry. He should have known better than that. How had he ever imagined the Road would permit him to make any money?

Anger was not in him yet; no rousing of the blind, white-hot wrath that leaps to the attack with prehensile fingers, moved him. The blow merely crushed, staggered, confused.

He stepped aside to give place to a coatless man in a pink shirt, who entered, carrying in his hands an automatic door-closing apparatus.

" Where does this go? " inquired the man.

Dyke sat down for a moment on a seat that had been removed from a worn-out railway car to do duty in Ruggles's office. On the back of a yellow envelope he made some vague figures with a stump of blue pencil, multiplying, subtracting, perplexing himself with many errors.

S. Behrman, the clerk, and the man with the door-closing apparatus involved themselves in a long argument, gazing intently at the top panel of the door. The man who had come to fix the apparatus was unwilling to guarantee it, unless a sign was put on the outside of the door, warning incomers that the door was self-closing. This sign would cost fifteen cents extra.

" But you didn't say anything about this when the thing was ordered," declared S. Behrman. " No, I won't pay it, my friend. It's an overcharge."

" You needn't think," observed the clerk, " that just because you are dealing with the Railroad you are going to work us."

Genslinger came in, accompanied by Delaney. S. Behrman and the clerk, abruptly dismissing the man with the door-closing machine, put themselves behind the counter and engaged in conversation with these two. Genslinger introduced Delaney. The buster had a string of horses he was shipping southward. No doubt he had come to make arrangements with the Railroad in the matter of stock cars. The conference of the four men was amicable in the extreme.

Dyke, studying the figures on the back of the envelope, came forward again. Absorbed only in his own distress, he ignored the editor and the cow-puncher.

" Say," he hazarded, " how about this? I make out——"

" We've told you what our rates are, Mr. Dyke," exclaimed the clerk angrily. " That's all the arrangement we will make. Take it or leave it." He turned again to Genslinger, giving the ex-engineer his back.

Dyke moved away and stood for a moment in the centre of the room, staring at the figures on the envelope.

" I don't see," he muttered, " just what I'm going to do. No, I don't see what I'm going to do at all."

Ruggles came in, bringing with him two other men in whom Dyke recognised dummy buyers of the Los Muertos and Osterman ranchos. They brushed by him, jostling his elbow, and as he went out of the door he heard them exchange jovial greetings with Delaney, Genslinger, and S. Behrman.

Dyke went down the stairs to the street and proceeded onward aimlessly in the direction of the Yosemite House, fingering the yellow envelope and looking vacantly at the sidewalk.

There was a stoop to his massive shoulders. His great arms dangled loosely at his sides, the palms of his hands open.

As he went along, a certain feeling of shame touched him. Surely his predicament must be apparent to every passer-by. No doubt, every one recognised the unsuccessful man in the very way he slouched along. The young girls in lawns, muslins, and garden hats, returning from the Post Office, their hands full of letters, must surely see in him the type of the failure, the bankrupt.

Then brusquely his tardy rage flamed up. By God, *no,* it was not his fault; he had made no mistake. His energy, industry, and foresight had been sound. He had been merely the object of a colossal trick, a sordid injustice, a victim of the insatiate greed of the monster, caught and choked by one of those millions of tentacles suddenly reaching up from below, from out the dark beneath his feet, coiling around his throat, throttling him, strangling him, sucking his blood. For a moment he thought of the courts, but instantly laughed at the idea. What court was immune from the power of the monster? Ah, the rage of helplessness, the fury of impotence! No help, no hope,—ruined in a brief instant—he a veritable giant, built of great sinews, powerful, in the full tide of his manhood, having all his health, all his wits. How could he now face his home? How could he tell his mother of this catastrophe? And Sidney—the little tad; how could he explain to her this wretchedness—how soften her disappointment? How keep the tears from out her eyes—how keep alive her confidence in him—her faith in his resources?

Bitter, fierce, ominous, his wrath loomed up in his heart. His fists gripped tight together, his teeth clenched. Oh, for a moment to have his hand upon the throat of S. Behrman, wringing the breath from him, wrenching out the red life of him—staining the street with the blood sucked from the veins of the People!

To the first friend that he met, Dyke told the tale of the tragedy, and to the next, and to the next. The affair went from mouth to mouth, spreading with electrical swiftness, overpassing and running ahead of Dyke himself, so that by the time he reached the lobby of the Yosemite House, he found his story awaiting him. A group formed about him. In his immediate vicinity business for the instant was suspended. The group swelled. One after another of his friends added themselves to it. Magnus Derrick joined it, and Annixter. Again and again, Dyke recounted the matter, beginning with the time when he was discharged from the same corporation's service for refusing to accept an unfair wage. His voice quivered with exasperation; his heavy frame shook with rage; his eyes were injected, bloodshot; his face flamed vermilion, while his deep bass rumbled throughout the running comments of his auditors like the thunderous reverberation of diapason.

From all points of view, the story was discussed by those who listened to him, now in the heat of excitement, now calmly, judicially. One verdict, however, prevailed. It was voiced by Annixter: "You're stuck. You can roar till you're black in the face, but you can't buck against the Railroad. There's nothing to be done."

"You can shoot the ruffian, you can shoot S. Behrman," clamoured one of the group. "Yes, sir; by the Lord, you can shoot him."

"Poor fool," commented Annixter, turning away.

Nothing to be done. No, there was nothing to be done—not one thing. Dyke, at last alone and driving his team out of the town, turned the business confusedly over in his mind from end to end. Advice, suggestion, even offers of financial aid had been showered upon him from all directions. Friends were not wanting who heatedly presented to his consideration all manner of ingenious plans, wonderful devices. They were worthless. The tentacle held fast. He was stuck.

By degrees, as his wagon carried him farther out into the country, and open empty fields, his anger lapsed, and the numbness of bewilderment returned. He could not look one hour ahead into the future; could formulate no plans even for the next day. He did not know what to do. He was stuck.

With the limpness and inertia of a sack of sand, the reins slipping loosely in his dangling fingers, his eyes fixed, staring between the horses' heads, he allowed himself to be carried aimlessly along. He resigned himself. What did he care? What was the use of going on? He was stuck.

The team he was driving had once belonged to the Los Muertos stables, and unguided as the horses were, they took the county road towards Derrick's ranch house. Dyke, all abroad, was unaware of the fact till, drawn by the smell of water, the horses halted by the trough in front of Caraher's saloon.

The ex-engineer dismounted, looking about him, realising where he was. So much the worse; it did not matter. Now that he had come so far it was as short to go home by this route as to return on his tracks. Slowly he unchecked the horses and stood at their heads, watching them drink.

"I don't see," he muttered, "just what I am going to do."

Caraher appeared at the door of his place, his red face, red beard, and flaming cravat standing sharply out from the shadow of the doorway. He called a welcome to Dyke.

"Hello, Captain."

Dyke looked up, nodding his head listlessly.

"Hello, Caraher," he answered.

"Well," continued the saloonkeeper, coming forward a step, "what's the news in town?"

Dyke told him. Caraher's red face suddenly took on a darker colour. The red glint in his eyes shot from under his eyebrows. Furious, he vented a rolling explosion of oaths.

"And now it's your turn," he vociferated. "They ain't after only the big wheat-growers, the rich men. By God, they'll even pick the poor man's pocket. Oh, they'll get their bellies full some day. It can't last forever: They'll wake up the wrong kind of man some morning, the man that's got guts in him, that will hit back when he's kicked and that will talk to 'em with a torch in one hand and a stick of dynamite in the other." He raised his clenched fists in the air. "So help me, God," he cried, "when I think it all over I go crazy, I see red.

Oh, if the people only knew their strength. Oh, if I could wake 'em up. There's not only Shelgrim, but there's others. All the magnates, all the butchers, all the blood-suckers, by the thousands. Their day will come, by God, it will."

By now, the ex-engineer and the bar-keeper had retired to the saloon back of the grocery to talk over the details of this new outrage. Dyke, still a little dazed, sat down by one of the tables, preoccupied, saying but little, and Caraher as a matter of course set the whiskey bottle at his elbow.

It happened that at this same moment, Presley, returning to Los Muertos from Bonneville, his pockets full of mail, stopped in at the grocery to buy some black lead for his bicycle. In the saloon, on the other side of the narrow partition, he overheard the conversation between Dyke and Caraher. The door was open. He caught every word distinctly.

" Tell us all about it, Dyke," urged Caraher.

For the fiftieth time Dyke told the story. Already it had crystallised into a certain form. He used the same phrases with each repetition, the same sentences, the same words. In his mind it became set. Thus he would tell it to any one who would listen from now on, week after week, year after year, all the rest of his life—" And I based my calculations on a two-cent rate. So soon as they saw I was to make money they doubled the tariff— all the traffic would bear—and I mortgaged to S. Behr-man—ruined me with a turn of the hand—stuck, cinched, and not one thing to be done."

As he talked, he drank glass after glass of whiskey, and the honest rage, the open, above-board fury of his mind coagulated, thickened, and sunk to a dull, evil hatred, a wicked, oblique malevolence. Caraher, sure now of winning a disciple, replenished his glass.

"Do you blame us now," he cried, "us others, the Reds? Ah, yes, it's all very well for your middle class to preach moderation. I could do it, too. You could do it, too, if your belly was fed, if your property was safe, if your wife had not been murdered, if your children were not starving. Easy enough then to preach law-abiding methods, legal redress, and all such rot. But how about *us?*" he vociferated. "Ah, yes, I'm a loud-mouthed rum-seller, ain't I? I'm a wild-eyed striker, ain't I? I'm a blood-thirsty anarchist, ain't I? Wait till you've seen your wife brought home to you with the face you used to kiss smashed in by a horse's hoof—killed by the Trust, as it happened to me. Then talk about moderation! And you, Dyke, black-listed engineer, discharged employee, ruined agriculturist, wait till you see your little tad and your mother turned out of doors when S. Behrman forecloses. Wait till you see 'em getting thin and white, and till you hear your little girl ask you why you all don't eat a little more and that she wants her dinner and you can't give it to her. Wait till you see—at the same time that your family is dying for lack of bread—a hundred thousand acres of wheat—millions of bushels of food—grabbed and gobbled by the Railroad Trust, and then talk of moderation. That talk is just what the Trust wants to hear. It ain't frightened of that. There's one thing only it does listen to, one thing it is frightened of—the people with dynamite in their hands,—six inches of plugged gaspipe. *That* talks."

Dyke did not reply. He filled another pony of whiskey and drank it in two gulps. His frown had lowered to a scowl, his face was a dark red, his head had sunk, bull-like, between his massive shoulders; without winking he gazed long and with troubled eyes at his knotted, muscular hands, lying open on the table before him, idle, their occupation gone.

Presley forgot his black lead. He listened to Caraher. Through the open door he caught a glimpse of Dyke's back, broad, muscled, bowed down, the great shoulders stooping.

The whole drama of the doubled freight rate leaped salient and distinct in the eye of his mind. And this was but one instance, an isolated case. Because he was near at hand he happened to see it. How many others were there, the length and breadth of the State? Constantly this sort of thing must occur—little industries choked out in their very beginnings, the air full of the death rattles of little enterprises, expiring unobserved in far-off counties, up in cañons and arroyos of the foothills, forgotten by every one but the monster who was daunted by the magnitude of no business, however great, who overlooked no opportunity of plunder, however petty, who with one tentacle grabbed a hundred thousand acres of wheat, and with another pilfered a pocketful of growing hops.

He went away without a word, his head bent, his hands clutched tightly on the cork grips of the handle bars of his bicycle. His lips were white. In his heart a blind demon of revolt raged tumultuous, shrieking blasphemies.

At Los Muertos, Presley overtook Annixter. As he guided his wheel up the driveway to Derrick's ranch house, he saw the master of Quien Sabe and Harran in conversation on the steps of the porch. Magnus stood in the doorway, talking to his wife.

Occupied with the press of business and involved in the final conference with the League's lawyers on the eve of the latter's departure for Washington, Annixter had missed the train that was to take him back to Guadalajara and Quien Sabe. Accordingly, he had accepted the Governor's invitation to return with him on his buckboard to Los Muertos, and before leaving Bonneville had telephoned to his ranch to have young Vacca bring the buckskin, by way of the Lower Road, to meet him at Los Muertos. He found her waiting there for him, but before going on, delayed a few moments to tell Harran of Dyke's affair.

"I wonder what he will do now?" observed Harran when his first outburst of indignation had subsided.

"Nothing," declared Annixter. "He's stuck."

"That eats up every cent of Dyke's earnings," Harran went on. "He has been ten years saving them. Oh, I told him to make sure of the Railroad when he first spoke to me about growing hops."

"I've just seen him," said Presley, as he joined the others. "He was at Caraher's. I only saw his back. He was drinking at a table and his back was towards me. But the man looked broken—absolutely crushed. It is terrible, terrible."

"He was at Caraher's, was he?" demanded Annixter.

"Yes."

"Drinking, hey?"

"I think so. Yes, I saw a bottle."

"Drinking at Caraher's," exclaimed Annixter, rancorously; "I can see *his* finish."

There was a silence. It seemed as if nothing more was to be said. They paused, looking thoughtfully on the ground.

In silence, grim, bitter, infinitely sad, the three men, as if at that moment actually standing in the bar-room of Caraher's roadside saloon, contemplated the slow sinking, the inevitable collapse and submerging of one of their companions, the wreck of a career, the ruin of an individual; an honest man, strong, fearless, upright, struck down by a colossal power, perverted by an evil influence, go reeling to his ruin.

"I see his finish," repeated Annixter. "Exit Dyke, and score another tally for S. Behrman, Shelgrim and Co."

He moved away impatiently, loosening the tie-rope with which the buckskin was fastened. He swung himself up.

"God for us all," he declared as he rode away, "and the devil take the hindmost. Good-bye, I'm going home. I still have one a little longer."

He galloped away along the Lower Road, in the direction of Quien Sabe, emerging from the grove of cypress and eucalyptus about the ranch house, and coming out upon the bare brown plain of the wheat land, stretching away from him in apparent barrenness on either hand.

It was late in the day, already his shadow was long upon the padded dust of the road in front of him. On ahead, a long ways off, and a little to the north, the venerable campanile of the Mission San Juan was glinting radiant in the last rays of the sun, while behind him, towards the north and west, the gilded dome of the courthouse at Bonneville stood silhouetted in purplish black against the flaming west. Annixter spurred the buckskin forward. He feared he might be late to his supper. He wondered if it would be brought to him by Hilma.

Hilma! The name struck across in his brain with a pleasant, glowing tremour. All through that day of activity, of strenuous business, the minute and cautious planning of the final campaign in the great war of the League and the Trust, the idea of her and the recollection of her had been the undercurrent of his thoughts. At last he was alone. He could put all other things behind him and occupy himself solely with her.

In that glory of the day's end, in that chaos of sunshine, he saw her again. Unimaginative, crude, direct, his fancy, nevertheless, placed her before him, steeped in sunshine, saturated with glorious light, brilliant, radiant, alluring. He saw the sweet simplicity of her carriage, the statuesque evenness of the contours of her figure, the single, deep swell of her bosom, the solid masses of her hair. He remembered the small contradictory suggestions of feminine daintiness he had so often remarked about her, her slim, narrow feet, the little steel buckles of her low shoes, the knot of black ribbon she had begun to wear of late on the back of her head, and he heard her voice, low-pitched, velvety, a sweet, murmuring huskiness that seemed to come more from her chest than from her throat.

The buckskin's hoofs clattered upon the gravelly flats of Broderson's Creek underneath the Long Trestle. Annixter's mind went back to the scene of the previous evening, when he had come upon her at this place. He set his teeth with anger and disappointment. Why had she not been able to understand? What was the matter with these women, always set upon this marrying notion? Was it not enough that he wanted her more than any other girl he knew and that she wanted him? She had said as much. Did she think she was going to be mistress of Quien Sabe? Ah, that was it. She was after his property, was for marrying him because of his money. His unconquerable suspicion of the woman, his innate distrust of the feminine element would not be done away with. What fathomless duplicity was hers, that she could appear so innocent. It was almost unbelievable; in fact, *was* it believable?

For the first time doubt assailed him. Suppose Hilma was indeed all that she appeared to be. Suppose it was not with her a question of his property, after all; it was a poor time to think of marrying him for his property when all Quien Sabe hung in the issue of the next few months. Suppose she had been sincere. But he caught himself up. Was he to be fooled by a feemale girl at this late date? He, Buck Annixter, crafty, hard-headed, a man of affairs? Not much. Whatever transpired he would remain the master.

He reached Quien Sabe in this frame of mind. But at this hour, Annixter, for all his resolutions, could no longer control his thoughts. As he stripped the saddle from the buckskin and led her to the watering trough by the stable corral, his heart was beating thick at the very notion of being near Hilma again. It was growing dark, but covertly he glanced here and there out of the corners of his eyes to see if she was anywhere about. Annixter—how, he could not tell—had become possessed of the idea that Hilma would not inform her parents of what had passed between them the previous evening under the Long Trestle. He had no idea that matters were at an end between himself and the young woman. He must apologise, he saw that clearly enough, must eat crow, as he told himself. Well, he would eat crow. He was not afraid of her any longer, now that she had made her confession to him. He would see her as soon as possible and get this business straightened out, and begin again from a new starting point. What he wanted with Hilma, Annixter did not define clearly in his mind. At one time he had known perfectly well what he wanted. Now, the goal of his desires had become vague. He could not say exactly what it was. He preferred that things should go forward without much idea of consequences; if consequences came, they would do so naturally enough, and of themselves; all that he positively knew was that Hilma occupied his thoughts morning, noon, and night; that he was happy when he was with her, and miserable when away from her.

The Chinese cook served his supper in silence. Annixter ate and drank and lighted a cigar, and after his meal sat on the porch of his house, smoking and enjoying the twilight. The evening was beautiful, warm, the sky one powder of stars. From the direction of the stables he heard one of the Portuguese hands picking a guitar.

But he wanted to see Hilma. The idea of going to bed without at least a glimpse of her became distasteful to him. Annixter got up and descending from the porch began to walk aimlessly about between the ranch buildings, with eye and ear alert. Possibly he might meet her somewheres.

The Trees' little house, toward which inevitably Annixter directed his steps, was dark. Had they all gone to bed so soon? He made a wide circuit about it, listening, but heard no sound. The door of the dairy-house stood ajar. He pushed it open, and stepped into the odorous darkness of its interior. The pans and deep cans of polished metal glowed faintly from the corners and from the walls. The smell of new cheese was pungent in his nostrils. Everything was quiet. There was nobody there. He went out again, closing the door, and stood for a moment in the space between the dairy-house and the new barn, uncertain as to what he should do next.

As he waited there, his foreman came out of the men's bunk house, on the other side of the kitchens, and crossed over toward the barn. "Hello, Billy," muttered Annixter as he passed.

"Oh, good evening, Mr. Annixter," said the other, pausing in front of him. "I didn't know you were back. By the way," he added, speaking as though the matter was already known to Annixter, "I see old man Tree and his family have left us. Are they going to be gone long? Have they left for good?"

"What's that?" Annixter exclaimed. "When did they go? Did all of them go, all three?"

"Why, I thought you knew. Sure, they all left on the afternoon train for San Francisco. Cleared out in a hurry—took all their trunks. Yes, all three went—the young lady, too. They gave me notice early this morning. They ain't ought to have done that. I don't know who I'm to get to run the dairy on such short notice. Do you know any one, Mr. Annixter?"

"Well, why in hell did you let them go?" vociferated Annixter. "Why didn't you keep them here till I got back? Why didn't you find out if they were going for good? I can't be everywhere. What do I feed you for if it ain't to look after things I can't attend to?"

He turned on his heel and strode away straight before him, not caring where he was going. He tramped out from the group of ranch buildings; holding on over the open reach of his ranch, his teeth set, his heels digging furiously into the ground. The minutes passed. He walked on swiftly, muttering to himself from time to time.

"Gone, by the Lord. Gone, by the Lord. By the Lord Harry, she's cleared out."

As yet his head was empty of all thought. He could not steady his wits to consider this new turn of affairs. He did not even try.

"Gone, by the Lord," he exclaimed. "By the Lord, she's cleared out."

He found the irrigating ditch, and the beaten path made by the ditch tenders that bordered it, and followed it some five minutes; then struck off at right angles over the rugged surface of the ranch land, to where a great white stone jutted from the ground. There he sat down, and leaning forward, rested his elbows on his knees, and looked out vaguely into the night, his thoughts swiftly readjusting themselves.

He was alone. The silence of the night, the infinite

repose of the flat, bare earth—two immensities—widened
around and above him like illimitable seas. A grey half-
light, mysterious, grave, flooded downward from the
stars.

Annixter was in torment. Now, there could be
no longer any doubt—now it was Hilma or nothing.
Once out of his reach, once lost to him, and the recollection of her assailed him with unconquerable vehemence.
Much as she had occupied his mind, he had never realised
till now how vast had been the place she had filled in his
life. He had told her as much, but even then he did not
believe it.

Suddenly, a bitter rage against himself overwhelmed
him as he thought of the hurt he had given her the previous evening. He should have managed differently.
How, he did not know, but the sense of the outrage he
had put upon her abruptly recoiled against him with
cruel force. Now, he was sorry for it, infinitely sorry,
passionately sorry. He had hurt her. He had brought
the tears to her eyes. He had so flagrantly insulted her
that she could no longer bear to breathe the same air
with him. She had told her parents all. She had left
Quien Sabe—had left him for good, at the very moment
when he believed he had won her. Brute, beast that he
was, he had driven her away.

An hour went by; then two, then four, then six. Annixter still sat in his place, groping and battling in a confusion of spirit, the like of which he had never felt before.
He did not know what was the matter with him. He
could not find his way out of the dark and out of the
turmoil that wheeled around him. He had had no experience with women. There was no precedent to guide
him. How was he to get out of this? What was the
clew that would set everything straight again?

That he would give Hilma up, never once entered his

head. Have her he would. She had given herself to him. Everything should have been easy after that, and instead, here he was alone in the night, wrestling with himself, in deeper trouble han ever, and Hilma farther than ever away from him.

It was true, he might have Hilma, even now, if he was willing to marry her. But marriage, to his mind, had been always a vague, most remote possibility, almost as vague and as remote as his death,—a thing that happened to some men, but that would surely never occur to him, or, if it did, it would be after long years had passed, when he was older, more settled, more mature— an event that belonged to the period of his middle life, distant as yet.

He had never faced the question of his marriage. He had kept it at an immense distance from him. It had never been a part of his order of things. He was not a marrying man.

But Hilma was an ever-present reality, as near to him as his right hand. Marriage was a formless, far distant abstraction. Hilma a tangible, imminent fact. Before he could think of the two as one; before he could consider the idea of marriage, side by side with the idea of Hilma, measureless distances had to be traversed, things as disassociated in his mind as fire and water, had to be fused together; and between the two he was torn as if upon a rack.

Slowly, by imperceptible degrees, the imagination, unused, unwilling machine, began to work. The brain's activity lapsed proportionately. He began to think less, and feel more. In that rugged composition, confused, dark, harsh, a furrow had been driven deep, a little seed planted, a little seed at first weak, forgotten, lost in the lower dark places of his character.

But as the intellect moved slower, its functions growing numb, the idea of self dwindled. Annixter no longer considered himself; no longer considered the notion of marriage from the point of view of his own comfort, his own wishes, his own advantage. He realised that in his new-found desire to make her happy, he was sincere. There was something in that idea, after all. To make some one happy—how about that now? It was worth thinking of.

Far away, low down in the east, a dim belt, a grey light began to whiten over the horizon. The tower of the Mission stood black against it. The dawn was coming. The baffling obscurity of the night was passing. Hidden things were coming into view.

Annixter, his eyes half-closed, his chin upon his fist, allowed his imagination full play. How would it be if he should take Hilma into his life, this beautiful young girl, pure as he now knew her to be; innocent, noble with the inborn nobility of dawning womanhood? An overwhelming sense of his own unworthiness suddenly bore down upon him with crushing force, as he thought of this. He had gone about the whole affair wrongly. He had been mistaken from the very first. She was infinitely above him. He did not want—he should not desire to be the master. It was she, his servant, poor, simple, lowly even, who should condescend to him.

Abruptly there was presented to his mind's eye a picture of the years to come, if he now should follow his best, his highest, his most unselfish impulse. He saw Hilma, his own, for better or for worse, for richer or for poorer, all barriers down between them, he giving himself to her as freely, as nobly, as she had given herself to him. By a supreme effort, not of the will, but of the emotion, he fought his way across that vast gulf that for a time had gaped between Hilma and the idea of his marriage. Instantly, like the swift blending of beautiful colours, like the harmony of beautiful chords of music, the two ideas melted into one, and in that moment into his harsh, unlovely world a new idea was born. Annixter stood suddenly upright, a mighty tenderness, a gentleness of spirit, such as he had never conceived of, in his heart strained, swelled, and in a moment seemed to burst. Out of the dark furrows of his soul, up from the deep rugged recesses of his being, something rose, expanding. He opened his arms wide. An immense happiness overpowered him. Actual tears came to his eyes. Without knowing why, he was not ashamed of it. This poor, crude fellow, harsh, hard, narrow, with his unlovely nature, his fierce truculency, his selfishness, his obstinacy, abruptly knew that all the sweetness of life, all the great vivifying eternal force of humanity had burst into life within him.

The little seed, long since planted, gathering strength quietly, had at last germinated.

Then as the realisation of this hardened into certainty, in the growing light of the new day that had just dawned for him, Annixter uttered a cry. Now at length, he knew the meaning of it all.

" Why—I—I, I *love* her," he cried. Never until then had it occurred to him. Never until then, in all his thoughts of Hilma, had that great word passed his lips.

It was a Memnonian cry, the greeting of the hard, harsh image of man, rough-hewn, flinty, granitic, uttering a note of joy, acclaiming the new risen sun.

By now it was almost day. The east glowed opalescent. All about him Annixter saw the land inundated with light. But there was a change. Overnight something had occurred. In his perturbation the change seemed to him, at first, elusive, almost fanciful, unreal. But now as the light spread, he looked again at the gigantic scroll of ranch lands unrolled before him from edge to edge of the horizon. The change was not fanciful. The change was real. The earth was no longer bare. The land was no longer barren,—no longer empty, no longer dull brown. All at once Annixter shouted aloud.

There it was, the Wheat, the Wheat! The little seed long planted, germinating in the deep, dark furrows of the soil, straining, swelling, suddenly in one night had burst upward to the light. The wheat had come up. It was there before him, around him, everywhere, illimitable, immeasurable. The winter brownness of the ground was overlaid with a little shimmer of green. The promise of the sowing was being fulfilled. The earth, the loyal mother, who never failed, who never disappointed, was keeping her faith again. Once more the strength of nations was renewed. Once more the force of the world was revivified. Once more the Titan, benignant, calm, stirred and woke, and the morning abruptly blazed into glory upon the spectacle of a man whose heart leaped exuberant with the love of a woman, and an exulting earth gleaming transcendent with the radiant magnificence of an inviolable pledge.

III

Presley's room in the ranch house of Los Muertos was in the second story of the building. It was a corner room; one of its windows facing the south, the other the east. Its appointments were of the simplest. In one angle was the small white painted iron bed, covered with a white counterpane. The walls were hung with a white paper figured with knots of pale green leaves, very gay and bright. There was a straw matting on the floor. White muslin half-curtains hung in the windows, upon the sills of which certain plants bearing pink waxen flowers of which Presley did not know the name, grew in oblong green boxes. The walls were unadorned, save by two pictures, one a reproduction of the " Reading from Homer," the other a charcoal drawing of the Mission of San Juan de Guadalajara, which Presley had made himself. By the east window stood the plainest of deal tables, innocent of any cloth or covering, such as might have been used in a kitchen. It was Presley's work table, and was invariably littered with papers, half-finished manuscripts, drafts of poems, notebooks, pens, half-smoked cigarettes, and the like. Near at hand, upon a shelf, were his books. There were but two chairs in the room—the straight backed wooden chair, that stood in front of the table, angular, upright, and in which it was impossible to take one's ease, and the long comfortable wicker steamer chair, stretching its length in front of the south window. Presley was immensely fond of this room. It amused and interested him to maintain its air of rigorous simplicity and freshness. He abhorred cluttered bric-a-brac and meaningless *objets d'art*. Once in so often he submitted his room to a vigorous inspection; setting it to rights, removing everything but the essentials, the few ornaments which, in a way, were part of his life.

His writing had by this time undergone a complete change. The notes for his great Song of the West, the epic poem he once had hoped to write he had flung aside, together with all the abortive attempts at its beginning. Also he had torn up a great quantity of "fugitive" verses, preserving only a certain half-finished poem, that he called "The Toilers." This poem was a comment upon the social fabric, and had been inspired by the sight of a painting he had seen in Cedarquist's art gallery. He had written all but the last verse.

On the day that he had overheard the conversation between Dyke and Caraher, in the latter's saloon, which had acquainted him with the monstrous injustice of the increased tariff, Presley had returned to Los Muertos, white and trembling, roused to a pitch of exaltation, the like of which he had never known in all his life. His wrath was little short of even Caraher's. He too "saw red"; a mighty spirit of revolt heaved tumultuous within him. It did not seem possible that this outrage could go on much longer. The oppression was incredible; the plain story of it set down in truthful statement of fact would not be believed by the outside world.

He went up to his little room and paced the floor with clenched fists and burning face, till at last, the repression of his contending thoughts all but suffocated him, and he flung himself before his table and began to write. For a time, his pen seemed to travel of itself; words came to him without searching, shaping themselves into phrases,—the phrases building themselves up to great,

forcible sentences, full of eloquence, of fire, of passion.
As his prose grew more exalted, it passed easily into the
domain of poetry. Soon the cadence of his paragraphs
settled to an ordered beat and rhythm, and in the end
Presley had thrust aside his journal and was once more
writing verse.

He picked up his incomplete poem of "The Toilers,"
read it hastily a couple of times to catch its swing, then
the Idea of the last verse—the Idea for which he so long
had sought in vain—abruptly springing to his brain,
wrote it off without so much as replenishing his pen with
ink. He added still another verse, bringing the poem to
a definite close, resuming its entire conception, and ending with a single majestic thought, simple, noble, dignified, absolutely convincing.

Presley laid down his pen and leaned back in his chair,
with the certainty that for one moment he had touched
untrod heights. His hands were cold, his head on fire,
his heart leaping tumultuous in his breast.

Now at last, he had achieved. He saw why he had
never grasped the inspiration for his vast, vague, *impersonal* Song of the West. At the time when he sought
for it, his convictions had not been aroused; he had not
then cared for the People. His sympathies had not been
touched. Small wonder that he had missed it. Now he
was of the People; he had been stirred to his lowest
depths. His earnestness was almost a frenzy. He
believed, and so to him all things were possible at
once.

Then the artist in him reasserted itself. He became
more interested in his poem, as such, than in the cause
that had inspired it. He went over it again, retouching
it carefully, changing a word here and there, and improving its rhythm. For the moment, he forgot the
People, forgot his rage, his agitation of the previous

hour, he remembered only that he had written a great poem.

Then doubt intruded. After all, was it so great? Did not its sublimity overpass a little the bounds of the ridiculous? Had he seen true? Had he failed again? He re-read the poem carefully; and it seemed all at once to lose force.

By now, Presley could not tell whether what he had written was true poetry or doggerel. He distrusted profoundly his own judgment. He must have the opinion of some one else, some one competent to judge. He could not wait; to-morrow would not do. He must know to a certainty before he could rest that night.

He made a careful copy of what he had written, and putting on his hat and laced boots, went down stairs and out upon the lawn, crossing over to the stables. He found Phelps there, washing down the buckboard.

"Do you know where Vanamee is to-day?" he asked the latter. Phelps put his chin in the air.

"Ask me something easy," he responded. "He might be at Guadalajara, or he might be up at Osterman's, or he might be a hundred miles away from either place. I know where he ought to be, Mr. Presley, but that ain't saying where the crazy gesabe is. He *ought* to be range-riding over east of Four, at the head waters of Mission Creek."

"I'll try for him there, at all events," answered Presley. "If you see Harran when he comes in, tell him I may not be back in time for supper."

Presley found the pony in the corral, cinched the saddle upon him, and went off over the Lower Road, going eastward at a brisk canter.

At Hooven's he called a "How do you do" to Minna, whom he saw lying in a slat hammock under the mammoth live oak, her foot in bandages; and then galloped on over the bridge across the irrigating ditch, wondering vaguely what would become of such a pretty girl as Minna, and if in the end she would marry the Portuguese foreman in charge of the ditching-gang. He told himself that he hoped she would, and that speedily. There was no lack of comment as to Minna Hooven about the ranches. Certainly she was a good girl, but she was seen at all hours here and there about Bonneville and Guadalajara, skylarking with the Portuguese farm hands of Quien Sabe and Los Muertos. She was very pretty; the men made fools of themselves over her. Presley hoped they would not end by making a fool of her.

Just beyond the irrigating ditch, Presley left the Lower Road, and following a trail that branched off southeasterly from this point, held on across the Fourth Division of the ranch, keeping the Mission Creek on his left. A few miles farther on, he went through a gate in a barbed wire fence, and at once engaged himself in a system of little arroyos and low rolling hills, that steadily lifted and increased in size as he proceeded. This higher ground was the advance guard of the Sierra foothills, and served as the stock range for Los Muertos. The hills were huge rolling hummocks of bare ground, covered only by wild oats. At long intervals, were isolated live oaks. In the cañons and arroyos, the chaparral and manzanita grew in dark olive-green thickets. The ground was honey-combed with gopher-holes, and the gophers themselves were everywhere. Occasionally a jack rabbit bounded across the open, from one growth of chaparral to another, taking long leaps, his ears erect. High overhead, a hawk or two swung at anchor, and once, with a startling rush of wings, a covey of quail flushed from the brush at the side of the trail.

On the hillsides, in thinly scattered groups were the cattle, grazing deliberately, working slowly toward the water-holes for their evening drink, the horses keeping to themselves, the colts nuzzling at their mothers' bellies, whisking their tails, stamping their unshod feet. But once in a remoter field, solitary, magnificent, enormous, the short hair curling tight upon his forehead, his small red eyes twinkling, his vast neck heavy with muscles, Presley came upon the monarch, the king, the great Durham bull, maintaining his lonely state, unapproachable, austere.

Presley found the one-time shepherd by a water-hole, in a far distant corner of the range. He had made his simple camp for the night. His blue-grey army blanket lay spread under a live oak, his horse grazed near at hand. He himself sat on his heels before a little fire of dead manzanita roots, cooking his coffee and bacon. Never had Presley conceived so keen an impression of loneliness as his crouching figure presented. The bald, bare landscape widened about him to infinity. Vanamee was a spot in it all, a tiny dot, a single atom of human organisation, floating endlessly on the ocean of an illimitable nature.

The two friends ate together, and Vanamee, having snared a brace of quails, dressed and then roasted them on a sharpened stick. After eating, they drank great refreshing draughts from the water-hole. Then, at length, Presley having lit his cigarette, and Vanamee his pipe, the former said:

"Vanamee, I have been writing again."

Vanamee turned his lean ascetic face toward him, his black eyes fixed attentively.

"I know," he said, "your journal."

"No, this is a poem. You remember, I told you about it once. 'The Toilers,' I called it."

"Oh, verse! Well, I am glad you have gone back to it. It is your natural vehicle."

"You remember the poem?" asked Presley. "It was unfinished."

"Yes, I remember it. There was better promise in it than anything you ever wrote. Now, I suppose, you have finished it."

Without reply, Presley brought it from out the breast pocket of his shooting coat. The moment seemed propitious. The stillness of the vast, bare hills was profound. The sun was setting in a cloudless brazier of red light; a golden dust pervaded all the landscape. Presley read his poem aloud. When he had finished, his friend looked at him.

"What have you been doing lately?" he demanded. Presley, wondering, told of his various comings and goings.

"I don't mean that," returned the other. "Something has happened to you, something has aroused you. I am right, am I not? Yes, I thought so. In this poem of yours, you have not been trying to make a sounding piece of literature. You wrote it under tremendous stress. Its very imperfections show that. It is better than a mere rhyme. It is an Utterance—a Message. It is Truth. You have come back to the primal heart of things, and you have seen clearly. Yes, it is a great poem."

"Thank you," exclaimed Presley fervidly. "I had begun to mistrust myself."

"Now," observed Vanamee, "I presume you will rush it into print. To have formulated a great thought, simply to have accomplished, is not enough."

"I think I am sincere," objected Presley. "If it is good it will do good to others. You said yourself it was a Message. If it has any value, I do not think it would be right to keep it back from even a very small and most indifferent public."

"Don't publish it in the magazines at all events," Vanamee answered. "Your inspiration has come *from* the People. Then let it go straight *to* the People—not the literary readers of the monthly periodicals, the rich, who would only be indirectly interested. If you must publish it, let it be in the daily press. Don't interrupt. I know what you will say. It will be that the daily press is common, is vulgar, is undignified; and I tell you that such a poem as this of yours, called as it is, 'The Toilers,' must be read *by* the Toilers. It *must be* common; it must be vulgarised. You must not stand upon your dignity with the People, if you are to reach them."

"That is true, I suppose," Presley admitted, "but I can't get rid of the idea that it would be throwing my poem away. The great magazine gives me such—a—background; gives me such weight."

"Gives *you* such weight, gives *you* such background. Is it *yourself* you think of? You helper of the helpless. Is that your sincerity? You must sink yourself; must forget yourself and your own desire of fame, of admitted success. It is your *poem*, your *message*, that must prevail,—not *you*, who wrote it. You preach a doctrine of abnegation, of self-obliteration, and you sign your name to your words as high on the tablets as you can reach, so that all the world may see, not the poem, but the poet. Presley, there are many like you. The social reformer writes a book on the iniquity of the possession of land, and out of the proceeds, buys a corner lot. The economist who laments the hardships of the poor, allows himself to grow rich upon the sale of his book."

But Presley would hear no further.

"No," he cried, "I know I am sincere, and to prove it to you, I will publish my poem, as you say, in the daily press, and I will accept no money for it."

They talked on for about an hour, while the evening

wore away. Presley very soon noticed that Vanamee was again preoccupied. More than ever of late, his silence, his brooding had increased. By and by he rose abruptly, turning his head to the north, in the direction of the Mission church of San Juan.

"I think," he said to Presley, "that I must be going."

"Going? Where to at this time of night?"

"Off there." Vanamee made an uncertain gesture toward the north. "Good-bye," and without another word he disappeared in the grey of the twilight. Presley was left alone wondering. He found his horse, and, tightening the girths, mounted and rode home under the sheen of the stars, thoughtful, his head bowed. Before he went to bed that night he sent "The Toilers" to the Sunday Editor of a daily newspaper in San Francisco.

Upon leaving Presley, Vanamee, his thumbs hooked into his empty cartridge belt, strode swiftly down from the hills of the Los Muertos stock-range and on through the silent town of Guadalajara. His lean, swarthy face, with its hollow cheeks, fine, black, pointed beard, and sad eyes, was set to the northward. As was his custom, he was bareheaded, and the rapidity of his stride made a breeze in his long, black hair. He knew where he was going. He knew what he must live through that night.

Again, the deathless grief that never slept leaped out of the shadows, and fastened upon his shoulders. It was scourging him back to that scene of a vanished happiness, a dead romance, a perished idyl,—the Mission garden in the shade of the venerable pear trees.

But, besides this, other influences tugged at his heart. There was a mystery in the garden. In that spot the night was not always empty, the darkness not always silent. Something far off stirred and listened to his cry, at times drawing nearer to him. At first this presence had been a matter for terror; but of late, as he felt it gradually drawing nearer, the terror had at long intervals given place to a feeling of an almost ineffable sweetness. But distrusting his own senses, unwilling to submit himself to such torturing, uncertain happiness, averse to the terrible confusion of spirit that followed upon a night spent in the garden, Vanamee had tried to keep away from the place. However, when the sorrow of his life reassailed him, and the thoughts and recollections of Angéle brought the ache into his heart, and the tears to his eyes, the temptation to return to the garden invariably gripped him close. There were times when he could not resist. Of themselves, his footsteps turned in that direction. It was almost as if he himself had been called.

Guadalajara was silent, dark. Not even in Solotari's was there a light. The town was asleep. Only the inevitable guitar hummed from an unseen 'dobe. Vanamee pushed on. The smell of the fields and open country, and a distant scent of flowers that he knew well, came to his nostrils, as he emerged from the town by way of the road that led on towards the Mission through Quien Sabe. On either side of him lay the brown earth, silently nurturing the implanted seed. Two days before it had rained copiously, and the soil, still moist, disengaged a pungent aroma of fecundity.

Vanamee, following the road, passed through the collection of buildings of Annixter's home ranch. Everything slept. At intervals, the aër-motor on the artesian well creaked audibly, as it turned in a languid breeze from the northeast. A cat, hunting field-mice, crept from the shadow of the gigantic barn and paused uncertainly in the open, the tip of her tail twitching. From within the barn itself came the sound of the friction of a heavy body and a stir of hoofs, as one of the dozing cows lay down with a long breath.

Vanamee left the ranch house behind him and proceeded on his way. Beyond him, to the right of the road, he could make out the higher ground in the Mission enclosure, and the watching tower of the Mission itself. The minutes passed. He went steadily forward. Then abruptly he paused, his head in the air, eye and ear alert. To that strange sixth sense of his, responsive as the leaves of the sensitive plant, had suddenly come the impression of a human being near at hand. He had neither seen nor heard, but for all that he stopped an instant in his tracks; then, the sensation confirmed, went on again with slow steps, advancing warily.

At last, his swiftly roving eyes lighted upon an object, just darker than the grey-brown of the night-ridden land. It was at some distance from the roadside. Vanamee approached it cautiously, leaving the road, treading carefully upon the moist clods of earth underfoot. Twenty paces distant, he halted.

Annixter was there, seated upon a round, white rock, his back towards him. He was leaning forward, his elbows on his knees, his chin in his hands. He did not move. Silent, motionless, he gazed out upon the flat, sombre land.

It was the night wherein the master of Quien Sabe wrought out his salvation, struggling with Self from dusk to dawn. At the moment when Vanamee came upon him, the turmoil within him had only begun. The heart of the man had not yet wakened. The night was young, the dawn far distant, and all around him the fields of upturned clods lay bare and brown, empty of all life, unbroken by a single green shoot.

For a moment, the life-circles of these two men, of so widely differing characters, touched each other, there in the silence of the night under the stars. Then silently Vanamee withdrew, going on his way, wondering at the trouble that, like himself, drove this hardheaded man of affairs, untroubled by dreams, out into the night to brood over an empty land.

Then speedily he forgot all else. The material world drew off from him. Reality dwindled to a point and vanished like the vanishing of a star at moonrise. Earthly things dissolved and disappeared, as a strange, unnamed essence flowed in upon him. A new atmosphere for him pervaded his surroundings. He entered the world of the Vision, of the Legend, of the Miracle, where all things were possible. He stood at the gate of the Mission garden.

Above him rose the ancient tower of the Mission church. Through the arches at its summit, where swung the Spanish queen's bells, he saw the slow-burning stars. The silent bats, with flickering wings, threw their dancing shadows on the pallid surface of the venerable façade.

Not the faintest chirring of a cricket broke the silence. The bees were asleep. In the grasses, in the trees, deep in the calix of punka flower and magnolia bloom, the gnats, the caterpillars, the beetles, all the microscopic, multitudinous life of the daytime drowsed and dozed. Not even the minute scuffling of a lizard over the warm, worn pavement of the colonnade disturbed the infinite repose, the profound stillness. Only within the garden, the intermittent trickling of the fountain made itself heard, flowing steadily, marking off the lapse of seconds, the progress of hours, the cycle of years, the inevitable march of centuries.

At one time, the doorway before which Vanamee now stood had been hermetically closed. But he, himself, had long since changed that. He stood before it for a moment, steeping himself in the mystery and romance of the place, then raising he latch, pushed open the gate, en-

tered, and closed it softly behind him.   He was in the
cloister garden.

The stars were out, strewn thick and close in the deep
blue of the sky, the milky way glowing like a silver veil.
Ursa Major wheeled gigantic in the north.   The great
nebula in Orion was a whorl of shimmering star dust.
Venus flamed a lambent disk of pale saffron, low over the
horizon.   From edge to edge of the world marched the
constellations, like the progress of emperors, and from the
innumerable glory of their courses a mysterious sheen of
diaphanous light disengaged itself, expanding over all the
earth, serene, infinite, majestic.

The little garden revealed itself but dimly beneath the
brooding light, only half emerging from the shadow.
The polished surfaces of the leaves of the pear trees
winked faintly back the reflected light as the trees just
stirred in the uncertain breeze.   A blurred shield of silver
marked the ripples of the fountain.   Under the flood of
dull blue lustre, the gravelled walks lay vague amid the
grasses, like webs of white satin on the bed of a lake.
Against the eastern wall the headstones of the graves, an
indistinct procession of grey cowls ranged themselves.

Vanamee crossed the garden, pausing to kiss the turf
upon Angéle's grave.   Then he approached the line of
pear trees, and laid himself down in their shadow, his
chin propped upon his hands, his eyes wandering over
the expanse of the little valley that stretched away from
the foot of the hill upon which the Mission was built.

Once again he summoned the Vision.   Once again he
conjured up the Illusion.   Once again, tortured with
doubt, racked with a deathless grief, he craved an Answer
of the night.   Once again, mystic that he was, he sent
his mind out from him across the enchanted sea of the
Supernatural. Hope, of what he did not know, roused up
within him.   Surely, on such a night as this, the hallu-

cination must define itself. Surely, the Manifestation must be vouchsafed.

His eyes closed, his will girding itself to a supreme effort, his senses exalted to a state of pleasing numbness, he called upon Angéle to come to him, his voiceless cry penetrating far out into that sea of faint, ephemeral light that floated tideless over the little valley beneath him. Then motionless, prone upon the ground, he waited.

Months had passed since that first night when, at length, an Answer had come to Vanamee. At first, startled out of all composure, troubled and stirred to his lowest depths, because of the very thing for which he sought, he resolved never again to put his strange powers to the test. But for all that, he had come a second night to the garden, and a third, and a fourth. At last, his visits were habitual. Night after night he was there, surrendering himself to the influences of the place, gradually convinced that something did actually answer when he called. His faith increased as the winter grew into spring. As the spring advanced and the nights became shorter, it crystallised into certainty. Would he have her again, his love, long dead? Would she come to him once more out of the grave, out of the night? He could not tell; he could only hope. All that he knew was that his cry found an answer, that his outstretched hands, groping in the darkness, met the touch of other fingers. Patiently he waited. The nights became warmer as the spring drew on. The stars shone clearer. The nights seemed brighter. For nearly a month after the occasion of his first answer nothing new occurred. Some nights it failed him entirely; upon others it was faint, illusive.

Then, at last, the most subtle, the barest of perceptible changes began. His groping mind far-off there, wandering like a lost bird over the valley, touched upon something again, touched and held it, and this time drew it a

single step closer to him. His heart beating, the blood
surging in his temples, he watched with the eyes of his
imagination, this gradual approach. What was coming
to him? Who was coming to him? Shrouded in the obscurity of the night, whose was the face now turned
towards his? Whose the footsteps that with such infinite slowness drew nearer to where he waited? He did
not dare to say.

His mind went back many years to that time before
the tragedy of Angéle's death, before the mystery of the
Other. He waited then as he waited now. But then he
had not waited in vain. Then, as now, he had seemed to
feel her approach, seemed to feel her drawing nearer and
nearer to their rendezvous. Now, what would hapen?
He did not know. He waited. He waited, hoping all
things. He waited, believing all things. He waited, enduring all things. He trusted in the Vision.

Meanwhile, as spring advanced, the flowers in the Seed
ranch began to come to life. Over the five hundred acres
whereon the flowers were planted, the widening growth
of vines and bushes spread like the waves of a green sea.
Then, timidly, colours of the faintest tints began to appear. Under the moonlight, Vanamee saw them expanding, delicate pink, faint blue, tenderest variations of
lavender and yellow, white shimmering with reflections
of gold, all subdued and pallid in the moonlight.

By degrees, the night became impregnated with the
perfume of the flowers. Illusive at first, evanescent as
filaments of gossamer; then as the buds opened, emphasising itself, breathing deeper, stronger. An exquisite mingling of many odours passed continually over
the Mission, from the garden of the Seed ranch, meeting
and blending with the aroma of its magnolia buds and
punka blossoms.

As the colours of the flowers of the Seed ranch deepened, and as their odours penetrated deeper and more distinctly, as the starlight of each succeeding night grew brighter and the air became warmer, the illusion defined itself. By imperceptible degrees, as Vanamee waited under the shadows of the pear trees, the Answer grew nearer and nearer. He saw nothing but the distant glimmer of the flowers. He heard nothing but the drip of the fountain. Nothing moved about him but the invisible, slow-passing breaths of perfume; yet he felt the approach of the Vision.

It came first to about the middle of the Seed ranch itself, some half a mile away, where the violets grew; shrinking, timid flowers, hiding close to the ground. Then it passed forward beyond the violets, and drew nearer and stood amid the mignonette, hardier blooms that dared look heavenward from out the leaves. A few nights later it left the mignonette behind, and advanced into the beds of white iris that pushed more boldly forth from the earth, their waxen petals claiming the attention. It advanced then a long step into the proud, challenging beauty of the carnations and roses; and at last, after many nights, Vanamee felt that it paused, as if trembling at its hardihood, full in the superb glory of the royal lilies themselves, that grew on the extreme border of the Seed ranch nearest to him. After this, there was a certain long wait. Then, upon a dark midnight, it advanced again. Vanamee could scarcely repress a cry. Now, the illusion emerged from the flowers. It stood, not distant, but unseen, almost at the base of the hill upon whose crest he waited, in a depression of the ground where the shadows lay thickest. It was nearly within earshot.

The nights passed. The spring grew warmer. In the daytime intermittent rains freshened all the earth. The flowers of the Seed ranch grew rapidly. Bud after bud burst forth, while those already opened expanded to full maturity. The colour of the Seed ranch deepened.

One night, after hours of waiting, Vanamee felt upon his cheek the touch of a prolonged puff of warm wind, breathing across the little valley from out the east. It reached the Mission garden and stirred the branches of the pear trees. It seemed veritably to be compounded of the very essence of the flowers. Never had the aroma been so sweet, so pervasive. It passed and faded, leaving in its wake an absolute silence. Then, at length, the silence of the night, that silence to which Vanamee had so long appealed, was broken by a tiny sound. Alert, half-risen from the ground, he listened; for now, at length, he heard something. The sound repeated itself. It came from near at hand, from the thick shadow at the foot of the hill. What it was, he could not tell, but it did not belong to a single one of the infinite similar noises of the place with which he was so familiar. It was neither the rustle of a leaf, the snap of a parted twig, the drone of an insect, the dropping of a magnolia blossom. It was a vibration merely, faint, elusive, impossible of definition; a minute notch in the fine, keen edge of stillness.

Again the nights passed. The summer stars became brighter. The warmth increased. The flowers of the Seed ranch grew still more. The five hundred acres of the ranch were carpeted with them.

At length, upon a certain midnight, a new light began to spread in the sky. The thin scimitar of the moon rose, veiled and dim behind the earth-mists. The light increased. Distant objects, until now hidden, came into view, and as the radiance brightened, Vanamee, looking down upon the little valley, saw a spectacle of incomparable beauty. All the buds of the Seed ranch had opened. The faint tints of the flowers had deepened, had asserted themselves. They challenged the eye. Pink became a royal red. Blue rose into purple. Yellow flamed into orange. Orange glowed golden and brilliant. The earth disappeared under great bands and fields of resplendent colour. Then, at length, the moon abruptly soared zenithward from out the veiling mist, passing from one filmy haze to another. For a moment there was a gleam of a golden light, and Vanamee, his eyes searching the shade at the foot of the hill, felt his heart suddenly leap, and then hang poised, refusing to beat. In that instant of passing light, something had caught his eye. Something that moved, down there, half in and half out of the shadow, at the hill's foot. It had come and gone in an instant. The haze once more screened the moonlight. The shade again engulfed the vision. What was it he had seen? He did not know. So brief had been that movement, the drowsy brain had not been quick enough to interpret the cipher message of the eye. Now it was gone. But something had been there. He had seen it. Was it the lifting of a strand of hair, the wave of a white hand, the flutter of a garment's edge? He could not tell, but it did not belong to any of those sights which he had seen so often in that place. It was neither the glancing of a moth's wing, the nodding of a windtouched blossom, nor the noiseless flitting of a bat. It was a gleam merely, faint, elusive, impossible of definition, an intangible agitation, in the vast, dim blur of the darkness.

And that was all. Until now no single real thing had occurred, nothing that Vanamee could reduce to terms of actuality, nothing he could put into words. The manifestation, when not recognisable to that strange sixth sense of his, appealed only to the most refined, the most delicate perception of eye and ear. It was all ephemeral, filmy, dreamy, the mystic forming of the Vision—the invisible developing a concrete nucleus, the starlight coagulating, the radiance of the flowers thickening to something actual; perfume, the most delicious fragrance, becoming a tangible presence.

But into that garden the serpent intruded. Though cradled in the slow rhythm of the dream, lulled by this beauty of a summer's night, heavy with the scent of flowers, the silence broken only by a rippling fountain, the darkness illuminated by a world of radiant blossoms, Vanamee could not forget the tragedy of the Other; that terror of many years ago,—that prowler of the night, that strange, fearful figure with the unseen face, swooping in there from out the darkness, gone in an instant, yet leaving behind the trail and trace of death and of pollution.

Never had Vanamee seen this more clearly than when leaving Presley on the stock range of Los Muertos, he had come across to the Mission garden by way of the Quien Sabe ranch.

It was the same night in which Annixter out-watched the stars, coming, at last, to himself.

As the hours passed, the two men, far apart, ignoring each other, waited for the Manifestation,—Annixter on the ranch, Vanamee in the garden.

Prone upon his face, under the pear trees, his forehead buried in the hollow of his arm, Vanamee lay motionless. For the last time, raising his head, he sent his voiceless cry out into the night across the multi-coloured levels of the little valley, calling upon the miracle, summoning the darkness to give Angéle back to him, resigning himself to the hallucination. He bowed his head upon his arm again and waited. The minutes passed. The fountain dripped steadily. Over the hills a haze of saffron light foretold the rising of the full moon. Nothing stirred. The silence was profound.

Then, abruptly, Vanamee's right hand shut tight upon his wrist. There—there it was. It began again, his invocation was answered. Far off there, the ripple formed again upon the still, black pool of the night. No sound, no sight; vibration merely, appreciable by some sublimated faculty of the mind as yet unnamed. Rigid, his nerves taut, motionless, prone on the ground, he waited.

It advanced with infinite slowness. Now it passed through the beds of violets, now through the mignonette. A moment later, and he knew it stood among the white iris. Then it left those behind. It was in the splendour of the red roses and carnations. It passed like a moving star into the superb abundance, the imperial opulence of the royal lilies. It was advancing slowly, but there was no pause. He held his breath, not daring to raise his head. It passed beyond the limits of the Seed ranch, and entered the shade at the foot of the hill below him. Would it come farther than this? Here it had always stopped hitherto, stopped for a moment, and then, in spite of his efforts, had slipped from his grasp and faded back into the night. But now he wondered if he had been willing to put forth his utmost strength, after all. Had there not always been an element of dread in the thought of beholding the mystery face to face? Had he not even allowed the Vision to dissolve, the Answer to recede into the obscurity whence it came?

But never a night had been so beautiful as this. It was the full period of the spring. The air was a veritable caress. The infinite repose of the little garden, sleeping under the night, was delicious beyond expression. It was a tiny corner of the world, shut off, discreet, distilling romance, a garden of dreams, of enchantments.

Below, in the little valley, the resplendent colourations of the million flowers, roses, lilies, hyacinths, carnations,

violets, glowed like incandescence in the golden light of
the rising moon. The air was thick with the perfume,
heavy with it, clogged with it. The sweetness filled the
very mouth. The throat choked with it. Overhead
wheeled the illimitable procession of the constellations.
Underfoot, the earth was asleep. The very flowers were
dreaming. A cathedral hush overlay all the land, and a
sense of benediction brooded low,—a divine kindliness
manifesting itself in beauty, in peace, in absolute repose.

It was a time for visions. It was the hour when
dreams come true, and lying deep in the grasses beneath
the pear trees, Vanamee, dizzied with mysticism, reaching up and out toward the supernatural, felt, as it were,
his mind begin to rise upward from out his body. He
passed into a state of being the like of which he had not
known before. He felt that his imagination was reshap-
ing itself, preparing to receive an impression never experienced until now. His body felt light to him, then it
dwindled, vanished. He saw with new eyes, heard with
new ears, felt with a new heart.

"Come to me," he murmured.

Then slowly he felt the advance of the Vision. It was
approaching. Every instant it drew gradually nearer.
At last, he was to see. It had left the shadow at the
base of the hill; it was on the hill itself. Slowly, steadily, it ascended the slope; just below him there, he heard
a faint stirring. The grasses rustled under the touch of
a foot. The leaves of the bushes murmured, as a hand
brushed against them; a slender twig creaked. The
sounds of approach were more distinct. They came
nearer. They reached the top of the hill. They were
within whispering distance.

Vanamee, trembling, kept his head buried in his arm.
The sounds, at length, paused definitely. The Vision
could come no nearer. He raised his head and looked.

The moon had risen. Its great shield of gold stood over the eastern horizon. Within six feet of Vanamee, clear and distinct, against the disk of the moon, stood the figure of a young girl. She was dressed in a gown of scarlet silk, with flowing sleeves, such as Japanese wear, embroidered with flowers and figures of birds worked in gold threads. On either side of her face, making three-cornered her round, white forehead, hung the soft masses of her hair of gold. Her hands hung limply at her sides. But from between her parted lips—lips of almost an Egyptian fulness—her breath came slow and regular, and her eyes, heavy lidded, slanting upwards toward the temples, perplexing, oriental, were closed. She was asleep.

From out this life of flowers, this world of colour, this atmosphere oppressive with perfume, this darkness clogged and cloyed, and thickened with sweet odours, she came to him. She came to him from out of the flowers, the smell of the roses in her hair of gold, the aroma and the imperial red of the carnations in her lips, the white-ness of the lilies, the perfume of the lilies, and the lilies' slender, balancing grace in her neck. Her hands disen-gaged the scent of the heliotrope. The folds of her scar-let gown gave off the enervating smell of poppies. Her feet were redolent of hyacinth. She stood before him, a Vision realised—a dream come true. She emerged from out the invisible. He beheld her, a figure of gold and pale vermilion, redolent of perfume, poised motionless in the faint saffron sheen of the new-risen moon. She, a creation of sleep, was herself asleep. She, a dream, was herself dreaming.

Called forth from out the darkness, from the grip of the earth, the embrace of the grave, from out the memory of corruption, she rose into light and life, divinely pure. Across that white forehead was no smudge, no trace of an earthly pollution—no mark of a terrestrial dishonour. He saw in her the same beauty of untainted innocence he had known in his youth. Years had made no difference with her. She was still young. It was the old purity that returned, the deathless beauty, the ever-renascent life, the eternal consecrated and immortal youth. For a few seconds, she stood there before him, and he, upon the ground at her feet, looked up at her, spellbound. Then, slowly she withdrew. Still asleep, her eyelids closed, she turned from him, descending the slope. She was gone.

Vanamee started up, coming, as it were, to himself, looking wildly about him. Sarria was there.

"I saw her," said the priest. "It was Angéle, the little girl, your Angéle's daughter. She is like her mother."

But Vanamee scarcely heard. He walked as if in a trance, pushing by Sarria, going forth from the garden. Angéle or Angéle's daughter, it was all one with him. It was She. Death was overcome. The grave vanquished. Life, ever-renewed, alone existed. Time was naught; change was naught; all things were immortal but evil; all things eternal but grief.

Suddenly, the dawn came; the east burned roseate toward the zenith. Vanamee walked on, he knew not where. The dawn grew brighter. At length, he paused upon the crest of a hill overlooking the ranchos, and cast his eye below him to the southward. Then, suddenly flinging up his arms, he uttered a great cry.

There it was. The Wheat! The Wheat! In the night it had come up. It was there, everywhere, from margin to margin of the horizon. The earth, long empty, teemed with green life. Once more the pendulum of the seasons swung in its mighty arc, from death back to life. Life out of death, eternity rising from out dissolution.

There was the lesson. Angéle was not the symbol, but the *proof* of immortality. The seed dying, rotting and corrupting in the earth; rising again in life unconquerable, and in immaculate purity,—Angéle dying as she gave birth to her little daughter, life springing from her death,—the pure, unconquerable, coming forth from the defiled. Why had he not had the knowledge of God? Thou fool, that which thou sowest is not quickened except it die. So the seed had died. So died Angéle. And that which thou sowest, thou sowest not that body that shall be, but bare grain. It may chance of wheat, or of some other grain. The wheat called forth from out the darkness, from out the grip of the earth, of the grave, from out corruption, rose triumphant into light and life. So Angéle, so life, so also the resurrection of the dead. It is sown in corruption. It is raised in incorruption. It is sown in dishonour. It is raised in glory. It is sown in weakness. It is raised in power. Death was swallowed up in Victory.

The sun rose. The night was over. The glory of the terrestrial was one, and the glory of the celestial was another. Then, as the glory of sun banished the lesser glory of moon and stars, Vanamee, from his mountain top, beholding the eternal green life of the growing Wheat, bursting its bonds, and in his heart exulting in his triumph over the grave, flung out his arms with a mighty shout:

"Oh, Death, where is thy sting? Oh, Grave, where is thy victory?"

IV

Presley's Socialistic poem, "The Toilers," had an enormous success. The editor of the Sunday supplement of the San Francisco paper to which it was sent, printed it in Gothic type, with a scare-head title so decorative as to be almost illegible, and furthermore caused the poem to be illustrated by one of the paper's staff artists in a most impressive fashion. The whole affair occupied an entire page. Thus advertised, the poem attracted attention. It was promptly copied in New York, Boston, and Chicago papers. It was discussed, attacked, defended, eulogised, ridiculed. It was praised with the most fulsome adulation; assailed with the most violent condemnation. Editorials were written upon it. Special articles, in literary pamphlets, dissected its rhetoric and prosody. The phrases were quoted,—were used as texts for revolutionary sermons, reactionary speeches. It was parodied; it was distorted so as to read as an advertisement for patented cereals and infants' foods. Finally, the editor of an enterprising monthly magazine reprinted the poem, supplementing it by a photograph and biography of Presley himself.

Presley was stunned, bewildered. He began to wonder at himself. Was he actually the "greatest American poet since Bryant"? He had had no thought of fame while composing "The Toilers." He had only been moved to his heart's foundations,—thoroughly in earnest, seeing clearly,—and had addressed himself to the poem's composition in a happy moment when words came easily to

him, and the elaboration of fine sentences was not difficult. Was it thus fame was achieved? For a while he was
tempted to cross the continent and go to New York and
there come unto his own, enjoying the triumph that
awaited him. But soon he denied himself this cheap reward. Now he was too much in earnest. He wanted
to help his People, the community in which he lived—
the little world of the San Joaquin, at grapples with the
Railroad. The struggle had found its poet. He told
himself that his place was here. Only the words of the
manager of a lecture bureau troubled him for a moment.
To range the entire nation, telling all his countrymen of
the drama that was working itself out on this fringe of
the continent, this ignored and distant Pacific Coast, rousing their interest and stirring them up to action—appealed to him. It might do great good. To devote himself to " the Cause," accepting no penny of remuneration;
to give his life to loosing the grip of the iron-hearted
monster of steel and steam would be beyond question
heroic. Other States than California had their grievances. All over the country the family of cyclops was
growing. He would declare himself the champion of the
People in their opposition to the Trust. He would be
an apostle, a prophet, a martyr of Freedom.

But Presley was essentially a dreamer, not a man of
affairs. He hesitated to act at this precise psychological
moment, striking while the iron was yet hot, and while he
hesitated, other affairs near at hand began to absorb his
attention.

One night, about an hour after he had gone to bed, he
was awakened by the sound of voices on the porch of the
ranch house, and, descending, found Mrs. Dyke there
with Sidney. The ex-engineer's mother was talking to
Magnus and Harran, and crying as she talked. It
seemed that Dyke was missing. He had gone into town

early that afternoon with the wagon and team, and was to have been home for supper. By now it was ten o'clock and there was no news of him. Mrs. Dyke told how she first had gone to Quien Sabe, intending to telephone from there to Bonneville, but Annixter was in San Francisco, and in his absence the house was locked up, and the overseer, who had a duplicate key, was himself in Bonneville. She had telegraphed three times from Guadalajara to Bonneville for news of her son, but without result. Then, at last, tortured with anxiety, she had gone to Hooven's, taking Sidney with her, and had prevailed upon "Bismarck" to hitch up and drive her across Los Muertos to the Governor's, to beg him to telephone into Bonneville, to know what had become of Dyke.

While Harran rang up Central in town, Mrs. Dyke told Presley and Magnus of the lamentable change in Dyke.

"They have broken my son's spirit, Mr. Derrick," she said. "If you were only there to see. Hour after hour, he sits on the porch with his hands lying open in his lap, looking at them without a word. He won't look me in the face any more, and he don't sleep. Night after night, he has walked the floor until morning. And he will go on that way for days together, very silent, without a word, and sitting still in his chair, and then, all of a sudden, he will break out—oh, Mr. Derrick, it is terrible— into an awful rage, cursing, swearing, grinding his teeth, his hands clenched over his head, stamping so that the house shakes, and saying that if S. Behrman don't give him back his money, he will kill him with his two hands. But that isn't the worst, Mr. Derrick. He goes to Mr. Caraher's saloon now, and stays there for hours, and listens to Mr. Caraher. There is something on my son's mind; I know there is—something that he and Mr. Caraher have talked over together, and I can't find out what it is. Mr. Caraher is a bad man, and my son has fallen under his influence." The tears filled her eyes. Bravely, she turned to hide them, turning away to take Sidney in her arms, putting her head upon the little girl's shoulder.

"I—I haven't broken down before, Mr. Derrick," she said, "but after we have been so happy in our little house, just us three—and the future seemed so bright—oh, God will punish the gentlemen who own the railroad for being so hard and cruel."

Harran came out on the porch, from the telephone, and she interrupted herself, fixing her eyes eagerly upon him.

"I think it is all right, Mrs. Dyke," he said, reassuringly. "We know where he is, I believe. You and the little tad stay here, and Hooven and I will go after him."

About two hours later, Harran brought Dyke back to Los Muertos in Hooven's wagon. He had found him at Caraher's saloon, very drunk.

There was nothing maudlin about Dyke's drunkenness. In him the alcohol merely roused the spirit of evil, vengeful, reckless.

As the wagon passed out from under the eucalyptus trees about the ranch house, taking Mrs. Dyke, Sidney, and the one-time engineer back to the hop ranch, Presley leaning from his window heard the latter remark:

"Caraher is right. There is only one thing they listen to, and that's dynamite."

The following day Presley drove Magnus over to Guadalajara to take the train for San Francisco. But after he had said good-bye to the Governor, he was moved to go on to the hop ranch to see the condition of affairs in that quarter. He returned to Los Muertos overwhelmed with sadness and trembling with anger. The hop ranch that he had last seen in the full tide of prosperity was almost a ruin. Work had evidently been abandoned long since. Weeds were already choking the vines. Everywhere the poles sagged and drooped. Many had even fallen, dragging the vines with them, spreading them over the ground in an inextricable tangle of dead leaves, decaying tendrils, and snarled string. The fence was broken; the unfinished storehouse, which never was to see completion, was a lamentable spectacle of gaping doors and windows—a melancholy skeleton. Last of all, Presley had caught a glimpse of Dyke himself, seated in his rocking chair on the porch, his beard and hair unkempt, motionless, looking with vague eyes upon his hands that lay palm upwards and idle in his lap.

Magnus on his way to San Francisco was joined at Bonneville by Osterman. Upon seating himself in front of the master of Los Muertos in the smoking-car of the train, this latter, pushing back his hat and smoothing his bald head, observed:

"Governor, you look all frazeled out. Anything wrong these days?"

The other answered in the negative, but, for all that, Osterman was right. The Governor had aged suddenly. His former erectness was gone, the broad shoulders stooped a little, the strong lines of his thin-lipped mouth were relaxed, and his hand, as it clasped over the yellowed ivory knob of his cane, had an unwonted tremulousness not hitherto noticeable. But the change in Magnus was more than physical. At last, in the full tide of power, President of the League, known and talked of in every county of the State, leader in a great struggle, consulted, deferred to as the "Prominent Man," at length attaining that position, so long and vainly sought for, he yet found no pleasure in his triumph, and little but bitterness in life. His success had come by devious methods, had been reached by obscure means.

He was a briber. He could never forget that. To

further his ends, disinterested, public-spirited, even phil-
anthropic as those were, he had connived with knavery,
he, the politician of the old school, of such rigorous integrity, who had abandoned a "career" rather than compromise with honesty. At this eleventh hour, involved
and entrapped in the fine-spun web of a new order of
things, bewildered by Osterman's dexterity, by his volubility and glibness, goaded and harassed beyond the point
of reason by the aggression of the Trust he fought, he
had at last failed. He had fallen; he had given a bribe.
He had thought that, after all, this would make but little
difference with him. The affair was known only to
Osterman, Broderson, and Annixter; they would not
judge him, being themselves involved. He could still
preserve a bold front; could still hold his head high. As
time went on the affair would lose its point.

But this was not so. Some subtle element of his character had forsaken him. He felt it. He knew it. Some
certain stiffness that had given him all his rigidity, that
had lent force to his authority, weight to his dominance,
temper to his fine, inflexible hardness, was diminishing
day by day. In the decisions which he, as President of the League, was called upon to make so
often, he now hesitated. He could no longer be arrogant, masterful, acting upon his own judgment, independent of opinion. He began to consult his lieutenants,
asking their advice, distrusting his own opinions. He
made mistakes, blunders, and when those were brought
to his notice, took refuge in bluster. He knew it to be
bluster—knew that sooner or later his subordinates would
recognise it as such. How long could he maintain his
position? So only he could keep his grip upon the lever
of control till the battle was over, all would be well.
If not, he would fall, and, once fallen, he knew that now,
briber that he was, he would never rise again.

He was on his way at this moment to the city to consult with Lyman as to a certain issue of the contest between the Railroad and the ranchers, which, of late, had been brought to his notice.

When appeal had been taken to the Supreme Court by the League's Executive Committee, certain test cases had been chosen, which should represent all the lands in question. Neither Magnus nor Annixter had so appealed, believing, of course, that their cases were covered by the test cases on trial at Washington. Magnus had here blundered again, and the League's agents in San Francisco had written to warn him that the Railroad might be able to take advantage of a technicality, and by pretending that neither Quien Sabe nor Los Muertos were included in the appeal, attempt to put its dummy buyers in possession of the two ranches before the Supreme Court handed down its decision. The ninety days allowed for taking this appeal were nearly at an end and after then the Railroad could act. Osterman and Magnus at once decided to go up to the city, there joining Annixter (who had been absent from Quien Sabe for the last ten days), and talk the matter over with Lyman. Lyman, because of his position as Commissioner, might be cognisant of the Railroad's plans, and, at the same time, could give sound legal advice as to what was to be done should the new rumour prove true.

"Say," remarked Osterman, as the train pulled out of the Bonneville station, and the two men settled themselves for the long journey, "say Governor, what's all up with Buck Annixter these days? He's got a bean about something, sure."

"I had not noticed," answered Magnus. "Mr. Annixter has been away some time lately. I cannot imagine what should keep him so long in San Francisco."

"That's it," said Osterman, winking. "Have three

guesses. Guess right and you get a cigar. I guess
g-i-r-l spells Hilma Tree. And a little while ago she quit
Quien Sabe and hiked out to 'Frisco. So did Buck. Do
I draw the cigar? It's up to you."

"I have noticed her," observed Magnus. "A fine
figure of a woman. She would make some man a good
wife."

"Hoh! Wife! Buck Annixter marry! Not much.
He's gone a-girling at last, old Buck! It's as funny as
twins. Have to josh him about it when I see him, sure."

But when Osterman and Magnus at last fell in with
Annixter in the vestibule of the Lick House, on Montgomery Street, nothing could be got out of him. He was
in an execrable humour. When Magnus had broached
the subject of business, he had declared that all business
could go to pot, and when Osterman, his tongue in his
cheek, had permitted himself a most distant allusion to a
feemale girl, Annixter had cursed him for a " busy-face "
so vociferously and tersely, that even Osterman was
cowed.

" Well," insinuated Osterman, " what are you dallying
'round 'Frisco so much for? "

" Cat fur, to make kitten-breeches," retorted Annixter
with oracular vagueness.

Two weeks before this time, Annixter had come up to
the city and had gone at once to a certain hotel on Bush
Street, behind the First National Bank, that he knew was
kept by a family connection of the Trees. In his con-
jecture that Hilma and her parents would stop here, he
was right. Their names were on the register. Ignoring
custom, Annixter marched straight up to their rooms,
and before he was well aware of it, was " eating crow "
before old man Tree.

Hilma and her mother were out at the time. Later on,
Mrs. Tree returned alone, leaving Hilma to spend the

day with one of her cousins who lived far out on Stanyan Street in a little house facing the park.

Between Annixter and Hilma's parents, a reconciliation had been effected, Annixter convincing them both of his sincerity in wishing to make Hilma his wife. Hilma, however, refused to see him. As soon as she knew he had followed her to San Francisco she had been unwilling to return to the hotel and had arranged with her cousin to spend an indefinite time at her house.

She was wretchedly unhappy during all this time; would not set foot out of doors, and cried herself to sleep night after night. She detested the city. Already she was miserably homesick for the ranch. She remembered the days she had spent in the little dairy-house, happy in her work, making butter and cheese; skimming the great pans of milk, scouring the copper vessels and vats, plunging her arms, elbow deep, into the white curds; coming and going in that atmosphere of freshness, cleanliness, and sunlight, gay, singing, supremely happy just because the sun shone. She remembered her long walks toward the Mission late in the afternoons, her excursions for cresses underneath the Long Trestle, the crowing of the cocks, the distant whistle of the passing trains, the faint sounding of the Angelus. She recalled with infinite longing the solitary expanse of the ranches, the level reaches between the horizons, full of light and silence; the heat at noon, the cloudless iridescence of the sunrise and sunset. She had been so happy in that life! Now, all those days were passed. This crude, raw city, with its crowding houses all of wood and tin, its blotting fogs, its uproarious trade winds, disturbed and saddened her. There was no outlook for the future.

At length, one day, about a week after Annixter's arrival in the city, she was prevailed upon to go for a walk in the park. She went alone, putting on for the first time the little hat of black straw with its puff of white silk her mother had bought for her, a pink shirtwaist, her belt of imitation alligator skin, her new skirt of brown cloth, and her low shoes, set off with their little steel buckles.

She found a tiny summer house, built in Japanese fashion, around a diminutive pond, and sat there for a while, her hands folded in her lap, amused with watching the goldfish, wishing—she knew not what.

Without any warning, Annixter sat down beside her. She was too frightened to move. She looked at him with wide eyes that began to fill with tears.

"Oh," she said, at last, "oh—I didn't know."

"Well," exclaimed Annixter, "here you are at last. I've been watching that blamed house till I was afraid the policeman would move me on. By the Lord," he suddenly cried, "you're pale. You—you, Hilma, do you feel well?"

"Yes—I am well," she faltered.

"No, you're not," he declared. "I know better. You are coming back to Quien Sabe with me. This place don't agree with you. Hilma, what's all the matter? Why haven't you let me see you all this time? Do you know—how things are with me? Your mother told you, didn't she? Do you know how sorry I am? Do you know that I see now that I made the mistake of my life there, that time, under the Long Trestle? I found it out the night after you went away. I sat all night on a stone out on the ranch somewhere and I don't know exactly what happened, but I've been a different man since then. I see things all different now. Why, I've only begun to live since then. I know what love means now, and instead of being ashamed of it, I'm proud of it. If I never was to see you again I would be glad I'd lived through that night, just the same. I just woke up that night.

I'd been absolutely and completely selfish up to the moment I realised I really loved you, and now, whether you'll let me marry you or not, I mean to live—I don't know, in a different way. I've *got* to live different. I—well—oh, I can't make you understand, but just loving you has changed my life all around. It's made it easier to do the straight, clean thing. I want to do it, it's fun doing it. Remember, once I said I was proud of being a hard man, a driver, of being glad that people hated me and were afraid of me? Well, since I've loved you I'm ashamed of it all. I don't want to be hard any more, and nobody is going to hate me if I can help it. I'm happy and I want other people so. I love you," he suddenly exclaimed; " I love you, and if you will forgive me, and if you will come down to such a beast as I am, I want to be to you the best a man can be to a woman, Hilma. Do you understand, little girl? I want to be your husband."

Hilma looked at the goldfishes through her tears.

"Have you got anything to say to me, Hilma?" he asked, after a while.

"I don't know what you want me to say," she murmured.

"Yes, you do," he insisted. "I've followed you 'way up here to hear it. I've waited around in these beastly, draughty picnic grounds for over a week to hear it. You know what I want to hear, Hilma."

"Well—I forgive you," she hazarded.

"That will do for a starter," he answered. "But that's not *it*."

"Then, I don't know what."

"Shall I say it for you?"

She hesitated a long minute, then:

"You mightn't say it right," she replied.

"**Trust me for that. Shall I say it for you, Hilma?**"

"I don't know what you'll say."

"I'll say what you are thinking of. Shall I say it?"

There was a very long pause. A goldfish rose to the surface of the little pond, with a sharp, rippling sound. The fog drifted overhead. There was nobody about.

"No," said Hilma, at length. "I—I—I can say it for myself. I—" All at once she turned to him and put her arms around his neck. "Oh, *do* you love me?" she cried. "Is it really true? Do you mean every word of it? And you are sorry and you *will* be good to me if I will be your wife? You will be my dear, dear husband?"

The tears sprang to Annixter's eyes. He took her in his arms and held her there for a moment. Never in his life had he felt so unworthy, so undeserving of this clean, pure girl who forgave him and trusted his spoken word and believed him to be the good man he could only wish to be. She was so far above him, so exalted, so noble that he should have bowed his forehead to her feet, and instead, she took him in her arms, believing him to be good, to be her equal. He could think of no words to say. The tears overflowed his eyes and ran down upon his cheeks. She drew away from him and held him a second at arm's length, looking at him, and he saw that she, too, had been crying.

"I think," he said, "we are a couple of softies."

"No, no," she insisted. "I want to cry and want you to cry, too. Oh, dear, I haven't a handkerchief."

"Here, take mine."

They wiped each other's eyes like two children and for a long time sat in the deserted little Japanese pleasure house, their arms about each other, talking, talking, talking.

On the following Saturday they were married in an uptown Presbyterian church, and spent the week of their

honeymoon at a small, family hotel on Sutter Street. As
a matter of course, they saw the sights of the city together. They made the inevitable bridal trip to the Cliff
House and spent an afternoon in the grewsome and
made-to-order beauties of Sutro's Gardens; they went
through Chinatown, the Palace Hotel, the park museum—
where Hilma resolutely refused to believe in the Egyptian mummy—and they drove out in a hired hack to the
Presidio and the Golden Gate.

On the sixth day of their excursions, Hilma abruptly
declared they had had enough of " playing out," and must
be serious and get to work.

This work was nothing less than the buying of the
furniture and appointments for the rejuvenated ranch
house at Quien Sabe, where they were to live. Annixter
had telegraphed to his overseer to have the building re-
painted, replastered, and reshingled and to empty the
rooms of everything but the telephone and safe. He also
sent instructions to have the dimensions of each room
noted down and the result forwarded to him. It was the
arrival of these memoranda that had roused Hilma to
action.

Then ensued a most delicious week. Armed with
formidable lists, written by Annixter on hotel envelopes,
they two descended upon the department stores of the
city, the carpet stores, the furniture stores. Right and
left they bought and bargained, sending each consignment as soon as purchased to Quien Sabe. Nearly an
entire car load of carpets, curtains, kitchen furniture,
pictures, fixtures, lamps, straw matting, chairs, and the
like were sent down to the ranch, Annixter making a
point that their new home should be entirely equipped by
San Francisco dealers.

The furnishings of the bedroom and sitting-room were
left to the very last. For the former, Hilma bought a

"set" of pure white enamel, three chairs, a washstand and bureau, a marvellous bargain of thirty dollars, discovered by wonderful accident at a "Friday Sale." The bed was a piece by itself, bought elsewhere, but none the less a wonder. It was of brass, very brave and gay, and actually boasted a canopy! They bought it complete, just as it stood in the window of the department store, and Hilma was in an ecstasy over its crisp, clean, muslin curtains, spread, and shams. Never was there such a bed, the luxury of a princess, such a bed as she had dreamed about her whole life.

Next the appointments of the sitting-room occupied her—since Annixter, himself, bewildered by this astonishing display, unable to offer a single suggestion himself, merely approved of all she bought. In the sitting-room was to be a beautiful blue and white paper, cool straw matting, set off with white wool rugs, a stand of flowers in the window, a globe of goldfish, rocking chairs, a sewing machine, and a great, round centre table of yellow oak whereon should stand a lamp covered with a deep shade of crinkly red tissue paper. On the walls were to hang several pictures—lovely affairs, photographs from life, all properly tinted—of choir boys in robes, with beautiful eyes; pensive young girls in pink gowns, with flowing yellow hair, drooping over golden harps; a coloured reproduction of "Rouget de Lisle, Singing the Marseillaise," and two "pieces" of wood carving, representing a quail and a wild duck, hung by one leg in the midst of game bags and powder horns,—quite masterpieces, both.

At last everything had been bought, all arrangements made, Hilma's trunks packed with her new dresses, and the tickets to Bonneville bought.

"We'll go by the Overland, by Jingo," declared Annixter across the table to his wife, at their last meal in the hotel where they **had** been stopping; "no way trains or locals for us, hey?"

"But we reach Bonneville at *such* an hour," protested Hilma. "Five in the morning!"

"Never mind," he declared, "we'll go home in *Pullman's*, Hilma. I'm not going to have any of those slobs in Bonneville say I didn't know how to do the thing in style, and we'll have Vacca meet us with the team. No, sir, it is Pullman's or nothing. When it comes to buying furniture, I don't shine, perhaps, but I know what's due my wife."

He was obdurate, and late one afternoon the couple boarded the Transcontinental (the crack Overland Flyer of the Pacific and Southwestern) at the Oakland mole. Only Hilma's parents were there to say good-bye. Annixter knew that Magnus and Osterman were in the city, but he had laid his plans to elude them. Magnus, he could trust to be dignified, but that goat Osterman, one could never tell what he would do next. He did not propose to start his journey home in a shower of rice.

Annixter marched down the line of cars, his hands encumbered with wicker telescope baskets, satchels, and valises, his tickets in his mouth, his hat on wrong side foremost, Hilma and her parents hurrying on behind him, trying to keep up. Annixter was in a turmoil of nerves lest something should go wrong; catching a train was always for him a little crisis. He rushed ahead so furiously that when he had found his Pullman he had lost his party. He set down his valises to mark the place and charged back along the platform, waving his arms.

"Come on," he cried, when, at length, he espied the others. "We've no more time."

He shouldered and urged them forward to where he had set his valises, only to find one of them gone. Instantly he raised an outcry. Aha, a fine way to treat passengers! There was P. and S. W. management for you. He would, by the Lord, he would—but the porter appeared in the vestibule of the car to placate him. He had already taken his valises inside.

Annixter would not permit Hilma's parents to board the car, declaring that the train might pull out any moment. So he and his wife, following the porter down the narrow passage by the stateroom, took their places and, raising the window, leaned out to say good-bye to Mr. and Mrs. Tree. These latter would not return to Quien Sabe. Old man Tree had found a business chance awaiting him in the matter of supplying his relative's hotel with dairy products. But Bonneville was not too far from San Francisco; the separation was by no means final.

The porters began taking up the steps that stood by the vestibule of each sleeping-car.

"Well, have a good time, daughter," observed her father; "and come up to see us whenever you can."

From beyond the enclosure of the depot's reverberating roof came the measured clang of a bell.

"I guess we're off," cried Annixter. "Good-bye, Mrs. Tree."

"Remember your promise, Hilma," her mother hastened to exclaim, "to write every Sunday afternoon."

There came a prolonged creaking and groan of straining wood and iron work, all along the length of the train. They all began to cry their good-byes at once. The train stirred, moved forward, and gathering slow headway, rolled slowly out into the sunlight. Hilma leaned out of the window and as long as she could keep her mother in sight waved her handkerchief. Then at length she sat back in her seat and looked at her husband.

"Well," she said.

"Well," echoed Annixter, "happy?" for the tears rose in her eyes.

She nodded energetically, smiling at him bravely.

"You look a little pale," he declared, frowning uneasily; "feel well?"

"Pretty well."

Promptly he was seized with uneasiness.

"But not *all* well, hey? Is that it?"

It was true that Hilma had felt a faint tremour of seasickness on the ferry-boat coming from the city to the Oakland mole. No doubt a little nausea yet remained with her. But Annixter refused to accept this explanation. He was distressed beyond expression.

"Now you're going to be sick," he cried anxiously.

"No, no," she protested, "not a bit."

"But you said you didn't feel very well. Where is it you feel sick?"

"I don't know. I'm not sick. Oh, dear me, why will you bother?"

"Headache?"

"Not the least."

"You feel tired, then. That's it. No wonder, the way I've rushed you 'round to-day."

"Dear, I'm *not* tired, and I'm *not* sick, and I'm all *right*."

"No, no; I can tell. I think we'd best have the berth made up and you lie down."

"That would be perfectly ridiculous."

"Well, where is it you feel sick? Show me; put your hand on the place. Want to eat something?"

With elaborate minuteness, he cross-questioned her, refusing to let the subject drop, protesting that she had dark circles under her eyes; that she had grown thinner.

"Wonder if there's a doctor on board," he murmured, looking uncertainly about the car. "Let me see your tongue. I know—a little whiskey is what you want, that and some pru——"

"No, no, *no*," she exclaimed. "I'm as well as I ever was in all my life. Look at me. Now, tell me, do I look like a sick lady?"

He scrutinised her face distressfully.

"Now, don't I look the picture of health?" she challenged.

"In a way you do," he began, "and then again——"

Hilma beat a tattoo with her heels upon the floor, shutting her fists, the thumbs tucked inside. She closed her eyes, shaking her head energetically.

"I won't listen, I won't listen, I won't listen," she cried.

"But, just the same——"

"Gibble—gibble—gibble," she mocked. "I won't listen, I won't listen." She put a hand over his mouth. "Look, here's the dining-car waiter, and the first call for supper, and your wife is hungry."

They went forward and had supper in the diner, while the long train, now out upon the main line, settled itself to its pace, the prolonged, even gallop that it would hold for the better part of the week, spinning out the miles as a cotton spinner spins thread.

It was already dark when Antioch was left behind. Abruptly the sunset appeared to wheel in the sky and readjusted itself to the right of the track behind Mount Diablo, here visible almost to its base. The train had turned southward. Neroly was passed, then Brentwood, then Byron. In the gathering dusk, mountains began to build themselves up on either hand, far off, blocking the horizon. The train shot forward, roaring. Between the mountains the land lay level, cut up into farms, ranches. These continually grew larger; growing wheat began to appear, billowing in the wind of the train's passage. The mountains grew higher, the land richer, and by the time the moon rose, the train was well into the northernmost limits of the valley of the San Joaquin.

Annixter had engaged an entire section, and after he and his wife went to bed had the porter close the upper berth. Hilma sat up in bed to say her prayers, both hands over her face, and then kissing Annixter good-night, went to sleep with the directness of a little child, holding his hand in both her own.

Annixter, who never could sleep on the train, dozed and tossed and fretted for hours, consulting his watch and time-table whenever there was a stop; twice he rose to get a drink of ice water, and between whiles was for-ever sitting up in the narrow berth, stretching himself and yawning, murmuring with uncertain relevance:

"Oh, Lord! Oh-h-h *Lord!*"

There were some dozen other passengers in the car—a lady with three children, a group of school-teachers, a couple of drummers, a stout gentleman with whiskers, and a well-dressed young man in a plaid travelling cap, whom Annixter had observed before supper time read-ing Daudet's "Tartarin" in the French.

But by nine o'clock, all these people were in their berths. Occasionally, above the rhythmic rumble of the wheels, Annixter could hear one of the lady's children fidgeting and complaining. The stout gentleman snored monotonously in two notes, one a rasping bass, the other a prolonged treble. At intervals, a brakeman or the pas-senger conductor pushed down the aisle, between the curtains, his red and white lamp over his arm. Looking out into the car Annixter saw in an end section where the berths had not been made up, the porter, in his white duck coat, dozing, his mouth wide open, his head on his shoulder.

The hours passed. Midnight came and went. Annixter, checking off the stations, noted their passage of Modesto, Merced, and Madeira. Then, after another broken nap, he lost count. He wondered where they were. Had they reached Fresno yet? Raising the window curtain, he made a shade with both hands on either side of his face and looked out. The night was thick, dark, clouded over. A fine rain was falling, leaving horizontal streaks on the glass of the outside window. Only the faintest grey blur indicated the sky. Everything else was impenetrable blackness.

"I think sure we must have passed Fresno," he muttered. He looked at his watch. It was about half-past three. "If we have passed Fresno," he said to himself, "I'd better wake the little girl pretty soon. She'll need about an hour to dress. Better find out for sure."

He drew on his trousers and shoes, got into his coat, and stepped out into the aisle. In the seat that had been occupied by the porter, the Pullman conductor, his cash box and car-schedules before him, was checking up his berths, a blue pencil behind his ear.

"What's the next stop, Captain?" inquired Annixter, coming up. "Have we reached Fresno yet?"

"Just passed it," the other responded, looking at Annixter over his spectacles.

"What's the next stop?"

"Goshen. We will be there in about forty-five minutes."

"Fair black night, isn't it?

"Black as a pocket. Let's see, you're the party in upper and lower 9."

Annixter caught at the back of the nearest seat, just in time to prevent a fall, and the conductor's cash box was shunted off the surface of the plush seat and came clanking to the floor. The Pintsch lights overhead vibrated with blinding rapidity in the long, sliding jar that ran through the train from end to end, and the momentum of its speed suddenly decreasing, all but pitched the conductor from his seat. A hideous ear-splitting rasp made itself heard from the clamped-down Westinghouse gear underneath, and Annixter knew that the wheels had ceased to revolve and that the train was sliding forward upon the motionless flanges.

"Hello, hello," he exclaimed, "what's all up now?"

"Emergency brakes," declared the conductor, catching up his cash box and thrusting his papers and tickets into it. "Nothing much; probably a cow on the track."

He disappeared, carrying his lantern with him.

But the other passengers, all but the stout gentleman, were awake; heads were thrust from out the curtains, and Annixter, hurrying back to Hilma, was assailed by all manner of questions.

"What was that?"

"Anything wrong?"

"What's up, anyways?"

Hilma was just waking as Annixter pushed the curtain aside.

"Oh, I was so frightened. What's the matter, dear?" she exclaimed.

"I don't know," he answered. "Only the emergency brakes. Just a cow on the track, I guess. Don't get scared. It isn't anything."

But with a final shriek of the Westinghouse appliance, the train came to a definite halt.

At once the silence was absolute. The ears, still numb with the long-continued roar of wheels and clashing iron, at first refused to register correctly the smaller noises of the surroundings. Voices came from the other end of the car, strange and unfamiliar, as though heard at a great distance across the water. The stillness of the night outside was so profound that the rain, dripping from the car roof upon the road-bed underneath, was as distinct as the ticking of a clock.

"Well, we've sure stopped," observed one of the drummers.

"What is it?" asked Hilma again. "Are you sure there's nothing wrong?"

"Sure," said Annixter.

Outside, underneath their window, they heard the sound of hurried footsteps crushing into the clinkers by the side of the ties. They passed on, and Annixter heard some one in the distance shout:

"Yes, on the other side."

Then the door at the end of their car opened and a brakeman with a red beard ran down the aisle and out upon the platform in front. The forward door closed. Everything was quiet again. In the stillness the fat gentleman's snores made themselves heard once more.

The minutes passed; nothing stirred. There was no sound but the dripping rain. The line of cars lay immobilised and inert under the night. One of the drummers, having stepped outside on the platform for a look around, returned, saying:

"There sure isn't any station anywheres about and no siding. Bet you they have had an accident of some kind."

"Ask the porter."

"I did. He don't know."

"Maybe they stopped to take on wood or water, or something."

"Well, they wouldn't use the emergency brakes for that, would they? Why, this train stopped almost in her own length. Pretty near slung me out the berth. Those were the emergency brakes. I heard some one say so."

From far out towards the front of the train, near the

locomotive, came the sharp, incisive report of a revolver;
then two more almost simultaneously; then, after a long
interval, a fourth.

"Say, that's *shooting*. By God, boys, they're shooting.
Say, this is a hold-up."

Instantly a white-hot excitement flared from end to end
of the car. Incredibly sinister, heard thus in the night,
and in the rain, mysterious, fearful, those four pistol
shots started confusion from out the sense of security
like a frightened rabbit hunted from her burrow. Wide-
eyed, the passengers of the car looked into each other's
faces. It had come to them at last, this, they had so
often read about. Now they were to see the real thing,
now they were to face actuality, face this danger of the
night, leaping in from out the blackness of the roadside,
masked, armed, ready to kill. They were facing it now.
They were held up.

Hilma said nothing, only catching Annixter's hand,
looking squarely into his eyes.

"Steady, little girl," he said. "They can't hurt you.
I won't leave you. By the Lord," he suddenly exclaimed,
his excitement getting the better of him for a moment.
"By the Lord, it's a hold-up."

The school-teachers were in the aisle of the car, in
night gown, wrapper, and dressing sack, huddled together
like sheep, holding on to each other, looking to the men,
silently appealing for protection. Two of them were
weeping, white to the lips.

"Oh, oh, oh, it's terrible. Oh, if they only won't hurt
me."

But the lady with the children looked out from her
berth, smiled reassuringly, and said:

"I'm not a bit frightened. They won't do anything to
us if we keep quiet. I've my watch and jewelry all ready
for them in my little black bag, see?"

She exhibited it to the passengers. Her children were all awake. They were quiet, looking about them with eager faces, interested and amused at this surprise. In his berth, the fat gentleman with whiskers snored profoundly.

"Say, I'm going out there," suddenly declared one of the drummers, flourishing a pocket revolver.

His friend caught his arm.

"Don't make a fool of yourself, Max," he said.

"They won't come near us," observed the well-dressed young man; "they are after the Wells-Fargo box and the registered mail. You won't do any good out there."

But the other loudly protested. No; he was going out. He didn't propose to be buncoed without a fight. He wasn't any coward.

"Well, you don't go, that's all," said his friend, angrily. "There's women and children in this car. You ain't going to draw the fire here."

"Well, that's to be thought of," said the other, allowing himself to be pacified, but still holding his pistol.

"Don't let him open that window," cried Annixter sharply from his place by Hilma's side, for the drummer had made as if to open the sash in one of the sections that had not been made up.

"Sure, that's right," said the others. "Don't open any windows. Keep your head in. You'll get us all shot if you aren't careful."

However, the drummer had got the window up and had leaned out before the others could interfere and draw him away.

"Say, by jove," he shouted, as he turned back to the car, "our engine's gone. We're standing on a curve and you can see the end of the train. She's gone, I tell you. Well, look for yourself."

In spite of their precautions, one after another, his

friends looked out. Sure enough, the train was without a locomotive.

"They've done it so we can't get away," vociferated the drummer with the pistol. "Now, by jiminy-Christmas, they'll come through the cars and stand us up. They'll be in here in a minute. *Lord! What was that?*"

From far away up the track, apparently some half-mile ahead of the train, came the sound of a heavy explosion. The windows of the car vibrated with it.

"Shooting again."

"That isn't shooting," exclaimed Annixter. "They've pulled the express and mail car on ahead with the engine and now they are dynamiting her open."

"That must be it. Yes, sure, that's just what they are doing."

The forward door of the car opened and closed and the school-teachers shrieked and cowered. The drummer with the revolver faced about, his eyes bulging. However, it was only the train conductor, hatless, his lantern in his hand. He was soaked with rain. He appeared in the aisle.

"Is there a doctor in this car?" he asked.

Promptly the passengers surrounded him, voluble with questions. But he was in a bad temper.

"I don't know anything more than you," he shouted angrily. "It was a hold-up. I guess you know that, don't you? Well, what more do you want to know? I ain't got time to fool around. They cut off our express car and have cracked it open, and they shot one of our train crew, that's all, and I want a doctor."

"Did they shoot him—kill him, do you mean?"

"Is he hurt bad?"

"Did the men get away?"

"Oh, shut up, will you all?" exclaimed the conductor.

"What do I know? Is there a *doctor* in this car, that's what I want to know?"

The well-dressed young man stepped forward.

"I'm a doctor," he said.

"Well, come along then," returned the conductor, in a surly voice, "and the passengers in this car," he added, turning back at the door and nodding his head menacingly, "will go back to bed and *stay* there. It's all over and there's nothing to see."

He went out, followed by the young doctor.

Then ensued an interminable period of silence. The entire train seemed deserted. Helpless, bereft of its engine, a huge, decapitated monster it lay, half-way around a curve, rained upon, abandoned.

There was more fear in this last condition of affairs, more terror in the idea of this prolonged line of sleepers, with their nickelled fittings, their plate glass, their upholstery, vestibules, and the like, loaded down with people, lost and forgotten in the night and the rain, than there had been when the actual danger threatened.

What was to become of them now? Who was there to help them? Their engine was gone; they were helpless. What next was to happen?

Nobody came near the car. Even the porter had disappeared. The wait seemed endless, and the persistent snoring of the whiskered gentleman rasped the nerves like the scrape of a file.

"Well, how long are we going to stick here now?" began one of the drummers. "Wonder if they hurt the engine with their dynamite?"

"Oh, I know they will come through the car and rob us," wailed the school-teachers.

The lady with the little children went back to bed, and Annixter, assured that the trouble was over, did likewise.

But nobody slept. From berth to berth came the sound of suppressed voices talking it all over, formulating conjectures. Certain points seemed to be settled upon, no one knew how, as indisputable. The highwaymen had been four in number and had stopped the train by pulling the bell cord. A brakeman had attempted to interfere and had been shot. The robbers had been on the train all the way from San Francisco. The drummer named Max remembered to have seen four "suspicious-looking characters" in the smoking-car at Lathrop, and had intended to speak to the conductor about them. This drummer had been in a hold-up before, and told the story of it over and over again.

At last, after what seemed to have been an hour's delay, and when the dawn had already begun to show in the east, the locomotive backed on to the train again with a reverberating jar that ran from car to car. At the jolting, the school-teachers screamed in chorus, and the whiskered gentleman stopped snoring and thrust his head from his curtains, blinking at the Pintsch lights. It appeared that he was an Englishman.

"I say," he asked of the drummer named Max, "I say, my friend, what place is this?"

The others roared with derision.

"We were *held up,* sir, that's what we were. We were held up and you slept through it all. You missed the show of your life."

The gentleman fixed the group with a prolonged gaze. He said never a word, but little by little he was convinced that the drummers told the truth. All at once he grew wrathful, his face purpling. He withdrew his head angrily, buttoning his curtains together in a fury. The cause of his rage was inexplicable, but they could hear him resettling himself upon his pillows with exasperated movements of his head and shoulders. In a few moments the deep bass and shrill treble of his snoring once more sounded through the car.

At last the train got under way again, with useless warning blasts of the engine's whistle. In a few moments it was tearing away through the dawn at a wonderful speed, rocking around curves, roaring across culverts, making up time.

And all the rest of that strange night the passengers, sitting up in their unmade beds, in the swaying car, lighted by a strange mingling of pallid dawn and trembling Pintsch lights, rushing at break-neck speed through the misty rain, were oppressed by a vision of figures of terror, far behind them in the night they had left, masked, armed, galloping toward the mountains, pistol in hand, the booty bound to the saddle bow, galloping, galloping on, sending a thrill of fear through all the country side.

The young doctor returned. He sat down in the smoking-room, lighting a cigarette, and Annixter and the drummers pressed around him to know the story of the whole affair.

"The man is dead," he declared; "the brakeman. He was shot through the lungs twice. They think the fellow got away with about five thousand in gold coin."

"The fellow? Wasn't there four of them?"

"No; only one. And say, let me tell you, he had his nerve with him. It seems he was on the roof of the express car all the time, and going as fast as we were, he jumped from the roof of the car down on to the coal on the engine's tender, and crawled over that and held up the men in the cab with his gun, took their guns from 'em and made 'em stop the train. Even ordered 'em to use the emergency gear, seems he knew all about it. Then he went back and uncoupled the express car himself.

While he was doing this, a brakeman—you remember that brakeman that came through here once or twice— had a red mustache."

" *That* chap?"

" Sure. Well, as soon as the train stopped, this brakeman guessed something was wrong and ran up, saw the fellow cutting off the express car and took a couple of shots at him, and the fireman says the fellow didn't even take his hand off the coupling-pin; just turned around as cool as how-do-you-do and *nailed* the brakeman right there. They weren't five feet apart when they began shooting. The brakeman had come on him unexpected, had no idea he was so close."

" And the express messenger, all this time?"

" Well, he did his best. Jumped out with his repeating shot-gun, but the fellow had him covered before he could turn round. Held him up and took his gun away from him. Say, you know I call that nerve, just the same. One man standing up a whole train-load, like that. Then, as soon as he'd cut the express car off, he made the engineer run her up the track about half a mile to a road crossing, *where he had a horse tied.* What do you think of that? Didn't he have it all figured out close? And when he got there, he dynamited the safe and got the Wells-Fargo box. He took five thousand in gold coin; the messenger says it was railroad money that the company were sending down to Bakersfield to pay off with. It was in a bag. He never touched the registered mail, nor a whole wad of greenbacks that were in the safe, but just took the coin, got on his horse, and lit out. The engineer says he went to the east'ard."

" He got away, did he?"

" Yes, but they think they'll get him. He wore a kind of mask, but the brakeman recognised him positively. We got his ante-mortem statement. The brakeman said the fellow had a grudge against the road. He was a discharged employee, and lives near Bonneville."

"Dyke, by the Lord!" exclaimed Annixter.

"That's the name," said the young doctor.

When the train arrived at Bonneville, forty minutes behind time, it landed Annixter and Hilma in the midst of the very thing they most wished to avoid—an enormous crowd. The news that the Overland had been held up thirty miles south of Fresno, a brakeman killed and the safe looted, and that Dyke alone was responsible for the night's work, had been wired on ahead from Fowler, the train conductor throwing the despatch to the station agent from the flying train.

Before the train had come to a standstill under the arched roof of the Bonneville depot, it was all but taken by assault. Annixter, with Hilma on his arm, had almost to fight his way out of the car. The depot was black with people. S. Behrman was there, Delaney, Cyrus Ruggles, the town marshal, the mayor. Genslinger, his hat on the back of his head, ranged the train from cab to rear-lights, note-book in hand, interviewing, questioning, collecting facts for his extra. As Annixter descended finally to the platform, the editor, alert as a black-and-tan terrier, his thin, osseous hands quivering with eagerness, his brown, dry face working with excitement, caught his elbow.

"Can I have your version of the affair, Mr. Annixter?"

Annixter turned on him abruptly.

"Yes!" he exclaimed fiercely. "You and your gang drove Dyke from his job because he wouldn't work for starvation wages. Then you raised freight rates on him and robbed him of all he had. You ruined him and drove him to fill himself up with Caraher's whiskey. He's only taken back what you plundered him of, and now you're going to hound him over the State, hunt him down like a wild animal, and bring him to the gallows at San Quentin. That's *my* version of the affair, Mister Gen- slinger, but it's worth your subsidy from the P. and S. W. to print it."

There was a murmur of approval from the crowd that stood around, and Genslinger, with an angry shrug of one shoulder, took himself away.

At length, Annixter brought Hilma through the crowd to where young Vacca was waiting with the team. How- ever, they could not at once start for the ranch, Annix- ter wishing to ask some questions at the freight office about a final consignment of chairs. It was nearly eleven o'clock before they could start home. But to gain the Upper Road to Quien Sabe, it was necessary to traverse all of Main Street, running through the heart of Bonne- ville.

The entire town seemed to be upon the sidewalks. By now the rain was over and the sun shining. The story of the hold-up—the work of a man whom every one knew and liked—was in every mouth. How had Dyke come to do it? Who would have believed it of him? Think of his poor mother and the little tad. Well, after all, he was not so much to blame; the railroad people had brought it on themselves. But he had shot a man to death. Ah, that was a serious business. Good-natured, big, broad-shouldered, jovial Dyke, the man they knew, with whom they had shaken hands only yesterday, yes, and drank with him. He had shot a man, killed him, had stood there in the dark and in the rain while they were asleep in their beds, and had killed a man. Now where was he? Instinctively eyes were turned east- ward, over the tops of the houses, or down vistas of side streets to where the foot-hills of the mountains rose dim and vast over the edge of the valley. He was in amongst them, somewhere, in all that pile of blue crests and purple cañons he was hidden away. Now for weeks of searching, false alarms, clews, trailings, watchings, all the thrill and heart-bursting excitement of a man-hunt. Would he get away? Hardly a man on the sidewalks of the town that day who did not hope for it.

As Annixter's team trotted through the central portion of the town, young Vacca pointed to a denser and larger crowd around the rear entrance of the City Hall. Fully twenty saddle horses were tied to the iron rail underneath the scant, half-grown trees near by, and as Annixter and Hilma drove by, the crowd parted and a dozen men with revolvers on their hips pushed their way to the curbstone, and, mounting their horses, rode away at a gallop.

"It's the posse," said young Vacca.

Outside the town limits the ground was level. There was nothing to obstruct the view, and to the north, in the direction of Osterman's ranch, Vacca made out another party of horsemen, galloping eastward, and beyond these still another.

"There're the other posses," he announced. "That further one is Archie Moore's. He's the sheriff. He came down from Visalia on a special engine this morning."

When the team turned into the driveway to the ranch house, Hilma uttered a little cry, clasping her hands joyfully. The house was one glitter of new white paint, the driveway had been freshly gravelled, the flower-beds replenished. Mrs. Vacca and her daughter, who had been busy putting on the finishing touches, came to the door to welcome them.

"What's this case here?" asked Annixter, when, after helping his wife from the carry-all, his eye fell upon a wooden box of some three by five feet that stood on the porch and bore the red Wells-Fargo label.

"It came here last night, addressed to you, sir," exclaimed Mrs. Vacca. "We were sure it wasn't any of your furniture, so we didn't open it."

"Oh, maybe it's a wedding present," exclaimed Hilma, her eyes sparkling.

"Well, maybe it is," returned her husband. "Here, m' son, help me in with this."

Annixter and young Vacca bore the case into the sitting-room of the house, and Annixter, hammer in hand, attacked it vigorously. Vacca discreetly withdrew on signal from his mother, closing the door after him. Annixter and his wife were left alone.

"Oh, hurry, hurry," cried Hilma, dancing around him.

"I want to see what it is. Who do you suppose could have sent it to us? And so heavy, too. What *do* you think it can be?"

Annixter put the claw of the hammer underneath the edge of the board top and wrenched with all his might. The boards had been clamped together by a transverse bar and the whole top of the box came away in one piece. A layer of excelsior was disclosed, and on it a letter addressed by typewriter to Annixter. It bore the trade-mark of a business firm of Los Angeles. Annixter glanced at this and promptly caught it up before Hilma could see, with an exclamation of intelligence.

"Oh, I know what this is," he observed, carelessly trying to restrain her busy hands. "It isn't anything. Just some machinery. Let it go."

But already she had pulled away the excelsior. Underneath, in temporary racks, were two dozen Winchester repeating rifles.

"Why—what—what—" murmured Hilma blankly.

"Well, I told you not to mind," said Annixter. "It isn't anything. Let's look through the rooms."

"But you said you knew what it was," she protested,

bewildered. "You wanted to make believe it was machinery. Are you keeping anything from me? Tell me what it all means. Oh, why are you getting—these?"

She caught his arm, looking with intense eagerness into his face. She half understood already. Annixter saw that.

"Well," he said, lamely, "*you* know—it may not come to anything at all, but you know—well, this League of ours—suppose the Railroad tries to jump Quien Sabe or Los Muertos or any of the other ranches—we made up our minds—the Leaguers have—that we wouldn't let it. That's all."

"And I thought," cried Hilma, drawing back fearfully from the case of rifles, "and I thought it was a wedding present."

And that was their home-coming, the end of their bridal trip. Through the terror of the night, echoing with pistol shots, through that scene of robbery and murder, into this atmosphere of alarms, a man-hunt organising, armed horsemen silhouetted against the horizons, cases of rifles where wedding presents should have been, Annixter brought his young wife to be mistress of a home he might at any moment be called upon to defend with his life.

The days passed. Soon a week had gone by. Magnus Derrick and Osterman returned from the city without any definite idea as to the Corporation's plans. Lyman had been reticent. He knew nothing as to the progress of the land cases in Washington. There was no news. The Executive Committee of the League held a perfunctory meeting at Los Muertos at which nothing but routine business was transacted. A scheme put forward by Osterman for a conference with the railroad managers fell through because of the refusal of the company to treat with the ranchers upon any other basis than

that of the new grading. It was impossible to learn
whether or not the company considered Los Muertos,
Quien Sabe, and the ranches around Bonneville covered
by the test cases then on appeal.

Meanwhile there was no decrease in the excitement
that Dyke's hold-up had set loose over all the county.
Day after day it was the one topic of conversation, at
street corners, at cross-roads, over dinner tables, in office,
bank, and store. S. Behrman placarded the town with a
notice of $500.00 reward for the ex-engineer's capture,
dead or alive, and the express company supplemented
this by another offer of an equal amount. The country
was thick with parties of horsemen, armed with rifles
and revolvers, recruited from Visalia, Goshen, and the
few railroad sympathisers around Bonneville and Guad-
lajara. One after another of these returned, empty-
handed, covered with dust and mud, their horses exhausted, to be met and passed by fresh posses starting
out to continue the pursuit. The sheriff of Santa Clara
County sent down his bloodhounds from San José—
small, harmless-looking dogs, with a terrific bay—to help
in the chase. Reporters from the San Francisco papers
appeared, interviewing every one, sometimes even accom-
panying the searching bands. Horse hoofs clattered over
the roads at night; bells were rung, the " Mercury " issued extra after extra; the bloodhounds bayed, gun butts
clashed on the asphalt pavements of Bonneville; acci-
dental discharges of revolvers brought the whole town
into the street; farm hands called to each other across
the fences of ranch-divisions—in a word, the country-
side was in an uproar.

And all to no effect. The hoof-marks of Dyke's horse
had been traced in the mud of the road to within a quarter of a mile of the foot-hills and there irretrievably lost.
Three days after the hold-up, a sheep-herder was found

who had seen the highwayman on a ridge in the higher mountains, to the northeast of Taurusa. And that was absolutely all. Rumours were thick, promising clews were discovered, new trails taken up, but nothing transpired to bring the pursuers and pursued any closer together. Then, after ten days of strain, public interest began to flag. It was believed that Dyke had succeeded in getting away. If this was true, he had gone to the southward, after gaining the mountains, and it would be his intention to work out of the range somewhere near the southern part of the San Joaquin, near Bakersfield. Thus, the sheriffs, marshals, and deputies decided. They had hunted too many criminals in these mountains before not to know the usual courses taken. In time, Dyke *must* come out of the mountains to get water and provisions. But this time passed, and from not one of the watched points came any word of his appearance. At last the posses began to disband. Little by little the pursuit was given up.

Only S. Behrman persisted. He had made up his mind to bring Dyke in. He succeeded in arousing the same degree of determination in Delaney—by now, a trusted aide of the Railroad—and of his own cousin, a real estate broker, named Christian, who knew the mountains and had once been marshal of Visalia in the old stock-raising days. These two went into the Sierras, accompanied by two hired deputies, and carrying with them a month's provisions and two of the bloodhounds loaned by the Santa Clara sheriff.

On a certain Sunday, a few days after the departure of Christian and Delaney, Annixter, who had been reading "David Copperfield" in his hammock on the porch of the ranch house, put down the book and went to find Hilma, who was helping Louisa Vacca set the table for dinner. He found her in the dining-room, her hands full of the gold-bordered china plates, only used on special occasions and which Louisa was forbidden to touch.

His wife was more than ordinarily pretty that day. She wore a dress of flowered organdie over pink sateen, with pink ribbons about her waist and neck, and on her slim feet the low shoes she always affected, with their smart, bright buckles. Her thick, brown, sweet-smelling hair was heaped high upon her head and set off with a bow of black velvet, and underneath the shadow of its coils, her wide-open eyes, rimmed with the thin, black line of her lashes, shone continually, reflecting the sunlight. Marriage had only accentuated the beautiful maturity of Hilma's figure—now no longer precocious—defining the single, deep swell from her throat to her waist, the strong, fine amplitude of her hips, the sweet, feminine undulation of her neck and shoulders. Her cheeks were pink with health, and her large round arms carried the piled-up dishes with never a tremour. Annixter, observant enough where his wife was concerned, noted how the reflection of the white china set a glow of pale light underneath her chin.

"Hilma," he said, "I've been wondering lately about things. We're so blamed happy ourselves it won't do for us to forget about other people who are down, will it? Might change our luck. And I'm just likely to forget that way, too. It's my nature."

His wife looked up at him joyfully. Here was the new Annixter, certainly.

"In all this hullabaloo about Dyke," he went on, "there's some one nobody ain't thought about at all. That's *Mrs.* Dyke—and the little tad. I wouldn't be surprised if they were in a hole over there. What do you say we drive over to the hop ranch after dinner and see if she wants anything?"

Hilma put down the plates and came around the table and kissed him without a word.

As soon as their dinner was over, Annixter had the carry-all hitched up, and, dispensing with young Vacca, drove over to the hop ranch with Hilma.

Hilma could not keep back the tears as they passed through the lamentable desolation of the withered, brown vines, symbols of perished hopes and abandoned effort, and Annixter swore between his teeth.

Though the wheels of the carry-all grated loudly on the roadway in front of the house, nobody came to the door nor looked from the windows. The place seemed tenantless, infinitely lonely, infinitely sad.

Annixter tied the team, and with Hilma approached the wide-open door, scuffling and tramping on the porch to attract attention. Nobody stirred. A Sunday stillness pervaded the place. Outside, the withered hop-leaves rustled like dry paper in the breeze. The quiet was ominous. They peered into the front room from the doorway, Hilma holding her husband's hand. Mrs. Dyke was there. She sat at the table in the middle of the room, her head, with its white hair, down upon her arm. A clutter of unwashed dishes were strewed over the red and white tablecloth. The unkempt room, once a marvel of neatness, had not been cleaned for days. Newspapers, Genslinger's extras and copies of San Francisco and Los Angeles dailies were scattered all over the room. On the table itself were crumpled yellow telegrams, a dozen of them, a score of them, blowing about in the draught from the door. And in the midst of all this disarray, surrounded by the published accounts of her son's crime, the telegraphed answers to her pitiful appeals for tidings fluttering about her head, the highwayman's mother, worn out, abandoned and forgotten, slept through the stillness of the Sunday afternoon.

Neither Hilma nor Annixter ever forgot their interview with Mrs. Dyke that day. Suddenly waking, she had caught sight of Annixter, and at once exclaimed eagerly:

"Is there any news?"

For a long time afterwards nothing could be got from her. She was numb to all other issues than the one question of Dyke's capture. She did not answer their questions nor reply to their offers of assistance. Hilma and Annixter conferred together without lowering their voices, at her very elbow, while she looked vacantly at the floor, drawing one hand over the other in a persistent, maniacal gesture. From time to time she would start suddenly from her chair, her eyes wide, and as if all at once realising Annixter's presence, would cry out:

"Is there any news?"

"Where is Sidney, Mrs. Dyke?" asked Hilma for the fourth time. "Is she well? Is she taken care of?"

"Here's the last telegram," said Mrs. Dyke, in a loud, monotonous voice. "See, it says there is no news. He didn't do it," she moaned, rocking herself back and forth, drawing one hand over the other, "he didn't do it, he didn't do it, he didn't do it. I don't know where he is."

When at last she came to herself, it was with a flood of tears. Hilma put her arms around the poor, old woman, as she bowed herself again upon the table, sobbing and weeping.

"Oh, my son, my son," she cried, "my own boy, my only son! If I could have died for you to have prevented this. I remember him when he was little. Such a splendid little fellow, so brave, so loving, with never an unkind thought, never a mean action. So it was all his life. We were never apart. It was always 'dear little son,' and 'dear mammy' between us—never once was he unkind, and he loved me and was the gentlest son to me. And he was a *good* man. He is now, he is now. They don't understand him. They are not even sure that he did this. He never meant it. They don't know my son. Why, he wouldn't have hurt a kitten. Everybody loved him. He was driven to it. They hounded him down, they wouldn't let him alone. He was not right in his mind. They hounded him to it," she cried fiercely, "they hounded him to it. They drove him and goaded him till he couldn't stand it any longer, and now they mean to kill him for turning on them. They are hunting him with dogs; night after night I have stood on the porch and heard the dogs baying far off. They are tracking my boy with dogs like a wild animal. May God never forgive them." She rose to her feet, terrible, her white hair unbound. "May God punish them as they deserve, may they never prosper—on my knees I shall pray for it every night—may their money be a curse to them, may their sons, their first-born, only sons, be taken from them in their youth."

But Hilma interrupted, begging her to be silent, to be quiet. The tears came again then and the choking sobs. Hilma took her in her arms.

"Oh, my little boy, my little boy," she cried. "My only son, all that I had, to have come to this! He was not right in his mind or he would have known it would break my heart. Oh, my son, my son, if I could have died for you."

Sidney came in, clinging to her dress, weeping, imploring her not to cry, protesting that they never could catch her papa, that he would come back soon. Hilma took them both, the little child and the broken-down old woman, in the great embrace of her strong arms, and they all three sobbed together.

Annixter stood on the porch outside, his back turned, looking straight before him into the wilderness of dead vines, his teeth shut hard, his lower lip thrust out.

" I hope S. Behrman is satisfied with all this," he muttered. " I hope he is satisfied now, damn his soul!"

All at once an idea occurred to him. He turned about
and reëntered the room.

" Mrs. Dyke," he began, " I want you and Sidney to
come over and live at Quien Sabe. I know—you can't
make me believe that the reporters and officers and
officious busy-faces that pretend to offer help just so as
they can satisfy their curiosity aren't nagging you to
death. I want you to let me take care of you and the
little tad till all this trouble of yours is over with.
There's plenty of place for you. You can have the
house my wife's people used to live in. You've got
to look these things in the face. What are you going
to do to get along? You must be very short of money.
S. Behrman will foreclose on you and take the whole
place in a little while, now. I want you to let me help
you, let Hilma and me be good friends to you. It
would be a privilege."

Mrs. Dyke tried bravely to assume her pride, insisting
that she could manage, but her spirit was broken. The
whole affair ended unexpectedly, with Annixter and
Hilma bringing Dyke's mother and little girl back to
Quien Sabe in the carry-all.

Mrs. Dyke would not take with her a stick of furniture
nor a single ornament. It would only serve to remind her
of a vanished happiness. She packed a few clothes of her
own and Sidney's in a little trunk, Hilma helping her,
and Annixter stowed the trunk under the carry-all's back
seat. Mrs. Dyke turned the key in the door of the house
and Annixter helped her to her seat beside his wife. They
drove through the sear, brown hop vines. At the angle
of the road Mrs. Dyke turned around and looked back at
the ruin of the hop ranch, the roof of the house just
showing above the trees. She never saw it again.

As soon as Annixter and Hilma were alone, after their return to Quien Sabe—Mrs. Dyke and Sidney having been installed in the Trees' old house—Hilma threw her arms around her husband's neck.

"Fine," she exclaimed, "oh, it was fine of you, dear, to think of them and to be so good to them. My husband is such a *good* man. So unselfish. You wouldn't have thought of being kind to Mrs. Dyke and Sidney a little while ago. You wouldn't have thought of them at all. But you did now, and it's just because you love me true, isn't it? Isn't it? And because it's made you a better man. I'm so proud and glad to think it's so. It is so, isn't it? Just because you love me true."

"You bet it is, Hilma," he told her.

As Hilma and Annixter were sitting down to the supper which they found waiting for them, Louisa Vacca came to the door of the dining-room to say that Harran Derrick had telephoned over from Los Muertos for Annixter, and had left word for him to ring up Los Muertos as soon as he came in.

"He said it was important," added Louisa Vacca.

"Maybe they have news from Washington," suggested Hilma.

Annixter would not wait to have supper, but telephoned to Los Muertos at once. Magnus answered the call. There was a special meeting of the Executive Committee of the League summoned for the next day, he told Annixter. It was for the purpose of considering the new grain tariff prepared by the Railroad Commissioners. Lyman had written that the schedule of this tariff had just been issued, that he had not been able to construct it precisely according to the wheat-growers' wishes, and that he, himself, would come down to Los Muertos and explain its apparent discrepancies. Magnus said Lyman would be present at the session.

Annixter, curious for details, forbore, nevertheless, to question. The connection from Los Muertos to Quien Sabe was made through Bonneville, and in those troublesome times no one could be trusted. It could not be known who would overhear conversations carried on over the lines. He assured Magnus that he would be on hand.

The time for the Committee meeting had been set for seven o'clock in the evening, in order to accommodate Lyman, who wrote that he would be down on the evening train, but would be compelled, by pressure of business, to return to the city early the next morning.

At the time appointed, the men composing the Committee gathered about the table in the dining-room of the Los Muertos ranch house. It was almost a reproduction of the scene of the famous evening when Osterman had proposed the plan of the Ranchers' Railroad Commission. Magnus Derrick sat at the head of the table, in his buttoned frock coat. Whiskey bottles and siphons of soda-water were within easy reach. Presley, who by now was considered the confidential friend of every member of the Committee, lounged as before on the sofa, smoking cigarettes, the cat Nathalie on his knee. Besides Magnus and Annixter, Osterman was present, and old Broderson and Harran; Garnet from the Ruby Rancho and Gethings of the San Pablo, who were also members of the Executive Committee, were on hand, preoccupied, bearded men, smoking black cigars, and, last of all, Dabney, the silent old man, of whom little was known but his name, and who had been made a member of the Committee, nobody could tell why.

" My son Lyman should be here, gentlemen, within at least ten minutes. I have sent my team to meet him at Bonneville," explained Magnus, as he called the meeting to order. " The Secretary will call the roll."

Osterman called the roll, and, to fill in the time, read

over the minutes of the previous meeting. The treasurer was making his report as to the funds at the disposal of the League when Lyman arrived.

Magnus and Harran went forward to meet him, and the Committee rather awkwardly rose and remained standing while the three exchanged greetings, the members, some of whom had never seen their commissioner, eyeing him out of the corners of their eyes.

Lyman was dressed with his usual correctness. His cravat was of the latest fashion, his clothes of careful design and unimpeachable fit. His shoes, of patent leather, reflected the lamplight, and he carried a drab overcoat over his arm. Before being introduced to the Committee, he excused himself a moment and ran to see his mother, who waited for him in the adjoining sitting-room. But in a few moments he returned, asking pardon for the delay.

He was all affability; his protruding eyes, that gave such an unusual, foreign appearance to his very dark face, radiated geniality. He was evidently anxious to please, to produce a good impression upon the grave, clumsy farmers before whom he stood. But at the same time, Presley, watching him from his place on the sofa, could imagine that he was rather nervous. He was too nimble in his cordiality, and the little gestures he made in bringing his cuffs into view and in touching the ends of his tight, black mustache with the ball of his thumb were repeated with unnecessary frequency.

"Mr. Broderson, my son, Lyman, my eldest son. Mr. Annixter, my son, Lyman."

The Governor introduced him to the ranchers, proud of Lyman's good looks, his correct dress, his ease of manner. Lyman shook hands all around, keeping up a flow of small talk, finding a new phrase for each member, complimenting Osterman, whom he already knew, upon his talent for organisation, recalling a mutual acquaintance to the mind of old Broderson. At length, however, he sat down at the end of the table, opposite his brother. There was a silence.

Magnus rose to recapitulate the reasons for the extra session of the Committee, stating again that the Board of Railway Commissioners which they—the ranchers—had succeeded in seating had at length issued the new schedule of reduced rates, and that Mr. Derrick had been obliging enough to offer to come down to Los Muertos in person to acquaint the wheat-growers of the San Joaquin with the new rates for the carriage of their grain.

But Lyman very politely protested, addressing his father punctiliously as "Mr. Chairman," and the other ranchers as "Gentlemen of the Executive Committee of the League." He had no wish, he said, to disarrange the regular proceedings of the Committee. Would it not be preferable to defer the reading of his report till "new business" was called for? In the meanwhile, let the Committee proceed with its usual work. He understood the necessarily delicate nature of this work, and would be pleased to withdraw till the proper time arrived for him to speak.

"Good deal of backing and filling about the reading of a column of figures," muttered Annixter to the man at his elbow.

Lyman "awaited the Committee's decision." He sat down, touching the ends of his mustache.

"Oh, play ball," growled Annixter.

Gethings rose to say that as the meeting had been called solely for the purpose of hearing and considering the new grain tariff, he was of the opinion that routine business could be dispensed with and the schedule read at once. It was so ordered.

Lyman rose and made a long speech. Voluble as Osterman himself, he, nevertheless, had at his command a vast number of ready-made phrases, the staples of a political speaker, the stock in trade of the commercial lawyer, which rolled off his tongue with the most persuasive fluency. By degrees, in the course of his speech, he began to insinuate the idea that the wheat-growers had never expected to settle their difficulties with the Railroad by the work of a single commission; that they had counted upon a long, continued campaign of many years, railway commission succeeding railway commission, before the desired low rates should be secured; that the present Board of Commissioners was only the beginning and that too great results were not expected from them. All this he contrived to mention casually, in the talk, as if it were a foregone conclusion, a matter understood by all.

As the speech continued, the eyes of the ranchers around the table were fixed with growing attention upon this well-dressed, city-bred young man, who spoke so fluently and who told them of their own intentions. A feeling of perplexity began to spread, and the first taint of distrust invaded their minds.

" But the good work has been most auspiciously inaugurated," continued Lyman. "Reforms so sweeping as the one contemplated cannot be accomplished in a single night. Great things grow slowly, benefits to be permanent must accrue gradually. Yet, in spite of all this, your commissioners have done much. Already the phalanx of the enemy is pierced, already his armour is dinted. Pledged as were your commissioners to an average ten per cent. reduction in rates for the carriage of grain by the Pacific and Southwestern Railroad, we have rigidly adhered to the demands of our constituency, we have obeyed the People. The main problem has not yet been completely solved; that is for later, when we shall have gathered sufficient strength to attack the enemy in his very stronghold; *but an average ten per cent. cut has been made all over the State.* We have made a great advance, have taken a great step forward, and if the work is carried ahead, upon the lines laid down by the present commissioners and their constituents, there is every reason to believe that within a very few years equitable and stable rates for the shipment of grain from the San Joaquin Valley to Stockton, Port Costa, and tidewater will be permanently imposed."

"Well, hold on," exclaimed Annixter, out of order and ignoring the Governor's reproof, "hasn't your commission reduced grain rates in the San Joaquin?"

"We have reduced grain rates by ten per cent. all over the State," rejoined Lyman. "Here are copies of the new schedule."

He drew them from his valise and passed them around the table.

"You see," he observed, "the rate between Mayfield and Oakland, for instance, has been reduced by twenty-five cents a ton."

"Yes—but—but—" said old Broderson, "it is rather unusual, isn't it, for wheat in that district to be sent to Oakland?"

"Why, look here," exclaimed Annixter, looking up from the schedule, "where is there any reduction in rates in the San Joaquin—from Bonneville and Guadalajara, for instance? I don't see as you've made any reduction at all. Is this right? Did you give me the right schedule?"

"Of course, *all* the points in the State could not be covered at once," returned Lyman. "We never expected, you know, that we could cut rates in the San Joaquin the very first move; that is for later. But you will see we made very material reductions on shipments from the

upper Sacramento Valley; also the rate from Ione to
Marysville has been reduced eighty cents a ton."

" Why, rot," cried Annixter, " no one ever ships wheat
that way."

" The Salinas rate," continued Lyman, " has been lowered seventy-five cents; the St. Helena rate fifty cents,
and please notice the very drastic cut from Red Bluff,
north, along the Oregon route, to the Oregon State
Line."

" Where not a carload of wheat is shipped in a year,"
commented Gethings of the San Pablo.

" Oh, you will find yourself mistaken there, Mr.
Gethings," returned Lyman courteously. " And for the
matter of that, a low rate would stimulate wheat-
production in that district."

The order of the meeting was broken up, neglected;
Magnus did not even pretend to preside. In the growing
excitement over the inexplicable schedule, routine was not
thought of. Every one spoke at will.

" Why, Lyman," demanded Magnus, looking across the
table to his son, " is this schedule correct? You have not
cut rates in the San Joaquin at all. We—these gentlemen here and myself, we are no better off than we were
before we secured your election as commissioner."

" We were pledged to make an average ten per cent.
cut, sir——"

" It *is* an average ten per cent. cut," cried Osterman.
" Oh, yes, that's plain. It's an average ten per cent. cut
all right, but you've made it by cutting grain rates between points where practically no grain is shipped.
We, the wheat-growers in the San Joaquin, where all
the wheat is grown, are right where we were before.
The Railroad won't lose a nickel. By Jingo, boys," he
glanced around the table, " I'd like to know what this
means."

"The Railroad, if you come to that," returned Lyman, "has already lodged a protest against the new rate."

Annixter uttered a derisive shout.

"A protest! That's good, that is. When the P. and S. W. objects to rates it don't 'protest,' m' son. The first you hear from Mr. Shelgrim is an injunction from the courts preventing the order for new rates from taking effect. By the Lord," he cried angrily, leaping to his feet, "I would like to know what all this means, too. Why didn't you reduce our grain rates? What did we elect you for?"

"Yes, what did we elect you for?" demanded Osterman and Gethings, also getting to their feet.

"Order, order, gentlemen," cried Magnus, remembering the duties of his office and rapping his knuckles on the table. "This meeting has been allowed to degenerate too far already."

"You elected us," declared Lyman doggedly, "to make an average ten per cent. cut on grain rates. We have done it. Only because you don't benefit at once, you object. It makes a difference whose ox is gored, it seems."

"Lyman!"

It was Magnus who spoke. He had drawn himself to his full six feet. His eyes were flashing direct into his son's. His voice rang with severity.

"Lyman, what does this mean?"

The other spread out his hands.

"As you see, sir. We have done our best. I warned you not to expect too much. I told you that this question of transportation was difficult. You would not wish to put rates so low that the action would amount to confiscation of property."

"Why did you not lower rates in the valley of the San Joaquin?"

"That was not a *prominent* issue in the affair," responded Lyman, carefully emphasising his words. "I understand, of course, it was to be approached *in time*. The main point was *an average ten per cent. reduction*. Rates *will* be lowered in the San Joaquin. The ranchers around Bonneville will be able to ship to Port Costa at equitable rates, but so radical a measure as that cannot be put through in a turn of the hand. We must study——"

"You *knew* the San Joaquin rate *was* an issue," shouted Annixter, shaking his finger across the table. "What do we men who backed you care about rates up in Del Norte and Siskiyou Counties? Not a whoop in hell. It was the San Joaquin rate we were fighting for, and we elected you to reduce that. You didn't do it and you don't intend to, and, by the Lord Harry, I want to know why."

"You'll know, sir——" began Lyman.

"Well, I'll tell you why," vociferated Osterman. "I'll tell you why. It's because we have been sold out. It's because the P. and S. W. have had their spoon in this boiling. It's because our commissioners have betrayed us. It's because we're a set of damn fool farmers and have been cinched again."

Lyman paled under his dark skin at the direct attack. He evidently had not expected this so soon. For the fraction of one instant he lost his poise. He strove to speak, but caught his breath, stammering.

"What have you to say, then?" cried Harran, who, until now, had not spoken.

"I have this to say," answered Lyman, making head as best he might, "that this is no proper spirit in which to discuss business. The Commission has fulfilled its obligations. It has adjusted rates to the best of its ability. We have been at work for two months on the preparation of this schedule——"

" That's a lie," shouted Annixter, his face scarlet;
" that's a lie. That schedule was drawn in the offices of
the Pacific and Southwestern and you know it. It's a
scheme of rates made for the Railroad and by the Railroad and you were bought over to put your name to it."

There was a concerted outburst at the words. All the
men in the room were on their feet, gesticulating and
vociferating.

" Gentlemen, gentlemen," cried Magnus, " are we
schoolboys, are we ruffians of the street? "

" We're a set of fool farmers and we've been betrayed,"
cried Osterman.

" Well, what have you to say? What have you to
say? " persisted Harran, leaning across the table toward
his brother. " For God's sake, Lyman, you've got *some*
explanation."

" You've misunderstood," protested Lyman, white and
trembling. " You've misunderstood. You've expected
too much. Next year,—next year,—soon now, the Commission will take up the—the Commission will consider
the San Joaquin rate. We've done our best, that is all."

" Have you, sir? " demanded Magnus.

The Governor's head was in a whirl; a sensation,
almost of faintness, had seized upon him. Was it possible? Was it possible?

" Have you done your best? " For a second he compelled Lyman's eye. The glances of father and son
met, and, in spite of his best efforts, Lyman's eyes wavered. He began to protest once more, explaining the
matter over again from the beginning. But Magnus did
not listen. In that brief lapse of time he was convinced
that the terrible thing had happened, that the unbelievable had come to pass. It was in the air. Between father
and son, in some subtle fashion, the truth that was a lie
stood suddenly revealed. But even then Magnus would

not receive it. Lyman do this! His son, his eldest son, descend to this! Once more and for the last time he turned to him and in his voice there was that ring that compelled silence.

"Lyman," he said, "I adjure you—I—I demand of you as you are my son and an honourable man, explain yourself. What is there behind all this? It is no longer as Chairman of the Committee I speak to you, you a member of the Railroad Commission. It is your father who speaks, and I address you as my son. Do you understand the gravity of this crisis; do you realise the responsibility of your position; do you not see the importance of this moment? Explain yourself."

"There is nothing to explain."

"You have not reduced rates in the San Joaquin? You have not reduced rates between Bonneville and tidewater?"

"I repeat, sir, what I said before. An average ten per cent. cut——"

"Lyman, answer me, yes or no. Have you reduced the Bonneville rate?"

"It could not be done so soon. Give us time. We ——"

"Yes or no! By God, sir, do you dare equivocate with me? Yes or no; have you reduced the Bonneville rate?"

"No."

"And answer *me*," shouted Harran, leaning far across the table, "answer *me*. Were you paid by the Railroad to leave the San Joaquin rate untouched?"

Lyman, whiter than ever, turned furious upon his brother.

"Don't you dare put that question to me again."

"No, I won't," cried Harran, "because I'll *tell* you to your villain's face that you *were* paid to do it."

On the instant the clamour burst forth afresh. Still

on their feet, the ranchers had, little by little, worked around the table, Magnus alone keeping his place. The others were in a group before Lyman, crowding him, as it were, to the wall, shouting into his face with menacing gestures. The truth that was a lie, the certainty of a trust betrayed, a pledge ruthlessly broken, was plain to every one of them.

"By the Lord! men have been shot for less than this," cried Osterman. "You've sold us out, you, and if you ever bring that dago face of yours on a level with mine again, I'll slap it."

"Keep your hands off," exclaimed Lyman quickly, the aggressiveness of the cornered rat flaming up within him. "No violence. Don't you go too far."

"How much were you paid? How much were you paid?" vociferated Harran.

"Yes, yes, what was your price?" cried the others. They were beside themselves with anger; their words came harsh from between their set teeth; their gestures were made with their fists clenched.

"You know the Commission acted in good faith," retorted Lyman. "You know that all was fair and above board."

"Liar," shouted Annixter; "liar, bribe-eater. You were bought and paid for," and with the words his arm seemed almost of itself to leap out from his shoulder. Lyman received the blow squarely in the face and the force of it sent him staggering backwards toward the wall. He tripped over his valise and fell half way, his back supported against the closed door of the room. Magnus sprang forward. His son had been struck, and the instincts of a father rose up in instant protest; rose for a moment, then forever died away in his heart. He checked the words that flashed to his mind. He lowered his upraised arm. No, he had but one son. The poor, staggering creature with the fine clothes, white face, and blood-streaked lips was no longer his. A blow could not dishonour him more than he had dishonoured himself.

But Gethings, the older man, intervened, pulling Annixter back, crying:

"Stop, this won't do. Not before his father."

"I am no father to this man, gentlemen," exclaimed Magnus. "From now on, I have but one son. You, sir," he turned to Lyman, "you, sir, leave my house."

Lyman, his handkerchief to his lips, his smart cravat in disarray, caught up his hat and coat. He was shaking with fury, his protruding eyes were blood-shot. He swung open the door.

"Ruffians," he shouted from the threshold, "ruffians, bullies. Do your own dirty business yourselves after this. I'm done with you. How is it, all of a sudden you talk about honour? How is it that all at once you're so clean and straight? You weren't so particular at Sacramento just before the nominations. How was the Board elected? I'm a bribe-eater, am I? Is it any worse than *giving* a bribe? Ask Magnus Derrick what he thinks about that. Ask him how much he paid the Democratic bosses at Sacramento to swing the convention."

He went out, slamming the door.

Presley followed. The whole affair made him sick at heart, filled him with infinite disgust, infinite weariness. He wished to get away from it all. He left the dining-room and the excited, clamouring men behind him and stepped out on the porch of the ranch house, closing the door behind him. Lyman was nowhere in sight. Presley was alone. It was late, and after the lamp-heated air of the dining-room, the coolness of the night was delicious, and its vast silence, after the noise and fury of the committee meeting, descended from the stars like a benediction. Presley stepped to the edge of the porch, looking off to southward.

And there before him, mile after mile, illimitable, covering the earth from horizon to horizon, lay the Wheat. The growth, now many days old, was already high from the ground. There it lay, a vast, silent ocean, shimmering a pallid green under the moon and under the stars; a mighty force, the strength of nations, the life of the world. There in the night, under the dome of the sky, it was growing steadily. To Presley's mind, the scene in the room he had just left dwindled to paltry insignificance before this sight. Ah, yes, the Wheat—it was over this that the Railroad, the ranchers, the traitor false to his trust, all the members of an obscure conspiracy, were wrangling. As if human agency could affect this colossal power! What were these heated, tiny squabbles, this feverish, small bustle of mankind, this minute swarming of the human insect, to the great, majestic, silent ocean of the Wheat itself! Indifferent, gigantic, resistless, it moved in its appointed grooves. Men, Liliputians, gnats in the sunshine, buzzed impudently in their tiny battles, were born, lived through their little day, died, and were forgotten; while the Wheat, wrapped in Nirvanic calm, grew steadily under the night, alone with the stars and with God.

V

Jack-rabbits were a pest that year and Presley occasionally found amusement in hunting them with Harran's half-dozen greyhounds, following the chase on horseback. One day, between two and three months after Lyman's visit to Los Muertos, as he was returning toward the ranch house from a distant and lonely quarter of Los Muertos, he came unexpectedly upon a strange sight.

Some twenty men, Annixter's and Osterman's tenants, and small ranchers from east of Guadalajara—all members of the League—were going through the manual of arms under Harran Derrick's supervision. They were all equipped with new Winchester rifles. Harran carried one of these himself and with it he illustrated the various commands he gave. As soon as one of the men under his supervision became more than usually proficient, he was told off to instruct a file of the more backward. After the manual of arms, Harran gave the command to take distance as skirmishers, and when the line had opened out so that some half-dozen feet intervened between each man, an advance was made across the field, the men stooping low and snapping the hammers of their rifles at an imaginary enemy.

The League had its agents in San Francisco, who watched the movements of the Railroad as closely as was possible, and some time before this, Annixter had received word that the Marshal and his deputies were coming down to Bonneville to put the dummy buyers of his ranch in possession. The report proved to be but the first of many false alarms, but it had stimulated the League to unusual activity, and some three or four hundred men were furnished with arms and from time to time were drilled in secret.

Among themselves, the ranchers said that if the Railroad managers did not believe they were terribly in earnest in the stand they had taken, they were making a fatal mistake.

Harran reasserted this statement to Presley on the way home to the ranch house that same day. Harran had caught up with him by the time he reached the Lower Road, and the two jogged homeward through the miles of standing wheat.

"They may jump the ranch, Pres," he said, "if they try hard enough, but they will never do it while I am alive. By the way," he added, "you know we served notices yesterday upon S. Behrman and Cy. Ruggles to quit the country. Of course, they won't do it, but they won't be able to say they didn't have warning."

About an hour later, the two reached the ranch house, but as Harran rode up the driveway, he uttered an exclamation.

"Hello," he said, "something is up. That's Genslinger's buckboard."

In fact, the editor's team was tied underneath the shade of a giant eucalyptus tree near by. Harran, uneasy under this unexpected visit of the enemy's friend, dismounted without stabling his horse, and went at once to the dining-room, where visitors were invariably received. But the dining-room was empty, and his mother told him that Magnus and the editor were in the "office." Magnus had said they were not to be disturbed.

Earlier in the afternoon, the editor had driven up to the porch and had asked Mrs. Derrick, whom he found reading a book of poems on the porch, if he could see

Magnus. At the time, the Governor had gone with Phelps to inspect the condition of the young wheat on Hooven's holding, but within half an hour he returned, and Genslinger had asked him for a " few moments' talk in private."

The two went into the " office," Magnus locking the door behind him.

" Very complete you are here, Governor," observed the editor in his alert, jerky manner, his black, bead-like eyes twinkling around the room from behind his glasses. " Telephone, safe, ticker, account-books—well, that's progress, isn't it? Only way to manage a big ranch these days. But the day of the big ranch is over. As the land appreciates in value, the temptation to sell off small holdings will be too strong. And then the small holding can be cultivated to better advantage. I shall have an editorial on that some day."

" The cost of maintaining a number of small holdings," said Magnus, indifferently, " is, of course, greater than if they were all under one management."

" That may be, that may be," rejoined the other.

There was a long pause. Genslinger leaned back in his chair and rubbed a knee. Magnus, standing erect in front of the safe, waited for him to speak.

" This is an unfortunate business, Governor," began the editor, " this misunderstanding between the ranchers and the Railroad. I wish it could be adjusted. *Here* are two industries that *must* be in harmony with one another, or we all go to pot."

" I should prefer not to be interviewed on the subject, Mr. Genslinger," said Magnus.

" Oh, no, oh, no. Lord love you, Governor, I don't want to interview you. We all know how *you* stand."

Again there was a long silence. Magnus wondered what this little man, usually so garrulous, could want of him. At length, Genslinger began again. He did not look at Magnus, except at long intervals.

"About the present Railroad Commission," he remarked. "That was an interesting campaign you conducted in Sacramento and San Francisco."

Magnus held his peace, his hands shut tight. Did Genslinger know of Lyman's disgrace? Was it for this he had come? Would the story of it be the leading article in to-morrow's *Mercury?*

"An interesting campaign," repeated Genslinger, slowly; "a very interesting campaign. I watched it with every degree of interest. I saw its every phase, Mr. Derrick."

"The campaign was not without its interest," admitted Magnus.

"Yes," said Genslinger, still more deliberately, "and some phases of it were—more interesting than others, as, for instance, let us say the way in which you—personally—secured the votes of certain chairmen of delegations—*need* I particularise further? Yes, those men—the way you got their votes. Now, *that* I should say, Mr. Derrick, was the most interesting move in the whole game—to you. Hm, curious," he murmured, musingly. "Let's see. You deposited two one-thousand dollar bills and four five-hundred dollar bills in a box—three hundred and eight was the number—in a box in the Safety Deposit Vaults in San Francisco, and then—let's see, you gave a key to this box to each of the gentlemen in question, and after the election the box was empty. Now, I call that interesting—curious, because it's a new, safe, and highly ingenious method of bribery. How did you happen to think of it, Governor?"

"Do you know what you are doing, sir?" Magnus burst forth. "Do you know what you are insinuating, here, in my own house?"

" Why, Governor," returned the editor, blandly, " I'm not *insinuating* anything. I'm talking about what I *know*."

" It's a lie."

Genslinger rubbed his chin reflectively.

" Well," he answered, " you can have a chance to prove it before the Grand Jury, if you want to."

" My character is known all over the State," blustered Magnus. " My politics are pure politics. My—— "

" No one needs a better reputation for pure politics than the man who sets out to be a briber," interrupted Genslinger, " and I might as well tell you, Governor, that you can't shout me down. I can put my hand on the two chairmen you bought before it's dark to-day. I've had their depositions in my safe for the last six weeks. We could make the arrests to-morrow, if we wanted. Governor, you sure did a risky thing when you went into that Sacramento fight, an awful risky thing. Some men can afford to have bribery charges preferred against them, and it don't hurt one little bit, but *you*—Lord, it would *bust* you, Governor, bust you dead. I know all about the whole shananigan business from A to Z, and if you don't believe it—here," he drew a long strip of paper from his pocket, " here's a galley proof of the story."

Magnus took it in his hands. There, under his eyes, scare-headed, double-leaded, the more important clauses printed in bold type, was the detailed account of the " deal " Magnus had made with the two delegates. It was pitiless, remorseless, bald. Every statement was substantiated, every statistic verified with Genslinger's meticulous love for exactness. Besides all that, it had the ring of truth. It was exposure, ruin, absolute annihilation.

" That's about correct, isn't it? " commented Genslinger, as Derrick finished reading. Magnus did not reply. "I think it is correct enough," the editor continued. "But I thought it would only be fair to you to let you see it before it was published."

The one thought uppermost in Derrick's mind, his one impulse of the moment was, at whatever cost, to preserve his dignity, not to allow this man to exult in the sight of one quiver of weakness, one trace of defeat, one suggestion of humiliation. By an effort that put all his iron rigidity to the test, he forced himself to look straight into Genslinger's eyes.

"I congratulate you," he observed, handing back the proof, "upon your journalistic enterprise. Your paper will sell to-morrow."

"Oh, I don't know as I want to publish this story," remarked the editor, indifferently, putting away the galley. "I'm just like that. The fun for me is running a good story to earth, but once I've got it, I lose interest. And, then, I wouldn't like to see you—holding the position you do, President of the League and a leading man of the county—I wouldn't like to see a story like this smash you over. It's worth more to you to keep it out of print than for me to put it in. I've got nothing much to gain but a few extra editions, but you—Lord, you would lose everything. Your committee was in the deal right enough. But your League, all the San Joaquin Valley, everybody in the State believes the commissioners were fairly elected."

"Your story," suddenly exclaimed Magnus, struck with an idea, "will be thoroughly discredited just so soon as the new grain tariff is published. I have means of knowing that the San Joaquin rate—the issue upon which the board was elected—is not to be touched. Is it likely the ranchers would secure the election of a board that plays them false?"

"Oh, we know all about that," answered Genslinger,

smiling. "You thought you were electing Lyman easily. You thought you had got the Railroad to walk right into your trap. You didn't understand how you could pull off your deal so easily. Why, Governor, *Lyman was pledged to the Railroad two years ago.* He was *the one particular* man the corporation wanted for commissioner. And your people elected him—saved the Railroad all the trouble of campaigning for him. And you can't make any counter charge of bribery there. No, sir, the corporation don't use such amateurish methods as that. Confidentially and between us two, all that the Railroad has done for Lyman, in order to attach him to their interests, is to promise to back him politically in the next campaign for Governor. It's too bad," he continued, dropping his voice, and changing his position. "It really is too bad to see good men trying to bunt a stone wall over with their bare heads. You couldn't have won at any stage of the game. I wish I could have talked to you and your friends before you went into that Sacramento fight. I could have told you then how little chance you had. When will you people realise that you can't buck against the Railroad? Why, Magnus, it's like me going out in a paper boat and shooting peas at a battleship."

"Is that all you wished to see me about, Mr. Genslinger?" remarked Magnus, bestirring himself. "I am rather occupied to-day."

"Well," returned the other, "you know what the publication of this article would mean for you." He paused again, took off his glasses, breathed on them, polished the lenses with his handkerchief and readjusted them on his nose. "I've been thinking, Governor," he began again, with renewed alertness, and quite irrelevantly, "of enlarging the scope of the 'Mercury.' You see, I'm midway between the two big centres of the State, San Francisco and Los Angeles, and I want to extend the 'Mer-

cury's ' sphere of influence as far up and down the valley
as I can. I want to illustrate the paper. You see, if I had
a photo-engraving plant of my own, I could do a good
deal of outside jobbing as well, and the investment would
pay ten per cent. But it takes money to make money. I
wouldn't want to put in any dinky, one-horse affair. I
want a good plant. I've been figuring out the business.
Besides the plant, there would be the expense of a high
grade paper. Can't print half-tones on anything but
coated paper, and that *costs*. Well, what with this and
with that and running expenses till the thing began to
pay, it would cost me about ten thousand dollars, and I
was wondering if, perhaps, you couldn't see your way
clear to accommodating me."

"Ten thousand?"

"Yes. Say five thousand down, and the balance
within sixty days."

Magnus, for the moment blind to what Genslinger
had in mind, turned on him in astonishment.

"Why, man, what security could *you* give me for such
an amount?"

"Well, to tell the truth," answered the editor, "I
hadn't thought much about securities. In fact, I believed
you would see how greatly it was to your advantage to
talk business with me. You see, I'm not going to print
this article about you, Governor, and I'm not going to let
it get out so as any one else can print it, and it seems to
me that one good turn deserves another. You understand?"

Magnus understood. An overwhelming desire suddenly took possession of him to grip this blackmailer by
the throat, to strangle him where he stood; or, if not, at
least to turn upon him with that old-time terrible anger,
before which whole conventions had once cowered. But
in the same moment the Governor realised this was not

to be. Only its righteousness had made his wrath terrible; only the justice of his anger had made him feared. Now the foundation was gone from under his feet; he had knocked it away himself. Three times feeble was he whose quarrel was unjust. Before this country editor, this paid speaker of the Railroad, he stood, convicted. The man had him at his mercy. The detected briber could not resent an insult. Genslinger rose, smoothing his hat.

"Well," he said, "of course, you want time to think it over, and you can't raise money like that on short notice. I'll wait till Friday noon of this week. We begin to set Saturday's paper at about four, Friday afternoon, and the forms are locked about two in the morning. I hope," he added, turning back at the door of the room, "that you won't find anything disagreeable in your Saturday morning 'Mercury,' Mr. Derrick."

He went out, closing the door behind him, and in a moment, Magnus heard the wheels of his buckboard grating on the driveway.

The following morning brought a letter to Magnus from Gethings, of the San Pueblo ranch, which was situated very close to Visalia. The letter was to the effect that all around Visalia, upon the ranches affected by the regrade of the Railroad, men were arming and drilling, and that the strength of the League in that quarter was undoubted. "But to refer," continued the letter, "to a most painful recollection. You will, no doubt, remember that, at the close of our last committee meeting, specific charges were made as to fraud in the nomination and election of one of our commissioners, emanating, most unfortunately, from the commissioner himself. These charges, my dear Mr. Derrick, were directed at yourself. How the secrets of the committee have been noised about, I cannot understand. You may be, of course, assured of my own unquestioning confidence and loyalty. However, I regret exceedingly to state not only that the rumour of the charges referred to above is spreading in this district, but that also they are made use of by the enemies of the League. It is to be deplored that some of the Leaguers themselves—you know, we number in our ranks many small farmers, ignorant Portuguese and foreigners—have listened to these stories and have permitted a feeling of uneasiness to develop among them. Even though it were admitted that fraudulent means had been employed in the elections, which, of course, I personally do not admit, I do not think it would make very much difference in the confidence which the vast majority of the Leaguers repose in their chiefs. Yet we have so insisted upon the probity of our position as opposed to Railroad chicanery, that I believe it advisable to quell this distant suspicion at once; to publish a denial of these rumoured charges would only be to give them too much importance. However, can you not write me a letter, stating exactly how the campaign was conducted, and the commission nominated and elected? I could show this to some of the more disaffected, and it would serve to allay all suspicion on the instant. I think it would be well to write as though the initiative came, not from me, but from yourself, ignoring this present letter. I offer this only as a suggestion, and will confidently endorse any decision you may arrive at."

The letter closed with renewed protestations of confidence.

Magnus was alone when he read this. He put it carefully away in the filing cabinet in his office, and wiped the sweat from his forehead and face. He stood for one moment, his hands rigid at his sides, his fists clinched.

"This is piling up," he muttered, looking blankly at the opposite wall. "My God, this is piling up. What am I to do?"

Ah, the bitterness of unavailing regret, the anguish of compromise with conscience, the remorse of a bad deed done in a moment of excitement. Ah, the humiliation of detection, the degradation of being caught, caught like a schoolboy pilfering his fellows' desks, and, worse than all, worse than all, the consciousness of lost self-respect, the knowledge of a prestige vanishing, a dignity impaired, knowledge that the grip which held a multitude in check was trembling, that control was wavering, that command was being weakened. Then the little tricks to deceive the crowd, the little subterfuges, the little pretences that kept up appearances, the lies, the bluster, the pose, the strut, the gasconade, where once was iron authority; the turning of the head so as not to see that which could not be prevented; the suspicion of suspicion, the haunting fear of the Man on the Street, the uneasiness of the direct glance, the questioning as to motives— why had this been said, what was meant by that word, that gesture, that glance?

Wednesday passed, and Thursday. Magnus kept to himself, seeing no visitors, avoiding even his family. How to break through the mesh of the net, how to regain the old position, how to prevent discovery? If there were only some way, some vast, superhuman effort by which he could rise in his old strength once more, crushing Lyman with one hand, Genslinger with the other, and for one more moment, the last, to stand supreme again, indomitable, the leader; then go to his death, triumphant at the end, his memory untarnished, his fame undimmed. But the plague-spot was in himself, knitted forever into the fabric of his being. Though Genslinger should be silenced, though Lyman should be crushed, though even the League should overcome the Railroad, though he should be the acknowledged leader of a resplendent victory, yet the plague-spot would remain. There was no success for him now. However conspicuous the outward achievement, he, he himself, Magnus Derrick, had failed, miserably and irredeemably.

Petty, material complications intruded, sordid considerations. Even if Genslinger was to be paid, where was the money to come from? His legal battles with the Railroad, extending now over a period of many years, had cost him dear; his plan of sowing all of Los Muertos to wheat, discharging the tenants, had proved expensive, the campaign resulting in Lyman's election had drawn heavily upon his account. All along he had been relying upon a " bonanza crop " to reimburse him. It was not believable that the Railroad would " jump " Los Muertos, but if this should happen, he would be left without resources. Ten thousand dollars! Could he raise the amount? Possibly. But to pay it out to a blackmailer! To be held up thus in road-agent fashion, without a single means of redress! Would it not cripple him financially? Genslinger could do his worst. He, Magnus, would brave it out. Was not his character above suspicion?

Was it? This letter of Gethings's. Already the murmur of uneasiness made itself heard. Was this not the thin edge of the wedge? How the publication of Genslinger's story would drive it home! How the spark of suspicion would flare into the blaze of open accusation! There would be investigations. Investigation! There was terror in the word. He could not stand investigation. Magnus groaned aloud, covering his head with his clasped hands. Briber, corrupter of government, ballot-box stuffer, descending to the level of back-room politicians, of bar-room heelers, he, Magnus Derrick, statesman of the old school, Roman in his iron integrity, abandoning a career rather than enter the " new politics," had, in one moment of weakness, hazarding all, even honour, on a single stake, taking great chances to achieve great results, swept away the work of a lifetime.

Gambler that he was, he had at last chanced his highest stake, his personal honour, in the greatest game of his life, and had lost.

It was Presley's morbidly keen observation that first noticed the evidence of a new trouble in the Governor's face and manner. Presley was sure that Lyman's defection had not so upset him. The morning after the committee meeting, Magnus had called Harran and Annie Derrick into the office, and, after telling his wife of Lyman's betrayal, had forbidden either of them to mention his name again. His attitude towards his prodigal son was that of stern, unrelenting resentment. But now, Presley could not fail to detect traces of a more deepseated travail. Something was in the wind. The times were troublous. What next was about to happen? What fresh calamity impended?

One morning, toward the very end of the week, Presley woke early in his small, white-painted iron bed. He hastened to get up and dress. There was much to be done that day. Until late the night before, he had been at work on a collection of some of his verses, gathered from the magazines in which they had first appeared. Presley had received a liberal offer for the publication of these verses in book form. " The Toilers " was to be included in this book, and, indeed, was to give it its name —" The Toilers and Other Poems." Thus it was that, until the previous midnight, he had been preparing the collection for publication, revising, annotating, arranging. The book was to be sent off that morning.

But also Presley had received a typewritten note from Annixter, inviting him to Quien Sabe that same day. Annixter explained that it was Hilma's birthday, and that he had planned a picnic on the high ground of his ranch, at the headwaters of Broderson Creek. They were to go in the carry-all, Hilma, Presley, Mrs. Dyke, Sidney, and himself, and were to make a day of it. They would leave Quien Sabe at ten in the morning. Presley had at once resolved to go. He was immensely fond of Annixter—more so than ever since his marriage with Hilma and the astonishing transformation of his character. Hilma, as well, was delightful as Mrs. Annixter; and Mrs. Dyke and the little tad had always been his friends. He would have a good time.

But nobody was to go into Bonneville that morning with the mail, and if he wished to send his manuscript, he would have to take it in himself. He had resolved to do this, getting an early start, and going on horseback to Quien Sabe, by way of Bonneville.

It was barely six o'clock when Presley sat down to his coffee and eggs in the dining-room of Los Muertos. The day promised to be hot, and for the first time, Presley had put on a new khaki riding suit, very English-looking, though in place of the regulation top-boots, he wore his laced knee-boots, with a great spur on the left heel. Harran joined him at breakfast, in his working clothes of blue canvas. He was bound for the irrigating ditch to see how the work was getting on there.

" How is the wheat looking? " asked Presley.

" Bully," answered the other, stirring his coffee. " The Governor has had his ususal luck. Practically, every acre of the ranch was sown to wheat, and everywhere the stand is good. I was over on Two, day before yesterday, and if nothing happens, I believe it will go thirty sacks to the acre there. Cutter reports that there are spots on Four where we will get forty-two or three. Hooven, too, brought up some wonderful fine ears for me to look at. The grains were just beginning to show. Some of the ears carried twenty grains. That means nearly forty bushels of wheat to every acre. I call it a bonanza year."

"Have you got any mail?" said Presley, rising. "I'm going into town."

Harran shook his head, and took himself away, and Presley went down to the stable-corral to get his pony.

As he rode out of the stable-yard and passed by the ranch house, on the driveway, he was surprised to see Magnus on the lowest step of the porch.

"Good morning, Governor," called Presley. "Aren't you up pretty early?"

"Good morning, Pres, my boy." The Governor came forward and, putting his hand on the pony's withers, walked along by his side.

"Going to town, Pres?" he asked.

"Yes, sir. Can I do anything for you, Governor?"

Magnus drew a sealed envelope from his pocket.

"I wish you would drop in at the office of the *Mercury* for me," he said, "and see Mr. Genslinger personally, and give him this envelope. It is a package of papers, but they involve a considerable sum of money, and you must be careful of them. A few years ago, when our enmity was not so strong, Mr. Genslinger and I had some business dealings with each other. I thought it as well just now, considering that we are so openly opposed, to terminate the whole affair, and break off relations. We came to a settlement a few days ago. These are the final papers. They must be given to him in person, Presley. You understand."

Presley cantered on, turning into the county road, and holding northward by the mammoth watering tank and Broderson's popular windbreak. As he passed Caraher's, he saw the saloon-keeper in the doorway of his place, and waved him a salutation which the other returned.

By degrees, Presley had come to consider Caraher in

a more favourable light. He found, to his immense astonishment, that Caraher knew something of Mill and Ba-
kounin, not, however, from their books, but from extracts and quotations from their writings, reprinted in the
anarchistic journals to which he subscribed. More than
once, the two had held long conversations, and from
Caraher's own lips, Presley heard the terrible story of the
death of his wife, who had been accidentally killed by
Pinkertons during a "demonstration" of strikers. It
invested the saloon-keeper, in Presley's imagination, with
all the dignity of the tragedy. He could not blame
Caraher for being a "red." He even wondered how it
was the saloon-keeper had not put his theories into practice, and adjusted his ancient wrong with his "six inches
of plugged gas-pipe." Presley began to conceive of the
man as a "character."

"You wait, Mr. Presley," the saloon-keeper had once
said, when Presley had protested against his radical ideas.
"You don't know the Railroad yet. Watch it and its
doings long enough, and you'll come over to my way of
thinking, too."

It was about half-past seven when Presley reached
Bonneville. The business part of the town was as yet
hardly astir; he despatched his manuscript, and then hurried to the office of the "Mercury." Genslinger, as he
feared, had not yet put in appearance, but the janitor of
the building gave Presley the address of the editor's
residence, and it was there he found him in the act of
sitting down to breakfast. Presley was hardly courteous
to the little man, and abruptly refused his offer of a drink.
He delivered Magnus's envelope to him and departed.

It had occurred to him that it would not do to present
himself at Quien Sabe on Hilma's birthday, empty-
handed, and, on leaving Genslinger's house, he turned
his pony's head toward the business part of the town

again pulling up in front of the jeweller's, just as the clerk was taking down the shutters.

At the jeweller's, he purchased a little brooch for Hilma, and at the cigar stand in the lobby of the Yosemite House, a box of superfine cigars, which, when it was too late, he realised that the master of Quien Sabe would never smoke, holding, as he did, with defiant inconsistency, to miserable weeds, black, bitter, and flagrantly doctored, which he bought, three for a nickel, at Guadalajara.

Presley arrived at Quien Sabe nearly half an hour behind the appointed time; but, as he had expected, the party were in no way ready to start. The carry-all, its horses covered with white fly-nets, stood under a tree near the house, young Vacca dozing on the seat. Hilma and Sidney, the latter exuberant with a gayety that all but brought the tears to Presley's eyes, were making sandwiches on the back porch. Mrs. Dyke was nowhere to be seen, and Annixter was shaving himself in his bedroom.

This latter put a half-lathered face out of the window as Presley cantered through the gate, and waved his razor with a beckoning motion.

"Come on in, Pres," he cried. "Nobody's ready yet. You're hours ahead of time."

Presley came into the bedroom, his huge spur clinking on the straw matting. Annixter was without coat, vest, or collar, his blue silk suspenders hung in loops over either hip, his hair was disordered, the crown lock stiffer than ever.

"Glad to see you, old boy," he announced, as Presley came in. "No, don't shake hands, I'm all lather. Here, find a chair, will you? I won't be long."

"I thought you said ten o'clock," observed Presley, sitting down on the edge of the bed.

"Well, I did, but——"

"But, then again, in a way, you didn't, hey?" his friend interrupted.

Annixter grunted good-humouredly, and turned to strop his razor. Presley looked with suspicious disfavour at his suspenders.

"Why is it," he observed, "that as soon as a man is about to get married, he buys himself pale blue suspenders, silk ones? Think of it. You, Buck Annixter, with sky-blue, silk suspenders. It ought to be a strap and a nail."

"Old fool," observed Annixter, whose repartee was the heaving of brick bats. "Say," he continued, holding the razor from his face, and jerking his head over his shoulder, while he looked at Presley's reflection in his mirror; "say, look around. Isn't this a nifty little room? We refitted the whole house, you know. Notice she's all painted?"

"I have been looking around," answered Presley, sweeping the room with a series of glances. He forebore criticism. Annixter was so boyishly proud of the effect that it would have been unkind to have undeceived him. Presley looked at the marvellous, department-store bed of brass, with its brave, gay canopy; the mill-made washstand, with its pitcher and bowl of blinding red and green china, the straw-framed lithographs of symbolic female figures against the multi-coloured, new wall-paper; the inadequate spindle chairs of white and gold; the sphere of tissue paper hanging from the gas fixture, and the plumes of pampas grass tacked to the wall at artistic angles, and overhanging two astonishing oil paintings, in dazzling golden frames.

"Say, how about those paintings, Pres?" inquired Annixter a little uneasily. "I don't know whether they're good or not. They were painted by a three-fingered Chinaman in Monterey, and I got the lot for thirty dollars, frames thrown in. Why, I think the frames alone are worth thirty dollars."

"Well, so do I," declared Presley. He hastened to change the subject.

"Buck," he said, "I hear you've brought Mrs. Dyke and Sidney to live with you. You know, I think that's rather white of you."

"Oh, rot, Pres," muttered Annixter, turning abruptly to his shaving.

"And you can't fool me, either, old man," Presley continued. "You're giving this picnic as much for Mrs. Dyke and the little tad as you are for your wife, just to cheer them up a bit."

"Oh, pshaw, you make me sick."

"Well, that's the right thing to do, Buck, and I'm as glad for your sake as I am for theirs. There was a time when you would have let them all go to grass, and never so much as thought of them. I don't want to seem to be officious, but you've changed for the better, old man, and I guess I know why. She—" Presley caught his friend's eye, and added gravely, "She's a good woman, Buck."

Annixter turned around abruptly, his face flushing under its lather.

"Pres," he exclaimed, "she's made a man of me. I was a machine before, and if another man, or woman, or child got in my way, I rode 'em down, and I never *dreamed* of anybody else but myself. But as soon as I woke up to the fact that I really loved her, why, it was glory hallelujah all in a minute, and, in a way, I kind of loved everybody then, and wanted to be everybody's friend. And I began to see that a fellow can't live *for* himself any more than he can live *by* himself. He's got to think of others. If he's got brains, he's got to think for the poor ducks that haven't 'em, and not give 'em a boot in the backsides because they happen to be stupid; and if he's got money, he's got to help those that are busted, and if he's got a house, he's got to think of those that ain't got anywhere to go. I've got a whole lot of ideas since I began to love Hilma, and just as soon as I can, I'm going to get in and *help* people, and I'm going to keep to that idea the rest of my natural life. That ain't much of a religion, but it's the best I've got, and Henry Ward Beecher couldn't do any more than that. And it's all come about because of Hilma, and because we cared for each other."

Presley jumped up, and caught Annixter about the shoulders with one arm, gripping his hand hard. This absurd figure, with dangling silk suspenders, lathered chin, and tearful eyes, seemed to be suddenly invested with true nobility. Beside this blundering struggle to do right, to help his fellows, Presley's own vague schemes, glittering systems of reconstruction, collapsed to ruin, and he himself, with all his refinement, with all his poetry, culture, and education, stood, a bungler at the world's workbench.

"You're all *right,* old man," he exclaimed, unable to think of anything adequate. "You're all right. That's the way to talk, and here, by the way, I brought you a box of cigars."

Annixter stared as Presley laid the box on the edge of the washstand.

"Old fool," he remarked, "what in hell did you do that for?"

"Oh, just for fun."

"I suppose they're rotten stinkodoras, or you wouldn't give 'em away."

"This cringing gratitude—" Presley began.

"Shut up," shouted Annixter, and the incident was closed.

Annixter resumed his shaving, and Presley lit a cigarette.

" Any news from Washington ? " he queried.

" Nothing that's any good," grunted Annixter. " Hello," he added, raising his head, " there's somebody in a hurry for sure."

The noise of a horse galloping so fast that the hoof-beats sounded in one uninterrupted rattle, abruptly made itself heard. The noise was coming from the direction of the road that led from the Mission to Quien Sabe. With incredible swiftness, the hoof-beats drew nearer. There was that in their sound which brought Presley to his feet. Annixter threw open the window.

" Runaway," exclaimed Presley.

Annixter, with thoughts of the Railroad, and the " jumping " of the ranch, flung his hand to his hip pocket.

" What is it, Vacca ? " he cried.

Young Vacca, turning in his seat in the carryall, was looking up the road. All at once, he jumped from his place, and dashed towards the window.

" Dyke," he shouted. " Dyke, it's Dyke."

While the words were yet in his mouth, the sound of the hoof-beats rose to a roar, and a great, bell-toned voice shouted :

" Annixter, Annixter, Annixter ! "

It was Dyke's voice, and the next instant he shot into view in the open square in front of the house.

" Oh, my God ! " cried Presley.

The ex-engineer threw the horse on its haunches, springing from the saddle ; and, as he did so, the beast collapsed, shuddering, to the ground. Annixter sprang from the window, and ran forward, Presley following.

There was Dyke, hatless, his pistol in his hand, a gaunt, terrible figure, the beard immeasurably long, the cheeks fallen in, the eyes sunken. His clothes ripped and torn by weeks of flight and hiding in the chaparral, were ragged beyond words, the boots were shreds of leather, bloody to the ankle with furious spurring.

"Annixter," he shouted, and again, rolling his sunken eyes, " Annixter. Annixter! "

" Here, here," cried Annixter.

The other turned, levelling his pistol.

" Give me a horse, give me a horse, quick, do you hear? Give me a horse, or I'll shoot."

" Steady, steady. That won't do. You know me, Dyke. We're friends here."

The other lowered his weapon.

" I know, I know," he panted. " I'd forgotten. I'm unstrung, Mr. Annixter, and I'm running for my life. They're not ten minutes behind me."

" Come on, come on," shouted Annixter, dashing stablewards, his suspenders flying.

" Here's a horse."

" Mine? " exclaimed Presley. " He wouldn't carry you a mile."

Annixter was already far ahead, trumpeting orders.

" The buckskin," he yelled. " Get her out, Billy. Where's the stable-man? Get out that buckskin. Get out that saddle."

Then followed minutes of furious haste, Presley, Annixter, Billy the stable-man, and Dyke himself, darting hither and thither about the yellow mare, buckling, strapping, cinching, their lips pale, their fingers trembling with excitement.

" Want anything to eat? " Annixter's head was under the saddle flap as he tore at the cinch. " Want anything to eat? Want any money? Want a gun? "

" Water," returned Dyke. " They've watched every spring. I'm killed with thirst."

" There's the hydrant. Quick now."

" I got as far as the Kern River, but they turned me back," he said between breaths as he drank.

" Don't stop to talk."

" My mother, and the little tad——"

" I'm taking care of them. They're stopping with me."

" Here? "

" You won't see 'em; by the Lord, you won't. You'll get away. Where's that back cinch strap, *Billy?* God damn it, are you going to let him be shot before he can get away? Now, Dyke, up you go. She'll kill herself running before they can catch you."

" God bless you, Annixter. Where's the little tad? Is she well, Annixter, and the mother? Tell them——"

" Yes, yes, yes. All clear, Pres? Let her have her own gait, Dyke. You're on the best horse in the county now. Let go her head, Billy. Now, Dyke,—shake hands? You bet I will. That's all right. Yes, God bless you. Let her go. You're *off*."

Answering the goad of the spur, and already quivering with the excitement of the men who surrounded her, the buckskin cleared the stable-corral in two leaps; then, gathering her legs under her, her head low, her neck stretched out, swung into the road from out the driveway, disappearing in a blur of dust.

With the agility of a monkey, young Vacca swung himself into the framework of the artesian well, clambering aloft to its very top. He swept the country with a glance.

" Well? " demanded Annixter from the ground. The others cocked their heads to listen.

" I see him; I see him! " shouted Vacca. " He's going like the devil. He's headed for Guadalajara."

" Look back, up the road, toward the Mission. Anything there? "

The answer came down in a shout of apprehension.

"There's a party of men. Three or four—on horse-back. There's dogs with 'em. They're coming this way. Oh, I can hear the dogs. And, say, oh, say, there's an-other party coming down the Lower Road, going towards Guadalajara, too. They got guns. I can see the shine of the barrels. And, oh, Lord, say, there's three more men on horses coming down on the jump from the hills on the Los Muertos stock range. They're making towards Guadalajara. And I can hear the courthouse bell in Bonneville ringing. Say, the whole county is up."

As young Vacca slid down to the ground, two small black-and-tan hounds, with flapping ears and lolling tongues, loped into view on the road in front of the house. They were grey with dust, their noses were to the ground. At the gate where Dyke had turned into the ranch house grounds, they halted in confusion a mo-ment. One started to follow the highwayman's trail to-wards the stable corral, but the other, quartering over the road with lightning swiftness, suddenly picked up the new scent leading on towards Guadalajara. He tossed his head in the air, and Presley abruptly shut his hands over his ears.

Ah, that terrible cry! deep-toned, reverberating like the bourdon of a great bell. It was the trackers exult-ing on the trail of the pursued, the prolonged, raucous howl, eager, ominous, vibrating with the alarm of the tocsin, sullen with the heavy muffling note of death. But close upon the bay of the hounds, came the gallop of horses. Five men, their eyes upon the hounds, their rifles across their pommels, their horses reeking and black with sweat, swept by in a storm of dust, glinting hoofs, and streaming manes.

"That was Delaney's gang," exclaimed Annixter. "I saw him."

" The other was that chap Christian," said Vacca, " S. Behrman's cousin. He had two deputies with him; and the chap in the white slouch hat was the sheriff from Visalia."

" By the Lord, they aren't far behind," declared Annixter.

As the men turned towards the house again they saw Hilma and Mrs. Dyke in the doorway of the little house where the latter lived. They were looking out, bewildered, ignorant of what had happened. But on the porch of the Ranch house itself, alone, forgotten in the excitement, Sidney—the little tad—stood, with pale face and serious, wide-open eyes. She had seen everything, and had understood. She said nothing. Her head inclined towards the roadway, she listened to the faint and distant baying of the dogs.

Dyke thundered across the railway tracks by the depot at Guadalajara not five minutes ahead of his pursuers. Luck seemed to have deserted him. The station, usually so quiet, was now occupied by the crew of a freight train that lay on the down track; while on the up line, near at hand and headed in the same direction, was a detached locomotive, whose engineer and fireman recognized him, he was sure, as the buckskin leaped across the rails.

He had had no time to formulate a plan since that morning, when, tortured with thirst, he had ventured near the spring at the headwaters of Broderson Creek, on Quien Sabe, and had all but fallen into the hands of the posse that had been watching for that very move. It was useless now to regret that he had tried to foil pursuit by turning back on his tracks to regain the mountains east of Bonneville. Now Delaney was almost on him. To distance that posse, was the only thing to be thought of now. It was no longer a question of hiding till pursuit should flag; they had driven him out from the shelter of the mountains, down into this populous countryside, where an enemy might be met with at every turn of the road. Now it was life or death. He would either escape or be killed. He knew very well that he would never allow himself to be taken alive. But he had no mind to be killed—to turn and fight—till escape was blocked. His one thought was to leave pursuit behind.

Weeks of flight had sharpened Dyke's every sense. As he turned into the Upper Road beyond Guadalajara, he saw the three men galloping down from Derrick's stock range, making for the road ahead of him. They would cut him off there. He swung the buckskin about. He must take the Lower Road across Los Muertos from Guadalajara, and he must reach it before Delaney's dogs and posse. Back he galloped, the buckskin measuring her length with every leap. Once more the station came in sight. Rising in his stirrups, he looked across the fields in the direction of the Lower Road. There was a cloud of dust there. From a wagon? No, horses on the run, and their riders were armed! He could catch the flash of gun barrels. They were all closing in on him, converging on Guadalajara by every available road. The Upper Road west of Guadalajara led straight to Bonneville. That way was impossible. Was he in a trap? Had the time for fighting come at last?

But as Dyke neared the depot at Guadalajara, his eye fell upon the detached locomotive that lay quietly steaming on the up line, and with a thrill of exultation, he remembered that he was an engineer born and bred. Delaney's dogs were already to be heard, and the roll of hoofs on the Lower Road was dinning in his ears, as he leaped from the buckskin before the depot. The train crew scattered like frightened sheep before him, but Dyke ignored them. His pistol was in his hand as, once more on foot, he sprang toward the lone engine.

"Out of the cab," he shouted. "Both of you. Quick, or I'll kill you both."

The two men tumbled from the iron apron of the tender as Dyke swung himself up, dropping his pistol on the floor of the cab and reaching with the old instinct for the familiar levers.

The great compound hissed and trembled as the steam was released, and the huge drivers stirred, turning slowly on the tracks. But there was a shout. Delaney's posse, dogs and men, swung into view at the turn of the road, their figures leaning over as they took the curve at full speed. Dyke threw everything wide open and caught up his revolver. From behind came the challenge of a Winchester. The party on the Lower Road were even closer than Delaney. They had seen his manœuvre, and the first shot of the fight shivered the cab windows above the engineer's head.

But spinning futilely at first, the drivers of the engine at last caught the rails. The engine moved, advanced, travelled past the depot and the freight train, and gathering speed, rolled out on the track beyond. Smoke, black and boiling, shot skyward from the stack; not a joint that did not shudder with the mighty strain of the steam; but the great iron brute—one of Baldwin's newest and best—came to call, obedient and docile as soon as ever the great pulsing heart of it felt a master hand upon its levers. It gathered its speed, bracing its steel muscles, its thews of iron, and roared out upon the open track, filling the air with the rasp of its tempest-breath, blotting the sunshine with the belch of its hot, thick smoke. Already it was lessening in the distance, when Delaney, Christian, and the sheriff of Visalia dashed up to the station.

The posse had seen everything.

"Stuck. Curse the luck!" vociferated the cow-puncher.

But the sheriff was already out of the saddle and into the telegraph office.

"There's a derailing switch between here and Pixley, isn't there?" he cried.

"Yes."

"Wire ahead to open it. We'll derail him there. Come on;" he turned to Delaney and the others. They sprang into the cab of the locomotive that was attached to the freight train.

"Name of the State of California," shouted the sheriff to the bewildered engineer. "Cut off from your train."

The sheriff was a man to be obeyed without hesitating. Time was not allowed the crew of the freight train for debating as to the right or the wrong of requisitioning the engine, and before anyone thought of the safety or danger of the affair, the freight engine was already flying out upon the down line, hot in pursuit of Dyke, now far ahead upon the up track.

"I remember perfectly well there's a derailing switch between here and Pixley," shouted the sheriff above the roar of the locomotive. "They use it in case they have to derail runaway engines. It runs right off into the country. We'll pile him up there. Ready with your guns, boys."

"If we should meet another train coming up on this track——" protested the frightened engineer.

"Then we'd jump or be smashed. Hi! look! There he is." As the freight engine rounded a curve, Dyke's engine came into view, shooting on some quarter of a mile ahead of them, wreathed in whirling smoke.

"The switch ain't much further on," clamoured the engineer. "You can see Pixley now."

Dyke, his hand on the grip of the valve that controlled the steam, his head out of the cab window, thundered on. He was back in his old place again; once more he was the engineer; once more he felt the engine quiver under him; the familiar noises were in his ears; the familiar buffeting of the wind surged, roaring at his face; the familiar odours of hot steam and smoke reeked in his nostrils, and on either side of him, parallel panoramas, the two halves of the landscape sliced, as it were, in two by the clashing wheels of his engine, streamed by in green and brown blurs.

He found himself settling to the old position on the cab seat, leaning on his elbow from the window, one hand on the controller. All at once, the instinct of the pursuit that of late had become so strong within him, prompted him to shoot a glance behind. He saw the other engine on the down line, plunging after him, rocking from side to side with the fury of its gallop. Not yet had he shaken the trackers from his heels; not yet was he out of the reach of danger. He set his teeth and, throwing open the fire-door, stoked vigorously for a few moments. The indicator of the steam gauge rose; his speed increased; a glance at the telegraph poles told him he was doing his fifty miles an hour. The freight engine behind him was never built for that pace. Barring the terrible risk of accident, his chances were good.

But suddenly—the engineer dominating the highwayman—he shut off his steam and threw back his brake to the extreme notch. Directly ahead of him rose a semaphore, placed at a point where evidently a derailing switch branched from the line. The semaphore's arm was dropped over the track, setting the danger signal that showed the switch was open.

In an instant, Dyke saw the trick. They had meant to smash him here; had been clever enough, quick-witted enough to open the switch, but had forgotten the automatic semaphore that worked simultaneously with the movement of the rails. To go forward was certain destruction. Dyke reversed. There was nothing for it but to go back. With a wrench and a spasm of all its metal fibres, the great compound braced itself, sliding with rigid wheels along the rails. Then, as Dyke applied the reverse, it drew back from the greater danger, returning towards the less. Inevitably now the two engines, one on the up, the other on the down line, must meet and pass each other.

Dyke released the levers, reaching for his revolver. The engineer once more became the highwayman, in peril of his life. Now, beyond all doubt, the time for fighting was at hand.

The party in the heavy freight engine, that lumbered after in pursuit, their eyes fixed on the smudge of smoke on ahead that marked the path of the fugitive, suddenly raised a shout.

"He's stopped. He's broke down. Watch, now, and see if he jumps off."

"Broke *nothing*. *He's coming back.* Ready, now, he's got to pass us."

The engineer applied the brakes, but the heavy freight locomotive, far less mobile than Dyke's flyer, was slow to obey. The smudge on the rails ahead grew swiftly larger.

"He's coming. He's coming—look out, there's a shot. He's shooting already."

A bright, white sliver of wood leaped into the air from the sooty window sill of the cab.

"Fire on him! Fire on him!"

While the engines were yet two hundred yards apart, the duel began, shot answering shot, the sharp staccato reports punctuating the thunder of wheels and the clamour of steam.

Then the ground trembled and rocked; a roar as of heavy ordnance developed with the abruptness of an explosion. The two engines passed each other, the men firing the while, emptying their revolvers, shattering wood, shivering glass, the bullets clanging against the metal work as they struck and struck and struck. The men leaned from the cabs towards each other, frantic with excitement, shouting curses, the engines rocking, the steam roaring; confusion whirling in the scene like the whirl of a witch's dance, the white clouds of steam, the black eddies from the smokestack, the blue wreaths from the hot mouths of revolvers, swirling together in a blinding maze of vapour, spinning around them, dazing them, dizzying them, while the head rang with hideous clamour and the body twitched and trembled with the leap and jar of the tumult of machinery.

Roaring, clamouring, reeking with the smell of powder and hot oil, spitting death, resistless, huge, furious, an abrupt vision of chaos, faces, rage-distorted, peering through smoke, hands gripping outward from sudden darkness, prehensile, malevolent; terrible as thunder, swift as lightning, the two engines met and passed.

"He's hit," cried Delaney. "I know I hit him. He can't go far now. After him again. He won't dare go through Bonneville."

It was true. Dyke had stood between cab and tender throughout all the duel, exposed, reckless, thinking only of attack and not of defence, and a bullet from one of the pistols had grazed his hip. How serious was the wound he did not know, but he had no thought of giving up. He tore back through the depot at Guadalajara in a storm of bullets, and, clinging to the broken window ledge of his cab, was carried towards Bonneville, on over the Long Trestle and Broderson Creek and through the open country between the two ranches of Los Muertos and Quien Sabe.

But to go on to Bonneville meant certain death. Be-

fore, as well as behind him, the roads were now blocked.
Once more he thought of the mountains. He resolved to
abandon the engine and make another final attempt to get
into the shelter of the hills in the northernmost corner of
Quien Sabe. He set his teeth. He would not give in.
There was one more fight left in him yet. Now to try
the final hope.

He slowed the engine down, and, reloading his revolver, jumped from the platform to the road. He looked
about him, listening. All around him widened an ocean
of wheat. There was no one in sight.

The released engine, alone, unattended, drew slowly
away from him, jolting ponderously over the rail joints.
As he watched it go, a certain indefinite sense of abandonment, even in that moment, came over Dyke. His last
friend, that also had been his first, was leaving him. He
remembered that day, long ago, when he had opened the
throttle of his first machine. To-day, it was leaving him
alone, his last friend turning against him. Slowly it was
going back towards Bonneville, to the shops of the Railroad, the camp of the enemy, that enemy that had ruined
him and wrecked him. For the last time in his life, he
had been the engineer. Now, once more, he became the
highwayman, the outlaw against whom all hands were
raised, the fugitive skulking in the mountains, listening
for the cry of dogs.

But he would not give in. They had not broken him
yet. Never, while he could fight, would he allow S. Behrman the triumph of his capture.

He found his wound was not bad. He plunged into the
wheat on Quien Sabe, making northward for a division
house that rose with its surrounding trees out of the
wheat like an island. He reached it, the blood squelching
in his shoes. But the sight of two men, Portuguese
farm-hands, staring at him from an angle of the barn,

abruptly roused him to action. He sprang forward with peremptory commands, demanding a horse.

At Guadalajara, Delaney and the sheriff descended from the freight engine.

"Horses now," declared the sheriff. "He won't go into Bonneville, that's certain. He'll leave the engine between here and there, and strike off into the country. We'll follow after him now in the saddle. Soon as he leaves his engine, *he's* on foot. We've as good as got him now."

Their horses, including even the buckskin mare that Dyke had ridden, were still at the station. The party swung themselves up, Delaney exclaiming, "Here's *my* mount," as he bestrode the buckskin.

At Guadalajara, the two bloodhounds were picked up again. Urging the jaded horses to a gallop, the party set off along the Upper Road, keeping a sharp lookout to right and left for traces of Dyke's abandonment of the engine.

Three miles beyond the Long Trestle, they found S. Behrman holding his saddle horse by the bridle, and looking attentively at a trail that had been broken through the standing wheat on Quien Sabe. The party drew rein.

"The engine passed me on the tracks further up, and empty," said S. Behrman. "Boys, I think he left her here."

But before anyone could answer, the bloodhounds gave tongue again, as they picked up the scent.

"That's him," cried S. Behrman. "Get on, boys."

They dashed forward, following the hounds. S. Behrman laboriously climbed to his saddle, panting, perspiring, mopping the roll of fat over his coat collar, and turned in after them, trotting along far in the rear, his great stomach and tremulous jowl shaking with the horse's gait.

"What a day," he murmured. "What a day."

Dyke's trail was fresh, and was followed as easily as if made on new-fallen snow. In a short time, the posse swept into the open space around the division house. The two Portuguese were still there, wide-eyed, terribly excited.

Yes, yes, Dyke had been there not half an hour since, had held them up, taken a horse and galloped to the northeast, towards the foothills at the headwaters of Broderson Creek.

On again, at full gallop, through the young wheat, trampling it under the flying hoofs; the hounds hot on the scent, baying continually; the men, on fresh mounts, secured at the division house, bending forward in their saddles, spurring relentlessly. S. Behrman jolted along far in the rear.

And even then, harried through an open country, where there was no place to hide, it was a matter of amazement how long a chase the highwayman led them. Fences were passed; fences whose barbed wire had been slashed apart by the fugitive's knife. The ground rose under foot; the hills were at hand; still the pursuit held on. The sun, long past the meridian, began to turn earthward. Would night come on before they were up with him?

"Look! Look! There he is! Quick, there he goes!"

High on the bare slope of the nearest hill, all the posse, looking in the direction of Delaney's gesture, saw the figure of a horseman emerge from an arroyo, filled with chaparral, and struggle at a labouring gallop straight up the slope. Suddenly, every member of the party shouted aloud. The horse had fallen, pitching the rider from the saddle. The man rose to his feet, caught at the bridle, missed it and the horse dashed on alone. The man, pausing for a second, looked around, saw the chase drawing nearer, then, turning back, disappeared in the chaparral. Delaney raised a great whoop.

"We've got you now."

Into the slopes and valleys of the hills dashed the band of horsemen, the trail now so fresh that it could be easily discerned by all. On and on it led them, a furious, wild scramble straight up the slopes. The minutes went by. The dry bed of a rivulet was passed; then another fence; then a tangle of manzanita; a meadow of wild oats, full of agitated cattle; then an arroyo, thick with chaparral and scrub oaks, and then, without warning, the pistol shots ripped out and ran from rider to rider with the rapidity of a gatling discharge, and one of the deputies bent forward in the saddle, both hands to his face, the blood jetting from between his fingers.

Dyke was there, at bay at last, his back against a bank of rock, the roots of a fallen tree serving him as a rampart, his revolver smoking in his hand.

"You're under arrest, Dyke," cried the sheriff. "It's not the least use to fight. The whole country is up."

Dyke fired again, the shot splintering the foreleg of the horse the sheriff rode.

The posse, four men all told—the wounded deputy having crawled out of the fight after Dyke's first shot—fell back after the preliminary fusillade, dismounted, and took shelter behind rocks and trees. On that rugged ground, fighting from the saddle was impracticable. Dyke, in the meanwhile, held his fire, for he knew that, once his pistol was empty, he would never be allowed time to reload.

"Dyke," called the sheriff again, "for the last time, I summon you to surrender."

Dyke did not reply. The sheriff, Delaney, and the man named Christian conferred together in a low voice. Then Delaney and Christian left the others, making a wide detour up the sides of the arroyo, to gain a position to the left and somewhat to the rear of Dyke.

But it was at this moment that S. Behrman arrived. It could not be said whether it was courage or carelessness that brought the Railroad's agent within reach of Dyke's revolver. Possibly he was really a brave man; possibly occupied with keeping an uncertain seat upon the back of his labouring, scrambling horse, he had not noticed that he was so close upon that scene of battle. He certainly did not observe the posse lying upon the ground behind sheltering rocks and trees, and before anyone could call a warning, he had ridden out into the open, within thirty paces of Dyke's intrenchment.

Dyke saw. There was the arch-enemy; the man of all men whom he most hated; the man who had ruined him, who had exasperated him and driven him to crime, and who had instigated tireless pursuit through all those past terrible weeks. Suddenly, inviting death, he leaped up and forward; he had forgotten all else, all other considerations, at the sight of this man. He would die, gladly, so only that S. Behrman died before him.

" I've got *you*, anyway," he shouted, as he ran forward.

The muzzle of the weapon was not ten feet from S. Behrman's huge stomach as Dyke drew the trigger. Had the cartridge exploded, death, certain and swift, would have followed, but at this, of all moments, the revolver missed fire.

S. Behrman, with an unexpected agility, leaped from the saddle, and, keeping his horse between him and Dyke, ran, dodging and ducking, from tree to tree. His first shot a failure, Dyke fired again and again at his enemy, emptying his revolver, reckless of consequences. His every shot went wild, and before he could draw his knife, the whole posse was upon him.

Without concerted plans, obeying no signal but the

promptings of the impulse that snatched, unerring, at opportunity—the men, Delaney and Christian from one side, the sheriff and the deputy from the other, rushed in. They did not fire. It was Dyke alive they wanted. One of them had a riata snatched from a saddle-pommel, and with this they tried to bind him.

The fight was four to one—four men with law on their side, to one wounded freebooter, half-starved, exhausted by days and nights of pursuit, worn down with loss of sleep, thirst, privation, and the grinding, nerve-racking consciousness of an ever-present peril.

They swarmed upon him from all sides, gripping at his legs, at his arms, his throat, his head, striking, clutching, kicking, falling to the ground, rolling over and over, now under, now above, now staggering forward, now toppling back.

Still Dyke fought. Through that scrambling, struggling group, through that maze of twisting bodies, twining arms, straining legs, S. Behrman saw him from moment to moment, his face flaming, his eyes bloodshot, his hair matted with sweat. Now he was down, pinned under, two men across his legs, and now half-way up again, struggling to one knee. Then upright again, with half his enemies hanging on his back. His colossal strength seemed doubled; when his arms were held, he fought bull-like with his head. A score of times, it seemed as if they were about to secure him finally and irrevocably, and then he would free an arm, a leg, a shoulder, and the group that, for the fraction of an instant, had settled, locked and rigid, on its prey, would break up again as he flung a man from him, reeling and bloody, and he himself twisting, squirming, dodging, his great fists working like pistons, backed away, dragging and carrying the others with him.

More than once, he loosened almost every grip, and

for an instant stood nearly free, panting, rolling his eyes, his clothes torn from his body, bleeding, dripping with sweat, a terrible figure, nearly free. The sheriff, under his breath, uttered an exclamation:

" By God, he'll get away yet."

S. Behrman watched the fight complacently.

" That all may show obstinacy," he commented, " but it don't show common sense."

Yet, however Dyke might throw off the clutches and fettering embraces that encircled him, however he might disintegrate and scatter the band of foes that heaped themselves upon him, however he might gain one instant of comparative liberty, some one of his assailants always hung, doggedly, blindly to an arm, a leg, or a foot, and the others, drawing a second's breath, closed in again, implacable, unconquerable, ferocious, like hounds upon a wolf.

At length, two of the men managed to bring Dyke's wrists close enough together to allow the sheriff to snap the handcuffs on. Even then, Dyke, clasping his hands, and using the handcuffs themselves as a weapon, knocked down Delaney by the crushing impact of the steel brace-lets upon the cow-puncher's forehead. But he could no longer protect himself from attacks from behind, and the riata was finally passed around his body, pinioning his arms to his sides. After this it was useless to resist.

The wounded deputy sat with his back to a rock, hold-ing his broken jaw in both hands. The sheriff's horse, with its splintered foreleg, would have to be shot. De-laney's head was cut from temple to cheekbone. The right wrist of the sheriff was all but dislocated. The other deputy was so exhausted he had to be helped to his horse. But Dyke was taken.

He himself had suddenly lapsed into semi-unconscious-ness, unable to walk. They sat him on the buckskin, S.

Behrman supporting him, the sheriff, on foot, leading the horse by the bridle. The little procession formed, and descended from the hills, turning in the direction of Bonneville. A special train, one car and an engine, would be made up there, and the highwayman would sleep in the Visalia jail that night.

Delaney and S. Behrman found themselves in the rear of the cavalcade as it moved off. The cow-puncher turned to his chief:

"Well, captain," he said, still panting, as he bound up his forehead; "well—we *got* him."

VI

Osterman cut his wheat that summer before any of the other ranchers, and as soon as his harvest was over organized a jack-rabbit drive. Like Annixter's barn-dance, it was to be an event in which all the country-side should take part. The drive was to begin on the most western division of the Osterman ranch, whence it would proceed towards the southeast, crossing into the northern part of Quien Sabe—on which Annixter had sown no wheat— and ending in the hills at the headwaters of Broderson Creek, where a barbecue was to be held.

Early on the morning of the day of the drive, as Harran and Presley were saddling their horses before the stables on Los Muertos, the foreman, Phelps, remarked:

"I was into town last night, and I hear that Christian has been after Ruggles early and late to have him put him in possession here on Los Muertos, and Delaney is doing the same for Quien Sabe."

It was this man Christian, the real estate broker, and cousin of S. Behrman, one of the main actors in the drama of Dyke's capture, who had come forward as a purchaser of Los Muertos when the Railroad had re-graded its holdings on the ranches around Bonneville.

"He claims, of course," Phelps went on, "that when he bought Los Muertos of the Railroad he was guaranteed possession, and he wants the place in time for the harvest."

"That's almost as thin," muttered Harran as he thrust the bit into his horse's mouth, "as Delaney buying Annixter's Home ranch. That slice of Quien Sabe, according to the Railroad's grading, is worth about ten thousand dollars; yes, even fifteen, and I don't believe Delaney is worth the price of a good horse. Why, those people don't even *try* to preserve appearances. Where would Christian find the money to buy Los Muertos? There's no one man in all Bonneville rich enough to do it. Damned rascals! as if we didn't see that Christian and Delaney are S. Behrman's right and left hands. Well, he'll get 'em cut off," he cried with sudden fierceness, " if he comes too near the machine."

" How is it, Harran," asked Presley as the two young men rode out of the stable yard, " how is it the Railroad gang can do anything before the Supreme Court hands down a decision? "

" Well, you know how they talk," growled Harran. " They have claimed that the cases taken up to the Supreme Court were not test cases as *we* claim they *are*, and that because neither Annixter nor the Governor appealed, they've lost their cases by default. It's the rottenest kind of sharp practice, but it won't do any good. The League is too strong. They won't dare move on us yet awhile. Why, Pres, the moment they'd try to jump any of these ranches around here, they would have six hundred rifles cracking at them as quick as how-do-you-do. Why, it would take a regiment of U. S. soldiers to put any one of us off our land. No, sir; they know the League means business this time."

As Presley and Harran trotted on along the county road they continually passed or overtook other horsemen, or buggies, carry-alls, buck-boards or even farm wagons, going in the same direction. These were full of the farming people from all the country round about Bonneville, on their way to the rabbit drive—the same people seen at the barn-dance—in their Sunday finery, the girls in muslin frocks and garden hats, the men with linen dusters over their black clothes; the older women in prints and dotted calicoes. Many of these latter had already taken off their bonnets—the day was very hot—and pinning them in newspapers, stowed them under the seats. They tucked their handkerchiefs into the collars of their dresses, or knotted them about their fat necks, to keep out the dust. From the axle trees of the vehicles swung carefully covered buckets of galvanised iron, in which the lunch was packed. The younger children, the boys with great frilled collars, the girls with ill-fitting shoes cramping their feet, leaned from the sides of buggy and carry-all, eating bananas and " macaroons," staring about with ox-like stolidity. Tied to the axles, the dogs followed the horses' hoofs with lolling tongues coated with dust.

The California summer lay blanket-wise and smothering over all the land. The hills, bone-dry, were browned and parched. The grasses and wild-oats, sear and yellow, snapped like glass filaments under foot. The roads, the bordering fences, even the lower leaves and branches of the trees, were thick and grey with dust. All colour had been burned from the landscape, except in the irrigated patches, that in the waste of brown and dull yellow glowed like oases.

The wheat, now close to its maturity, had turned from pale yellow to golden yellow, and from that to brown. Like a gigantic carpet, it spread itself over all the land. There was nothing else to be seen but the limitless sea of wheat as far as the eye could reach, dry, rustling, crisp and harsh in the rare breaths of hot wind out of the southeast.

As Harran and Presley went along the county road, the number of vehicles and riders increased. They overtook and passed Hooven and his family in the former's farm wagon, a saddled horse tied to the back board. The little Dutchman, wearing the old frock coat of Magnus Derrick, and a new broad-brimmed straw hat, sat on the front seat with Mrs. Hooven. The little girl Hilda, and the older daughter Minna, were behind them on a board laid across the sides of the wagon. Presley and Harran stopped to shake hands.

"Say," cried Hooven, exhibiting an old, but extremely well kept, rifle, "say, bei Gott, me, I tek some schatz at dose rebbit, you bedt. Ven he hef shtop to run und sit oop soh, bei der hind laigs on, I oop mit der guhn und—bing! *I* cetch um."

"The marshals won't allow you to shoot, Bismarck," observed Presley, looking at Minna.

Hooven doubled up with merriment.

"Ho! dot's hell of some fine joak. Me, *I'm one oaf dose mairschell mine-selluf*," he roared with delight, beating his knee. To his notion, the joke was irresistible. All day long, he could be heard repeating it. "Und Mist'r Praicelie, he say, ' Dose mairschell woand led you schoot, Bismarck,' und *me*, ach Gott, *me*, aindt I mine-selluf one oaf dose mairschell? "

As the two friends rode on, Presley had in his mind the image of Minna Hooven, very pretty in a clean gown of pink gingham, a cheap straw sailor hat from a Bonneville store on her blue black hair. He remembered her very pale face, very red lips and eyes of greenish blue,—a pretty girl certainly, always trailing a group of men behind her. Her love affairs were the talk of all Los Muertos.

"I hope that Hooven girl won't go to the bad," Presley said to Harran.

"Oh, she's all right," the other answered. "There's nothing vicious about Minna, and I guess she'll marry that foreman on the ditch gang, right enough."

" Well, as a matter of course, she's a good girl," Presley hastened to reply, " only she's too pretty for a poor girl, and too sure of her prettiness besides. That's the kind," he continued, " who would find it pretty easy to go wrong if they lived in a city."

Around Caraher's was a veritable throng. Saddle horses and buggies by the score were clustered underneath the shed or hitched to the railings in front of the watering trough. Three of Broderson's Portuguese tenants and a couple of workmen from the Railroad shops in Bonneville were on the porch, already very drunk.

Continually, young men, singly or in groups, came from the door-way, wiping their lips with sidelong gestures of the hand. The whole place exhaled the febrile bustle of the saloon on a holiday morning.

The procession of teams streamed on through Bonneville, reënforced at every street corner. Along the Upper Road from Quien Sabe and Guadalajara came fresh auxiliaries, Spanish-Mexicans from the town itself,—swarthy young men on capering horses, dark-eyed girls and matrons, in red and black and yellow, more Portuguese in brand-new overalls, smoking long thin cigars. Even Father Sarria appeared.

" Look," said Presley, " there goes Annixter and Hilma. He's got his buckskin back." The master of Quien Sabe, in top laced boots and campaign hat, a cigar in his teeth, followed along beside the carry-all. Hilma and Mrs. Derrick were on the back seat, young Vacca driving. Harran and Presley bowed, taking off their hats.

" Hello, hello, Pres," cried Annixter, over the heads of the intervening crowd, standing up in his stirrups and waving a hand, " Great day! What a mob, hey? Say, when this thing is over and everybody starts to walk into the barbecue, come and have lunch with us. I'll look for you, you and Harran. Hello, Harran, where's the Governor?"

"He didn't come to-day," Harran shouted back, as the crowd carried him further away from Annixter. "Left him and old Broderson at Los Muertos."

The throng emerged into the open country again, spreading out upon the Osterman ranch. From all directions could be seen horses and buggies driving across the stubble, converging upon the rendezvous. Osterman's Ranch house was left to the eastward; the army of the guests hurrying forward—for it began to be late—to where around a flag pole, flying a red flag, a vast crowd of buggies and horses was already forming. The marshals began to appear. Hooven, descending from the farm wagon, pinned his white badge to his hat brim and mounted his horse. Osterman, in marvellous riding clothes of English pattern, galloped up and down upon his best thoroughbred, cracking jokes with everybody, chaffing, joshing, his great mouth distended in a perpetual grin of amiability.

"Stop here, stop here," he vociferated, dashing along in front of Presley and Harran, waving his crop. The procession came to a halt, the horses' heads pointing eastward. The line began to be formed. The marshals perspiring, shouting, fretting, galloping about, urging this one forward, ordering this one back, ranged the thousands of conveyances and cavaliers in a long line, shaped like a wide open crescent. Its wings, under the command of lieutenants, were slightly advanced. Far out before its centre Osterman took his place, delighted beyond expression at his conspicuousness, posing for the gallery, making his horse dance.

"Wail, aindt dey gowun to gommence den bretty soohn," exclaimed Mrs. Hooven, who had taken her husband's place on the forward seat of the wagon.

"I never was so warm," murmured Minna, fanning herself with her hat. All seemed in readiness. For miles over the flat expanse of stubble, curved the interminable lines of horses and vehicles. At a guess, nearly five thousand people were present. The drive was one of the largest ever held. But no start was made; immobilized, the vast crescent stuck motionless under the blazing sun. Here and there could be heard voices uplifted in jocular remonstrance.

"Oh, I say, get a move on, somebody."

"*All* aboard."

"Say, I'll take root here pretty soon."

Some took malicious pleasure in starting false alarms.

"Ah, *here* we go."

"Off, at last."

"We're off."

Invariably these jokes fooled some one in the line. An old man, or some old woman, nervous, hard of hearing, always gathered up the reins and started off, only to be hustled and ordered back into the line by the nearest marshal. This manœuvre never failed to produce its effect of hilarity upon those near at hand. Everybody laughed at the blunderer, the joker jeering audibly.

"Hey, come back here."

"Oh, he's easy."

"Don't be in a hurry, Grandpa."

"Say, you want to drive all the rabbits yourself."

Later on, a certain group of these fellows started a huge "josh."

"Say, that's what we're waiting for, the 'do-funny.'"

"The do-funny?"

"Sure, you can't drive rabbits without the 'do-funny.'"

"What's the do-funny?"

"Oh, say, she don't know what the do-funny is. We can't start without it, sure. Pete went back to get it."

" Oh, you're joking me, there's no such thing."

" Well, aren't we *waiting* for it? "

" Oh, look, look," cried some women in a covered rig. " See, they are starting already 'way over there."

In fact, it did appear as if the far extremity of the line was in motion. Dust rose in the air above it.

" They *are* starting. Why don't we start? "

" No, they've stopped. False alarm."

" They've not, either. Why don't we move? "

But as one or two began to move off, the nearest marshal shouted wrathfully:

" Get back there, get back there."

" Well, they've started over there."

" Get back, I tell you."

" Where's the ' do-funny ? ' "

" Say, we're going to miss it all. They've all started over there."

A lieutenant came galloping along in front of the line, shouting:

" Here, what's the matter here? Why don't you start? "

There was a great shout. Everybody simultaneously uttered a prolonged " Oh-h."

" We're off."

" Here we go for sure this time."

" Remember to keep the alignment," roared the lieutenant. " Don't go too fast."

And the marshals, rushing here and there on their sweating horses to points where the line bulged forward, shouted, waving their arms: " Not too fast, not too fast. . . . Keep back here. . . . Here, keep closer together here. Do you want to let all the rabbits run back between you? "

A great confused sound rose into the air,—the creaking of axles, the jolt of iron tires over the dry clods, the click of brittle stubble under the horses' hoofs, the barking of dogs, the shouts of conversation and laughter.

The entire line, horses, buggies, wagons, gigs, dogs, men and boys on foot, and armed with clubs, moved slowly across the fields, sending up a cloud of white dust, that hung above the scene like smoke. A brisk gaiety was in the air. Everyone was in the best of humor, calling from team to team, laughing, skylarking, joshing. Garnett, of the Ruby Rancho, and Gethings, of the San Pablo, both on horseback, found themselves side by side. Ignoring the drive and the spirit of the occasion, they kept up a prolonged and serious conversation on an expected rise in the price of wheat. Dabney, also on horseback, followed them, listening attentively to every word, but hazarding no remark.

Mrs. Derrick and Hilma sat in the back seat of the carry-all, behind young Vacca. Mrs. Derrick, a little disturbed by such a great concourse of people, frightened at the idea of the killing of so many rabbits, drew back in her place, her young-girl eyes troubled and filled with a vague distress. Hilma, very much excited, leaned from the carry-all, anxious to see everything, watching for rabbits, asking innumerable questions of Annixter, who rode at her side.

The change that had been progressing in Hilma, ever since the night of the famous barn-dance, now seemed to be approaching its climax; first the girl, then the woman, last of all the Mother. Conscious dignity, a new element in her character, developed. The shrinking, the timidity of the girl just awakening to the consciousness of sex, passed away from her. The confusion, the troublous complexity of the woman, a mystery even to herself, disappeared. Motherhood dawned, the old simplicity of her maiden days came back to her. It was no longer a simplicity of ignorance, but of supreme knowledge, the simplicity of the perfect, the simplicity of greatness. She looked the world fearlessly in the eyes. At last, the confusion of her ideas, like frightened birds, re-settling, adjusted itself, and she emerged from the trouble calm, serene, entering into her divine right, like a queen into the rule of a realm of perpetual peace.

And with this, with the knowledge that the crown hung poised above her head, there came upon Hilma a gentleness infinitely beautiful, infinitely pathetic; a sweetness that touched all who came near her with the softness of a caress. She moved surrounded by an invisible atmosphere of Love. Love was in her wide-opened brown eyes, Love—the dim reflection of that descending crown poised over her head—radiated in a faint lustre from her dark, thick hair. Around her beautiful neck, sloping to her shoulders with full, graceful curves, Love lay encircled like a necklace—Love that was beyond words, sweet, breathed from her parted lips. From her white, large arms downward to her pink finger-tips—Love, an invisible electric fluid, disengaged itself, subtle, alluring. In the velvety huskiness of her voice, Love vibrated like a note of unknown music.

Annixter, her uncouth, rugged husband, living in this influence of a wife, who was also a mother, at all hours touched to the quick by this sense of nobility, of gentleness and of love, the instincts of a father already clutching and tugging at his heart, was trembling on the verge of a mighty transformation. The hardness and inhumanity of the man was fast breaking up. One night, returning late to the Ranch house, after a compulsory visit to the city, he had come upon Hilma asleep. He had never forgotten that night. A realization of his boundless happiness in this love he gave and received, the thought that Hilma *trusted* him, a knowledge of his own unworthiness, a vast and humble thankfulness that his

God had chosen him of all men for this great joy, had brought him to his knees for the first time in all his troubled, restless life of combat and aggression. He prayed, he knew not what,—vague words, wordless thoughts, resolving fiercely to do right, to make some return for God's gift thus placed within his hands.

Where once Annixter had thought only of himself, he now thought only of Hilma. The time when this thought of another should broaden and widen into thought of *Others*, was yet to come; but already it had expanded to include the unborn child—already, as in the case of Mrs. Dyke, it had broadened to enfold another child and another mother bound to him by no ties other than those of humanity and pity. In time, starting from this point it would reach out more and more till it should take in all men and all women, and the intolerant selfish man, while retaining all of his native strength, should become tolerant and generous, kind and forgiving.

For the moment, however, the two natures struggled within him. A fight was to be fought, one more, the last, the fiercest, the attack of the enemy who menaced his very home and hearth, was to be resisted. Then, peace attained, arrested development would once more proceed.

Hilma looked from the carry-all, scanning the open plain in front of the advancing line of the drive.

" Where are the rabbits? " she asked of Annixter. " I don't see any at all."

" They are way ahead of us yet," he said. " Here, take the glasses."

He passed her his field glasses, and she adjusted them.

" Oh, yes," she cried, " I see. I can see five or six, but oh, so far off."

" The beggars run 'way ahead, at first."

" I should say so. See them run,—little specks. **Every**

now and then they sit up, their ears straight up, in the air."

"Here, look, Hilma, there goes one close by."

From out of the ground apparently, some twenty yards distant, a great jack sprang into view, bounding away with tremendous leaps, his black-tipped ears erect. He disappeared, his grey body losing itself against the grey of the ground.

"Oh, a big fellow."

"Hi, yonder's another."

"Yes, yes, oh, look at him run."

From off the surface of the ground, at first apparently empty of all life, and seemingly unable to afford hiding place for so much as a field-mouse, jack-rabbits started up at every moment as the line went forward. At first, they appeared singly and at long intervals; then in twos and threes, as the drive continued to advance. They leaped across the plain, and stopped in the distance, sitting up with straight ears, then ran on again, were joined by others; sank down flush to the soil—their ears flattened; started up again, ran to the side, turned back once more, darted away with incredible swiftness, and were lost to view only to be replaced by a score of others.

Gradually, the number of jacks to be seen over the expanse of stubble in front of the line of teams increased. Their antics were infinite. No two acted precisely alike. Some lay stubbornly close in a little depression between two clods, till the horses' hoofs were all but upon them, then sprang out from their hiding-place at the last second. Others ran forward but a few yards at a time, refusing to take flight, scenting a greater danger before them than behind. Still others, forced up at the last moment, doubled with lightning alacrity in their tracks, turning back to scuttle between the teams, taking desperate chances. As often as this occurred, it was the signal for a great uproar.

"Don't let him get through; don't let him get through."

"Look out for him, there he goes."

Horns were blown, bells rung, tin pans clamorously beaten. Either the jack escaped, or confused by the noise, darted back again, fleeing away as if his life depended on the issue of the instant. Once even, a bewildered rabbit jumped fair into Mrs. Derrick's lap as she sat in the carry-all, and was out again like a flash.

"Poor frightened thing," she exclaimed; and for a long time afterward, she retained upon her knees the sensation of the four little paws quivering with excitement, and the feel of the trembling furry body, with its wildly beating heart, pressed against her own.

By noon the number of rabbits discernible by Annixter's field glasses on ahead was far into the thousands. What seemed to be ground resolved itself, when seen through the glasses, into a maze of small, moving bodies, leaping, ducking, doubling, running back and forth—a wilderness of agitated ears, white tails and twinkling legs. The outside wings of the curved line of vehicles began to draw in a little; Osterman's ranch was left behind, the drive continued on over Quien Sabe.

As the day advanced, the rabbits, singularly enough, became less wild. When flushed, they no longer ran so far nor so fast, limping off instead a few feet at a time, and crouching down, their ears close upon their backs. Thus it was, that by degrees the teams began to close up on the main herd. At every instant the numbers increased. It was no longer thousands, it was tens of thousands. The earth was alive with rabbits.

Denser and denser grew the throng. In all directions nothing was to be seen but the loose mass of the moving jacks. The horns of the crescent of teams began to con-

tract. Far off the corral came into sight. The disintegrated mass of rabbits commenced, as it were, to solidify,
to coagulate. At first, each jack was some three feet distant from his nearest neighbor, but this space diminished
to two feet, then to one, then to but a few inches. The
rabbits began leaping over one another.

Then the strange scene defined itself. It was no longer
a herd covering the earth. It was a sea, whipped into
confusion, tossing incessantly, leaping, falling, agitated
by unseen forces. At times the unexpected tameness of
the rabbits all at once vanished. Throughout certain
portions of the herd eddies of terror abruptly burst forth.
A panic spread; then there would ensue a blind, wild
rushing together of thousands of crowded bodies, and a
furious scrambling over backs, till the scuffing thud of
innumerable feet over the earth rose to a reverberating
murmur as of distant thunder, here and there pierced
by the strange, wild cry of the rabbit in distress.

The line of vehicles was halted. To go forward now
meant to trample the rabbits under foot. The drive came
to a standstill while the herd entered the corral. This
took time, for the rabbits were by now too crowded to
run. However, like an opened sluice-gate, the extending
flanks of the entrance of the corral slowly engulfed the
herd. The mass, packed tight as ever, by degrees diminished, precisely as a pool of water when a dam is
opened. The last stragglers went in with a rush, and the
gate was dropped.

"Come, just have a look in here," called Annixter.

Hilma, descending from the carry-all and joined by
Presley and Harran, approached and looked over the
high board fence.

"Oh, did you ever see anything like that?" she exclaimed.

The corral, a really large enclosure, had proved all too

small for the number of rabbits collected by the drive. Inside it was a living, moving, leaping, breathing, twisting mass. The rabbits were packed two, three, and four feet deep. They were in constant movement; those beneath struggling to the top, those on top sinking and disappearing below their fellows. All wildness, all fear of man, seemed to have entirely disappeared. Men and boys reaching over the sides of the corral, picked up a jack in each hand, holding them by the ears, while two reporters from San Francisco papers took photographs of the scene. The noise made by the tens of thousands of moving bodies was as the noise of wind in a forest, while from the hot and sweating mass there rose a strange odor, penetrating, ammoniacal, savouring of wild life.

On signal, the killing began. Dogs that had been brought there for that purpose when let into the corral refused, as had been half expected, to do the work. They snuffed curiously at the pile, then backed off, disturbed, perplexed. But the men and boys—Portuguese for the most part—were more eager. Annixter drew Hilma away, and, indeed, most of the people set about the barbecue at once.

In the corral, however, the killing went forward. Armed with a club in each hand, the young fellows from Guadalajara and Bonneville, and the farm boys from the ranches, leaped over the rails of the corral. They walked unsteadily upon the myriad of crowding bodies underfoot, or, as space was cleared, sank almost waist deep into the mass that leaped and squirmed about them. Blindly, furiously, they struck and struck. The Anglo-Saxon spectators round about drew back in disgust, but the hot, degenerated blood of Portuguese, Mexican, and mixed Spaniard boiled up in excitement at this wholesale slaughter.

But only a few of the participants of the drive cared

to look on. All the guests betook themselves some quarter of a mile farther on into the hills.

The picnic and barbecue were to be held around the spring where Broderson Creek took its rise. Already two entire beeves were roasting there; teams were hitched, saddles removed, and men, women, and children, a great throng, spread out under the shade of the live oaks. A vast confused clamour rose in the air, a babel of talk, a clatter of tin plates, of knives and forks. Bottles were uncorked, napkins and oil-cloths spread over the ground. The men lit pipes and cigars, the women seized the occasion to nurse their babies.

Osterman, ubiquitous as ever, resplendent in his boots and English riding breeches, moved about between the groups, keeping up an endless flow of talk, cracking jokes, winking, nudging, gesturing, putting his tongue in his cheek, never at a loss for a reply, playing the goat.

"That josher, Osterman, always at his monkey-shines, but a good fellow for all that; brainy too. Nothing stuck up about him either, like Magnus Derrick."

"Everything all right, Buck?" inquired Osterman, coming up to where Annixter, Hilma and Mrs. Derrick were sitting down to their lunch.

"Yes, yes, everything right. But we've no corkscrew."

"No screw-cork—no scare-crow? Here you are," and he drew from his pocket a silver-plated jack-knife with a cork-screw attachment.

Harran and Presley came up, bearing between them a great smoking, roasted portion of beef just off the fire. Hilma hastened to put forward a huge china platter.

Osterman had a joke to crack with the two boys, a joke that was rather broad, but as he turned about, the words almost on his lips, his glance fell upon Hilma herself, whom he had not seen for more than two months.

She had handed Presley the platter, and was now sitting with her back against the tree, between two boles of the roots. The position was a little elevated and the supporting roots on either side of her were like the arms of a great chair—a chair of state. She sat thus, as on a throne, raised above the rest, the radiance of the unseen crown of motherhood glowing from her forehead, the beauty of the perfect woman surrounding her like a glory.

And the josh died away on Osterman's lips, and unconsciously and swiftly he bared his head. Something was passing there in the air about him that he did not understand, something, however, that imposed reverence and profound respect. For the first time in his life, embarrassment seized upon him, upon this joker, this wearer of clothes, this teller of funny stories, with his large, red ears, bald head and comic actor's face. He stammered confusedly and took himself away, for the moment abstracted, serious, lost in thought.

By now everyone was eating. It was the feeding of the People, elemental, gross, a great appeasing of appetite, an enormous quenching of thirst. Quarters of beef, roasts, ribs, shoulders, haunches were consumed, loaves of bread by the thousands disappeared, whole barrels of wine went down the dry and dusty throats of the multitude. Conversation lagged while the People ate, while hunger was appeased. Everybody had their fill. One ate for the sake of eating, resolved that there should be nothing left, considering it a matter of pride to exhibit a clean plate.

After dinner, preparations were made for games. On a flat plateau at the top of one of the hills the contestants were to strive. There was to be a footrace of young girls under seventeen, a fat men's race, the younger fellows were to put the shot, to compete in the running broad jump, and the standing high jump, in the hop, skip, and step and in wrestling.

Presley was delighted with it all. It was Homeric, this feasting, this vast consuming of meat and bread and wine, followed now by games of strength. An epic simplicity and directness, an honest Anglo-Saxon mirth and innocence, commended it. Crude it was; coarse it was, but no taint of viciousness was here. These people were good people, kindly, benignant even, always readier to give than to receive, always more willing to help than to be helped. They were good stock. Of such was the backbone of the nation—sturdy Americans everyone of them. Where else in the world round were such strong, honest men, such strong, beautiful women?

Annixter, Harran, and Presley climbed to the level plateau where the games were to be held, to lay out the courses, and mark the distances. It was the very place where once Presley had loved to lounge entire afternoons, reading his books of poems, smoking and dozing. From this high point one dominated the entire valley to the south and west. The view was superb. The three men paused for a moment on the crest of the hill to consider it.

Young Vacca came running and panting up the hill after them, calling for Annixter.

"Well, well, what is it?"

"Mr. Osterman's looking for you, sir, you and Mr. Harran. Vanamee, that cow-boy over at Derrick's, has just come from the Governor with a message. I guess it's important."

"Hello, what's up now?" muttered Annixter, as they turned back.

They found Osterman saddling his horse in furious haste. Near-by him was Vanamee holding by the bridle an animal that was one lather of sweat. A few of the picnickers were turning their heads curiously in that direction. Evidently something of moment was in the wind.

"What's all up?" demanded Annixter, as he and Harran, followed by Presley, drew near.

"There's hell to pay," exclaimed Osterman under his breath. "Read that. Vanamee just brought it."

He handed Annixter a sheet of note paper, and turned again to the cinching of his saddle.

"We've got to be quick," he cried. "They've stolen a march on us."

Annixter read the note, Harran and Presley looking over his shoulder.

"Ah, it's them, is it," exclaimed Annixter.

Harran set his teeth. "Now for it," he exclaimed.

"They've been to your place already, Mr. Annixter," said Vanamee. "I passed by it on my way up. They have put Delaney in possession, and have set all your furniture out in the road."

Annixter turned about, his lips white. Already Presley and Harran had run to their horses.

"Vacca," cried Annixter, "where's Vacca? Put the saddle on the buckskin, *quick*. Osterman, get as many of the League as are here together at *this* spot, understand. I'll be back in a minute. I must tell Hilma this."

Hooven ran up as Annixter disappeared. His little eyes were blazing, he was dragging his horse with him.

"Say, dose fellers come, hey? Me, I'm alretty, see I hev der guhn."

"They've jumped the ranch, little girl," said Annixter, putting one arm around Hilma. "They're in our house now. I'm off. Go to Derrick's and wait for me there."

She put her arms around his neck.

"You're going?" she demanded.

"I must. Don't be frightened. It will be all right. Go to Derrick's and—good-bye."

She said never a word. She looked once long into his eyes, then kissed him on the mouth.

Meanwhile, the news had spread. The multitude rose to its feet. Women and men, with pale faces, looked at each other speechless, or broke forth into inarticulate exclamations. A strange, unfamiliar murmur took the place of the tumultuous gaiety of the previous moments. A sense of dread, of confusion, of impending terror weighed heavily in the air. What was now to happen?

When Annixter got back to Osterman, he found a number of the Leaguers already assembled. They were all mounted. Hooven was there and Harran, and besides these, Garnett of the Ruby ranch and Gethings of the San Pablo, Phelps the foreman of Los Muertos, and, last of all, Dabney, silent as ever, speaking to no one. Presley came riding up.

" Best keep out of this, Pres," cried Annixter.

" Are we ready? " exclaimed Gethings.

" Ready, ready, we're all here."

" *All*. Is this all of us? " cried Annixter. " Where are the six hundred men who were going to rise when this happened? "

They had wavered, these other Leaguers. Now, when the actual crisis impended, they were smitten with confusion. Ah, no, they were not going to stand up and be shot at just to save Derrick's land. They were not armed. What did Annixter and Osterman take them for? No, sir ; the Railroad had stolen a march on them. After all his big talk Derrick had allowed them to be taken by surprise. The only thing to do was to call a meeting of the Executive Committee. That was the only thing. As for going down there with no weapons in their hands, *no*, sir. That was asking a little *too* much.

" Come on, then, boys," shouted Osterman, turning his

back on the others. "The Governor says to meet him at
Hooven's. We'll make for the Long Trestle and strike
the trail to Hooven's there."

They set off. It was a terrible ride. Twice during the
scrambling descent from the hills, Presley's pony fell
beneath him. Annixter, on his buckskin, and Osterman,
on his thoroughbred, good horsemen both, led the others,
setting a terrific pace. The hills were left behind. Broderson Creek was crossed and on the levels of Quien
Sabe, straight through the standing wheat, the nine
horses, flogged and spurred, stretched out to their utmost. Their passage through the wheat sounded like the
rip and tear of a gigantic web of cloth. The landscape on
either hand resolved itself into a long blur. Tears came
to the eyes, flying pebbles, clods of earth, grains of wheat
flung up in the flight, stung the face like shot. Osterman's thoroughbred took the second crossing of Broderson's Creek in a single leap. Down under the Long
Trestle tore the cavalcade in a shower of mud and
gravel; up again on the further bank, the horses blowing
like steam engines; on into the trail to Hooven's, single
file now, Presley's pony lagging, Hooven's horse bleeding at the eyes, the buckskin, game as a fighting cock,
catching her second wind, far in the lead now, distancing
even the English thoroughbred that Osterman rode.

At last Hooven's unpainted house, beneath the enormous live oak tree, came in sight. Across the Lower
Road, breaking through fences and into the yard around
the house, thundered the Leaguers. Magnus was waiting
for them.

The riders dismounted, hardly less exhausted than their
horses.

"Why, where's all the men?" Annixter demanded of
Magnus.

"Broderson is here and Cutter," replied the Governor,

"no one else. I thought *you* would bring more men with you."

"There are only nine of us."

"And the six hundred Leaguers who were going to rise when this happened!" exclaimed Garnett, bitterly.

"Rot the League," cried Annixter. "It's gone to pot —went to pieces at the first touch."

"We have been taken by surprise, gentlemen, after all," said Magnus. "Totally off our guard. But there are eleven of us. It is enough."

"Well, what's the game? Has the marshal come? How many men are with him?"

"The United States marshal from San Francisco," explained Magnus, "came down early this morning and stopped at Guadalajara. We learned it all through our friends in Bonneville about an hour ago. They telephoned me and Mr. Broderson. S. Behrman met him and provided about a dozen deputies. Delaney, Ruggles, and Christian joined them at Guadalajara. They left Guadalajara, going towards Mr. Annixter's ranch house on Quien Sabe. They are serving the writs in ejectment and putting the dummy buyers in possession. They are armed. S. Behrman is with them."

"Where are they now?"

"Cutter is watching them from the Long Trestle. They returned to Guadalajara. They are there now."

"Well," observed Gethings, "from Guadalajara they can only go to two places. Either they will take the Upper Road and go on to Osterman's next, or they will take the Lower Road to Mr. Derrick's."

"That is as I supposed," said Magnus. "That is why I wanted you to come here. From Hooven's, here, we can watch both roads simultaneously."

"Is anybody on the lookout on the Upper Road?"

"Cutter. He is on the Long Trestle."

"Say," observed Hooven, the instincts of the old-time soldier stirring him, "say, dose feller pretty demn schmart, I tink. We got to put some picket way oudt bei der Lower Roadt alzoh, und he tek dose glassus Mist'r Ennixt'r got bei um. Say, look at dose irregation ditsch. Dot ditsch he run righd across *both* dose road, hey? Dat's some fine entrenchment, you bedt. We fighd um from dose ditsch."

In fact, the dry irrigating ditch was a natural trench, admirably suited to the purpose, crossing both roads as Hooven pointed out and barring approach from Guadalajara to all the ranches save Annixter's—which had already been seized.

Gethings departed to join Cutter on the Long Trestle, while Phelps and Harran, taking Annixter's field glasses with them, and mounting their horses, went out towards Guadalajara on the Lower Road to watch for the marshal's approach from that direction.

After the outposts had left them, the party in Hooven's cottage looked to their weapons. Long since, every member of the League had been in the habit of carrying his revolver with him. They were all armed and, in addition, Hooven had his rifle. Presley alone carried no weapon.

The main room of Hooven's house, in which the Leaguers were now assembled, was barren, poverty-stricken, but tolerably clean. An old clock ticked vociferously on a shelf. In one corner was a bed, with a patched, faded quilt. In the centre of the room, straddling over the bare floor, stood a pine table. Around this the men gathered, two or three occupying chairs, Annixter sitting sideways on the table, the rest standing.

"I believe, gentlemen," said Magnus, "that we can go through this day without bloodshed. I believe not one shot need be fired. The Railroad will not force the issue, will not bring about actual fighting. When the marshal realises that we are thoroughly in earnest, thoroughly determined, I am convinced that he will withdraw."

There were murmurs of assent.

"Look here," said Annixter, "if this thing can by any means be settled peaceably, I say let's do it, so long as we don't give in."

The others stared. Was this Annixter who spoke— the Hotspur of the League, the quarrelsome, irascible fellow who loved and sought a quarrel? Was it Annixter, who now had been the first and only one of them all to suffer, whose ranch had been seized, whose household possessions had been flung out into the road?

"When you come right down to it," he continued, "killing a man, no matter what he's done to you, is a serious business. I propose we make one more attempt to stave this thing off. Let's see if we can't get to talk with the marshal himself; at any rate, warn him of the danger of going any further. Boys, let's not fire the first shot. What do you say?"

The others agreed unanimously and promptly; and old Broderson, tugging uneasily at his long beard, added:

"No—no—no violence, no *unnecessary* violence, that is. I should hate to have innocent blood on my hands— that is, if it *is* innocent. I don't know, that S. Behrman —ah, he is a—a—surely he had innocent blood on *his* head. That Dyke affair, terrible, terrible; but then Dyke *was* in the wrong—driven to it, though; the Railroad did drive him to it. I want to be fair and just to every-body——"

"There's a team coming up the road from Los Muertos," announced Presley from the door.

"Fair and just to everybody," murmured old Broderson, wagging his head, frowning perplexedly. "I don't want to—to—to harm anybody unless they harm me."

"Is the team going towards Guadalajara?" enquired Garnett, getting up and coming to the door.

"Yes, it's a Portuguese, one of the garden truck men."

"We must turn him back," declared Osterman. "He can't go through here. We don't want him to take any news on to the marshal and S. Behrman."

"I'll turn him back," said Presley.

He rode out towards the market cart, and the others, watching from the road in front of Hooven's, saw him halt it. An excited interview followed. They could hear the Portuguese expostulating volubly, but in the end he turned back.

"Martial law on Los Muertos, isn't it?" observed Osterman. "Steady all," he exclaimed as he turned about, "here comes Harran."

Harran rode up at a gallop. The others surrounded him.

"I saw them," he cried. "They are coming this way. S. Behrman and Ruggles are in a two-horse buggy. All the others are on horseback. There are eleven of them. Christian and Delaney are with them. Those two have rifles. I left Hooven watching them."

"Better call in Gethings and Cutter right away," said Annixter. "We'll need all our men."

"I'll call them in," Presley volunteered at once. "Can I have the buckskin? My pony is about done up."

He departed at a brisk gallop, but on the way met Gethings and Cutter returning. They, too, from their elevated position, had observed the marshal's party leaving Guadalajara by the Lower Road. Presley told them of the decision of the Leaguers not to fire until fired upon.

"All right," said Gethings. "But if it comes to a gun-fight, that means it's all up with at least one of us. Delaney never misses his man."

When they reached Hooven's again, they found that the Leaguers had already taken their position in the ditch. The plank bridge across it had been torn up. Magnus, two long revolvers lying on the embankment in front of him, was in the middle, Harran at his side. On either side, some five feet intervening between each man, stood the other Leaguers, their revolvers ready. Dabney, the silent old man, had taken off his coat.

"Take your places between Mr. Osterman and Mr. Broderson," said Magnus, as the three men rode up. "Presley," he added, "I forbid you to take any part in this affair."

"Yes, keep him out of it," cried Annixter from his position at the extreme end of the line. "Go back to Hooven's house, Pres, and look after the horses," he added. "This is no business of yours. And keep the road behind us clear. Don't let *any one* come near, not *any one*, understand?"

Presley withdrew, leading the buckskin and the horses that Gethings and Cutter had ridden. He fastened them under the great live oak and then came out and stood in the road in front of the house to watch what was going on.

In the ditch, shoulder deep, the Leaguers, ready, watchful, waited in silence, their eyes fixed on the white shimmer of the road leading to Guadalajara.

"Where's Hooven?" enquired Cutter.

"I don't know," Osterman replied. "He was out watching the Lower Road with Harran Derrick. Oh, Harran," he called, "isn't Hooven coming in?"

"I don't know what he is waiting for," answered Harran. "He was to have come in just after me. He thought maybe the marshal's party might make a feint in this direction, then go around by the Upper Road, after all. He wanted to watch them a little longer. But he ought to be here now."

"Think he'll take a shot at them on his own account?"

"Oh, no, he wouldn't do that."

"Maybe they took him prisoner."

"Well, that's to be thought of, too."

Suddenly there was a cry. Around the bend of the road in front of them came a cloud of dust. From it emerged a horse's head.

"Hello, hello, there's something."

"Remember, we are not to fire first."

"Perhaps that's Hooven; I can't see. Is it? There only seems to be one horse."

"Too much dust for one horse."

Annixter, who had taken his field glasses from Harran, adjusted them to his eyes.

"That's not them," he announced presently, "nor Hooven either. That's a cart." Then after another moment, he added, "The butcher's cart from Guadalajara."

The tension was relaxed. The men drew long breaths, settling back in their places.

"Do we let him go on, Governor?"

"The bridge is down. He can't go by and we must not let him go back. We shall have to detain him and question him. I wonder the marshal let him pass."

The cart approached at a lively trot.

"Anybody else in that cart, Mr. Annixter?" asked Magnus. "Look carefully. It may be a ruse. It is strange the marshal should have let him pass."

The Leaguers roused themselves again. Osterman laid his hand on his revolver.

"No," called Annixter, in another instant, "no, there's only one man in it."

The cart came up, and Cutter and Phelps, clambering from the ditch, stopped it as it arrived in front of the party.

"Hey—what—what?" exclaimed the young butcher, pulling up. "Is that bridge broke?"

But at the idea of being held, the boy protested at top voice, badly frightened, bewildered, not knowing what was to happen next.

"No, no, I got my meat to deliver. Say, you let me go. Say, I ain't got nothing to do with you."

He tugged at the reins, trying to turn the cart about. Cutter, with his jack-knife, parted the reins just back of the bit.

"You'll stay where you are, m' son, for a while. We're not going to hurt you. But you are not going back to town till we say so. Did you pass anybody on the road out of town?"

In reply to the Leaguers' questions, the young butcher at last told them he had passed a two-horse buggy and a lot of men on horseback just beyond the railroad tracks. They were headed for Los Muertos.

"That's them, all right," muttered Annixter. "They're coming by this road, sure."

The butcher's horse and cart were led to one side of the road, and the horse tied to the fence with one of the severed lines. The butcher, himself, was passed over to Presley, who locked him in Hooven's barn.

"Well, what the devil," demanded Osterman, "has become of Bismarck?"

In fact, the butcher had seen nothing of Hooven. The minutes were passing, and still he failed to appear.

"What's he up to, anyways?"

"Bet you what you like, they caught him. Just like that crazy Dutchman to get excited and go too near. You can always depend on Hooven to lose his head."

Five minutes passed, then ten. The road towards Guadalajara lay empty, baking and white under the sun.

"Well, the marshal and S. Behrman don't seem to be in any hurry, either."

"Shall I go forward and reconnoitre, Governor?" asked Harran.

But Dabney, who stood next to Annixter, touched him on the shoulder and, without speaking, pointed down the road. Annixter looked, then suddenly cried out:

"Here comes Hooven."

The German galloped into sight, around the turn of the road, his rifle laid across his saddle. He came on rapidly, pulled up, and dismounted at the ditch.

"Dey're commen," he cried, trembling with excitement. "I watch um long dime bei der side oaf der roadt in der busches Dey shtop bei der gate oder side der relroadt trecks and talk long dime mit one n'udder. Den dey gome on. Dey're gowun sure do zum monkey-doodle pizeness. Me, I see Gritschun put der kertridges in his guhn. I tink dey gowun to gome *my* blace first. Dey gowun to try put me off, tek my home, bei Gott."

"All right, get down in here and keep quiet, Hooven. Don't fire unless——"

"Here they are."

A half-dozen voices uttered the cry at once.

There could be no mistake this time. A buggy, drawn by two horses, came into view around the curve of the road. Three riders accompanied it, and behind these, seen at intervals in a cloud of dust were two—three— five—six others.

This, then, was S. Behrman with the United States marshal and his posse. The event that had been so long in preparation, the event which it had been said would never come to pass, the last trial of strength, the last fight between the Trust and the People, the direct, brutal grapple of armed men, the law defied, the Government ignored, behold, here it was close at hand.

Osterman cocked his revolver, and in the profound silence that had fallen upon the scene, the click was plainly audible from end to end of the line.

"Remember our agreement, gentlemen," cried Magnus, in a warning voice. "Mr. Osterman, I must ask you to let down the hammer of your weapon."

No one answered. In absolute quiet, standing motionless in their places, the Leaguers watched the approach of the marshal.

Five minutes passed. The riders came on steadily. They drew nearer. The grind of the buggy wheels in the grit and dust of the road, and the prolonged clatter of the horses' feet began to make itself heard. The Leaguers could distinguish the faces of their enemies.

In the buggy were S. Behrman and Cyrus Ruggles, the latter driving. A tall man in a frock coat and slouched hat—the marshal, beyond question—rode at the left of the buggy; Delaney, carrying a Winchester, at the right. Christian, the real estate broker, S. Behrman's cousin, also with a rifle, could be made out just behind the marshal. Back of these, riding well up, was a group of horsemen, indistinguishable in the dust raised by the buggy's wheels.

Steadily the distance between the Leaguers and the posse diminished.

"Don't let them get too close, Governor," whispered Harran.

When S. Behrman's buggy was about one hundred yards distant from the irrigating ditch, Magnus sprang out upon the road, leaving his revolvers behind him. He beckoned Garnett and Gethings to follow, and the three ranchers, who, with the exception of Broderson, were the oldest men present, advanced, without arms, to meet the marshal.

Magnus cried aloud:

" Halt where you are."

From their places in the ditch, Annixter, Osterman,
Dabney, Harran, Hooven, Broderson, Cutter, and
Phelps, their hands laid upon their revolvers, watched
silently, alert, keen, ready for anything.

At the Governor's words, they saw Ruggles pull
sharply on the reins. The buggy came to a standstill, the
riders doing likewise. Magnus approached the marshal,
still followed by Garnett and Gethings, and began to
speak. His voice was audible to the men in the ditch, but
his words could not be made out. They heard the marshal reply quietly enough and the two shook hands. Delaney came around from the side of the buggy, his horse
standing before the team across the road. He leaned
from the saddle, listening to what was being said, but
made no remark. From time to time, S. Behrman and
Ruggles, from their seats in the buggy, interposed a
sentence or two into the conversation, but at first, so far
as the Leaguers could discern, neither Magnus nor the
marshal paid them any attention. They saw, however,
that the latter repeatedly shook his head and once they
heard him exclaim in a loud voice:

" I only know my duty, Mr. Derrick."

Then Gethings turned about, and seeing Delaney close
at hand, addressed an unheard remark to him. The cow-
puncher replied curtly and the words seemed to anger
Gethings. He made a gesture, pointing back to the
ditch, showing the intrenched Leaguers to the posse.
Delaney appeared to communicate the news that the
Leaguers were on hand and prepared to resist, to the
other members of the party. They all looked toward
the ditch and plainly saw the ranchers there, standing to
their arms.

But meanwhile Ruggles had addressed himself more
directly to Magnus, and between the two an angry dis-

cussion was going forward. Once even Harran heard his father exclaim:

" The statement is a lie and no one knows it better than yourself."

" Here," growled Annixter to Dabney, who stood next him in the ditch, " those fellows are getting too close. Look at them edging up. Don't Magnus see that ? "

The other members of the marshal's force had come forward from their places behind the buggy and were spread out across the road. Some of them were gathered about Magnus, Garnett, and Gethings; and some were talking together, looking and pointing towards the ditch. Whether acting upon signal or not, the Leaguers in the ditch could not tell, but it was certain that one or two of the posse had moved considerably forward. Besides this, Delaney had now placed his horse between Magnus and the ditch, and two others riding up from the rear had followed his example. The posse surrounded the three ranchers, and by now, everybody was talking at once.

" Look here," Harran called to Annixter, " this won't do. I don't like the looks of this thing. They all seem to be edging up, and before we know it they may take the Governor and the other men prisoners."

" They ought to come back," declared Annixter.

" Somebody ought to tell them that those fellows are creeping up."

By now, the angry argument between the Governor and Ruggles had become more heated than ever. Their voices were raised; now and then they made furious gestures.

" They ought to come back," cried Osterman. " We couldn't shoot now if anything should happen, for fear of hitting them."

"Well, it sounds as though something were going to happen pretty soon."

They could hear Gethings and Delaney wrangling furiously; another deputy joined in.

"I'm going to call the Governor back," exclaimed Annixter, suddenly clambering out of the ditch.

"No, no," cried Osterman, "keep in the ditch. They can't drive us out if we keep here."

Hooven and Harran, who had instinctively followed Annixter, hesitated at Osterman's words and the three halted irresolutely on the road before the ditch, their weapons in their hands.

"Governor," shouted Harran, "come on back. You can't do anything."

Still the wrangle continued, and one of the deputies, advancing a little from out the group, cried out:

"Keep back there! Keep back there, you!"

"Go to hell, will you?" shouted Harran on the instant. "You're on my land."

"Oh, come back here, Harran," called Osterman. "That ain't going to do any good."

"There—listen," suddenly exclaimed Harran. "The Governor is calling us. Come on; I'm going."

Osterman got out of the ditch and came forward, catching Harran by the arm and pulling him back.

"He didn't call. Don't get excited. You'll ruin everything. Get back into the ditch again."

But Cutter, Phelps, and the old man Dabney, misunderstanding what was happening, and seeing Osterman leave the ditch, had followed his example. All the Leaguers were now out of the ditch, and a little way down the road, Hooven, Osterman, Annixter, and Harran in front, Dabney, Phelps, and Cutter coming up from behind.

"Keep back, you," cried the deputy again.

In the group around S. Behrman's buggy, Gethings and Delaney were yet quarrelling, and the angry debate between Magnus, Garnett, and the marshal still continued.

Till this moment, the real estate broker, Christian, had taken no part in the argument, but had kept himself in the rear of the buggy. Now, however, he pushed forward. There was but little room for him to pass, and, as he rode by the buggy, his horse scraped his flank against the hub of the wheel. The animal recoiled sharply, and, striking against Garnett, threw him to the ground. Delaney's horse stood between the buggy and the Leaguers gathered on the road in front of the ditch; the incident, indistinctly seen by them, was misinterpreted.

Garnett had not yet risen when Hooven raised a great shout:

" *Hoch, der Kaiser! Hoch, der Vaterland!* "

With the words, he dropped to one knee, and sighting his rifle carefully, fired into the group of men around the buggy.

Instantly the revolvers and rifles seemed to go off of themselves. Both sides, deputies and Leaguers, opened fire simultaneously. At first, it was nothing but a confused roar of explosions; then the roar lapsed to an irregular, quick succession of reports, shot leaping after shot; then a moment's silence, and, last of all, regular as clock-ticks, three shots at exact intervals. Then stillness.

Delaney, shot through the stomach, slid down from his horse, and, on his hands and knees, crawled from the road into the standing wheat. Christian fell backward from the saddle toward the buggy, and hung suspended in that position, his head and shoulders on the wheel, one stiff leg still across his saddle. Hooven, in attempting to rise from his kneeling position, received a rifle ball squarely in the throat, and rolled forward upon his face. Old Broderson, crying out, " Oh, they've shot me, boys," staggered sideways, his head bent, his hands rigid at his sides, and fell into the ditch. Osterman, blood running from his mouth and nose, turned about and walked back. Presley helped him across the irrigating ditch and Osterman laid himself down, his head on his folded arms. Harran Derrick dropped where he stood, turning over on his face, and lay motionless, groaning terribly, a pool of blood forming under his stomach. The old man Dabney, silent as ever, received his death, speechless. He fell to his knees, got up again, fell once more, and died without a word. Annixter, instantly killed, fell his length to the ground, and lay without movement, just as he had fallen, one arm across his face.

VII

On their way to Derrick's ranch house, Hilma and Mrs. Derrick heard the sounds of distant firing.

"Stop!" cried Hilma, laying her hand upon young Vacca's arm. "Stop the horses. Listen, what was that?"

The carry-all came to a halt and from far away across the rustling wheat came the faint rattle of rifles and revolvers.

"Say," cried Vacca, rolling his eyes, "oh, say, they're fighting over there."

Mrs. Derrick put her hands over her face.

"Fighting," she cried, "oh, oh, it's terrible. Magnus is there—and Harran."

"Where do you think it is?" demanded Hilma.

"That's over toward Hooven's."

"I'm going. Turn back. Drive to Hooven's, quick."

"Better not, Mrs. Annixter," protested the young man. "Mr. Annixter said we were to go to Derrick's. Better keep away from Hooven's if there's trouble there. We wouldn't get there till it's all over, anyhow."

"Yes, yes, let's go home," cried Mrs. Derrick, "I'm afraid. Oh, Hilma, I'm afraid."

"Come with me to Hooven's then."

"There, where they are fighting? Oh, I couldn't. I—I can't. It would be all over before we got there as Mr. Vacca says."

"Sure," repeated young Vacca.

"Drive to Hooven's," commanded Hilma. "If you

won't, I'll walk there." She threw off the lap-robes, preparing to descend. "And you," she exclaimed, turning to Mrs. Derrick, "how *can* you—when Harran and your husband may be—may—are in danger."

Grumbling, Vacca turned the carry-all about and drove across the open fields till he reached the road to Guadalajara, just below the Mission.

"Hurry!" cried Hilma.

The horses started forward under the touch of the whip. The ranch houses of Quien Sabe came in sight.

"Do you want to stop at the house?" inquired Vacca over his shoulder.

"No, no; oh, go faster—make the horses run."

They dashed through the houses of the Home ranch.

"Oh; oh," cried Hilma suddenly, "look, look there. Look what they have done."

Vacca pulled the horses up, for the road in front of Annixter's house was blocked.

A vast, confused heap of household effects was there —chairs, sofas, pictures, fixtures, lamps. Hilma's little home had been gutted; everything had been taken from it and ruthlessly flung out upon the road, everything that she and her husband had bought during that wonderful week after their marriage. Here was the white enamelled "set" of the bedroom furniture, the three chairs, washstand and bureau,—the bureau drawers falling out, spilling their contents into the dust; there were the white wool rugs of the sitting-room, the flower stand, with its pots all broken, its flowers wilting; the cracked goldfish globe, the fishes already dead; the rocking chair, the sewing machine, the great round table of yellow oak, the lamp with its deep shade of crinkly red tissue paper, the pretty tinted photographs that had hung on the wall— the choir boys with beautiful eyes, the pensive young girls in pink gowns—the pieces of wood carving that represented quails and ducks, and, last of all, its curtains of crisp, clean muslin, cruelly torn and crushed—the bed, the wonderful canopied bed so brave and gay, of which Hilma had been so proud, thrust out there into the common road, torn from its place, from the discreet intimacy of her bridal chamber, violated, profaned, flung out into the dust and garish sunshine for all men to stare at, a mockery and a shame.

To Hilma it was as though something of herself, of her person, had been thus exposed and degraded; all that she held sacred pilloried, gibbeted, and exhibited to the world's derision. Tears of anguish sprang to her eyes, a red flame of outraged modesty overspread her face.

"Oh," she cried, a sob catching her throat, "oh, how could they do it?" But other fears intruded; other greater terrors impended.

"Go on," she cried to Vacca, "go on quickly."

But Vacca would go no further. He had seen what had escaped Hilma's attention, two men, deputies, no doubt, on the porch of the ranch house. They held possession there, and the evidence of the presence of the enemy in this raid upon Quien Sabe had daunted him.

"No, sir," he declared, getting out of the carry-all, "I ain't going to take you anywhere where you're liable to get hurt. Besides, the road's blocked by all this stuff. You can't get the team by."

Hilma sprang from the carry-all.

"Come," she said to Mrs. Derrick.

The older woman, trembling, hesitating, faint with dread, obeyed, and Hilma, picking her way through and around the wreck of her home, set off by the trail towards the Long Trestle and Hooven's.

When she arrived, she found the road in front of the German's house, and, indeed, all the surrounding yard, crowded with people. An overturned buggy lay on the side of the road in the distance, its horses in a tangle of harness, held by two or three men. She saw Caraher's buckboard under the live oak and near it a second buggy which she recognised as belonging to a doctor in Guadalajara.

"Oh, what has happened; oh, what has happened?" moaned Mrs. Derrick.

"Come," repeated Hilma. The young girl took her by the hand and together they pushed their way through the crowd of men and women and entered the yard.

The throng gave way before the two women, parting to right and left without a word.

"Presley," cried Mrs. Derrick, as she caught sight of him in the doorway of the house, "oh, Presley, what has happened? Is Harran safe? Is Magnus safe? Where are they?"

"Don't go in, Mrs. Derrick," said Presley, coming forward, "don't go in."

"Where is my husband?" demanded Hilma.

Presley turned away and steadied himself against the jamb of the door.

Hilma, leaving Mrs. Derrick, entered the house. The front room was full of men. She was dimly conscious of Cyrus Ruggles and S. Behrman, both deadly pale, talking earnestly and in whispers to Cutter and Phelps. There was a strange, acrid odour of an unfamiliar drug in the air. On the table before her was a satchel, surgical instruments, rolls of bandages, and a blue, oblong paper box full of cotton. But above the hushed noises of voices and footsteps, one terrible sound made itself heard—the prolonged, rasping sound of breathing, half choked, laboured, agonised.

"Where is my husband?" she cried. She pushed the men aside. She saw Magnus, bareheaded, three or four men lying on the floor, one half naked, his body swathed in white bandages; the doctor in shirt sleeves, on one knee beside a figure of a man stretched out beside him.

Garnett turned a white face to her.

" Where is my husband?"

The other did not reply, but stepped aside and Hilma saw the dead body of her husband lying upon the bed. She did not cry out. She said no word. She went to the bed, and sitting upon it, took Annixter's head in her lap, holding it gently between her hands. Thereafter she did not move, but sat holding her dead husband's head in her lap, looking vaguely about from face to face of those in the room, while, without a sob, without a cry, the great tears filled her wide-opened eyes and rolled slowly down upon her cheeks.

On hearing that his wife was outside, Magnus came quickly forward. She threw herself into his arms.

" Tell me, tell me," she cried, " is Harran—is——"

" We don't know yet," he answered. " Oh, Annie——"

Then suddenly the Governor checked himself. He, the indomitable, could not break down now.

" The doctor is with him," he said; " we are doing all we can. Try and be brave, Annie. There is always hope. This is a terrible day's work. God forgive us all."

She pressed forward, but he held her back.

" No, don't see him now. Go into the next room. Garnett, take care of her."

But she would not be denied. She pushed by Magnus, and, breaking through the group that surrounded her son, sank on her knees beside him, moaning, in compassion and terror.

Harran lay straight and rigid upon the floor, his head propped by a pillow, his coat that had been taken off spread over his chest. One leg of his trousers was soaked through and through with blood. His eyes were half-closed, and with the regularity of a machine, the eyeballs twitched and twitched. His face was so white that it made his yellow hair look brown, while from his opened mouth, there issued that loud and terrible sound of guttering, rasping, laboured breathing that gagged and choked and gurgled with every inhalation.

" Oh, Harrie, Harrie," called Mrs. Derrick, catching at one of his hands.

The doctor shook his head.

" He is unconscious, Mrs. Derrick."

" Where was he—where is—the—the——"

" Through the lungs."

" Will he get well? Tell me the truth."

" I don't know, Mrs. Derrick."

She had all but fainted, and the old rancher, Garnett, half-carrying, half-leading her, took her to the one adjoining room—Minna Hooven's bedchamber. Dazed, numb with fear, she sat down on the edge of the bed, rocking herself back and forth, murmuring:

" Harrie, Harrie, oh, my son, my little boy."

In the outside room, Presley came and went, doing what he could to be of service, sick with horror, trembling from head to foot.

The surviving members of both Leaguers and deputies—the warring factions of the Railroad and the People—mingled together now with no thought of hostility. Presley helped the doctor to cover Christian's body. S. Behrman and Ruggles held bowls of water while Osterman was attended to. The horror of that dreadful business had driven all other considerations from the mind. The sworn foes of the last hour had no thought of anything but to care for those whom, in their fury, they had shot down. The marshal, abandoning for that day the attempt to serve the writs, departed for San Francisco.

The bodies had been brought in from the road where

they fell. Annixter's corpse had been laid upon the bed;
those of Dabney and Hooven, whose wounds had all been
in the face and head, were covered with a tablecloth.
Upon the floor, places were made for the others. Cutter
and Ruggles rode into Guadalajara to bring out the
doctor there, and to telephone to Bonneville for others.

Osterman had not at any time since the shooting, lost
consciousness. He lay upon the floor of Hooven's house,
bare to the waist, bandages of adhesive tape reeved about
his abdomen and shoulder. His eyes were half-closed.
Presley, who looked after him, pending the arrival of a
hack from Bonneville that was to take him home, knew
that he was in agony.

But this poser, this silly fellow, this cracker of jokes,
whom no one had ever taken very seriously, at the last
redeemed himself. When at length, the doctor had arrived, he had, for the first time, opened his eyes.

" I can wait," he said.   " Take Harran first."

And when at length, his turn had come, and while the
sweat rolled from his forehead as the doctor began probing for the bullet, he had reached out his free arm and
taken Presley's hand in his, gripping it harder and
harder, as the probe entered the wound. His breath
came short through his nostrils; his face, the face of a
comic actor, with its high cheek bones, bald forehead,
and salient ears, grew paler and paler, his great slit of a
mouth shut tight, but he uttered no groan.

When the worst anguish was over and he could find
breath to speak, his first words had been:

" Were any of the others badly hurt?"

As Presley stood by the door of the house after bringing in a pail of water for the doctor, he was aware of a
party of men who had struck off from the road on the
other side of the irrigating ditch and were advancing
cautiously into the field of wheat. He wondered what it

meant and Cutter, coming up at that moment, Presley
asked him if he knew.

"It's Delaney," said Cutter. "It seems that when he
was shot he crawled off into the wheat. They are looking for him there."

Presley had forgotten all about the buster and had
only a vague recollection of seeing him slide from his
horse at the beginning of the fight. Anxious to know
what had become of him, he hurried up and joined the
party of searchers.

"We better look out," said one of the young men,
"how we go fooling around in here. If he's alive yet
he's just as liable as not to think we're after him and
take a shot at us."

"I guess there ain't much fight left in him," another
answered. "Look at the wheat here."

"Lord! He's bled like a stuck pig."

"Here's his hat," abruptly exclaimed the leader of the
party. "He can't be far off. Let's call him."

They called repeatedly without getting any answer,
then proceeded cautiously. All at once the men in advance stopped so suddenly that those following car-
romed against them. There was an outburst of exclamation.

"Here he is!"

"Good Lord! Sure, that's him."

"Poor fellow, poor fellow."

The cow-puncher lay on his back, deep in the wheat,
his knees drawn up, his eyes wide open, his lips brown.
Rigidly gripped in one hand was his empty revolver.

The men, farm hands from the neighbouring ranches,
young fellows from Guadalajara, drew back in instinctive
repulsion. One at length ventured near, peering down
into the face.

"Is he dead?" inquired those in the rear.

" *I* don't know."

" Well, put your hand on his heart."

" No! I—I don't want to."

" What you afraid of ? "

" Well, I just don't want to touch him, that's all. It's bad luck. *You* feel his heart."

" You can't always tell by that."

" How can you tell, then? Pshaw, you fellows make me sick. Here, let me get there. I'll do it."

There was a long pause, as the other bent down and laid his hand on the cow-puncher's breast.

" Well? "

" I can't tell. Sometimes I think I feel it beat and sometimes I don't. I never saw a dead man before."

" Well, you can't tell by the heart."

" What's the good of talking so blame much. Dead or not, let's carry him back to the house."

Two or three ran back to the road for planks from the broken bridge. When they returned with these a litter was improvised, and throwing their coats over the body, the party carried it back to the road. The doctor was summoned and declared the cow-puncher to have been dead over half an hour.

" What did I tell you? " exclaimed one of the group.

" Well, I never said he wasn't dead," protested the other. " I only said you couldn't always tell by whether his heart beat or not."

But all at once there was a commotion. The wagon containing Mrs. Hooven, Minna, and little Hilda drove up.

" Eh, den, my men," cried Mrs. Hooven, wildly interrogating the faces of the crowd. " Whadt has happun? Sey, den, dose vellers, hev dey hurdt my men, eh, whadt? "

She sprang from the wagon, followed by Minna with

Hilda in her arms. The crowd bore back as they advanced, staring at them in silence.

"Eh, whadt has happun, whadt has happun?" wailed Mrs. Hooven, as she hurried on, her two hands out before her, the fingers spread wide. "Eh, Hooven, eh, my men, are you alle righdt?"

She burst into the house. Hooven's body had been removed to an adjoining room, the bedroom of the house, and to this room Mrs. Hooven—Minna still at her heels—proceeded, guided by an instinct born of the occasion. Those in the outside room, saying no word, made way for them. They entered, closing the door behind them, and through all the rest of that terrible day, no sound nor sight of them was had by those who crowded into and about that house of death. Of all the main actors of the tragedy of the fight in the ditch, they remained the least noted, obtruded themselves the least upon the world's observation. They were, for the moment, forgotten.

But by now Hooven's house was the centre of an enormous crowd. A vast concourse of people from Bonneville, from Guadalajara, from the ranches, swelled by the thousands who had that morning participated in the rabbit drive, surged about the place; men and women, young boys, young girls, farm hands, villagers, townspeople, ranchers, railroad employees, Mexicans, Spaniards, Portuguese. Presley, returning from the search for Delaney's body, had to fight his way to the house again.

And from all this multitude there rose an indefinable murmur. As yet, there was no menace in it, no anger. It was confusion merely, bewilderment, the first long-drawn "oh!" that greets the news of some great tragedy. The people had taken no thought as yet. Curiosity was their dominant impulse. Every one wanted to see what had been done; failing that, to hear of it, and failing that, to be near the scene of the affair. The crowd of people packed the road in front of the house for nearly a quarter of a mile in either direction. They balanced themselves upon the lower strands of the barbed wire fence in their effort to see over each others' shoulders; they stood on the seats of their carts, buggies, and farm wagons, a few even upon the saddles of their riding horses. They crowded, pushed, struggled, surged forward and back without knowing why, converging incessantly upon Hooven's house.

When, at length, Presley got to the gate, he found a carry-all drawn up before it. Between the gate and the door of the house a lane had been formed, and as he paused there a moment, a group of Leaguers, among whom were Garnett and Gethings, came slowly from the door carrying old Broderson in their arms. The doctor, bareheaded and in his shirt sleeves, squinting in the sunlight, attended them, repeating at every step:

" Slow, slow, take it easy, gentlemen."

Old Broderson was unconscious. His face was not pale, no bandages could be seen. With infinite precautions, the men bore him to the carry-all and deposited him on the back seat; the rain flaps were let down on one side to shut off the gaze of the multitude.

But at this point a moment of confusion ensued. Presley, because of half a dozen people who stood in his way, could not see what was going on. There were exclamations, hurried movements. The doctor uttered a sharp command and a man ran back to the house, returning on the instant with the doctor's satchel. By this time, Presley was close to the wheels of the carry-all and could see the doctor inside the vehicle bending over old Broderson.

" Here it is, here it is," exclaimed the man who had been sent to the house.

"I won't need it," answered the doctor, "he's dying now."

At the words a great hush widened throughout the throng near at hand. Some men took off their hats.

"Stand back," protested the doctor quietly, "stand back, good people, please."

The crowd bore back a little. In the silence, a woman began to sob. The seconds passed, then a minute. The horses of the carry-all shifted their feet and whisked their tails, driving off the flies. At length, the doctor got down from the carry-all, letting down the rain-flaps on that side as well.

"Will somebody go home with the body?" he asked. Gethings stepped forward and took his place by the driver. The carry-all drove away.

Presley reëntered the house. During his absence it had been cleared of all but one or two of the Leaguers, who had taken part in the fight. Hilma still sat on the bed with Annixter's head in her lap. S. Behrman, Ruggles, and all the railroad party had gone. Osterman had been taken away in a hack and the tablecloth over Dabney's body replaced with a sheet. But still unabated, agonised, raucous, came the sounds of Harran's breathing. Everything possible had already been done. For the moment it was out of the question to attempt to move him. His mother and father were at his side, Magnus, with a face of stone, his look fixed on those persistently twitching eyes, Annie Derrick crouching at her son's side, one of his hands in hers, fanning his face continually with the crumpled sheet of an old newspaper.

Presley on tip-toes joined the group, looking on attentively. One of the surgeons who had been called from Bonneville stood close by, watching Harran's face, his arms folded.

"How is he?" Presley whispered.

"He won't live," the other responded.

By degrees the choke and gurgle of the breathing became more irregular and the lids closed over the twitching eyes. All at once the breath ceased. Magnus shot an inquiring glance at the surgeon.

"He is dead, Mr. Derrick," the surgeon replied.

Annie Derrick, with a cry that rang through all the house, stretched herself over the body of her son, her head upon his breast, and the Governor's great shoulders bowed never to rise again.

"God help me and forgive me," he groaned.

Presley rushed from the house, beside himself with grief, with horror, with pity, and with mad, insensate rage. On the porch outside Caraher met him.

"Is he—is he—" began the saloon-keeper.

"Yes, he's dead," cried Presley. "They're all dead, murdered, shot down, dead, dead, all of them. Whose turn is next?"

"That's the way they killed my wife, Presley."

"Caraher," cried Presley, "give me your hand. I've been wrong all the time. The League is wrong. All the world is wrong. You are the only one of us all who is right. I'm with you from now on. *By God, I too, I'm a Red!*"

In course of time, a farm wagon from Bonneville arrived at Hooven's. The bodies of Annixter and Harran were placed in it, and it drove down the Lower Road towards the Los Muertos ranch houses.

The bodies of Delaney and Christian had already been carried to Guadalajara and thence taken by train to Bonneville.

Hilma followed the farm wagon in the Derricks' carry-all, with Magnus and his wife. During all that ride none of them spoke a word. It had been arranged that, since Quien Sabe was in the hands of the Railroad, Hilma

should come to Los Muertos. To that place also
Annixter's body was carried.

Later on in the day, when it was almost evening, the
undertaker's black wagon passed the Derricks' Home
ranch on its way from Hooven's and turned into the
county road towards Bonneville. The initial excitement
of the affair of the irrigating ditch had died down; the
crowd long since had dispersed. By the time the wagon
passed Caraher's saloon, the sun had set. Night was
coming on.

And the black wagon went on through the darkness,
unattended, ignored, solitary, carrying the dead body of
Dabney, the silent old man of whom nothing was known
but his name, who made no friends, whom nobody knew
or spoke to, who had come from no one knew whence and
who went no one knew whither.

Towards midnight of that same day, Mrs. Dyke was
awakened by the sounds of groaning in the room next to
hers. Magnus Derrick was not so occupied by Harran's
death that he could not think of others who were in distress, and when he had heard that Mrs. Dyke and Sidney,
like Hilma, had been turned out of Quien Sabe, he had
thrown open Los Muertos to them.

"Though," he warned them, "it is precarious hospi-
tality at the best."

Until late, Mrs. Dyke had sat up with Hilma, comforting her as best she could, rocking her to and fro in
her arms, crying with her, trying to quiet her, for once
having given way to her grief, Hilma wept with a terrible anguish and a violence that racked her from head to
foot, and at last, worn out, a little child again, had
sobbed herself to sleep in the older woman's arms, and
as a little child, Mrs. Dyke had put her to bed and had
retired herself.

Aroused a few hours later by the sounds of a distress

that was physical, as well as mental, Mrs. Dyke hurried into Hilma's room, carrying the lamp with her.

Mrs. Dyke needed no enlightenment. She woke Presley and besought him to telephone to Bonneville at once, summoning a doctor. That night Hilma in great pain suffered a miscarriage.

Presley did not close his eyes once during the night; he did not even remove his clothes. Long after the doctor had departed and that house of tragedy had quieted down, he still remained in his place by the open window of his little room, looking off across the leagues of growing wheat, watching the slow kindling of the dawn. Horror weighed intolerably upon him. Monstrous things, huge, terrible, whose names he knew only too well, whirled at a gallop through his imagination, or rose spectral and grisly before the eyes of his mind. Harran dead, Annixter dead, Broderson dead, Osterman, perhaps, even at that moment dying. Why, these men had made up his world. Annixter had been his best friend, Harran, his almost daily companion; Broderson and Osterman were familiar to him as brothers. They were all his associates, his good friends, the group was his environment, belonging to his daily life. And he, standing there in the dust of the road by the irrigating ditch, had seen them shot. He found himself suddenly at his table, the candle burning at his elbow, his journal before him, writing swiftly, the desire for expression, the craving for outlet to the thoughts that clamoured tumultuous at his brain, never more insistent, more imperious. Thus he wrote:

" Dabney dead, Hooven dead, Harran dead, Annixter dead, Broderson dead, Osterman dying, S. Behrman alive, successful; the Railroad in possession of Quien Sabe. I saw them shot. Not twelve hours since I stood there at the irrigating ditch. Ah, that terrible moment of horror

and confusion! powder smoke—flashing pistol barrels—
blood stains—rearing horses—men staggering to their
death—Christian in a horrible posture, one rigid leg high
in the air across his saddle—Broderson falling sideways
into the ditch—Osterman laying himself down, his head
on his arms, as if tired, tired out. These things, I have
seen them. The picture of this day's work is from hence-
forth part of my mind, part of *me*. They have done it,
S. Behrman and the owners of the railroad have done
it, while all the world looked on, while the people of
these United States looked on. Oh, come now and try
your theories upon us, us of the ranchos, us, who have
suffered, us, who *know*. Oh, talk to *us* now of the
'rights of Capital,' talk to *us* of the Trust, talk to *us* of
the 'equilibrium between the classes.' Try your ingenious ideas upon us. *We Know*. I cannot tell whether or
not your theories are excellent. I do not know if your
ideas are plausible. I do not know how practical is your
scheme of society. I do not know if the Railroad has a
right to our lands, but I *do* know that Harran is dead,
that Annixter is dead, that Broderson is dead, that Hooven is dead, that Osterman is dying, and that S. Behrman
is alive, successful, triumphant; that he has ridden into
possession of a principality over the dead bodies of five
men shot down by his hired associates.

"I can see the outcome. The Railroad will prevail.
The Trust will overpower us. Here in this corner of a
great nation, here, on the edge of the continent, here, in
this valley of the West, far from the great centres, isolated, remote, lost, the great iron hand crushes life from
us, crushes liberty and the pursuit of happiness from us,
and our little struggles, our moment's convulsion of
death agony causes not one jar in the vast, clashing machinery of the nation's life; a fleck of grit in the wheels,
perhaps, a grain of sand in the cogs—the momentary

creak of the axle is the mother's wail of bereavement, the wife's cry of anguish—and the great wheel turns, spinning smooth again, even again, and the tiny impediment of a second, scarce noticed, is forgotten. Make the people believe that the faint tremour in their great engine is a menace to its function? What a folly to think of it. Tell them of the danger and they will laugh at you. Tell them, five years from now, the story of the fight between the League of the San Joaquin and the Railroad and it will not be believed. What! a pitched battle between Farmer and Railroad, a battle that cost the lives of seven men? Impossible, it could not have happened. Your story is fiction—is exaggerated.

" Yet it is Lexington—God help us, God enlighten us, God rouse us from our lethargy—it is Lexington; farmers with guns in their hands fighting for Liberty. Is our State of California the only one that has its ancient and hereditary foe? Are there no other Trusts between the oceans than this of the Pacific and Southwestern Railroad? Ask yourselves, you of the Middle West, ask yourselves, you of the North, ask yourselves, you of the East, ask yourselves, you of the South—ask yourselves, every citizen of every State from Maine to Mexico, from the Dakotas to the Carolinas, have you not the monster in your boundaries? If it is not a Trust of transportation, it is only another head of the same Hydra. Is not our death struggle typical? Is it not one of many, is it not symbolical of the great and terrible conflict that is going on everywhere in these United States? Ah, you people, blind, bound, tricked, betrayed, can you not see it? Can you not see how the monsters have plundered your treasures and holding them in the grip of their iron claws, dole them out to you only at the price of your blood, at the price of the lives of your wives and your little children? You give your babies to Moloch for the loaf of bread you have kneaded yourselves. You offer your starved wives to Juggernaut for the iron nail you have yourselves compounded."

He spent the night over his journal, writing down such thoughts as these or walking the floor from wall to wall, or, seized at times with unreasoning horror and blind rage, flinging himself face downward upon his bed, vowing with inarticulate cries that neither S. Behrman nor Shelgrim should ever live to consummate their triumph.

Morning came and with it the daily papers and news. Presley did not even glance at the "Mercury." Bonneville published two other daily journals that professed to voice the will and reflect the temper of the people and these he read eagerly.

Osterman was yet alive and there were chances of his recovery. The League—some three hundred of its members had gathered at Bonneville over night and were patrolling the streets and, still resolved to keep the peace, were even guarding the railroad shops and buildings. Furthermore, the Leaguers had issued manifestoes, urging all citizens to preserve law and order, yet summoning an indignation meeting to be convened that afternoon at the City Opera House.

It appeared from the newspapers that those who obstructed the marshal in the discharge of his duty could be proceeded against by the District Attorney on information or by bringing the matter before the Grand Jury. But the Grand Jury was not at that time in session, and it was known that there were no funds in the marshal's office to pay expenses for the summoning of jurors or the serving of processes. S. Behrman and Ruggles in interviews stated that the Railroad withdrew entirely from the fight; the matter now, according to them, was between the Leaguers and the United States Government; they washed their hands of the whole business.

The ranchers could settle with Washington. But it seemed that Congress had recently forbade the use of troops for civil purposes; the whole matter of the League-Railroad contest was evidently for the moment to be left in *statu quo*.

But to Presley's mind the most important piece of news that morning was the report of the action of the Railroad upon hearing of the battle.

Instantly Bonneville had been isolated. Not a single local train was running, not one of the through trains made any halt at the station. The mails were not moved. Further than this, by some arrangement difficult to understand, the telegraph operators at Bonneville and Guadalajara, acting under orders, refused to receive any telegrams except those emanating from railway officials. The story of the fight, the story creating the first impression, was to be told to San Francisco and the outside world by S. Behrman, Ruggles, and the local P. and S. W. agents.

An hour before breakfast, the undertakers arrived and took charge of the bodies of Harran and Annixter. Presley saw neither Hilma, Magnus, nor Mrs. Derrick. The doctor came to look after Hilma. He breakfasted with Mrs. Dyke and Presley, and from him Presley learned that Hilma would recover both from the shock of her husband's death and from her miscarriage of the previous night.

"She ought to have her mother with her," said the physician. "She does nothing but call for her or beg to be allowed to go to her. I have tried to get a wire through to Mrs. Tree, but the company will not take it, and even if I could get word to her, how could she get down here? There are no trains."

But Presley found that it was impossible for him to stay at Los Muertos that day. Gloom and the shadow of tragedy brooded heavy over the place. A great silence pervaded everything, a silence broken only by the subdued coming and going of the undertaker and his assistants. When Presley, having resolved to go into Bonneville, came out through the doorway of the house, he found the undertaker tying a long strip of crape to the bell-handle.

Presley saddled his pony and rode into town. By this time, after long hours of continued reflection upon one subject, a sombre brooding malevolence, a deep-seated desire of revenge, had grown big within his mind. The first numbness had passed off; familiarity with what had been done had blunted the edge of horror, and now the impulse of retaliation prevailed. At first, the sullen anger of defeat, the sense of outrage, had only smouldered, but the more he brooded, the fiercer flamed his rage. Sudden paroxysms of wrath gripped him by the throat; abrupt outbursts of fury injected his eyes with blood. He ground his teeth, his mouth filled with curses, his hands clenched till they grew white and bloodless. Was the Railroad to triumph then in the end? After all those months of preparation, after all those grandiloquent resolutions, after all the arrogant presumption of the League! The League! what a farce; what had it amounted to when the crisis came? Was the Trust to crush them all so easily? Was S. Behrman to swallow Los Muertos? S. Behrman! Presley saw him plainly, huge, rotund, white; saw his jowl tremulous and obese, the roll of fat over his collar sprinkled with sparse hairs, the great stomach with its brown linen vest and heavy watch chain of hollow links, clinking against the buttons of imitation pearl. And this man was to crush Magnus Derrick—had already stamped the life from such men as Harran and Annixter. This man, in the name of the Trust, was to grab Los Muertos as he had grabbed Quien Sabe, and after Los

Muertos, Broderson's ranch, then Osterman's, then others, and still others, the whole valley, the whole State.

Presley beat his forehead with his clenched fist as he rode on.

" No," he cried, " no, kill him, kill him, kill him with my hands."

The idea of it put him beside himself. Oh, to sink his fingers deep into the white, fat throat of the man, to clutch like iron into the great puffed jowl of him, to wrench out the life, to batter it out, strangle it out, to pay him back for the long years of extortion and oppression, to square accounts for bribed jurors, bought judges, corrupted legislatures, to have justice for the trick of the Ranchers' Railroad Commission, the charlatanism of the " ten per cent. cut," the ruin of Dyke, the seizure of Quien Sabe, the murder of Harran, the assassination of Annixter!

It was in such mood that he reached Caraher's. The saloon-keeper had just opened his place and was standing in his doorway, smoking his pipe. Presley dismounted and went in and the two had a long talk.

When, three hours later, Presley came out of the saloon and rode on towards Bonneville, his face was very pale, his lips shut tight, resolute, determined. His manner was that of a man whose mind is made up.

The hour for the mass meeting at the Opera House had been set for one o'clock, but long before noon the street in front of the building and, in fact, all the streets in its vicinity, were packed from side to side with a shifting, struggling, surging, and excited multitude. There were few women in the throng, but hardly a single male inhabitant of either Bonneville or Guadalajara was absent. Men had even come from Visalia and Pixley. It was no longer the crowd of curiosity seekers that had thronged around Hooven's place by the irrigating ditch;

the People were no longer confused, bewildered. A full realisation of just what had been done the day before was clear now in the minds of all. Business was suspended; nearly all the stores were closed. Since early morning the members of the League had put in an appearance and rode from point to point, their rifles across their saddle pommels. Then, by ten o'clock, the streets had begun to fill up, the groups on the corners grew and merged into one another; pedestrians, unable to find room on the sidewalks, took to the streets. Hourly the crowd increased till shoulders touched and elbows, till free circulation became impeded, then congested, then impossible. The crowd, a solid mass, was wedged tight from store front to store front. And from all this throng, this single unit, this living, breathing organism—the People—there rose a droning, terrible note. It was not yet the wild, fierce clamour of riot and insurrection, shrill, high pitched; but it was a beginning, the growl of the awakened brute, feeling the iron in its flank, heaving up its head with bared teeth, the throat vibrating to the long, indrawn snarl of wrath.

Thus the forenoon passed, while the people, their bulk growing hourly vaster, kept to the streets, moving slowly backward and forward, oscillating in the grooves of the thoroughfares, the steady, low-pitched growl rising continually into the hot, still air.

Then, at length, about twelve o'clock, the movement of the throng assumed definite direction. It set towards the Opera House. Presley, who had left his pony at the City livery stable, found himself caught in the current and carried slowly forward in its direction. His arms were pinioned to his sides by the press, the crush against his body was all but rib-cracking, he could hardly draw his breath. All around him rose and fell wave after wave of faces, hundreds upon hundreds, thousands upon thousands, red, lowering, sullen. All were set in one direction and slowly, slowly they advanced, crowding closer, till they almost touched one another. For reasons that were inexplicable, great, tumultuous heavings, like ground-swells of an incoming tide, surged over and through the multitude. At times, Presley, lifted from his feet, was swept back, back, back, with the crowd, till the entrance of the Opera House was half a block away; then, the returning billow beat back again and swung him along, gasping, staggering, clutching, till he was landed once more in the vortex of frantic action in front of the foyer. Here the waves were shorter, quicker, the crushing pressure on all sides of his body left him without strength to utter the cry that rose to his lips; then, suddenly the whole mass of struggling, stamping, fighting, writhing men about him seemed, as it were, to rise, to lift, multitudinous, swelling, gigantic. A mighty rush dashed Presley forward in its leap. There was a moment's whirl of confused sights, congested faces, opened mouths, bloodshot eyes, clutching hands; a moment's outburst of furious sound, shouts, cheers, oaths; a moment's jam wherein Presley veritably believed his ribs must snap like pipestems and he was carried, dazed, breathless, helpless, an atom on the crest of a storm-driven wave, up the steps of the Opera House, on into the vestibule, through the doors, and at last into the auditorium of the house itself.

There was a mad rush for places; men disdaining the aisle, stepped from one orchestra chair to another, striding over the backs of seats, leaving the print of dusty feet upon the red plush cushions. In a twinkling the house was filled from stage to topmost gallery. The aisles were packed solid, even on the edge of the stage itself men were sitting, a black fringe on either side of the footlights.

35

The curtain was up, disclosing a half-set scene,—the flats, leaning at perilous angles,—that represented some sort of terrace, the pavement, alternate squares of black and white marble, while red, white, and yellow flowers were represented as growing from urns and vases. A long, double row of chairs stretched across the scene from wing to wing, flanking a table covered with a red cloth, on which was set a pitcher of water and a speaker's gavel.

Promptly these chairs were filled up with members of the League, the audience cheering as certain well-known figures made their appearance—Garnett of the Ruby ranch, Gethings of the San Pablo, Keast of the ranch of the same name, Chattern of the Bonanza, elderly men, bearded, slow of speech, deliberate.

Garnett opened the meeting; his speech was plain, straightforward, matter-of-fact. He simply told what had happened. He announced that certain resolutions were to be drawn up. He introduced the next speaker.

This one pleaded for moderation. He was conservative. All along he had opposed the idea of armed resistance except as the very last resort. He "deplored" the terrible affair of yesterday. He begged the people to wait in patience, to attempt no more violence. He informed them that armed guards of the League were, at that moment, patrolling Los Muertos, Broderson's, and Osterman's. It was well known that the United States marshal confessed himself powerless to serve the writs. There would be no more bloodshed.

"We have had," he continued, "bloodshed enough, and I want to say right here that I am not so sure but what yesterday's terrible affair might have been avoided. A gentleman whom we all esteem, who from the first has been our recognised leader, is, at this moment, mourning the loss of a young son, killed before his eyes. God knows that I sympathise, as do we all, in the affliction of our President. I am sorry for him. My heart goes out to him in this hour of distress, but, at the same time, the position of the League must be defined. We owe it to ourselves, we owe it to the people of this county. The League armed for the very purpose of preserving the peace, not of breaking it. We believed that with six hundred armed and drilled men at our disposal, ready to muster at a moment's call, we could so overawe any attempt to expel us from our lands that such an attempt would not be made until the cases pending before the Supreme Court had been decided. If when the enemy appeared in our midst yesterday they had been met by six hundred rifles, it is not conceivable that the issue would have been forced. No fight would have ensued, and to-day we would not have to mourn the deaths of four of our fellow-citizens. A mistake has been made and we of the League must not be held responsible."

The speaker sat down amidst loud applause from the Leaguers and less pronounced demonstrations on the part of the audience.

A second Leaguer took his place, a tall, clumsy man, half-rancher, half-politician.

"I want to second what my colleague has just said," he began. "This matter of resisting the marshal when he tried to put the Railroad dummies in possession on the ranches around here, was all talked over in the committee meetings of the League long ago. It never was our intention to fire a single shot. No such absolute authority as was assumed yesterday was delegated to anybody. Our esteemed President is all right, but we all know that he is a man who loves authority and who likes to go his own gait without accounting to anybody. We—the rest of us Leaguers—never were informed as to what was going on. We supposed, of course, that watch was being

kept on the Railroad so as we wouldn't be taken by surprise as we were yesterday. And it seems no watch was
kept at all, or if there was, it was mighty ineffective.
Our idea was to forestall any movement on the part of
the Railroad and then when we knew the marshal was
coming down, to call a meeting of our Executive Committee and decide as to what should be done. We ought
to have had time to call out the whole League. Instead
of that, what happens? While we're all off chasing rabbits, the Railroad is allowed to steal a march on us and
when it is too late, a handful of Leaguers is got together
and a fight is precipitated and our men killed. *I'm* sorry
for our President, too. No one is more so, but I want to
put myself on record as believing he did a hasty and in-
considerate thing. If he had managed right, he could
have had six hundred men to oppose the Railroad and
there would not have been any gun fight or any killing.
He *didn't* manage right and there *was* a killing and I
don't see as how the League ought to be held responsible.
The idea of the League, the whole reason why it was
organised, was to protect *all* the ranches of this valley
from the Railroad, and it looks to me as if the lives of our
fellow-citizens had been sacrificed, not in defending *all*
of our ranches, but just in defence of one of them—Los
Muertos—the one that Mr. Derrick owns."

The speaker had no more than regained his seat when
a man was seen pushing his way from the back of the
stage towards Garnett. He handed the rancher a note,
at the same time whispering in his ear. Garnett read the
note, then came forward to the edge of the stage, holding
up his hand. When the audience had fallen silent he
said:

"I have just received sad news. Our friend and
fellow-citizen, Mr. Osterman, died this morning between
eleven and twelve o'clock."

Instantly there was a roar. Every man in the building rose to his feet, shouting, gesticulating. The roar increased, the Opera House trembled to it, the gas jets in the lighted chandeliers vibrated to it. It was a raucous howl of execration, a bellow of rage, inarticulate, deafening.

A tornado of confusion swept whirling from wall to wall and the madness of the moment seized irresistibly upon Presley. He forgot himself; he no longer was master of his emotions or his impulses. All at once he found himself upon the stage, facing the audience, flaming with excitement, his imagination on fire, his arms uplifted in fierce, wild gestures, words leaping to his mind in a torrent that could not be withheld.

"One more dead," he cried, "one more. Harran dead, Annixter dead, Broderson dead, Dabney dead, Osterman dead, Hooven dead; shot down, killed, killed in the defence of their homes, killed in the defence of their rights, killed for the sake of liberty. How long must it go on? How long must we suffer? Where is the end; what is the end? How long must the iron-hearted monster feed on our life's blood? How long must this terror of steam and steel ride upon our necks? Will you never be satisfied, will you never relent, you, our masters, you, our lords, you, our kings, you, our task-masters, you, our Pharoahs. Will you never listen to that command '*Let My people go*'? Oh, that cry ringing down the ages. Hear it, hear it. It is the voice of the Lord God speaking in his prophets. Hear it, hear it—'Let My people go!' Rameses heard it in his pylons at Thebes, Cæsar heard it on the Palatine, the Bourbon Louis heard it at Versailles, Charles Stuart heard it at Whitehall, the white Czar heard it in the Kremlin,—'*Let My people go.*' It is the cry of the nations, the great voice of the centuries; everywhere it is raised. The voice of God is the voice of the People. The people cry out 'Let us, the People, God's people, go.' You, our masters, you, our kings, you, our tyrants, don't you hear us? Don't you hear God speaking in us? Will you never let us go? How long at length will you abuse our patience? How long will you drive us? How long will you harass us? Will nothing daunt you? Does nothing check you? Do you not know that to ignore our cry too long is to wake the Red Terror? Rameses refused to listen to it and perished miserably. Cæsar refused to listen and was stabbed in the Senate House. The Bourbon Louis refused to listen and died on the guillotine; Charles Stuart refused to listen and died on the block; the white Czar refused to listen and was blown up in his own capital. Will you let it come to that? Will you drive us to it? We who boast of our land of freedom, we who live in the country of liberty?

"Go on as you have begun and it *will* come to that. Turn a deaf ear to that cry of 'Let My people go' too long and another cry will be raised, that you cannot choose but hear, a cry that you cannot shut out. It will be the cry of the man on the street, the '*à la Bastille*' that wakes the Red Terror and unleashes Revolution. Harassed, plundered, exasperated, desperate, the people will turn at last as they have turned so many, many times before. You, our lords, you, our task-masters, you, our kings; you have caught your Samson, you have made his strength your own. You have shorn his head; you have put out his eyes; you have set him to turn your millstones, to grind the grist for your mills; you have made him a shame and a mock. Take care, oh, as you love your lives, take care, lest some day calling upon the Lord his God he reach not out his arms for the pillars of your temples."

The audience, at first bewildered, confused by this unexpected invective, suddenly took fire at his last words. There was a roar of applause; then, more significant than mere vociferation, Presley's listeners, as he began to speak again, grew suddenly silent. His next sentences were uttered in the midst of a profound stillness.

"They own us, these task-masters of ours; they own our homes, they own our legislatures. We cannot escape from them. There is no redress. We are told we can defeat them by the ballot-box. They own the ballot-box. We are told that we must look to the courts for redress; they own the courts. We know them for what they are,—ruffians in politics, ruffians in finance, ruffians in law, ruffians in trade, bribers, swindlers, and tricksters. No outrage too great to daunt them, no petty larceny too small to shame them; despoiling a government treasury of a million dollars, yet picking the pockets of a farm hand of the price of a loaf of bread.

"They swindle a nation of a hundred million and call it Financiering; they levy a blackmail and call it Commerce; they corrupt a legislature and call it Politics; they bribe a judge and call it Law; they hire blacklegs to carry out their plans and call it Organisation; they prostitute the honour of a State and call it Competition.

"And this is America. We fought Lexington to free ourselves; we fought Gettysburg to free others. Yet the yoke remains; we have only shifted it to the other shoulder. We talk of liberty—oh, the farce of it, oh, the folly of it! We tell ourselves and teach our children that we have achieved liberty, that we no longer need fight for it. Why, the fight is just beginning and so long as our conception of liberty remains as it is to-day, it will continue.

"For we conceive of Liberty in the statues we raise to her as a beautiful woman, crowned, victorious, in bright armour and white robes, a light in her uplifted hand—a serene, calm, conquering goddess. Oh, the farce of it, oh, the folly of it! Liberty is *not* a crowned goddess, beautiful, in spotless garments, victorious, supreme. Liberty is the Man In the Street, a terrible figure, rushing through powder smoke, fouled with the mud and ordure of the gutter, bloody, rampant, brutal, yelling curses, in one hand a smoking rifle, in the other, a blazing torch.

"Freedom is *not* given free to any who ask; Liberty is not born of the gods. She is a child of the People, born in the very height and heat of battle, born from death, stained with blood, grimed with powder. And she grows to be not a goddess, but a Fury, a fearful figure, slaying friend and foe alike, raging, insatiable, merciless, the Red Terror."

Presley ceased speaking. Weak, shaking, scarcely knowing what he was about, he descended from the stage. A prolonged explosion of applause followed, the Opera House roaring to the roof, men cheering, stamping, waving their hats. But it was not intelligent applause. Instinctively as he made his way out, Presley knew that, after all, he had not once held the hearts of his audience. He had talked as he would have written; for all his scorn of literature, he had been literary. The men who listened to him, ranchers, country people, store-keepers, attentive though they were, were not once sympathetic. Vaguely they had felt that here was something which other men—more educated—would possibly consider eloquent. They applauded vociferously but perfunctorily, in order to appear to understand.

Presley, for all his love of the people, saw clearly for one moment that he was an outsider to their minds. He had not helped them nor their cause in the least; he never would.

Disappointed, bewildered, ashamed, he made his way slowly from the Opera House and stood on the steps outside, thoughtful, his head bent.

He had failed, thus he told himself.   In that moment of crisis, that at the time he believed had been an inspiration, he had failed.   The people would not consider him, would not believe that he could do them service.   Then suddenly he seemed to remember.   The resolute set of his lips returned once more.   Pushing his way through the crowded streets, he went on towards the stable where he had left his pony.

Meanwhile, in the Opera House, a great commotion had occurred.   Magnus Derrick had appeared.

Only a sense of enormous responsibility, of gravest duty could have prevailed upon Magnus to have left his house and the dead body of his son that day.   But he was the President of the League, and never since its organisation had a meeting of such importance as this one been held.   He had been in command at the irrigating ditch the day before.   It was he who had gathered the handful of Leaguers together.   It was he who must bear the responsibility of the fight.

When he had entered the Opera House, making his way down the central aisle towards the stage, a loud disturbance had broken out, partly applause, partly a meaningless uproar.   Many had pressed forward to shake his hand, but others were not found wanting who, formerly his staunch supporters, now scenting opposition in the air, held back, hesitating, afraid to compromise themselves by adhering to the fortunes of a man whose actions might be discredited by the very organisation of which he was the head.

Declining to take the chair of presiding officer which Garnett offered him, the Governor withdrew to an angle of the stage, where he was joined by Keast.

This one, still unalterably devoted to Magnus, acquainted him briefly with the tenor of the speeches that had been made.

"I am ashamed of them, Governor," he protested indignantly, "to lose their nerve now! To fail you now! it makes my blood boil. If you had succeeded yesterday, if all had gone well, do you think we would have heard of any talk of 'assumption of authority,' or 'acting without advice and consent'? As if there was any time to call a meeting of the Executive Committee. If you hadn't acted as you did, the whole county would have been grabbed by the Railroad. Get up, Governor, and bring 'em all up standing. Just tear 'em all to pieces, show 'em that you are the head, the boss. That's what they need. That killing yesterday has shaken the nerve clean out of them."

For the instant the Governor was taken all aback. What, his lieutenants were failing him? What, he was to be questioned, interpolated upon yesterday's "irrepressible conflict"? Had disaffection appeared in the ranks of the League—at this, of all moments? He put from him his terrible grief. The cause was in danger. At the instant he was the President of the League only, the chief, the master. A royal anger surged within him, a wide, towering scorn of opposition. He would crush this disaffection in its incipiency, would vindicate himself and strengthen the cause at one and the same time. He stepped forward and stood in the speaker's place, turning partly toward the audience, partly toward the assembled Leaguers.

"Gentlemen of the League," he began, "citizens of Bonneville——"

But at once the silence in which the Governor had begun to speak was broken by a shout. It was as though his words had furnished a signal. In a certain quarter of the gallery, directly opposite, a man arose, and in a voice partly of derision, partly of defiance, cried out:

"How about the bribery of those two delegates at

Sacramento? Tell us about that. That's what we want to hear about."

A great confusion broke out. The first cry was repeated not only by the original speaker, but by a whole group of which he was but a part. Others in the audience, however, seeing in the disturbance only the clamour of a few Railroad supporters, attempted to howl them down, hissing vigorously and exclaiming:

"Put 'em out, put 'em out."

"Order, order," called Garnett, pounding with his gavel. The whole Opera House was in an uproar.

But the interruption of the Governor's speech was evidently not unpremeditated. It began to look like a deliberate and planned attack. Persistently, doggedly, the group in the gallery vociferated:

"Tell us how you bribed the delegates at Sacramento. Before you throw mud at the Railroad, let's see if you are clean yourself."

"Put 'em out, put 'em out."

"Briber, briber—Magnus Derrick, unconvicted briber! Put *him* out."

Keast, beside himself with anger, pushed down the aisle underneath where the recalcitrant group had its place and, shaking his fist, called up at them:

"You were paid to break up this meeting. If you have anything to say, you will be afforded the opportunity, but if you do not let the gentleman proceed, the police will be called upon to put you out."

But at this, the man who had raised the first shout leaned over the balcony rail, and, his face flaming with wrath, shouted:

"*Yah!* talk to me of your police. Look out we don't call on them first to arrest your President for bribery. You and your howl about law and justice and corruption! Here"—he turned to the audience—"read about him, read the story of how the Sacramento convention was bought by Magnus Derrick, President of the San Joaquin League. Here's the facts printed and proved."

With the words, he stooped down and from under his seat dragged forth a great package of extra editions of the "Bonneville Mercury," not an hour off the presses. Other equally large bundles of the paper appeared in the hands of the surrounding group. The strings were cut and in handfuls and armfuls the papers were flung out over the heads of the audience underneath. The air was full of the flutter of the newly printed sheets. They swarmed over the rim of the gallery like clouds of monstrous, winged insects, settled upon the heads and into the hands of the audience, were passed swiftly from man to man, and within five minutes of the first outbreak every one in the Opera House had read Genslinger's detailed and substantiated account of Magnus Derrick's "deal" with the political bosses of the Sacramento convention.

Genslinger, after pocketing the Governor's hush money, had "sold him out."

Keast, one quiver of indignation, made his way back upon the stage. The Leaguers were in wild confusion. Half the assembly of them were on their feet, bewildered, shouting vaguely. From proscenium wall to foyer, the Opera House was a tumult of noise. The gleam of the thousands of the "Mercury" extras was like the flash of white caps on a troubled sea.

Keast faced the audience.

"Liars," he shouted, striving with all the power of his voice to dominate the clamour, " liars and slanderers. Your paper is the paid organ of the corporation. You have not one shadow of proof to back you up. Do you choose this, of all times, to heap your calumny upon the head of an honourable gentleman, already prostrated by your murder of his son? Proofs—we demand your proofs!"

"We've got the very assemblymen themselves," came back the answering shout. "Let Derrick speak. Where is he hiding? If this is a lie, let him deny it. Let *him* *disprove* the charge."

"Derrick, Derrick," thundered the Opera House.

Keast wheeled about. Where was Magnus? He was not in sight upon the stage. He had disappeared. Crowding through the throng of Leaguers, Keast got from off the stage into the wings. Here the crowd was no less dense. Nearly every one had a copy of the "Mercury." It was being read aloud to groups here and there, and once Keast overheard the words, "Say, I wonder if this is true, after all?"

"Well, and even if it was," cried Keast, turning upon the speaker, "we should be the last ones to kick. In any case, it was done for our benefit. It elected the Ranchers' Commission."

"A lot of benefit we got out of the Ranchers' Commission," retorted the other.

"And then," protested a third speaker, "that ain't the way to do—if he *did* do it—bribing legislatures. Why, we were bucking against corrupt politics. We couldn't afford to be corrupt."

Keast turned away with a gesture of impatience. He pushed his way farther on. At last, opening a small door in a hallway back of the stage, he came upon Magnus.

The room was tiny. It was a dressing-room. Only two nights before it had been used by the leading actress of a comic opera troupe which 'had played for three nights at Bonneville. A tattered sofa and limping toilet table occupied a third of the space. The air was heavy with the smell of stale grease paint, ointments, and sachet.

Faded photographs of young women in tights and gauzes ornamented the mirror and the walls. Underneath the sofa was an old pair of corsets. The spangled skirt of a pink dress, turned inside out, hung against the wall.

And in the midst of such environment, surrounded by an excited group of men who gesticulated and shouted in his very face, pale, alert, agitated, his thin lips pressed tightly together, stood Magnus Derrick.

"Here," cried Keast, as he entered, closing the door behind him, "where's the Governor? Here, Magnus, I've been looking for you. The crowd has gone wild out there. You've got to talk 'em down. Come out there and give those blacklegs the lie. They are saying you are hiding."

But before Magnus could reply, Garnett turned to Keast.

"Well, that's what we want him to do, and he won't do it."

"Yes, yes," cried the half-dozen men who crowded around Magnus, "yes, that's what we want him to do."

Keast turned to Magnus.

"Why, what's all this, Governor?" he exclaimed. "You've *got* to answer that. Hey? why don't you give 'em the lie?"

"I—I," Magnus loosened the collar about his throat, "it is a lie. I will not stoop—I would not—would be— it would be beneath my—my—it would be beneath me."

Keast stared in amazement. Was this the Great Man, the Leader, indomitable, of Roman integrity, of Roman valour, before whose voice whole conventions had quailed? Was it possible he was *afraid* to face those hired villifiers?

"Well, how about this?" demanded Garnett suddenly. "It *is* a lie, isn't it? That Commission was elected honestly, wasn't it?"

"How dare you, sir!" Magnus burst out. "How dare you question me—call me to account! Please understand, sir, that I tolerate——"

"Oh, quit it!" cried a voice from the group. "You can't scare us, Derrick. That sort of talk was well enough once, but it don't go any more. We want a yes or no answer."

It was gone—that old-time power of mastery, that faculty of command. The ground crumbled beneath his feet. Long since it had been, by his own hand, undermined. Authority was gone. Why keep up this miserable sham any longer? Could they not read the lie in his face, in his voice? What a folly to maintain the wretched pretence! He had failed. He was ruined. Harran was gone. His ranch would soon go; his money was gone. Lyman was worse than dead. His own honour had been prostituted. Gone, gone, everything he held dear, gone, lost, and swept away in that fierce struggle. And suddenly and all in a moment the last remaining shells of the fabric of his being, the sham that had stood already wonderfully long, cracked and collapsed.

"Was the Commission honestly elected?" insisted Garnett. "Were the delegates—did you bribe the delegates?"

"We were obliged to shut our eyes to means," faltered Magnus. "There was no other way to—" Then suddenly and with the last dregs of his resolution, he concluded with: "Yes, I gave them two thousand dollars each."

"Oh, hell! Oh, my God!" exclaimed Keast, sitting swiftly down upon the ragged sofa.

There was a long silence. A sense of poignant embarrassment descended upon those present. No one knew what to say or where to look. Garnett, with a laboured attempt at nonchalance, murmured:

"I see. Well, that's what I was trying to get at. Yes, I see."

"Well," said Gethings at length, bestirring himself, "I guess *I'll* go home."

There was a movement. The group broke up, the men making for the door. One by one they went out. The last to go was Keast. He came up to Magnus and shook the Governor's limp hand.

"Good-bye, Governor," he said. "I'll see you again pretty soon. Don't let this discourage you. They'll come around all right after a while. So long."

He went out, shutting the door.

And seated in the one chair of the room, Magnus Derrick remained a long time, looking at his face in the cracked mirror that for so many years had reflected the painted faces of soubrettes, in this atmosphere of stale perfume and mouldy rice powder.

It had come—his fall, his ruin. After so many years of integrity and honest battle, his life had ended here— in an actress's dressing-room, deserted by his friends, his son murdered, his dishonesty known, an old man, broken, discarded, discredited, and abandoned.

Before nightfall of that day, Bonneville was further excited by an astonishing bit of news. S. Behrman lived in a detached house at some distance from the town, surrounded by a grove of live oak and eucalyptus trees. At a little after half-past six, as he was sitting down to his supper, a bomb was thrown through the window of his dining-room, exploding near the doorway leading into the hall. The room was wrecked and nearly every window of the house shattered. By a miracle, S. Behrman, himself, remained untouched.

VIII

On a certain afternoon in the early part of July, about a month after the fight at the irrigating ditch and the mass meeting at Bonneville, Cedarquist, at the moment opening his mail in his office in San Francisco, was genuinely surprised to receive a visit from Presley.

"Well, upon my word, Pres," exclaimed the manufacturer, as the young man came in through the door that the office boy held open for him, "upon my word, have you been sick? Sit down, my boy. Have a glass of sherry. I always keep a bottle here."

Presley accepted the wine and sank into the depths of a great leather chair near by.

"Sick?" he answered. "Yes, I have been sick. I'm sick now. I'm gone to pieces, sir."

His manner was the extreme of listlessness—the listlessness of great fatigue. "Well, well," observed the other. "I'm right sorry to hear that. What's the trouble, Pres?"

"Oh, nerves mostly, I suppose, and my head, and insomnia, and weakness, a general collapse all along the line, the doctor tells me. 'Over-cerebration,' he says; 'over-excitement.' I fancy I rather narrowly missed brain fever."

"Well, I can easily suppose it," answered Cedarquist gravely, "after all you have been through."

Presley closed his eyes—they were sunken in circles of dark brown flesh—and pressed a thin hand to the back of his head.

"It is a nightmare," he murmured. "A frightful night-mare, and it's not over yet. You have heard of it all only through the newspaper reports. But down there, at Bonneville, at Los Muertos—oh, you can have no idea of it, of the misery caused by the defeat of the ranchers and by this decision of the Supreme Court that dis-possesses them all. We had gone on hoping to the last that we would win there. We had thought that in the Supreme Court of the United States, at least, we could find justice. And the news of its decision was the worst, last blow of all. For Magnus it was the last—positively the very last."

"Poor, poor Derrick," murmured Cedarquist. "Tell me about him, Pres. How does he take it? What is he going to do?"

"It beggars him, sir. He sunk a great deal more than any of us believed in his ranch, when he resolved to turn off most of the tenants and farm the ranch himself. Then the fight he made against the Railroad in the Courts and the political campaign he went into, to get Lyman on the Railroad Commission, took more of it. The money that Genslinger blackmailed him of, it seems, was about all he had left. He had been gambling—you know the Governor—on another bonanza crop this year to recoup him. Well, the bonanza came right enough—just in time for S. Behrman and the Railroad to grab it. Mag-nus is ruined."

"What a tragedy! what a tragedy!" murmured the other. "Lyman turning rascal, Harran killed, and now this; and all within so short a time—all at the *same* time, you might almost say."

"If it had only killed him," continued Presley; "but that is the worst of it."

"How the worst?"

"I'm afraid, honestly, I'm afraid it is going to turn

his wits, sir. It's broken him; oh, you should see him, you should see him. A shambling, stooping, trembling old man, in his dotage already. He sits all day in the dining-room, turning over papers, sorting them, tying them up, opening them again, forgetting them—all fumbling and mumbling and confused. And at table sometimes he forgets to eat. And, listen, you know, from the house we can hear the trains whistling for the Long Trestle. As often as that happens the Governor seems to be—oh, I don't know, frightened. He will sink his head between his shoulders, as though he were dodging something, and he won't fetch a long breath again till the train is out of hearing. He seems to have conceived an abject, unreasoned terror of the Railroad."

"But he will have to leave Los Muertos now, of course?"

"Yes, they will all have to leave. They have a fortnight more. The few tenants that were still on Los Muertos are leaving. That is one thing that brings me to the city. The family of one of the men who was killed—Hooven was his name—have come to the city to find work. I think they are liable to be in great distress, unless they have been wonderfully lucky, and I am trying to find them in order to look after them."

"You need looking after yourself, Pres."

"Oh, once away from Bonneville and the sight of the ruin there, I'm better. But I intend to go away. And that makes me think, I came to ask you if you could help me. If you would let me take passage on one of your wheat ships. The Doctor says an ocean voyage would set me up."

"Why, certainly, Pres," declared Cedarquist. "But I'm sorry you'll have to go. We expected to have you down in the country with us this winter."

Presley shook his head.

"No," he answered. "I must go. Even if I had all my health, I could not bring myself to stay in California just now. If you can introduce me to one of your captains——"

"With pleasure. When do you want to go? You may have to wait a few weeks. Our first ship won't clear till the end of the month."

"That would do very well. Thank you, sir."

But Cedarquist was still interested in the land troubles of the Bonneville farmers, and took the first occasion to ask:

"So, the Railroad are in possession on most of the ranches?"

"On all of them," returned Presley. "The League went all to pieces, so soon as Magnus was forced to resign. The old story—they got quarrelling among themselves. Somebody started a compromise party, and upon that issue a new president was elected. Then there were defections. The Railroad offered to lease the lands in question to the ranchers—the ranchers who owned them," he exclaimed bitterly, "and because the terms were nominal—almost nothing—plenty of the men took the chance of saving themselves. And, of course, once signing the lease, they acknowledged the Railroad's title. But the road would not lease to Magnus. S. Behrman takes over Los Muertos in a few weeks now."

"No doubt, the road made over their title in the property to him," observed Cedarquist, "as a reward of his services."

"No doubt," murmured Presley wearily. He rose to go.

"By the way," said Cedarquist, "what have you on hand for, let us say, Friday evening? Won't you dine with us then? The girls are going to the country Monday of next week, and you probably won't see them again for some time if you take that ocean voyage of yours."

"I'm afraid I shall be very poor company, sir," hazarded Presley. "There's no 'go,' no life in me at all these days. I am like a clock with a broken spring."

"Not broken, Pres, my boy," urged the other, "only run down. Try and see if we can't wind you up a bit. Say that we can expect you. We dine at seven."

"Thank you, sir. Till Friday at seven, then."

Regaining the street, Presley sent his valise to his club (where he had engaged a room) by a messenger boy, and boarded a Castro Street car. Before leaving Bonneville, he had ascertained, by strenuous enquiry, Mrs. Hooven's address in the city, and thitherward he now directed his steps.

When Presley had told Cedarquist that he was ill, that he was jaded, worn out, he had only told half the truth. Exhausted he was, nerveless, weak, but this apathy was still invaded from time to time with fierce incursions of a spirit of unrest and revolt, reactions, momentary returns of the blind, undirected energy that at one time had prompted him to a vast desire to acquit himself of some terrible deed of readjustment, just what, he could not say, some terrifying martyrdom, some awe-inspiring immolation, consummate, incisive, conclusive. He fancied himself to be fired with the purblind, mistaken heroism of the anarchist, hurling his victim to destruction with full knowledge that the catastrophe shall sweep him also into the vortex it creates.

But his constitutional irresoluteness obstructed his path continually; brain-sick, weak of will, emotional, timid even, he temporised, procrastinated, brooded; came to decisions in the dark hours of the night, only to abandon them in the morning.

Once only he had *acted*. And at this moment, as he

was carried through the windy, squalid streets, he trembled at the remembrance of it. The horror of "what might have been" incompatible with the vengeance whose minister he fancied he was, oppressed him. The scene perpetually reconstructed itself in his imagination. He saw himself under the shade of the encompassing trees and shrubbery, creeping on his belly toward the house, in the suburbs of Bonneville, watching his chances, seizing opportunities, spying upon the lighted windows where the raised curtains afforded a view of the interior. Then had come the appearance in the glare of the gas of the figure of the man for whom he waited. He saw himself rise and run forward. He remembered the feel and weight in his hand of Caraher's bomb—the six inches of plugged gas pipe. His upraised arm shot forward. There was a shiver of smashed window-panes, then—a void—a red whirl of confusion, the air rent, the ground rocking, himself flung headlong, flung off the spinning circumference of things out into a place of terror and vacancy and darkness. And then after a long time the return of reason, the consciousness that his feet were set upon the road to Los Muertos, and that he was fleeing terror-stricken, gasping, all but insane with hysteria. Then the never-to-be-forgotten night that ensued, when he descended into the pit, horrified at what he supposed he had done, at one moment ridden with remorse, at another raging against his own feebleness, his lack of courage, his wretched, vacillating spirit. But morning had come, and with it the knowledge that he had failed, and the baser assurance that he was not even remotely suspected. His own escape had been no less miraculous than that of his enemy, and he had fallen on his knees in inarticulate prayer, weeping, pouring out his thanks to God for the deliverance from the gulf to the very brink of which his feet had been drawn.

After this, however, there had come to Presley a deep-rooted suspicion that he was—of all human beings, the most wretched—a failure. Everything to which he had set his mind failed—his great epic, his efforts to help the people who surrounded him, even his attempted destruction of the enemy, all these had come to nothing. Girding his shattered strength together, he resolved upon one last attempt to live up to the best that was in him, and to that end had set himself to lift out of the despair into which they had been thrust, the bereaved family of the German, Hooven.

After all was over, and Hooven, together with the seven others who had fallen at the irrigating ditch, was buried in the Bonneville cemetery, Mrs. Hooven, asking no one's aid or advice, and taking with her Minna and little Hilda, had gone to San Francisco—had gone to find work, abandoning Los Muertos and her home forever. Presley only learned of the departure of the family after fifteen days had elapsed.

At once, however, the suspicion forced itself upon him that Mrs. Hooven—and Minna, too for the matter of that—country-bred, ignorant of city ways, might easily come to grief in the hard, huge struggle of city life. This suspicion had swiftly hardened to a conviction, acting at last upon which Presley had followed them to San Francisco, bent upon finding and assisting them.

The house to which Presley was led by the address in his memorandum book was a cheap but fairly decent hotel near the power house of the Castro Street cable. He inquired for Mrs. Hooven.

The landlady recollected the Hoovens perfectly.

"German woman, with a little girl-baby, and an older daughter, sure. The older daughter was main pretty. Sure I remember them, but they ain't here no more. They left a week ago. I had to ask them for their room.

As it was, they owed a week's room-rent. Mister, I can't afford——"

"Well, do you know where they went? Did you hear what address they had their trunk expressed to?"

"Ah, yes, their trunk," vociferated the woman, clapping her hands to her hips, her face purpling. "Their trunk, ah, sure. I got their trunk, and what are you going to do about it? I'm holding it till I get my money. What have you got to say about it? Let's hear it."

Presley turned away with a gesture of discouragement, his heart sinking. On the street corner he stood for a long time, frowning in trouble and perplexity. His suspicions had been only too well founded. So long ago as a week, the Hoovens had exhausted all their little store of money. For seven days now they had been without resources, unless, indeed, work had been found; "and what," he asked himself, "what work in God's name could they find to do here in the city?"

Seven days! He quailed at the thought of it. Seven days without money, knowing not a soul in all that swarming city. Ignorant of city life as both Minna and her mother were, would they even realise that there were institutions built and generously endowed for just such as they? He knew them to have their share of pride, the dogged sullen pride of the peasant; even if they knew of charitable organisations, would they, could they bring themselves to apply there? A poignant anxiety thrust itself sharply into Presley's heart. Where were they now? Where had they slept last night? Where breakfasted this morning? Had there even been any breakfast this morning? Had there even been any bed last night? Lost, and forgotten in the plexus of the city's life, what had befallen them? Towards what fate was the ebb tide of the streets drifting them?

Was this to be still another theme wrought out by iron

hands upon the old, the world-old, world-wide keynote? How far were the consequences of that dreadful day's work at the irrigating ditch to reach? To what length was the tentacle of the monster to extend?

Presley returned toward the central, the business quarter of the city, alternately formulating and dismissing from his mind plan after plan for the finding and aiding of Mrs. Hooven and her daughters. He reached Montgomery Street, and turned toward his club, his imagination once more reviewing all the causes and circumstances of the great battle of which for the last eighteen months he had been witness.

All at once he paused, his eye caught by a sign affixed to the wall just inside the street entrance of a huge office building, and smitten with an idea, stood for an instant motionless, upon the sidewalk, his eyes wide, his fists shut tight.

The building contained the General Office of the Pacific and Southwestern Railroad. Large though it was, it nevertheless, was not pretentious, and during his visits to the city, Presley must have passed it, unheeding, many times.

But for all that it was the stronghold of the enemy— the centre of all that vast ramifying system of arteries that drained the life-blood of the State; the nucleus of the web in which so many lives, so many fortunes, so many destinies had been enmeshed. From this place— so he told himself—had emanated that policy of extortion, oppression and injustice that little by little had shouldered the ranchers from their rights, till, their backs to the wall, exasperated and despairing they had turned and fought and died. From here had come the orders to S. Behrman, to Cyrus Ruggles and to Genslinger, the orders that had brought Dyke to a prison, that had killed Annixter, that had ruined Magnus, that had corrupted

Lyman. Here was the keep of the castle, and here, be-hind one of those many windows, in one of those many offices, his hand upon the levers of his mighty engine, sat the master, Shelgrim himself.

Instantly, upon the realisation of this fact an ungovern-able desire seized upon Presley, an inordinate curiosity. Why not see, face to face, the man whose power was so vast, whose will was so resistless, whose potency for evil so limitless, the man who for so long and so hope-lessly they had all been fighting. By reputation he knew him to be approachable; why should he not then approach him? Presley took his resolution in both hands. If he failed to act upon this impulse, he knew he would never act at all. His heart beating, his breath coming short, he entered the building, and in a few moments found him-self seated in an ante-room, his eyes fixed with hypnotic intensity upon the frosted pane of an adjoining door, whereon in gold letters was inscribed the word, "*Presi-dent.*"

In the end, Presley had been surprised to find that Shelgrim was still in. It was already very late, after six o'clock, and the other offices in the building were in the act of closing. Many of them were already deserted. At every instant, through the open door of the ante-room, he caught a glimpse of clerks, office boys, book-keepers, and other employees hurrying towards the stairs and elevators, quitting business for the day. Shelgrim, it seemed, still remained at his desk, knowing no fatigue, requiring no leisure.

"What time does Mr. Shelgrim usually go home?" inquired Presley of the young man who sat ruling forms at the table in the ante-room.

"Anywhere between half-past six and seven," the other answered, adding, "Very often he comes back in the evening."

And the man was seventy years old. Presley could not repress a murmur of astonishment. Not only mentally, then, was the President of the P. and S. W. a giant. Seventy years of age and still at his post, holding there with the energy, with a concentration of purpose that would have wrecked the health and impaired the mind of many men in the prime of their manhood.

But the next instant Presley set his teeth.

"It is an ogre's vitality," he said to himself. "Just so is the man-eating tiger strong. The man should have energy who has sucked the life-blood from an entire People."

A little electric bell on the wall near at hand trilled a warning. The young man who was ruling forms laid down his pen, and opening the door of the President's office, thrust in his head, then after a word exchanged with the unseen occupant of the room, he swung the door wide, saying to Presley:

"Mr. Shelgrim will see you, sir."

Presley entered a large, well lighted, but singularly barren office. A well-worn carpet was on the floor, two steel engravings hung against the wall, an extra chair or two stood near a large, plain, littered table. That was absolutely all, unless he excepted the corner washstand, on which was set a pitcher of ice water, covered with a clean, stiff napkin. A man, evidently some sort of manager's assistant, stood at the end of the table, leaning on the back of one of the chairs. Shelgrim himself sat at the table.

He was large, almost to massiveness. An iron-grey beard and a mustache that completely hid the mouth covered the lower part of his face. His eyes were a pale blue, and a little watery; here and there upon his face were moth spots. But the enormous breadth of the shoulders was what, at first, most vividly forced itself upon Presley's notice. Never had he seen a broader man; the neck, however, seemed in a manner to have settled into the shoulders, and furthermore they were humped and rounded, as if to bear great responsibilities, and great abuse.

At the moment he was wearing a silk skull-cap, pushed to one side and a little awry, a frock coat of broadcloth, with long sleeves, and a waistcoat from the lower buttons of which the cloth was worn and, upon the edges, rubbed away, showing the metal underneath. At the top this waistcoat was unbuttoned and in the shirt front disclosed were two pearl studs.

Presley, uninvited, unnoticed apparently, sat down. The assistant manager was in the act of making a report. His voice was not lowered, and Presley heard every word that was spoken.

The report proved interesting. It concerned a book-keeper in the office of the auditor of disbursements. It seems he was at most times thoroughly reliable, hard-working, industrious, ambitious. But at long intervals the vice of drunkenness seized upon the man and for three days rode him like a hag. Not only during the period of this intemperance, but for the few days imme-diately following, the man was useless, his work un-trustworthy. He was a family man and earnestly strove to rid himself of his habit; he was, when sober, valuable. In consideration of these facts, he had been pardoned again and again.

"You remember, Mr. Shelgrim," observed the man-ager, "that you have more than once interfered in his behalf, when we were disposed to let him go. I don't think we can do anything with him, sir. He promises to reform continually, but it is the same old story. This last time we saw nothing of him for four days. Hon-estly, Mr. Shelgrim, I think we ought to let Tentell out.

We can't afford to keep him. He is really losing us too much money. Here's the order ready now, if you care to let it go."

There was a pause. Presley all attention, listened breathlessly. The assistant manager laid before his President the typewritten order in question. The silence lengthened; in the hall outside, the wrought-iron door of the elevator cage slid to with a clash. Shelgrim did not look at the order. He turned his swivel chair about and faced the windows behind him, looking out with unseeing eyes. At last he spoke:

" Tentell has a family, wife and three children. . . . How much do we pay him? "

" One hundred and thirty."

" Let's double that, or say two hundred and fifty. Let's see how that will do."

" Why—of course—if you say so, but really, Mr. Shelgrim——"

" Well, we'll try that, anyhow."

Presley had not time to readjust his perspective to this new point of view of the President of the P. and S. W. before the assistant manager had withdrawn. Shelgrim wrote a few memoranda on his calendar pad, and signed a couple of letters before turning his attention to Presley. At last, he looked up and fixed the young man with a direct, grave glance. He did not smile. It was some time before he spoke. At last, he said:

" Well, sir."

Presley advanced and took a chair nearer at hand. Shelgrim turned and from his desk picked up and consulted Presley's card. Presley observed that he read without the use of glasses.

" You," he said, again facing about, " you are the young man who wrote the poem called ' The Toilers.' "

" Yes, sir."

"It seems to have made a great deal of talk. I've read it, and I've seen the picture in Cedarquist's house, the picture you took the idea from."

Presley, his senses never more alive, observed that, curiously enough, Shelgrim did not move his body. His arms moved, and his head, but the great bulk of the man remained immobile in its place, and as the interview proceeded and this peculiarity emphasised itself, Presley began to conceive the odd idea that Shelgrim had, as it were, placed his body in the chair to rest, while his head and brain and hands went on working independently. A saucer of shelled filberts stood near his elbow, and from time to time he picked up one of these in a great thumb and forefinger and put it between his teeth.

"I've seen the picture called 'The Toilers,'" continued Shelgrim, "and of the two, I like the picture better than the poem."

"The picture is by a master," Presley hastened to interpose.

"And for that reason," said Shelgrim, "it leaves nothing more to be said. You might just as well have kept quiet. There's only one best way to say anything. And what has made the picture of 'The Toilers' great is that the artist said in it the *best* that could be said on the subject."

"I had never looked at it in just that light," observed Presley. He was confused, all at sea, embarrassed. What he had expected to find in Shelgrim, he could not have exactly said. But he had been prepared to come upon an ogre, a brute, a terrible man of blood and iron, and instead had discovered a sentimentalist and an art critic. No standards of measurement in his mental equipment would apply to the actual man, and it began to dawn upon him that possibly it was not because these standards were different in kind, but that they were lamentably deficient in size. He began to see that here was the man not only great, but large; many-sided, of vast sympathies, who understood with equal intelligence, the human nature in an habitual drunkard, the ethics of a masterpiece of painting, and the financiering and operation of ten thousand miles of railroad.

" I had never looked at it in just that light," repeated Presley. " There is a great deal in what you say."

" If I am to listen," continued Shelgrim, " to that kind of talk, I prefer to listen to it first hand. I would rather listen to what the great French painter has to say, than to what *you* have to say about what he has already said."

His speech, loud and emphatic at first, when the idea of what he had to say was fresh in his mind, lapsed and lowered itself at the end of his sentences as though he had already abandoned and lost interest in that thought, so that the concluding words were indistinct, beneath the grey beard and mustache. Also at times there was the faintest suggestion of a lisp.

" I wrote that poem," hazarded Presley, " at a time when I was terribly upset. I live," he concluded, " or did live on the Los Muertos ranch in Tulare County—Magnus Derrick's ranch."

" The Railroad's ranch *leased* to Mr. Derrick," observed Shelgrim.

Presley spread out his hands with a helpless, resigned gesture.

" And," continued the President of the P. and S. W. with grave intensity, looking at Presley keenly, " I suppose you believe I am a grand old rascal."

" I believe," answered Presley, " I am persuaded——" He hesitated, searching for his words.

" Believe this, young man," exclaimed Shelgrim, laying a thick powerful forefinger on the table to emphasise his words, " try to believe this—to begin with—*that Rail-roads build themselves.* Where there is a demand sooner or later there will be a supply. Mr. Derrick, does he grow his wheat? The Wheat grows itself. What does he count for? Does he supply the force? What do I count for? Do I build the Railroad? You are dealing with forces, young man, when you speak of Wheat and the Railroads, not with men. There is the Wheat, the supply. It must be carried to feed the People. There is the demand. The Wheat is one force, the Railroad, another, and there is the law that governs them—supply and demand. Men have only little to do in the whole business. Complications may arise, conditions that bear hard on the individual—crush him maybe—*but the Wheat will be carried to feed the people* as inevitably as it will grow. If you want to fasten the blame of the affair at Los Muertos on any one person, you will make a mistake. Blame conditions, not men."

" But—but," faltered Presley, " you are the head, you control the road."

" You are a very young man. Control the road! Can I stop it? I can go into bankruptcy if you like. But otherwise if I run my road, as a business proposition, I can do nothing. I can *not* control it. It is a force born out of certain conditions, and I—no man—can stop it or control it. Can your Mr. Derrick stop the Wheat growing? He can burn his crop, or he can give it away, or sell it for a cent a bushel—just as I could go into bankruptcy—but otherwise his Wheat must grow. Can any one stop the Wheat? Well, then no more can I stop the Road."

Presley regained the street stupefied, his brain in a whirl. This new idea, this new conception dumfounded him. Somehow, he could not deny it. It rang with the clear reverberation of truth. Was no one, then, to blame for the horror at the irrigating ditch? Forces, conditions, laws of supply and demand—were these then the enemies, after all? Not enemies; there was no malevolence in Nature. Colossal indifference only, a vast trend toward appointed goals. Nature was, then, a gigantic engine, a vast cyclopean power, huge, terrible, a leviathan with a heart of steel, knowing no compunction, no forgiveness, no tolerance; crushing out the human atom standing in its way, with nirvanic calm, the agony of destruction sending never a jar, never the faintest tremour through all that prodigious mechanism of wheels and cogs.

He went to his club and ate his supper alone, in gloomy agitation. He was sombre, brooding, lost in a dark maze of gloomy reflections. However, just as he was rising from the table an incident occurred that for the moment roused him and sharply diverted his mind.

His table had been placed near a window and as he was sipping his after-dinner coffee, he happened to glance across the street. His eye was at once caught by the sight of a familiar figure. Was it Minna Hooven? The figure turned the street corner and was lost to sight; but it had been strangely like. On the moment, Presley had risen from the table and, clapping on his hat, had hurried into the streets, where the lamps were already beginning to shine.

But search though he would, Presley could not again come upon the young woman, in whom he fancied he had seen the daughter of the unfortunate German. At last, he gave up the hunt, and returning to his club—at this hour almost deserted—smoked a few cigarettes, vainly attempted to read from a volume of essays in the library, and at last, nervous, distraught, exhausted, retired to his bed.

But none the less, Presley had not been mistaken. The

girl whom he had tried to follow had been indeed Minna Hooven.

When Minna, a week before this time, had returned to the lodging house on Castro Street, after a day's unsuccessful effort to find employment, and was told that her mother and Hilda had gone, she was struck speechless with surprise and dismay. She had never before been in any town larger than Bonneville, and now knew not which way to turn nor how to account for the disappearance of her mother and little Hilda. That the landlady was on the point of turning them out, she understood, but it had been agreed that the family should be allowed to stay yet one more day, in the hope that Minna would find work. Of this she reminded the landlady. But this latter at once launched upon her such a torrent of vituperation, that the girl was frightened to speechless submission.

"Oh, oh," she faltered, "I know. I am sorry. I know we owe you money, but where did my mother go? I only want to find her."

"Oh, I ain't going to be bothered," shrilled the other. "How do I know?"

The truth of the matter was that Mrs. Hooven, afraid to stay in the vicinity of the house, after her eviction, and threatened with arrest by the landlady if she persisted in hanging around, had left with the woman a note scrawled on an old blotter, to be given to Minna when she returned. This the landlady had lost. To cover her confusion, she affected a vast indignation, and a turbulent, irascible demeanour.

"I ain't going to be bothered with such cattle as you," she vociferated in Minna's face. "I don't know where your folks is. Me, I only have dealings with honest people. I ain't got a word to say so long as the rent is paid. But when I'm soldiered out of a week's lodging, then

I'm done. You get right along now. *I* don't know you.
I ain't going to have my place get a bad name by having
any South of Market Street chippies hanging around.
You get along, or I'll call an officer."

Minna sought the street, her head in a whirl. It was
about five o'clock. In her pocket was thirty-five cents,
all she had in the world. What now?

All at once, the Terror of the City, that blind, unreasoned fear that only the outcast knows, swooped upon
her, and clutched her vulture-wise, by the throat.

Her first few days' experience in the matter of finding
employment, had taught her just what she might expect
from this new world upon which she had been thrown.
What was to become of her? What was she to do, where
was she to go? Unanswerable, grim questions, and now
she no longer had herself to fear for. Her mother and
the baby, little Hilda, both of them equally unable to look
after themselves, what was to become of them, where
were they gone? Lost, lost, all of them, herself as well.
But she rallied herself, as she walked along. The idea
of her starving, of her mother and Hilda starving, was
out of all reason. Of course, it would not come to that,
of course not. It was not thus that starvation came.
Something would happen, of course, it would—in time.
But meanwhile, meanwhile, how to get through this approaching night, and the next few days. That was the
thing to think of just now.

The suddenness of it all was what most unnerved her.
During all the nineteen years of her life, she had never
known what it meant to shift for herself. Her father
had always sufficed for the family; he had taken care of
her, then, all of a sudden, her father had been killed,
her mother snatched from her. Then all of a sudden
there was no help anywhere. Then all of a sudden a
terrible voice demanded of her, " Now just what can

you do to keep yourself alive?" Life faced her; she looked the huge stone image squarely in the lustreless eyes.

It was nearly twilight. Minna, for the sake of avoiding observation—for it seemed to her that now a thousand prying glances followed her—assumed a matter-of-fact demeanour, and began to walk briskly toward the business quarter of the town.

She was dressed neatly enough, in a blue cloth skirt with a blue plush belt, fairly decent shoes, once her mother's, a pink shirt waist, and jacket and a straw sailor. She was, in an unusual fashion, pretty. Even her troubles had not dimmed the bright light of her pale, greenish-blue eyes, nor faded the astonishing redness of her lips, nor hollowed her strangely white face. Her blue-black hair was trim. She carried her well-shaped, well-rounded figure erectly. Even in her distress, she observed that men looked keenly at her, and sometimes after her as she went along. But this she noted with a dim sub-conscious faculty. The real Minna, harassed, terrified, lashed with a thousand anxieties, kept murmuring under her breath:

"What shall I do, what shall I do, oh, what shall I do, now?"

After an interminable walk, she gained Kearney Street, and held it till the well-lighted, well-kept neighbourhood of the shopping district gave place to the vice-crowded saloons and concert halls of the Barbary Coast. She turned aside in avoidance of this, only to plunge into the purlieus of Chinatown, whence only she emerged, panic-stricken and out of breath, after a half hour of never-to-be-forgotten terrors, and at a time when it had grown quite dark.

On the corner of California and Dupont streets, she stood a long moment, pondering.

" I *must* do something," she said to herself. " I must do *something*."

She was tired out by now, and the idea occurred to her to enter the Catholic church in whose shadow she stood, and sit down and rest. This she did. The evening service was just being concluded. But long after the priests and altar boys had departed from the chancel, Minna still sat in the dim, echoing interior, confronting her desperate situation as best she might.

Two or three hours later, the sexton woke her. The church was being closed; she must leave. Once more, chilled with the sharp night air, numb with long sitting in the same attitude, still oppressed with drowsiness, confused, frightened, Minna found herself on the pavement. She began to be hungry, and, at length, yielding to the demand that every moment grew more imperious, bought and eagerly devoured a five-cent bag of fruit. Then, once more she took up the round of walking.

At length, in an obscure street that branched from Kearney Street, near the corner of the Plaza, she came upon an illuminated sign, bearing the inscription, "Beds for the Night, 15 and 25 cents."

Fifteen cents! Could she afford it? It would leave her with only that much more, that much between herself and a state of privation of which she dared not think; and, besides, the forbidding look of the building frightened her. It was dark, gloomy, dirty, a place suggestive of obscure crimes and hidden terrors. For twenty minutes or half an hour, she hesitated, walking twice and three times around the block. At last, she made up her mind. Exhaustion such as she had never known, weighed like lead upon her shoulders and dragged at her heels. She must sleep. She could not walk the streets all night. She entered the door-way under the sign, and found her way up a filthy flight of stairs. At the top,

a man in a blue checked " jumper " was filling a lamp behind a high desk. To him Minna applied.

"I should like," she faltered, "to have a room—a bed
for the night. One of those for fifteen cents will be good
enough, I think."

"Well, this place is only for men," said the man, looking up from the lamp.

"Oh," said Minna, "oh—I—I didn't know."

She looked at him stupidly, and he, with equal stu-
pidity, returned the gaze. Thus, for a long moment, they
held each other's eyes.

"I—I didn't know," repeated Minna.

"Yes, it's for men," repeated the other.

She slowly descended the stairs, and once more came
out upon the streets.

And upon those streets that, as the hours advanced,
grew more and more deserted, more and more silent,
more and more oppressive with the sense of the bitter
hardness of life towards those who have no means of
living, Minna Hooven spent the first night of her struggle to keep her head above the ebb-tide of the city's sea,
into which she had been plunged.

Morning came, and with it renewed hunger. At this
time, she had found her way uptown again, and towards
ten o'clock was sitting upon a bench in a little park full
of nurse-maids and children. A group of the maids
drew their baby-buggies to Minna's bench, and sat
down, continuing a conversation they had already begun. Minna listened. A friend of one of the maids had
suddenly thrown up her position, leaving her "madame"
in what would appear to have been deserved embarrassment.

"Oh," said Minna, breaking in, and lying with sudden
unwonted fluency, "I am a nurse-girl. I am out of a
place. Do you think I could get that one?"

The group turned and fixed her—so evidently a country girl—with a supercilious indifference.

"Well, you might try," said one of them. "Got good references?"

"References?" repeated Minna blankly. She did not know what this meant.

"Oh, Mrs. Field ain't the kind to stick about references," spoke up the other, "she's that soft. Why, anybody could work her."

"I'll go there," said Minna. "Have you the address?" It was told to her.

"Lorin," she murmured. "Is that out of town?"

"Well, it's across the Bay."

"Across the Bay."

"Um. You're from the country, ain't you?"

"Yes. How—how do I get there? Is it far?"

"Well, you take the ferry at the foot of Market Street, and then the train on the other side. No, it ain't very far. Just ask any one down there. They'll tell you."

It was a chance; but Minna, after walking down to the ferry slips, found that the round trip would cost her twenty cents. If the journey proved fruitless, only a dime would stand between her and the end of everything. But it was a chance; the only one that had, as yet, presented itself. She made the trip.

And upon the street-railway cars, upon the ferryboats, on the locomotives and way-coaches of the local trains, she was reminded of her father's death, and of the giant power that had reduced her to her present straits, by the letters, P. and S. W. R. R. To her mind, they occurred everywhere. She seemed to see them in every direction. She fancied herself surrounded upon every hand by the long arms of the monster.

Minute after minute, her hunger gnawed at her. She could not keep her mind from it. As she sat on the boat, she found herself curiously scanning the faces of the passengers, wondering how long since such a one had breakfasted, how long before this other should sit down to lunch.

When Minna descended from the train, at Lorin on the other side of the Bay, she found that the place was one of those suburban towns, not yet become fashionable, such as may be seen beyond the outskirts of any large American city. All along the line of the railroad thereabouts, houses, small villas—contractors' ventures— were scattered, the advantages of suburban lots and sites for homes being proclaimed in seven-foot letters upon mammoth bill-boards close to the right of way.

Without much trouble, Minna found the house to which she had been directed, a pretty little cottage, set back from the street and shaded by palms, live oaks, and the inevitable eucalyptus. Her heart warmed at the sight of it. Oh, to find a little niche for herself here, a home, a refuge from those horrible city streets, from the rat of famine, with its relentless tooth. How she would work, how strenuously she would endeavour to please, how patient of rebuke she would be, how faithful, how conscientious. Nor were her pretensions altogether false; upon her, while at home, had devolved almost continually the care of the baby Hilda, her little sister. She knew the wants and needs of children.

Her heart beating, her breath failing, she rang the bell set squarely in the middle of the front door.

The lady of the house herself, an elderly lady, with pleasant, kindly face, opened the door. Minna stated her errand.

"But I have already engaged a girl," she said.

"Oh," murmured Minna, striving with all her might to maintain appearances. "Oh—I thought perhaps—" She turned away.

"I'm sorry," said the lady. Then she added, "Would you care to look after so many as three little children, and help around in light housework between whiles?"

"Yes, ma'am."

"Because my sister—she lives in North Berkeley, above here—she's looking for a girl. Have you had lots of experience? Got good references?"

"Yes, ma'am."

"Well, I'll give you the address. She lives up in North Berkeley."

She turned back into the house a moment, and returned, handing Minna a card.

"That's where she lives—careful not to *blot* it, child, the ink's wet yet—you had better see her."

"Is it far? Could I walk there?"

"My, no; you better take the electric cars, about six blocks above here."

When Minna arrived in North Berkeley, she had no money left. By a cruel mistake, she had taken a car going in the wrong direction, and though her error was rectified easily enough, it had cost her her last five-cent piece. She was now to try her last hope. Promptly it crumbled away. Like the former, this place had been already filled, and Minna left the door of the house with the certainty that her chance had come to naught, and that now she entered into the last struggle with life—the death struggle —shorn of her last pitiful defence, her last safeguard, her last penny.

As she once more resumed her interminable walk, she realised she was weak, faint; and she knew that it was the weakness of complete exhaustion, and the faintness of approaching starvation. Was this the end coming on? Terror of death aroused her.

"I *must*, I *must* do something, oh, anything. I must have something to eat."

At this late hour, the idea of pawning her little jacket occurred to her, but now she was far away from the city and its pawnshops, and there was no getting back.

She walked on. An hour passed. She lost her sense of direction, became confused, knew not where she was going, turned corners and went up by-streets without knowing why, anything to keep moving, for she fancied that so soon as she stood still, the rat in the pit of her stomach gnawed more eagerly.

At last, she entered what seemed to be, if not a park, at least some sort of public enclosure. There were many trees; the place was beautiful; well-kept roads and walks led sinuously and invitingly underneath the shade. Through the trees upon the other side of a wide expanse of turf, brown and sear under the summer sun, she caught a glimpse of tall buildings and a flagstaff. The whole place had a vaguely public, educational appearance, and Minna guessed, from certain notices affixed to the trees, warning the public against the picking of flowers, that she had found her way into the grounds of the State University. She went on a little further. The path she was following led her, at length, into a grove of gigantic live oaks, whose lower branches all but swept the ground. Here the grass was green, the few flowers in bloom, the shade very thick. A more lovely spot she had seldom seen. Near at hand was a bench, built around the trunk of the largest live oak, and here, at length, weak from hunger, exhausted to the limits of her endurance, despairing, abandoned, Minna Hooven sat down to enquire of herself what next she could do.

But once seated, the demands of the animal—so she could believe—became more clamorous, more insistent. To eat, to rest, to be safely housed against another night, above all else, these were the things she craved; and the craving within her grew so mighty that she crisped her poor, starved hands into little fists, in an agony of desire, while the tears ran from her eyes, and the sobs rose thick from her breast and struggled and strangled in her aching throat.

But in a few moments Minna was aware that a woman, apparently of some thirty years of age, had twice passed along the walk in front of the bench where she sat, and now, as she took more notice of her, she remembered that she had seen her on the ferry-boat coming over from the city.

The woman was gowned in silk, tightly corseted, and wore a hat of rather ostentatious smartness. Minna became convinced that the person was watching her, but before she had a chance to act upon this conviction she was surprised out of all countenance by the stranger coming up to where she sat and speaking to her.

" Here is a coincidence," exclaimed the new-comer, as she sat down; " surely you are the young girl who sat opposite me on the boat. Strange I should come across you again. I've had you in mind ever since."

On this nearer view Minna observed that the woman's face bore rather more than a trace of enamel and that the atmosphere about was impregnated with sachet. She was not otherwise conspicuous, but there was a certain hardness about her mouth and a certain droop of fatigue in her eyelids which, combined with an indefinite self-confidence of manner, held Minna's attention.

" Do you know," continued the woman, " I believe you are in trouble. I thought so when I saw you on the boat, and I think so now. Are you? Are you in trouble? You're from the country, ain't you?"

Minna, glad to find a sympathiser, even in this chance acquaintance, admitted that she was in distress; that she had become separated from her mother, and that she was indeed from the country.

"I've been trying to find a situation," she hazarded in conclusion, "but I don't seem to succeed. I've never been in a city before, except Bonneville."

"Well, it *is* a coincidence," said the other. "I know I wasn't drawn to you for nothing. I am looking for just such a young girl as you. You see, I live alone a good deal and I've been wanting to find a nice, bright, sociable girl who will be a sort of *companion* to me. Understand? And there's something about you that I like. I took to you the moment I saw you on the boat. Now shall we talk this over?"

Towards the end of the week, one afternoon, as Presley was returning from his club, he came suddenly face to face with Minna upon a street corner.

"Ah," he cried, coming toward her joyfully. "Upon my word, I had almost given you up. I've been looking everywhere for you. I was afraid you might not be getting along, and I wanted to see if there was anything I could do. How are your mother and Hilda? Where are you stopping? Have you got a good place?"

"I don't know where mamma is," answered Minna. "We got separated, and I never have been able to find her again."

Meanwhile, Presley had been taking in with a quick eye the details of Minna's silk dress, with its garniture of lace, its edging of velvet, its silver belt-buckle. Her hair was arranged in a new way and on her head was a wide hat with a flare to one side, set off with a gilt buckle and a puff of bright blue plush. He glanced at her sharply.

"Well, but—but how are you getting on?" he demanded.

Minna laughed scornfully.

"I?" she cried. "Oh, *I've* gone to hell. It was either that or starvation."

Presley regained his room at the club, white and trembling. Worse than the worst he had feared had happened. He had not been soon enough to help. He had failed again. A superstitious fear assailed him that he was, in a manner, marked; that he was foredoomed to fail. Minna had come—had been driven to this; and he, acting too late upon his tardy resolve, had not been able to prevent it. Were the horrors, then, never to end? Was the grisly spectre of consequence to forever dance in his vision? Were the results, the far-reaching results of that battle at the irrigating ditch to cross his path forever? When would the affair be terminated, the incident closed? Where was that spot to which the tentacle of the monster could not reach?

By now, he was sick with the dread of it all. He wanted to get away, to be free from that endless misery, so that he might not see what he could no longer help. Cowardly he now knew himself to be. He thought of himself only with loathing.

Bitterly self-contemptuous that he could bring himself to a participation in such trivialities, he began to dress to keep his engagement to dine with the Cedarquists.

He arrived at the house nearly half an hour late, but before he could take off his overcoat, Mrs. Cedarquist appeared in the doorway of the drawing-room at the end of the hall. She was dressed as if to go out.

"My *dear* Presley," she exclaimed, her stout, overdressed body bustling toward him with a great rustle of silk. "I never was so glad. You poor, dear poet, you are thin as a ghost. You need a better dinner than I can give you, and that is just what you are to have."

"Have I blundered?" Presley hastened to exclaim. "Did not Mr. Cedarquist mention Friday evening?"

"No, no, no," she cried; "it was he who blundered. *You* blundering in a social amenity! Preposterous! No; Mr. Cedarquist forgot that we were dining out ourselves to-night, and when he told me he had asked you here for the same evening, I fell upon the man, my dear, I did actually, tooth and nail. But I wouldn't hear of his wiring you. I just dropped a note to our hostess, asking if I could not bring you, and when I told her who you *were*, she received the idea with, oh, *empressement*. So, there it is, all settled. Cedarquist and the girls are gone on ahead, and you are to take the old lady like a dear, dear poet. I believe I hear the carriage. *Allons! En voiture!*"

Once settled in the cool gloom of the coupé, odorous of leather and upholstery, Mrs. Cedarquist exclaimed:

"And I've never told you who you were to dine with; oh, a personage, really. Fancy, you will be in the camp of your dearest foes. You are to dine with the Gerard people, one of the Vice-Presidents of your *bête noir*, the P. and S. W. Railroad."

Presley started, his fists clenching so abruptly as to all but split his white gloves. He was not conscious of what he said in reply, and Mrs. Cedarquist was so taken up with her own endless stream of talk that she did not observe his confusion.

"Their daughter Honora is going to Europe next week; her mother is to take her, and Mrs. Gerard is to have just a few people to dinner—very informal, you know—ourselves, you and, oh, I don't know, two or three others. Have you ever seen Honora? The prettiest little thing, and will she be rich? Millions, I would not dare say how many. *Tiens. Nous voici.*"

The coupé drew up to the curb, and Presley followed Mrs. Cedarquist up the steps to the massive doors of the great house. In a confused daze, he allowed one of the footmen to relieve him of his hat and coat; in a daze he rejoined Mrs. Cedarquist in a room with a glass roof, hung with pictures, the art gallery, no doubt, and in a

daze heard their names announced at the entrance of another room, the doors of which were hung with thick,
blue curtains.

He entered, collecting his wits for the introductions
and presentations that he foresaw impended.

The room was very large, and of excessive loftiness.
Flat, rectagonal pillars of a rose-tinted, variegated marble,
rose from the floor almost flush with the walls, finishing
off at the top with gilded capitals of a Corinthian design,
which supported the ceiling. The ceiling itself, instead
of joining the walls at right angles, curved to meet them,
a device that produced a sort of dome-like effect. This
ceiling was a maze of golden involutions in very high relief, that adjusted themselves to form a massive framing
for a great picture, nymphs and goddesses, white doves,
golden chariots and the like, all wreathed about with
clouds and garlands of roses. Between the pillars around
the sides of the room were hangings of silk, the design—
of a Louis Quinze type—of beautiful simplicity and fault-
less taste. The fireplace was a marvel. It reached from
floor to ceiling; the lower parts, black marble, carved into crouching Atlases, with great muscles that upbore
the superstructure. The design of this latter, of a kind
of purple marble, shot through with white veinings, was
in the same style as the design of the silk hangings. In
its midst was a bronze escutcheon, bearing an undeci-
pherable monogram and a Latin motto. Andirons of
brass, nearly six feet high, flanked the hearthstone.

The windows of the room were heavily draped in sombre brocade and *écru* lace, in which the initials of the
family were very beautifully worked. But directly opposite the fireplace, an extra window, lighted from the adjoining conservatory, threw a wonderful, rich light into
the apartment. It was a Gothic window of stained glass,
very large, the centre figures being armed warriors, Par-

sifal and Lohengrin; the one with a banner, the other with
a swan. The effect was exquisite, the window a veritable masterpiece, glowing, flaming, and burning with a
hundred tints and colours—opalescent, purple, wine-
red, clouded pinks, royal blues, saffrons, violets so dark
as to be almost black.

Under foot, the carpet had all the softness of texture of
grass; skins (one of them of an enormous polar bear)
and rugs of silk velvet were spread upon the floor. A
Renaissance cabinet of ebony, many feet taller than Presley's head, and inlaid with ivory and silver, occupied one
corner of the room, while in its centre stood a vast table
of Flemish oak, black, heavy as iron, massive. A faint
odour of sandalwood pervaded the air. From the conservatory near-by, came the splashing of a fountain. A
row of electric bulbs let into the frieze of the walls between the golden capitals, and burning dimly behind hem-
ispheres of clouded glass, threw a subdued light over the
whole scene.

Mrs. Gerard came forward.

"This is Mr. Presley, of course, our new poet of whom
we are all so proud. I was so afraid you would be unable to come. You have given me a real pleasure in allowing me to welcome you here."

The footman appeared at her elbow.

"Dinner is served, madame," he announced.

———

When Mrs. Hooven had left the boarding-house on
Castro Street, she had taken up a position on a neighbouring corner, to wait for Minna's reappearance. Little Hilda, at this time hardly more than six years of age,
was with her, holding to her hand.

Mrs. Hooven was by no means an old woman, but
hard work had aged her. She no longer had any claim
to good looks. She no longer took much interest in her

personal appearance. At the time of her eviction from the Castro Street boarding-house, she wore a faded black bcnnet, garnished with faded artificial flowers of dirty pink. A plaid shawl was about her shoulders. But this day of misfortune had set Mrs. Hooven adrift in even worse condition than her daughter. Her purse, containing a miserable handful of dimes and nickels, was in her trunk, and her trunk was in the hands of the landlady. Minna had been allowed such reprieve as her thirty-five cents would purchase. The destitution of Mrs. Hooven and her little girl had begun from the very moment of her eviction.

While she waited for Minna, watching every street car and every approaching pedestrian, a policeman appeared, asked what she did, and, receiving no satisfactory reply, promptly moved her on.

Minna had had little assurance in facing the life struggle of the city. Mrs. Hooven had absolutely none. In her, grief, distress, the pinch of poverty, and, above all, the nameless fear of the turbulent, fierce life of the streets, had produced a numbness, an embruted, sodden, silent, speechless condition of dazed mind, and clogged, unintelligent speech. She was dumb, bewildered, stupid, animated but by a single impulse. She clung to life, and to the life of her little daughter Hilda, with the blind tenacity of purpose of a drowning cat.

Thus, when ordered to move on by the officer, she had silently obeyed, not even attempting to explain her situation. She walked away to the next street-crossing. Then, in a few moments returned, taking up her place on the corner near the boarding-house, spying upon the approaching cable cars, peeping anxiously down the length of the sidewalks.

Once more, the officer ordered her away, and once more, unprotesting, she complied. But when for the third time the policeman found her on the forbidden spot, he had lost his temper. This time when Mrs. Hooven departed, he had followed her, and when, bewildered, persistent, she had attempted to turn back, he caught her by the shoulder.

"Do you want to get arrested, hey?" he demanded. "Do you want me to lock you up? Say, do you, speak up?"

The ominous words at length reached Mrs. Hooven's comprehension. Arrested! She was to be arrested. The countrywoman's fear of the Jail nipped and bit eagerly at her unwilling heels. She hurried off, thinking to return to her post after the policeman should have gone away. But when, at length, turning back, she tried to find the boarding-house, she suddenly discovered that she was on an unfamiliar street. Unwittingly, no doubt, she had turned a corner. She could not retrace her steps. She and Hilda were lost.

"Mammy, I'm tired," Hilda complained.

Her mother picked her up.

"Mammy, where're we gowun, mammy?"

Where, indeed? Stupefied, Mrs. Hooven looked about her at the endless blocks of buildings, the endless procession of vehicles in the streets, the endless march of pedestrians on the sidewalks. Where was Minna; where was she and her baby to sleep that night? How was Hilda to be fed?

She could not stand still. There was no place to sit down; but one thing was left, walk.

Ah, that *via dolorosa* of the destitute, that *chemin de la croix* of the homeless. Ah, the mile after mile of granite pavement that *must* be, *must* be traversed. Walk they must. Move, they must; onward, forward, whither they cannot tell; why, they do not know. Walk, walk, walk with bleeding feet and smarting joints; walk with aching back and trembling knees; walk, though the senses grow giddy with fatigue, though the eyes droop with sleep, though every nerve, demanding rest, sets in motion its tiny alarm of pain. Death is at the end of that devious, winding maze of paths, crossed and re-crossed and crossed again. There is but one goal to the *via dolorosa;* there is no escape from the central chamber of that labyrinth. Fate guides the feet of them that are set therein. Double on their steps though they may, weave in and out of the myriad corners of the city's streets, return, go forward, back, from side to side, here, there, anywhere, dodge, twist, wind, the central chamber where Death sits is reached inexorably at the end.

Sometimes leading and sometimes carrying Hilda, Mrs. Hooven set off upon her objectless journey. Block after block she walked, street after street. She was afraid to stop, because of the policemen. As often as she so much as slackened her pace, she was sure to see one of these terrible figures in the distance, watching her, so it seemed to her, waiting for her to halt for the frac-tion of a second, in order that he might have an excuse to arrest her.

Hilda fretted incessantly.

"Mammy, where're we gowun? Mammy, I'm tired." Then, at last, for the first time, that plaint that stabbed the mother's heart:

"Mammy, I'm hungry."

"Be qui-ut, den," said Mrs. Hooven. "Bretty soon we'll hev der subber."

Passers-by on the sidewalk, men and women in the great six o'clock homeward march, jostled them as they went along. With dumb, dull curiousness, she looked into one after another of the limitless stream of faces, and she fancied she saw in them every emotion but pity. The faces were gay, were anxious, were sorrowful, were

mirthful, were lined with thought, or were merely flat
and expressionless, but not one was turned toward her
in compassion. The expressions of the faces might be
various, but an underlying callousness was discoverable
beneath every mask. The people seemed removed from
her immeasurably; they were infinitely above her. What
was she to them, she and her baby, the crippled outcasts
of the human herd, the unfit, not able to survive, thrust
out on the heath to perish?

To beg from these people did not yet occur to her.
There was no pride, however, in the matter. She would
have as readily asked alms of so many sphinxes.

She went on. Without willing it, her feet carried her
in a wide circle. Soon she began to recognise the houses;
she had been in that street before. Somehow, this was
distasteful to her; so, striking off at right angles, she
walked straight before her for over a dozen blocks. By
now, it was growing darker. The sun had set. The
hands of a clock on the power-house of a cable line
pointed to seven. No doubt, Minna had come long before
this time, had found her mother gone, and had—just
what had she done, just what *could* she do? Where was
her daughter now? Walking the streets herself, no
doubt. What was to become of Minna, pretty girl that
she was, lost, houseless and friendless in the maze of
these streets? Mrs. Hooven, roused from her lethargy,
could not repress an exclamation of anguish. Here was
misfortune indeed; here was calamity. She bestirred herself, and remembered the address of the boarding-house.
She might inquire her way back thither. No doubt, by
now the policeman would be gone home for the night.
She looked about. She was in the district of modest
residences, and a young man was coming toward her,
carrying a new garden hose looped around his shoulder.

"Say, Meest'r; say, blease——"

The young man gave her a quick look and passed on, hitching the coil of hose over his shoulder. But a few paces distant, he slackened in his walk and fumbled in his vest pocket with his fingers. Then he came back to Mrs. Hooven and put a quarter into her hand.

Mrs. Hooven stared at the coin stupefied. The young man disappeared. He thought, then, that she was begging. It had come to that; she, independent all her life, whose husband had held five hundred acres of wheat land, had been taken for a beggar. A flush of shame shot to her face. She was about to throw the money after its giver. But at the moment, Hilda again exclaimed:

"Mammy, I'm hungry."

With a movement of infinite lassitude and resigned acceptance of the situation, Mrs. Hooven put the coin in her pocket. She had no right to be proud any longer. Hilda must have food.

That evening, she and her child had supper at a cheap restaurant in a poor quarter of the town, and passed the night on the benches of a little uptown park.

Unused to the ways of the town, ignorant as to the customs and possibilities of eating-houses, she spent the whole of her quarter upon supper for herself and Hilda, and had nothing left wherewith to buy a lodging.

The night was dreadful; Hilda sobbed herself to sleep on her mother's shoulder, waking thereafter from hour to hour, to protest, though wrapped in her mother's shawl, that she was cold, and to enquire why they did not go to bed. Drunken men snored and sprawled near at hand. Towards morning, a loafer, reeking of alcohol, sat down beside her, and indulged in an incoherent soliloquy, punctuated with oaths and obscenities. It was not till far along towards daylight that she fell asleep.

She awoke to find it broad day. Hilda—mercifully—

slept. Her mother's limbs were stiff and lame with cold
and damp; her head throbbed. She moved to another
bench which stood in the rays of the sun, and for a long
two hours sat there in the thin warmth, till the moisture
of the night that clung to her clothes was evaporated.

A policeman came into view. She woke Hilda, and
carrying her in her arms, took herself away.

"Mammy," began Hilda as soon as she was well
awake; "Mammy, I'm hungry. I want mein breakfast."

"Sure, sure, soon now, leedle tochter."

She herself was hungry, but she had but little thought
of that. How was Hilda to be fed? She remembered
her experience of the previous day, when the young
man with the hose had given her money. Was it so
easy, then, to beg? Could charity be had for the asking?
So it seemed; but all that was left of her sturdy inde-
pendence revolted at the thought. *She* beg! *She* hold
out the hand to strangers!

"Mammy, I'm hungry."

There was no other way. It must come to that in the
end. Why temporise, why put off the inevitable? She
sought out a frequented street where men and women
were on their way to work. One after another, she let
them go by, searching their faces, deterred at the very
last moment by some trifling variation of expression, a
firm set mouth, a serious, level eyebrow, an advancing
chin. Then, twice, when she had made a choice, and
brought her resolution to the point of speech, she
quailed, shrinking, her ears tingling, her whole being
protesting against the degradation. Every one must be
looking at her. Her shame was no doubt the object of
an hundred eyes.

"Mammy, I'm hungry," protested Hilda again.

She made up her mind. What, though, was she to
say? In what words did beggars ask for assistance?

She tried to remember how tramps who had appeared at her back door on Los Muertos had addressed her; how and with what formula certain mendicants of Bonneville had appealed to her. Then, having settled upon a phrase, she approached a whiskered gentleman with a large stomach, walking briskly in the direction of the town.

"Say, den, please hellup a boor womun."

The gentleman passed on.

"Perhaps he doand hear me," she murmured.

Two well-dressed women advanced, chattering gayly.

"Say, say, den, please hellup a boor womun."

One of the women paused, murmuring to her companion, and from her purse extracted a yellow ticket which she gave to Mrs. Hooven with voluble explanations. But Mrs. Hooven was confused, she did not understand. What could the ticket mean? The women went on their way.

The next person to whom she applied was a young girl of about eighteen, very prettily dressed.

"Say, say, den, please hellup a boor womun."

In evident embarrassment, the young girl paused and searched in her little pocketbook.

"I think I have—I think—I have just ten cents here somewhere," she murmured again and again.

In the end, she found a dime, and dropped it into Mrs. Hooven's palm.

That was the beginning. The first step once taken, the others became easy. All day long, Mrs. Hooven and Hilda followed the streets, begging, begging. Here it was a nickel, there a dime, here a nickel again. But she was not expert in the art, nor did she know where to buy food the cheapest; and the entire day's work resulted only in barely enough for two meals of bread, milk, and a wretchedly cooked stew. Tuesday night found the pair once more shelterless.

Once more, Mrs. Hooven and her baby passed the

night on the park benches. But early on Wednesday morning, Mrs. Hooven found herself assailed by sharp pains and cramps in her stomach. What was the cause she could not say; but as the day went on, the pains increased, alternating with hot flushes over all her body, and a certain weakness and faintness. As the day went on, the pain and the weakness increased. When she tried to walk, she found she could do so only with the greatest difficulty. Here was fresh misfortune. To beg, she must walk. Dragging herself forward a half-block at a time, she regained the street once more. She succeeded in begging a couple of nickels, bought a bag of apples from a vender, and, returning to the park, sank exhausted upon a bench.

Here she remained all day until evening, Hilda alternately whimpering for her bread and milk, or playing languidly in the gravel walk at her feet. In the evening, she started out again. This time, it was bitter hard. Nobody seemed inclined to give. Twice she was " moved on " by policemen. Two hours' begging elicited but a single dime. With this, she bought Hilda's bread and milk, and refusing herself to eat, returned to the bench— the only home she knew—and spent the night shivering with cold, burning with fever.

From Wednesday morning till Friday evening, with the exception of the few apples she had bought, and a quarter of a loaf of hard bread that she found in a greasy newspaper—scraps of a workman's dinner—Mrs. Hooven had nothing to eat. In her weakened condition, begging became hourly more difficult, and such little money as was given her, she resolutely spent on Hilda's bread and milk in the morning and evening.

By Friday afternoon, she was very weak, indeed. Her eyes troubled her. She could no longer see distinctly, and at times there appeared to her curious figures, huge crystal goblets of the most graceful shapes, floating and swaying in the air in front of her, almost within arm's reach. Vases of elegant forms, made of shimmering glass, bowed and courtesied toward her. Glass bulbs took graceful and varying shapes before her vision, now rounding into globes, now evolving into hour-glasses, now twisting into pretzel-shaped convolutions.

"Mammy, I'm hungry," insisted Hilda, passing her hands over her face. Mrs. Hooven started and woke. It was Friday evening. Already the street lamps were being lit.

"Gome, den, leedle girl," she said, rising and taking Hilda's hand. "Gome, den, we go vind subber, hey?"

She issued from the park and took a cross street, directly away from the locality where she had begged the previous days. She had had no success there of late. She would try some other quarter of the town. After a weary walk, she came out upon Van Ness Avenue, near its junction with Market Street. She turned into the avenue, and went on toward the Bay, painfully traversing block after block, begging of all whom she met (for she no longer made any distinction among the passers-by).

"Say, say, den, blease hellup a boor womun."

"Mammy, mammy, I'm hungry."

It was Friday night, between seven and eight. The great deserted avenue was already dark. A sea fog was scudding overhead, and by degrees descending lower. The warmth was of the meagerest, and the street lamps, birds of fire in cages of glass, fluttered and danced in the prolonged gusts of the trade wind that threshed and weltered in the city streets from off the ocean.

———

Presley entered the dining-room of the Gerard mansion with little Miss Gerard on his arm. The other guests had preceded them—Cedarquist with Mrs.

Gerard; a pale-faced, languid young man (introduced to Presley as Julian Lambert) with Presley's cousin Beatrice, one of the twin daughters of Mr. and Mrs. Cedarquist; his brother Stephen, whose hair was straight as an Indian's, but of a pallid straw color, with Beatrice's sister; Gerard himself, taciturn, bearded, rotund, loud of breath, escorted Mrs. Cedarquist. Besides these, there were one or two other couples, whose names Presley did not remember.

The dining-room was superb in its appointments. On three sides of the room, to the height of some ten feet, ran a continuous picture, an oil painting, divided into long sections by narrow panels of black oak. The painting represented the personages in the *Romaunt de la Rose*, and was conceived in an atmosphere of the most delicate, most ephemeral allegory. One saw young chevaliers, blue-eyed, of elemental beauty and purity; women with crowns, gold girdles, and cloudy wimples; young girls, entrancing in their loveliness, wearing snow-white kerchiefs, their golden hair unbound and flowing, dressed in white samite, bearing armfuls of flowers; the whole procession defiling against a background of forest glades, venerable oaks, half-hidden fountains, and fields of asphodel and roses.

Otherwise, the room was simple. Against the side of the wall unoccupied by the picture stood a sideboard of gigantic size, that once had adorned the banquet hall of an Italian palace of the late Renaissance. It was black with age, and against its sombre surfaces glittered an array of heavy silver dishes and heavier cut-glass bowls and goblets.

The company sat down to the first course of raw Blue Point oysters, served upon little pyramids of shaved ice, and the two butlers at once began filling the glasses of the guests with cool Haut Sauterne.

Mrs. Gerard, who was very proud of her dinners, and never able to resist the temptation of commenting upon them to her guests, leaned across to Presley and Mrs. Cedarquist, murmuring, "Mr. Presley, do you find that Sauterne too cold? I always believe it is so *bourgeois* to keep such a delicate wine as Sauterne on the ice, and to ice Bordeaux or Burgundy—oh, it is nothing short of a crime."

"This is from your own vineyard, is it not?" asked Julian Lambert. "I think I recognise the bouquet."

He strove to maintain an attitude of *fin gourmet*, unable to refrain from comment upon the courses as they succeeded one another.

Little Honora Gerard turned to Presley:

"You know," she explained, "Papa has his own vineyards in southern France. He is so particular about his wines; turns up his nose at California wines. And I am to go there next summer. Ferrières is the name of the place where our vineyards are, the dearest village!"

She was a beautiful little girl of a dainty porcelain type, her colouring low in tone. She wore no jewels, but her little, undeveloped neck and shoulders, of an exquisite immaturity, rose from the tulle bodice of her first *décolleté* gown.

"Yes," she continued; "I'm to go to Europe for the first time. Won't it be gay? And I am to have my own *bonne,* and Mamma and I are to travel—so many places, Baden, Homburg, Spa, the Tyrol. Won't it be gay?"

Presley assented in meaningless words. He sipped his wine mechanically, looking about that marvellous room, with its subdued saffron lights, its glitter of glass and silver, its beautiful women in their elaborate toilets, its deft, correct servants; its array of tableware—cut glass, chased silver, and Dresden crockery. It was Wealth, in all its outward and visible forms, the signs of an opulence so great that it need never be husbanded. It was the home of a railway "Magnate," a Railroad King. For this, then, the farmers paid. It was for this that S. Behrman turned the screw, tightened the vise. It was for this that Dyke had been driven to outlawry and a jail. It was for this that Lyman Derrick had been bought, the Governor ruined and broken, Annixter shot down, Hooven killed.

The soup, *purée à la Derby,* was served, and at the same time, as *hors d'œuvres,* ortolan patties, together with a tiny sandwich made of browned toast and thin slices of ham, sprinkled over with Parmesan cheese. The wine, so Mrs. Gerard caused it to be understood, was Xeres, of the 1815 vintage.

Mrs. Hooven crossed the avenue. It was growing late. Without knowing it, she had come to a part of the city that experienced beggars shunned. There was nobody about. Block after block of residences stretched away on either hand, lighted, full of people. But the sidewalks were deserted.

"Mammy," whimpered Hilda. "I'm tired, carry me."

Using all her strength, Mrs. Hooven picked her up and moved on aimlessly.

Then again that terrible cry, the cry of the hungry child appealing to the helpless mother:

"Mammy, I'm hungry."

"Ach, Gott, leedle girl," exclaimed Mrs. Hooven, holding her close to her shoulder, the tears starting from her eyes. "Ach, leedle tochter. Doand, doand, doand. You praik my hairt. I cen't vind any subber. We got noddings to eat, noddings, noddings."

"When do we have those bread'n milk again, Mammy?"

" To-morrow — soon — py-and-py, Hilda.   I doand know what pecome oaf us now, what pecome oaf my leedle babby."

She went on, holding Hilda against her shoulder with one arm as best she might, one hand steadying herself against the fence railings along the sidewalk. At last, a solitary pedestrian came into view, a young man in a top hat and overcoat, walking rapidly. Mrs. Hooven held out a quivering hand as he passed her.

" Say, say, den, Meest'r, blease hellup a boor womun."
The other hurried on.

The fish course was *grenadins* of bass and small salmon, the latter stuffed, and cooked in white wine and mushroom liquor.

" I have read your poem, of course, Mr. Presley," observed Mrs. Gerard.   " ' The Toilers,' I mean.   What a sermon you read us, you dreadful young man.   I felt that I ought at once to ' sell all that I have and give to the poor.'   Positively, it did stir me up.   You may congratulate yourself upon making at least one convert. Just because of that poem Mrs. Cedarquist and I have started a movement to send a whole shipload of wheat to the starving people in India.   Now, you horrid *réactionnaire*, are you satisfied? "

" I am very glad," murmured Presley.

" But I am afraid," observed Mrs. Cedarquist, "that we may be too late.   They are dying so fast, those poor people.   By the time our ship reaches India the famine may be all over."

" One need never be afraid of being ' too late ' in the matter of helping the destitute," answered Presley. " Unfortunately, they are always a fixed quantity. ' The poor ye have always with you.' "

" How very clever that is," said Mrs. Gerard.

Mrs. Cedarquist tapped the table with her fan in mild applause.

"Brilliant, brilliant," she murmured, "epigrammatical."

"Honora," said Mrs. Gerard, turning to her daughter, at that moment in conversation with the languid Lambert, "Honora, *entends-tu, ma chérie, l'esprit de notre jeune Lamartine.*"

———

Mrs. Hooven went on, stumbling from street to street, holding Hilda to her breast. Famine gnawed incessantly at her stomach; walk though she might, turn upon her tracks up and down the streets, back to the avenue again, incessantly and relentlessly the torture dug into her vitals. She was hungry, hungry, and if the want of food harassed and rended her, full-grown woman that she was, what must it be in the poor, starved stomach of her little girl? Oh, for some helping hand now, oh, for one little mouthful, one little nibble! Food, food, all her wrecked body clamoured for nourishment; anything to numb those gnawing teeth—an abandoned loaf, hard, mouldered; a half-eaten fruit, yes, even the refuse of the gutter, even the garbage of the ash heap. On she went, peering into dark corners, into the areaways, anywhere, everywhere, watching the silent prowling of cats, the intent rovings of stray dogs. But she was growing weaker; the pains and cramps in her stomach returned. Hilda's weight bore her to the pavement. More than once a great giddiness, a certain wheeling faintness all but overcame her. Hilda, however, was asleep. To wake her would only mean to revive her to the consciousness of hunger; yet how to carry her further? Mrs. Hooven began to fear that she would fall with her child in her arms. The terror of a collapse upon those cold pavements glistening with fog-damp roused her; she must make an effort to get through the night. She rallied all her strength, and pausing a moment to shift the weight of her baby to the other arm, once more set off through the night. A little while later she found on the edge of the sidewalk the peeling of a banana. It had been trodden upon and it was muddy, but joyfully she caught it up.

"Hilda," she cried, "wake oop, leedle girl. See, loog den, dere's somedings to eat. Look den, hey? Dat's goot, ain't it? Zum bunaner."

But it could not be eaten. Decayed, dirty, all but rotting, the stomach turned from the refuse, nauseated.

"No, no," cried Hilda, "that's not good. I can't eat it. Oh, Mammy, please gif me those bread'n milk."

By now the guests of Mrs. Gerard had come to the entrées—Londonderry pheasants, escallops of duck, and *rissolettes à la pompadour*. The wine was Château Latour.

All around the table conversations were going forward gayly. The good wines had broken up the slight restraint of the early part of the evening and a spirit of good humour and good fellowship prevailed. Young Lambert and Mr. Gerard were deep in reminiscences of certain mutual duck-shooting expeditions. Mrs. Gerard and Mrs. Cedarquist discussed a novel—a strange mingling of psychology, degeneracy, and analysis of erotic conditions—which had just been translated from the Italian. Stephen Lambert and Beatrice disputed over the merits of a Scotch collie just given to the young lady. The scene was gay, the electric bulbs sparkled, the wine flashing back the light. The entire table was a vague glow of white napery, delicate china, and glass as brilliant as crystal. Behind the guests the serving-men came and went, filling the glasses continually, changing the covers, serving the entrées, managing the dinner without interruption, confusion, or the slightest unnecessary noise.

But Presley could find no enjoyment in the occasion. From that picture of feasting, that scene of luxury, that atmosphere of decorous, well-bred refinement, his thoughts went back to Los Muertos and Quien Sabe and the irrigating ditch at Hooven's. He saw them fall, one by one, Harran, Annixter, Osterman, Broderson, Hooven. The clink of the wine glasses was drowned in the explosion of revolvers. The Railroad might indeed be a force only, which no man could control and for which no man was responsible, but his friends had been killed, but years of extortion and oppression had wrung money from all the San Joaquin, money that had made possible this very scene in which he found himself. Because Magnus had been beggared, Gerard had become Railroad King; because the farmers of the valley were poor, these men were rich.

The fancy grew big in his mind, distorted, caricatured, terrible. Because the farmers had been killed at the irrigation ditch, these others, Gerard and his family, fed full. They fattened on the blood of the People, on the blood of the men who had been killed at the ditch. It was a half-ludicrous, half-horrible "dog eat dog," an unspeakable cannibalism. Harran, Annixter, and Hooven were being devoured there under his eyes. These dainty women, his cousin Beatrice and little Miss Gerard, frail, delicate; all these fine ladies with their small fingers and slender necks, suddenly were transfigured in his tortured mind into harpies tearing human flesh. His head swam with the horror of it, the terror of it. Yes, the People *would* turn some day, and turning, rend those who now preyed upon them. It would be "dog eat dog" again, with positions reversed, and he saw for one instant of time that splendid house sacked to its foundations, the

tables overturned, the pictures torn, the hangings blazing, and Liberty, the red-handed Man in the Street,
grimed with powder smoke, foul with the gutter, rush
yelling, torch in hand, through every door.

At ten o'clock Mrs. Hooven fell.

Luckily she was leading Hilda by the hand at the time
and the little girl was not hurt. In vain had Mrs.
Hooven, hour after hour, walked the streets. After a
while she no longer made any attempt to beg; nobody
was stirring, nor did she even try to hunt for food with
the stray dogs and cats. She had made up her mind to
return to the park in order to sit upon the benches there,
but she had mistaken the direction, and following up
Sacramento Street, had come out at length, not upon the
park, but upon a great vacant lot at the very top of the
Clay Street hill. The ground was unfenced and rose
above her to form the cap of the hill, all overgrown with
bushes and a few stunted live oaks. It was in trying to
cross this piece of ground that she fell. She got upon
her feet again.

"Ach, Mammy, did you hurt yourself?" asked Hilda.

"No, no."

"Is that house where we get those bread'n milk?"

Hilda pointed to a single rambling building just visible in the night, that stood isolated upon the summit of
the hill in a grove of trees.

"No, no, dere aindt no braid end miluk, leedle tochter."

Hilda once more began to sob.

"Ach, Mammy, please, *please*, I want it. I'm hungry."

The jangled nerves snapped at last under the tension,
and Mrs. Hooven, suddenly shaking Hilda roughly, cried
out:

"Stop, stop. Doand say ut egen, you. My Gott, you
kill me yet."

But quick upon this came the reaction. The mother caught her little girl to her, sinking down upon her knees, putting her arms around her, holding her close.

"No, no, gry all so mudge es you want. Say dot you are hongry. Say ut egen, say ut all de dime, ofer end ofer egen. Say ut, poor, starfing, leedle babby. Oh, mein poor, leedle tochter. My Gott, oh, I go crazy bretty soon, I guess. I cen't hellup you. I cen't ged you noddings to eat, noddings, noddings. Hilda, we gowun to die togedder. Put der arms roundt me, soh, tighd, leedle babby. We gowun to die, we gowun to vind Popper. We aindt gowun to be hongry eny more."

"Vair we go now?" demanded Hilda.

"No places. Mommer's soh tiredt. We stop heir, leedle while, end rest."

Underneath a large bush that afforded a little shelter from the wind, Mrs. Hooven lay down, taking Hilda in her arms and wrapping her shawl about her. The infinite, vast night expanded gigantic all around them. At this elevation they were far above the city. It was still. Close overhead whirled the chariots of the fog, galloping landward, smothering lights, blurring outlines. Soon all sight of the town was shut out; even the solitary house on the hilltop vanished. There was nothing left but grey, wheeling fog, and the mother and child, alone, shivering in a little strip of damp ground, an island drifting aimlessly in empty space.

Hilda's fingers touched a leaf from the bush and instinctively closed upon it and carried it to her mouth.

"Mammy," she said, "I'm eating those leaf. Is those good?"

Her mother did not reply.

"You going to sleep, Mammy?" inquired Hilda, touching her face.

Mrs. Hooven roused herself a little.

"Hey? Vat you say? Asleep? Yais, I guess I wass asleep."

Her voice trailed unintelligibly to silence again. She was not, however, asleep. Her eyes were open. A grateful numbness had begun to creep over her, a pleasing semi-insensibility. She no longer felt the pain and cramps of her stomach, even the hunger was ceasing to bite.

———

"These stuffed artichokes are delicious, Mrs. Gerard," murmured young Lambert, wiping his lips with a corner of his napkin. "Pardon me for mentioning it, but your dinner must be my excuse."

"And this asparagus—since Mr. Lambert has set the bad example," observed Mrs. Cedarquist, "so delicate, such an exquisite flavour. How *do* you manage?"

"We get all our asparagus from the southern part of the State, from one particular ranch," explained Mrs. Gerard. "We order it by wire and get it only twenty hours after cutting. My husband sees to it that it is put on a special train. It stops at this ranch just to take on our asparagus. Extravagant, isn't it, but I simply cannot eat asparagus that has been cut more than a day."

"Nor I," exclaimed Julian Lambert, who posed as an epicure. "I can tell to an hour just how long asparagus has been picked."

"Fancy eating ordinary market asparagus," said Mrs. Gerard, "that has been fingered by Heaven knows how many hands."

———

"Mammy, mammy, wake up," cried Hilda, trying to push open Mrs. Hooven's eyelids, at last closed. "Mammy, don't. You're just trying to frighten me."

Feebly Hilda shook her by the shoulder. At last Mrs. Hooven's lips stirred. Putting her head down, Hilda distinguished the whispered words:

"I'm sick. Go to schleep. . . . Sick. . . . Noddings to eat."

The dessert was a wonderful preparation of alternate layers of biscuit glacés, ice cream, and candied chestnuts.

"Delicious, is it not?" observed Julian Lambert, partly to himself, partly to Miss Cedarquist. "This *Moscovite fouetté*—upon my word, I have never tasted its equal."

"And you should know, shouldn't you?" returned the young lady.

"Mammy, mammy, wake up," cried Hilda. "Don't sleep so. I'm frightenedt."

Repeatedly she shook her; repeatedly she tried to raise the inert eyelids with the point of her finger. But her mother no longer stirred. The gaunt, lean body, with its bony face and sunken eye-sockets, lay back, prone upon the ground, the feet upturned and showing the ragged, worn soles of the shoes, the forehead and grey hair beaded with fog, the poor, faded bonnet awry, the poor, faded dress soiled and torn.

Hilda drew close to her mother, kissing her face, twining her arms around her neck. For a long time, she lay that way, alternately sobbing and sleeping. Then, after a long time, there was a stir. She woke from a doze to find a police officer and two or three other men bending over her. Some one carried a lantern. Terrified, smitten dumb, she was unable to answer the questions put to her. Then a woman, evidently a mistress of the house on the top of the hill, arrived and took Hilda in her arms and cried over her.

"I'll take the little girl," she said to the police officer.

" But the mother, can you save her? Is she too far gone?"

" I've sent for a doctor," replied the other.

Just before the ladies left the table, young Lambert raised his glass of Madeira. Turning towards the wife of the Railroad King, he said:

" My best compliments for a delightful dinner."

The doctor who had been bending over Mrs. Hooven, rose.

" It's no use," he said; " she has been dead some time—exhaustion from starvation."

IX

On Division Number Three of the Los Muertos ranch the wheat had already been cut, and S. Behrman on a certain morning in the first week of August drove across the open expanse of stubble toward the southwest, his eyes searching the horizon for the feather of smoke that would mark the location of the steam harvester. However, he saw nothing. The stubble extended onward apparently to the very margin of the world.

At length, S. Behrman halted his buggy and brought out his field glasses from beneath the seat. He stood up in his place and, adjusting the lenses, swept the prospect to the south and west. It was the same as though the sea of land were, in reality, the ocean, and he, lost in an open boat, were scanning the waste through his glasses, looking for the smoke of a steamer, hull down, below the horizon. "Wonder," he muttered, "if they're working on Four this morning?"

At length, he murmured an "Ah" of satisfaction. Far to the south into the white sheen of sky, immediately over the horizon, he made out a faint smudge—the harvester beyond doubt.

Thither S. Behrman turned his horse's head. It was all of an hour's drive over the uneven ground and through the crackling stubble, but at length he reached the harvester. He found, however, that it had been halted. The sack sewers, together with the header-man, were stretched on the ground in the shade of the machine, while the engineer and separator-man were pottering about a portion of the works.

"What's the matter, Billy?" demanded S. Behrman reining up.

The engineer turned about.

"The grain is heavy in here. We thought we'd better increase the speed of the cup-carrier, and pulled up to put in a smaller sprocket."

S. Behrman nodded to say that was all right, and added a question.

"How is she going?"

"Anywheres from twenty-five to thirty sacks to the acre right along here; nothing the matter with *that* I guess."

"Nothing in the world, Bill."

One of the sack sewers interposed:

"For the last half hour we've been throwing off three bags to the minute."

"That's good, that's good."

It was more than good; it was "bonanza," and all that division of the great ranch was thick with just such wonderful wheat. Never had Los Muertos been more generous, never a season more successful. S. Behrman drew a long breath of satisfaction. He knew just how great was his share in the lands which had just been absorbed by the corporation he served, just how many thousands of bushels of this marvellous crop were his property. Through all these years of confusion, bickerings, open hostility and, at last, actual warfare he had waited, nursing his patience, calm with the firm assurance of ultimate success. The end, at length, had come; he had entered into his reward and saw himself at last installed in the place he had so long, so silently coveted; saw himself chief of a principality, the Master of the Wheat.

The sprocket adjusted, the engineer called up the gang and the men took their places. The fireman stoked vigorously, the two sack sewers resumed their posts on the sacking platform, putting on the goggles that kept the chaff from their eyes. The separator-man and header-man gripped their levers.

The harvester, shooting a column of thick smoke straight upward, vibrating to the top of the stack, hissed, clanked, and lurched forward. Instantly, motion sprang to life in all its component parts; the header knives, cutting a thirty-six foot swath, gnashed like teeth; beltings slid and moved like smooth flowing streams; the separator whirred, the agitator jarred and crashed; cylinders, augers, fans, seeders and elevators, drapers and chaff-carriers clattered, rumbled, buzzed, and clanged. The steam hissed and rasped; the ground reverberated a hollow note, and the thousands upon thousands of wheat stalks sliced and slashed in the clashing shears of the header, rattled like dry rushes in a hurricane, as they fell inward, and were caught up by an endless belt, to disappear into the bowels of the vast brute that devoured them.

It was that and no less. It was the feeding of some prodigious monster, insatiable, with iron teeth, gnashing and threshing into the fields of standing wheat; devouring always, never glutted, never satiated, swallowing an entire harvest, snarling and slobbering in a welter of warm vapour, acrid smoke, and blinding, pungent clouds of chaff. It moved belly-deep in the standing grain, a hippopotamus, half-mired in river ooze, gorging rushes, snorting, sweating; a dinosaur wallowing through thick, hot grasses, floundering there, crouching, grovelling there as its vast jaws crushed and tore, and its enormous gullet swallowed, incessant, ravenous, and inordinate.

S. Behrman, very much amused, changed places with one of the sack sewers, allowing him to hold his horse while he mounted the sacking platform and took his place. The trepidation and jostling of the machine shook him till his teeth chattered in his head. His ears were shocked and assaulted by a myriad-tongued clamour, clashing steel, straining belts, jarring woodwork, while the impalpable chaff powder from the separators settled like dust in his hair, his ears, eyes, and mouth.

Directly in front of where he sat on the platform was the chute from the cleaner, and from this into the mouth of a half-full sack spouted an unending gush of grain, winnowed, cleaned, threshed, ready for the mill.

The pour from the chute of the cleaner had for S. Behrman an immense satisfaction. Without an instant's pause, a thick rivulet of wheat rolled and dashed tumultuous into the sack. In half a minute—sometimes in twenty seconds—the sack was full, was passed over to the second sewer, the mouth reeved up, and the sack dumped out upon the ground, to be picked up by the wagons and hauled to the railroad.

S. Behrman, hypnotised, sat watching that river of grain. All that shrieking, bellowing machinery, all that gigantic organism, all the months of labour, the ploughing, the planting, the prayers for rain, the years of preparation, the heartaches, the anxiety, the foresight, all the whole business of the ranch, the work of horses, of steam, of men and boys, looked to this spot—the grain chute from the harvester into the sacks. Its volume was the index of failure or success, of riches or poverty. And at this point, the labour of the rancher ended. Here, at the lip of the chute, he parted company with his grain, and from here the wheat streamed forth to feed the world. The yawning mouths of the sacks might well stand for the unnumbered mouths of the People, all agape for food; and here, into these sacks, at first so lean, so flaccid, attenuated like starved stomachs, rushed the living stream

of food, insistent, interminable, filling the empty, fattening the shrivelled, making it sleek and heavy and solid.

Half an hour later, the harvester stopped again. The
men on the sacking platform had used up all the sacks.
But S. Behrman's foreman, a new man on Los Muertos,
put in an appearance with the report that the wagon
bringing a fresh supply was approaching.

"How is the grain elevator at Port Costa getting on,
sir?"

"Finished," replied S. Behrman.

The new master of Los Muertos had decided upon
accumulating his grain in bulk in a great elevator at the
tide-water port, where the grain ships for Liverpool and
the East took on their cargoes. To this end, he had
bought and greatly enlarged a building at Port Costa,
that was already in use for that purpose, and to this
elevator all the crop of Los Muertos was to be carried.
The P. and S. W. made S. Behrman a special rate.

"By the way," said S. Behrman to his superintendent,
"we're in luck. Fallon's buyer was in Bonneville yesterday. He's buying for Fallon and for Holt, too. I
happened to run into him, and I've sold a ship load."

"A ship load!"

"Of Los Muertos wheat. He's acting for some Indian
Famine Relief Committee—lot of women people up in
the city—and wanted a whole cargo. I made a deal with
him. There's about fifty thousand tons of disengaged
shipping in San Francisco Bay right now, and ships are
fighting for charters. I wired McKissick and got a long
distance telephone from him this morning. He got me a
barque, the 'Swanhilda.' She'll dock day after to-
morrow, and begin loading."

"Hadn't I better take a run up," observed the superintendent, "and keep an eye on things?"

"No," answered S. Behrman, "I want you to stop

down here, and see that those carpenters hustle the work in the ranch house. Derrick will be out by then. You see this deal is peculiar. I'm not selling to any middle-man—not to Fallon's buyer. He only put me on to the thing. I'm acting direct with these women people, and I've got to have some hand in shipping this stuff myself. But I made my selling figure cover the price of a charter. It's a queer, mixed-up deal, and I don't fancy it much, but there's boodle in it. I'll go to Port Costa myself."

A little later on in the day, when S. Behrman had satisfied himself that his harvesting was going forward favourably, he reëntered his buggy and driving to the County Road turned southward towards the Los Muertos ranch house. He had not gone far, however, before he became aware of a familiar figure on horseback, jogging slowly along ahead of him. He recognised Presley; he shook the reins over his horse's back and very soon ranging up by the side of the young man passed the time of day with him.

"Well, what brings you down here again, Mr. Presley?" he observed. "I thought we had seen the last of you."

"I came down to say good-bye to my friends," answered Presley shortly.

"Going away?"

"Yes—to India."

"Well, upon my word. For your health, hey?"

"Yes."

"You *look* knocked up," asserted the other. "By the way," he added, "I suppose you've heard the news?"

Presley shrank a little. Of late the reports of disasters had followed so swiftly upon one another that he had begun to tremble and to quail at every unexpected bit of information.

"What news do you mean?" he asked.

"About Dyke. He has been convicted. The judge sentenced him for life."

For life! Riding on by the side of this man through the ranches by the County Road, Presley repeated these words to himself till the full effect of them burst at last upon him.

Jailed for life! No outlook. No hope for the future. Day after day, year after year, to tread the rounds of the same gloomy monotony. He saw the grey stone walls, the iron doors; the flagging of the "yard" bare of grass or trees—the cell, narrow, bald, cheerless; the prison garb, the prison fare, and round all the grim granite of insuperable barriers, shutting out the world, shutting in the man with outcasts, with the pariah dogs of society, thieves, murderers, men below the beasts, lost to all decency, drugged with opium, utter reprobates. To this, Dyke had been brought, Dyke, than whom no man had been more honest, more courageous, more jovial. This was the end of him, a prison; this was his final estate, a criminal.

Presley found an excuse for riding on, leaving S. Behrman behind him. He did not stop at Caraher's saloon, for the heat of his rage had long since begun to cool, and dispassionately, he saw things in their true light. For all the tragedy of his wife's death, Caraher was none the less an evil influence among the ranchers, an influence that worked only to the inciting of crime. Unwilling to venture himself, to risk his own life, the anarchist saloon-keeper had goaded Dyke and Presley both to murder; a bad man, a plague spot in the world of the ranchers, poisoning the farmers' bodies with alcohol and their minds with discontent.

At last, Presley arrived at the ranch house of Los Muertos. The place was silent; the grass on the lawn was half dead and over a foot high; the beginnings of weeds showed here and there in the driveway. He tied his horse to a ring in the trunk of one of the larger eucalyptus trees and entered the house.

Mrs. Derrick met him in the dining-room. The old look of uneasiness, almost of terror, had gone from her wide-open brown eyes. There was in them instead, the expression of one to whom a contingency, long dreaded, has arrived and passed. The stolidity of a settled grief, of an irreparable calamity, of a despair from which there was no escape was in her look, her manner, her voice. She was listless, apathetic, calm with the calmness of a woman who knows she can suffer no further.

"We are going away," she told Presley, as the two sat down at opposite ends of the dining table. "Just Magnus and myself—all there is left of us. There is very little money left; Magnus can hardly take care of himself, to say nothing of me. I must look after him now. We are going to Marysville."

"Why there?"

"You see," she explained, "it happens that my old place is vacant in the Seminary there. I am going back to teach—literature." She smiled wearily. "It is beginning all over again, isn't it? Only there is nothing to look forward to now. Magnus is an old man already, and I must take care of him."

"He will go with you, then," Presley said, "that will be some comfort to you at least."

"I don't know," she said slowly, "you have not seen Magnus lately."

"Is he—how do you mean? Isn't he any better?"

"Would you like to see him? He is in the office. You can go right in."

Presley rose. He hesitated a moment, then:

"Mrs. Annixter," he asked, "Hilma—is she still with you? I should like to see her before I go."

"Go in and see Magnus," said Mrs. Derrick. "I will tell her you are here."

Presley stepped across the stone-paved hallway with the glass roof, and after knocking three times at the office door pushed it open and entered.

Magnus sat in the chair before the desk and did not look up as Presley entered. He had the appearance of a man nearer eighty than sixty. All the old-time erectness was broken and bent. It was as though the muscles that once had held the back rigid, the chin high, had softened and stretched. A certain fatness, the obesity of inertia, hung heavy around the hips and abdomen, the eye was watery and vague, the cheeks and chin unshaven and unkempt, the grey hair had lost its forward curl towards the temples and hung thin and ragged around the ears. The hawk-like nose seemed hooked to meet the chin; the lips were slack, the mouth half-opened.

Where once the Governor had been a model of neatness in his dress, the frock coat buttoned, the linen clean, he now sat in his shirt sleeves, the waistcoat open and showing the soiled shirt. His hands were stained with ink, and these, the only members of his body that yet appeared to retain their activity, were busy with a great pile of papers,—oblong, legal documents, that littered the table before him. Without a moment's cessation, these hands of the Governor's came and went among the papers, deft, nimble, dexterous.

Magnus was sorting papers. From the heap upon his left hand he selected a document, opened it, glanced over it, then tied it carefully, and laid it away upon a second pile on his right hand. When all the papers were in one pile, he reversed the process, taking from his right hand to place upon his left, then back from left to right again, then once more from right to left. He spoke no word, he sat absolutely still, even his eyes did not move, only his hands, swift, nervous, agitated, seemed alive.

"Why, how are you, Governor?" said Presley, coming forward. Magnus turned slowly about and looked at him and at the hand in which he shook his own.

"Ah," he said at length, "Presley . . . yes."

Then his glance fell, and he looked aimlessly about upon the floor.

"I've come to say good-bye, Governor," continued Presley, "I'm going away."

"Going away . . . yes, why it's Presley. Good-day, Presley."

"Good-day, Governor. I'm going away. I've come to say good-bye."

"Good-bye?" Magnus bent his brows, "what are you saying good-bye for?"

"I'm going away, sir."

The Governor did not answer. Staring at the ledge of the desk, he seemed lost in thought. There was a long silence. Then, at length, Presley said:

"How are you getting on, Governor?"

Magnus looked up slowly.

"Why it's Presley," he said. "How do you do, Presley."

"Are you getting on all right, sir?"

"Yes," said Magnus after a while, "yes, all right. I am going away. I've come to say good-bye. No—" He interrupted himself with a deprecatory smile, "*you* said *that,* didn't you?"

"Well, you are going away, too, your wife tells me."

"Yes, I'm going away. I can't stay on . . ." he hesitated a long time, groping for the right word, "I can't stay on—on—what's the name of this place?"

"Los Muertos," put in Presley.

"No, it isn't. Yes, it is, too, that's right, Los Muertos. I don't know where my memory has gone to of late."

"Well, I hope you will be better soon, Governor."

As Presley spoke the words, S. Behrman entered the room, and the Governor sprang up with unexpected agility and stood against the wall, drawing one long breath after another, watching the railroad agent with intent eyes.

S. Behrman saluted both men affably and sat down near the desk, drawing the links of his heavy watch chain through his fat fingers.

"There wasn't anybody outside when I knocked, but I heard your voice in here, Governor, so I came right in. I wanted to ask you, Governor, if my carpenters can begin work in here day after to-morrow. I want to take down that partition there, and throw this room and the next into one. I guess that will be O. K., won't it? You'll be out of here by then, won't you?"

There was no vagueness about Magnus's speech or manner now. There was that same alertness in his demeanour that one sees in a tamed lion in the presence of its trainer.

"Yes, yes," he said quickly, "you can send your men here. I will be gone by to-morrow."

"I don't want to seem to hurry you, Governor."

"No, you will not hurry me. I am ready to go now."

"Anything I can do for you, Governor?"

"Nothing."

"Yes, there is, Governor," insisted S. Behrman. "I think now that all is over we ought to be good friends. I think I can do something for you. We still want an assistant in the local freight manager's office. Now, what do you say to having a try at it? There's a salary of fifty a month goes with it. I guess you must be in need of money now, and there's always the wife to support; what do you say? Will you try the place?"

Presley could only stare at the man in speechless wonder. What was he driving at? What reason was there back of this new move, and why should it be made thus openly and in his hearing? An explanation occurred to him. Was this merely a pleasantry on the part of S. Behrman, a way of enjoying to the full his triumph; was he testing the completeness of his victory, trying to see just how far he could go, how far beneath his feet he could push his old-time enemy?

"What do you say?" he repeated. "Will you try the place?"

"You—you *insist?*" inquired the Governor.

"Oh, I'm not insisting on anything," cried S. Behrman. "I'm offering you a place, that's all. Will you take it?"

"Yes, yes, I'll take it."

"You'll come over to our side?"

"Yes, I'll come over."

"You'll have to turn 'railroad,' understand?"

"I'll turn railroad."

"Guess there may be times when you'll have to take orders from me."

"I'll take orders from you."

"You'll have to be loyal to railroad, you know. No funny business."

"I'll be loyal to the railroad."

"You would like the place then?"

"Yes."

S. Behrman turned from Magnus, who at once resumed his seat and began again to sort his papers.

"Well, Presley," said the railroad agent: "I guess I won't see you again."

"I hope not," answered the other.

"Tut, tut, Presley, you know you can't make me angry."

He put on his hat of varnished straw and wiped his fat forehead with his handkerchief. Of late, he had grown fatter than ever, and the linen vest, stamped with a multitude of interlocked horseshoes, strained tight its imitation pearl buttons across the great protuberant stomach.

Presley looked at the man a moment before replying. But a few weeks ago he could not thus have faced the great enemy of the farmers without a gust of blind rage blowing tempestuous through all his bones. Now, however, he found to his surprise that his fury had lapsed to a profound contempt, in which there was bitterness, but no truculence. He was tired, tired to death of the whole business.

"Yes," he answered deliberately, "I am going away. You have ruined this place for me. I couldn't live here where I should have to see you, or the results of what you have done, whenever I stirred out of doors."

"Nonsense, Presley," answered the other, refusing to become angry. "That's foolishness, that kind of talk; though, of course, I understand how you feel. I guess it was you, wasn't it, who threw that bomb into my house?"

"It was."

"Well, that don't show any common sense, Presley," returned S. Behrman with perfect aplomb. "What could you have gained by killing me?"

"Not so much probably as you have gained by killing Harran and Annixter. But that's all passed now. You're safe from *me*." The strangeness of this talk, the oddity of the situation burst upon him and he laughed aloud. "It don't seem as though you could be brought to book, S. Behrman, by anybody, or by any means, does it? They can't get at you through the courts,—the law can't get you, Dyke's pistol missed fire for just your benefit, and you even escaped Caraher's six inches of plugged gas pipe. Just what are we going to do with you?"

"Best give it up, Pres, my boy," returned the other. "I guess there ain't anything can touch me. Well, Magnus," he said, turning once more to the Governor. "Well, I'll think over what you say, and let you know if I can get the place for you in a day or two. You see," he added, "you're getting pretty old, Magnus Derrick."

Presley flung himself from the room, unable any longer to witness the depths into which Magnus had fallen. What other scenes of degradation were enacted in that room, how much further S. Behrman carried the humiliation, he did not know. He suddenly felt that the air of the office was choking him.

He hurried up to what once had been his own room. On his way he could not but note that much of the house was in disarray, a great packing-up was in progress; trunks, half-full, stood in the hallways, crates and cases in a litter of straw encumbered the rooms. The servants came and went with armfuls of books, ornaments, articles of clothing.

Presley took from his room only a few manuscripts and note-books, and a small valise full of his personal effects; at the doorway he paused and, holding the knob of the door in his hand, looked back into the room a very long time.

He descended to the lower floor and entered the dining-room. Mrs. Derrick had disappeared. Presley stood for a long moment in front of the fireplace, looking about the room, remembering the scenes that he had witnessed there—the conference when Osterman had first suggested the fight for Railroad Commissioner and then later the attack on Lyman Derrick and the sudden revelation of that inconceivable treachery. But as he stood considering these things a door to his right opened and Hilma entered the room.

Presley came forward, holding out his hand, all unable to believe his eyes. It was a woman, grave, dignified, composed, who advanced to meet him. Hilma was dressed in black, the cut and fashion of the gown severe, almost monastic. All the little feminine and contradictory daintinesses were nowhere to be seen. Her statuesque calm evenness of contour yet remained, but it was the calmness of great sorrow, of infinite resignation. Beautiful she still remained, but she was older. The seriousness of one who has gained the knowledge of the world—knowledge of its evil—seemed to envelope her. The calm gravity of a great suffering past, but not forgotten, sat upon her. Not yet twenty-one, she exhibited the demeanour of a woman of forty.

The one-time amplitude of her figure, the fulness of hip and shoulder, the great deep swell from waist to throat were gone. She had grown thinner and, in consequence, seemed unusually, almost unnaturally tall. Her neck was slender, the outline of her full lips and round chin was a little sharp; her arms, those wonderful, beautiful arms of hers, were a little shrunken. But her eyes were as wide open as always, rimmed as ever by the thin, intensely black line of the lashes and her brown, fragrant hair was still thick, still, at times, glittered and coruscated in the sun. When she spoke, it was with the old-time velvety huskiness of voice that Annixter had learned to love so well.

"Oh, it is you," she said, giving him her hand. "You were good to want to see me before you left. I hear that you are going away."

She sat down upon the sofa.

"Yes," Presley answered, drawing a chair near to her, "yes, I felt I could not stay—down here any longer. I am going to take a long ocean voyage. My ship sails in a few days. But you, Mrs. Annixter, what are you going to do? Is there any way I can serve you?"

"No," she answered, "nothing. Papa is doing well. We are living here now."

"You are well?"

She made a little helpless gesture with both her hands, smiling very sadly.

"As you see," she answered.

As he talked, Presley was looking at her intently. Her dignity was a new element in her character and the certain slender effect of her figure, emphasised now by the long folds of the black gown she wore, carried it almost superbly. She conveyed something of the impression of a queen in exile. But she had lost none of her womanliness; rather, the contrary. Adversity had softened her, as well as deepened her. Presley saw that very clearly. Hilma had arrived now at her perfect maturity; she had known great love and she had known great grief, and the woman that had awakened in her with her affection for Annixter had been strengthened and infinitely ennobled by his death.

What if things had been different? Thus, as he conversed with her, Presley found himself wondering. Her sweetness, her beautiful gentleness, and tenderness were almost like palpable presences. It was almost as if a caress had been laid softly upon his cheek, as if a gentle hand closed upon his. Here, he knew, was sympathy; here, he knew, was an infinite capacity for love.

Then suddenly all the tired heart of him went out towards her. A longing to give the best that was in him to the memory of her, to be strong and noble because of her, to reshape his purposeless, half-wasted life with her nobility and purity and gentleness for his inspiration leaped all at once within him, leaped and stood firm, hardening to a resolve stronger than any he had ever known.

For an instant he told himself that the suddenness of this new emotion must be evidence of its insincerity. He was perfectly well aware that his impulses were abrupt and of short duration. But he knew that this was not sudden. Without realising it, he had been from the first drawn to Hilma, and all through these last terrible days, since the time he had seen her at Los Muertos, just after the battle at the ditch, she had obtruded continually upon his thoughts. The sight of her to-day, more beautiful than ever, quiet, strong, reserved, had only brought matters to a culmination.

"Are you," he asked her, "are you so unhappy, Hilma, that you can look forward to no more brightness in your life?"

"Unless I could forget—forget my husband," she answered, "how can I be happy? I would rather be unhappy in remembering him than happy in forgetting him. He was my whole world, literally and truly. Nothing seemed to count before I knew him, and nothing can count for me now, after I have lost him."

"You think now," he answered, "that in being happy again you would be disloyal to him. But you will find after a while—years from now—that it need not be so. The part of you that belonged to your husband can always keep him sacred, that part of you belongs to him and he to it. But you are young; you have all your life to live yet. Your sorrow need not be a burden to you. If you consider it as you should—as you *will* some day, believe me—it will only be a great help to you. It will make you more noble, a truer woman, more generous."

"I think I see," she answered, "and I never thought about it in that light before."

"I want to help you," he answered, "as you have

helped me. I want to be your friend, and above all things I do not want to see your life wasted. I am going away and it is quite possible I shall never see you again, but you will always be a help to me."

"I do not understand," she answered, "but I know you mean to be very, very kind to me. Yes, I hope when you come back—if you ever do—you will still be that. I do not know why you should want to be so kind, unless— yes, of course—you were my husband's dearest friend."

They talked a little longer, and at length Presley rose.

"I cannot bring myself to see Mrs. Derrick again," he said. "It would only serve to make her very unhappy. Will you explain that to her? I think she will understand."

"Yes," answered Hilma. "Yes, I will."

There was a pause. There seemed to be nothing more for either of them to say. Presley held out his hand.

"Good-bye," she said, as she gave him hers.

He carried it to his lips.

"Good-bye," he answered. "Good-bye and may God bless you."

He turned away abruptly and left the room.

But as he was quietly making his way out of the house, hoping to get to his horse unobserved, he came suddenly upon Mrs. Dyke and Sidney on the porch of the house. He had forgotten that since the affair at the ditch, Los Muertos had been a home to the engineer's mother and daughter.

"And you, Mrs. Dyke," he asked as he took her hand, "in this break-up of everything, where do you go?"

"To the city," she answered, "to San Francisco. I have a sister there who will look after the little tad."

"But you, how about yourself, Mrs. Dyke?"

She answered him in a quiet voice, monotonous, ex- pressionless:

"I am going to die very soon, Mr. Presley. There is no reason why I should live any longer. My son is in prison for life, everything is over for me, and I am tired, worn out."

"You mustn't talk like that, Mrs. Dyke," protested Presley, "nonsense; you will live long enough to see the little tad married." He tried to be cheerful. But he knew his words lacked the ring of conviction. Death already overshadowed the face of the engineer's mother. He felt that she spoke the truth, and as he stood there speaking to her for the last time, his arm about little Sidney's shoulder, he knew that he was seeing the beginnings of the wreck of another family and that, like Hilda Hooven, another baby girl was to be started in life, through no fault of hers, fearfully handicapped, weighed down at the threshold of existence with a load of disgrace. Hilda Hooven and Sidney Dyke, what was to be their histories? the one, sister of an outcast; the other, daughter of a convict. And he thought of that other young girl, the little Honora Gerard, the heiress of millions, petted, loved, receiving adulation from all who came near to her, whose only care was to choose from among the multitude of pleasures that the world hastened to present to her consideration.

"Good-bye," he said, holding out his hand.

"Good-bye."

"Good-bye, Sidney."

He kissed the little girl, clasped Mrs. Dyke's hand a moment with his; then, slinging his satchel about his shoulders by the long strap with which it was provided, left the house, and mounting his horse rode away from Los Muertos never to return.

Presley came out upon the County Road. At a little distance to his left he could see the group of buildings where once Broderson had lived. These were being remodelled, at length, to suit the larger demands of the New Agriculture. A strange man came out by the road gate; no doubt, the new proprietor. Presley turned away, hurrying northwards along the County Road by the mammoth watering-tank and the long wind-break of poplars.

He came to Caraher's place. There was no change here. The saloon had weathered the storm, indispensable to the new as well as to the old régime. The same dusty buggies and buckboards were tied under the shed, and as Presley hurried by he could distinguish Caraher's voice, loud as ever, still proclaiming his creed of annihilation.

Bonneville Presley avoided. He had no associations with the town. He turned aside from the road, and crossing the northwest corner of Los Muertos and the line of the railroad, turned back along the Upper Road till he came to the Long Trestle and Annixter's,—Silence, desolation, abandonment.

A vast stillness, profound, unbroken, brooded low over all the place. No living thing stirred. The rusted windmill on the skeleton-like tower of the artesian well was motionless; the great barn empty; the windows of the ranch house, cook house, and dairy boarded up. Nailed upon a tree near the broken gateway was a board, white painted, with stencilled letters,· bearing the inscription:

"Warning. ALL PERSONS FOUND TRESPASSING ON THESE PREMISES WILL BE PROSECUTED TO THE FULLEST EXTENT OF THE LAW. By order P. and S. W. R. R."

As he had planned, Presley reached the hills by the head waters of Broderson's Creek late in the afternoon. Toilfully he climbed them, reached the highest crest, and turning about, looked long and for the last time at all the reach of the valley unrolled beneath him. The land of the ranches opened out forever and forever under the stimulus of that measureless range of vision. The whole gigantic sweep of the San Joaquin expanded Titanic before the eye of the mind, flagellated with heat, quivering and shimmering under the sun's red eye. It was the season after the harvest, and the great earth, the mother, after its period of reproduction, its pains of labour, delivered of the fruit of its loins, slept the sleep of exhaustion in the infinite repose of the colossus, benignant, eternal, strong, the nourisher of nations, the feeder of an entire world.

And as Presley looked there came to him strong and true the sense and the significance of all the enigma of growth. He seemed for one instant to touch the explanation of existence. Men were nothings, mere animalculæ, mere ephemerides that fluttered and fell and were forgotten between dawn and dusk. Vanamee had said there was no death. But for one second Presley could go one step further. Men were naught, death was naught, life was naught; FORCE only existed—FORCE that brought men into the world, FORCE that crowded them out of it to make way for the succeeding generation, FORCE that made the wheat grow, FORCE that garnered it from the soil to give place to the succeeding crop.

It was the mystery of creation, the stupendous miracle of re-creation; the vast rhythm of the seasons, measured, alternative, the sun and the stars keeping time as the eternal symphony of reproduction swung in its tremendous cadences like the colossal pendulum of an almighty machine—primordial energy flung out from the hand of the Lord God himself, immortal, calm, infinitely strong.

But as he stood thus looking down upon the great valley he was aware of the figure of a man, far in the distance, moving steadily towards the Mission of San Juan.

The man was hardly more than a dot, but there was something unmistakably familiar in his gait; and besides this, Presley could fancy that he was hatless. He touched his pony with his spur. The man was Vanamee beyond all doubt, and a little later Presley, descending the maze of cow-paths and cattle-trails that led down towards the Broderson Creek, overtook his friend.

Instantly Presley was aware of an immense change. Vanamee's face was still that of an ascetic, still glowed with the rarefied intelligence of a young seer, a half-inspired shepherd-prophet of Hebraic legends; but the shadow of that great sadness which for so long had brooded over him was gone; the grief that once he had fancied deathless was, indeed, dead, or rather swallowed up in a victorious joy that radiated like sunlight at dawn from the deep-set eyes, and the hollow, swarthy cheeks. They talked together till nearly sundown, but to Presley's questions as to the reasons for Vanamee's happiness, the other would say nothing. Once only he allowed himself to touch upon the subject.

"Death and grief are little things," he said. "They are transient. Life must be before death, and joy before grief. Else there are no such things as death or grief. These are only negatives. Life is positive. Death is only the absence of life, just as night is only the absence of day, and if this is so, there is no such thing as death. There is only life, and the suppression of life, that we, foolishly, say is death. 'Suppression,' I say, not extinction. I do not say that life returns. Life never departs. Life simply *is*. For certain seasons, it is hidden in the dark, but is that death, extinction, annihilation? I take it, thank God, that it is not. Does the grain of wheat, hidden for certain seasons in the dark, die? The grain we think is dead *resumes again;* but how? Not as one grain, but as twenty. So all life. Death is only real for all the detritus of the world, for all the sorrow, for all the injustice, for all the grief. Presley, the good never dies; evil dies, cruelty, oppression, selfishness, greed—these die; but nobility, but love, but sacrifice, but generosity, but truth, thank God for it, small as they are, difficult as it is to discover them—these live forever, these are eternal. You are all broken, all cast down by what you have seen in this valley, this hopeless struggle, this apparently hopeless despair. Well, the end is not yet. What is it that remains after all is over, after the dead are buried and the hearts are broken? Look at it all from the vast height of humanity—'the greatest good to the greatest numbers.' What remains? Men perish, men are corrupted, hearts are rent asunder, but what remains untouched, unassailable, undefiled? Try to find that, not only in this, but in every crisis of the world's life, and you will find, if your view be large enough, that it is *not* evil, but good, that in the end remains."

There was a long pause. Presley, his mind full of new thoughts, held his peace, and Vanamee added at length:

"I believed Angéle dead. I wept over her grave; mourned for her as dead in corruption. She has come back to me, more beautiful than ever. Do not ask me any further. To put this story, this idyl, into words, would, for me, be a profanation. This must suffice you. Angéle has returned to me, and I am happy. *Adios.*"

He rose suddenly. The friends clasped each other's hands.

"We shall probably never meet again," said Vanamee; "but if these are the last words I ever speak to you, listen to them, and remember them, because I know I speak the truth. Evil is short-lived. Never judge of the whole round of life by the mere segment you can see. The whole is, in the end, perfect."

Abruptly he took himself away. He was gone. Presley, alone, thoughtful, his hands clasped behind him, passed on through the ranches—here teeming with ripened wheat—his face set from them forever.

Not so Vanamee. For hours he roamed the countryside, now through the deserted cluster of buildings that had once been Annixter's home; now through the rustling and, as yet, uncut wheat of Quien Sabe! now treading the slopes of the hills far to the north, and again following the winding courses of the streams. Thus he spent the night.

At length, the day broke, resplendent, cloudless. The night was passed. There was all the sparkle and effervescence of joy in the crystal sunlight as the dawn expanded roseate, and at length flamed dazzling to the zenith when the sun moved over the edge of the world and looked down upon all the earth like the eye of God the Father.

At the moment, Vanamee stood breast-deep in the wheat in a solitary corner of the Quien Sabe rancho. He turned eastward, facing the celestial glory of the day and sent his voiceless call far from him across the golden grain out towards the little valley of flowers.

Swiftly the answer came. It advanced to meet him. The flowers of the Seed ranch were gone, dried and parched by the summer's sun, shedding their seed by handfuls to be sown again and blossom yet another time. The Seed ranch was no longer royal with colour. The roses, the lilies, the carnations, the hyacinths, the poppies, the violets, the mignonette, all these had vanished, the little valley was without colour; where once it had exhaled the most delicious perfume, it was now odourless. Under the blinding light of the day it stretched to its hillsides, bare, brown, unlovely. The romance of the place had vanished, but with it had vanished the Vision.

It was no longer a figment of his imagination, a creature of dreams that advanced to meet Vanamee. It was Reality—it was Angéle in the flesh, vital, sane, material, who at last issued forth from the entrance of the little valley. Romance had vanished, but better than romance was here. Not a manifestation, not a dream, but her very self. The night was gone, but the sun had risen; the flowers had disappeared, but strong, vigorous, noble, the wheat had come.

In the wheat he waited for her. He saw her coming. She was simply dressed. No fanciful wreath of tuberoses was about her head now, no strange garment of red and gold enveloped her now. It was no longer an ephemeral illusion of the night, evanescent, mystic, but a simple country girl coming to meet her lover. The vision of the night had been beautiful, but what was it compared to this? Reality was better than Romance. The simple honesty of a loving, trusting heart was better than a legend of flowers, an hallucination of the moonlight. She came nearer. Bathed in sunlight, he saw her face to face, saw her hair hanging in two straight plaits on either side of her face, saw the enchanting fulness of her lips, the strange, balancing movement of her head upon her slender neck. But now she was no longer asleep. The wonderful eyes, violet blue, heavy-lidded, with their perplexing, oriental slant towards the temples, were wide open and fixed upon his.

From out the world of romance, out of the moonlight and the star sheen, out of the faint radiance of the lilies and the still air heavy with perfume, she had at last come to him. The moonlight, the flowers, and the dream were all vanished away. Angéle was realised in the Wheat. She stood forth in the sunlight, a fact, and no longer a fancy.

He ran forward to meet her and she held out her arms

to him. He caught her to him, and she, turning her face
to his, kissed him on the mouth.

"I love you, I love you," she murmured.

.　　.　　.　　.　　.　　.

Upon descending from his train at Port Costa, S.
Behrman asked to be directed at once to where the bark
"Swanhilda" was taking on grain. Though he had
bought and greatly enlarged his new elevator at this port,
he had never seen it. The work had been carried on
through agents, S. Behrman having far too many and
more pressing occupations to demand his presence and
attention. Now, however, he was to see the concrete
evidence of his success for the first time.

He picked his way across the railroad tracks to the
line of warehouses that bordered the docks, numbered
with enormous Roman numerals and full of grain in
bags.

The sight of these bags of grain put him in mind of
the fact that among all the other shippers he was practically alone in his way of handling his wheat. They
handled the grain in bags; he, however, preferred it in
the bulk. Bags were sometimes four cents apiece, and
he had decided to build his elevator and bulk his grain
therein, rather than to incur this expense. Only a small
part of his wheat—that on Number Three division—
had been sacked. All the rest, practically two-thirds
of the entire harvest of Los Muertos, now found
itself warehoused in his enormous elevator at Port
Costa.

To a certain degree it had been the desire of observing
the working of his system of handling the wheat in bulk
that had drawn S. Behrman to Port Costa. But the more
powerful motive had been curiosity, not to say down-
right sentiment. So long had he planned for this day of
triumph, so eagerly had he looked forward to it, that

now, when it had come, he wished to enjoy it to its fullest extent, wished to miss no feature of the disposal of the crop. He had watched it harvested, he had watched it hauled to the railway, and now would watch it as it poured into the hold of the ship, would even watch the ship as she cleared and got under way.

He passed through the warehouses and came out upon the dock that ran parallel with the shore of the bay. A great quantity of shipping was in view, barques for the most part, Cape Horners, great, deep sea tramps, whose iron-shod forefeet had parted every ocean the world round from Rangoon to Rio Janeiro, and from Melbourne to Christiania. Some were still in the stream, loaded with wheat to the Plimsoll mark, ready to depart with the next tide. But many others laid their great flanks alongside the docks and at that moment were being filled by derrick and crane with thousands upon thousands of bags of wheat. The scene was brisk; the cranes creaked and swung incessantly with a rattle of chains; stevedores and wharfingers toiled and perspired; boatswains and dock-masters shouted orders, drays rumbled, the water lapped at the piles; a group of sailors, painting the flanks of one of the great ships, raised an occasional chanty; the trade wind sang aeolian in the cordages, filling the air with the nimble taint of salt. All around were the noises of ships and the feel and flavor of the sea.

S. Behrman soon discovered his elevator. It was the largest structure discernible, and upon its red roof, in enormous white letters, was his own name. Thither, between piles of grain bags, halted drays, crates and boxes of merchandise, with an occasional pyramid of salmon cases, S. Behrman took his way. Cabled to the dock, close under his elevator, lay a great ship with lofty masts and great spars. Her stern was toward him as he approached, and upon it, in raised golden letters, he could read the words "Swanhilda—Liverpool."

He went aboard by a very steep gangway and found the mate on the quarter deck. S. Behrman introduced himself.

"Well," he added, "how are you getting on?"

"Very fairly, sir," returned the mate, who was an Englishman. "We'll have her all snugged down tight by this time, day after to-morrow. It's a great saving of time shunting the stuff in her like that, and three men can do the work of seven."

"I'll have a look 'round, I believe," returned S. Behrman.

"Right—oh," answered the mate with a nod.

S. Behrman went forward to the hatch that opened down into the vast hold of the ship. A great iron chute connected this hatch with the elevator, and through it was rushing a veritable cataract of wheat.

It came from some gigantic bin within the elevator itself, rushing down the confines of the chute to plunge into the roomy, gloomy interior of the hold with an incessant, metallic roar, persistent, steady, inevitable. No men were in sight. The place was deserted. No human agency seemed to be back of the movement of the wheat. Rather, the grain seemed impelled with a force of its own, a resistless, huge force, eager, vivid, impatient for the sea.

S. Behrman stood watching, his ears deafened with the roar of the hard grains against the metallic lining of the chute. He put his hand once into the rushing tide, and the contact rasped the flesh of his fingers and like an undertow drew his hand after it in its impetuous dash.

Cautiously he peered down into the hold. A musty odour rose to his nostrils, the vigorous, pungent aroma

of the raw cereal. It was dark. He could see nothing;
but all about and over the opening of the hatch the air
was full of a fine, impalpable dust that blinded the eyes
and choked the throat and nostrils.

As his eyes became used to the shadows of the cavern
below him, he began to distinguish the grey mass of the
wheat, a great expanse, almost liquid in its texture,
which, as the cataract from above plunged into it, moved
and shifted in long, slow eddies. As he stood there, this
cataract on a sudden increased in volume. He turned
about, casting his eyes upward toward the elevator to
discover the cause. His foot caught in a coil of rope, and
he fell headforemost into the hold.

The fall was a long one and he struck the surface of
the wheat with the sodden impact of a bundle of damp
clothes. For the moment he was stunned. All the breath
was driven from his body. He could neither move nor
cry out. But, by degrees, his wits steadied themselves
and his breath returned to him. He looked about and
above him. The daylight in the hold was dimmed and
clouded by the thick, chaff-dust thrown off by the pour
of grain, and even this dimness dwindled to twilight at a
short distance from the opening of the hatch, while the
remotest quarters were lost in impenetrable blackness.
He got upon his feet only to find that he sunk ankle deep
in the loose packed mass underfoot.

" Hell," he muttered, " here's a fix."

Directly underneath the chute, the wheat, as it poured
in, raised itself in a conical mound, but from the sides
of this mound it shunted away incessantly in thick layers, flowing in all directions with the nimbleness of water.
Even as S. Behrman spoke, a wave of grain poured
around his legs and rose rapidly to the level of his knees.
He stepped quickly back. To stay near the chute would
soon bury him to the waist.

No doubt, there was some other exit from the hold, some companion ladder that led up to the deck. He scuffled and waded across the wheat, groping in the dark with outstretched hands. With every inhalation he choked, filling his mouth and nostrils more with dust than with air. At times he could not breathe at all, but gagged and gasped, his lips distended. But search as he would, he could find no outlet to the hold, no stairway, no companion ladder. Again and again, staggering along in the black darkness, he bruised his knuckles and forehead against the iron sides of the ship. He gave up the attempt to find any interior means of escape and returned laboriously to the space under the open hatchway. Already he could see that the level of the wheat was raised.

"God," he said, "this isn't going to do at all." He uttered a great shout. "Hello, on deck there, somebody. For God's sake."

The steady, metallic roar of the pouring wheat drowned out his voice. He could scarcely hear it himself above the rush of the cataract. Besides this, he found it impossible to stay under the hatch. The flying grains of wheat, spattering as they fell, stung his face like wind-driven particles of ice. It was a veritable torture; his hands smarted with it. Once he was all but blinded. Furthermore, the succeeding waves of wheat, rolling from the mound under the chute, beat him back, swirling and dashing against his legs and knees, mounting swiftly higher, carrying him off his feet.

Once more he retreated, drawing back from beneath the hatch. He stood still for a moment and shouted again. It was in vain. His voice returned upon him, unable to penetrate the thunder of the chute, and horrified, he discovered that so soon as he stood motionless upon the wheat, he sank into it. Before he knew it, he

was knee-deep again, and a long swirl of grain sweeping
outward from the ever-breaking, ever-reforming pyramid
below the chute, poured around his thighs, immobolising
him.

A frenzy of terror suddenly leaped to life within him.
The horror of death, the Fear of The Trap, shook him
like a dry reed. Shouting, he tore himself free of the
wheat and once more scrambled and struggled towards
the hatchway. He stumbled as he reached it and fell directly beneath the pour. Like a storm of small shot, mer-
cilessly, pitilessly, the unnumbered multitude of hurtling
grains flagellated and beat and tore his flesh. Blood
streamed from his forehead and, thickening with the
powder-like chaff-dust, blinded his eyes. He struggled
to his feet once more. An avalanche from the cone of
wheat buried him to his thighs. He was forced back and
back and back, beating the air, falling, rising, howling
for aid. He could no longer see; his eyes, crammed with
dust, smarted as if transfixed with needles whenever he
opened them. His mouth was full of the dust, his lips
were dry with it; thirst tortured him, while his outcries
choked and gagged in his rasped throat.

And all the while without stop, incessantly, inexorably,
the wheat, as if moving with a force all its own, shot
downward in a prolonged roar, persistent, steady, inevitable.

He retreated to a far corner of the hold and sat down
with his back against the iron hull of the ship and tried
to collect his thoughts, to calm himself. Surely there
must be some way of escape; surely he was not to die
like this, die in this dreadful substance that was neither
solid nor fluid. What was he to do? How make himself
heard?

But even as he thought about this, the cone under the
chute broke again and sent a great layer of grain rippling

and tumbling toward him. It reached him where he sat
and buried his hand and one foot.

He sprang up trembling and made for another corner.
"By God," he cried, "by God, I must think of something pretty quick!"

Once more the level of the wheat rose and the grains
began piling deeper about him. Once more he retreated.
Once more he crawled staggering to the foot of the cataract, screaming till his ears sang and his eyeballs strained
in their sockets, and once more the relentless tide drove
him back.

Then began that terrible dance of death; the man
dodging, doubling, squirming, hunted from one corner to
another, the wheat slowly, inexorably flowing, rising,
spreading to every angle, to every nook and cranny. It
reached his middle. Furious and with bleeding hands
and broken nails, he dug his way out to fall backward,
all but exhausted, gasping for breath in the dust-
thickened air. Roused again by the slow advance of the
tide, he leaped up and stumbled away, blinded with the
agony in his eyes, only to crash against the metal hull
of the vessel. He turned about, the blood streaming from
his face, and paused to collect his senses, and with a
rush, another wave swirled about his ankles and knees.
Exhaustion grew upon him. To stand still meant to sink;
to lie or sit meant to be buried the quicker; and all this
in the dark, all this in an air that could scarcely be
breathed, all this while he fought an enemy that could
not be gripped, toiling in a sea that could not be stayed.

Guided by the sound of the falling wheat, S. Behrman
crawled on hands and knees toward the hatchway. Once
more he raised his voice in a shout for help. His bleeding
throat and raw, parched lips refused to utter but a wheez-
ing moan. Once more he tried to look toward the one
patch of faint light above him. His eye-lids, clogged with

chaff, could no longer open. The Wheat poured about his waist as he raised himself upon his knees.

Reason fled. Deafened with the roar of the grain, blinded and made dumb with its chaff, he threw himself forward with clutching fingers, rolling upon his back, and lay there, moving feebly, the head rolling from side to side. The Wheat, leaping continuously from the chute, poured around him. It filled the pockets of the coat, it crept up the sleeves and trouser legs, it covered the great, protuberant stomach, it ran at last in rivulets into the distended, gasping mouth. It covered the face.

Upon the surface of the Wheat, under the chute, nothing moved but the Wheat itself. There was no sign of life. Then, for an instant, the surface stirred. A hand, fat, with short fingers and swollen veins, reached up, clutching, then fell limp and prone. In another instant it was covered. In the hold of the " Swanhilda " there was no movement but the widening ripples that spread flowing from the ever-breaking, ever-reforming cone; no sound, but the rushing of the Wheat that continued to plunge incessantly from the iron chute in a prolonged roar, persistent, steady, inevitable.

CONCLUSION

The "Swanhilda" cast off from the docks at Port Costa two days after Presley had left Bonneville and the ranches and made her way up to San Francisco, anchoring in the stream off the City front. A few hours after her arrival, Presley, waiting at his club, received a despatch from Cedarquist to the effect that she would clear early the next morning and that he must be aboard of her before midnight.

He sent his trunks aboard and at once hurried to Cedarquist's office to say good-bye. He found the manufacturer in excellent spirits.

"What do you think of Lyman Derrick now, Presley?" he said, when Presley had sat down. "He's in the new politics with a vengeance, isn't he? And our own dear Railroad openly acknowledges him as their candidate. You've heard of his canvass."

"Yes, yes," answered Presley. "Well, he knows his business best."

But Cedarquist was full of another idea: his new venture—the organizing of a line of clipper wheat ships for Pacific and Oriental trade—was prospering.

"The 'Swanhilda' is the mother of the fleet, Pres. I had to buy her, but the keel of her sister ship will be laid by the time she discharges at Calcutta. We'll carry our wheat into Asia yet. The Anglo-Saxon started from there at the beginning of everything and it's manifest destiny that he must circle the globe and fetch up where he began his march. You are up with procession, Pres, going to India this way in a wheat ship that flies American colours. By the way, do you know where the money is to come from to build the sister ship of the 'Swanhilda'? From the sale of the plant and scrap iron of the Atlas Works. Yes, I've given it up definitely, that business. The people here would not back me up. But I'm working off on this new line now. It may break me, but we'll try it on. You know the 'Million Dollar Fair' was formally opened yesterday. There is," he added with a wink, "a Midway Pleasance in connection with the thing. Mrs. Cedarquist and our friend Hartrath 'got up a subscription' to construct a figure of California—heroic size—out of dried apricots. I assure you," he remarked with prodigious gravity, "it is a real work of art and quite a 'feature' of the Fair. Well, good luck to you, Pres. Write to me from Honolulu, and *bon voyage*. My respects to the hungry Hindoo. Tell him 'we're coming, Father Abraham, a hundred thousand more.' Tell the men of the East to look out for the men of the West. The irrepressible Yank is knocking at the doors of their temples and he will want to sell 'em carpet-sweepers for their harems and electric light plants for their temple shrines. Good-bye to you."

"Good-bye, sir."

"Get fat yourself while you're about it, Presley," he observed, as the two stood up and shook hands.

"There shouldn't be any lack of food on a wheat ship. Bread enough, surely."

"Little monotonous, though. 'Man cannot live by bread alone.' Well, you're really off. Good-bye."

"Good-bye, sir."

And as Presley issued from the building and stepped out into the street, he was abruptly aware of a great wagon shrouded in white cloth, inside of which a bass drum was being furiously beaten. On the cloth, in great letters, were the words:

" Vote for Lyman Derrick, Regular Republican Nominee for Governor of California."

    *   *   *   *   *   *

The " Swanhilda " lifted and rolled slowly, majestically on the ground swell of the Pacific, the water hissing and boiling under her forefoot, her cordage vibrating and droning in the steady rush of the trade winds. It was drawing towards evening and her lights had just been set. The master passed Presley, who was leaning over the rail smoking a cigarette, and paused long enough to remark:

" The land yonder, if you can make it out, is Point Gordo, and if you were to draw a line from our position now through that point and carry it on about a hundred miles further, it would just about cross Tulare County not very far from where you used to live."

" I see," answered Presley, " I see. Thanks. I am glad to know that."

The master passed on, and Presley, going up to the quarter deck, looked long and earnestly at the faint line of mountains that showed vague and bluish above the waste of tumbling water.

Those were the mountains of the Coast range and beyond them was what once had been his home. Bonneville was there, and Guadalajara and Los Muertos and Quien Sabe, the Mission of San Juan, the Seed ranch, Annixter's desolated home and Dyke's ruined hop-fields.

Well, it was all over now, that terrible drama through which he had lived. Already it was far distant from him; but once again it rose in his memory, portentous, sombre, ineffaceable. He passed it all in review from the day of his first meeting with Vanamee to the day of his parting with Hilma. He saw it all—the great sweep of country opening to view from the summit of the hills at the head waters of Broderson's Creek; the barn dance at Annixter's, the harness room with its jam of furious men; the quiet garden of the Mission; Dyke's house, his flight upon the engine, his brave fight in the chaparral; Lyman Derrick at bay in the dining-room of the ranch house; the rabbit drive; the fight at the irrigating ditch, the shouting mob in the Bonneville Opera House.

The drama was over. The fight of Ranch and Railroad had been wrought out to its dreadful close. It was true, as Shelgrim had said, that forces rather than men had locked horns in that struggle, but for all that the men of the Ranch and not the men of the Railroad had suffered. Into the prosperous valley, into the quiet community of farmers, that galloping monster, that terror of steel and steam had burst, shooting athwart the horizons, flinging the echo of its thunder over all the ranches of the valley, leaving blood and destruction in its path.

Yes, the Railroad had prevailed. The ranches had been seized in the tentacles of the octopus; the iniquitous burden of extortionate freight rates had been imposed like a yoke of iron. The monster had killed Harran, had killed Osterman, had killed Broderson, had killed Hooven. It had beggared Magnus and had driven him to a state of semi-insanity after he had wrecked his honour in the vain attempt to do evil that good might come. It had enticed Lyman into its toils to pluck from him his manhood and his honesty, corrupting him and poisoning him beyond redemption; it had hounded Dyke from his legitimate employment and had made of him a highwayman and criminal. It had cast forth Mrs. Hooven to starve to death upon the City streets. It had driven Minna to prostitution. It had slain Annixter at the very moment when painfully and manfully he had at last achieved his own salvation and stood forth resolved to do right, to act unselfishly and to live for others. It had widowed Hilma in the very dawn of her happiness. It had killed the very babe within the mother's womb, strangling life ere yet it had been born, stamping out the spark ordained by God to burn through all eternity.

What then was left? Was there no hope, no outlook for the future, no rift in the black curtain, no glimmer through the night? Was good to be thus overthrown? Was evil thus to be strong and to prevail? Was nothing left?

Then suddenly Vanamee's words came back to his mind. What was the larger view, what contributed the greatest good to the greatest numbers? What was the full round of the circle whose segment only he beheld? In the end, the ultimate, final end of all, what was left? Yes, good issued from this crisis, untouched, unassailable, undefiled.

Men—motes in the sunshine—perished, were shot down in the very noon of life, hearts were broken, little children started in life lamentably handicapped; young girls were brought to a life of shame; old women died in the heart of life for lack of food. In that little, isolated group of human insects, misery, death, and anguish spun like a wheel of fire.

But the WHEAT *remained.* Untouched, unassailable, undefiled, that mighty world-force, that nourisher of nations, wrapped in Nirvanic calm, indifferent to the human swarm, gigantic, resistless, moved onward in its appointed grooves. Through the welter of blood at the irrigation ditch, through the sham charity and shallow philanthropy of famine relief committees, the great harvest of Los Muertos rolled like a flood from the Sierras to the Himalayas to feed thousands of starving scarecrows on the barren plains of India.

Falseness dies; injustice and oppression in the end of everything fade and vanish away. Greed, cruelty, selfishness, and inhumanity are short-lived; the individual suffers, but the race goes on. Annixter dies, but in a far distant corner of the world a thousand lives are saved. The larger view always and through all shams, all wickednesses, discovers the Truth that will, in the end, prevail, and all things, surely, inevitably, resistlessly work together for good.

SUGGESTIONS FOR
FURTHER READING

OTHER WORKS BY FRANK NORRIS
Yvernelle. Philadelphia, 1892.
Moran of the Lady Letty. New York, 1898. English title *Shanghaied*,
    London, 1899.
McTeague: A Story of San Francisco. New York, 1899.
Blix. New York, 1899.
The Pit. New York, 1903.
The Responsibilities of the Novelist and Other Literary Essays. New
    York, 1903.
A Deal in Wheat and Other Stories of the New and Old West. New
    York, 1903.
Vandover and the Brute. New York, 1914.

COLLECTED EDITIONS
The Complete Works of Frank Norris. Seven volumes. New York,
    1903.
The Argonaut Manuscript Limited Edition of Frank Norris's Works.
    Ten volumes. Garden City, 1928.
The Complete Works of Frank Norris. Ten volumes. Port Washington,
    New York, 1967. (A reprint of the Argonaut Edition.)

ANTHOLOGIES
Frank Norris, Collected Writings Hitherto Unpublished in Book Form.
    With an introduction by Charles G. Norris. Volume Ten of the
    Argonaut Edition of 1928.
*Frank Norris of "The Wave"; Stories and Sketches from the San Fran-
    cisco Weekly, 1893 to 1897*. Foreword by Charles G. Norris.
    Introduction by Oscar Lewis. San Francisco, 1931.
The Letters of Frank Norris. Edited by Franklin Walker. San Fran-
    cisco, 1956.

The Literary Criticism of Frank Norris. Edited by Donald Pizer. Austin, 1964.

BIBLIOGRAPHY AND REFERENCE

Crisler, Jesse S., and Joseph R. McElrath, Jr., *Frank Norris, A Reference Guide.* Boston, 1974.

Hill, John S. *The Merrill Checklist of Frank Norris.* Columbus, Ohio, 1970.

Lohf, Kenneth A., and Eugene P. Sheehy, *Frank Norris, A Bibliography.* Los Gatos, California, 1959.

BIOGRAPHY

Norris, Charles Gilman. *Frank Norris, 1870–1902: An Intimate Sketch of the Man Who Was Universally Acclaimed the Greatest American Writer of His Generation.* New York, 1914.

Richards, Grant. *Author Hunting by an Old Literary Sports Man.* New York, 1934.

Walker, Franklin Dickerson. *Frank Norris, a Biography.* Garden City, 1932. Reprinted 1963.

CRITICISM

Ahnebrink, Lars. *The Influence of Émile Zola on Frank Norris.* Upsala, 1947.

———. *The Beginnings of Naturalism in American Fiction.* New York, 1961.

Brooks, Van Wyck. *The Confident Years, 1885–1915.* New York, 1952.

Cargill, Oscar. *Intellectual America.* New York, 1941.

Chase, Richard Volney. *The American Novel and Its Tradition.* Garden City, 1957.

Davison, Richard Allan, editor. *The Merrill Studies in The Octopus.* Columbus, Ohio, 1969.

Dillingham, William B. *Frank Norris, Instinct and Art.* Lincoln, 1969.

Garland, Hamlin. *Companions on the Trail.* New York, 1931.

Geismar, Maxwell David. *Rebels and Ancestors, The American Novel, 1890–1915.* Boston, 1953.

Graham, Don. *The Fiction of Frank Norris, The Aesthetic Context.* Columbus and London, 1978.

Graham, Don, editor. *Critical Essays on Frank Norris*. Boston, 1980.

Hicks, Granville. *The Great Tradition: An Interpretation of American Literature Since the Civil War*. New York, 1933.

Hofstadter, Richard. *The Age of Reform*. New York, 1955.

Kazin, Alfred. *On Native Grounds: An Interpretation of Modern American Prose Literature*. New York, 1942.

Lutwack, Leonard. *Heroic Fiction: The Epic Tradition and American Novels of the Twentieth Century*. Carbondale, Illinois, 1970.

Lynn, Kenneth S. *The Dream of Success*. Boston, 1955.

——. *Visions of America: Eleven Literary Historical Essays*. Westport, Conn., 1973.

Marchand, Ernest. *Frank Norris, A Study*. Stanford, 1942.

Marx, Leo. *The Machine in the Garden: Technology and the Pastoral Ideal in America*. New York, 1964.

Parrington, Vernon Louis. *Main Currents in American Thought*. New York, 1930.

Pizer, Donald. *The Novels of Frank Norris*. Bloomington, 1966.

Spiller, Robert E. *The Cycle of American Literature*. New York, 1955.

Taylor, Walter Fuller. *The Economic Novel in America*. Chapel Hill, 1942.

Wolcutt, Charles Child. *American Literary Naturalism, A Divided Stream*. Minneapolis, 1966.

ARTICLES

Bixler, Paul H. "Frank Norris's Literary Reputation," *American Literature*, 6 (1934), 109–121.

Burns, Stuart L. "The Rapist in Frank Norris's *The Octopus*," *American Literature*, 42 (1971), 567–569.

Davison, Richard Allan. "An Undiscovered Early Review of Norris' *Octopus*," *Western American Literature*, 3 (1968), 147–151.

Dobie, Charles Caldwell. "Frank Norris, or, Up from Culture," *American Mercury*, 13 (1928), 412–424.

Folsom, James K. "Social Darwinism or Social Protest? The 'Philosophy' of *The Octopus*," *Modern Fiction Studies*, 8 (1962–63), 393–400.

Graham, D. B. "Studio Art in *The Octopus*," *American Literature*, 44 (1973), 657–666.

Hoffman, Charles G. "Norris and the Responsibility of the Novelist," *South Atlantic Quarterly*, 54 (1955), 508–515.

Howells, William Dean. "Frank Norris," *North American Review,* 175 (1902), 769–778.

Isani, Mukhtar Ali. "Jack London on Norris' *The Octopus,*" *American Literary Realism,* 6 (1973), 66–69.

Martin, Willard E. "The Establishment of the Order of Printings in Books Printed from Plates: Illustrated in Frank Norris's *The Octopus,*" *American Literature,* 5 (1933), 17–28.

McKee, Irving. "Notable Memorials to Mussel Slough," *Pacific Historical Review,* 17 (1948), 19–27.

Meyer, George W. "A New Interpretation of *The Octopus,*" *College English,* 4 (1943), 351–359.

Piper, Henry Dan. "Frank Norris and Scott Fitzgerald," *Huntington Library Quarterly,* 19 (1956), 393–400.

Pizer, Donald. "The Concept of Nature in Frank Norris' *The Octopus,*" *American Quarterly,* 14 (1962), 73–80.

———. "Synthetic Criticism and Frank Norris: Or, Mr. Marx, Mr. Taylor, and *The Octopus,*" *American Literature,* 34 (1963), 532–541.

Reninger, H. Willard. "Norris Explains *The Octopus:* a Correlation of His Theory and Practice," *American Literature,* 12 (1940), 218–227.

Walker, Don D. "The Western Naturalism of Frank Norris," *Western American Literature,* 2 (1967), 14–29.

Walker, Philip. "*The Octopus* and Zola: a New Look," *Symposium,* 21 (1967), 155–165.

FURTHER REFERENCES

Norris, Frank. *Collection of Correspondence and Papers and Material Relating to Him.* Eight volumes. The Bancroft Library of the University of California at Berkeley.